THE TASMANIAN TALES

OMNIBUS EDITION

JENNIFER SCOULLAR

PILYARA PRESS

ISBN: 978-1-925827-43-9
Pilyara Press
Melbourne

ALSO BY JENNIFER SCOULLAR

Brumby's Run (The Wild Australia Stories - book 1)

Currawong Creek (The Wild Australia Stories - book 2)

Billabong Bend (The Wild Australia Stories - book 3)

Turtle Reef (The Wild Australia Stories - book 4)

Journey's End (The Wild Australia Stories - book 5)

Wasp Season (The Wild Australia Stories - book 6)

Fortune's Son (The Tasmanian Tales - book 1)

THE LOST VALLEY

THE TASMANIAN TALES 2

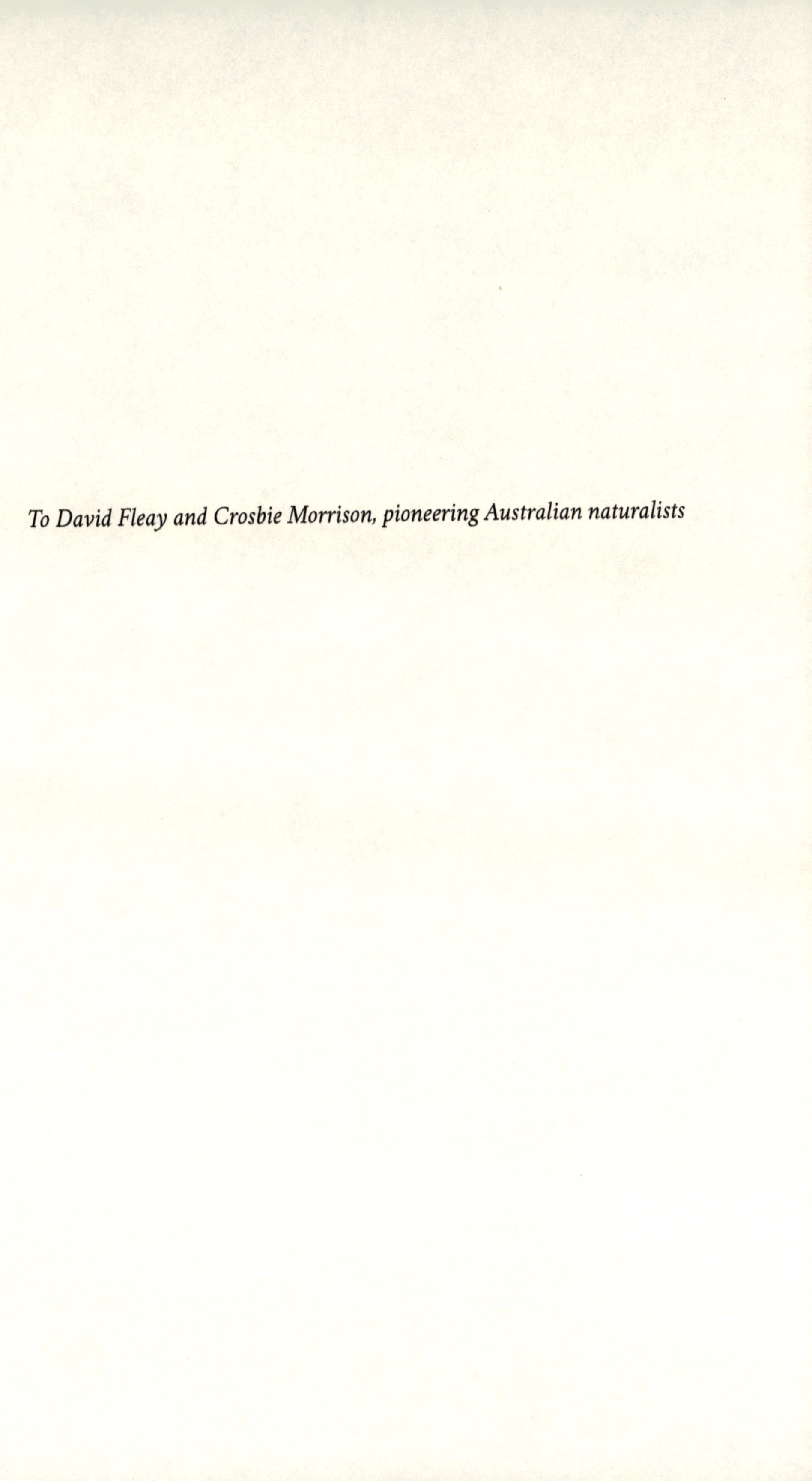

To David Fleay and Crosbie Morrison, pioneering Australian naturalists

PROLOGUE

H*obart, 1929 —*

Mr Robert Abbott, close friend of the Premier and Hobart's most prominent businessman, was forty-one-years old when he took a rifle and shot his wife in the head. He then turned the gun on himself.

Robert had planned his crime. The twins away at boarding school. Staff with the night off. A very special 20th wedding anniversary celebration at home with Helen, just the two of them. Crystal vases stood crammed with roses. A silver ice bucket held his wife's preferred brand of French champagne. They feasted on oysters and poached salmon in the garden as the sun went down.

After dinner, they danced in the drawing room to a carefully arranged play-list. A mix of their favourites, up tempo at first. *Putting On The Ritz. Happy Days Are Here Again.* Helen loved Charles King. Then a little jazz and ragtime. He showed off his moves, and her face flushed with pleasure as he swirled her about in her lilac dress. How beautiful she was. His wife could still foxtrot with the best of them, although her Charleston lacked some of its former, youthful energy. Helen's breath came in little pants and her generous bosom heaved as he stopped to change the record.

As the night wound down, the music grew slower and more tender. 'I love you, Robbie,' she whispered, as they waltzed cheek-to-cheek to strains of *Don't Ever Leave Me* and Gershwin's *Feeling Sentimental*. It was an unseasonably warm evening for a Tasmanian early spring. The heady scent of jasmine wafted through the open window, so evocative of a lifetime spent together in this house. Robert breathed in a great draught of sweet air. This was as fine an evening as had ever been. So fine, he almost changed his mind.

CHAPTER 1

Ten-year-old Tom Abbott and his brother Harry walked in slow motion down the aisle of St Mary's cathedral. Tom had never liked churches, and he especially hated this one. With its frightening frescoes of frowning saints, booming organ music and those twin coffins at the front that, according to Reverend Russell, contained his dead mother and father. Which was which? The coffins looked the same, and neither he nor Harry had been allowed to look inside. Tom desperately wanted a chance to see his parents again, especially Mama. What if she wasn't dead in there? What if she needed help?

The long, black boxes, engraved with crosses, bore heavy brass handles and were strewn with flowers. Tom couldn't stop staring; couldn't stop worrying. Mama was scared of small spaces and Papa? He was so tall, surely he'd hit his head?

The boys came to a halt, causing a traffic jam of mourners. Mrs Boyle nudged them forward. Harry tried to escape down the aisle while Tom ran up to the first coffin and struggled to raise the lid. A man pulled him away, handing him back to his scolding governess.

Grandma Bertha hurried over, chins wobbling, large nose turning red. 'Control your charges, Mrs Boyle. This is a funeral, not a playground!'

'I want to see them,' yelled Tom, squirming free. 'I want to see my parents.'

Grandma Bertha grabbed his arm in a vice-like grip. She shoved Tom and Harry along the front row and pushed them into their seats. 'Stay here and don't move,' she hissed. 'We are in God's house. God is all-seeing and all-knowing. He will punish you boys severely for any further misbehaviour.'

Tom looked at his brother and an understanding passed between them. Grandma's threat was an empty one. If Mama and Papa were dead, hadn't God already done his worst? Tom started to cry.

Isabelle Abbott approached St Mary's with shaky steps. The imposing, sandstone cathedral, built in the gothic style, was too grand, too public for her personal sorrow. A gloomy sheet of cloud lay over everything. Raindrops dripped down her veil and off her nose. She loved rain in the ranges, but here in Hobart? It just emphasised the tragedy of the occasion. Mothers should not bury their sons.

She stumbled as a wave of anguish stole the strength from her legs. This ordeal was almost beyond her. Isabelle steadied herself and searched the crowd, hoping to spot Thomas and Henry, Robert's twin boys. She hadn't seen them for six long years, but the children were nowhere in sight.

Isabelle had insisted on coming to the funeral alone. That was a mistake. She suddenly longed for a friendly face, someone to share the burden of her grief. Robert's father was dead and her daughters lived in England. None of the Abbotts would welcome her; far from it. Not the black sheep of the family. Not the dishonourable woman who'd abandoned her husband to run off with the fabulously wealthy Colonel Lucas Buchanan, the undisputed love of her life. He'd died two years ago, breaking her heart. Leaving Isabelle alone at Binburra, their beautiful but remote estate in the Tasmanian highlands, with only a yard man and housekeeper for company.

And now her son and daughter-in-law were gone too, laid to rest together at this shared funeral, as requested in a recent caveat to Robbie's will. Isabelle had spoken to the police. An intruder, they'd said. A mysterious intruder, bursting into Abbott House and blasting the life from her beautiful Robbie and his wife. But Isabelle knew better. That open verdict returned by the coroner? A cover-up to protect the reputation of the Abbott name.

Robbie had confided something on that last visit home, the first in years by her estranged son. Such a fine-looking man. Intelligent brown eyes. Tall, with even features and a proud bearing, just like his father. They'd sat in those woven wicker chairs on the verandah, beneath the scrambling mountain blueberry vine. Drinking tea. Taking in the view of Binburra's wild ranges. For the longest time nobody spoke. Robert seemed to be gathering courage for something.

'Wall Street,' he'd said finally. 'The crash. What do you know of it?'

'I read the papers,' said Isabelle. 'But I don't pay too much attention.' He bowed his head, like when he was a little boy and something had confused him. 'Why should I, Robbie? New York is so far away.'

He surprised her by leaning over and briefly squeezing her hand. 'You don't understand. It's a new world, Mother, a global economy. Everything's connected these days.' She studied his face. Robert had always been hard to read, so it shocked her to see open anguish in his eyes. 'The stock market was booming for years, with investors making money hand-over-fist.' He gazed into his cup and frowned, as if he was reading the tea leaves and didn't like what he saw. 'I got caught up in the excitement, I suppose. Over-borrowing against my assets. Buying on margin, just ten percent down.'

'On margin?'

'The new economy – buy now and pay later. Everyone jumped on the bandwagon, but now ...' Was that a tear? 'My shares are worthless. I can't repay the loans.' His voice broke. 'My house of cards is tumbling down around me, Mama. I'll be wiped out.'

Mama. He hadn't called her that since he was fifteen years old.

She tried to reassure him. 'You have the mine, Robbie, and the timber mills. The shipyard, the sheep stations. Surely you can trade your way out of trouble?'

'Not with a depression looming.'

'Let me help.'

His face hardened. 'Do you really think I'd take the Colonel's money?'

'Don't be ridiculous, Robbie. It's my money now, and anyway he'd want you to have it.'

Robbie shook his head and it pained her to see the hurt on his face. She started to protest, but he shushed her gently and rose to leave. To Isabelle's surprise he kissed her goodbye. 'I've always loved you, Mama, in spite of everything. I've always loved you.'

Her heart leaped with hope, convinced these words marked the beginning of a reconciliation. A fresh start with her son. A chance to see her grandchildren.

She'd never understood Robbie. A month later he was dead.

If she'd grasped the significance of that final visit. If she'd done something, maybe this nightmare wouldn't have happened. Loud organ music soared through the grand cathedral doors. Lost in the anonymous sea of mourners, grief threatened to overwhelm her.

A woman approached and laid a consoling hand on her arm. Isabelle didn't recognise her at first, not until she lifted her veil – Bertha Barr, Helen's mother. They'd never been friends, far from it, but she recognised the sorrow in those hollow eyes. It was the same as in her own. The sorrow of a mother who'd lost a child.

'My dear Isabelle.' Bertha couldn't conceal the cry in her voice.

Isabelle's mouth went dry and a terrible guilt shook her body. Did Bertha know that Robbie had killed her daughter? Did she guess?

'It's been a long time,' said Bertha. 'How dreadful that this dark day should be the one to bring us together.' She hooked her arm into Isabelle's and together they entered the church.

So many people. Even in this cavernous cathedral, some wouldn't find a seat. Bertha led her past the other mourners to the front row. A mutter rose from those nearby as Isabelle sat down, loud enough to be heard through the organ music. Some disapproving shakes of the head followed. To hell with them. Robbie was her only son. Who had more right to be there than she did?

Bertha touched her arm and pointed down the row. Isabelle drew in a quick breath. Two boys. Thomas and Henry.

A choir led endless hymns and a minister boomed out bible readings. They were supposed to comfort – all that talk of dwelling in God's house and the resurrection of the body – but they meant nothing, said nothing about who Robbie was. Isabelle didn't listen to the worthless words. Instead she focused on the splendid stained-glass window above the altar, flooding the cathedral with beauty and light. Robbie had an eye for architecture. He'd approve of the design. The five, elegant lancets depicting scenes from the scriptures. The exquisite tracery.

At last the service was over. Isabelle glanced across to where she'd seen the boys, but they'd vanished. She rose unsteadily to her feet, determined to slip away before disappointment and sorrow entirely stole the strength from her legs.

Bertha laid a supportive hand on Isabelle's back. 'Come with us to the cemetery.'

She shook her head. 'I can't bear it.'

'Come to the house then, later.' Something in Bertha's expression gave her pause. 'Please, Isabelle. The rest of the family will be attending a private wake. It will just be the two of us. I've an important matter to discuss with you.'

Abbott House. Isabelle shuddered as she passed through its heavy oak door. The stately Victorian home hadn't changed; the façade still ugly and overly-ornate, the atmosphere inside still cold. She and her children had lived in this house for the final years of her marriage to

Edward Abbott. Years of misery. Years of enduring Edward's lies and infidelities and addictions, until she'd found the courage to free herself. Until Luke had swept back into her life.

Bertha led her to the drawing room, called for tea and indicated a chair. Isabelle perched herself on the edge, preparing for a swift exit, ready to express her condolences one more time and escape. Bertha fiddled with her spectacles as the room grew increasingly claustrophobic. Isabelle couldn't stand it. She didn't need to be cooped up here with another mother's grief. She had enough of her own. Why ever had she agreed to this?

Isabelle rose to leave.

'It's about the twins.'

She sat back down.

'I don't know how much you knew about Robert's financial affairs …' The hesitation and raised inflection said that Bertha knew a great deal. 'It seems they were complicated; a lot of money tied up in the stock market. In the meantime, well, the twins have outstanding school fees and can't return to Scotch College until the estate is settled.' Bertha leaned forward. 'I'd love to have them, of course, but they can be a handful and with my health …' She affected a cough. Isabelle remembered why she didn't like Bertha. 'I wondered if they might stay with you in the country for a while?'

Isabelle swallowed hard. Had she misheard? For years she'd been desperate to see her grandsons and be part of their lives. The whole Abbott clan, including her own son, Robbie, had thwarted her at every turn. She wasn't a suitable influence, apparently. She might warp their tender moral fibre. Yet now? The twins were being offered to her like a pair of unwanted puppies.

Bertha seemed to mistake her shocked silence for reluctance. 'Only for the time being, my dear Isabelle. Until Robert's money comes through.' She heaved a great sigh. 'There's really nobody else.'

Isabelle watched Thomas and Henry climb from the back seat of the great, grey Buick; a hulking car that looked out of place beneath the graceful blue gums lining Binburra's driveway. The boys shuffled their feet and stole sideways glances at her. They looked older than she'd expected, with their pressed suits and neat Scotch College hair-cuts. Like little men instead of children.

Rex and Shadow, the resident Newfoundland dogs, trotted up and inspected them. The children shrank back.

'They're perfectly friendly,' said Isabelle. Thomas and Henry did not look convinced. 'I'll put them away. Until you get used to them.'

When she returned, the driver was taking two small suitcases from the trunk.

'Is that all they have?' she asked.

'Yes, madam, apart from this.' He handed her an envelope. 'A letter from their governess.' And with that the car lumbered away.

The twins weren't identical, but looked very much alike. One of them smiled at her. Taller than his brother, hair lighter, dark blonde. He pointed to the letter. 'Don't believe everything you read, Miss.'

She felt a stab of shame. Was that Thomas or Henry? It had been such a long time since she'd seen them. She couldn't very well ask. What sort of grandmother doesn't know her own grandchildren?

Isabelle put the letter in her pocket. She'd have to guess. The odds were fifty-fifty after all.

'I'm your grandmother, Henry, and you don't need to call me Miss.'

'I'm Tom.' He pointed to the other boy. 'That's Henry.'

'Don't call me that.' Henry kept his eyes firmly fixed on the ground. 'Papa calls me Harry; everyone does.' He rubbed the back of his neck. 'How long do we have to stay here?'

'I don't know, Harry,' said Isabelle. 'Some weeks I think.'

'What do we call you, then?' asked Tom. 'We can't call you Grandma. We already have one of those.' He made a face. 'One's enough.'

Isabelle stifled a laugh. 'Call me Nana.'

The boys exchanged an unreadable look. Harry had sharper

features than his brother, his skin a shade darker, his eyes wary and watchful.

'I'm sorry about your mother and father,' she said, knowing how inadequate her words were. She was grateful, in that moment, for the lie Bertha had told them about the manner of their parents' death. A violent intruder was heartbreaking, but it was something a ten-year-old could understand. Nobody, let alone a child, could understand one parent murdering another. Yet the rumours would undoubtedly be swirling around town. At least here in the remote Binburra Ranges, more than a hundred miles from Hobart, the boys would be shielded from that ugliness.

Harry's guarded expression slipped and his eyes brimmed with tears. He knuckled them away as Tom wrapped an arm around his shoulder.

Isabelle wanted to hug them both, but sensed it was too soon. 'I'm delighted you children are here. I'll try my very best to make you happy.'

Harry frowned. 'Looks like the middle of nowhere to me.' A mere mumble, but Isabelle had sharp ears.

'What about you, Tom? What do you think of Binburra?'

Tom ventured a look around, at the gracious homestead perched halfway up the hill. At the looming mountains and encroaching forest. A flock of green rosellas landed in the branches above him, and chittered a greeting. His face split into a grin. 'I think it's bonzer, Miss. Just bonzer.'

Tom pulled the covers up to his chin as Isabelle leaned over and made the blanket snug. Nobody had ever tucked him into bed except his mother. That sweet memory threatened to overwhelm him. This new grandmother didn't smell of perfume though, like Mama did. She smelt of freshly baked bread, and cut grass and wood-smoke.

'Shall I read you a story?'

Silence.

'Have you had enough supper?'

'Yes, Miss.'

'Not Miss, Tom. Nana.' She smoothed the paisley eiderdown. 'Is there anything you *do* want?'

'Yes, Miss.' He hesitated a moment. 'Could Harry sleep in here with me?'

'If he wants to.'

'Rex and Shadow as well? They don't look like dogs, do they? They look like bears.'

She smiled in that kind way his mother had. 'Let me see what I can do.'

Tom opened the curtains and gazed out across the ranges, bathed in bright moonshine. 'It's not so bad here.'

Harry patted Rex who was lying, watchful, by his bed, and joined Tom at the window. He put his lucky gold nugget on the window-sill – the one Papa had given him, the one he always kept in his pocket. It shone in the faint light. Tom ran a finger over its gleaming surface, and his brother snatched it away.

If only Tom had something from their old life too. Something more than clothes and shoes. His teddy perhaps, though Grandma Bertha said he was too big for that nonsense. Or a lock of Mama's hair. Tom closed his eyes and her face appeared, so vivid and real he felt he could almost touch it. When he tried, she vanished like a half-remembered dream.

Harry took a penknife from his pocket and carved a word into the sill. *Papa.* 'Do you miss him terribly? I miss Papa so much, I think I'll die.'

Tom looked at his toes, feeling ashamed. The truth was, he missed his mother most. Her sweet smile and quiet voice. The touch of her hand. She and Tom had shared a special bond. Papa, on the other hand, had always liked Harry best. It made sense. Harry was good at everything that Papa cared about; algebra and geometry and building things. He was fascinated by how they crushed ore at the mine, and how they cut logs at the mill. He loved to spend time at the shipyard.

By contrast, Tom felt like a disappointment. He'd rather read a book than take an engine apart. He excelled at English, yet failed arithmetic. He liked chasing dragonflies by the pond and watching baby magpies learn to fly in the garden. *Why can't you be more like your brother?* was his father's constant mantra.

Harry kissed his lucky nugget. 'When I grow up, I'm going to track down the man who murdered Mama and Papa. I'm going to kill him.'

Tom put his arm around his brother. Poor Harry. Papa had been his whole world. It was easier for Tom; he hadn't loved Papa so completely. There was one good thing, at least. He couldn't let his father down any more.

CHAPTER 3

Isabelle walked the phone away from the desk as far as the cord would allow. She peered around the corner of the library to make sure the boys weren't in earshot. 'No, of course I don't mind. I love having them, but what about school? They've been here for weeks now.'

Bertha's voice sounded thin and tinny on the other end of the line. 'Things haven't worked out with Scotch College.'

Oh. Isabelle could imagine what *things* hadn't worked out. The bank manager had been in touch with her about the boys' trust accounts. Robert had apparently cleaned them out along with the rest, cobbling together what money he could to pay failed funds and margin calls. An elaborate but doomed juggling act.

'The twins won't be returning for their final term?'

'I'm afraid not, unless … unless you're prepared to pay their fees yourself? I imagine the Colonel left you generously provided for.'

Bertha was right. Isabelle could afford to cover the costs, but it was the last thing she wanted to do. A disgrace, how sons of privilege were packed off to mainland boarding schools at such tender ages. Torn from the people they loved. Delivered into the hands of strangers. Her own son had been abandoned in such a way. He'd grown mistrustful and closed off because of it.

Silence stretched down the line. 'Perhaps you could teach them yourself for the remainder of this year, then,' said Bertha, a hint of irritation in her voice. 'We're only talking one term, and I'm well aware of the fine reputation you held as Principal of Campbell College.'

'That was thirty years ago.'

She could hear Bertha breathing, planning her words. 'My dear Isabelle, if you won't pay their fees, and home-schooling isn't possible, I believe Hills End has a public school ...'

What? Things were worse than she thought. In the entire history of the family, no Abbott child had ever attended a public school.

'Leave it with me,' said Isabelle. 'Would you like to talk to the boys?'

'Next time, perhaps. Ernest and I are on our way out.'

Bertha ended the call and Isabelle sat down to think. Until now she'd had no clue how long the boys might be with her. She'd been frightened some nameless chauffeur might whisk them away any day. She hadn't dared to hope it might be a more permanent arrangement.

These past two months, having the twins, had been one of the happiest times of her life. Since being widowed, Isabelle had retreated into herself, becoming more and more reclusive - losing interest in the bush restoration work that she and Luke had once been so passionate about. Fourteen years ago, together with a dedicated band of conservationists, they fought for Tasmania's first national parks at Mount Field and the Freycinet Peninsula. Cradle Mountain-Lake St Clair soon followed. Heady days of bitter struggles, hard disappointments and some spectacular successes. She'd been a fearless warrior for Tasmania's forests back then, like her father before her.

Then came Luke's terrible illness. The proud, vibrant man she adored, wasting away in a fog of pain. He faced his death with the same courage and fortitude with which he lived his life. If it was possible, Isabelle loved him even more because of it. And as she nursed him through those final months, as a choking cancer stole the breath from his lungs, her vital force faded along with his.

By the time he died, she was a hollow shell. For months she spoke to no one. Her passion for conservation - her very passion for life itself - had died with Luke. She withdrew from her position with the Royal Society. Latest copies of the *British Natural History* magazine lay unread in the library along with *Field Naturalist* newsletters and scientific journals. When subscriptions ran out, she failed to renew. What was the point? At sixty she didn't have the energy to fight and, without Luke, her work seemed empty.

Since the boys' arrival, that was changing. She'd read the letter from their governess with its dire assessment of the *devilish pair*. Rude, irreverent, defiant. This was true. Old George, the yard man, had threatened more than once to tan their hides. Unpredictable and quarrelsome. Mrs Mills, the housekeeper, was forever shouting at them. Harry was prone to tantrums and black days of grief. Robbie's death seemed to have hit him particularly hard.

So yes, the twins were incorrigible, but they were also clever and funny and charming. Filled with the kind of youthful exuberance that she'd forgotten existed. Brimming with curiosity and ideas and original thoughts. Tom and Harry, with their wonder at the world, were bringing her steadily back to life.

Of course it wasn't a one-way street. Between nannies and boarding school and summer camps, the boys had been starved of love. A child's heart needed feeding as well as his stomach. Their persistent, troublesome behaviour was a cry for attention and a rebellion against a lonely and highly regimented life.

Yet here, in the shadow of Binburra's wild ranges, the boys were free to simply *be*. Riding and rabbiting. Hiking and camping with the dogs in the forest. Fashioning weapons: swords and shields from bush timber. Bows and arrows from saplings. Acting out elaborate battles that could last from daybreak until dusk. They swam and fished. They built boats and yabby ponds. They grew their hair long, played tricks on Old George and turned nut-brown in the sun.

Isabelle herself had enjoyed such a childhood and understood how there hardly seemed enough hours in the day. She demanded little from them, other than they be home for dinner. She endured their tempers, forgave them when they needed it, listened patiently when they talked. Adored them beyond measure.

The boys were very different. It was impossible to believe that two months ago she couldn't tell them apart. Tom was easier to warm to than Harry. Harry was smart and sure with a razor-sharp wit, but he was also secretive and suspicious of her love. By contrast Tom had a kind of open, naive honesty that was most appealing. As was his interest in nature. It was Tom who drew her back to the library, exploring the natural history collection with an enthusiasm far beyond his years. He collected feathers and insects, tempted her into bush rambles, asked questions about devils and eagles and native tigers.

'Tigers? They used to be at Binburra,' said Isabelle, 'but a wicked bounty scheme wiped them out. I doubt you'd find a single thylacine between here and Hobart.'

'I'd like to go looking,' said Tom. 'I bet I'd find one, too, and if I did, guess what?' He put a finger to his lips. 'I'd never tell a soul.'

Isabelle smiled. Cut from the same cloth as his grandfather. The thought of losing him, of losing either of the boys, had filled her with dread. And now it seemed her fears were groundless. Thanks mainly, she supposed, to Tasmania's gloomy financial outlook. Robert wasn't the only victim of Wall Street. The papers were filled with stories of ruined financiers pitching themselves out of windows and off buildings and bridges. Shock waves from the crash reverberated internationally, crippling economies, threatening to plunge the entire world into chaos. Here in Tasmania unemployment was already at twenty-five percent and rising. As the depression took hold, it seemed nobody wanted to take on two extra mouths, especially an unruly pair of penniless orphans like Tom and Harry. Nobody except Isabelle.

CHAPTER 4

After six years of living at Binburra, Tom still couldn't pick his favourite season. Was it lazy summer? Long, sun-drenched days. Building dams on the creek to a chorus of currawongs. Swimming and launching homemade boats. Was it vivid autumn, when the turning beeches clothed the range in rich tapestries of red and gold? Or perhaps icy winter? Skiing the upper slopes, snow spume flying. Knowing the profound silence of Binburra's glittering mountains.

Sixteen year old Tom gazed out of the library window to the bottlebrush, alive with bees. No, spring was the most magical time of the year. Nesting eagles. Streams running high with snowmelt. A ten-thousand-year-old forest renewing itself, just waiting to be explored. He shifted, restless in his seat. The sparkling morning beckoned, yet he faced a day indoors. A day of history and arithmetic presided over by Mr Hancock, their deadly dull tutor. Yesterday he'd kept them in for hours to complete a week of unfinished homework. A crime, letting sunny days go to waste like that.

Last night, Harry said he'd come up with a plan to get rid of Mr Hancock, but he wouldn't share it. There was a time when they'd shared everything. When they'd been best friends, running wild in the vast wilderness on their doorstep. A time when they would never have kept secrets from each other. That was changing. As they grew older, a strand of strangeness, of separateness, was coming between them.

Harry came in with a sack slung over his shoulder, and dumped it at his feet.

Tom poked it with his foot. Something squirmed inside. 'Is that what I think it is?'

Harry's face broke into a slow grin.

'I thought we were just going to have a bit of fun,' said Tom. 'Fill his desk with wombat turds, or molasses or something. You always go too far.'

'We need to chase this clown off, right?'

'My oath,' said Tom. 'If he makes me *enunciate my vowels* one more time, I'll strangle him myself.'

'But he's more stubborn than the others. It'll take more than molasses.'

Harry picked up the bag and untied its neck. The thrashing creature slid into the open drawer of Mr Hancock's desk, and landed among the rulers and fountain pens. It coiled its tail around a stapler, flattened its neck, cobra-like, and raised its head. Tom admired the reptile's sleek olive scales and bright yellow bands. The most beautiful tiger snake he'd ever seen. With an explosive hiss the snake feigned a strike, and the boys sprang back. Then it poured itself into the recesses of the drawer and vanished from sight.

'Quick,' whispered Harry. 'He's coming.'

Mr Hancock had been their tutor for six months now – a record. He was an intense, bookish man, not many years older than them. This was his first teaching position and he seemed inordinately proud of the appointment. Being more determined than his predecessors, Mr Hancock was not easily put off. None of the boys' usual tricks had worked. Not caps under the typewriter ribbon so it went off like a machine gun when he used it. Not glue in the ink wells or dead fish under the floor boards to stink out his room. They'd gone so far as abandoning him in the bush during a nature walk, but he'd found his way home.

Tom and his brother sat quietly, giving the tutor their full attention. Hancock's eyes darted around. He was clearly suspicious of this good behaviour. A knot of tension formed in the room. He settled very slowly on his seat, as if an electric shock might accompany the move. Tom sat forward in his chair and the knot of tension drew tighter.

'Good morning boys.'

'Good morning sir,' they chorused.

Hancock licked his lips and sat back in his chair. 'We're having an English test today.' He rummaged around in his bag. 'Now where did I put your papers?'

'Maybe they're in the desk?' said Harry.

Hancock gave him a knowing look and tapped the desktop. 'That would be rather unwise, wouldn't it? There's no lock on this drawer.'

Tom glanced at Harry in disbelief. Did Hancock really think they cared enough to steal his stupid test and then study for it?

'Here we are.' He distributed the papers and a sharpened pencil each. 'You have one hour.'

Tom looked at the first few questions:

1. *Give the rule for the use of the subjunctive mood.*
2. *Define integer, fraction, interest, discount, power, and root.*
3. *Write a sentence containing a noun used as an attribute, a verb in the perfect tense potential mood, and a proper adjective.*

Argh! Was it possible to make his favourite subject any more boring? Nana's lessons were altogether different; she made English come alive. Reading the great romantic poets like Coleridge and Wordsworth. The kind of poetry that made Tom want to walk by the sea, or soar like a bird or fall in love. Studying Shakespeare's bloody tales of murder and revenge. Dickens and Kipling. Even practical Harry was enchanted by Mowgli's *Jungle Book* adventures.

Tom finished reading. He'd rather set himself on fire than answer these ridiculous questions. Doodling on the test instead, he went back to thinking about the snake in the desk. Hancock was a pompous, dreary buffoon, but he didn't deserve to be bitten by a tiger snake.

Tom put up his hand, ignoring his brother's poisonous stare. 'Mr Hancock, there's a snake in your desk.'

'You won't get out of this test by making up silly stories, Tom.'

Now Harry put up his hand. 'Sir, the lead in my pencil's broken. May I please have another?' Hancock opened the drawer and reached inside.

'Don't,' yelled Tom. 'Stop!'

Too late. Hancock howled, clutched his right arm and scrambled backwards. His face turned ghostly white as the snake reared up before him, then vanished back into the desk.

Tom dashed forward. 'Sir, you need to lie flat.' He pulled the groaning tutor to the floor. 'Stay still, sir. Harry, go get Nana.'

His brother didn't move, wearing an expression of half-horror, half-fascination.

'Harry, go!'

Harry finally ran from the room.

Beads of moisture appeared on Mr Hancock's brow, turning to a slick sheen of sweat. 'I can't feel my arm.' His breathing was laboured. 'I'm going to die, aren't I? I know I am.'

'Nah, you'll be right,' soothed Tom. 'There's an antidote.'

He spoke with a confidence he did not feel. It was true there was a new cure, specifically designed for tiger snake bites, made from their own venom. Binburra was part of a snake-catching program that sent dozens of the reptiles to Hobart laboratories for milking. But where was the nearest dose of the finished product? At the doctor's surgery perhaps, in Hills End? Miles away. Tom's skin felt clammy. He wet his lips and tried to reassure the moaning man. This would be touch and go.

Tom stood beside Harry on the verandah as old George drove away with Mr Hancock, who was lying prone on the back seat. Nana waved the car goodbye, then climbed the timber steps with a flushed face and wild eyes. Tom couldn't ever remember seeing his grandmother really angry before, not until today.

She glared at them, then paced up and down the railing, as if she didn't trust herself to speak. Mr Hancock's vomit stained her trousers, and the pins had come out of her hair. It fell around her face in an untidy, grey cloud. Nana suddenly looked very old.

'I can't believe you two. If I hadn't had some anti-venom in the fridge …' She turned to Harry. 'I suppose this was your idea?'

Harry stiffened. 'That's right, blame me.'

She turned to Tom. 'Will I have more luck with you, then? Was this your doing?'

Harry shot him a warning glance.

'The truth now. No lying to protect Harry.'

Tom thought quickly. How often had loyalty made him take the fall for his brother? But not this time. 'It wasn't me.'

Harry rounded on him. 'You knew though.'

'Yeah, about a minute before you put the snake in the desk.'

'Why didn't you warn Mr Hancock, Tom?'

'I did. I just waited too long, that's all, and by then it was too late.'

'Well, at least you tried. Off you go, while I decide what to do with your brother.'

Tom stayed put, not wanting to miss the fireworks.

'It's not fair.' Harry's voice rose a few notches. 'Tom wanted Mr Hancock gone as much as I did. You always play favourites, Nana.'

'That's not true …'

'It damn well is. I hate it here. I wish Papa was alive. He wasn't like you, Nana. Papa couldn't be bothered with Tom. He said Tom was a good for nothing, and I reckon he was right.'

'Apologise to your brother this instant.'

Harry glared at her, a defiant tilt to his chin. He bounded from the verandah, three steps at a time, and ran off towards the stables.

Nana sighed and scrubbed a hand across her eyes. 'Oh, Tom, your brother didn't mean it.'

He shrugged. There was a time, mere weeks ago, when Harry's outburst would have cut deep. But Tom no longer cared about his father's opinion – of him, or anything else. He'd overheard Nana talking with Grandma Bertha on the phone, and what he'd learned changed everything. He'd found his father out. Nana put a hand on his shoulder, and he turned to hug her. She felt slight in his arms, like the wind might blow her away.

'I'm sorry about Mr Hancock,' he said. 'Will he be all right?'

She managed a faint smile. 'I believe we treated him in time.'

He brushed a fly from her green silk blouse. It reminded him of one his mother used to wear. 'Would you like a pot of tea?'

'Thank you, Tom.' She patted his hand. 'Then see if you can find your brother for me. Tell him I love him. Tell him to come home.'

He took his grandmother her tea, and went to the library to rescue the snake from the desk. Using a homemade catching stick, Tom coaxed it from the drawer and expertly dropped it into an old chaff bag. He released it in the bush behind the stables.

Buster, Harry's bay gelding, wasn't in the yards. Tom saddled his own horse and set off into the mountains, homing in on his twin with the sixth sense they'd always shared. Hoofprints in the damp earth confirmed his hunch. Harry was headed for the cliffs above Binburra falls.

CHAPTER 5

Isabelle held her teacup with both hands, but couldn't keep it steady. Time to admit defeat. Teaching the twins at Binburra had never been her preference. She'd tried to convince the Abbott clan they'd be better off at the local school, where they could mix with other children. Reminding Bertha that she herself had suggested it in the beginning.

'Oh, my dear, you must be mistaken,' Bertha had said. 'As the boys' guardian, I couldn't possibly allow it. No Abbott child has ever had a public education. You must teach them yourself, Isabelle. I have complete faith in you.'

Complete faith. This from a woman who'd kept Isabelle from her grandsons for years. The hypocrisy was breathtaking.

She'd enlisted a string of tutors, but none had lasted long. The twins were intelligent, gifted students, and this year had gained their intermediate equivalency certificates with high marks. However they did love to play pranks on their unsuspecting teachers. As they grew older, the scale of their mischief escalated alarmingly. Last month, Mr Hancock had spent a freezing night lost in the bush after the boys gave him the slip. This incident with the snake, though, was by far the most dangerous. It might take a fair sum of money to buy Mr Hancock's silence.

More tea lay in the rose-patterned saucer than in the cup. She gave up her balancing act and put the teacup down with trembling hands. No, it couldn't go on like this. She didn't have the energy any more. The twins were running wild here at Binburra. Sixteen-years-old and living in grand isolation, with no social life. No way to make their own friends, or lead their own lives.

The boys' former camaraderie was turning into an unhealthy rivalry, and the chip Harry had always worn on his shoulder was growing fast. Sometimes the way he looked at Tom gave her a chill – all that veiled hostility. This angry, adolescent Harry wasn't easy to love.

She shut her eyes, picturing the two lost little souls who'd arrived six years earlier. For Tom, Binburra had been a place of healing after tragedy. By contrast, Harry had never really recovered from the loss of his parents, especially his father.

Isabelle took her tea into the parlour. She opened the sideboard, where she kept her photograph albums, and flipped through the pages. An image of Harry on his eleventh birthday caught her eye, taken with her old box Brownie camera. The tip of his tongue showed from between his teeth as he glued together a model yacht. The picture of concentration. Such a clever boy, with a knack for building things, especially boats. What a shame Robbie had lost the family shipyard. Harry would have loved working there.

He tinkered endlessly with motors and helped Old George keep the farm machinery running. A whizz with electricity and engines, rigging up all sorts of mostly useful inventions. An automatic hay-lift for the loft. An electric chick incubator. Even a stream-driven dynamo to generate power. He possessed a boundless curiosity about how things worked, and once received a serious electric shock while investigating the wiring under the house.

And here was a photo of Tom at the same age – dressed in that silly home-made bird costume with canvas wings outstretched and hope shining in his eyes. She smiled at the memory. Five minutes later he'd taken a running jump off the haystack. A leap of faith. Biting the dust hadn't dented his passion for flying.

Tom devoured books about aviation, collected toy planes and made mail-order Meccano and balsa wood kits, including twelve different World War I biplanes. It wasn't enough for him to cram full every shelf. Tom wanted them to fly. In his bedroom he built an elaborate, overhead web of cotton and fuse wire, organising his planes into dramatic scenes of combat.

He knew everything there was to know about World War I flying aces like the Red Baron and Australia's own Roderick Dallas and Robert A Little.

'When I grow up I'll be a pilot too,' he'd say. 'I'll finally know how an eagle feels.'

Isabelle didn't doubt him for a moment. Tom might be an optimist, a dreamer with his head and his heart in the clouds, but there was an indefinable sense of destiny about the boy.

She wished her father could have known him. Daniel Campbell had been one of Tasmania's greatest naturalists and a pioneering member of the Royal Society, the oldest scientific organisation in Australia. He'd had a special love for birds, too, especially owls and eagles. How he would have loved Tom.

Isabelle took a deep breath. Decision time. The boys needed a circuit breaker and so did she. Time to broaden their horizons as her own dear mother had done for her. Time to take them to Hobart, so they could learn about the world beyond Binburra's boundaries.

A plan formed in her mind. They could stay at Coomalong, Isabelle's old family home next to Campbell College, where she'd once been Principal. Isabelle remained on the board. She'd donated her house to the school on condition that it be used not only for lessons, but as accommodation for scholarship girls. Harry and Tom would be able to attend classes and mix with people their own age. She would have a respite from the burden of their education.

It would be an adventure for them all.

CHAPTER 6

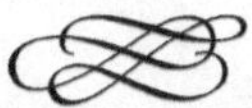

Tom and Flame, his eager chestnut mare, pounded up the waterfall track under the bluest of skies. He tried to look on the bright side. If all went well, Mr Hancock would recover and never come back. Nana and Harry would calm down. He'd escaped the hated school room into a perfect spring day and wouldn't have to sit that stupid test.

He slowed Flame to a walk as they reached the falls and tackled the rocky climb to the clifftop. Flame's hooves struck sparks from the flinty stones as she scrambled up the perilous path. Harry hadn't nursed his horse in the same way. He'd taken the slope at a gallop. Dislodged rocks told the story of his frantic ascent.

When Tom reached the top he spotted Harry standing on a granite overhang above the falls, throwing stones into the foaming water. His bay gelding, tethered nearby, whinnied and held up a forefoot. Tom dismounted and examined its leg. The pastern and cannon bone felt hot and swollen.

'You've lamed Buster.'

'Go to hell,' yelled Harry.

Tom rubbed the gelding between the ears and slipped off his

bridle. 'Go home, boy.' He waved his hat and Buster trotted off, limping.

'Hey,' called Harry as his horse vanished into the forest. 'What the fuck are you doing?'

'You can't ride that horse.' Tom joined his brother at the head of the falls and picked up a handful of stones. He lobbed one into the pool sixty feet below. 'Nana sent me to fetch you back. I reckon she's forgiven you.'

'Forgiven me?' Harry's voice burned with anger. 'What about me forgiving her?'

'What for?'

'For making everything my fault. For treating me like crap all these years. Take her birthday. I saved my pocket money for ages to buy her a brooch. I've hardly ever seen her wear it. But you? You give her a half-dead quoll you just find out in the bush, yet she loves that quoll more than anything. It has the run of her room, sleeps on her bed, and it didn't cost you a penny.'

'You should know that Nana's not a great one for jewellery. And anyway, with her, it's not about the money.'

'Then what is it about?' said Harry. 'I fix things for her like the toaster and the iron. Keep that clapped out tractor running. I even invented an oil-heated drum in the shed to dry wet laundry when it's raining. You? You just moon about in the bush looking at birds. Or build those stupid gliders that always crash.' He flexed his fingers, eyes cold as flint. 'For some reason she still thinks the sun shines out of your arse.'

Harry had conveniently forgotten about how much trouble he'd caused Nana. He'd forgotten about the war of attrition he'd waged against their teachers and how often Tom had unfairly shared the blame. He'd forgotten about his tempers and black moods. But otherwise he was right. Harry was far more useful than Tom around Binburra, at least in a practical sense.

Tom threw another stone, mulling over his brother's words. He almost felt sorry for Harry, understanding all too well the pain of feeling second best in the eyes of someone you loved. It left a sharp icicle of damage in your heart.

'Come on,' said Tom. 'I'll double-bunk you home.'

'I'm not going home.' Harry's eyes blazed with the power of a long-smouldering resentment, suddenly fanned into flames. 'I'm sick of her playing favourites, and I'm sick of you.'

'Fine, walk then.'

'I meant what I said about Papa.' Harry's tone was taunting now, his legs planted wide. 'I bet he wished you'd never been born. I bet Papa never even wanted you.'

'Who cares what Father wanted?'

As Tom walked away, a blinding pain exploded at the back of his head. The rock bounced off and cartwheeled down the cliff. Harry bent down to pick up another. Tom tackled his brother, wrestled the rock from his hand, then sat on him. 'You think Father was so perfect, don't you?' said Tom. 'Some sort of saint? Well, I know different.'

'What the hell do you mean?' Harry's voice came in short, angry pants.

Tom swore under his breath, and let his brother up. 'Forget it. Forget I said anything.'

He turned to go, but in a flash Harry was upon him. 'You can't talk about Papa like that.'

Caught off guard, Tom lost his balance and fell hard on his back. The two of them rarely fought. Harry had long ago learned he was no match for his heavier, stronger brother, but something was different about him today. A new ferocity lay behind his pummelling fists. When Tom raised his hands to guard his face, Harry sent a blow to his stomach, hard enough to wind him.

Then Harry's hands were around his neck, thumbs pressed against his throat.

Anger rose in Tom like a hot tide, threatening to engulf them both. He exploded like a spring released, hurling Harry back to the edge of the waterfall. Tom scrambled to his feet. 'Want to know why I don't care any more? Want to know the truth about Papa?' He stood over his fallen brother, eyes wild. 'There was no armed robber at our house. We've been lied to all along. Father shot Mama, and then he shot himself.'

'Bullshit.' Sunlight glinted off Harry's tears.

'It damn well isn't. I heard Nana talking about it on the phone. Father killed himself and Mama because he was ashamed. He lost everything, even your precious shipyard. He lost the family fortune and couldn't face people. That's the kind of man he was – a coward who murdered our mother and abandoned us. That's exactly how much he loved you.'

Time stood still. Then a jagged cry, barely human, escaped Harry. It pierced Tom's heart, and all the rage leaked out of him. What had he done? He was stronger than Harry, and hadn't loved Father so fiercely. He should have protected his brother from the awful truth. Yet in one mean, hate-filled moment he'd used it as a weapon against him. Fear for Harry gripped him. A fear he wouldn't survive the pain of knowing. Tom squeezed his eyes shut, willing time to go backwards. Desperate to take back his cruel words.

A sudden, blinding pain tore through him as Harry's knee crashed into his groin. Tom caught a glimpse of his brother's eyes, black and murderous, before stumbling back and tripping on a tanglefoot beech that clung to the edge of the overhang. Tom snatched at it with both hands, feeling himself slipping, losing his footing. Suddenly he was dangling; treading air. All that kept him from sliding into the abyss was the shallow-rooted tree, its branches slick with spray from the falls.

'Harry.' His heart thumped madly. His legs scrambled for a foothold but found none. 'Help!'

Hands reached down for him, grasping his wrists. 'I've got you, Tom. Hang onto me. Let go of the tree.'

It went against every instinct. His fingers inched towards Harry's arm, loath to forgo their hold on the branch. He steeled himself, gulped down a breath and transferred his grip. The sun in his eyes meant he couldn't see Harry's face. For a long moment he hung there, suspended in space, anchored to his brother for better or worse.

Harry opened his fingers and Tom slipped into the void.

CHAPTER 7

Tom seemed to be falling forever, as in a dream, merging with the rushing cascade. He bounced off boulders and snags on the way down, but felt nothing – not yet. If he could just spread his wings and soar up through the rainbow spray, like the spine-tailed swifts that nested on these cliffs. If he could be a bird …

Reprieve from pain ended when he smacked into the rocky pool at the base of the falls. The impact knocked the wind from his lungs, a small blessing. It stopped him gasping for breath beneath the water, when his mind was still spinning, when his body felt impossibly heavy.

Tom surfaced by instinct and struck out for the bank. His right arm didn't work and each breath was torture. He hauled himself into the shallows left-handed, and with agonising slowness, crawled onto the river sand. Blood oozed from his many cuts. He vomited, light-headed, struggling to think. Struggling to accept what his brother had done. How was Harry feeling? Sick at heart? Frightened? Maybe he felt nothing; maybe he was happy. Tom vomited again, growing more and more dizzy. Would Harry come for him? And if he did, would it be to help? With this last, frightening thought, Tom's vision faded and darkness descended.

. . .

Tom woke in a world of hurt. A round moon sailed high in the sky. His breath came in shallow pants and the pain in his arm made him scream when he tried to move. Tom gritted his teeth, dragged himself to the dark water and drank. With the help of a low branch he pulled himself to his feet, stiff with an agony more than physical. The agony of knowing his brother had left him to die.

Tom's injuries had stiffened. Each inch of him ached. Raw skin showed through his shredded clothes, crusted with dried blood. Each step was an agony, but his legs moved when ordered to and moonlight showed the way. He could do this. He had to do this. With a groan, Tom shuffled off down the waterfall track.

Hours later, a light appeared in the gloom ahead. At first he thought the flash was inside his lids, a prelude to fainting. But there were hoofbeats, and someone calling. A sudden fear came over him and he stumbled into the trees.

The hoofbeats drew nearer. 'Harry! Tom!' Old George's voice.

'Here,' yelled Tom, drag-footing his way back onto the track. 'I'm here.'

Tom opened his eyes. Morning sun streamed through the window. He was in his own bed, unsure of how he got there, unable to remember anything after Old George found him. He knew one thing though – he was grateful to be alive.

His hurting was down to a dull throb. Tom peeked under the covers. Someone had cut off his torn clothes and taped up his torso. His wounds were cleaned and dressed, and his right arm lay stiff and heavy in plaster.

'Thank God, Tom.' He hadn't seen Nana standing there by his pillow. 'I've been frantic with worry.'

He pulled the sheet higher, embarrassed to be naked underneath.

When he tried to sit up, a sharp spasm gripped him and made him gasp.

'Lie down,' she said. 'Try not to move. You have a broken arm and broken ribs.'

Nana gently raised his head and held two pills and a cup of lemonade to his lips. She smelt sweet, like roses. Like his mother.

'This will help with the pain.' He swallowed the pills in one gulp, drained the cup dry and asked for another. Nana placed the softest kiss on his forehead. 'I should never have sent you off like that. You must have been thrown from your horse, Tom. Flame came home without you.'

'Is she all right?' he asked through fat lips. Talking hurt his jaw.

'Listen to you.' Nana smiled and smoothed his hair. 'Flame's fine, Tom. Now, tell me what happened. What do you remember?'

He closed his eyes, head hurting, his mind a fog of confusion. Part of him wanted to scream out what Harry had done, wanted the world to know, wanted to make him pay. Yet the instinct to protect his brother remained strong, ingrained in his being. Tom licked his swollen lips, but no spit would come. What to do? A small voice said this was his fault too. He'd provoked Harry, telling him about Father like that.

'Tom?'

An expectant silence stretched between them.

'Ask Harry,' he said at last, unable to meet her eye.

'Oh, my poor darling, you don't know, do you? Your brother's still missing. His horse came in after midnight without him.' She dabbed his cut face with a washer dipped in warm water and Dettol. He tried not to flinch. 'Listen, Tom, this is important.' She reached for his hand. 'Did you find Harry yesterday? Do you know where he might be?'

He turned away.

'Look at me, Tom. Buster came home lame and he's lost his bridle. Harry's out there somewhere, probably hurt. You have to think.'

'Sorry, Nana, I can't remember.' His voice broke into a sob. 'I can't remember anything.'

. . .

Tom dozed on and off all morning, thinking about Harry and listening to the sounds coming through the window; the grind of car engines, the clip-clop of hooves, the mutter of strange voices and barking dogs. A waste of everybody's time. They wouldn't find Harry if he didn't want to be found.

The corner clock had chimed twelve when Nana brought in a bowl of steaming chicken soup and a plate of buttered toast. The town police sergeant followed her into the room; a stout, middle-aged man with a ginger beard.

'Sergeant Murphy's coordinating the search for Harry,' she said. 'He has some questions.'

Murphy cast a curious eye over Tom. 'So you and your brother had a blue before he took off up the mountain.' The clock ticked out the seconds. 'Were you still angry when you went after him?'

'That was my fault,' said Nana. 'I sent Tom to find Harry.'

Murphy frowned. 'What happened out there, son? Where's your brother?'

Tom began to shiver.

'He doesn't remember.' Nana laid an eiderdown over him. 'He must have hit his head.'

'If you don't mind, I'd like to speak to your grandson alone.' Nana crossed her arms and shook her head. Murphy glared at her, pulled a chair up to the bed and settled his square frame into it. 'You're pretty beat up, son. You and Harry get into a fight out there?'

Nana stepped forward. 'Sergeant, anyone can see the boy's been thrown from his horse.'

'Maybe so.' Murphy leaned forward and tipped Tom's head a little further back on the pillow. 'But no fall caused those thumb marks around his neck, or these knuckle-shaped bruises.' He fetched a hand mirror from the dresser and held it up for Tom. 'Take a gander at yourself, son.'

Tom drew in a sharp breath, causing a white-hot pain to rip through him. He didn't recognise his reflection. Eyes rimmed in black. Lips split and crusted with scabbed blood. Nose smashed and swollen

... and those tell-tale bruises. The story of Harry's flying fists was written all over his face.

'With you looking like this, well, it makes me wonder how young Harry ended up.' Murphy's mouth turned up in a cold smile. 'You might be able to fool your grandmother, son, but we both know you and your brother got into it.'

'That's quite enough, Sergeant.' Nana drew herself up to her full height. 'My grandson is not on trial here.'

Murphy stood up. 'All right, I'll go.' His eyes bored into Tom's one last time. 'Are you sure there's nothing more?'

Tom was torn, the blood rushing in his ears. It would be so simple, the sergeant was standing right there. Why not tell the truth, clear himself of blame, and save everyone this pointless search for the supposedly injured Harry?

'Your soup's getting cold.' Nana fussed around, arranging his lunch on a tray and helping him sit up a little.

Murphy sensed Tom's ambivalence and placed an encouraging hand on his shoulder. 'Help us out here.'

Tom's mind froze. Did he really want Nana to know the truth? How he'd mocked Harry with the awful reality of their parents' deaths? Leaving that part out would be worse than lying. If not for his cruel taunts, Harry would never have dropped him off a cliff.

'Speak up, son.'

'Sorry,' said Tom. 'I can't remember.'

Disappointment and concern clouded his grandmother's face. He wished he had the courage to reassure her about his brother. Harry wasn't the bushman Tom was, but he could live rough for a while. He'd come home when he was fed up with bush tucker and cold nights.

Harry held out for three days. Then, one morning, Nana came running into Tom's room where he still lay, too bruised and sore to move.

'He's home, Tom.' She couldn't stop smiling. 'Harry's home.'

Tom craned his neck to see around her. His brother stood in the doorway, clothes filthy and torn.

'Tom's been so worried about you,' said Nana.

Harry approached the bed with halting steps and dark, unreadable eyes.

'Glad you're home,' said Tom. He hadn't meant to say it. He'd meant to be angry, but the words just slipped out.

'We're all glad you're home.' Nana wrapped her arms around Harry. He barely tolerated the embrace, standing stiff and unyielding. 'Come on, you can catch up with Tom later, dear. The doctor's on his way to check you over, and you need something to eat.'

Tom held his nose. 'Make him take a bath while you're at it.'

Two hours later, Harry was back. Tom studied his stony face, wanting to ask if he was surprised to find him alive. 'The whole town's been searching for you,' he said instead. 'Where'd you go?'

'Upstream.' Harry shuffled his feet. 'Nearly starved to death. Couldn't even snare a bloody rabbit.'

'What did you tell Nana?'

'That I fell off Buster and got lost.' Harry gulped hard. 'What did you tell her?'

'That I can't remember.'

Harry exhaled and rubbed his sunburnt neck. 'Didn't mean to let you go, mate. I couldn't hold on.' He plucked at the cream counterpane with his fingers, the same fingers that had let Tom plunge into the abyss. 'You're a tough bugger, tougher than me. I told myself you'd fall in the water. I told myself you'd be all right.'

Tom sagged back on his pillows. He knew Harry, knew the darkness in him. The same darkness was in himself. Buried a little deeper perhaps, but it was there. Why else did he taunt Harry with a truth so guaranteed to hurt?

'I shouldn't have left you like that. It was a mongrel thing to do.' Harry looked him straight in the eye. 'I'm sorry.'

Tom sat up, ignoring the pain of his cracked ribs. Had he

misheard? Harry was never sorry, no matter what. His brother based this principle on one of Father's oft-repeated PG Wodehouse quotes. *It is a good rule in life never to apologise. The right sort of people do not want apologies, and the wrong sort take a mean advantage of them.* Harry took everything their father had said to heart, with the literal interpretation of a child.

Tom snatched at the precious apology like a man overboard snatching for a life buoy. Eager to believe. In a hurry to forgive.

The knot of tension in the room unravelled. 'How's that dickhead, Hancock?' asked Harry.

'He'll be good as new, apparently.'

Harry pulled up a chair to the bed. 'I guess he won't be coming back.'

'Guess not.'

They talked about small things. Would Nana be foolish enough to engage another tutor? How long before Tom could use his arm again? Would he still be able to chop wood? Harry's time on the mountain.

'I found a new eagle nest, chicks and all. Once you're out of that bed, I'll show you.'

Their father remained the great unmentioned. Tom wanted to leave the subject alone. He'd have got up and walked out if he could. They tiptoed around the issue for a few more minutes, but Harry was gearing up to talk about him. It showed in his nervous eyes, and how his tongue flicked around his lips. 'What you said about Papa,' he said at last. 'About what he did ...' His words ground to a halt.

'I won't take it back,' said Tom. 'I know what I heard.'

Harry held up his hand. 'The thing is, I think I already knew. Not sure how. Just a feeling.'

Tom stared at his brother. All these years of putting Father on a pedestal, of being his defender and champion. How could he do that if he suspected?

'I miss him every day,' said Harry, his voice breaking. 'I loved Mama, you know that, but I still love Papa too, despite what he did. It's killing me.' He fixed Tom with troubled eyes. 'Do you love him?'

Tom tried to recall his father's face, but it was a mere blur. Mama's lovely image swam before him instead; the sunny smile and gentle eyes, the soft curl of her copper-coloured hair. She seemed so real, he could almost smell her rose perfume, almost hear her kind voice.

'Well?' said Harry. 'Do you love Papa?'

'Not any more.' It felt good to say it out loud, like he was free of something. 'You shouldn't love him either, Harry. Father doesn't deserve it.'

For an instant his brother's eyes flashed with something akin to hatred. It happened so quickly Tom might have imagined it. A small fear squirmed in his stomach as he remembered hands around his throat.

The next moment Harry was smiling and shaking his head. 'Wish I could see the world like you do, mate. Black and white. Good and bad – mostly good. My world's a hell of a lot more complicated.'

'Knock, knock.' Nana came in with scones. 'There's jam and cream, just how you like, Tom, and Mrs Mills is bringing up a pot of tea.' She set the tray down. 'That's enough talk for now, boys. You both need your rest.'

'I'll only go,' said Harry, 'if there are more scones in the kitchen.'

Tom watched him leave, his mind awhirl. So, all this time, Harry had a feeling that their father had committed a terrible crime. Tom started to shiver. He'd had no such feeling. What he'd learned in that overheard conversation had come as a complete shock, an utter heartbreak. Tom closed his eyes and faced the wall, wishing he could unhear every ugly word.

CHAPTER 8

'Hurry up, Harry,' called Isabelle. 'There's a long drive ahead of us.'

She climbed into the passenger seat of Miriam, their red Ford roadster; a present from Luke shortly before he died. She loved Miriam like one of the family, despite her quirks. An engine that hammered like an aeroplane on take-off, emitting clouds of scalding steam. Impossible gears. Dodgy brakes that meant you had to go downhill in reverse to help slow her down.

But Miriam had her strengths. Navigating rocky roads and managing mud. Crossing shallow streams and climbing hills with ease. When Binburra suffered one of its frequent power blackouts, Old George would remove one of her wheels, fasten a pulley to the hub and make a flat belt to drive the water pump and generator.

Tom honked the horn, and Harry heaved his bag into the back seat. 'How come he gets to drive?'

'Your turn on the way home,' said Isabelle.

Harry frowned and got in. 'Wait.' He flung the door open and raced for the house, returning with the elaborate red speedboat he'd built from broken toys and old clock parts. The intricate mechanism

43

powered it along faster than any shop-bought wind-up boat. He wrapped it in a linen sheet and stowed it carefully on the back seat.

Miriam back-fired with a deafening bang and Isabelle laughed aloud, brimming with optimism. Here was a chance to put their recent dramas behind them. The snake and Mr Hancock. Tom's unexplained injuries – his arm still wasn't right. Harry's mysterious disappearance. Something awful had happened out there in the bush; something the boys refused to talk about. Whatever it was had fractured their bond, and made her feel excluded. This trip might help bring them all closer together.

Harry wanted to visit the Battery Point shipyards and go to a cricket match at Bellerive Oval. Tom wanted to visit the museum and Cambridge Aerodrome. Isabelle wanted to see a play and attend meetings of the Royal Society again. Everybody wanted to see a movie. Nobody wanted to see Grandma Bertha.

Tom whooped as they headed for the gate. 'Hold onto your hat, Nana. Hobart, here we come!'

~

Isabelle found her key and opened the door wide. 'Welcome to Coomalong.' Tom and Harry stood in the front hall. 'Go on, you two, take a look around.' They dropped their bags and bounded up the stairs.

She hadn't been to Coomalong since Robert's funeral. Visits here were bittersweet affairs. Isabelle had grown up in this gracious old home in Sandy Bay, living here until she was twelve; the happiest childhood imaginable. Her father had founded Campbell College in the old wool store next door, offering working-class children – both boys and girls – a low-cost, progressive education.

Later on she'd lived here with her beloved Colonel Buchanan, known to all as the wealthy South African diamond tycoon who'd arrived in Tasmania one day and whisked Isabelle away from her husband. There was nobody left alive who knew the truth – that they'd met as children, right here, when he was a poor boy attending the school next door.

So many memories. She looked down at her wedding ring, twisted it in her fingers. Her hands didn't look like they belonged to her, with their wrinkles and age spots. Isabelle rarely looked in the mirror anymore, but her hands were an unavoidable reminder that she was in the autumn of her life. There were things the twins had a right to know before she died.

Emma Starr threw off her neat navy pinafore, kicked off her shoes and fastened her wavy, red hair into a ponytail. The morning shift at *À La Mode* Fashions and Haberdashery had lasted longer than usual, and now she was going to be late. Not even time for lunch. Argh. She'd have to grab an apple from her stinky bag and eat it on the way. Emma opened the bottom drawer of her dresser and pulled out a pair of boy's dungarees and a blue serge work shirt.

She was about to slip her petticoat off, when she stopped. Heavy footsteps sounded in the corridor outside. Who could it be? All the other girls had gone home for the holidays.

The door burst open and Emma screamed. A boy, about her own age, and here she was dressed in nothing but her underwear. She took another look at him, despite her fright. Handsome, distractingly so. Tall and well-built with lightly tanned skin, golden hair and wide brown eyes that he now politely averted.

'Sorry, Miss.' He seemed as shocked as she was.

Good grief, here was another one, peering over the first boy's shoulder – good-looking as well, a little darker with bolder eyes. He started to laugh and held his nose. 'What smells?'

Emma burned with embarrassment. She grabbed a throw rug from the bed and used it to cover herself. The boy in front had turned bright red, while the one behind tried to push past into the room.

'Shove off, Harry,' said the first boy. They backed out and closed the door.

Emma quickly pulled on her shirt and buttoned it up. It was way too big for her. That fact hadn't bothered her before, but now she regretted having to go downstairs looking like a shapeless sack of potatoes. She pulled her dungarees on over her petticoat, no longer trusting that the room would afford her any privacy. Hefting her duffel bag with both hands, Emma hurried out to the landing and peered over the banister.

The boys were standing together with an old lady at the foot of the staircase.

'You've been holding out on us, Nana,' said the darker boy with a grin. 'You didn't say there were girls.'

'Girls?'

'Yes, indeed, and half-dressed ones at that.' He wagged a finger at Tom. 'Who's a naughty boy, then? My brother should learn to mind his manners.'

'You said we could look around, Nana,' said Tom. 'How was I supposed to know she was in there?'

The old lady spotted Emma at the top of the stairs, and gave a welcoming wave. 'Come down, my dear. It seems my grandsons owe you an apology.'

Emma descended with hesitant steps, dragging the duffel bag behind her.

'I'm Mrs Isabelle Buchanan,' said the old woman. 'And your name, dear?'

'Emma Starr.' She pushed a wayward strand of hair behind her ear, wishing her bag didn't smell. They probably thought it was her.

Mrs Buchanan was apparently too polite to mention it. Instead, she said, 'This is Tom and Harry.'

The flame was leaving Tom's cheeks. 'Sorry for barging in on you like that, Miss.'

'Mrs Woolhouse didn't tell me about you,' said Mrs Buchanan. 'Otherwise I'd never have let the boys go wandering about like that. She said the girls had gone home for the holidays.'

'I got a job in a dress shop instead,' said Emma, 'so I can send money back to my mum.'

Mrs Buchanan looked her up and down and smiled. 'Must be a funny kind of dress shop.'

Emma hitched up her dungarees. 'Oh, I've finished my shift, Miss.' She tugged at her duffel, anxious to get away. The bag fell on its side, spilling the contents. Carrots, bread, apples, slimy sausages. Half a skinned rabbit. An entire chicken.

Emma's hand flew to her mouth. Then she was on her knees, trying to stuff the food back into the bag. Tom knelt down to help.

'Boys, take our bags upstairs,' said Mrs Buchanan. 'Emma and I need to have a little talk.'

Mrs Buchanan escorted Emma to the library and closed the door behind them. 'Did that food come from Coomalong's kitchen?'

'The bread was mouldy, Miss, and I didn't think the carrots and apples would last.'

'And the meat?'

'It's going off. Cook left it in the ice box when she left for the holidays, Miss. She must have forgotten about it.'

'Did you have permission to take food from the kitchen, Emma?'

'Please, Miss, being at this school means the world to me. If you tell, I could lose my scholarship.' She tightened her belt and hitched up her loose trousers. 'The kitchen's closed until next term. The food was just going to waste.'

'I see.' Mrs Buchanan steered Emma to a chair and took a seat opposite. 'I want to help you, dear, but you have to be honest with me. What do you mean to do with all that food? You do realise that rotten meat will make people sick, and mouldy bread too. Is it for your mother?'

'No, Miss. My mum lives in Launceston.'

'Were you going to sell it, perhaps?'

'Take food and then sell it?' Emma was shocked. 'That would be like stealing, Miss.'

Mrs Buchanan smiled. 'Very well. Put the carrots and apples back in the pantry, and I'll say no more about it. But you must throw the meat and bread out.'

Emma had no choice but to return some of the food to the kitchen.

What a waste. She repacked her bag under Mrs Buchanan's watchful eye. 'Can I go now?'

'Yes, Emma. I hope that food was meant for a good cause.'

'Oh yes, Miss. The best cause ever.' Emma escaped through the double doors, hoping to quietly duck out the back way. No such luck. The boys were standing outside the library as if they'd been waiting for her. Tom hung back, a faint flush back in his cheeks. She kept looking at him, while trying not to. He was even more handsome at second glance. So well-defined, all straight lines – straight back, straight nose, straight jaw, straight teeth. Was that a little dimple in his chin?

Harry glanced at Tom then back to her. His face wasn't as square as his brother's, his jaw not so pronounced, but his eyes were sharp and clever. They seemed to be weighing her up. 'Did my grandmother read you the riot act, Emma?' Harry paused for an instant before saying her name, giving it an odd emphasis as if he enjoyed saying it.

'She was very understanding.'

'Good to hear,' said Harry. 'Where are you going ... all dolled up like that?'

There was sufficient humour behind the sarcasm to temper her irritation. 'None of your business ... Harry.' She picked up the smelly duffel.

Tom stepped forward and put his hand beside hers on the handles. 'Let me help.' She should say no, yet his shy smile disarmed her, and she liked how his strong hand brushed against hers. 'I've got it,' he said. Slowly she let go.

Harry shook his head. 'First you barge into her room while she's in her underwear, and now you want to play the gentleman?'

'I'm sure Emma can manage.' Nobody had noticed Mrs Buchanan come out of the library. Tom put the bag down. 'My grandsons and I will be staying here for a while, my dear.'

Emma stifled a small groan. Staying, why? She'd been looking forward to having Coomalong all to herself over the holidays. Who were these people?

'We'll take the west wing,' said Mrs Buchanan, 'and I'll have the caretaker put a lock on your door to ensure your privacy.'

'Thank you, Miss. Goodbye, Miss.'

Emma grabbed the bag and headed for the front door. At least it wasn't so heavy now. She glanced at the clock on the way out. Great, she'd miss her tram.

Emma ran from the tram stop to the Beaumaris Zoo Tea Gardens and paused to catch her breath. Even from here she could hear Bagheera, the black panther, roaring his discontent. Always hungry that one. The rabbit wasn't much, but it was for him.

Since Arthur Reid, the curator, had taken ill, the animals never got enough food. The depression had hit the zoo hard, and without Arthur to fight for funding, Hobart Council had slashed his budget and staff. The main gates were closed in order to save the cost of employing Arthur's daughter, Alison, as a turnstile attendant. Now entry was via the kiosk, with the tea room ladies selling tickets.

Emma entered the kiosk, fished the sixpence from her pocket and offered it to Betty, behind the counter.

'Put that away,' said Betty, looking around to be sure nobody heard. 'It's a crime, them making you pay each time, and at adult prices too. Considering all you do, it's the council should be paying you.'

Emma thanked Betty and slipped the coin back into her pocket. It would buy a loaf of bread for the possums, or a small bag of oats. She picked up her duffel.

'Wait a minute, love.' Betty smiled and handed her an apple. 'For that pretty macaw. It's my favourite.' She waved a handkerchief in front of her face. 'Now get that bag outside before it stinks out my tea shop.'

Emma slipped through the door leading to the zoo, where a few visitors were wandering about the exhibits. Bagheera called again. He'd have to wait his turn. Betty wasn't the only one with a favourite.

Emma passed the lions and bears. She passed the monkey-house, aviaries and water bird pond.

When she reached the devils' pen, she found Alison laying down fresh straw. Emma had never seen her looking so thin and tired. Alison paused her work, leaning on her rake. 'Thank God you're here, Emma. John's quit. Says he hasn't been paid for weeks. I could really use an extra pair of hands.' The male devil loped up to the fence, nose twitching. Alison wiped her dirty hands on her overalls. 'He can smell whatever you have in that bag.'

'Sorry, boy, it's not for you.' Emma moved the bag away from the wire, and entered the enclosure. 'Let me do that.' Alison gave her a grateful smile, and relinquished the rake. 'How's your father?' asked Emma.

'Not good. He couldn't work at all today. The pain wears him down.'

Arthur Reid had lost an eye some years ago defending the aviary birds from a night-time thief. A malignant, inoperable growth now mushroomed from his empty socket. Alison had become the de facto full-time curator, looking after the animals' welfare, the grounds and managing the zoo accounts – all in an unpaid capacity. Bruce Lipscombe, Superintendent of Reserves, didn't believe it was a job for a woman, despite her being the only person suitably qualified.

Alison chatted as Emma finished spreading the clean straw. 'Did you see that story in the paper? No? There's a new push on in parliament to declare thylacines a protected species.'

'That's wonderful.'

'I suppose so. Way too late, if you ask me,' said Alison. 'They interviewed somebody called Frank for the article. Said he used to work here at the zoo. Funny thing is, I've never heard of him.'

Emma laughed. 'What did this Frank have to say?'

'You won't believe it. He said he looked after our Tasmanian tiger, and that she was a male called Benjamin.'

Emma put a hand on her hip. 'Where on earth did that come from?'

'Beats me,' said Alison. 'But the name has stuck. All week I've had people come in wanting to see Benjamin. I didn't know who they meant at first. They wouldn't believe me when I said our tiger was a young female.'

Emma spread the last of the straw and put down the rake. She looked longingly at the pen gate.

'Go on with you,' said Alison. 'Say hello to Karma for me, and let her into her den. When you're ready, meet me at the possums. John didn't fix their cage before he left. It's up to us now.'

The last Tasmanian tiger lived in a wire enclosure, shaded by an elm tree, opposite the deer and kangaroo paddocks at Beaumaris Zoo. It was just down the hill from the Reids' caretaker cottage. Emma found Karma endlessly pacing the fence, as usual. Such a pretty creature. About the size of a collie, but slimmer, with sixteen dark stripes gracing her soft russet fur. Head like a wolf. Tail muscular and tapered like a kangaroo's.

Emma took the chicken from the bag and entered the small enclosure. 'Look what I have.'

Karma stepped around her and kept pacing, a faraway look in her large, brown eyes. It always broke Emma's heart a little to see the young thylacine. The other large carnivores had been born in zoos. Kahn, the Bengal tiger. The lions. Bagheera. They, at least, knew no other life. However, Karma had been captured as an adult only last year. Snared in the wild forests of the remote Florentine Valley. Trussed up and carted by pack horse to Tyenna. From there she'd been caged and railed to Hobart, never to know freedom or another of her kind again.

The animal gently bumped Emma and continued her aimless marching. 'Stop,' said Emma. She reached out to stroke Karma, trailing her hand along a dark stripe, running her fingers through the dense, soft fur; more like possum than dog.

Karma ran to the door of her den and made a small coughing

noise, her way of asking Emma to open it. To ensure the animals remained on display for visitors during the day, they were locked out of their sleeping quarters. What torment this caused the mainly nocturnal thylacine, Emma could only imagine.

'Look, Papa,' said a small boy, pointing through the wire. 'It's Benjamin. Doesn't he look fierce.' As if on cue, Karma hissed and opened her jaws wide. The boy shrank back.

Emma put the chook on the ground.

'Good,' said the father. 'Feeding time.'

Karma sniffed the carcass and wrinkled her nose. Thylacines weren't scavengers, like devils. They were fastidious feeders who preferred to kill afresh each day. It had taken a long time before hunger convinced Karma to eat the dead rabbits and chickens that were standard zoo fare. This smelly, plucked chook was a poorer offering than most, but budget cuts had reduced her ration and Karma was ravenous. She seized it in her powerful jaws.

A gasp came from the watching family. 'Oh, he gives me the shivers, he does,' said the mother. 'Aren't you scared to be in there, love? I hear them tigers are vicious brutes.'

Emma ignored her. Instead she opened the door to the den, and Karma vanished inside to eat her meal in peace.

'Hey,' complained the father. 'We were watching him.'

'Sorry.' Emma slipped out the gate with her bag. 'I have to go.'

She hurried off to give Bagheera his half rabbit, the lions their sausages and the macaw his apple. She divided the bread between the water birds and cleaned out their pond. Then she'd help Alison fix the possum pen until it was time for the last tram to Sandy Bay. A lot to do, after her busy day at *À La Mode* Fashions, but she didn't mind the extra work. Emma loved being at the zoo. She'd grown up on a dairy farm outside Launceston, surrounded by animals. When Dad died, the family had moved into town, leaving their dogs, cats, cows and ponies behind. She'd missed them terribly, having always felt more at ease with animals than people.

If she didn't have to work at the dress shop next morning, she'd happily crawl into Karma's den and spend the night with the lonely tiger. Emma hated the idea of going home to Coomalong with that nosy Mrs Buchanan staying there. And those boys. A picture of Tom's square face came into her mind. Wide-set brown eyes, thick blonde hair and that little dimple in his chin. He'd seen her in her underwear. A small flush came over her. Maybe going home tonight wouldn't be so bad after all.

Tom opened his suitcase and began putting away his clothes. The spacious bedroom, with its wide casement windows overlooking the garden, was far grander than the one next door. When he chose it he'd expected an argument, but Harry took the smaller room without a murmur. It wasn't like him to defer like that. It made Tom suspicious.

On opening a drawer for his socks, he found the previous occupant had left something behind; a woman's slip, cream silk with satin ribbon shoulder straps. He ran the smooth fabric through his fingers. Whose was it? Emma's? The charming image of her standing in nothing but her petticoat was burned into his brain. He had little experience with the opposite sex, having gone straight from a boys' boarding school to the wilds of Binburra, but recently he'd become fascinated by girls in a way he didn't quite understand.

Back home, people viewed the eccentric, reclusive Isabelle Buchanan and her grandsons with a mixture of curiosity and apprehension. Although she lived a simple life, it was rumoured the Colonel had left Nana a fortune when he died. It was also rumoured that she was a witch, a godless woman who made healing potions from native herbs and mushrooms. A woman who talked to animals, and kept devils as pets. A woman who'd buried the Colonel somewhere out in the wilderness, in unhallowed ground, with neither priest nor prayer to help him on his final journey.

This horrified the god-fearing, church-going people of Hills End. The lure of two handsome young heirs wasn't enough. Local girls were encouraged to steer clear of them, although farmers' wives secretly came to Binburra with sick dogs or lambs, and children brought orphaned and injured wildlife. Nana was a gifted healer.

However, few visitors ever stayed for long, and none of them were like Emma. The prospect of living in the same house as a real life girl was tantalising, especially such a pretty one. When he closed his eyes she appeared before him; glossy auburn curls, the smooth curve of her forehead, the heart-shaped face and full lips. How would it feel to kiss her?

Tom finished unpacking and went downstairs to the kitchen. He was starving and it was way past lunchtime. Apart from a few wizened apples, there wasn't much to eat. Emma had probably cleared out the pantry. Whatever did she mean to do with all that food?

He tossed an apple in the air and caught it. Time to find Nana, go shopping and stock up that kitchen.

They'd been at Coomalong a week now. Tom, who loved the peace and quiet of the mountains, found Hobart bewildering. Long-ago memories of life there, life before Binburra, were filtered by the rosy lens of childhood: picnics on Mt Wellington, hot cocoa on cold winter nights, golden afternoons spent with Mama in the garden. Home had been a haven from hated boarding school; a place of security and calm. But this time round Hobart wasn't like that at all. It was filled with movement and noise and strange smells. Shops and factories everywhere. So many cars on the roads and people on the streets. Where was everybody going in such a hurry?

His brother, on the other hand, was in his element. Back at Binburra, Tom was the one who knew the country best, the one who excelled at bushcraft and was at home in the vast mountain wilderness. But here in Hobart, the tables were turned. Harry was made for city life. He was at home here, finding his way around and getting to know people; the one who looked sharp and grown-up in new clothes, two-toned Oxford shoes and a black fedora. He wore brilliantine in his hair and sneaked out at night. He'd had a call this morning, from a girl too. When Tom answered the telephone a voice had purred, 'Is that you, Harry? It's Celeste. I had ever so nice a time yesterday.'

Harry disappeared each morning to the Battery Point shipyards, a half hour walk away. Twice he'd *borrowed* Miriam to get there, causing Nana to hide the car keys.

'What if you get caught?' Tom had said that morning. 'You're not even seventeen, you don't have a licence.'

'Don't I?' Harry extracted an official-looking piece of paper from his pocket titled *License For Driver Of Motor Vehicle* in the name of Henry Edward Abbott, aged 21. 'It gets me into the Sunset Jazz Club, too.'

'Twenty-one?' Tom shook his head, impressed in spite of himself. 'How'd you manage that?'

Harry tapped his nose. 'It's not what you know, little brother. It's who you know.'

Little brother. How Tom hated the smug way his brother said that; older by five minutes, was all.

'Now, if I'm right,' said Harry, 'and Nana has hidden the keys in her blue hat box, I'll be off.' He punched Tom playfully on the arm. 'Don't wait up, little brother.' Harry bounded upstairs briefly, returned and slipped out the back door. A minute later Miriam back-fired like a rifle shot, and the sound of her motor faded into the distance.

Nana, who didn't feel well again, was lying down in the parlour and listening to the morning news on the wireless. A little hard of hearing these days, she had it turned up loud, and probably wouldn't hear the car leave. Tom wasn't about to tell her. The last thing he wanted was to be stuck there all day while Nana complained about his brother.

He went to the morning room window, pulled aside the lace

curtain and looked longingly down the empty road. He missed the way things used to be, the time when Harry would have invited him along, and he would have been glad to go. They'd have gotten into a few scrapes, had a few laughs. Not any more. The distance between them yawned wider every day.

Tom dropped the curtain and wandered around the room, at a loss – an unfamiliar feeling. At Binburra there was always so much to do, and never enough hours in the day. Horses and forests and wide mountains right on his doorstep. But here? Some mornings he could hardly see the sky through low-hanging wood smoke. Thank goodness for Mount Wellington. The imposing timbered peak, dusted with snow, towered four thousand feet above the town. A reminder that even here, in the heart of Hobart, the wild was never far away.

If he knew his way around Hobart like Harry did, he'd go to the aerodrome for the day. He and Nana had gone there last week, spending a glorious few hours spotting planes. He'd seen two Gipsy Moths and an assortment of sleek monoplanes. The beautiful DH89 Dragon, a short-haul biplane made by the legendary de Havilland company. A Lockheed Altair, the same model as the *Lady Southern Cross* in which Charles Kingsford Smith had flown from Australia to America only last year – the very first eastward crossing of the Pacific Ocean by air.

Tom took photographs and recorded each aircraft carefully in his notebook. No plane impressed him more than *Miss Hobart*, a twelve-seater that had commenced a daily mail and passenger service between Hobart and Melbourne. It held the record for flying Bass Strait in under two hours. He imagined piloting the airliner, mastering its four powerful engines, speeding above the clouds.

Unfortunately, the aerodrome was miles away on the other side of the Derwent River, and he wasn't sure yet how to navigate the trams, buses and ferries required to get there. A wave of emptiness washed over him. Who'd have thought he could be so lonely in a city full of people? He didn't want to stay in Hobart. He didn't want to start school at Campbell College. He could see himself now – the odd one out in a room full of strangers. Putting up with his brother, who'd either be charming everybody or raising hell. Either way, Harry would be the centre of attention.

Tom went to the kitchen and helped himself to bread and cheese for breakfast. The cook only came in the afternoon. He missed old Mrs Mills. She might be grumpy and cuff him about the ears sometimes, but she cooked great bacon and eggs. He'd even welcome one of their strange conversations about the coming Martian invasion. She seemed to think H.G. Wells' *War Of The Worlds* had been an accurate prediction of the future.

The only bright spot on the horizon was Emma. He checked the longcase clock in the corner. It would be hours before she'd be home from work. Spending time with her was high on his wish list, but she always disappeared after lunch, dressed in those old clothes. Emma was friendly enough in a distant kind of way - and seemed to have forgiven him for bursting into her bedroom – but she was shy, and he was shy. It didn't make for easy communication.

His confident brother fared better, gently teasing Emma about her clothes and pack-rat habits in the kitchen, provoking conversations. Emma didn't exactly open up, but Harry could generally make her smile. Tom hadn't even summoned the courage to talk to her. Today would be different.

Tom cut himself another hunk of bread and headed to the library – the very best thing about Coomalong. He plucked a novel from the shelf, drawn by the cover and title, hoping *The Maltese Falcon* really was about birds.

The book wasn't about birds after all, but it was still a rip-roaring story. Tom cast himself in the role of Sam Spade; smart and unflinching, solver of riddles, able to take care of himself in any situation. The sort of man that beautiful women came to for help.

So engrossed was he in his reading that he missed Emma coming home. By the time he heard her in the kitchen and went to investigate, she'd already changed out of her work clothes. He watched her poking about in the cupboards, collecting odds and ends of food like always. He tried to imagine her as the glamorous Miss Wonderly from his novel. Both had red hair, long legs and eyes of emerald green, but there the resemblance ended.

In the last scene he'd read, Miss Wonderly wore a clinging red gown, silk stockings and scarlet lipstick that emphasised her pale, powdered complexion. By contrast, Emma wore a man's shirt way too big for her and baggy trousers. She wasn't a woman. She was a lanky, freckled girl with a shiny face and sunburnt nose.

Emma wrapped a piece of bacon in brown paper and shot him a worried look. 'You won't tell your grandmother, will you?'

Tom opened the refrigerator and added another piece of bacon and two cooked sausages to her parcel. 'If she asks, I'll say I ate them.' He handed over half a loaf of bread. 'Eggs? They any use to you?'

She nodded, white teeth sparkling in the crescent of her shy smile.

He bundled up four eggs in brown paper. 'Lemons? No, how about dried apricots?'

Emma nodded, and he wrapped up two handfuls. She reached for them.

'Not so fast,' he said, channelling Sam Spade. 'You can have the food if I can come with you.'

'Come with me?' Emma stared at him. 'Why would you want to do that?'

'I don't know.' Tom traced a knot in the timber of the table with his finger. 'Maybe I'm curious. Maybe I'm bored.' He looked up, meeting her direct gaze. 'Maybe I like you.'

Emma's cheeks flushed pink, but she did not look away. He could see her turning the idea over. Delightful, the way her nose crinkled when she was thinking.

It seemed to take forever, but at last her eyes smiled. 'You really want to come?'

'I really want to come.'

Emma opened her smelly old duffel bag and packed the food inside. 'Then what are we waiting for?'

'Why didn't you tell me?' said Tom, as he and Emma fed bread and apricots to three excited Macaques.

'These are hard times.' Emma held the hand of the smallest monkey through the wire. It kissed her fingers. 'Some people think food is wasted on animals when so many people are going hungry.'

'Not me.' Tom buttoned up his coat as it started to rain. 'Not Nana. She's the biggest animal lover in the world. You should see the menagerie we have at home.'

Emma's eyes grew round. 'What sort of animals?'

'All sorts. People bring us sick puppies and kittens and lambs. Native wildlife too: wallabies, wombats, magpies. We released three orphan devils just before we came to Hobart. I gave Nana a baby quoll for her birthday. It's all grown up now, and keeps the stable free of rats, but it still sleeps in her bedroom. She left the window open when we left so it can get in.'

Emma's mouth curled into a smile. 'I love quolls. We had them on the farm. They used to eat our chickens. Dad put poison down but I always got rid of the baits.'

'You and my grandmother have a lot in common,' said Tom. 'Come on, what else can you show me?'

Tom marvelled over an assortment of exotic creatures, including lions, a Bengal tiger and a beautiful black panther. Fascinated as he was, he was also saddened. Cages were clean, but bare, and the animals were obviously hungry. The panther lapped up four eggs in a bowl within seconds, and looked hopefully around for more.

'When does he get his dinner?' said Tom, wishing he had something more to offer.

Emma scratched the panther behind the ears, and a rumbling purr started in his throat. 'Bagheera only gets fed every second day. It's all the zoo can afford.'

The lions roared in vain as they passed by. Ducks and swans squabbled over crusts of bread. An eagle huddled on a narrow perch near the top of its cage, as close to the sky as it could reach, feathers fluffed against the cold wind.

They came to a pair of devils who lay curled together at the back of their pen, which was exposed to the weather. Squat black creatures, the size of small dogs, with large heads and muscular builds.

'Poor things,' said Tom. 'Locked out like that. Let's open the door to their den.'

'We can't.' Emma checked her watch. 'Not until the zoo closes. People want to see them. Thank goodness it's stopped raining.' She called to the dozing devils who took their time waking up. The bigger one stretched, shook his wet fur and sniffed the air. Emma called again, and pulled two dead rats from her bag followed by a squashed cat. It looked suspiciously like the one Harry had run over two days ago in the lane behind Coomalong.

Emma dropped the cat and a rat through the door. The devils pounced on them with a sudden ferocity, scrapping fiercely over the meagre meal. The smaller animal was getting the worst of the fight.

'Daisy,' called Emma. 'Over here.' She poked the last rat through the wire netting a little further down the fence. Daisy raced over, snatched it and carried it away.

'Give them the bacon,' said Tom.

'No, the bacon is for someone else.'

They came to the next pen, and Tom stopped short. His scalp prickled at the sight of the animal within – a native tiger. The strangest feeling came over him; a mixture of joy and sorrow. The tiger ignored them, eyes fixed on some point in the distance, and continued its restless pacing.

Tom had seen photos and drawings of native tigers, more correctly known as thylacines, but no two-dimensional image could have prepared him for the sight of this living animal.

'Meet Karma,' whispered Emma. She slipped inside the pen. The tiger paused to lick her hand, then resumed its lonely march.

There was something other-worldly about Karma, so much like a wolf yet so unlike one at the same time. These large marsupial carnivores, once common enough to be killed as pests, were now rare, almost mythical, creatures. Tom had lived half his life in a region once famed for its tigers, and the idea of them had quickly captured his imagination. His great-grandfather, the renowned naturalist Daniel Campbell, had kept live specimens in the past, and written natural history essays about their lives. Tom had read them all, as well as anything else he could find on the subject.

He often browsed John Gould's classic 1863 tome, *The Mammals Of Australia*, mesmerised by the prints of two thylacines; their dark, slanted eyes and keen expressions. Gould's dire prediction about the native tigers' future was burned into his brain.

When the comparatively small island of Tasmania becomes more densely populated, and its primitive forests are intersected with roads from the eastern to the western coast, the numbers of this singular animal will speedily diminish, extermination will have full sway, and it will then, like the Wolf in England and Scotland, be recorded as an animal of the past...

Tom fervently hoped Gould was wrong. He'd spent weeks searching Binburra's mountains, but never found any sign of them. Not a flash of striped hide in the bracken. Not a cosy den lined with soft ferns. Not even tracks. Wild dogs, yes, but not tigers. He'd been fooled in the beginning. 'I found tiger prints,' Tom had announced proudly to his grandmother when he was twelve.

For an exciting moment Nana's eyes lit up. 'Where?'

'Near the road on the other side of our neighbours' fence. I think they were following a flock of sheep.'

Nana's face fell. 'Not tigers, I'm afraid. Dogs.'

'How do you know?'

She led him to the library and took a box from the shelf. 'These are my father's – your great-grandfather's – field notes. I helped him write them up.' It took her a while to find the right page – comparative sketches of thylacine and dog prints. 'Drawn from life,' she said. 'From when we kept a trio of tigers right here at Binburra. I used to play with them.'

Tom was captivated, full of questions. It took some time before she could bring him back to the drawings.

'Take a good look, darling. Which ones look most like the tracks you saw?'

He inspected the sketches and felt a surge of disappointment. Nana was right. The prints he'd seen were missing the distinctive, heel-to-toe indents of tiger tracks.

'I'm sorry, Tom. Tigers, if there are any left, would never come down to the lowlands; they'd never come so close to human habitation.'

This comment had prompted him to explore ever higher into Binburra's mountains, right up to where forest met sky, and trees grew too close together for horse and rider to pass. Years of searching, and never a trace. Yet here in the middle of Hobart, exposed to the elements in this humble pen, where people walked past with half a glance – here was a living example of Tasmania's rarest creature. Such a sad and unlikely miracle.

'Give me the bacon,' said Emma, waving him back. 'No, don't come in.' The tiger fixed Tom with dark eyes, and its jaws yawned impossibly wide. 'That's a warning. Pass it through the gate. Karma doesn't like strangers. She went a scientist last year when he was taking photographs … bit him on the bottom.'

Tom grinned, and handed her the meat. Two people stopped to watch, then two more. Then a family. Karma sniffed the offering, wrinkled her nose, then gently took it from Emma's hand and went to stand by the door of her den.

'She wants me to let her in.' Emma frowned and checked her watch. 'But it's too early.'

Tom stared at Karma in dismay, looking so lost and out of place in her concrete cage. He wanted to rescue her, steal her away to the wild ranges where she belonged.

'That dog looks mean,' said a small girl as Karma gave up all hopes of privacy and lay down in the farthest corner to eat. 'Look how sharp his teeth are.'

'Not a dog, sweety,' said the mother. 'His name is Benjamin Tiger.'

Tom shot Emma a questioning look.

She shrugged. 'It's a long story.'

. . .

Tom spent the rest of the afternoon cleaning pens, preparing meals and feeding animals. The poor quality of the animals' meals surprised him. Half the fruit and vegetables on offer were mouldy. The meat wasn't much better, all bone and fat and gristle, and not enough of it. No wonder Emma took food to supplement their diets.

He looked at her with a newfound admiration. Emma was an amazing, compassionate girl with an independent spirit. Much like Nana might have been as a young woman. Beautiful too, despite her dungarees and work shirt; maybe because of them. So much herself.

Emma stopped chopping carrots and wiped her forehead with the back of her hand. She looked done in.

'Those men back there, weeding the garden. They must work here. Can't they help you?' said Tom.

Emma snorted. 'They're sussos, worse than useless. Here under sufferance, working for welfare. That lot couldn't care less about the animals. All they do is smoke, lean on their rakes and try to chat me up. Sometimes there seem to be more sussos around here than animals.'

'Who's in charge?' he asked as they tossed Bagheera a bony chicken carcass, already stripped of meat.

'Alison Reid and her father.' She pointed to a cottage outside the fence on the edge of the zoo. 'They live over there. Arthur's quite ill. Alison has taken the day off to give her mother a break from caring for him.'

Emma turned back towards Tom, just as he took a step forward. Only inches apart now. She smelled earthy and sweet, looked so lovely, so natural. Softly freckled cheeks. Windblown hair caressing her neck. The soft swell of breasts beneath her shirt. The temptation was too great. He pulled her to him and kissed her.

Tom had often wondered what a kiss might feel like, but his imagination hadn't even come close. This kiss was a revelation. How could he have possibly imagined its heat, and power? He'd closed his eyes without realising, lost in a dizzy explosion of desire. And she felt it too. He knew by their twin racing hearts, the way she kissed him back, the giddy pleasure in her bright green eyes when he finally let her go. A soft, musical sigh escaped her lips.

'You don't have to do this alone anymore, Em.' Tom brushed her hair behind her ear. 'You can count on me to help from now on – my grandmother too.'

Her smile slipped and she gave him a strange look. 'Until you go back to Hills End.'

'Well, yes.'

His elation leaked away as Emma checked her watch, and wouldn't meet his gaze. 'Come on,' she said. 'Time to let the animals into their night pens before the zoo closes.'

'What a wonderful thing for Emma to do. She should have told me,' said Nana, when Tom got home. 'I would have happily donated food for the zoo. Let me talk to her.'

Tom watched Nana climb the staircase to Emma's room. Half way up she paused and held a hand to her heart. After a few moments she continued, but without her usual brisk energy.

He couldn't stop thinking about what Emma had said. *Until you go back to Hills End.* He'd been looking forward to that day. Not any more. Not now that he was in love.

The next few days were the happiest of Tom's life. Afternoons with Emma at the zoo. Coming home together. Sharing hopes and dreams as they held hands on the tram. Snatching time alone after dinner. When it got late, and they finally had to drag themselves away from each other, Tom lay sleepless in his bed for hours, mind brimming with Emma.

It was Friday morning and Tom had spent a restless night punctuated by dreams of Binburra that left him homesick. He rose at sunrise, grabbed some bread and cheese and slipped out the back gate. A windy late-spring day beckoned. He strolled through the chilly streets to the harbour and along the foreshore of Sullivan's Cove. Smelling the salty sea-spray. Watching the tide come in. Hearing the wild cry of gulls from beyond the breakwater. Hobart's civilised façade ended at the ocean's edge – an oddly comforting thought.

Tom walked past the yacht club. Past grand old houses along the esplanade. Past cottages of seafarers and shipbuilders. Past rows of sandstone warehouses at Salamanca Place and Constitution Dock. All the way to the shipyards of Battery Point.

The wharf was abuzz, despite the early hour. Sail-makers and coopers went about their trades. The air throbbed with the ring of blacksmiths' hammers, the growl of red-glowing rivet guns and the clash of chisels and welders. Cranes angled crazily against the pale sky. Dozens of boats, in various stages of construction and maintenance, lined the waterfront. Some mere skeletons. Some almost complete, shiny with fresh paint and the promise of adventure. Others rocked to and fro on their moorings, dancing to the rhythm of the waves. The morning harbour was an exciting place. No wonder Harry loved it here.

Tom wandered past the slips and dry docks of various shipbuilders until he came to the gates of Abbott & Son – the shipyard his father had lost in the stock market crash. It still bore their family name, a name that had stood for quality Tasmanian boat building for more than a century.

'One day, I'll buy the yard back,' Harry had told him. 'I'll make it bigger and better than ever.' Tom didn't doubt it. When his brother set his mind to something, he rarely failed.

Tom sat on a bollard to eat his bread and cheese, watching the aerial acrobatics of shearwaters and terns soaring over the harbour. A flotilla of pelicans sailed by. And there, right above him, a wandering albatross. It caught a high crosswind and wheeled away. Tom watched the giant seabird until it became a mere speck on the horizon, then disappeared altogether. The old yearning gripped him. Boats were fun, but nothing could beat the joy of flight.

Was his brother here somewhere? Maybe he was still with Celeste. Tom had seen her last night, hanging around on the street outside the house, waiting for Harry. A different creature altogether from his shy, serious Emma. Buxom with a blonde bob, glamourous in the glow of a streetlight. Wearing rouge, and lipstick, and a skirt above her knee. Looking at least eighteen. How the hell did Harry do it? Tom grinned and decided to stick around for a while, to see if he showed up. Maybe he'd pluck up the courage to ask him.

Time slipped away. Tom was enjoying the hustle and bustle of the wharves. Men measuring sails. The smell of turpentine and tar. Ship chandlers making deliveries. Tallow and twine. Barrels of oil. Cages of ducks and chickens. The sun sailed high in the sky before Tom gave up waiting for Harry and headed back along the foreshore, lost once more in thoughts of Emma. That first, delicious kiss and all those that had followed. His brother could keep Celeste and others like her. Emma was the girl for Tom, and he wanted to be home when she got back from work.

Twenty minutes later, Tom slipped in the back gate to find Nana standing out on the porch, watching for him. 'I'm glad you're back. Come to the parlour. We need to talk.'

'Go home? Why?' said Tom. 'I thought we were staying in Hobart until Christmas.'

'I've been doing a great deal of thinking,' said Nana. 'You know my health hasn't been the best lately, and there's something important I want to show you, back at Binburra.'

He wasn't sure if the tremor in her voice was from illness or emotion.

'Somewhere special I need to take you, before I get too old. And anyway, I thought you couldn't wait to get back?'

Tom wasn't sure what to say. Last night he'd dreamed of Binburra. Its upland button-grass clearings and stands of beech. Its pure, strong mornings, and the special clarity of light that meant you could see forever. The eagle from Hobart Zoo was there with him; free from its dingy cage, feathers shining, flying high towards the sun. And Karma, lounging on a fallen King Billy pine tree, gracing the elemental landscape, back where she belonged. He'd woken to a powerful longing for home, but what about Emma? He loved her. He wouldn't leave her. Not for Nana. Not for anyone.

Nana saw through his confusion, as she always did. 'Emma received a telegram this morning. Bad news, I'm afraid. Her mother has had a major stroke.' She put a hand on his shoulder. 'Emma left for Launceston an hour ago. She asked me to say goodbye.'

Tom couldn't get his head around the news. 'What about her scholarship?'

'The College will keep it open as long as they can. Emma's one of their most talented students, but apparently there's nobody else to care for her mother. Mrs Starr requires 'round the clock nursing. Life can be so unfair.'

This was more than unfair. Tom could hear Emma's voice in his head, full of determination and hope for the future. 'I'm not going to be a shop girl forever. I'm going to be a doctor and find a cure for Mum's arthritis. It's in her fingers and makes it hard for her to sew. Doctors earn lots of money, so she won't even have to sew if she doesn't want to. She can be a lady of leisure.'

'Sorry, Tom. I gather you've grown rather fond of her.'

Tom did not feel like discussing his feelings for Emma with his grandmother. 'Harry and I were supposed to start school here. What about our education?'

Nana smiled. 'That's the first time I've known you to be worried about your education.'

Tom couldn't see the funny side.

'I'll engage a tutor,' she said.

'After what happened to the last one?'

'I'm sure we'll be able to keep a suitable teacher, without Harry to cause trouble.'

'Without Harry?' Nana was making less and less sense.

'Hasn't he told you? Your brother won't be coming home with us. He's found himself a position at one of the shipyards.'

Oh. Tom bit his lip so hard it hurt. So that's why Harry had let him have the best bedroom. He hadn't planned on staying long. It came as a wrench to think his twin hadn't wanted to share his plans. 'Has he landed a job with Abbott & Son?'

'Sadly no, although of course that was his preference. Harry will work at the next yard – Purton & Featherby. An apprentice ship-wright with accommodation at the wharf. Harry can follow his passion and forge a career at the same time. Doing a man's job, a hard day's work, knowing the pride of earning a wage. Perhaps it will make him grow up, although I don't know what Bertha will say about him taking up a trade and not finishing school.' Nana sighed and gave Tom a heartfelt hug. 'It's a shock, I know, but just between us, Harry's such a tearaway. Sometimes he's too much for me.'

For me too, thought Tom, recalling that terrifying night at the waterfall. The strange sensation of falling through space. A sudden shiver passed through him, the kind Nana said was caused by someone walking over your future grave. He cast the feeling aside, missing Harry already, despite everything. He could see past his brother's faults, knew the pain that lived at the core of him. And they'd always been together. Always.

'What about you, Tom? What do you want to do? You don't have to go on to university, in spite of what Grandma Bertha says.' Nana patted his hand. 'We could ask around at the aero club, find you an engineering apprenticeship or something similar for next year?'

His heart leaped at the possibility. Spending his days surrounded by planes. Understanding them from the inside out. Learning to fly.

'What about you, Nana? You'd be all alone again.'

'You're a good boy, Tom. A fine boy. I'd hate to lose you, but I'd be a selfish old woman to stand in your way.' A series of dry, hacking coughs stole her breath.

Tom jumped to his feet. 'Stay there. I'll make you some of that special tea.' Nana nodded, still unable to speak.

Tom filled the kettle in the kitchen and put it on the gas range. He found the ginger jar, sliced up a few pieces and dropped them into Nana's favourite blue teapot. All in slow motion. He needed time to think. His initial enthusiasm for staying in Hobart was slipping away. So much had changed in the space of one morning. It would be lonely here with Emma gone and Harry caught up in a new life.

And he would miss Nana. She wasn't well. The numerous doctor appointments hadn't seemed to help. If anything, her cough was worse than ever. A surge of love claimed him. His grandmother had been there for him at the darkest point in his life; been there when everyone else turned away. Well, now she needed him, and he wasn't about to let her down.

The whistling kettle jolted him from his thoughts. He poured boiling water into the pot, added a dipper of honey, took the tray into the parlour and poured Nana a cuppa.

She indicated the teapot. 'Aren't you having one?'

He made a face. 'There's not enough money in Hobart for me to drink ginger tea.'

She laughed and took a sip. 'Ah, that's good.'

'What about the zoo?' said Tom. 'Those animals will be in trouble without Emma.'

'I've already been to see Arthur Reid, the curator. A wonderful man. Such a shame about his eye. Do you know Hobart Council refuses to help with his medical fees, even though he was injured in the course of duty?' She pursed her lips in disapproval. 'I've arranged for a sum of money to be deposited into the zoo's account on a monthly basis. It will allow him to feed the animals properly, and employ an experienced person to assist his daughter, Alison.'

'Does Emma know?'

'I told her before she left. It seemed to be a great comfort to her.' Nana fixed warm, knowing eyes on him. 'She asked me to say goodbye. Emma seems very fond of you, too.' She took a small envelope from her pocket and handed it over. He thought about opening it later, in private, but couldn't wait.

My darling Tom. Forgive me for leaving in such haste. I will never forget you. Love Emma.'

Tom fought back tears.

Nana's breath grew more laboured. Her face turned pale and she started to cough. After a few more sips of tea the coughing subsided. Tom studied his grandmother's face. In her youth she'd been a great beauty, pursued by two of Tasmania's wealthiest men. More than a hint of that beauty remained in her classic features, her regal bearing, her full, wavy hair that still retained some of its chestnut colour. In her emerald eyes.

Mama had been the only person in his family to defend Nana's decision to leave her husband. 'Who knows what is in another's heart?' she said one day, after Grandma Bertha embarked on a bitter tirade against his grandmother. 'Love is mysterious and strange, Tom. It lies where it falls, and does not always obey the rules we lay down for it.'

Tom poured Nana more tea.

'Thank you dear. You always know exactly how to make me feel better.'

Her heartfelt words sealed his decision. 'I don't want to stay in Hobart.' He leaned over and kissed her cheek. 'Let's go home.'

CHAPTER 11

The sky was a melancholy blanket of grey, the day unseasonably cold for late spring. A rag-tag pack of dogs chased after the taxi as it turned the corner into Emma's street, spraying a fan of mud over a pair of unfortunate pedestrians.

Emma's stomach churned with mixed emotions. Looking forward to seeing Mum, fearful about what she would find. 'There it is,' she said. 'Number thirty-five.'

They pulled up beside the drooping wire fence of her family home. After the grandeur of Coomalong, the rundown house was a depressing sight. The front gate hung from one hinge. A few shreds of white paint still clung to the weatherboards. Weeds sprouted from rusty gutters that sagged from the corrugated iron roof. Straggly geraniums bordered an overgrown square of buffalo grass. The waratah she loved was leafless and brown, its stark skeleton as dead as her dreams.

Emma had hoped to arrive home unnoticed, but no such luck. The neighbourhood was out in force today. Kids riding dilapidated bikes up and down the slushy street. Mr Wren mending a letter box. The Harper clan drinking beer and smoking out on their porch, although it wasn't even twelve o'clock.

Everybody stopped what they were doing as Emma climbed from the car. The driver fetched her suitcase from the boot, then tipped his cap in farewell.

Old Mrs Phipps was waiting at the gate next door, almost like she knew Emma was coming. 'Here she is, hoity toity as you like,' she announced in a loud voice. 'Thinks she's too good to come home and look after her poor sick mother.'

Emma ignored her and hurried through the gate. How she hated that woman. Ever since they'd moved from the farm to Sparrow Lane, she'd made life a misery. If Emma read a book in the garden, Mrs Phipps would lean over the fence and say 'Look at her, miss la-de-da. Lazy so-and-so.' If Emma planted flower bulbs, Mrs Phipps would snort and say, 'Stupid girl. Your poor ma can't eat daffodils. You should be growing potatoes.' When Emma dug a potato patch, Mrs Phipps shook her head and scoffed, 'Everyone knows you can't grow potatoes in this soil.'

Emma couldn't think of anything she'd said or done to invite such hostility. Although Mrs Phipps was the worst offender, others also seemed to resent her. The general consensus of opinion was that she had tickets on herself.

'Take no notice,' her mother would say. 'They're a miserable bunch around here and misery loves company. When they see a bright girl like you, full of potential? Well, folks get jealous. They want to drag you down to their level.'

'Nobody seems to have a problem with Tim and Jacky.'

'They're boys,' Mum had said simply. 'Boys are allowed to aim above their station.'

Emma had burned with the unfairness of it. *I'll show them just how far I can go.* She'd studied hard, constantly topping her class.

'No point keeping that one at school,' Mrs Phipps told Mum. 'With your poor husband in the grave, you need to send her out to work. She'll only go and get married, and all that learning will be wasted.'

'Maybe she will, and maybe she won't,' said Mum. 'But whatever happens, I don't believe education is ever wasted. It broke my heart when I had to leave school to find a job. I won't disappoint my daughter that way.'

When Emma won a scholarship to Campbell College, Mum urged her on. Saying how proud Dad would have been. Never once questioning her daughter's ambition to be a doctor. Never once doubting her. Mum was her rock, her anchor, her safe place to fall.

Emma pushed through the rickety gate, mouth dry as sawdust. Licking her lips didn't help. No spit would come. Her steps slowed as she neared the front door. Maybe if she wished hard enough, maybe she could make it so nothing had changed. Her mother would be baking scones in the kitchen. Or doing the mending she took in to make a living since Dad died. Maybe Mum would be sitting by the window watching for Emma to come, a *Women's Weekly* on her knee and a smile on her face.

'What are you waiting for, you silly girl?' called Mrs Phipps.

Emma turned to see a host of curious eyes and a wave of panic claimed her. She rushed onto the porch and tried the door. Unlocked, as usual. Her mother always said they had nothing worth stealing.

'Mum?' The door opened into the familiar musty hallway, its fading floral wallpaper peeling in the corners. 'Tim? Jacky?'

Emma's brother Jack came in from the kitchen – an athletic, red-haired young man whose square, freckled face lit up at the sight of her. 'Good to see you, little sis.' He enfolded her in a long bear hug.

'How's Mum?' she asked when Jack finally let her go. His happiness seeped away. He looked as grim as she'd ever seen him. It frightened her.

'It's bad, Em. Real bad. She can't walk, can't talk, can't feed herself. You even need to remind her to swallow.'

'What does the doctor say?' A sudden shame hit her. The car had dropped her off ten minutes ago. Ten whole minutes, and she still hadn't seen Mum. Still hadn't summoned up the courage. 'Where is she?'

Jack nodded towards the lounge room.

Her mother lay on a bed by the window. Someone had moved the couch out to make room. Food scraps clung to her chin, and something dark stained her blouse. Emma's nose wrinkled at the smell. The odour of urine vied with that of disinfectant, and something else, something fetid and dank.

'Mum?' Emma reached for her hand, a hand she knew as well as her own. It remained stiff and unyielding. Cold too. The whole room was cold. 'Mum?' Louder this time.

Her mother moved her head a fraction and called out; a guttural, animal sound. Emma stared, too shocked to react. Then she felt something, a light pressure on her fingers.

'Oh, Mum.' She choked back a sob. 'We'll get you well again. Whatever it takes, I promise.'

Jack backed out of the room.

'Where are you going?' said Emma.

'I promised Bluey we'd catch up this arvo.' He reversed more quickly.

'Hang on, Jacky.' Emma released her mother's hand and hurried after him.'You can't leave me alone with Mum.'

'You'll be right.' He pulled on his coat. 'Mrs Shaw'll be here at five to show you the ropes, how to help her with the toilet and that.' He put on his hat.

'I just got home, haven't even unpacked my bag and you want to throw me in the deep end?'

'Jesus, sis, I've been doing this by myself for three days straight. Sleeping in the chair beside her. Feeding her. Even helping her … you know, when Mrs Shaw got drunk and didn't show. Don't know who was more embarrassed; me or Mum.'

'What about Tim?'

'You know Timmy, dodges anything hard. He did give me some money to pay for Mrs Shaw, though. Tim and his wife have only been 'round here once. He got so worked up when he saw Mum, so upset, you'd think he was the one stuck in that bed for life.'

'Is that what the doctor said? That Mum won't get better?'

'He told me to pray.' Jack gave the faintest shrug, as if sorrow weighed down his shoulders. He took off his hat and wrung it in his hands. 'There ain't no treatment.'

No treatment. The awful words echoed around Emma's head. She felt as paralysed as her mother. It wasn't possible; there must be something she could do to help. She'd promised Mum.

Jack seemed close to tears now. He suddenly looked much younger than his eighteen years, much younger than she felt. 'Go on,' she said, taking pity. 'Go see Bluey. I'll be all right.'

'Thanks, sis.' He gave her a ghost of a smile. 'I'll be back by six. Don't worry about tea. I'll get fish and chips to celebrate you being home. I bet Mum could even eat them without making a mess.'

He wrapped Emma in another one of his great hugs, and escaped through the door before she could change her mind.

Emma went back into the lounge room, pulled up a chair beside her mother and started talking. Mum always loved to hear about her life in Hobart. She told her about Campbell College, and her classmates and the dress shop. About Alison and the zoo and the animals. She took hold of her hand, hoping to feel that squeeze again, however slight. Hoping for some sign her mother could hear her. Nothing.

Emma took a deep breath. 'There's a boy I like, Mum – Tom. He has a twin brother. They come from a very good family.'

Surely this news would get her attention. Mum always wanted to know if she'd met anybody nice. 'Make sure he's rich, sweetheart,' she would say. 'I loved your father, of course I did, but it was a hard life on the farm. Miles from anywhere, living off the land. I want more for my girl.'

Emma had roundly resented this advice. She'd loved their simple life back on the farm, as much as she hated moving to the filthy backstreets of Launceston. She missed the space and hills and fresh air. She missed the trees and animals and birds. She missed the wildflowers in spring, the taste of warm, frothy milk straight from the cow, and the vegetable garden that kept them amply supplied with fresh produce all year round. They could barely coax a single potato from Sparrow Lane's exhausted soil.

A low groan came from the bed.

'Mum?' Emma leaned across and looked deeply into her eyes, desperate for some sign of the woman she knew and loved. Her mother's eyes remained eerily unfocused, fixed on something nobody else could see. If she was in there, it was impossible to tell.

The dam finally burst and Emma crumpled into a blubbering mess. The worst thing, the thing that made her ashamed, was that her tears weren't just for her mother. They were for herself as well.

Emma couldn't breathe. She pulled the curtains aside and opened the grimy window. The chilly blast of air was like a blast of cold reality. There'd be no return to Hobart. No romance with Tom. No working at the zoo. No resuming the scholarship. Her chance of a higher education lay trampled in the wake of this tragedy. How could she leave her mother in this foul, stuffy room, dressed in soiled clothes and lying in her own filth? How could she abandon her to the tender mercies of drunken Mrs Shaw, and of 18-year-old Jack who meant well but was in way over his head? Tim wouldn't be any help. Jack was right about their older brother. Timid Timmy, they used to call him – a boy who seemed to have been born frightened of the world. He'd grown into a man who ran from responsibility and closed his eyes to the hardships of life. Jack's account of Tim's visit rang true. Mum's plight would have scared the hell out of him.

Emma wiped away the tears from her cheek. She may be the youngest – barely seventeen – but there was no getting away from it. She was also the best candidate to care for Mum.

A crush of painful memories tumbled in. The giddy excitement of opening the letter offering her the scholarship. Her first wide-eyed day in Hobart. Meeting the principal, Mrs Woolhouse.

'So you want to be a doctor? You're one of the brightest, most talented scholarship girls we've ever had here at Campbell College. There's absolutely no reason why you shouldn't achieve your goal. We have high hopes for you.'

What a shock it had been, being recognised for her brain by people other than her parents. And what a delight. She hadn't dared to dream of such a thing, yet there she was, shaking the Principal's hand, receiving the sort of accolades that she'd thought impossible for home-schooled farm girls. Her life in Hobart had been perfect. Her studies, her cosy room at Coomalong, the elegant library. Alison, and her work with the animals at the zoo. Arthur Reid had even promised her a paid, part-time job at the zoo when she finished school. A job that would have seen her through university until she finished her medical degree. Such bitter-sweet thoughts. She'd been going to find a cure for arthritis. It suddenly seemed a foolish and trivial ambition. Arthritis was the least of her mother's problems.

Wind rattled the roof as the rain began in earnest. It came in sideways, spraying Emma's face, but she was too numb to feel it. It was time to stop feeling sorry for herself. Time to pack her things away, light a fire, find Mum some clean clothes to wear.

'I'm going out for some wood,' she said. 'Is there anything I can do for you first?'

Emma was almost glad Mum couldn't answer. She knew what she'd say. Her mother's voice sounded in her mind, clear as a bell. 'Yes, you daft child. You know exactly what you can do for me. You can leave here and get your behind back to Hobart, quick smart.'

In some ways it was as if Tom had never left Binburra, as if his time in Hobart had been a dream. He loved being back. Spring turned into summer, and the ranges had never looked more beautiful. Waratahs and leatherwood flowered in the valleys. Honeyeaters hovered among the crimson bottlebrush and two half-grown eaglets peered down from their eyrie, perched two hundred feet above him in a mountain ash. Higher up in the hills, dramatic grass-tree spears, patterned with multitudes of creamy flowers, reached for the sky,. Higher still, and the slopes were clothed with lemon-scented boronia and silver snow daisies.

He rode Flame into the wilderness, as before. Followed new paths into the forest. He explored crystal tarns, where platypus played, and plump spotted trout were so plentiful they almost caught themselves. He scaled craggy clifftops he'd never climbed before. There was always something fresh to discover in these mountains.

Yet in other ways, everything had changed. He missed Emma terribly, each minute of the day. He didn't even have a photo. And he missed Harry. Where was he living? What was he doing? In some ways, his brother was more present in his absence. Tom viewed things in terms of how they related to Harry. He went fishing, and compared his catch to the number of fish Harry caught when they were last together at the lake. He went swimming and, in his mind's eye, saw Harry launching his latest creation: that sleek clockwork speedboat – a masterpiece of engineering. He couldn't pass the waterfall without a shudder.

In his loneliness, Tom daydreamed about Hobart. Here at Binburra, surrounded by a vast wilderness, the capital city and its bustling crowds seemed a world away. Remembering his time there made it seem more real. He thought about the aerodrome, where the magnificent planes he'd seen in books were transformed into shiny reality. He thought about the zoo, and of Karma endlessly pacing her prison. Whenever Tom rode into the mountains, he imagined her there with him, poised on a fallen log or bounding after the little pademelon wallabies in a grassy clearing. He couldn't get those images out of his head.

He couldn't get Emma out of his head either. The taste of her lips. Her serious face and funny clothes. Her love and compassion for the zoo animals. Her standing in her underwear with her mouth open. Unanswerable questions plagued him. How was she managing back in Launceston? He didn't even have an address. How was her mother? Tom had no idea about strokes, or how disabling they were. Would Emma be able to resume her scholarship, realise her ambition and become a doctor? It frustrated him to think that he might never know.

Their return to Binburra coincided with his grandmother's remarkable return to health. Colour came back to her cheeks, and her eyes shone with a restless energy Tom hadn't seen before. Her nagging cough persisted, but she pushed through it. Her appetite was back.

'Can't remember when you last ate two eggs,' said a beaming Mrs Mills as Nana lingered over her breakfast toast. She ate slowly, but seemed determined to devour every last crumb. She went for longer and longer walks in the bush with the dogs. She started riding again, appropriating Harry's bay gelding Buster, as her own horse was quite old now. Tom always rode with her, fearful she might take a fall alone in the mountains. Her enthusiasm surprised him. He'd barely seen her on a horse since he arrived at Binburra.

'What's got into Nana?' Tom asked Mrs Mills one morning, as Nana disappeared out the back door with the dogs.

'Says she's got a special tonic.' Mrs Mills chuckled. 'Whatever it is, I could sure use some.'

Tom stumbled across the identity of Nana's special tonic a few days later – three dusty cases of *Vin Tonique Mariani* at the back of the cart shed. Tom examined one of the squat bottles with its French language label. He gave it a shake. The liquid inside looked like red wine. He found a colourful leaflet inside the crate labelled *Popular French Tonic Wine*. It showed a risqué image of a scantily clad young woman, pouring herself a glass while she danced. Beneath, in smaller letters, it read *Fortifies and Refreshes Body & Brain. Restores Health and Vitality.*

'Leftover from my late husband's illness,' said Nana when he asked. 'It brought him great comfort towards the end, and works marvellously well for me as a restorative.'

He couldn't argue with that. The stuff was a miracle cure.

Nana didn't get him a tutor. 'You're seventeen, Tom. Time to decide what you want to do with your life. Next year I'm sending you back to Hobart. You could finish school and aim for university, or take up an apprenticeship like your brother. But this time I won't be coming with you.'

A shiver of excitement and anticipation ran through him. Nana was right. He needed to make his own way in the world, beyond Binburra's remote boundaries. Reconnect with Emma and forge a life for himself, like Harry was doing. With Nana well again, he could leave without guilt.

'Don't make any hasty decisions,' said Nana. 'Think it through. However, in the meantime, remember I said there's something special I want us to do together? Well, it's time. I want us to go camping in the ranges. We'll be away for a week or more.

'Camping?' He and Harry had never gone camping with Nana before. 'You're just full of surprises. Are you sure you're well enough?'

'Look at all I've been doing lately. Do I seem ill?'

Tom grinned. 'You've been in training for this trip, haven't you?'

'Precisely so. We leave the day after tomorrow.'

They set off on horseback at first light. As they started up the water-fall track, Old George joined them on Nana's old horse. Excited to be out of her paddock and included for once, the grey mare whinnied and pranced like a filly.

Tom cast Nana a puzzled look.

'The way will soon grow too rough for horses,' she explained. 'We'll need George to take them back to the homestead for us.'

Just as she said, in a few hours they had to leave their mounts behind. Tom waved goodbye to George as he disappeared back down the track with the horses. Nana had already marched off uphill. Just where was she taking him with such tireless determination?

Upwards, ever upwards, Nana and Tom forged into the rugged ranges. The going grew tougher as the forest grew thicker. Criss-crossed fallen trees blocked their path, like a giant had been playing an immense game of pick up sticks. The ancient, downed trunks formed homes for a dazzling array of mosses, ferns, and flowers.

'Look,' said Nana as they climbed across a creek beneath a canopy of sassafras and celery-topped pine. An orchid twined around a myrtle twig overhanging the water. Fragrant sprays of purple and white blossom dangled down, catching the muted sunlight.

'A butterfly orchid,' said Tom in a whisper. 'I've never seen one.' Despite his knowledge of these ranges, he had not passed this way before.

It was almost dark before Nana halted beside a rocky spring where two mountain gullies met. She didn't speak. Although it was summer, the chill of a highland night was already seeping into Tom's bones.

'I'll set up camp and light a fire.' He pointed to a fallen tree. 'Sit down and rest.'

Nana gave him a grateful smile and shrugged off her backpack. She pulled her jacket tight around her and sank down on the log. Looking limp, staring at nothing, taking slow, deep breaths – the very picture of exhaustion. Tom couldn't believe the pace she'd set all day, and the strength she'd shown. What was pushing her?

Tom filled up the billy and canteens at the spring. Nana produced a bottle of Vin Mariani from her pack and, to Tom's delight, a block of Cadbury's chocolate. She eased herself off her log and rubbed her back. Then she filled her mug with a generous portion of tonic and took a great swig.

Tom cleared a flat spot and arranged a ring of stones for their campfire.

Nana handed him some squares of chocolate. 'I'll collect kindling.'

Tom opened his mouth to protest, but thought better of it. Nana wouldn't thank him for taking over. She was too proud. Instead he rushed to set up camp before she got back. Laying out swags. Chopping wood. Selecting a stout backlog which would burn all night.

When Nana returned with a supply of sticks, Tom got the fire going and put the billy on. He could see Nana looking around for something else to do. 'Sit down and keep the fire going, Nana.' He grabbed his rifle. 'I'll try my luck shooting bunnies. Better than bully beef.'

Half an hour later he returned with two rabbits, expertly skinned and gutted. Soon they were roasting on a spit resting between two forked sticks, beside a pot of boiling potatoes.

Tom relaxed by the fire, sipping sweet billy tea and turning the rabbits. Nana dozed off in the warm glow, with her back against a tree. He carefully covered her with a blanket, then sat down, waiting for the meal to cook. There was no hurry. Wild rabbits took time to turn tender.

It was ages since Tom had camped out like this. Everyday worries fled. He'd forgotten the peace of it, how wilderness stripped away cares and longings. A flock of green rosellas chattered in the branches above him as they settled down to roost. The sinking sun flamed one last time through a filigree of leaves, then dropped from the sky. Night fell quickly in the highlands, and the forest dissolved into mystery.

Tom was no longer curious about where they were going, or why they were going there. It was enough to be on the journey.

On the fourth day they reached a limestone canyon, framed by towering cliffs like jagged battlements. A natural fortress.

'Welcome to *Loongana Warraroong*,' whispered Nana. 'Pass of the Tiger. No one alive knows about this place apart from me, and now, you.'

The birds fell silent as they went by, and the air hung heavy with stillness. The rock walls were honeycombed with caves, and a stream ran through the pass, here wide and shining, there dwindling to a chain of rocky pools. They followed its course until it fell in a silver ribbon down a bottomless cliff.

Tom climbed onto a rock shelf above the waterfall. From his vantage point he saw the pass was really a little hanging valley, suspended above an immense, natural amphitheatre.

'A long-vanished ice river carved out this canyon,' said Nana, 'on its way down to the main glacier.' She pointed to the scene below them: giant trees, virgin forests and green clearings stretching as far as the eye could see. 'Your great-grandfather Daniel called this, *a place hidden from everything but sky.*'

Tom tried to imagine how it would have looked eons ago – a vast glittering ice world. He wished he could share this place with Emma. How she would love it.

'Once upon a time, a track led down the escarpment to a lost valley where the first people hunted teeming game and walked for weeks without reaching its limit. Then an earthquake blocked the way, sealing off the valley.'

Tom offered his hand, and pulled Nana up to stand beside him on the ledge. High above them, an eagle wheeled across the blue face of the sky. They stood for the longest time, absorbing the majesty of the scene.

Nana turned to him with bright eyes. 'What do you think?'

'It's magical,' he said. 'Like I've stepped back in time.'

They retraced their steps. Nana stopped beside a twisted Huon pine. Tom gazed up in amazement. He'd never seen one so tall. 'It must be a thousand years old.'

Nana stroked its knotted bark. 'Imagine the things this tree has seen.' She took out the torches from his pack, and pointed to a nearby cave. 'That one.'

Tom followed her inside and waited for his eyes to adjust. Nana seemed to be searching for something at her feet. She trained her torch on the ground and rubbed it with her boot. Something gleamed beneath the dirt. She knelt down, spat on a handkerchief and scrubbed at the rock floor. To his astonishment a square brass plate emerged from the dust.

After a moment or two he could read the inscription. *In loving memory of Luke Tyler and his loyal dog Bear. My heart is forever yours. Bluebell.*

'Who put it here?' asked Tom. 'Who's Luke Tyler?'

Darkness and silence yawned between them. Tom lifted his torch, startled to see tears in her eyes. 'Nana, what is it?' He put a steadying hand on her arm.

She managed a smile, and raised her own torch high, training it on the walls. Eerie images appeared from the gloom; dozens of drawings, hand-prints and concentric circles. Nana pulled him further in. A manmade tunnel opened up at the rear of the cave, shored up with stout timbers. Tom investigated. After ten feet or so, the way was impassable, choked with rocks.

Nana pointed to the roof and Tom drew in a quick breath. The painted likeness of a thylacine gazed down on them.

'Lord, it does my poor heart good to be in this place again,' said

Nana with a deep, joyful sigh. 'We'll camp here tonight. There's much I need to tell you.'

Tom caught three plump trout for dinner, collected wood and warrigal greens, lit a fire and laid out their swags. He burned with curiosity. Who was Bluebell? Who built the tunnel and where did it lead? But Nana had retreated into herself.

'Later,' she said, when he pressed her. 'We'll talk later.'

When they'd eaten, Nana finally began. 'I am Bluebell,' she said. 'I set that plaque in tribute to Luke Tyler, the great love of my life. Luke was your grandfather, Tom. The truth is that you and Harry are not Abbotts at all.' Her voice grew fierce. 'Not one drop of their damn blood flows in your veins.'

'I don't understand …'

'We adored each other, Luke and I, although it was a forbidden love affair. I became pregnant with his child when I was just sixteen, younger than you are now. That child was Robert, your father.'

Tom's skin prickled.

'I was forced to marry Edward Abbott so the baby would be legitimate, and in any case, I believed Luke had died in a rock fall, right here in this cave. But I was wrong. His dog died, but Luke cheated death and came back to me. He came back to me as Colonel Lucas Buchanan. I didn't leave my devoted husband to run off with a rich diamond tycoon, although that's what people think. I left a loveless marriage to be with your grandfather, Tom. To be with the only man I'd ever loved.'

Tom knuckled tears from his eyes, although he didn't know he was crying.

Nana threw a log on the fire, and a flurry of sparks lit up the rough walls. She poured herself a mug of Vin Mariani. 'It's a lot to take in.'

The understatement of the year. Conflicting feelings surged through him. Disbelief led the tide. Perhaps Nana was lying or confused somehow? Shame followed hard on its heels. He'd never met anyone as honest and straightforward as his grandmother, nor anyone with a finer mind. And there was the plaque, and her sure knowledge of this place. So if Nana told the truth, what then? It meant she'd never abandoned her family, quite the opposite. She wasn't the heartless black sheep that she'd been painted.

'You say Luke Tyler returned as Colonel Buchanan,' said Tom. 'Did no one else know his true identity?'

'A few people.' Nana took a big swig of tonic. 'Your mother and father knew.'

Tom gasped. That explained why Mama had always defended Nana. But it didn't explain his father's open hostility. 'When Harry and I were small, Papa said you were wicked to leave. Papa said the Colonel was a monster who'd lured you away. If the Colonel was his true father, why did Papa hate him so?'

Nana's sigh held all the sadness of the ages. 'Your father was fifteen years old when he learned the truth of his paternity. Edward Abbott was the only father he'd ever known. Edward had not been a good husband to me, but he'd been a loving father to Robbie. They were very close.'

'How did the Colonel feel about that?'

'It devastated him. He tried to reach out to Robbie, tried to build a relationship with his son, but Robbie wouldn't have it. It was all too late. Robbie blamed Luke and me for breaking up his family. He never forgave us.'

Tom tipped out his cold tea and held out the mug. 'Can I have some of your tonic?'

Nana smiled and held out the bottle. 'Just this once.'

They talked long into the night. Tom wanted to know all about his grandfather – the mysterious Colonel Buchanan. The years slipped from Nana's face as she told him astounding stories; stories of heroism, bravery and adventures in far off lands.

Tom had always been proud of his link to Daniel Campbell: Nana's father, Tasmania's foremost naturalist, and a man ahead of his time. Daniel was a founding member of the Royal Society. He spoke out for the protection of thylacines when farmers still shot them as pests. He purchased Binburra back in 1883 specifically to protect its flora and fauna. And now Tom discovered that, as a boy, the Colonel had been Daniel's protégé.

'Luke dedicated his life to advancing my father's work,' said Nana. She laid a hand on Tom's arm. 'You remind me very much of the Colonel. He would have cherished you.'

Tom felt like singing. A missing piece of his life had fallen into place. Papa might have loved Harry best. Papa might have thought that a boy with his head in the clouds would amount to nothing. But that's not what Tom's grandfather would have thought. The Colonel would have loved him; Nana said so. And that love, the love of a dead grandfather whom he'd never met, suddenly meant the world to him. It eased the pain of Papa's rejection, the loss of his mother, and his brother's disloyalty. It made him feel important and strong, like he could do anything.

An odd cry echoed through the night.

'What was that?' asked Tom.

'It's late, my dear,' said Nana. 'We all need some rest.'

When Tom woke the next morning, Nana was up and cooking breakfast.

'Are we heading home today?' he asked, stifling a yawn. He'd lain awake long into the night, processing all he'd learned, and hadn't had much sleep.

'Tomorrow,' she said. 'I've more to show you.'

Tom shook his head and chased baked beans around his plate with a spoon. 'Whatever it is, it won't beat last night.'

Nana gave him an odd smile. 'Don't be so sure.'

After they'd tidied the camp, Tom stepped through the cave mouth to greet the day.

'Come back,' called Nana. 'You're going the wrong way.'

When he returned Nana handed him work gloves and a torch. She shone her own torch into the dark tunnel at the rear of the cave, and beckoned for Tom to follow her in. 'Right. Let's get to work.' Nana picked up a stone and moved it aside.

'We can't move an entire rockfall by hand,' said Tom, gazing at the impenetrable wall that blocked their way. 'Who knows? It could be ten feet thick.'

'It could be,' she said. 'But it's not. It's only two stones wide.'

'How can you know that?'

Nana picked up another small rock, put it aside, and slowly straightened her back 'Because your grandfather and I built it ourselves.'

Tom grinned and shook his head. Would Nana ever stop surprising him? 'Go back to the camp and sit down,' he told her. 'I'll do this.'

An hour later, the way was clear. Tom shone his torch into the darkness as Nana marched into the tunnel. At the back of the cave, Tom stopped short. He was growing used to surprises, but this was astonishing. Crude stone steps led downwards through a recess in the rock.

'A passage to the lost valley.' Nana took a swig of her tonic. 'Never thought I'd have the privilege of coming here again.'

It was a slow and dangerous descent. A little stream ran down through the rocks, making the path slick underfoot, and they slipped more than once. Tom led the way, so if Nana tripped he would break her fall.

Glow worms, clustered on the walls and ceiling in their thousands, provided a spectacular display – myriad blue lights resembling stars in the night sky. Tiny bats, disturbed from their rocky roosts, fluttered and whirled about their faces before vanishing into the darkness. Nana seemed unfazed, but it took all of Tom's nerve not to flinch.

When they finally emerged at the base of the cliff, a pristine valley stretched before them. A crystal-clear creek bubbled through patches of virgin rainforest: myrtle, leatherwood and sassafras. Huon and King Billy pine – trees that had never felt the bite of an axe. Some rose a hundred feet high, with trunks of impressive girth. They must have been ancient. Tracts of stringybark and swamp gums bordered broad grassy clearings where kangaroos and pademelons grazed.

A flock of gang-gang cockatoos fed noisily on ripe seed pods in the blackwood canopy and right at Tom's feet, a brilliant blue-crowned fairy wren led his troop of plainer wives in search of insects. A pair of butcher birds, Tasmania's most sublime songsters, piped a duet, magnified by the cathedral-like acoustics of the surrounding cliffs. Tom slowly exhaled. Nature and the physical landscape had come together to create a scene of unforgettable splendour.

Nana sank down on a fallen log in the shade, plainly exhausted, but wearing a rapturous smile. Tom joined her, offering the water canteen before taking a long draught himself. They sat that way, side by side, for the longest time, stunned into silence by the beauty of their surrounds.

'So, this is what you came all this way to show me,' Tom murmured at last. 'It's spectacular. Who else knows about this place?'

Nana's smile slipped. 'Nobody else alive, and it must stay that way.'

'Why?' said Tom. 'We're on Binburra land, yes? The valley is safe. In any case, it's too remote to log.'

Nana's expression was unreadable. 'Come on.' She hauled herself up with the help of a low-hanging branch. 'There's more.'

Tom clapped his hand to his head and laughed. 'Of course there is.'

They followed the course of the creek upstream, sometimes paddling in the cool water to soothe their aching feet. The creek wound its way around the base of canyon walls that soared impossibly high. A trick of the light blended cliff tops with sky. Tom stopped and gazed up in sheer wonder.

'Do you know what your grandfather used to say?' whispered Nana. 'He said you couldn't tell where earth ended and heaven began.'

Tom felt a thrill of excitement – to be walking in the steps of his grandfather, to be hearing his words. To be sharing the same hallowed reverence for this place.

After an hour or so they reached a pretty pool at the bottom of the falls. The silver cascade fractured into rainbows of spray when it broke on the rocks, the falling water singing a song all its own. Nana leaned on the walking stick he'd made her, staring at a wide recess at the base of the cliff with a faraway expression on her face and sweat beading her brow.

'Let's stop here for lunch,' he said, worried she might be suffering from heat stroke.

Nana took a swig of tonic. 'Not yet.'

They travelled for another hour, as the temperature climbed higher. Tom couldn't believe his grandmother's endurance. Even he was flagging. Where on earth were they going? It was no use asking. She was breathing too hard to talk, waving away his questions.

'This is it,' said Nana at last, indicating a cave that looked no different from a dozen others they'd passed. 'Fortune Cave.' In they went, passing from sunlight to shadow.

Nana trained her torch on the rear wall. Pick-axe marks. She poured a little water from her canteen onto the scored rock, then rubbed the moist surface with her sleeve. A shining vein of gold gleamed in the beam of light. 'This is a valley of gold, Tom.'

His eyes widened as he trailed his fingers along the bright seam.

'Nobody can find out about this,' she said, her voice low and urgent as if someone might hear.

'Not even Harry?'

'Especially not Harry.'

They ate lunch in the coolness of the cave mouth. Tom wanted to hear everything. 'How do you know about this cave?'

'Luke discovered it.' Nana pushed a stray lock of hair from her face. 'In 1887 state parliament passed a bounty scheme that sealed the fate of our native tigers. They were already rare, and now the remaining animals would be shot and snared into oblivion. My father released three orphans into this remote valley, hoping to protect them. Hoping they might breed with the few remaining tigers that lived here. He appointed Luke as their guardian, charged with keeping them safe and supervising their reintroduction to the wild.'

'What happened?' asked Tom, transfixed. 'Did they survive?'

'So many questions.' Nana closed her eyes, looking completely done in.

'Sorry, Nana. Sit there and rest for a while.'

She managed a smile and hauled herself to her feet with the help of a low branch. 'Come on, slowcoach.'

An hour later Nana stopped again. She seemed to be searching for something beside the stream. He examined the ground and caught his breath. Animal tracks bearing a tell-tale, heel-to-toe groove in the sand - the magical groove he thought he'd never ever see. Tiger tracks. Tom glanced up in disbelief and Nana's eyes crinkled into a smile.

'Does that answer your question?' Happy tears shone on her dust-smudged cheeks and she seemed suddenly girlish. 'That cry we heard last night? I'd recognise it anywhere. They're here, Tom. They're still here.'

It was nearly dark before they arrived back at their camp at the top of the cliff. The gruelling climb from the valley had taken them three times as long as the descent, and Tom had half-carried his grand-mother on the final stretch. He lit the fire and prepared a meal, while Nana lay on her swag, dishevelled and dog-tired. Her cough had returned, and not even liberal doses of tonic could settle it. But her eyes burned bright with joy and the deep satisfaction of having achieved the difficult goal she'd set herself.

During dinner they were both lost in private thought. Afterwards Nana produced another block of chocolate. 'Now you know why I had to bring you here. I couldn't let this knowledge die with me.'

'You're not going to die, Nana.'

She patted his hand. 'We all die one day, Tom. So with that in mind, I'm charging you with the guardianship of the tigers and this valley, just as my father charged Luke all those years ago. Passing the baton. They must always be protected.'

'What about Harry?'

'Harry is a wonderful, clever boy, and I love him dearly, but there is temptation here, Tom, buried in these cliffs and underground. Would you really trust your brother with that knowledge?'

Tom pictured Harry with his lucky golden nugget, turning it over and over in his hand. The loving way he stroked it; the jealous way he guarded it. Nana was right, perhaps more right than she knew, as she was unaware that they knew the truth about their parents' death. That tragedy had taught Tom that worshipping wealth would only lead to heartbreak. It had taught Harry the exact opposite. In his grief, he believed the loss of family wealth had led to disaster. He didn't blame their father. He blamed the stock market crash, as if the tumbling figures on Wall Street had somehow pulled that trigger themselves.

'It will never happen to me,' he'd told Tom more than once. 'I'm going to rebuild the Abbott fortune, take back what is rightfully ours. I swear I will, for Papa and for Mama. Just wait and see.'

Tom didn't doubt him for a second. Instead he pitied him. Following in his father's footsteps, chasing the money god - these things would not make his confused, grief-stricken brother happy. One day, perhaps, he'd make Harry understand, but until then he'd be proud to guard Nana's secret.

CHAPTER 13

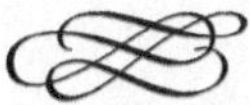

It was tough for the Starr family, making ends meet after Emma's father died. Moving from the farm. Finding their feet in town without a male breadwinner. Tim, the eldest, had married a local woman and found work at the foundry, but his financial contributions were few and far between. His wife, Jane, seemed resentful of Tim's family, and begrudged giving them money. The small sum Mum earned from mending was barely enough to pay rent and bills. They sometimes ran out of food, and their rundown house was collapsing around them. But now, with Mum incapacitated and Emma bound to the house as her caregiver, life wasn't just difficult - it was impossible.

Emma had no savings from her job at the Hobart dress shop. She'd sent every spare penny home to her mother. And now the money Mrs Campbell had so generously given her was almost gone. She'd let Mrs Shaw go, saving that expense, but doctors cost money.

When she approached Tim, he covered his ears. 'Poor Mum. Don't tell me. I can't bear to hear it.'

Tim's wife was a tall, stylish woman with straight black hair that she always wore up, along with a haughty expression. At thirty, she was eight years older than Tim. Some had unkindly suggested that she'd only married him for fear of being left on the shelf. This was no doubt part of the truth, but not all of it. They seemed genuinely fond of each other, and Jane was protective of her sensitive husband – in some ways more mother than wife.

A talented seamstress, Jane had begun work at the woollen mills at fourteen. Her skill with the needle was quickly noticed, and she'd worked her way up to the position of head dressmaker for *Trés Chic*, Launceston's most fashionable boutique. Despite the depression, the business still plied a good trade among the well-heeled. With no children, and with both Tim and his wife working, Emma had expected her brother to willingly pitch in.

She hadn't counted on jealous Jane, however, and Jane was well and truly in charge of her husband. 'Why come around here, crying poor and bringing him such gloomy news?' she'd said. 'Tim loves his mother, but he's not a strong man. You know how much her illness upsets him. I must ask you to wait until you have something positive to report, Emma, before you visit us again. Then you will be most welcome.' She passed over a few shillings. 'To tide you over. We don't have any more.'

Emma thanked her and said goodbye to Tim, who was close to tears. She was stunned by the unfairness of their response, and vowed to herself that she would not be back. At least Tim wasn't living at home. He wasn't costing Emma anything.

Jack, on the other hand, was a constant drain on her dwindling finances.

'Get yourself some steady work,' said Emma in exasperation.

'I'm trying, sis,' he said gloomily. 'I've been to the brewery, brickworks, sawmills, joinery, abattoirs – every bloody place. There's three dozen blokes waiting in line for each spot, even at the stinking tanneries down by the river. I tell you, sis, there ain't a single job going in this whole damn town.'

Emma didn't doubt him. It was hard to miss the growing face of poverty and unemployment in Launceston. Families standing confused and bewildered on footpaths outside the rented homes they could no longer afford. Swagmen tramping the streets looking for work. Women, old and young, haunting pubs and bars, prepared to sell their bodies to feed their children. It made Emma sick to think how desperate someone would have to be to do that.

The Great Depression had hit their island state even harder than the rest of Australia. She'd heard Premier Ogilvie talking last week on the radio. Unemployment in Tasmania was a disaster, he'd said, with more than one in three breadwinners out of work. Jack's best hope for a real chance in life was to leave Launceston and go to Hobart or even the mainland. Perhaps join the military or merchant marines. Emma wanted very much for him to have a future, but how would she cope without him?

Jack was the one there to help when they had to lift Mum. When they had to turn her, and wash her and dress her bed sores. When they had to remind her to chew and swallow, and clean up her vomit when she ate too quickly. Jack was a good and generous person. If he got the odd day's work, he handed over his meagre pay to Emma. How could she say no when he wanted threepence here or sixpence there? He deserved the odd treat: a bet with the boys or a bit of tobacco. He had a right to his youth. As for her mother, she didn't seem to be improving, but neither was she getting worse

Emma had dispensed with the old doctor, the one who couldn't help Mum and just told them to pray. This new one was better, an optimist. Dr Dennisdeen explained things properly. 'A stroke happens when blood flow to a portion of the brain is diminished by a blood clot or broken blood vessel. As with heart attacks, the lack of oxygenated blood can lead to tissue death. When brain cells die, symptoms occur in parts of the body that those brain cells control. Sudden weakness, paralysis, numbness of the face or limbs. That's why stroke victims may have difficulty thinking, moving, and some-times even breathing.'

'Is there any treatment?' asked Emma.

'Rehabilitation can greatly improve outcomes for patients. I have a particular interest in this field, and believe other parts of the brain can be encouraged to take over from the damaged cells. It's just a theory, but it explains why certain stroke victims recover a reasonable quality of life. Eileen's disability is indeed a severe one, but there is always hope. I'd like to prepare an exercise program for your mother, if you're willing of course. This will mean a lot of work for you, I'm afraid.'

Anything was worth a try. Emma followed the doctor's instructions with meticulous care, frequently changing Mum's position in bed, and passively exercising her arms and legs. To begin with her muscles were stiff, resisting movement, but thanks to persistent stretching, they gradually loosened up. With Mum unable to speak, it was hard for Emma to know if she was hurting her or not. Still, if there was a chance it might help, it had to be done.

Emma took special care to exercise Mum's hands, stroking them and opening her fingers dozens of times a day. Splints and sandbags kept her legs straight, and cushions under her arms did the same for her shoulders. All designed to prevent the crippling deformities that plagued many stroke victims.

Weeks passed. In quiet moments Emma thought about Tom, and how he'd helped her at the zoo, and the dimple in his chin, and that first, magical kiss. And how she loved him. If she closed her eyes she could taste the salt on his skin, feel his beating heart, and the press of his hard, muscled body against her. Hear his husky whisper, 'There's no one like you, Em. You're one in a million.' But she didn't allow herself to go there often. It was too sad, too painful.

Christmas day arrived, as bright and clear a day as Emma had ever seen. A breeze blew away the pall that so often enveloped the town, and she could smell the faraway forest. Jack pushed their mother's bed closer to the open window.

Emma wasn't feeling festive, far from it, but Mum always loved this special time of year, so Emma had decided to make an effort. Jack put up a blue gum branch in the lounge room where Mum could see, and they decorated it with berries and gumnuts, holly leaves and wildflowers. Emma fashioned a star for the top out of hat wire, wound around fragrant sprigs of creamy Christmas Bush blossom. She sewed up little bags made from a worn out pillowcase, and filled them with flowering lavender as gifts. She dipped into her fast-dwindling reserves to buy boiled lollies for the table, and mixed fruit for a pudding.

Jack came home with eggs and a fat cockerel that looked suspiciously like the one belonging to Mrs Phipps; the one that always woke her at four in the morning. Jacky grinned as he handed his offerings over. Emma usually frowned at bandicooting – the pilfering of food from home gardens – but for once she turned a blind eye. Here came a proper Christmas dinner, and the bones would make a nourishing stock. Jack had even managed a pint of milk – frothy, fresh and straight, Emma guessed, from the Harper's house cow.

Tim and Jane came by with half a ham and a bottle of brandy. Jane could make Emma feel inferior without saying a word. By the clever re-use of samples and seconds, she always managed to dress like a lady. Today was no exception. She wore a smart, two-piece number: fine cotton broadcloth, in a navy and white polka-dot print. Kick pleats. White pique collar. Emma wondered how she herself might look in such a stylish outfit, instead of her frayed blouse, more grey than white, shapeless beige skirt and scuffed shoes.

Tim seemed very cheerful to see Mum looking clean and well cared for. Her cheeks had filled out, thanks to Emma's dedicated feeding, and her neatly-cut red hair shone with health. Emma had even bought a green satin ribbon to tie it back. Tim mistook the result of his sister's devotion for an improvement in his mother's condition.

'I bought you some soap, Mum,' he said, unwrapping the present on her bed. 'And a bag of oranges.' He spoke in a loud, slow, exaggerated way, as if Mum was deaf or demented.

There was a pair of scented candles for Emma and a pocket-knife for Jack. She couldn't help wishing Tim hadn't wasted his money on presents. Emma would have much preferred the cash. But as they enjoyed a fine meal of ham, roast chicken and vegetables, followed by a slightly raw plum pudding and custard, her mood lifted. She sipped a small glass of brandy, pretending Dad was down at the dairy, and Mum was picking parsley in the garden. It could almost be the old days, back at the farm.

As her guests were leaving, Tim took her aside and gave her a final present; a pretty tapestry purse containing five florins. 'You're doing a wonderful job with Mum.' He kissed her cheek, and she glowed with pleasure. 'I have some good news. Jane is expecting. You're going to be an auntie.'

'Congratulations.' He'd once confided to Emma that he thought a pregnancy might never happen.

'It means money will be tight, though,' said Tim. 'We can't keep carrying you like this.'

It was like she'd been slapped. This was Jane talking, not her brother, but it still hurt. 'Carrying me? Maybe you *should* be carrying me, since I'm barely seventeen years old. But the truth is I've only seen you three times since I've been home. The last time Jane told me to stay away, and I've honoured that request. I've used up every penny of my own money caring for Mum, and the pittance Jacky's earned as well. I've no idea how we'll manage in the new year.'

'Send the lazy little sod out to work,' said Tim.

'Leave Jacky alone.' Emma's voice rose a notch, and she could feel the sharp sting of tears. 'He's been a marvellous help, and is doing his very best to find a job. It's not his fault there are none to be had.' She couldn't help herself. She began to cry.

Tim looked horrified and Emma sniffed back her tears. This was Christmas after all, and she didn't want to spoil it. 'If you could find Jacky work at the foundry it would make all the difference.'

Tim shook his head. 'With this downturn they're more likely to be laying men off than putting them on. You're so very mature, Em. Perhaps you'd have a better chance of finding work than Jack would.'

'But I couldn't leave Mum.'

'She seems better,' said Tim. 'Surely Jack could take care of her during the day?' He took two shillings from his pocket and added it to the purse. 'You're doing a great job with Mum, by the way. Thank you.'

Emma gave him a heartfelt hug. To be appreciated was the best Christmas present she could have wished for.

. . .

The new year was ushered in with an almighty heatwave that knocked everybody flat. Thank goodness Tim had paid the overdue electricity bill (behind Jane's back), so that Mum could have her fan. Even so, the lounge room was like an oven. It must be awfully boring and lonely, sitting there day after day in the hot room with nothing to do. If only she could afford a little wireless for Mum to listen to.

One evening Emma brought out the thick mutton broth, chock full of sieved vegetables, that was her mother's mainstay. 'Open up,' said Emma, the spoon hovering outside Mum's lips like she was a baby. Emma had learned the trick. Gently pinch Mum's cheek to open her mouth, then quickly massage her throat to get her to swallow before she choked.

Just as Emma went to touch her cheek, Mum opened her mouth. Emma almost dropped the spoon in surprise. After a few mouthfuls her mother was swallowing without a reminder. 'That's wonderful, Mum.' Emma tried to contain her excitement. 'You'll be well in no time.'

Emma called Dr Dennisdeen from a neighbour's house to tell him the good news. He came straight away, gave Mum a thorough examination and turned to Emma with a satisfied expression. 'There is an encouraging response in her reflexes, particularly on the right side. Just keep doing what you're doing and I shall see you next week.'

Emma opened her new purse. The doctor held up his hand. 'No charge for today. I'm impressed with your mother's progress, and it's mainly thanks to you. Such dedication in one so young. You'd make an excellent nurse.'

'I'd make an excellent doctor.' Emma hadn't meant to say it out loud. It had just slipped out.

Dr Dennisdeen smiled at her. 'Indeed you would, my dear.' He snapped his bag shut. 'Indeed you would.'

As the year wore on, Emma came closer and closer to running out of money. She turned Tim's suggestion over in her mind daily, the suggestion that she should try to find a job herself. In the end she didn't have any choice. Financial ruin lay just around the corner. So each day she dressed in her most presentable clothes and did the rounds. She tried everywhere: bakers, hairdressers, grocers. Jewellers and watchmakers. Furniture makers, potters, the church school. She had no more luck than Jacky, other than one indecent proposal and a priest who suggested she become a nun.

In March, it finally happened. There was no money left to pay for electricity or gas. No money to pay the greengrocer. No money to pay the milkman.

'Can't hand this over til you settle the account, love,' said the butcher as he wrapped her weekly order of mutton and soup bones in newspaper. Emma trailed her toe in the sawdust strewn floor, then left the shop empty-handed.

'You must find a job tomorrow,' she told Jack. 'Mum had the last of the stew for lunch. We can't let her starve.'

'I don't want us to starve either, sis,' he said. 'But I won't find a job just because you tell me to. Don't we have anything left?'

'Four pounds, but that's for the rent. We can't touch it.'

'Go and see Tim and Jane, then.'

Emma had vowed never to ask those two for help again, but Jack was right. She couldn't afford to be proud any more. 'I'll go tonight,' she said. 'I won't ring first. You'll need to look after Mum.'

She found Tim in the front garden, mowing the lawn with a push mower. A sign on the front gate read *Bide-A-While*. Jane had inherited the little cottage when her parents died, so they didn't even pay rent. A scene of domestic bliss; sun setting behind the roses, the sweet smell of cut grass, a jug of iced tea on the vine-draped porch. It wasn't fair. Why couldn't Mum live like this, instead of in the squalor of Sparrow Lane?

'I told you, Em,' Tim said when she asked him. 'I can't hand over any more money. My wife would be livid.'

'You'll have to,' she said. 'Jacky and I can't get work. We've looked all over. If you don't bail us out, Mum will be evicted.' Tim nervously licked his lips. 'I suppose I'll just have to bring her here,' said Emma. 'Have you got room for me and Jacky too?'

Jane caught sight of them through the window, and hurried out. 'Hello Emma.' She frowned at Tim. 'What's going on?'

'Ah, my sister … is looking for work. She was wondering if you could recommend her for a job at the boutique?'

'Out of the question—' began Jane.

'Otherwise Tim's mum will get evicted and we'll all have to move in here … with you,' said Emma. She smiled grimly as Jane's mouth dropped open. That had shut her up.

'My dear Emma, I believe you worked at a dress shop in Hobart. Would they give you a reference?'

'I suppose so, yes.'

'Very well, I shall talk to Monsieur Dupont tomorrow and see if there's an opening.'

Jane was true to her word. She dropped by the next day to give Emma the good news. 'You have an appointment at *Tres Chic* tomorrow afternoon at three. Don't be late.' Jane looked her up and down with a frown. Emma hadn't been expecting company. She was wearing her zoo garb – an oversized man's shirt and baggy trousers. 'Come home with me, dear. I'll lend you a dress for the interview. Monsieur Dupont is most particular.'

Emma checked on Mum, then she and Jane took the short bus ride back to the cottage. Jane disappeared into her bedroom and returned with a smart belted dress of burgundy cotton with a scatter-dot print. 'Try it on.'

Emma did as she was told.

Jane frowned. 'Hmm. I'll need to take it in here, and here … Don't lose any more weight,' she warned, as if Emma was deliberately getting skinny just to be annoying. Jane went into the front room to make the alterations, leaving Emma standing in the kitchen in her underwear.

'Try it on again,' said Jane when she emerged. 'Much better, and you'll need these.' She produced a pair of modern, grey suede platform pumps. 'And these.' She handed Emma a pill box hat and a pair of salmon pink gloves. 'No, not like that. Tilt it.' Jane expertly secured the hat on the side of Emma's head with pins, then extracted two pounds from her purse. 'Take this. Tim told me you've been caught short. Call it an advance on your first pay. I expect it to be repaid promptly.'

'Thank you,' said Emma. 'Can I wear this home?'

'Of course not.'

Emma loved her new frock. She paraded in front of the small cracked mirror in Mum's old bedroom, seeing only bits of herself at a time, trying to get a sense of how she looked as a whole. The dress had a frilled neckline, and flattering cape-effect collar with organdie trim. The cotton voile fabric was soft and sheer, and felt wonderful against her skin. She'd never felt more grown-up and sophisticated.

'Look Mum,' she said, as she twirled by the window in the lounge room. 'Look at my new dress. I'm a grand lady on my way to a garden party, or maybe the Melbourne Cup.'

Was it her imagination, or did her mother's eyes flutter in response?

The proprietor of *Très Chic*, Monsieur Dupont, was a short, balding widower in his fifties, and lived in a flat above his shop. He had stumpy legs, porcine eyes and a mouth too wide for his face. Nevertheless, he managed to look dapper in a dark, silk suit. He peered at Emma short-sightedly before finding his horn-rimmed spectacles.

'Good afternoon, sir,' she began nervously. 'My sister-in-law, Mrs Jane Starr, says you're looking for a retail assistant.'

Monsieur Dupont looked her up and down. 'Do you have experience?' He spoke with a French accent, but Jane said it was fake. She said he'd been born Melvyn Spriggs in Fingal, the son of emancipated convicts. He'd been a sanitary plumber until he was forty, when a bachelor uncle he'd never met died in Wales, leaving him a large estate and making him a wealthy man. Melvyn had bought the boutique, practiced the accent, called himself Monsieur Dupont and the transformation from fixing toilets to fashion aficionado was complete.

Emma told him about her work at *À la Mode Fashions* in Hobart, and gave him the phone number of her employer.

'How old are you, mademoiselle?'

'Seventeen.'

His lips began to twitch. 'I think you'll do perfectly.'

'You mean I have the job?'

Monsieur Dupont took a pipe down from the shelf, filled it with tobacco and lit it. He puffed three times before answering Emma's question, as if he enjoyed making her wait. 'Three pounds per week, and extra for overtime,' he said at last. 'I'll see you tomorrow morning at nine o'clock sharp.'

Three pounds a week. She hadn't expected so much. Rejection after rejection, and now this. It seemed too easy. 'I might not be available for overtime, Monsieur Dupont. I'm caring for my sick mother.'

His tongue darted out from between his teeth. 'A certain amount of overtime is non-negotiable, Mademoiselle Starr. Of course, if that doesn't suit—'

'No, no. That suits perfectly. Thank you for the opportunity.'

Emma left the shop at a measured, ladylike walk, maintaining self-control just long enough to get past the front window. Then she pulled off her hat and gloves and went running down the street, laughing with relief. She couldn't wait to get home to tell Jacky and Mum.

Emma arrived at *Trés Chic* the next morning close to tears. To save money on the bus fare, and because it didn't look like rain, she'd decided to walk the two miles to work. What a misjudgement. High gusts of wind seemed to come from nowhere, playing havoc with her carefully coiffed hair. Worse was to come. The heavens opened ten minutes into her trip, and when Emma arrived half an hour later she looked and felt like a drowned rat.

Her damp dress clung to her figure in a most embarrassing way, and when she attempted to fix her bedraggled hair, Emma realised she'd lost Jane's smart pill box hat in the gale. She looked down at her suede shoes which, being a size too small, had blistered both her heels. They were caked in mud. Her sister-in-law would be furious.

Emma extracted a handkerchief from her bag and cleaned them off as best she could, with the help of a puddle of water. It would have to do. Utterly humiliating, yet when she caught a glimpse of her reflection in the window glass, Emma was pleasantly surprised. She didn't look nearly as bad as she'd imagined. In fact, she looked rather smart. Determined to make the best of things, Emma took a deep breath, held her head high and marched inside.

. . .

For the first few weeks Emma couldn't have been happier. The regular income made a world of difference. She bought Mum that wireless and a few hens for fresh eggs. She enjoyed her work at the boutique, where the clients wore beautiful clothes and had lovely manners. The garments she sold were high end, and far more costly than at *À La Mode*, but otherwise her duties were similar. There was one main difference, however, one that both flattered and terrified her. Monsieur Dupont wanted her to model clothes for clients.

'You have the perfect figure for a clothes horse, Emma. Tall and slim. Shapely legs and, ah, well-developed for one so young. My vain customers will see you in their chosen gowns and imagine themselves equally beautiful, *mais oui?*'

His eyes lingered on her chest and she tried to put aside a creeping sense of unease. She'd heard rumours about Monsieur Dupont pressing his attentions upon girls in the stock room, but that hadn't been Emma's experience. She sometimes caught him watching her, but he'd never been inappropriate. This was no time for prudishness or false modesty. Models earned more than shop girls.

The first few times she burned with embarrassment, stumbling in high heels as nerves got the better of her. But after a while she grew to enjoy wearing such a wide variety of gorgeous clothes. Clients loved her, eager to buy the garments she modelled. '*Bon travail*, mademoiselle,' whispered Monsieur Dupont, as a customer ordered two of the same gown in different colours. 'You have an enchanting combination of innocence and elegance that is utterly irresistible.' Emma became his go-to model, especially for the younger styles.

Late one afternoon when the boutique had closed to the public, a client came in for a private viewing. Afterwards Emma was changing out of a beaded blouson gown in the dressing room when Monsieur Dupont walked in. She was wearing nothing but a brassiere and knickers. She spun around and reached for her own dress, but before she could he was upon her, forcing kisses on her mouth, neck and shoulders, whispering how lovely she was.

When she tried to pull away, he grabbed her arm hard and snaked his hand between her legs. She twisted free and stood panting in the corner, filled with revulsion and ready to defend herself.

'Mademoiselle,' said Monsieur Dupont, his face turned red. 'We both know you're not as innocent as you pretend. If you wish to continue working for me, we must come to an arrangement. I am a man like any other, a man with needs, and you are a beautiful girl. If you please me, you will find me most generous.'

Emma pulled on her dress and fled. Whatever was she to do? She couldn't ask her mother. Maybe Jane would help?

'You stupid, selfish girl,' said Jane, when Emma tearfully confessed her ordeal. 'I went to a great deal of trouble to get you that job. These are difficult times, Emma. Plenty of girls would be grateful to have a gentleman such as Monsieur Dupont wanting to look after them. Think of what it might mean to your mother.'

'You knew,' said Emma as the truth dawned. 'You offered me up to that bastard like a sacrifice.'

'Don't be so melodramatic. A little slap and tickle in return for the largesse of a wealthy man. It seems like a splendid arrangement to me, one you are in no position to refuse.'

Emma shook her head in disbelief. Should she go to Tim, tell him what a monster he'd married? She could imagine his shock and disappointment. He strived so hard to ignore the harsh realities of this world, but he wouldn't turn a blind eye to this betrayal, no matter how his wife tried to deny it.

Jane seemed to read her mind. 'And don't you go crying to your brother, Emma. He's not a worldly man. He may not appreciate the benefits of Monsieur Dupont's proposal the way I do.' A spark of fear flickered in her eyes, and her tone grew plaintive. 'You know how happy he is about the baby. Please don't spoil it for him.'

'You're a real piece of work,' said Emma, as she swept out the cottage door.

And to think her sister-in-law had once made her feel inferior.

Never again. Jane was the lowest of the low, and she pitied her soon-to-be niece or nephew for having to endure such a mother.

However, in one respect, Jane was right. What good would it do to tear Tim's marriage apart, especially now, with a baby on the way? What would it accomplish, apart from exposing Jane for the witch she was. Emma could see it now. Tim would tell Jack, who in turn would tell his friends, humiliating Emma even further. Her brothers would confront Monsieur Dupont. Jack would start a fight. Jane would lose her job, leaving the young family vulnerable if the foundry should let Tim go.

Emma crossed the street, so lost in thought that a car had to brake to avoid her. She barely heard the blaring horn. It was intolerable, bearing this burden alone.

By the time Emma turned the corner into Sparrow Lane, she'd made her decision. What real choice was there? She couldn't afford to lose her job. No, she would persevere at the boutique a while longer, try to handle the situation herself. Who knew? Perhaps Monsieur Dupont would search his conscience and regret his vile actions in the morning.

Emma turned up the next day for work as usual, sick with apprehension. She tried to pretend that nothing had happened, giving her boss a wide berth, desperate to avoid being alone with him.

Monsieur Dupont's behaviour towards her remained scrupulously polite, although his eyes often followed her around the room, making her skin crawl. She agonised over what had happened, wondering if she'd overreacted, maybe even dreamed the whole thing. However the broad bruise changing colour on her arm brought the truth home.

Weeks passed without incident and Emma began to relax. With a regular wage coming in, life had become easier in so many ways. Mum continued to progress, eating independently and consistently returning a hand squeeze with one of her own. Her eyes could focus on Emma's face now, and Dr Dennisdeen was becoming more positive about her prospects for recovery.

'You have done an excellent job in these vital, early weeks, Emma. I'm keeping a diary about your mother's case. Rehabilitation medicine is a fascinating new specialty, being pioneered by a truly wonderful American, Frank Krusen. He runs the physical medicine department at the Mayo Clinic in Minnesota, and it's achieving some astonishing results. I have plans to establish a similar establishment in Hobart, devoted to the most advanced physiotherapy techniques for accident and stroke victims. Polio too. With any luck, I'll have it up and running by next year.'

'Would that be a good place for my mother?'

'Indeed it would.' Dr Dennisdeen beamed at Emma, clearly excited to be talking about his future plans. 'But in the meantime, I want to extend Eileen's physical therapy here at home. You will need to attach two small pulleys to goose-neck pipes fitted over the head and the foot of her bed. Ordinary clothes line rope will do, with a two inch webbing for the hand and foot loops.'

'Will that help Mum?'

'Yes, and it will help you too,' said the doctor. 'Pulley therapy is less back-breaking for carers. It increases the range of limb motion and helps prevent bed sores. It also has the advantage that, over time, patients can progress to doing the exercises themselves.'

'You really think that's possible?'

Doctor Dennisdeen gave her an encouraging smile. 'I grow more hopeful by the day. Eileen is trapped in a body that doesn't work, but for all we know her mind is unaffected. Our job is to give your mother her life back.'

Emma felt a surge of hope so powerful it was hard to draw breath. Her mother would be well again, she was sure of it. She would do whatever it took to make that happen.

Emma's reprieve from Monsieur Dupont's lechery didn't last long. A month after his first attempt, he tried again. This time he made no physical advance; it was by way of a business proposition.

Late one afternoon, after rearranging the hats in the window display, Emma found him waiting for her in the stock room.

'Mademoiselle, a word if I may.' She looked around, and realised the rest of the staff had gone home. 'Firstly, let me apologise for the heavy-handed way I, ah, approached you last time. I see now that I took you by surprise.' Emma wondered where this was going. 'But do not think for a moment that I've changed my mind. Here is my proposal. No, don't go.' He moved to block her way. 'I will double your wage. I will open an account here in your name and pay it off each month. Within reason you may choose whatever apparel you want for yourself, aside from gowns in the Parisian range. My only condition is that you see nobody but me. In addition, I will engage you an excellent nurse for your mother.'

'A nurse?'

'I've spoken to Dr Dennisdeen. He informs me that a suitably qualified nurse, trained in the latest physiotherapy techniques, would greatly aid your mother's recovery.'

He moved one step closer and Emma moved one step back.

'In return you will be wholly available to me on Monday, Wednesday and Friday evenings. I shall give you a key to my flat upstairs, and you shall wait there for me after work. Discretion is, of course, essential. I may require you at other times, by arrangement.' He peered at her with piggy eyes. 'You have one week to decide. If this arrangement doesn't suit, you will be dismissed from your position here.' His face betrayed no expression as he calmly put on his coat. 'Goodnight. I'd thank you to lock up.' He turned to her as he reached the door, and tipped his hat. 'Remember, mademoiselle. One week.'

Emma couldn't remember how she got home. When Jack came into the kitchen, grinning like a fool, she was sitting at the table, still wearing her hat and gloves.

'Something wrong?' he said, when she didn't say hello. 'Is it Mum?' He ducked into the lounge room to check, then straight back out.

'Sorry I haven't done those exercises with her, but I've been out all afternoon.'

Emma wasn't listening, didn't even look at him.

'Sis.' He came closer. 'I'm trying to tell you something. I've got a job.'

This finally got her attention. 'A job?' She could smell beer on his breath. 'Why that's wonderful, Jacky.' If Jack had a job, maybe she could tell Monsieur Dupont where to stick his *arrangement*. 'How? Where?'

'You won't believe this. It's got to do with you and your boss in a roundabout way.' She felt a creeping fear. 'I went to Patterson's pub for lunch with a few mates. Before you start, I used my race winnings from last week. You said I could do what I liked with that money.'

'Go on.'

'Well, this old bloke, Kevin, comes in and we get talking. He's in the rag trade, some kind of agent. Sells rolls of material – wool and silks and satins and such, along with suits and ladies' dresses. Just sold a swag of stuff to that boutique of yours, apparently. He goes every-where, he does; Melbourne, Sydney, even England and France. Turns out he's after a dogsbody, an apprentice like. Someone to drive him around, pick up samples, do deliveries. Someone who wants to learn the ropes.'

'And?'

'Well, he asks me if I know anyone who might be interested. So I say my sister is a model at *Trés Chic* and – you'll love this bit – that I was thinking of getting into the rag trade meself. He asks me your name, and says he's heard good things about you. Then he says, "If Monsieur Dupont thinks so highly of the sister, perhaps I should give the brother a go." And just like that, I got the job!' He gave a dramatic flourish and waited. 'Well, say something.'

'How did you meet this man again?'

'I told you, he came into the pub. It was fate, sis. All those empty tables, and for some reason, he sits down right next to me.'

Emma sensed a trap. Monsieur Dupont had organised this job for Jack. Did he think she would be grateful enough to sleep with him?

'There's one more thing.' He bent his head and shuffled his feet. 'I have to leave, sis. Tomorrow, for Hobart. Like I said, this bloke lives and works on the road. After that we're sailing to Melbourne.' He looked up, trying to look sorry and not succeeding. 'I've never been to Melbourne.'

'What about Mum?' she said, thinking aloud. 'When I'm at work.'

'Maybe, between the two of us, we could afford to hire someone. I don't mean that old drunk, Mrs Shaw. I mean a proper trained nurse. How expensive do you reckon that would be?'

Way outside their budget, that was for certain. 'Where did that idea come from, about the trained nurse I mean?'

'From Kevin. I told him about Mum and he suggested that's what we need. Kevin's a very easy bloke to talk to.'

Emma put her head in her hands.

'What's wrong, sis?'

'A headache is all. Let me go and lie down.'

Emma escaped with her racing thoughts to the bedroom. If Jack took the job and left Launceston, she'd be unable to manage Mum without a nurse. She'd have to take her boss up on his vile offer. Or she could tell Jack the job he was so excited about was really a ploy to get her into her boss's bed. It would destroy his self-confidence. It would also destroy the best opportunity he'd ever had, and ultimately lead to them all being jobless and evicted.

Emma tried to imagine what it would be like to be out on the street with a paralysed mother. No, she couldn't let it happen. Jack would have his job, Mum would have her nurse, and she would have her deal with the devil. Game, set and match to Monsieur Dupont.

For Emma, the next week felt like some sort of living death. She would give her boss what he wanted. What choice did she have? Life had backed her into a corner. But she would make him wait out the week he'd given her, and she would never think of him as Monsieur Dupont again. He was Melvyn to her now, though she didn't dare say it to his face. Melvyn Spriggs from Fingal; a sad, loathsome little coward who did not deserve his place on this good earth.

On the seventh day Melvyn confronted her. 'Have you made a decision, mademoiselle?'

'You leave me no choice,' she said. 'But before I agree, you must guarantee my mother will have her nurse, and my brother will have his job. Nothing happens until those arrangements are in place.'

Melvyn breathed hard, stared at her chest and licked his thick lips. 'Of course, my dear. I give my word. Whatever you want.' His tone was no longer commanding. It was eager, fawning even. So, she still had some power. He'd gone from bully to beggar. The change surprised her.

Melvyn was true to his word. Jack left, excited by the prospect of a steady job and his first trip across Bass Strait to Melbourne. Emma couldn't help but be pleased for him. A qualified nurse duly arrived and moved into Jack's old room. Emma hadn't expected round-the-clock help. Elsie Hopkins was a plump, matronly woman with a broad smile and sunny disposition. She'd come highly recommended by Dr Dennisdeen, and proved to be a godsend. Not only was she a dedicated and capable nurse, but she was also the sort of person who couldn't bear to be idle. Elsie cheerfully cooked up delicious, nourishing meals with the fresh produce that Emma could now afford. She tidied up while Emma was at work, and did some of the washing.

Best of all, she didn't treat Mum like she was unconscious or mentally deficient. Not like some people – Jane sprang to mind. Instead Elsie cheerfully chatted away as if they were best friends, telling Mum about her grown daughters in Sydney, and the grandchild she hardly ever got to see. Showing Mum the baby clothes she was knitting for the Red Cross, asking her opinion on colours and patterns.

'What do you think, Eileen? Lemon or white? And the bonnet ... striped or plain?'

Elsie was an enthusiastic member of the local library, and read aloud to Mum every day: Agatha Christie mysteries, *The Little House On The Prairie* series and the latest blockbusters like *Gone With The Wind*. Emma recalled Dr Dennisdeen's words. *For all we know Eileen's mind is unaffected.* Emma prayed this was true, but the horror of her mother being prisoner of a paralysed body remained. If Mum could indeed hear and understand everything going on around her, what a blessing Nurse Elsie's cheery company would be.

Emma missed Jack, but she didn't miss him constantly asking for money, and thrusting her into the role of parent, even though she was two years younger. Life at home was much happier and more peaceful than before.

There was nothing happy or peaceful about work however, or her despicable arrangement with Melvyn Spriggs. One morning, a week after Elsie arrived, Melvyn had called her into his office. 'Is the nurse I sent you working out?'

What to say? If she deemed Elsie unsuitable, she might put off the inevitable for a short time, while Melvyn arranged somebody else. But it would be a postponement, not a reprieve. And anyway, she loved having Elsie.

'The nurse is most helpful.'

'And the lad? Jack, your brother. He has taken up his traineeship?' She nodded and Melvyn stood up straighter, sucking in his belly as best he could. His fingers formed a steeple. 'I hope you're satisfied that I'm a man who keeps his promises.' He handed her a key on a silver chain set with a small opal, and lowered his voice to a whisper 'At five o'clock, go upstairs and let yourself in. Go to the bedroom where you'll find a garment laid out. Put it on and wait for me.'

Melvyn reached for her hand, and she forced herself to let him. Raising it to his flabby lips, he began to kiss her fingers, one by one. Filled with revulsion, she snatched her hand away.

'Ah.' He seemed undeterred. 'My little coquette likes to tease. No matter, you will be mine tonight.' He leaned in close. Close enough for her to smell his pipe tobacco breath. Close enough to see his wrinkles and enlarged pores and stained teeth. 'Don't worry. I will see that you have a good time, mademoiselle.'

At five o'clock Emma climbed the back stairs and let herself in. Melvyn's flat was crowded with lavish Parisienne-style furniture – or at least what Emma thought was Parisienne style furniture, based on the glossy French magazines downstairs. High pelmets, rich red drapes that pooled on the parquetry floor and an oversize gilt mirror. Cubist lamps, bronze figures of naked women and an art deco copper-and-glass chandelier. Fabulous art on the walls: prints by Matisse and Picasso. Emma liked each piece separately, but together they were too much, too fussy. Too try-hard.

She wandered around the overblown rooms, including the bedroom with its lacy scrap of cream silk lying on the gold damask counterpane. Was that what Melvyn expected her to wear? What was the point? She may as well be naked. Yet the thought of losing her job and Elsie was enough to persuade her.

Emma took off her dress, hung it up carefully, put on the lace teddy and looked in the mirror. She shuddered to think of Melvyn seeing her like that. A memory flashed by, of another day when she was standing in her underwear. A day with Tom looking on, making her blush. Tom, with his brilliant brown eyes, blazing with an overwhelming, irresistible vitality. Why couldn't she be waiting for him instead?

Time dragged on. This must be how Marie Antoinette felt before her execution. Then, the sound of the front door opening. Emma froze. Before she had time to think, Melvyn was upon her. He tore off the teddy without a word and shoved her back on the bed. She closed her eyes, trying to block out his hot, clammy hands kneading her breasts and the ragged sound of his panting breath.

Every instinct screamed to fight him off. To gouge her fingers into his eye sockets, knee him in the groin and escape. But she couldn't. She was paralysed, just like her mother. So instead Emma lay, still as death, going deeper and deeper into shock. He flopped his fat belly on top, forced Emma's legs apart with his knee, and tried to shove himself into her. Grunting and sweating. Harder and harder, and harder still until he forced his way inside. She felt a distant pain, as if through a thick fog. A pain that didn't belong to her. And as she lay suffocating under Melvyn Spriggs flabby, bucking body, she thought of Tom and began to cry.

CHAPTER 16

Tom filed into the paymaster's office behind the other men, excited to receive his first pay packet. He'd begun the new year working at the Hobart Aero Club as a trainee civil aviation mechanic, living at Cambridge Aerodrome, sleeping in a humble dorm with five other apprentices. Lumpy bunks, thin blankets and stodgy, tasteless food, but Tom didn't mind. It had been like his birthday every day, investigating the innermost workings of a dizzying array of aircraft, learning the secrets of flight in a satisfying nuts-and-bolts way.

The problem was that Tom didn't only want to know how planes worked. He wanted to fly them himself, guide them through the heavens, leave his earthbound existence behind. It would be next year at least before he could transfer to a pilot training course, and even then, entry wasn't guaranteed.

So he'd applied for a Royal Australian Air Force flying cadetship. Technically he was a year too young, but he'd talked to Harry and, hey presto, he had a shiny new birth certificate proclaiming him to be eighteen years old. Applying for the RAAF was the first thing Tom had ever done that seemed to impress his brother.

'An air force pilot?' Harry whistled through his teeth. 'Papa would have been proud.'

Tom bit his tongue at the mention of their father. There was so much that Harry didn't know about their heritage, about the past. A privilege to think Nana had chosen him as secret keeper, but also a burden.

The panel interview had been exhaustive but maddeningly vague. *We mark candidates on general promise and fitness for service*, they'd said. How could you quantify *general promise*? He had no idea how he'd done. The entrance exam on physics, physical science and mathematics was more to his liking, and he'd achieved a high score.

'A letter for you, Tom,' said the paymaster as he distributed the wages. The man toyed with it, taking an agonising amount of time to hand it over, piquing the interest of the others. 'Not planning on leaving us so soon, are you, son?'

Tom snatched the letter, taking a deep breath as he spotted the Air Board insignia in the corner. Unwilling to open it in front of an audience, he retreated to his empty dorm room, extracted the note from the envelope with shaky fingers, then whooped aloud with joy. He'd been selected for the RAAF's No. 1 Flying Training School at Point Cook in Melbourne, and was to report there on the 20th of January, barely a week away.

A bolt of excitement coursed down Tom's spine as he looked out the dingy window to the sky of flawless blue. He couldn't remember a time when he hadn't longed to fly. When he hadn't been jealous of each bird, as it vanished into the sun; of each moth as it spiralled towards the moon. Not any more. He read the letter again and laughed aloud. This time it was his turn to defy gravity and soar to the stars.

Tom wished he could share the news with Emma, but without an address or phone number ... He'd tried everything to find out, even sneaking into the student records office at Campbell College to look at the files. But he'd been sprung. 'That's confidential information, I'm afraid.' Thereafter the door had remained firmly locked whenever the bursar or Principal's secretary were away. The awful truth was that he might never see Emma again.

Tom closed his eyes, imagining her serious smile and sweet face. She'd be thrilled for him, he knew she would be. Wherever Emma was, he hoped she was happy.

Tom spent a few days at Binburra before his ship sailed for Melbourne. His excitement was somewhat tempered when he saw his grandmother. She looked thinner than he remembered, and her cough had worsened. But she insisted she was fine, and her eyes shone with pride and joy as he told her his news.

On the day he left she gave him a thylacine pendant on a silver chain. 'Your grandfather gave this to me on our first wedding anniversary. He wore one too.'

Tom closed his hand over the small, shining figure. 'I'll call her Karma.'

'What an excellent name. She'll watch over you now, as she has always watched over me.' Tears filled his eyes and he hugged her tight. 'You've dreamed of this all your life,' said Nana, 'and it will be a glorious adventure. I just pray the world has learned its lesson, and there will not be another war.'

One fine morning a few days later, Tom lined up on the Point Cook parade ground with an assortment of other new cadets. Strangers, yes, but each knowing they shared something in common – a love of flight. There was already a certain camaraderie in the air.

That day passed in a whirl. Tom was shown his quarters and allocated a place in the mess hall. He was introduced to his instructors and, best of all, assigned a flight schedule. He couldn't wait to take off.

However, it didn't take long for the heady excitement of that first day to evaporate. The new cadets were *initiated* by the seniors that very night, while the officers turned a blind eye. Stripped, daubed with paint and tossed in the dam. Afterwards they were made to stand naked on a table and sing a song. A humiliating procedure apparently designed to 'knock any airs and graces out of you sorry little sods'.

In the coming days Tom struggled to adapt to a life of strict discipline; no easy thing for a boy from the bush. Endless backbreaking drills. A thousand rules. Two hours of compulsory sport daily. Fourteen-hour days, six days a week.

'At Point Cook we aim in one year to turn out officer pilots to the same standard as the RAF does in two,' said Flight Lieutenant Jock Allen, Tom's instructor. Working at the aerodrome had been easy compared to this, and a week passed with no sign of getting into a plane. There was plenty of theory though: twenty-three textbooks on subjects as wide-ranging as armaments, navigation, meteorology, navigation and the theory of flight.

In the hierarchy of the base, cadets were the lowest of the low, at everybody's beck and call. Expected to run messages for their superiors, clean their rooms, even shine their shoes. It didn't take long for Tom and the rest of the cadets to get their backs up.

'I swear, if that mangy corporal barks at me one more time, I'll deck him,' growled Stu Kennedy one day, after four hours of drill in the blazing sun. 'When in God's name will we get in the air?'

Stu was another country boy, from Cooma in the Snowy Mountains; a bit of a larrikin who in some ways reminded Tom of his brother. He and Tom were the two youngest cadets, and both shared a love of their mountain homes, swapping stories about the big skies and jutting peaks. The grand isolation. Talking to Stu helped ease Tom's impatience and homesickness.

The boys weren't long disappointed. Flying instruction began the following week. Tom was to train in a Tiger Moth. Hard to believe he'd be taking to the air in a plane made by de Havilland, the most innovative aviation manufacturer in the world.

His Moth was a single-engine, two seater biplane; yellow and black like its namesake. Jock jumped into the open cockpit. 'Hop in.'

Tom didn't need to be told twice, but to his great disappointment, they didn't leave the ground. He spent the next two hours taxiing around the runway, practising the controls.

'That's all for today, Abbott,' said Jock at last. 'Bring her back in.'

Tom gloomily headed for the hangar. At this rate he'd never take off, and he needed a certain number of dual flying hours before being allowed to go solo.

'Cheer up.' Jock smiled at his pupil's long face. 'You'll take her up tomorrow.'

Tomorrow seemed to take forever coming, but when it did, flying was everything Tom had dreamed of. Taxiing down the runway, gaining speed, the thrill of lift-off. The buzz of adrenaline and sense of total freedom. The view of earth from sky. The magical, supporting power of thin air beneath him. It was indeed a miracle.

However, it wasn't easy. Tom had blithely assumed he'd be a natural, and was surprised when he wasn't. In those first few weeks he found his pretty Moth had a mind of her own. 'I can't fly straight and level let alone bring her in properly,' he said to Stu one night over lamb shanks and mashed potato. 'Today I overshot the landing point twice and almost hit a fence. I swung like mad when taking off, jerked at the controls and Old Jock called me *rough and ham-fisted*.'

'You'll be right,' said Stu, who was flying an Avro Cadet, recently arrived from England; considered a superior training aircraft to the Tiger Moth and easier to fly. The pressure was on to go solo by ten hours of training, and it irked Tom that Stu had managed it after only seven.

But Tom wasn't far behind, soloing right on the course average of nine hours and forty minutes. The euphoria of that first flight without Jock knocked him sideways. He could barely bring himself to land, and returned to earth whistling and singing and jumping for joy.

After that his confidence surged, and he made swift progress. Six weeks later he could loop the loop, scream through the sky at one hundred miles an hour, and perform daredevil dives. This was living.

However, not for everybody. Point Cook had its fair share of mishaps and tragedies. Four months into their course, the first fatal training accident happened. On a windy day in April, nineteen-year-old Norman Chaplin, with twenty-five hours' flying time under his belt, was practising aerobatics when one wing crumpled coming out of a loop. The Gipsy Moth nosedived from a thousand feet. Norman had the courage and presence of mind to undo his belt, climb from the cockpit and jump. But his parachute became tangled in the plane.

Tom had liked Norman – a quiet, gentlemanly boy with whom he shared a bunkhouse – and the death hit him hard. Two days later Norman was buried with full ceremonial honours, and life at the base went on as before.

'Better than crippled for life,' said Stu. 'Have you seen the burned flyboys that came down in the war? Faces melted away. Hands burned off. You'd be better off dead, I reckon.'

Tom shuddered. For the first time it hit home what he was doing. Playing at being a fighter pilot, shooting imaginary enemies from the sky. Pretending to drop bombs - making the noise as he flew low over buildings and imagined them exploding into flames beneath him. All the cadets did it. Flying was a thrilling game, but where would it lead them? Nana's words rang in his ears. *I pray the world has learned its lesson, and there will not be another war.*

CHAPTER 17

Mum's progress was agonisingly slow – three steps forward, two steps back. But she was improving, and that was the only solace in Emma's grim existence. Going to work each day was a special kind of hell, especially on Mondays, Wednesdays and Fridays. But the other days were nearly as bad. Having to kowtow to Melvyn, call him *Monsieur*. Having to put up with his small familiarities, as if they shared something real between them.

Emma had tried her best to be discrete. Nothing could be more humiliating than her loathsome arrangement with Melvyn becoming public knowledge. However, rumours soon grew. She became an object of both contempt and envy among the other staff; a wicked combination that stripped her of friendships and ruined her reputation. Contempt for being an old man's slut, and envy for receiving his largesse. Melvyn treated Emma generously and it raised eyebrows. Thankfully her neighbours in Sparrow Lane hadn't caught wind of the scandal. They lived in the poorest quarter, moved in different circles, so the nightmare didn't follow her home. But Launceston was a small town. It was merely a matter of time.

Emma didn't blame her co-workers for despising her. She despised herself, and refused to think any more of Tom, or the fledgling love that she'd left behind in Hobart. That proud, innocent girl he'd known was dead. Risen in her place was a poor, sullied creature who allowed herself to be abused and manipulated; an unlovable wretch who deserved no respect. That other girl would never have got herself into this sort of trouble. Not the girl who won a scholarship to Campbell College and wanted to be a doctor. Not the girl who'd stolen Tom's heart. That girl would have had a clever plan to turn the tables on Melvyn.

Emma did think of Karma though, and the other zoo animals. How she longed to see them again, make sure they were being cared for. Find out how Alison was getting on. Karma often came to her in dreams, whispering in a soft, sad voice, 'Poor Emma, poor thing. As doomed and trapped as I am.'

A month passed, then two, then three, while each day Emma went through the motions. How she hated her life. If not for her mother, she may well have cast herself off the bridge at Cataract Gorge, as carelessly as one might cast away a scrap piece of paper. Commit her body to the cascade, where the wild South Esk river spilled into the Tamar. Let the current carry her to the river mouth, past the watchful eye of Low Head Lighthouse, and release her spirit into the vast, tumbling waters of Bass Strait.

Summer declined into autumn. Jack sent her letters almost every week, full of chatter about the places he'd been and the people he'd seen. Emma read them to her mother. "'I'm in Sydney. Hard to believe the size of the harbour here, and so blue you'd think it was painted. When Mum's well, you'll both have to come and see it for yourself.'"

He was a good boy, and it consoled her to know he was happy. A few shillings always fell out of the envelope - once even a pound note. She wanted to tell him not to bother; that she didn't need his money, but she could never bring herself to write back.

One Friday at work a buyer arrived; an important one apparently, by the way Melvyn fawned over him. 'Meet my top model,' he said, calling her over. 'Emma, this is Monsieur Angelo.'

Angelo was an attractive man. Mid-thirties. Tall and lean, with shiny blue-black hair and amused eyes. 'Please.' His gaze held hers.

'Call me Tony.' He reached for her hand, and drew it to his lips. 'Charmed.'

Emma felt a certain frisson when he touched her, and something unfamiliar stirred inside.

'Our friend here is considering an investment in *Trés Chic*, my dear.' Melvyn licked his greedy lips and puffed out his chest. 'It would mean opening new outlets in Hobart and Melbourne.' He peered at her triumphantly, hoping for some sign that she was impressed.

Emma turned her attention to the mannequins near the window.

When Emma let herself into the upstairs flat after work, Tony Angelo was waiting. A bottle of champagne stood in an ice bucket on the side table. He leaned back on the curved walnut sofa of cream leather, one long leg crossed over his knee, smoking a cigarette – the very picture of casual elegance.

Emma looked around for Melvyn.

'Monsieur Dupont isn't here.' Tony offered her a cigarette and she shook her head. 'He really is a revolting little man, Emma. How on earth do you put up with him?'

Emma wasn't sure what to say, but Melvyn's absence came as such a relief that she managed a shy smile. Tony stood, popped the champagne cork with a bang, poured two glasses and handed her one. 'Sit, please.'

She took a sip of the icy bubbles, and perched herself on the edge of the sofa.

'How old are you , Emma?'

'Seventeen, sir.'

Tony looked thoughtful. 'Do you know what your odious employer has promised me, Emma? A night with you in return for an investment in his business. What do you think of that?'

Emma weighed up the question. She wasn't really surprised. She already knew that no wickedness was beyond Melvyn Spriggs. Whatever else, it meant she would not have to submit to him tonight.

'What do I think?' she said. 'I think Melvyn is a monster – yes, that's his real name – but not because of any promise he made to you. He is a monster because he has coerced me into becoming his whore against my will. Whether I become your whore as well, sir, is of no concern to me.'

Emma finished her champagne. She liked the way the bubbles tingled as they slipped down her throat.

Tony refilled their glasses, and her eyes noticed the wedding ring on his left hand. 'I have no intention of forcing you, Emma. I'm content to drink champagne and enjoy your company.' His hand crept closer to her knee. 'That is, of course, unless you're … willing?'

Emma studied his features, so boldly handsome, and saw how much he wanted her. This was not Melvyn's stomach-turning brand of pitiful, panting need. This was the natural desire of a fit, healthy man for a woman. Just as the stallion back on the farm had desired his mares. And she realised the power she held, and that she wanted him too. Wanted to know what it felt like to be held in a real man's arms. What did she have to lose that wasn't already lost?

Emma swigged down her champagne. 'Yes, Tony. I am willing.' Still he hesitated. Slowly she unbuttoned the bodice of her dress. He watched her, hypnotised, as the swell of her pale breasts peeped through.

He put a hand around her waist, and drew her to him. 'So young,' he whispered. 'So lovely. So wasted on that preening old fool.'

During that wild night, Tony Angelo opened her eyes to the pleasures of the flesh. He taught her what he knew and she discovered much more for herself. How naïve she'd been, imagining that she might only enjoy sex with a man she loved and married. What a silly, childish notion. Tony was a skilful, considerate lover, strong and arousing – as different from bumbling, ham-fisted Melvyn as a cockroach was from a lion. But the two men had one thing in common; a powerful weakness for what she could offer them in bed. She must learn how to use that weakness. Use it to somehow wrest back her life.

· · ·

Emma lay lost in thought, as the faint light of dawn crept in the window. Trying to make sense of last night, and what she'd learned, and how it had changed her.

Staying all night in the flat was a first. Elsie was perfectly capable of looking after Mum, but Emma had always escaped at the first opportunity. So far Melvyn hadn't minded. He always fell asleep afterwards anyway, but lately he'd been angling for her to stay. 'An extra hour's sleep in the morning,' he'd offered, as if negotiating a pay rise. An extra, vile sexual encounter, more like it. The thought of waking up with Melvyn beside her made Emma ill, and how could she explain an overnight absence without exposing her shame to Elsie?

Tony stirred, and tried to wrap her in his arms. She shrugged him off, went to the bathroom, stood in the tub and turned on the shower. Hoping the hot water on her bare back could drum some answers into her. Tell her what she was supposed to do. Last night with Tony had made her current life even more unbearable. How could she stomach Melvyn now that she knew what a real man felt like?

Emma retrieved her clothes from the wardrobe, slipped into them and put up her hair. She checked her watch. Wearing the same dress as yesterday would no doubt inspire a fresh round of hateful gossip downstairs, but so what? Why should she care what they thought?

She was putting on the kettle in the kitchen when Tony appeared, wet skin shining from the shower, wearing nothing but a smile. He bounded over and pulled her in close for a kiss. For an awful moment she thought of how shocked her mother would be to know a naked man was taking such liberties. A few short months ago she herself would have been just as shocked. Emma cast the thought away. Too late for those sort of delicate sentiments where she was concerned.

'Where are you going?' said Tony, his voice husky with desire.

'Downstairs. Mind my hair.'

She twisted away from him, but he grasped her by the shoulders and sat her down at the table. 'Emma, sweetheart. Listen.' He licked his lips and glanced briefly at the roof, like he was thinking on his feet. 'I must see you again. Come to Hobart with me. I'll rent you an apartment. Lovely clothes, an allowance to buy pretty things. We'll paint the town red.'

How stupid did he think she was? She needed to get away, but not by swapping one trap for another. 'And your wife?' she said. 'Will she be there too?'

'Don't be like that, sweetheart.' He pouted like a thwarted child. 'Lily … Lily and I have an understanding. She won't get in our way.'

Poor Lily, thought Emma. Tony was another Melvyn, just younger and better-looking. Were all men the same? No, not Tom. He would never treat another person with such contempt.

'Come on,' he coaxed. 'You're something special, sweetheart. Any red-blooded man would give his eye teeth for a night like we just had. You don't want to stay here with that bloody old rogue, do you? Someone who was happy to pimp you out to make a deal?'

She studied his face, surprised at her own detachment. A plan was forming.

'Leave the old man behind,' he urged. 'Don't you want to come to Hobart?'

'Yes, but I have a sick mother, who must come with me.'

'Whoa,' he said. 'Mama's not part of this arrangement.'

'I don't want another *arrangement*,' said Emma. 'I want to be in control of my own life, make my own money – a great deal of it. Enough for my mother to go to an expensive rehabilitation hospital in Hobart.' She looked him coolly in the eye. 'Is there somewhere a girl like me could make that sort of money, Tony? I imagine a man like you might know these things.'

He shook his head. 'You don't know what you're saying. What kind of life would that be for a young girl?'

'What kind of life is this?' Emma shrugged. 'A whore is a whore.'

Tony took a step backwards, disappointment written large on his face, and something else. Sadness perhaps. Then he went to the desk and scribbled down a name, address and phone number. 'This lady may be able to help. She's always looking for talented girls. Models and … more. Tell her I sent you.' He took a wad of notes from his wallet. 'A contribution towards your mother's hospital fund.' He left the money on the desk, and added his business card. 'Call me when you get to Hobart.'

She put the card and money in her bag. Twenty pounds. More than enough to pay for her trip and cover Elsie's wages while she was away.

'Wait for me,' said Tony, throwing on some clothes.

Emma waited, quite looking forward to the stir when she came downstairs.

'Are you really going to invest in *Trés Chic*?' she asked.

'Not if you don't want me to.'

'I don't want you to.'

'Then I won't. It was touch and go anyway. Old Melvyn's been cooking the books.' He spun her around for a last, heart-thumping kiss. 'My God, sweetheart. You've bewitched me. I must see you again. Promise you'll call.'

When Melvyn saw Emma, he hurried over with what almost looked like shame in his eyes. 'My dear, I didn't sleep a wink.' He ran his tongue over his lips. Every staff member on the shop floor had stopped what they were doing and turned to watch. For once Melvyn didn't reprimand them for laziness. He didn't even seem to notice. 'Can we speak privately, *Mademoiselle*?'

They moved to his office.

'I may never forgive myself for last night,' he said. 'And for not warning you first. I assume that Monsieur Angelo, that he, ah—.'

'He did.'

'I see.' He sniffed, and sighed, looking decidedly miserable. 'Well, we must find a way to put this unpleasantness behind us. It was ultimately in a good cause, my dear, for your … cooperation will help seal his investment in the business. However, I could never countenance such a thing again. Frankly, I was green with jealousy. It was all I could do not to burst in and throw the cad out.'

Melvyn was sweating now. He pulled a silk handkerchief from his pocket and wiped his florid face. Then he extracted a little box from the desk drawer, and gave it to her.

'Open it.'

Inside was a gold ring, set with a brilliant blue stone in a cluster of diamonds.

'Hope you like sapphires, my dear. I got a great deal on this ring from a chap whose engagement fell through. His loss, our gain, eh?' He took Emma's hand and slipped it on her finger.

'You want to marry me?'

'When you're of age, yes. Make an honest woman of you.' She opened her mouth to speak and he held up his hand. 'Don't thank me, Emma. The truth is you are good for me. You make me feel young again.'

He leaned in to kiss her lips and she turned away. 'I'm tired,' she said, staring at the ring, wondering what it might be worth. 'May I take the rest of the day off?'

'In the circumstances I think that's fair. Tomorrow we shall announce our engagement, and set a wedding date.' He tried to kiss her again, and this time she endured it. He made a satisfied grunt in the back of his throat. 'Now, off with you. I have business to discuss with Monsieur Angelo.'

Emma decided to escape out the back way. With head held high, she marched past the shop girls, who were giggling and talking behind their hands. Past the other models who, along with trying on frocks for the morning showing, were also pointing at her and laughing. Past Jane in the cutting room, thick-waisted with child.

She did not say goodbye or look back. In the space of a few hours her life had utterly changed. She'd changed too. For better or worse, she didn't know yet.

When Emma arrived home, she went straight in to see her mother. Turning off the radio, Emma took her hand. 'I'm going away for a few days, Mum. To Hobart, to look for work. The boutique hasn't panned out.'

She felt Mum squeeze her fingers. It was happening more and more often lately.

'Elsie will look after you. I'll get Peggy from down the road to come in twice a day and give Elsie a hand turning you. You know Peg. She's a sweet girl, and strong too.'

Emma blinked back a tear. What was Mum feeling in that very second? Was she straining to connect with her fingers and toes? Was she struggling to get words out of her head and into her mouth? Or was she forever lost in a foggy brain, damaged beyond repair.

'Don't worry, Mum. When I find a job, you'll come with me to Hobart. Dr Dennisdeen has promised you a place in his new hospital. I'll get you the best care money can buy.'

That was the plan, anyway. Emma spent the rest of the day packing. She went shopping to stock the cupboards. She spoke to Elsie. 'I'll be employing you directly from now on,' she said, handing the surprised nurse ten pounds. Emma imagined Melvyn's pudgy face when she didn't show up for work in the morning. How could she? Tomorrow, she and her savings would be boarding a bus to Hobart.

CHAPTER 18

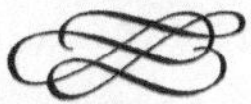

The bus trip was bittersweet. Three years ago a very different girl had waited at the same stop, caught the same rattly old bus, with the same chatty and cheerful driver. She'd sat in the very same seat at the front, with a good view of the road ahead, and excitedly told the driver about her scholarship to Campbell College. It seemed like a lifetime ago.

'Going back to school, Miss?' he asked, as the bus pulled away.

Back to school? 'That's right,' she said, wishing it were true. 'I've been home for a few days to see my mother. She hasn't been well.'

'That's no good.' He braked and honked as a pair of dogs raced across the road, chasing a terrified hen. 'Your mum doing better now, is she?'

'Much better, thank you.' Emma gave wishful thinking free rein. 'She'll be moving to Hobart soon. Getting a place near my school so we can be together.'

'That's great, love,' he said. 'Good old mum, eh?'

It seemed miraculous to Emma that the driver believed her. Surely he could tell she was no school girl? Surely, just by looking at her, he could see her shame?

. . .

The bus dropped Emma off outside the General Post Office on the corner of Elizabeth and Macquarie Streets. She checked the time on its grand clock tower, modelled after London's Big Ben. Almost one o'clock. She found a shop window, scrutinised her reflection and tidied her hair. In her blue cap-sleeved dress she might have been off to a tea party instead of a brothel. Emma picked up her small suitcase and sat on a bench to gather her thoughts, shivering under the cold winter sun. In different circumstances it would have been exciting to be back in Hobart. The clanging tramcars, the bustling crowds, all the pulse and vitality of Tasmania's biggest city. Happy memories crowded in. It was all she could do not to hop a Queens Domain tram to the zoo. Or maybe Campbell College. Would Harry still be there? And Tom?

The clock chimed the hour. Emma took a deep breath and pulled the scribbled address from her pocket. First things first. Right now she needed to ring Mrs Martha Finchley of Hampton Hall and tee up a job interview.

She found a public telephone and dialled the number with trembling fingers. The receptionist put her straight through.

'Ah, yes, Emma Starr,' said Mrs Finchley with an English accent. 'I've been expecting this call. You come highly recommended by Mr Tony Angelo, a valued client of ours.'

Emma wondered what form the recommendation had taken. *Emma's a talented girl* or *she's a great lay*.

'Can you be here in half an hour?' asked Mrs Finchley.

It was as simple as that. Emma thought back to her disheartening job search in Launceston earlier that year. Traipsing around the whole town, twice. Scoring only one interview with a lecherous shopkeeper who indecently propositioned her in the first five minutes. How shocked she'd been; how outraged. How she'd changed.

Emma looked in a shop window to check her hair. She tossed up whether or not it was worth the expense of a taxi, and decided it was. She needed to arrive looking her best, and she was flush with money, having sold Melvyn's ring to a Launceston jeweller before she caught the bus that morning. She tried to look into the future but drew a blank. Maybe Hampton Hall was a legitimate fashion house. Maybe it wasn't. It didn't really matter. If she was offered a job there, she'd take it.

The taxi dropped her off at an impressive sandstone and brick mansion in Runnymede St, Battery Point. An engraved sign on the wall behind the wrought iron gate read *Hampton Hall*, giving no hint of the nature of the establishment.

Emma smoothed her dress and knocked on the door. A maid opened it. She wore a tailored black dress and white apron, and looked very stylish. 'Yes?'

'I'm here to see Mrs Finchley. She's expecting me.'

The maid beckoned her into a wide reception lobby, with rich rugs on the floor, a grand piano in the corner and sparkling crystal chandeliers hanging from the vaulted ceiling. 'May I take your hat and coat?' Oil paintings decorated the wood-panelled walls. Glossy magazines such as *Vogue* and *C'est La Mode* lay on an intricately inlaid antique table by the chesterfield sofa. The place screamed of money. 'Wait here, please.'

The only indication that Hampton Hall might not be a high-end fashion house was the giant guard positioned at the base of the stairs. A mountain of a man. His broad coffee-coloured face cracked into a friendly smile when she looked at him.

Emma resisted the urge to inspect herself in the large gilt mirror. If her dress was wrinkled from the bus trip or her hair was mussed, it was too late to do anything about it. Instead she went over and over the story she'd practised in her head. Hands clammy with nerves. Worried that she'd be asked to give Melvyn as a reference.

When Mrs Finchley arrived, she wasn't at all what Emma expected. For some reason she'd imagined a tall, intimidating person with hard, calculating eyes and a haughty expression. But the plump, middle-aged woman who emerged from a side room reminded Emma of her mother. Expensively dressed, certainly; that gorgeous beaded gown must have been a Chanel original. But Mrs Finchley couldn't quite pull it off. She was too short, for one thing, barely five foot two. And her bosom was too generous, and her hips too wide for elegance.

'Emma, my darling girl.' Mrs Finchley wrapped her in a warm embrace, smelling comfortingly of cinnamon and talcum powder. 'Come with me, and we'll have a chat, shall we?'

When they passed the guard, Mrs Finchley introduced them. 'This is Kai, Emma, from Tonga. He keeps us all safe.'

She led Emma to a lavishly furnished sitting room.

'I believe you have a position vacant, Mrs Finchley. For a model, or—'

'All my girls call me Martha,' she said, as if Emma already worked there. She beamed so broadly that Emma couldn't help but smile back. 'You speak beautifully, Emma. An educated young woman. We love that here. Now, tell me about yourself. I know a little already. You're seventeen, you come from Launceston, and you have a sick mother.'

Tony had been true to his word. Martha gave her an encouraging smile, one of immense sympathy; a warm invitation to confide. The dam burst and her carefully rehearsed lines were forgotten in a rush of emotion. Emma told Martha everything. About the scholarship to Campbell College and her mother's stroke. About running out of money, and asking Jane for help, and Melvyn. About last night with Tony and how she couldn't stay in Launceston, and her resolve to somehow secure a place for her mother in Dr Dennisdeen's new hospital. She barely drew breath.

Martha let Emma talk, never once interrupting or trying to hurry her. At the end she patted her hand and offered a handkerchief. Emma blew her nose. 'My, you have had a time of it, haven't you? But you've done the right thing coming here, dear. I can help if you'll let me.'

Emma sniffed a few times, and balled the hanky in her hand. The maid came in and Martha asked her to bring tea. 'Do you know what kind of business I run, Emma?'

'A fashion house? It looks too grand to be a … to be a brothel.'

Martha stopped her. 'Brothel is such an ugly word. I prefer to call Hampton Hall a gentlemen's club — one that caters to the cream of Hobart society, I might add. We hold exclusive parties and put on regular fashion shows for our clients. My girls model the latest couture gowns and lingerie from London and Paris, and the gentlemen are able to purchase the outfits for their wives and girl-friends. They are also free to request private time with the models, who split their remuneration with the house on a fifty-fifty basis.'

Emma drew in a sharp breath. There it was. Martha hesitated, looking concerned. 'No, please go on,' said Emma, as the maid arrived with a tea tray.

'I was about to say that in a short time my best models can make a great deal of money. Enough to buy beautiful clothes, cars, apartments. Enough to achieve financial independence. My success is their success, Emma. Do you think you'd be interested in working for me?'

Emma tried to swallow, but her mouth was too dry. Martha seemed to understand, and poured her a cup of sweet, milky tea. Emma took a few sips. 'Would I ... would I do well here, do you think?'

'You'd be a favourite, Emma, a beautiful young woman such as yourself. But my gentlemen want more than a lovely face and nice figure. They can get that at many other places, and at far less expense. No, they also want a clever companion. Someone who'd be at home at the theatre or opera. Someone who speaks well and can hold a conversation. This is such an important aspect of what we offer here at Hampton Hall, that I employ tutors to teach the girls about politics and history and world affairs. Your obvious intelligence and education gives you a natural advantage.'

'I'll need to rent rooms, or a flat.'

Martha's eyes twinkled with kindness and something else. Admiration. 'You're thinking of your mother?'

Emma nodded. 'For her and a nurse, until she can get into that hospital.'

'You're a good girl, Emma, and your mother is lucky to have you. I could offer an advance if it helps, considering you already have an important client.'

'A client?'

'Tony Angelo. He's half in love with you already, dear. I doubt anybody else will get a look in.'

Emma smiled with relief. Thank God for Tony. 'Do I have the job then?'

'Yes, my darling girl. You have the job. Would you like to choose a new name? Most of my girls do.'

Give up her name? She could see the sense in it, but it felt wrong. Her parents had given her that name. It was a link to the person she'd been before. But no, she didn't deserve to keep it. Emma said the first name that popped into her head. 'Constance,' she said. 'Constance Stone.' The first woman to practise medicine in Australia. What a terrible irony.

'Very well, Constance. Welcome to the family.'

Emma would begin her duties — whatever that meant exactly — in a week's time. That would give her a chance to arrange Mum's accommodation and organise her trip to Hobart. A taxi all the way from Launceston was extravagant, but necessary, and she could afford it. With Tony's contribution, her own savings, Martha's generous advance and the money from selling Melvyn's ring, Emma had never been so rich in her life.

Martha showed Emma to her room; a large, beautifully appointed space with views of the harbour. 'I expect my girls to live in,' she said, 'but for you I shall make an exception. You may stay with your mother every Sunday, and return the next morning. If Tony Angelo requires you to sometimes stay away overnight, which I have no doubt he will, make sure you let me know first. I do worry about my girls.'

First impressions counted, and Emma couldn't help but like Martha. That opinion was echoed by the other models when they were called in to meet her. All seemed genuinely fond of the house madam.

'We're a family here at Hampton Hall,' said Martha. 'These girls will become your sisters, teachers and friends.'

'And Martha's our mother,' said one girl. 'There's nothing she wouldn't do for us.'

There was a general murmur of agreement from the assembled

women. Ranging in age from about twenty to forty, they were an exceptionally beautiful and sophisticated lot – not at all how she'd imagined.

Martha seemed to read her mind. 'My girls are not prostitutes, Constance, and neither will you be. They are paramours of wealthy, influential men. Seducing them with wit, wisdom and artistic talent, as much as with physical beauty. Diana here is a pianist of concert quality. Giselle, a gifted portrait painter. Anne has the voice of an angel, and the ear of the Premier.

You'll have the right to refuse any gentleman's request for companionship, and the freedom to conduct affairs as you see fit. The only house rule is – never fall in love. Never give away your power, Constance. You are to be a fabulous courtesan with the world at your feet – not one man's needy mistress.'

Emma felt a shiver of excitement, not unlike the day when Mrs Woolhouse first interviewed her at school. She took in the sumptuous surroundings, the elegant women, the startling promise of money and sex and sin. Hampton Hall was no Campbell College, but she'd be getting an education. If she kept her wits about her, if she maintained an open mind, life here could be a grand adventure.

Martha spent much of that afternoon helping Emma organise her affairs, giving her a map of Hobart so she could get her bearings. It listed local services such as a dentist and doctor. 'I require my girls to attend monthly medical appointments. Dr Chapman will discuss contraception and ways to protect your own health, along with that of your clients.' Martha even scoured the classifieds for rentals that might suit Emma's mother. 'Here's a place just down the road, and yes, it's downstairs.'

'Pricey,' said Emma, reading the advertisement. 'Can I afford it, do you think?'

'It'll be a doddle once you build a client list. Tony, and your advance, will cover the rent until then. I'm happy to sign the lease on your behalf, since you're not of legal age.'

Emma made an appointment to see it straight away. The furnished flat was just round the corner. Three large bedrooms with a modern kitchen that Elsie would love. The bathroom was small, but had a good-sized tub. Best of all, the lounge and main bedroom faced onto a park. She imagined her mother sitting by the open window, a stiff sea breeze tossing the trees, watching the leaves unfurl in spring. What a change from staring at their half-dead hedge.

'I'll take it,' she said to the hovering agent, feeling very grown up. 'Can I move in today?'

By five o'clock the flat was hers. Emma couldn't believe it. She used her brand new key to open the front door and put her suitcase in the smallest bedroom. She danced around the rooms, humming, looking in drawers, opening cupboards. She tested the gas heater. Everything was perfect. She put on her coat, hoping it wouldn't rain, and took the short walk to the harbour.

The sky was growing dark, but the waterfront was still a blaze of lights and activity. Ship's horns blared, stevedores hauled trolleys, fishing boats unloaded their catch – a favourite, familiar scene. She often used to walk here after school, and her feet started taking her down the path leading to Campbell College. Emma came to her senses when she reached the street stall with a sign saying *Best Fish & Chips In Tasmania*. A fair claim; she'd eaten there before. Emma joined the queue of three or four people. Having not eaten all day, the delicious smell of warm chips was making her stomach rumble. There was still one man in front of her when the heavens opened.

'Here, Miss.' He turned and gallantly offered his coat.

Emma was about to say thanks, but no thanks, when she stopped short. 'Harry?' At first he didn't seem to recognise her. 'It's me, Emma.'

His handsome face split into a broad grin as he held his coat over her head. 'Emma? Jesus, what happened to the smelly girl in men's trousers. You've turned into a real doll.'

The stall owner wrapped Harry's food in newspaper, and took Emma's order. She went to pay when it was ready, and Harry waved her purse away. 'I've got it, Em.' He took her arm and they ran for the cover of a street awning.

'I work at the shipyards, just round the corner,' he said, as they tucked into their meal and shared his bottle of lemonade. 'Are you back at school, then?'

She hesitated, the question bringing her back to earth with a thud. 'I'm a model now.'

Harry whistled approvingly as she nibbled her fish. He moved a little nearer and his thigh brushed hers. He lowered his voice and turned on his best Valentino eyes. His resemblance to Tom was painfully plain. 'Honestly Em, you look gorgeous.' Her insides tingled. 'Can I see you?' he asked. 'Take you to a movie or something?'

The crisp chip she was eating turned dry and floury in her mouth. Emma's appetite deserted her, replaced with an aching sense of loss. Her recent choices seemed suddenly wicked and bizarre, designed to cut her off from the simplest pleasures of an ordinary life. The warm flush of a tentative attraction. The skin-prickle of meeting a good-looking boy. Of wondering if he wanted to put his arm around her. Of wondering if he might try to kiss her, the way Tom had kissed her. *Can I see you?* Emma felt the sting of tears behind her eyes. She could never answer *yes* to that question again.

'Sorry,' she mumbled. 'I have to go.'

'Whoa, wait up. At least tell me where you're staying.'

'I can't.'

Harry's eyes narrowed. 'You're not still mooning over my brother, are you? Well, you're wasting your time, Em. Tom's off on the mainland, training to be a flyboy. He's forgotten all about us. Might never come back.'

'No!' The cry slipped out unawares. Tom leaving was for the best. She had to forget about him, but some small part of her, buried deep in her heart, must have still held out hope.

A brief scowl crossed Harry's face, but then the charm was back. 'You live round here?' She nodded without thinking. 'We're bound to run into each other again, just like we did today.' He reached for her hand and she brushed him away. 'Know what, Em? I'm not going to rest until I've cured you of my little brother.'

'Goodbye, Harry.' Emma hurried off into the rain, turning to see if he was following. If Harry or Tom ever found out about her new life, she'd simply curl up and die.

Emma had been looking forward to spending the first night in her very own place, but her encounter with Harry had ruined everything. He was right. They might accidentally run into each other, and she couldn't let that happen. There'd be no more fish and chips on the waterfront. No walks to the harbour she loved to watch the boats come in. As much as possible, she'd confine herself to the flat and Hampton Hall.

Emma changed out of her wet clothes, hung them to dry by the heater and stared miserably out the window. Already she felt trapped, hemmed in. The glow of a street lamp showed that the rain had stopped. A pressure was building inside, a terrible restless energy that could not be contained. She could not sit there for one more minute, alone with her thoughts and gazing into the gloom.

Emma unfolded the map Martha had given her. The zoo wasn't really that far; she could walk there in under an hour. It would be closed, of course, but just being near Karma would help ease her loneliness.

Emma put on her damp coat. She found the torch she kept in her bag, and slipped out into the darkness, just as the rain began again.

Emma stood shivering outside the zoo gates, listening to the wails and cries coming from inside. Something was wrong, very wrong. On a night so bitterly cold that she couldn't feel her face, the animals should be quietly sheltering in their sleeping quarters. Out of the weather; not howling like that.

She could hear the devils and lions. The baboons. Then, out of the blackness, came Karma's loud, coughing bark, repeated three times in quick succession. Emma froze. She knew that call. It was the one Karma made when she was locked out of her den, and there was a despairing quality to the sound that she'd never heard before. The rain redoubled its efforts, and Emma pulled the coat tight around her. Why on earth would Alison leave her charges exposed to this shocking weather?

Emma huddled as best she could in the shelter of the fence, determined not to leave until she could hear the animals were safely away. Time passed, but the desperate cries of the animals did not abate. Emma kept on waiting, with chattering teeth and water dripping off her nose. Not only was her face numb, but now she couldn't feel her feet either. She checked her watch — nine o'clock. Where the hell was Alison?

Suddenly a figure loomed out of the darkness. Emma lurched in fright, struggling to make her cramped legs move. She shone a torch into the stranger's face.

'Alison?'

'Emma? My God, what are you doing here?

'Waiting for the animals to be put away. Can't you hear them? They'll freeze to death.'

Alison burst into tears. Or maybe she'd already been crying, and Emma had mistaken her tears for raindrops, and her sobs for the moaning wind.

'Whatever's wrong?'

Alison drew her in for a long, heartfelt hug. 'You're soaked to the skin,' Alison said when she finally let go. 'Come back with me to the cottage, Emma, before you catch pneumonia.'

'What about the animals?' said Emma, shocked by her friend's uncharacteristic carelessness. 'Aren't you going into the zoo to help them?'

'I can't.' Her face crumpled in the glow of Emma's dying torch. The lion gave a heart-wrenching roar and Alison put her hands over her ears. 'They've taken away my keys.'

. . .

Ten minutes later Emma was sitting in the cottage, warming up in front of a meagre fire. Alison fussed about, tidying the table and making tea. 'We don't have any biscuits.'

'Never mind that,' said Emma. 'Come and sit down.'

Alison put a log on. 'I'm afraid that's the last of the wood.'

'For goodness sake, Alison. Tell me what's happened?'

She finally sat down. 'My father died before Christmas.'

'Oh no, I'm so sorry. He was a great man.'

'Thank you. Dad was very fond of you. He believed you'd make a fine zoologist.'

Emma squirmed inside, thinking how disappointed Arthur would be at the kind of life she'd chosen. 'What about the zoo? Aren't you the new curator?'

'Not me.' Alison looked grim. 'Guess who?'

'Not bloody Bruce Lipscombe?'

Alison nodded, and the story she proceeded to tell broke Emma's heart. 'The council said a woman couldn't run a zoo. First thing Bruce did was fire all the experienced staff, and employ only sussos. Second thing he did was cut off my stipend and take my keys away. Things are bad Emma, really bad. Animals are fed the wrong things, or not fed and watered at all. Food left to rot in filthy cages. They're permanently locked out of their dens without shelter, even on nights like this. You should see their poor coats: filthy and matted from the rain and cold.'

'How long has it been like that?' asked Emma.

'Six months. More and more animals are dying. Bagheera became ill, but Bruce wouldn't let me call a vet. "Can't afford it," he said. Lord knows what he does with Mrs Buchanan's monthly contributions. He doesn't spend it on the zoo, that's for sure. One morning I went in to find Bagheera had perished overnight.'

Emma's eyes clouded with tears.

'I was so desperate that I went over Bruce's head to the Town Clerk, begging for the keys so I could check the cages after hours, let the animals into their shelters and feed them properly. I argued that we had the last thylacine left in captivity, and they were too rare to ever find another one.'

'And?'

'I made things ten times worse. The Town Clerk reprimanded Bruce, and now he's so angry, he's throwing me and Mama out of the cottage. We have to leave, Emma. Abandon the animals to that monster.' She poured their tea with a trembling hand. 'Kahn died yesterday.'

'Oh no, not Kahn.' The young Bengal tiger had been Alison's pride and joy. Emma recalled his golden eyes and glorious striped coat. The sheer majesty of him.

'In the end he was just a bag of bones. I'm glad he's dead. At least he's free of his torture.'

Emma pressed a hand to the pain in her chest. Karma's call came again, fainter this time. Weaker.

Alison shuddered. 'I lie awake at night or wander around outside the zoo, listening to the animals calling for help. It's unbearable, Emma. Completely unbearable. But when I leave this place, the silence will be worse.'

CHAPTER 19

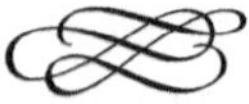

Tom was larking about one Monday morning, trying to steal one of Stu's breakfast sausages, when a senior came into the mess hall and held up an envelope. 'Telegram for Air Cadet Abbott.'

The distraction allowed him to snatch the snag.

'Oy.'

Tom ducked away, laughing, and went to fetch his telegram. On opening it the laughter died away and the sausage stuck in his throat. It was from Grandma Bertha.

I regret to say that your grandmother Mrs Isabelle Buchanan has died from a heart complaint stop Funeral ten o'clock St Paul's Church Hills End this Wed stop Deepest sympathies stop Mrs Bertha Cunningham.

Nana dead? Tom reread the telegram in disbelief. He'd received a letter from her just last week. She'd told him about the seeds she was raising in the greenhouse, the ones he'd collected for her last year. She'd told him about her quoll and the dogs and how sixty-seven-year-old George had become besotted with a widow in town. She'd sounded happy and upbeat, with no hint that she was unwell. Still, it was her way. She never wanted anybody to fuss, and he hadn't been home since January to see for himself. A lot could happen in six months. A lot had happened. His extraordinary, unique, most dearly loved Nana was dead. It seemed impossible.

Tom ran to his barracks as a kaleidoscope of memories ran through his head. That first day at Binburra, when she'd saved a shy, broken boy from his grief. A thousand fragments of a happy childhood lived in the light of her love and protection. That last magical trip to Tiger Pass, when Nana told him the secrets of his past, and bestowed upon him the guardianship of a lost valley.

He flung himself down on his bed as emptiness closed in. There was so much he wanted - no, *needed* - to share with Nana. He wasn't finished yet, nowhere near. She had to see him fly a plane. She had to see him graduate as a pilot. She had to be part of his future, a future that suddenly looked blank. His hands clenched weakly. Why the hell hadn't Nana told him how sick she was? Careless of his mates' curious looks, Tom sobbed into his pillow like a child. It was like losing his mother all over again.

Tom stood outside the modest church by the railway line, in the shadow of the Hills End gold mine. A far cry from the grandeur of St Mary's Cathedral, where he and Harry had farewelled their parents, but much more Nana's style. This simple rectangular building of brick and stone had served the people of Hills End as a place of worship for over eighty years. Generations of miners were buried in the little cemetery beyond the church yard. Now Nana would be buried there too.

Tom nervously entered the doorway. He recognised a few townsfolk, and spotted Old George and Mrs Mills seated to the side, but he didn't know most of the people. A woman hurried over to greet him. She had Nana's eyes. 'You must be Tom,' she said with a kind smile. 'Don't you look fine in your uniform? I'm your Aunt Clara, from England. Your brother's already here.'

She pointed to the front of the church. Harry was standing near the altar, staring blankly into space. Tom knew that look – the expression his brother wore when he was trying to hide his feelings. Tom went to join him.

'Hello little brother.' Harry looked him up and down. 'Where'd you rent the threads?'

Tom managed a fleeting smile. 'I can't believe she's gone. Nana was only sixty-six. That's not really old, is it? My mate's grandma is ninety.'

'She wouldn't have wanted to go on like she was,' said Harry. 'You should have seen her. Legs all swollen and she couldn't get out of bed, could hardly breathe. Only thing keeping her going was that Mariani wine. Full of cocaine, apparently. In the end her heart just gave out.'

'You were there?'

'Came home last Saturday for a visit, and Nana was so sick I had to stay. Auntie Clara arrived on Sunday. Mrs Mills sent her a telegram. Nana was upset when she found out. You know what she's like, not wanting to worry anybody. Said she wanted to be remembered the way she was when she was well.'

Harry's words lit a slow fuse. The more Tom considered them, the angrier he got. 'Why didn't somebody tell me?'

'What would have been the point? Do you think the RAAF would release you because of a sick grandma? What sort of dream world do you live in?'

'You could at least have let me know she was ill.'

Harry shrugged. 'Sorry, mate. I had my hands full.'

Tom turned his back on his brother, sat on a pew and tried to calm himself. The day of Nana's funeral was a time for sorrow, not anger. He should be happy that Nana had loved ones around for her last hours. She could so easily have died alone. Yet there was no rationality to his grief. Tom wished he'd been the one there instead of Harry. Wished he'd been the one to share those last precious days, and comfort her at the end.

Grandma Bertha came over, crying crocodile tears. Tom bristled. Why was she even there? 'My dear, dear boy.' She leaned in to kiss his cheek and he dodged away. 'Such a terrible loss. We're all bereft.' She spotted his aunt. 'There's darling Clara. I must offer my condolences on losing her mother.'

He shook his head as she hurried away. What a liar. Bertha hadn't visited them at Binburra once in the eight years since his parents died. Why was she pretending to care now?

Harry sat down next to him and nodded towards Bertha. 'Nauseating, isn't it?'

'What's her game?'

'Can't you guess? It's because of the will. If the Colonel left Nana even half of his fortune, we could all be filthy rich by the end of today. Guess old Bertha thinks we're worth sucking up to now.'

What a despicable woman. Tom wanted to throw Bertha out of the church then and there. Poor Mama, being raised by such a greedy, selfish person. She didn't deserve that. He wished for the millionth time that his mother was alive.

'How could anybody think about money at a time like this?'

Harry rolled his eyes. 'Why do you think half these people are here?

Everyone stood as the service commenced with a prayer. 'Dear Lord—'

Tom didn't bow his head or close his eyes. What had the Lord ever done for him, except take away the people he loved most in this life? His parents, Nana, Emma. Nana had loved Emma. Mama would have done too. How perfect his life could have been if the Lord had left him alone.

The prayer seemed never-ending. In his mind, Tom started going through his mates at Point Cook. As far as he knew, every one of them had a living mother. Plenty had grandmothers and girlfriends too. None had a murderer for a father.

Harry nudged him. 'Sit down. The prayer's over.'

The service droned on. Now the minister was telling a potted version of Nana's life. Where she was born and who her parents were. Where she grew up and her achievements as an educator and artist. But the story was incomplete. Scant mention was made of the second half of her life. A life spent conserving Tasmania's wilderness, and fighting for the creation of national parks. A life spent with Colonel Buchanan. Tom seethed inside. How dare they turn his grandmother's life into a lie.

Afterwards Tom and Harry acted as pall-bearers, helping to carry the coffin to the little cemetery beyond the churchyard.

'Our sister Isabelle has gone to her rest in the peace of Christ,' intoned the minister, as Nana was lowered into the ground. 'May the Lord welcome her to the table of God's children in heaven. With faith and hope in eternal life.'

Tom couldn't stand any more. He hurried off towards the church, fighting back tears. Harry followed him.

'How are the dogs?' asked Tom.

'Rex howled when she died,' said Harry. 'It was the damnedest thing.'

'Are you going back to the house?'

'We'll both go,' said Harry. 'You can catch up with Old George and Mrs Mills. We'll talk about the old days, get drunk.' He put a hand on Tom's shoulder. 'We both need that, I reckon. But first they'll read the will at the lawyer's office in town.'

'I don't care about that.'

'Really, little brother?' Harry lit a cigarette, and gave him a searching look. 'You don't care what happens to Binburra?'

Tom was gripped with a sudden fear. He'd been so blinded by grief, that he hadn't thought about the practicalities of Nana's death. 'Of course I care. What do you think will happen?'

'I think she'll leave Binburra to us,' said Harry. 'It's no use to Auntie Clara or Ann living in England. Ann didn't even make it back for the funeral. We're the ones who grew up there. It's the closest thing we have to a home.'

'I'll die if Grandma Bertha got her hands on it somehow.'

The mourners began wandering back from the graveyard. Harry flicked his cigarette to the ground, grinding it out with his heel. 'Guess we're about to find out.'

. . .

The office of Mr Bruce Billson LLB wasn't designed for so many people, and there weren't enough chairs. Tom, Harry, Clara, Bertha and her husband, Mrs Mills, Old George, and almost a dozen more who claimed to be relatives.

'Parasites,' whispered Harry. 'Crawling from the woodwork at the prospect of a handout.'

Mr Billson peered over his spectacles and thanked everybody for their attention. 'If you could all please sit down.' It was like a game of musical chairs as people tried to find a seat. Tom and Harry remained standing by the door. The solicitor produced a folded document sealed with red wax, along with a separate envelope. 'Mrs Buchanan has asked me, as executor of her estate, to read this letter before I move onto the terms of the will.' A hush fell on the room as he took a sheet of paper from the envelope.

'I write this letter by way of an explanation. There has long been speculation about my late husband's considerable wealth. As you know, the Colonel and I made conservation our life's work. We always wished that work to extend beyond our lifetimes, and thanks to blessed and fortunate circumstances, this has been possible.

It is not widely known that before he died, the Colonel founded a South African charity known as the Themba Trust. It was set up for two purposes. Firstly, to fund his network of private African game reserves. Secondly, to build and run schools in rural provinces, educating disadvantaged children and teaching local people how to coexist with wildlife such as elephants and lions.'

Mr Billson looked up at the sea of expectant faces and wet his lips.

'The Colonel arranged for profits from his South African mining interests to go to the Themba Trust.'

Grandma Bertha's disappointed gasp broke the silence. 'There's still Isabelle's own money,' her husband whispered, within earshot of Tom.

It almost seemed like Nana had heard him.

'I have recently set up my own charitable trust,' continued Mr Billson. *'The Binburra Conservation Foundation. Following my late husband's example, I am leaving the bulk of my estate to this trust.'*

Tom grinned with satisfaction. That would teach Bertha and the others like her. A confused murmur ran around the room, along with the sound shuffling of feet. Mr Billson paused until he had silence again.

'My dear daughters, Clara and Ann. You have grown into strong, accomplished women, with careers, husbands and families of your own. It is a great comfort to know that you are settled, financially independent, and in no need of my money.

My intrepid grandsons, Tom and Harry. You are the brightest of stars – clever and resourceful – with the world at your feet. You will be provided for, but too often I have seen young men lose their way when burdened with extravagant inheritances. I adore you both too much to let that happen.

Missing you all terribly,

With endless love,

Isabelle Buchanan.'

Mr Billson wiped his brow, and took a drink from the glass of water on the desk beside him. 'If there are no questions, I'll proceed to the formal provisions of the will.'

There were questions, but Mr Billson studiously ignored them. Harry leaned close and whispered, 'So much for us being filthy rich. I wonder what *provided for* means, exactly?'

Individual bequests came next. Fifty pounds to the Field Naturalist Club. Seventy pounds to the Hobart Museum. One hundred pounds for the Hills End State School. Two hundred pounds each for Old George and Mrs Mills, plus an annual stipend. Jewellery to Clara and Ann. And then, *'I give the sum of five thousand pounds free of all duties to each of my grandsons, Henry Edward Abbott and Thomas Daniel Abbott.'*

'Not a grand fortune,' whispered Harry. 'But not bad.'

'I also devise and bequeath to my grandson, Thomas Daniel Abbott, all my house and land known as Binburra, and contained in Certificate of title Volume 8949 Folio 009. I bequeath the remainder of my estate in full to the trustees of the Binburra Conservation Foundation.'

Mr Billson put down the document, and used a little cloth to clean his spectacles.

Harry shook his head, stood and stepped forward. 'What, so Tom gets Binburra?'

'That was your grandmother's wish, yes.'

'Show me.'

'I assure you—'

'Show me!' Mr Billson pointed out the clause. Harry read, and reread it, eyes darting from side to side, his breath coming in rapid pants. He glared accusingly at Tom. 'Did you know about this?'

'No, I swear—'

'I was the one there when she died.' Harry's voice rose as he addressed the room. 'The one watching Nana struggle to breathe, the one holding her hand at the end. Not bloody Tom.'

'That's because you didn't tell me.' Tom didn't want to cause a scene at Nana's funeral, didn't want to provoke his brother's famous temper, but some things needed saying. 'I'd have given anything to be there, but you kept me away.'

He'd expected Harry to blow up and storm about. But instead his brother's eyes filled with tears, and he hurried from the room.

Tom went after him. He followed Harry down the street, across the road, round the block. He followed him all the way to the railway station. Harry bought a ticket, moved onto the platform and sank down on a bench.

Tom sat beside him. 'I had nothing to do with what happened back there, Harry. Didn't have a clue.'

'I believe you, mate. You're too damned honest to pull off a scam like that.' He lit up a cigarette, and offered Tom one.

'I don't smoke.'

'Of course you don't.' They sat for a while in silence.

'Come back to the house,' said Tom, kicking at the timber boards. 'We can talk about it.'

'What's the point? Unless you're planning to give me my half of Binburra. Make things square.'

Tom scrubbed his hands over his eyes. Harry was right — it only seemed fair. But Nana's voice was ringing loud and clear in his head; the sacred trust she'd bestowed on him during that last, magical trek into the wilderness. *There is temptation here, Tom; buried in these cliffs and underground. Would you really trust your brother with that knowledge? I'm charging you with the guardianship of the tigers and this valley. They must always be protected.* That was why she'd left him Binburra. It suddenly made sense.

'I can't.' Tom hung his head. 'You don't understand—'

A train whistle sounded in the distance.

Harry's nostrils flared and he stood. 'What is it that I don't understand? That you were always her favourite? That now you can rub my nose in it?' He took a long drag on his fag. 'Is this some sort of payback? It's not my fault Papa didn't love you.'

Tom was determined to stay calm, but Harry had hit a chronically raw nerve, and the emotional pressure cooker of the funeral had taken its toll. 'That bastard killed our mother, but you don't give a fuck about that, do you? All you care about is wallowing in the past, and feeling sorry for yourself.'

Harry shirtfronted him, almost knocking him off his feet. Tom lashed out with his fist before he'd properly regained his balance, managing a glancing blow off Harry's chin.

Before either of them could do any real damage, the station master got in between them. 'You lads should be ashamed of yourselves. Now pick up your hats.' He cuffed Tom around the ears. 'You, especially, disrespecting your country's uniform like that. I've a good mind to report you for public brawling.'

Tom could see the train coming. What a mess he'd made of things. 'Harry, please come back to the house.'

'No, thanks.' He was breathing hard and staring at Tom with wild eyes.

'Please, Harry.' The train pulled into the station. 'Don't you have a bag or something at Binburra you need to get?'

'Tell Mrs Mills to send it on.' The train rattled and hissed to a halt. 'Oh, and Tom, I'll say hello to Emma for you.'

'Emma?'

'She's back in Hobart working as a model.' There was a malicious twist to his mouth. 'We're going together. I'm seeing rather a lot of her, if you catch my drift …'

Tom felt like he'd been struck. It was all he could do to keep from launching himself at Harry. 'I don't believe you.'

Harry shrugged. 'Suit yourself.' He opened a carriage door, jumped in and doffed his hat. 'Goodbye, little brother. If I see you again in this lifetime, it'll be way too soon.'

The train ground into motion. Tom felt the world shift beneath his feet as a vast emptiness claimed him. He clutched at Karma on the silver chain around his neck. How hollow life was, now everyone he loved was gone.

CHAPTER 20

Tom remained at Binburra for twenty-four hours after the funeral. Old George and Mrs Mills agreed to stay on as before, to care for the elderly dogs and be general caretakers.

'Can you water Nana's seedlings, and plant them out when they're ready, please George? And Mrs Mills, can you make sure Nana's bedroom window stays open for her quoll? And leave it a dish of chopped rabbit each night.'

'Lord knows I had this same conversation with your grandmother, just before she passed,' said Mrs Mills with a smile. 'Don't worry. I'll look after the wee mite.'

Tom returned to Point Cook subtly changed. His mates noticed it. His instructors, everybody. He'd always been a fair flyer, but now he became outstanding, displaying the sort of skill, courage and confidence that set him apart from his peers. 'What's happened to you?' asked Stu. 'Got the devil on your tail?'

His next flight evaluation deemed him to '*possess excellent technical skills, together with an uncommon natural aptitude. My one concern is that he flies with a certain reckless abandon that could prove hazardous to himself and his fellow pilots.'* Tom read the evaluation and laughed. What did they expect from a man with nothing to lose? He relentlessly practised aerobatics above a railway line so he could tell if he was coming out straight or not: stall turns, loops and vertical dives at one hundred and fifty miles per hour. Pushing himself to the limits of safety and earning himself the nickname of Mad Tom.

When the first term ended, he was the only cadet to stay on base during the three-week mid-year break. What else should he do? He couldn't bear the thought of Binburra without Nana. He had nowhere to go and nobody to miss him.

Tom spent his days swotting up on theory, picking his instructors' brains and cadging dual practice flights whenever he could in the Westland Wapitis. It took his mind both off his loneliness, and Harry's disturbing parting comment about Emma.

The cadets would be graduating to these single-engine biplane bombers in second term. Compared to Tiger Moths, the bigger, more powerful Wapitis were rumoured to be slow and clumsy. On the ground they needed to be manhandled by several men into flying position. However, Tom soon grew to love the grand, old aeroplanes. When the others returned for final term he had a head start, and was flying them solo after three hours.

Tom looked forward to the beginning of his advanced training. It would help keep his mind off Nana, and Harry and Emma. When he didn't stay busy, thoughts of them hijacked him at every turn. Far better to lose himself in the intricacies of formation flying, forced landings, dive-bombing and mid-air gunnery.

When he read in September that the last captive thylacine had died in Hobart zoo, he murmured a prayer for Karma and kissed her likeness on the silver chain around his neck. Then he volunteered to be the first cadet to go *under the hood.* A canvas cover was pulled over his cockpit to shut out the world. He couldn't see sideways, up or down; true instrument flying in readiness for night flights and heavy cloud cover. More and more they were training for the theatre of war.

Yet despite this new focus, and a rising political threat in Europe, Tom dismissed the chance of real military action. Hadn't they already had the war to end all wars? As he pushed himself towards perfection, his motivation was mastery for mastery's sake. And when Tom graduated at the top of his class; when he received his wings without any family to see or be proud, he had no sense of darker days to come.

The cadets had to nominate if they wished to stay with the RAAF, or join the Royal Air Force and go to England. Tom had originally chosen to stay, but when Nana died he'd changed his mind. Stu was going. They were best mates, and there was nothing left for him in Australia. He'd lost Emma. Harry sent his letters back marked *return to sender*. Tom's remaining family, such as it was, consisted of two aunts who lived in England.

'That's the shot,' said Stu. 'An easy life, beer and girls is what I've heard. We'll fly the best planes in the world and see the old country while we're at it.'

Tom went home with Stu to spend Christmas with his family. On January 9, 1937, along with twenty-three other Point Cook graduates, Tom and Stu boarded the ageing P&O liner *RMS Narkunda* that had been requisitioned by the Admiralty as a troopship. They stood waving on the deck, as well-wishers cheered and threw ribbons and streamers. Their great adventure had begun.

CHAPTER 21

Tom turned up his collar against the cold morning. After almost two years, he still wasn't used to the bleak British weather. He lit a cigarette, and walked past the stores and camp cinema and sick-bay, until he reached the officers' mess. Why had Flight Commander Percy Donovan summoned his pilots there on a Sunday morning?

The radio was turned up loud, and tuned to the BBC. 'Righto chaps. Grab a cuppa and gather round,' said Percy. 'Prepare for a broadcast of national importance.'

Tom fetched a hot drink and sat down to listen. He spotted Stu coming in the back door. The two Australians still insisted on wearing their dark blue RAAF uniforms, with RAF insignias attached. They stood out among their light-blue clad British companions.

Neville Chamberlain came on the air, an ominous sign. He declared that Germany had not met the deadline for withdrawal of its troops from Poland, as per Great Britain's demand. In a solemn voice, the Prime Minister announced that, as of September third, 'this country is at war with Germany.' Tom stiffened and a quiet cheer went up from some of the men. The national anthem sounded and they all stood to attention.

A thrill of excitement and fear ran through him. Europe had been on the brink for weeks. RAF squadrons from across the country were cancelling leave and moving to a war footing. Yet Tom was still dazed by the news. He glanced around at the faces of his young companions. They looked like boys, even with the moustaches they'd grown to make themselves look older. Despite their intensive training, none of them knew anything of real war, except for what they'd read in books. In one sense it was a relief for the waiting to be over. Up until now they'd been playing—albeit on a grand scale—and the game was about to change.

Tom felt for the solid presence of silver Karma in his pocket. She gave him a jolt of confidence, as always. What did he have to fear? He was the best flyer in the business, and everyone knew it. Recently promoted to squadron leader, sometimes even taking on flight commander duties.

For some reason, his father's face swam before him. Despite swearing to himself and Harry that he didn't care any more, he couldn't help wondering what Papa would think of his head-in-the-clouds son now? Just nineteen-years-old with a man's job ahead of him. Would he have finally been proud?

Tom fished Karma from his pocket and kissed her, like a Catholic kissing a rosary. He'd need all the help his lucky charm could give him.

None of them knew what to expect in the coming weeks. Would they be thrust straight into combat? Lose their best commanders to more experienced squadrons? Be split up? That would perhaps be the worst scenario, because they were like a family. Yet despite the declaration of war, they saw no action.

The papers called the long months after Germany's *blitzkrieg* attack on Poland 'the phoney war'. Christmas came and went, with nothing happening. Many of the children evacuated at the start of the war were returned to their families.

'Bloody hopeless,' said Stu, when they learned the British raids over Germany weren't dropping bombs, but propaganda leaflets. 'What are we trying to do, annoy them to death?'

Tom's frustration grew. He was a squadron commander, but all he seemed to be in charge of was waiting.

Then in March 1940 something happened to make the phoney war seem real. The squadron farewelled their Bristol Blenheim light bombers, and took delivery of a fleet of Spitfires. What a sensation; not even the ground crew could keep away. These high-performance, single-seater fighters were the best the RAF could offer, and were even faster than Hurricanes. They reached speeds of three hundred and fifty miles per hour, climbed to a height of four miles in nine minutes, and every pilot on the base dreamed of flying one.

Tom moved reverently around the first aircraft to arrive. He stroked its elegant, streamlined fuselage like a man in love. For the first time he felt they were a proper fighter squadron. He climbed into the tiny cockpit and let his hands trail over the controls, imagining swooping high in the air like a falcon. He'd never flown a Spitfire, but with the help of a few experienced pilots, it would be his job to convert the entire squadron in the space of a few weeks. The prospect didn't daunt him. Tom grinned, and went through the take-off drill in his head – RAFTP: radiator, airscrew, flaps, trim, petrol. He couldn't wait to get in the air.

On the same day in May that Churchill replaced Chamberlain, Germany ended the phoney war. They began their push on the Western Front. One hundred and thirty-five divisions streamed into Belgium and Holland, then France. The *Luftwaffe*, with three and a half thousand front-line aircraft, annihilated its opposition. With less than half as many planes, the RAF squadrons based in Europe were quickly overwhelmed, some all but wiped out in the space of a week. Nothing could halt the German advance, and thousands of allied soldiers were being squeezed towards Dunkirk on the coast. It became clear that if the English forces were to have any chance of survival, the navy would have to mount a rescue mission by sea. Operation Dynamo was born.

The navy didn't have enough destroyers available for the job, so they commandeered eight hundred private vessels: ferries, pleasure craft, motor cruisers, paddle-steamers, even little fishing boats – anything that could get across the channel to pick up troops.

RAF Fighter Command was given the task of defending this naval effort from the German bombers. The problem was, they'd already lost two hundred and fifty aircraft based at French airfields, along with many of their most seasoned pilots. Such heavy casualties resulted in corners being cut on training, and inexperienced pilots being drafted prematurely. It now fell to squadrons like Tom's to protect the ships, port and beaches of Dunkirk.

The night before their first sortie, Tom lay in bed, tense and wakeful in the room he shared with Stu, trying to envisage what they'd find across the channel. He knew the German army was surging like a tidal wave. He knew that hundreds of thousands of allied soldiers were trapped on the coast. Yet tomorrow morning's mission still felt like a training exercise. He couldn't imagine real-life struggle and suffering on such a grand scale.

Maybe it was just as well. Tom knew the odds. As squadron leader, he'd be taking his untried Spitfire pilots up against the battle-hardened veterans of the *Luftwaffe*. They'd have less than an hour to engage the enemy. Any longer and they'd run out of fuel. The two new men's only gunnery training on Spitfires had been ten rounds per gun, fired into the North Sea, which was hard to miss. They'd be out-numbered, out-skilled and out-resourced.

Tom got up, pulled on a coat and went outside. Stu was already there. Was he thinking about his mother back in Australia? Worrying how she'd feel if he died? Tom lit a cigarette. Perhaps he was the lucky one. Apart from his aunts, he'd leave nobody behind to mourn.

The two friends sat side by side on the step in silence. High above them, the moon tracked across the stars. Tom felt, as always, the irresistible tug of the sky.

. . .

At eight o'clock next morning the half-strength squadron – just six planes – was ready to go. Tom's nerves had been replaced by suppressed excitement and an overwhelming sense of responsibility for his men. He rubbed Karma in his pocket for luck.

'Where do you want my lot?' asked Stu, who would lead the three rear planes.

'Five hundred feet above,' said Tom. 'Stay between me and the sun. Mind your tails and no heroics.'

As Tom climbed onto the wing, he felt a nervous, unexpected urge to urinate. There was nothing for it but to piss on the grass in front of the ever-present ground crew. When he looked around, every other pilot was doing the same thing.

Soon Tom was strapped in the cockpit, leather helmet and goggles on, parachute stowed, radio ready and oxygen mask clipped in place. He signalled to the others and they took off, wheeling southwards. In minutes the English shoreline passed beneath their wings. They were headed for France, twisting their necks to scan the skies, flying escort over two destroyers sailing across the Channel.

Shortly before reaching the French coast they spotted enemy aircraft: two Messerschmitt 109 fighters guarding two JU 88 bombers flying low beneath them. They were heading for the British destroyers, and seemed unaware of the Spitfires above.

The enemy scattered when they realised the danger, and Tom went after the closest fighter: a grey plane bearing large, black crosses and swastikas on its tail. Marauding thoughts threatened Tom's resolve. How old was the German pilot, crouching low in his cockpit? Was this his first fight too? Did he love to loop and roll on bright mornings as Tom did, alone with his thoughts, reaching for heaven?

The German spotted Tom closing in, did a sharp stall turn and dived into a cloud. Tom dived after him, consumed now by the thrill of the chase and with no sense of danger. He fired a five-second burst from the wing-mounted guns, and emerged from the cloud to see the 109 losing altitude and streaming smoke and flame. His first hit! The pilot baled, but his parachute didn't open. He spiralled into a fatal free-fall from six thousand feet. Tom watched in horrid fascination.

The German seemed to take forever to hit the water, although it couldn't have been more than a minute. What was in his mind during those final moments? Did the seconds stretch, or shrink?

Tom shook his head to clear it. The other 109 was on his tail. Suddenly the air was filled with tracer fire, as if giant dragon claws were ripping through the sky. He dodged to the left and took cover in a cloud bank.

Dimly he saw a plane flying parallel and ahead of him. It seemed too big to be a Spitfire, but a RAF pilot had recently downed a Blenheim from his own squadron, and Tom had a horror of doing the same thing. No luck raising the others on the radio. They must all have their hands full.

Tom stalked the plane through the cloud until they emerged into a clear patch of sky. Bingo. A JU 88 bomber in his sights. Tom took it by surprise, opening fire with all eight guns at close range. Smoke and debris streamed from the fuselage and a sheet of flame licked at the engine. The rear-gunner attempted to defend, but it was too late. Tom was close enough to see the white faces of the four-man crew before the cockpit was engulfed in a fireball. He squirmed inside, horrified, feeling their pain. Against procedure he followed the stricken plane down until it slammed into the sea with a burst of white foam. Seconds later there was no sign that the bomber or its crew had ever existed.

Tom climbed back up in a state of bewilderment. In the space of twenty minutes he'd downed two enemy aircraft and killed five men. It seemed like some kind of dream. He called up the rest of the squadron. One by one they responded. Mick had taken down a Messerschmitt too. That was three out the four enemy aircraft accounted for, a terrific result for any mission, let alone their first. The second bomber had fled, leaving the destroyers to steam safely on to Dunkirk.

Tom called on the men to regroup. They still had enough fuel to do a quick sweep of the coast. He reached everyone except Stu. The damn fool had probably left his radio on transmit instead of receive again.

Joel's voice crackled over the radio. He was a wild young Canadian with barely ten hours experience in a Spitfire. 'Those other 109s almost had me, sir.'

'What other 109s?'

'Half a dozen Messerschmitts came in above me, sir. I took a little hit while escaping, and went into a spin. Stu drew their fire so I could get away. Man, you should have seen that boy fly.'

Tom's belly turned to ice. They tried to raise Stu again, and failed. Nobody had seen him since he'd sped away with a bunch of German fighters on his tail. Spitfires were faster than Messerschmitts, and Stu could outfly most men on the base, but still ... Tom sent someone to escort Joel and his wounded plane home. The rest of them spread out to search. No sign of a downed Spitfire. Tom felt sick, remembering how the trackless sea had swallowed the much larger German bomber without a trace.

They searched until low fuel forced them to return home, dog-tired and miserable. Tom sought permission to re-arm, refuel and keep searching. Permission denied. The next squadrons out would do what they could to find Stu. Shipping had also been alerted, but by now Tom had lost hope. There was no escaping the dark, swirling waters of the channel. He'd seen for himself how it swallowed men and planes whole.

Tom went to the room he shared with Stu. Everything was the same as when they'd left six hours earlier. The book Stu had been reading lay open on his bed. Now he'd never know how it ended. His towel, still damp, tossed on the window sill. A half-written letter to Dolly, his London girlfriend, lay on the table.

Tom wandered around the room in a daze. You'd think he'd be used to loss, but apparently he was a slow learner. How could Stu, who'd eaten a double serve of bacon and eggs for breakfast, who'd been so full of life – how could he be dead? Knowing Stu, he would have put up a hell of a fight before they got him. Never more would Tom have sympathy for the enemy. He couldn't wait to get back in the air to exact revenge.

He started to collect up his things. There'd be no sleeping in this room tonight – maybe never again. The long, depressing evening stretched ahead of him. As squadron leader it would be his job to write up the report, maybe even inform Stu's family. He sank down on Stu's bed, eyes filling with tears.

'Jeez mate, I didn't know you cared.'

Tom looked up. Was he imagining things? It was Stu, limping in, wearing a pair of trousers way too small for him, and an old-fashioned hounds-tooth jacket with leather patches at the elbow. Tom just stared, too shocked and delighted to speak.

Stu slumped down on a chair, face battered and bruised but wearing a wide smile. 'Aren't you going to say hello?'

'My God, mate. We thought you'd bought it.'

'Very nearly did,' said Stu, his voice shaky but strong. 'A lucky shot took me down, but not before I bailed in the channel. One of those little boats we were guarding fished me from the water and took me to Dover. I hitched a ride back here with a milk truck.'

Tom grinned. 'You haven't seen a doctor yet?'

'Nah, I'll be right, mate. Could kill a beer right now though.'

Tom ran to fetch the medicos, shouting to everyone he met, 'Stu's alive, he's alive!' He whispered a silent thank you to Karma in his pocket for delivering his best friend back to him. And a sudden, sure knowledge struck him. Let the Germans do the worst … As long as that lucky charm was in his pocket, they wouldn't be able to touch him. He had this war.

CHAPTER 22

Emma arranged the big bunch of flowers in the vase on the table beside her mother's wheelchair: tulips, daffodils, hyacinths and Dutch iris – blooms that could leave no doubt that spring had arrived. Emma would have preferred a native bouquet of waratahs and leatherwood, but Mum was a traditionalist.

Eileen managed a lop-sided smile. Six years since the stroke, and her mother had made tremendous progress. Therapists at Dr Dennisdeen's New Town Rehabilitation Hospital had worked with her as an inpatient at first, and later as an outpatient. Mum had painstakingly remastered the alphabet and could read simple texts. Using playing cards and numbered blocks, she'd learned how to count again. Emma was proud of how hard she tried with her daily memory exercises, along with her muscle and balance training.

Mum could walk now, with the help of a stick; feed herself, although handling cutlery was still a struggle. With young Jack away fighting in New Guinea, she listened non-stop to the wireless, eager for news of the war. She also loved listening to serials, plays and talent quests, and knew the times and days of the week of her favourite programs.

A speech therapist came by twice a week, although progress on that front had been depressingly slow. Dr Dennisdeen said that at six years out, not much more recovery could be expected.

But last week, a miracle had happened. Her mother had started to talk. Emma liked to think the change had been triggered by moving into this beautiful house. Mum was managing two-word sentences, speaking out of the side of her mouth, which made it hard for strangers, but Emma could understand her. Every word Mum uttered was like music to her ears, and proved beyond doubt that her mother's mind was still sharp.

Mum pointed to the wall calendar. 'Your birthday.'

Emma beamed. That's right, next week was her birthday. She looked around with satisfaction at the sunny room filled with light. At the adjoining bathroom, the elegant furniture and the French doors opening onto a private garden. The rest of the house was equally as impressive. A big, modern kitchen that Elsie loved. A study that could double as a guest room, and a garage for her new car. Even a small conservatory, where Mum could grow flowers. And since last week, this house was Emma's, the title in her name, and her name alone. Not bad for a single woman who hadn't yet turned twenty-four.

Maybe she'd get a kitten for Mum, to sit on her lap and keep her company. Emma had desperately missed that animal connection over the last few years. The Beaumaris Zoo had closed shortly after Karma died, and she'd scarcely patted so much as a puppy since. It had been too painful.

'Tomorrow I'll help you bake me a cake.' Emma kissed her mother. 'Right now, I have to go to work.'

Mum frowned. 'Work?'

'You know. I'm a nurse, at the hospital.'

Mum opened her mouth to speak, but only managed a grunt, tongue exploring her lips, like it hadn't felt them before. She looked slowly around the elegant room, and tried again. 'All this?'

A shiver of shame passed through Emma. Pretending to be a nurse had seemed like the perfect foil; a respectable profession, loosely linked to her long ago ambition of being a doctor, and it explained why she was away at night. Jack and Tim had never questioned her story. It hadn't occurred to Emma that her mother was not so gullible. Once Mum was finally well enough to ask questions, the lie might not be convincing. After all, how on earth could anyone afford this Battery Point sandstone terrace house on a nurse's wage?

Emma forced a smile and kissed her mother again. 'I won't be back tonight. See you tomorrow.'

She didn't have time to worry about it now. Tonight's fashion show at Hampton Hall was an important one. A contingent of high-ranking navy personnel was in town to oversee delivery of three naval vessels, built on commission at Hobart's shipyards, and Martha had pulled out all the stops. She always did where the military was concerned. 'Those boys put their lives on the line for us every day. The least we can do is show them a little gratitude.'

Tasmania was a long way from the main war in the Pacific, and even farther from Europe, yet people still felt vulnerable to attack, especially after an enemy minefield was discovered near the Derwent River entrance, thirty miles south of the Fort Direction gun batteries. And once a submarine-launched Japanese spy plane was spotted by hundreds of people flying south along the east coast.

The sighting sent a quiver of fear through Tasmania. The plane was too high to fire upon, and no fighters were available to intercept it. After that, anti-aircraft guns were positioned on nearby hills, and the papers were full of the threat. They warned that the Japanese had their eye on Hobart's harbour, one of the finest in the Pacific, and also on the Risdon Zinc Works. The plant produced half of the British Empire's zinc, vital for the production of munitions.

Hampton Hall was an enthusiastic supporter of the war effort. Martha knitted warm socks and scarves for the troops, and encouraged the others to do the same. She donated to the Red Cross. Whenever the call went out for useful materials, Martha would hold scrap drives. Patrons would often arrive with contributions of aluminium, rubber, paper and iron. Martha devised an evacuation plan and insisted on regular drills, interrupting everyone's business and prompting outrage from both the women and their clients.

'For heaven's sake,' said Diana, as she shivered on the street one freezing Hobart night, wearing nothing but a negligee and high heels. 'Can't we go back inside? This is Hobart, not London.'

'You'll thank me when the bombers come,' said Martha.

So it was little wonder that Martha showed a great deal of generosity to military men, offering discounts, splendid dinners and extra time with the women. Lieutenant or General, it didn't matter. All officers were treated with the same degree of kindness and respect, although she drew the line at enlisted men, arguing they wouldn't be able to afford the ladies of Hampton Hall anyway.

Emma arrived at work in plenty of time to pick up the *Mercury* on her way upstairs. After a shower, she lay on her bed with glue and a pair of scissors and went through the newspaper. Ever since Harry told her that Tom had joined the air force, she'd been keeping a scrap book. Stories about young Australian pilots serving in the RAF were popular, and she'd been able to roughly follow his progress.

After cutting his teeth at Dunkirk, Tom had received acclaim for becoming the first Aussie *Ace in a Day*, having downed five enemy aircraft on a single mission during the Battle of Britain. She scoured the papers for news, cutting out articles that mentioned Australian pilots and pasting them in her books. She had a whole stack of them tucked away in the top of her wardrobe. Most were filled with general news of the war, with one special book reserved only for news of Tom.

Giselle knocked on the door and came in without waiting for an invitation. 'Pining after your handsome flyboy again?' she said, as she noted the cut up bits of paper on the bed. 'Don't let Martha catch you. You know the rules.'

Emma jumped up in great excitement. 'Listen to this, Gissy.' She read, 'Local RAF Pilot awarded DFC. Tasmanian born RAF fighter pilot Thomas Abbott has been awarded the Distinguished Flying Cross for leadership and outstanding courage during flying operations over Germany. He has been promoted to Wing Commander, one of the youngest officers to hold that position.'

A grainy black and white photograph accompanied the article. Tom posed in front of his Spitfire, half-smiling and sporting a moustache. He looked much older than his twenty-four years. He also looked extraordinarily dashing and handsome in his uniform, yet still recognisably the boy she'd known back at Campbell College.

'Is that him? Let me see.' Emma handed over the paper. Giselle whistled. 'Now I know what all the fuss is about. No wonder you're stuck on him.'

'I'm not,' said Emma, snatching back the paper. 'He was a friend, that's all. A long time ago.'

Giselle raised her perfectly plucked brows. 'I'll have him then. He's a dish.'

'You know the rules. None of us can have him,' said Emma. 'Gissy, does it ever bother you that we can't, you know, have someone special, just for ourselves?'

'Are you going soft? Don't let Martha hear you talk like that. Anyway, what about Tony? He only has eyes for you, that one.'

It was true. When Tony was in town, he arrived like clockwork twice a week to whisk Emma away. He'd been doing it for years now, and they always went somewhere fabulous – Valentino's Jazz Club, a play at the Theatre Royal or a fine restaurant – before heading back to his Sandy Bay apartment, specially purchased for such occasions. He never saw the other girls. Her relationship with Tony sometimes felt like being married, or at least what Emma imagined being married might feel like.

After five years she'd come to understand Tony, and in some ways he was her closest friend. They talked of art, politics and the meaning of life long into the night, and afterwards made love as passionately as on that first day. He kept her supplied with tea, sugar, butter and meat, so she and her mother never felt the bite of the ration card. He took her on fashion buying trips to Sydney and Melbourne, wonderful trips where he always found time to show her the galleries and zoos. He discussed his business problems, using her as a sounding board and valuing her advice.

Yes, Tony told her everything – well nearly everything. He never talked about his personal life. Emma knew perfectly well that he had a wife and children living just around the corner from their apartment.

The few times Emma asked about them, she'd been met with stony silence and a disapproving frown. Tony's family was out of bounds. He had a whole other life, one that she was not privy to.

He often urged Emma to give up her work and become his full-time mistress. She had never been tempted. Tony might be special, but he wasn't special enough. She wanted more than half a man, and anyway, she didn't love him. In spite of everything, in spite of Martha and Hampton Hall and the number of men she'd known, deep down Emma still clung to a belief in romantic love. Still hoped for one person to share her life with, to love her the way her father had loved her mother. She still hoped for Tom.

Not in any realistic sense. Emma had long ago given up the idea of living a normal life, and in some ways she didn't want to. She had plenty of money to care for her mother, a lavish lifestyle, and the kind of independence that was rare for a woman, especially one from a poor background. Her love for Tom was a fantasy, the way a little girl might think of becoming a princess and living in a fairy-tale castle with her very own Prince Charming. She didn't really believe it would happen.

'Can I borrow this rouge?' asked Giselle, who was inspecting the makeup jars on Emma's marble dressing table.

'Go on,' said Emma, packing away her scrap book of dreams. 'And then clear out, will you? I have to get ready.'

At precisely six o'clock, Emma made her way to the dressing room on the ground floor. Vast open wardrobes held gowns and furs and shoes. Shelves groaned with hat boxes and jewellery cases. Martha was hovering as usual, choosing who would wear what, and helping the women into their clothes.

'This is your first outfit.' Martha draped a simple teal satin gown over Emma's arm, bias-cut to accentuate her curves.

Emma groaned inwardly. The gown was gorgeous, and the colour suited her red hair and green eyes. Not much chance of being over-looked tonight.

. . .

A bunch of out-of-town naval officers would hardly be in the market for ladies' couture, but Martha never skipped the fashion show. It lent a certain class to the evening, making clients feel their private arrangements were spontaneous dalliances with beautiful models, rather than paid sex.

The women were under no such illusions. Despite Martha's lofty talk of courtesans and paramours, Emma had long ago stopped pretending she was anything other than a high-class prostitute. The only difference between her and the miserable creatures walking the red light district was that she made more money and lived a comfortable life.

Emma awaited her turn on the catwalk. She wasn't looking forward to the evening ahead, making small talk with strangers, and then letting one of them take her to bed. She hurried her first showing, refusing to smile or make eye contact with the men. If she was lucky, nobody would choose her and she'd be free to retreat upstairs alone and update her scrap book with the latest news about Tom.

Martha buttonholed her as soon as she was back in the dressing room, before she had a chance to change into her next gown. 'A young gentleman noticed you immediately, Connie; wants you to meet him in the parlour for a drink. Handsome as the devil, he is too.'

A surge of irritation hit her. Why on earth did Martha think that would make any difference? Emma was sick of her pretending this place was something it wasn't.

'The fashion show isn't finished—'

'Never mind that.' Martha patted her hand. 'And leave the gown on, dear. It suits you so.'

Emma went to the parlour and glanced around. A man was sitting in the corner, smoking a cigarette. He wore a sharp suit, not a naval officer's uniform. Emma stopped dead. Harry.

She turned and fled.

'Wait.' Harry chased after her, and ran into Kai at the base of the stairs.

Emma slipped past, chest heaving, heart hammering against her ribs. Half-way up the staircase she stopped and turned.

Six foot six Kai had Harry by the collar of his shirt. He tried to squirm free, but it was useless. Nobody got past Kai. 'What you want me to do with him, Miss Connie?'

'Show the gentleman out, please.'

'I'll come back,' yelled Harry. 'Every night until you see me. If they won't let me in I'll wait outside. Please Emma. I don't want to hurt you. I just want to talk.'

Music was playing in the ballroom, meaning the fashion show was still in full swing. She hoped the band had drowned out the shouting. Emma fled upstairs to her room and slammed the door behind her. She went to the window and looked down to the street. There was Harry, leaning against a lamp post, smoking a cigarette, looking up at the house. Swiftly she pulled the curtain.

Emma poured herself a big glass of port from the cut-glass decanter on the table. She had to calm down, get some perspective on what had just happened. Why had she over-reacted like that? So Harry knew where she worked. That wasn't the end of the world, was it?

But a clawing fear crept up her back and gripped her by the throat. Her old and new life had collided tonight, right there in the down-stairs parlour. No good could come of that.

Harry was true to his word. Each night he was there outside Hampton Hall, always bearing some gift: a card, a book, flowers from some-body's garden; even chocolates, although how he found them during rationing was a mystery. Kai was forever chasing him away from the door, and she had to be careful that he didn't follow her home.

Martha was not happy. 'It lowers the tone of Hampton Hall, having that young man hanging about like a lovesick schoolboy. You know the rules, Constance. Don't fall in love.'

'I'm not in love,' she protested. 'I can't help it if someone has a crush on me, but I assure you, it's completely one-sided.'

The other women, however, found Harry and his devotion charming. It annoyed Emma no end. They accepted his gifts on her behalf. They took him hot drinks and offerings from the table, like he was a pet or something.

'Harry's there again,' said Giselle one evening as they were getting ready for the show. 'Standing in the rain.'

They both looked out the window. As they watched, Diana took Harry a pink umbrella to protect him from the downpour. 'Have pity on the poor boy,' urged Giselle. 'He's not so bad. He just wants to talk.'

'And you believe that?' Emma shimmied into her strapless gown of burgundy taffeta and frowned. Martha should have known better. The colour washed out her face, and the dress was too tight. She struggled with the side zipper, and it broke. 'Damn.'

'You know what?' said Giselle, still staring out the window. 'He looks a bit like that flyboy of yours.'

'Harry is Tom's brother.' Emma searched through the racks for another gown. 'They're twins.'

'Twins?' Giselle tutted loudly and shook her head. 'Fooling round with brothers? Connie, darling, has anyone told you you're playing with fire?'

Argh! It was maddening how everybody jumped to conclusions. 'I keep telling you, there's no fooling around. Tom's been in England since before the war, and I haven't seen Harry for years. Not until now.'

Giselle fixed her lipstick in the mirror. 'I think Martha could kick you out twice for falling in love with twins.'

'I'm *not* in love. You're talking nonsense.'

'So explain to me why one brother is waiting for you out in the pouring rain, and the top shelf of your wardrobe is a shrine to the other?'

'Shut up, Gissy.' Emma plucked a plain, blue velvet cocktail dress from its hanger and slipped it on.

The corners of Giselle's mouth turned up in a mocking smile. 'The lady doth protest too much, methinks.'

Emma rounded on her, shouting. 'I said shut up!'

Martha came into the room, looking suitably shocked. 'Girls, please. Whatever's going on here?' Giselle giggled and nodded towards the window. Martha peered out to the street below and scowled. 'I see. Constance, come with me, and why ever are you wearing that dress?'

A sullen Emma followed Martha to a private dressing room. 'Put a coat on, go out there, and speak to the boy. I don't care what you say to him, or how long it takes, but he must never come hanging around Hampton Hall again. Do you understand me?' There was a hard-steel edge to her voice that Emma had rarely heard before.

'Yes, Martha.'

'And if I discover you've been conducting some sort of illicit liaison behind my back—' Martha looked as outraged as a vicar finding his virginal daughter kissing a boy behind the alter. 'Well, in that case you'll need to find yourself another position.'

'That won't happen.'

She patted Emma's hand, and the old Martha was back. 'I'm extremely fond of you, dear, and would hate to lose you. Now, go and sort out your young man, eh? Will I send Kai with you?' Emma shook her head. 'Very well. You're excused from tonight's festivities until this is sorted. Don't let me down.'

Emma was getting a headache. What on earth was she going to say to Harry? She went upstairs to fetch her coat, thinking furiously. Harry was an unknown quantity, an undeniable threat, and Martha was right. She had to deal with him.

She'd had a couple of weeks now to come to terms with the fact that Harry knew what she did for a living. She'd been shell-shocked at first, sleepwalking through her days. Lying in bed at night, trying to imagine what Harry was thinking, and knowing that the truth would be far more salacious.

Embarrassing, certainly. Hurtful. Devastating even, but more devastating still if Harry decided to tell his brother. Emma's skin goose-bumped. The idea of Tom knowing that she sold herself to men for a living filled her with shame and dread. It would be almost as bad as her mother knowing. Perhaps Giselle had done her a favour, forcing this matter, bringing it to a head. Tonight she'd resolve the problem of Harry, one way or another, although right now she had no idea how that might happen.

Emma peeked out through her window, trying to remain out of sight, for Harry had worked out where her window was. Somehow he spotted her through the misty rain, and started singing *That Old Black Magic* at the top of his voice.

'Stop it,' she called. 'I'm coming down.'

Harry waved and fell silent. Thank God for that, thought Emma, as she slipped on sensible shoes and hurried downstairs before he started up again.

'Hello Constance,' he said with a grin as she emerged from the front door.

'What are you trying to do to me?'

'I just want to talk.' Harry attempted to hold the umbrella over her head, but she slapped him away. He looked ridiculous, standing there in his wet clothes, sodden shoes and pink parasol. Emma suddenly saw the funny side.

'Come on.' She took hold of his hand and led him down the street away from Hampton Hall. 'We can't stay here.'

The rain increased its intensity. She headed for her car that was parked around the corner – a big, blue Chevrolet of which she was inordinately proud. Emma unlocked it, snatched the umbrella away from him and opened the passenger side door. 'Get in.' She climbed into the driver's seat and started the car so the heater would work.

'Nice wheels,' said Harry, as he dripped water all over the floor.

Emma's teeth were chattering, whether from cold or nerves she didn't know. She leaned over, pulled the blanket off the back seat and wrapped herself in it. 'All right, you wanted to talk – so talk.'

'What happened, Em? Why are you working in that place?'

'Stop coming to Hampton Hall, Harry. You'll get me fired.'

'Would that be so bad?'

'Yes, it would be bad. My mother's had a stroke. I have to look after her, pay for therapists and a nurse. Exactly how do you expect me to do that without a job?'

'You could get another job.'

'Not one that pays enough.'

'I could help. Things are great for me, Em. I'm part owner of the shipyard now.' His voice rang with pride. 'I helped build those three harbour defence motor launches for the navy. Designed them myself, I did. That's why I was at Hampton Hall that night. Captain Scott took me along as a kind of thank you. I couldn't believe it when I saw you there.'

Emma changed the subject. 'If you love boats so much, why aren't you in the navy?'

'Lord knows I tried. I wanted nothing more than to join up and fight for Australia, especially with Tom off in England being a hero. But I couldn't, Em. Boatbuilders are a reserved occupation. We're not allowed to enlist.'

The bitterness in his voice was genuine, and she felt a strong and unexpected surge of compassion for her old friend, in spite of all the trouble he'd caused. For that's what Harry was, an old friend. One of a very few people who'd known her before everything changed. Sitting there, talking with him – it stirred up ghosts of her former life. Uncomfortable ghosts, certainly, but powerful ones too. Shadows of old ambitions, of wanting to go to university and become a doctor and save lives. She snatched at the memories, trying to hold on – but they vanished like half-remembered dreams.

'I want to see you,' said Harry. In the soft glow of the street lamp, his face bore a sudden resemblance to Tom.

'I can't.'

'What does your heart say?'

'I don't listen to it any more,' said Emma, but the truth was, quite unexpectedly, that she wanted to see him too. Harry was a link to who she used to be, and though there was no sense in it, she didn't want to lose that feeling.

'We could go to the movies,' he said. 'Next Monday night. What do you say?'

She had Mondays off. He probably already knew that. 'I won't stop working.'

'Didn't ask you to, did I?'

'Honestly, Harry, you're not the first man who's wanted to rescue me.'

'Musical versus comedy. *The Desert Song* versus *Mr Lucky*. You choose.'

And before she had time to properly think it through, her mouth was saying *Desert Song* like it had a mind of its own.

'Great. Should I pick you up at work?'

'No,' she said quickly. 'Never go there again.'

'Where then?'

She found a notepad in the glove box and scribbled down her address. 'My mother can't know what I do, obviously.'

He pulled a small box of chocolates from his great coat pocket. 'These are for you.'

'Thank you, Harry.' Emma took the rather squashed box from his hand. Back in the rarefied atmosphere of Hampton Hall there were always chocolates and sweets available for the women and their clients. Martha had connections everywhere, including at the Cadbury Factory in Claremont, which was the official supplier of chocolate to the Australian Armed Forces. She could usually find her way around any restrictions.

Yet Harry lived in the real world, a world of hard work and austerity and rationing. A world Emma no longer knew much about. He couldn't get luxuries whenever he wanted, so his humble offering meant a lot. As did the fact that she felt no judgement from him, no judgement at all. Only friendship. It was as sweet as it was surprising.

'Pick me up at six.' She whispered the words as if someone else might hear. 'Will you come in and meet my mother first? She'd like that.'

'Righto.' Harry flashed her his most winning smile. There it was again, that resemblance to Tom, tugging at her heartstrings. When he kissed her and took her in his arms, she didn't pull away.

CHAPTER 23

Hitler had surrendered and Britain was celebrating. The people had endured years of privation. Years of five inches of water in the bath, no bananas and the motto *make do and mend.* Half a million homes destroyed, hundreds of thousands dead, millions of lives disrupted – and now the horror was finally over.

When Tom and the rest of his squadron arrived from Biggin Hill for the victory party at London's fashionable Cable Club, they were greeted like rock stars – played in by the band and escorted to the exclusive VIP area beyond the red velvet cord.

Nobody had forgotten Prime Minister Churchill's stirring speech after the crucial air war during the Battle of Britain. *Never in the field of human conflict was so much owed by so many to so few.* Everybody knew the D-Day invasion of Normandy had relied on thousands of allied aircraft flying daring armed reconnaissance in the battlefield, firing rockets, dropping bombs and unleashing their machine guns against the might of the Luftwaffe. To the people of war-weary Britain, these brave young pilots were a symbol of the nation's courage and hope for the future. All wanted to share and celebrate their heroism.

Stu's new wife, Dolly, clutched his arm tighter as a bevy of beautiful women gathered around, however she was no match for his enthusiastic fans. They whisked him away, along with the rest of the squadron, to cheers, applause and countless requests for autographs.

Tom tried to excuse himself, daunted by a barrage of questions about the war and his part in it. That hell was the last thing he wanted to talk about. More than seventy thousand RAF personnel had died. Tonight's glorious moment of victory was bittersweet.

Tom had led a charmed life these past few years. It seemed the enemy couldn't touch him, but such good fortune did not extend to his comrades. A particular photo haunted him: his first day at the RAF base in 1937. Twenty-eight naive boy pilots, grinning for the camera, excited to be embarking on a new adventure – him and Stu among them. Of those, only eight lived to see this day. And although the war was over in Europe, it still raged in the Pacific, where Australian forces were fighting a desperate battle against Japan. Maybe he'd join that fight, he didn't know. But tonight he wanted to forget all that. He wanted to join in the celebrations of a joyful nation, and focus on a hard-won victory.

In spite of his resolve, the pressing crowd was becoming too much for Tom. The eagle-eyed *maître de* rescued him. 'Would you like to sit down, sir, and perhaps a drink?' He escorted Tom to a table at the side of the room, away from the throng, where a jug of ice water stood next to a bottle of French champagne in a silver bucket. 'If sir pleases, there's a young lady who would like to join you. May I show her to your table?'

Tom lit a cigarette. 'Be my guest.' One star-struck, grateful girl he could handle. It might even be fun.

Then he saw her. White-gold curls framed her face and rubies encircled her slender neck – a glittering beauty with skin the colour of warm honey. Magnetic eyes of cornflower blue, and that dress. A drift of simple, silver satin skimming her body, rippling with the rise and fall of her breasts.

Mesmerising. She half-smiled, lifted one perfect tanned shoulder, and when she did a little twirl, he knew it was just for him.

'Kitty Munro,' she said, extending an arm.

He kissed her hand, lips lingering a little longer than was customary. 'I'm—'

'I know who you are, Wing Commander Thomas Abbott. The more interesting question is, do you know who I am?'

She spoke with an American accent. Could he have met this ravishing vision before and forgotten? Tom racked his brain. Embarrassed by his failure to remember, perplexed as to why the most beautiful woman in the world was sitting at his table.

'It seems you have me at a disadvantage, Miss Munro.'

A middle-aged lady approached them, dripping in diamonds. Tom turned away, hoping she'd take the hint and leave. But it wasn't him she was interested in.

'Dear Kitty. I loved you in *The Moving Finger*. An absolutely stunning performance.' She held up an autograph book. 'Could I trouble you?' Kitty graciously inclined her head, and took up the pen. Several more people made the same request, and stood in line.

So she was an actress, a star of the stage perhaps, appearing in the West End. He'd never been to a swanky theatrical production before, but if Kitty was appearing in one, that would change, and quickly.

'Tell me about your latest play,' he said when the autograph hounds had gone. 'I'll get myself a ticket.'

She threw back her head and laughed; a charming, musical sound. 'You have no idea who I am, do you?'

Tom felt himself go red. 'They keep me pretty busy on the base,' he said, by way of apology. 'I don't often get up to London.'

The *maître de* returned to their table to pour the champagne, just as Kitty shuffled her chair a little closer, and put a hand on Tom's knee. A jolt of electricity shot through him, as more fans arrived to distract her.

The *maître de* raised his eyebrows and whispered in his ear. 'Miss Munro is a Hollywood star, sir. A box office sensation. She's in Britain filming her new movie, *Murder At The Ritz*.'

Tom murmured his thanks.

Kitty wrote a few autographs and shooed the other hopefuls away.

'I believe you're the first person I've met so far in London who hasn't seen my last movie, or at least pretended to have seen it.'

'My apologies, Miss Munro. As I said before—'

'No, No. Don't apologise. I find it quite charming.' She took a cigarette from a silver case and put it to her lips. He groped in his pocket for matches, all fumble fingers. She waited coolly for him to light it, cupping his hand in hers as he did.

Tom broke into a sweat and took a swig of champagne. Flying headlong into a squadron of Messerschmitts wasn't as daunting as this one, beautiful girl. Right through the war he'd kept his distance from women. He told himself that getting close to someone in wartime was irresponsible, but it was more than that. He'd lost too many people already, so he built a protective wall around his heart, one that he thought nobody could breach.

Many girls had tried, drawn to the dashing D-Day hero who'd become the toast of a nation. He'd been tempted a few times, especially by freckle-faced redheads who reminded him of Emma Starr. It must be true what they say about first love. Not only was Emma hard to forget, but she symbolised a time in his life before loss defined him. A time when his grandmother and brother were still in his life.

But Kitty Munro had broken through the wall in an instant, leaving him defenceless, at her mercy. Maybe it was because the strain of war was gone, and he wanted to smile and joke and laugh with this dazzling young woman. He wanted to tell her his secrets, and hear all of hers. He wanted to swing her into his arms, smell her fragrant hair and never let her go. It was as if she was already his lover. 'Care for this dance?'

She nodded. He led her to the dance floor and the other couples gave way. They were the centre of attention – the splendid airman and the glamourous Hollywood star. Someone snapped a flash snap of the pair, and security quickly bundled the photographer from the room. The band struck off in an especially romantic version of *As Time Goes By*, and Tom held her close. She felt so soft, so fragile, he was frightened she might break.

Stu and Dolly waltzed past, offering smiles, but he barely noticed them. 'Let's get out of here,' he whispered. Kitty seemed to be filled with the same breathless anticipation that had struck him down. The need to be alone with this woman was overwhelming.

They almost ran from the club, stopping to say goodbye to no one. They dodged cameras and well-wishers before hailing a taxi and collapsing into the blessed privacy of its back seat. 'The Savoy,' managed Kitty.

They kissed, and he exploded in a blinding flash of desire. Neither of them wanted to let the connection go, and they were still locked together when they arrived at the hotel. Tom paid the cabbie and the pair teetered onto the footpath, drunk with desire for each other. Cameras flashed in their faces as they hurried through the doors, hand in hand, assisted by two firm doormen who kept the photographers at bay.

Tom could barely get any air. 'Do you … do you want a drink at the bar?'

'I couldn't bear it,' breathed Kitty. 'Come to my suite.'

Tom didn't need to be asked twice. In one giant leap of faith, he abandoned the rigid controls cultivated during long years of war. Let go the shields, the protections, the denials that had allowed him to function in the fearful hell of battle. All fled into the shadows, banished by Kitty's blazing halo of light.

When they were finally alone, Kitty unbuttoned his coat, running her fingers over the medals and the flying cross on his lapel. She unbuttoned his shirt and laid her head against the corded muscles of his chest. 'I can hear your heart.'

He slipped the straps of her gown from her shoulders, with fingers that seemed too big and clumsy for the task. Kitty let down her hair, and gazed up at him with a flush on her cheek. He touched the soft swell of her breast. 'You're so very beautiful.'

Her bright blue eyes danced with pleasure. 'Take me to bed.' Her words carried with them a fizzing vitality that was almost palpable. Kitty was a force of nature, the most intensely alive person he'd ever met. In a moment they were naked together, Tom's hands exploring her perfect body. He grew so hard he feared he'd burst, but still he waited, eager for her to be ready too, for her to give him a sign. Finally she reached for him, pulling him close, guiding him home.

Hours later they lay spent and peaceful in each other's arms. Nothing could have prepared Tom for such joy. Kitty asked for champagne, so he fetched a bottle and poured two glasses, letting the bubbles slide down his parched throat.

She chattered away, telling him about her latest movie, and how much it meant and how cruel some critics could be. Tom wasn't really listening, not to the words anyway. He was listening to the sweet sound of her voice, the exotic twang, the husky musicality – and he knew he never wanted to be without it again.

He slid his arms around her. 'Marry me, Kitty.'

Her chatter ground to a halt. 'You don't mean that, Tom.'

'Try me.'

'I know nothing about you,' she said, as she fitted her smooth body to his. 'Other than you're a war hero, of course, and terribly attractive.'

'Isn't that enough?' Her lyrical laughter made him mad with happiness. 'All right then. What do you want to know?'

'Tell me anything.'

'My parents died in an accident when I was ten.'

'How awful!' She kissed his cheek.

'I have a twin brother.'

'Is he as handsome as you?'

'No.'

She giggled. 'Go on, tell me more. Impress me.'

'I own an estate in Tasmania. My grandmother left it to me. A big house with thousands of acres of land.'

'You do? An inheritance as well?'

'Absolutely.'

'How marvellous. I've always wanted to marry an heir.'

He smiled and held her tighter. 'Do you even know where Tasmania is?'

'Of course.' Her flawless forehead creased into a little frown. 'It's in Africa, isn't it? Do you have monkeys. I'd love to cuddle a monkey.'

Fantastic, she liked animals. 'Tasmania is part of Australia, sweetheart; an island state in the south. And no, we don't have monkeys. Will kangaroos do?'

'Kangaroos? I'll say they will. But Tom, are you sure?'

'Maybe this will convince you.' He kissed her, making such a thorough job of it that they were both dizzy. 'Now, how about I try again.' This time he knelt beside the bed and took hold of her hand. 'Kitty Munro, will you do me the honour of becoming my wife?'

'Yes.' She flung her arms around him, pressing her bare breasts against him like soft white pillows. 'Yes, I will. How the press will love us!'

CHAPTER 24

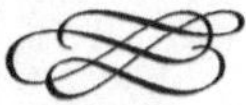

Emma hurried down the hallway to her mother's room, still in her dressing gown. She knocked hard on Elsie's door as she went in. 'Mama, Mama. Japan has surrendered.' Emma turned on the dressing table wireless and helped Mum to sit up in bed.

Elsie came in. 'Whatever's wrong?'

'Japan has surrendered. Jacky will be coming home. Listen. They're about to replay the Prime Minister's speech.'

A lively military march sounded from the speaker, and then came Ben Chifley's voice. *Fellow citizens, the war is over.*

Emma and Elsie joined hands and danced around the room. Even Mum managed a fine cheer. The news wasn't unexpected. Newspapers had been filled lately with articles about Allied success. Reports of American atom bombs flattening Hiroshima and Nagasaki had increased speculation about an imminent surrender. Troops in Darwin and New Guinea were apparently already celebrating, but Chifley's announcement made it official. Peace was at hand.

'Let's go into town,' said Elsie. 'Join in the celebrations.'

'Do you want to, Mum?' asked Emma. 'I can bring the car round the front, right by the door. Are you up for it?'

Her mother smiled, as widely as her wonky mouth would allow. 'Try to stop me.'

By ten-thirty they were in the car and ready to go. Emma was tucking a tartan rug around her mother's knee when she heard a knock on the window. Harry, wearing a silly party hat and waving a Union Jack flag.

She laughed and wound down the window. 'Isn't it marvellous?'

'The best,' he said, kissing her. 'And I have some marvellous news of my own. Let me in.'

'Yes, let him in,' said Mum. She was a big fan of Harry. He was exactly the type of man she had in mind for her daughter. Charming, hard-working and from a good family. The Abbott name was a well-known one.

Harry opened the back door, sat beside Elsie, and the four of them were off into town. It soon became clear that everyone had the same idea; men, women and children waving streamers, flags and noise-makers. The streets were packed with revellers all the way down Macquarie Street, to the Town Hall and beyond. Girls with linked arms danced around the rammed earth air-raid shelters in Franklin Square and painted the word *Peace* on walls and sandbags. Small boys climbed statues and lamp posts to see above the crowds.

'Drop Eileen and me off opposite the post office,' said Elsie. 'We'll go to that little tea room. Your mother can sit down, and we can watch all the fun from the window.'

'Are you sure?' said Emma, who was dying to join in the collective celebrations. 'What about you, Mum?'

'Go on,' her mother said. 'You two enjoy yourselves.'

Emma parked the car and took Harry's hand. 'What about your news?'

'That can wait.'

They melted into the laughing, cheering throng, buoyed by an immense shared joy that Emma had never felt before. The centre of Hobart was transformed into one, enormous street party. She lost track of the number of spontaneous kisses from strangers. There were no grumpy constables on corners, directing traffic. They'd all joined in the revelry, blowing their whistles and throwing their hats in the air. There were no harried clerks hurrying to the office, or impatient deliverymen backing vans into laneways. The city was at a standstill, except for the trams, with standing room only and smiling people spilling from the running boards.

A huge papier mâché figure, with the name *Hirohito* splashed across its chest, appeared from a third floor window. A man leaned out, wrapped the dummy in a Japanese flag, tightened a noose around its neck and let it fall. The crowd cheered as it swung three feet above the ground. Somebody set it alight, and people danced and sang while it burned.

The flaming effigy sent an uncomfortable prickle up Emma's spine. 'Let's find somewhere for a drink.'

They strolled down Elizabeth Street, past a man doing the highland fling. Past a woman whose little dogs were doing tricks to the applause of a gathering audience. Past thirty or forty people singing and dancing the hokey pokey. Harry joined in. 'Come on Em. Put your left foot in, and shake it all about.' He took hold of her hand and twirled her. 'Then you turn yourself around. That's what it's all about.'

They ran off laughing, hand in hand, until Harry ducked into a laneway. 'There's a little place down here. Wait a minute.' He ran back to the paperboy on the corner.

'There won't be anything about the war being over in there,' said Emma. 'You'll have to wait for tomorrow's edition.'

Harry folded the newspaper and followed her into the crowded cafe. He slipped something to the man behind the bar, who found them a table upstairs. 'Two beers, mate.'

This was exactly what she loved about being with Harry. This gritty place, with a fly buzzing at the window and a wonky-legged chair to sit on. The floor a little sticky, the beer a little warm, but filled with people living real lives. People putting aside their problems and differences to celebrate a shared hope for the future.

What a blessing that she hadn't slept at Hampton Hall last night. Martha would undoubtedly have arranged a hurried early opening. A party, with champagne cocktails and salmon appetisers. With wealthy businessmen and politicians who could buy whatever and whoever they wanted. Who'd never had to deal with rationing or risking their lives in battle, or being rejected by their lovely paid companions. She guessed some might even be sorry to see the end of the war, especially those invested in shipyards or munitions.

In the twelve months since she'd reconnected with Harry, her work at Hampton Hall had become more and more intolerable. She mightily resented having to hide him from Martha. She hated that Harry had to share her. He'd never thrown it in her face, and Emma suspected he was seeing other girls, but she hadn't asked. She wasn't that much of a hypocrite. Even so, Emma was finding it harder and harder to sleep with strangers.

Harry had opened her eyes to what a real relationship felt like, one based on friendship and mutual attraction instead of money. She'd turned her back on Tony Angelo, who once upon a time had seemed like her best friend. Now she knew better. She'd spotted him once in Macquarie Street, promenading with his family. It had shocked her to see how young and lovely his wife really was. He'd slipped an affectionate arm around her waist and they'd laughed at some joke or other, in the same way he might have done with her. Except it wasn't the same. It was more intimate and loving, she could see the difference now. And when he plucked their smiling baby from the pram, Emma had turned and fled, vowing to never see him again.

'A penny for them?' asked Harry.

'Never mind,' she said. 'How about something to eat? I'm starved, and after that we'd better get back to Mum.'

Harry sculled his beer. 'I'll see what I can do.'

Emma unfolded the newspaper, searching as always for war news relevant to Jack or Tom. On page three a photo stood out – it was Tom, pictured with a glamourous woman in a bridal gown. The caption read, *Actress Kitty Munro makes a charming study as she joins her husband, Wing Commander Thomas Abbott, in cutting their wedding cake.*

Emma didn't at first understand, so she read the article several times for clarification.

The marriage of RAF Wing Commander Thomas Abbott and Miss Kitty Munro took place yesterday in London. The Australian flying ace and his Hollywood film star wife have been inseparable since they met at a party on Victory in Europe day.

The wedding was attended by members of the RAF and many cinema notables. All admired the bride's elaborate gown of cream shot-silk over white taffeta. Wild excitement erupted outside the church, with police powerless to control the eager crowds intent on cheering the happy couple and their guests.

Could Tom really be married? And to an actress of all people, at a big celebrity wedding? It didn't sound like him at all. Emma thought back to the shy boy she'd met at Campbell College; so shy that he'd let Harry do all the talking, at least to begin with. The boy who loved to trek into the wilderness, with just his dogs and the mountains for company. Had he really changed so much?

Emma gazed at the photograph and let it burn itself into her brain. Tom's classically chiselled features, the warmth of his eyes, that chin dimple. He in turn was gazing at his bride. She'd turned to pose for the camera, wide eyes framed by long lashes, a rose-bud smile and perfect teeth. Kitty was a rare beauty, of that there was no doubt, and Tom was a man after all. A man who'd risked his life almost every day of the war and distinguished himself as a hero. A man who'd forgotten all about the red-haired girl he'd met years ago in Hobart. Why shouldn't he have changed? Lord knows she had.

Harry arrived, balancing a tray with two more beers and a plate of toasted sandwiches. She pushed the paper over to him. It was a long time before he spoke. 'Looks like my little brother's done all right for himself.'

She studied his face, a face that was trying too hard to look surprised. 'You knew.'

He rolled the paper up in his hand. 'Yeah, Tom sent me a telegram, though I never got back to him.'

'Your twin brother gets married and you didn't even send congratulations?'

'Something happened with me and Tom, Em. Years ago. It got

between us.' She asked the question with her eyes and he shook his head.

Emma shrugged and sipped her beer. 'Let's forget about Tom.' She was still more shaken than she cared to admit.

Harry lit a cigarette. 'Remember that marvellous news that I wanted to tell you?' He paused for greater effect.

'Go on, then.'

'I've done it, Em. Bought back Abbott & Son, our family shipyard. My father lost it in the depression and I swore to myself that I'd get it back.'

'But how?'

'Working double and triple shifts. Saving every penny for eight years. Talking a few other blokes into investing. Then last month I sold my shares in Purton & Featherby, and with my grandmother's inheritance ... well, the rest is history.' His face shone with pride, and he looked unbelievably handsome.

'That really is marvellous, Harry. What a magical day this is.' Emma threw her arms around him and kissed him until they were both breathless.

'There's more.' He knelt down, produced a small box from his pocket and offered it to her. 'Miss Emma Starr, will you marry me?'

A hush gradually fell on the room, as people realised what was happening. Emma froze in her chair. She had not expected a proposal.

'Go on, love,' called someone. 'Make him a happy man.'

But Emma was too stunned to speak.

Harry wet his lips and shuffled a little closer on his knees. 'We'll move into your place,' he whispered. 'Now I own the shipyard, I can support you *and* your Mum. You can stop working at that awful place.'

'It's not looking good, son.' A fat man at the next table chuckled and shook his head. 'Not if you're having to talk her into it.'

The crowd burst out laughing.

'Hush now,' said a middle-aged lady in a stars and stripes hat. 'Let the poor girl catch her breath.' Harry was going red and beginning to sweat. The lady gave Emma an encouraging smile. 'Now dear, put your young man out of his misery.'

The excitement in the room was infectious, bearing Emma along on a tide of enthusiasm and romance. 'Yes,' she said, at last. 'Yes, Harry, I'll marry you.'

A cheer raised the roof, and a flurry of hats flew through the air. Well-wishers helped Harry to his feet, shaking his hand.

'Congratulations, son,' said the fat man. 'What a way to start the peace.' He turned and yelled, 'Drinks are on me.'

Harry pulled up a chair beside her. 'We'll have the best, life, Em. I guarantee it.'

Emma nodded, resting against him, basking in the warm affection of this room full of strangers, all inspired by the simple promise of a man to a woman. She liked the weight of Harry's arm slung around her shoulder, and the happy lines on his face. She liked the prospect of leaving Hampton Hall, and the sound of her new name. Mrs Emma Abbott, a respectable married lady.

Harry began munching his way through the sandwiches. 'Want one?' But her stomach was too full of butterflies.

Emma finished her beer, and started on another, though she was already light-headed. Her mother would be thrilled. Mum loved Harry.

Yet a worm of doubt still squirmed somewhere inside. Mum might love Harry, but did she? She cared for him, certainly. Cared for him more than any other man she'd ever known, except for Tom, of course, and there was no future there. Idly she wondered if Harry had arranged for her to find out about his brother's wedding.

She took another swig of beer. Yes, she did love Harry, as well as someone like her could. After all, she'd spent the last seven years building a wall around her heart. She hadn't been allowed to love. She needed to give herself time, that was all. And as the umpteenth person stopped to congratulate her, the newspaper slipped from the table and the photo of Tom was trampled underfoot.

'Who the hell do they think they are?' Kitty tore the newspaper in half and threw herself back on the bed.

Tom pulled her to him. 'I told you not to read the reviews.'

She twisted in his arms, arching her body to get free in the most delicious way. He kissed the inside of her elbow and she dissolved into giggles. 'Tom, you are awful.'

He smothered her laughter with a kiss, pulled the sheet over their heads, and let passion sweep them away.

Tom lay perfectly relaxed, as he always did after they made love. Kitty dozed beside him, her head on his shoulder. Tom trailed his finger along the curve of her breast, overcome once again by how beautiful she was.

Married a year now, and it had been a tumultuous time. Kitty wasn't an easy person to live with – at times caring, charming, funny and a joy to be around. But she had darker moods when she was impulsive, erratic and critical. Prone to pique and violent fits of temper. But Tom looked for the best in people – the war hadn't changed that – and this optimism applied doubly to his wife. So he took Kitty as he found her, day to day, and loved her either way.

He couldn't really blame her for her moods, not at the moment. She'd had a stressful few weeks. Her latest movie – *Murder At The Ritz* – had been panned by the critics. Kitty played the daughter of a murdered financier. Her character was determined to track down those of her father's colleagues who'd plotted against him.

Her acting had been variously described as wooden, one-dimensional, clichéd and unconvincing. One review, that he'd thankfully managed to keep from Kitty, described the movie as 'a hackneyed, derivative copy of the classic Hollywood detective genre, that relies on Miss Munro's beauty to disguise her complete lack of talent.'

Tom tried to get up without waking her.

'Baby?' she said sleepily. 'I hate London. I want to go home.'

'California? I suppose we could. I'm due some leave.'

'Not Los Angeles, silly. You know what my family's like. You met them at the wedding.'

He had. It had cost him a fortune to fly them all out, and put them up at the Savoy.

'My stepfather thinks all actresses are whores,' said Kitty. 'Mum nags me about having babies, and my sisters are so jealous, they flirt with you and can't find one nice word to say to me.'

'They're not that bad.'

'They damn well are, and anyway, I meant *your* home, baby. Tasmania. We've been married almost a year, and I still haven't seen that big old estate of yours. Tell me about it.'

Kitty's question took Tom by surprise. He'd spent years trying not to think about Binburra. His last memories of home were Nana's funeral and that awful fight with Harry.

'Binburra's pretty remote,' he said, as he dressed in his uniform. 'Not really your style.'

Kitty hopped out of bed and brushed some lint from his shoulder. 'Maybe that's exactly what I need; rest and relaxation and mountain air before I start filming my next movie. There are mountains, aren't there?'

'Oh, there are mountains all right.' Scenes of home flashed through his mind. 'And forests as far as you can see, and air so pure, it's like breathing … champagne.'

'And kangaroos?'

'And kangaroos.'

'Sounds wonderful. Please, baby, let's go to Tasmania, just as soon as we can.' Her voice had dropped an octave, and she reached for his belt.

'Oh, no you don't,' said Tom, backing away but sorely tempted to stay. It was a long drive to Boscombe Down, a military aircraft testing site near Amesbury in Wiltshire. He wished Kitty would put some clothes on. 'I've got to get to work.' He reluctantly left for the garage.

Kitty had never expressed any interest in going to Tasmania before, and for some reason the prospect unsettled him. He tried to picture her drinking tea in Binburra's kitchen while Mrs Mills took a batch of scones from the oven. Riding a horse up the waterfall track. Hiking into the grandeur of Tiger Pass. He couldn't do it, couldn't imagine her there at all. His life was divided into two parts – before and after his grandmother's death, and Kitty belonged firmly to the second half.

He suspected the real reason for Kitty's change of heart. Since *Murder At The Ritz* had bombed at the box office, the studio had dropped her. She hadn't been given any official notice, nothing that would hit the papers. They simply hadn't contracted her for a new movie. Kitty had been offered other parts but had refused them all, complaining they were B-grade with terrible scripts, and would destroy her reputation. He didn't point out that *Murder At The Ritz* seemed to have effectively done that already.

Tom enjoyed the quiet life, flying planes by day and coming home to a wife who belonged just to him, instead of to the whole world. But Kitty loved to act. She loved the glamourous showbiz lifestyle and the adoration of her fans. He knew that when he met her, but they had to face facts. Right now they were living above their means. They couldn't afford to rent their furnished Kensington terrace much longer. He'd already spent most of his modest inheritance so that

Kitty could live the high life. Not that he minded. Money didn't matter to Tom, and he wanted his wife to be happy. But with a month's leave owing, it would be the perfect time to go home.

'Morning, Wing Commander,' said Flight Lieutenant Brand. 'Looking forward to going up in her, sir?'

The sleek DHC-1 Chipmunk looked just like Tom thought a modern airplane should look. He walked around her, admiring the low, tapered wings and narrow fuselage, which gave her the look of a small World War II fighter. He loved the enclosed tandem cockpit – complete with rear-sliding canopy – the aerodynamic lines, and her distinctive vertical fin; the signature of de Havilland designs.

'She's a beauty,' said Tom. 'A step up from what I learned to fly in, that's for sure.'

The Chipmunk was being developed as a replacement for the Tiger Moth, which had become too antiquated to continue as a basic trainer. Today Tom was taking this prototype model on a test flight.

'Ready when you are, sir.'

Tom briefly removed his new goggles. The leather was stiff and scratched his nose. He twisted them a few times to soften them before takeoff. It didn't help. Tom put them on anyway, climbed into the cockpit, and automatically felt for the silver Karma pendant around his neck. He'd forgotten to put it on after his shower. It wasn't in his pocket either. Tom's stomach sank. For a moment he considered cancelling the flight, but shook off the notion as superstitious nonsense. How could he stay on the ground when the blue sky beckoned?

Flight Lieutenant Brand waved him away, and Tom primed the engine. The Chipmunk literally started with a bang, and the smell of cordite from the cartridge-type starter. Takeoff was as smooth as silk. He pushed the irritating goggles high onto his forehead and nosed into the light breeze, daydreaming that he was seventeen again and going solo for the first time.

The Chippie was a delight to fly. Tom began thinking about what to say in the review he'd write later that morning. He flew 360 degree turns with varying amounts of bank in both directions. Even complicated manoeuvres were a breeze; the controls light and responsive, although the rudder was a little sensitive. The Chipmunk would not tolerate a ham-fisted pilot, and as such was an excellent trainer.

In fact it was so nicely balanced that, once set up with power and trim, it became the perfect flying classroom. Add more power and it pitched up and yawed to starboard; reduce power and it pitched down and yawed to port. Flaps down and it pitched down, flaps up and it pitched up. The Chipmunk was a true thoroughbred; the modern benchmark against which other light planes should be measured.

Tom decided to have some fun, looping and rolling high above the beautiful Wiltshire countryside. Flying the Chippie solo with an hour's fuel on a bright summer morning was an absolute joy.

It was only on his way back to the airfield that he noticed a problem – noises from the propeller, followed by an unusual vibration. He pulled back on the throttle, reducing speed, but the noise and vibration worsened. The blades began to wobble and bend, spinning more and more wildly.

Tom got on the radio. 'Trouble with propeller. Am using full left rudder. Keep airfield clear for emergency landing.'

As he signed off – disaster. One blade snapped off at the shaft with a tremendous bang and went spinning into the void. Tom instinctively ducked. Plenty of pilots had died when broken blades shot backwards into the cockpit.

'Mayday, mayday, mayday! Broken prop. Making forced landing.' Tom radioed his position and shut the plane down to stop the unbalanced propeller from tearing the engine from its mounts. He let his wartime experience come into play, looking for a place to do a dead-stick landing and glide to the ground.

Tom had learned long ago that during each moment in the air, sightseeing should include *there's one I can land on* thoughts. Keeping track had become second nature, almost a game, flying from one emergency field or clear roadway to the next, so he already had a mental map of the ground. The sparkling River Avon, wending its way through the countryside up ahead, helped him find his bearings.

Thankfully he had altitude and a light wind, so his options were good and his confidence rose. Tom considered trying to reach Boscombe Down, but he couldn't risk falling short and crashing into the town adjoining the airfield. For the same reason he couldn't use his parachute and abandon the plane, although he had enough height. No, Tom had made plenty of forced landings. He would bring the prototype Chipmunk down under control and intact.

The empty field looked perfect for his purpose; roughly the right size and shape with a slight uphill slope. Tom confirmed wind direction, reported his position and made his approach, mentally dividing the available landing distance into three and aiming at a point about one-third of the way along. A perfect approach and the Chipmunk was down, rushing along the rough ground on its fixed landing gear, rapidly losing speed.

It was then Tom saw it – a wide, grassy drainage channel that had been invisible from the air. He could only guess at its depth, and he was heading straight for it.

Tom struggled frantically to slide back the canopy and escaped the cockpit just as the plane flipped. Something cracked him on the head, knocking him sideways. A strong smell of fuel brought him to his senses. He stumbled to his feet and tried to run. But a deafening explosion and sheets of flame reached out to set him ablaze.

Tom's limbs would not work as he fell to the ground, enveloped in white heat. He couldn't open his eyes, or raise the scream in his throat.

Dimly, Tom became aware of willing arms rolling him on the cool green grass; of voices whispering words of comfort. 'You're all right, son. We've got buckets of water here, and the ambulance is on its way.'

They doused his smouldering body, clad in nothing now but burnt rags. Mercifully his clothes had offered some protection; thick over-alls over his uniform, a woollen jumper, leather gloves and three pairs of woolly socks under his flying boots.

But his eyes – in the strain of landing, Tom had forgotten to pull his goggles back down.

A stink was in his nose now, the most evil and terrifying of smells — his own burnt flesh. Tom shivered uncontrollably, nauseated and suddenly cold. As shock set in, blissful unconsciousness claimed him.

CHAPTER 26

Tom wasn't flying, he was falling; falling off a cliff into the sky, with the wind a dull, confusing roar in his ears. He reached for a hand that appeared before him, but it pulled away just as he thought he was safe. He screamed as Harry's grinning face mocked him from the clouds. He was hot now, too hot, on fire. Dear God, the pain; he couldn't bear it. Down and down he went, faster and faster. Past his horrified mother and frowning father. Past his weeping grandmother, who held his silver Karma out on a chain – too far away to reach.

A mirror floated past but he couldn't see himself – only a hideous mass of swollen burnt flesh that might have once been his face. And then Emma was there, smiling and dressed in boy's clothes two sizes too big, falling with him, holding his hands.

'Tom?' A woman's voice broke through the fog of sleep. 'Wake up, love.'

Emma? Tom tried to open his eyes. He tried to say her name but couldn't move his mouth. His whole face was painfully tight and stiff, and when he reached up to feel it, he found it swathed in bandages. He dredged his mind, but was unable to remember. What had happened to him? Why couldn't he move? Tom endured the agony of trying to sit, and discovered something extraordinary. His body hung in a kind of harness, a few inches above the bed.

'You've had an operation. Don't try to talk, love, and you won't be able to see for a while. I'm Wendy, the nurse who's come to change your dressings. But first, try to have a drink for me.'

A tube pressed against his lips and slipped into his raw, burning mouth. He gagged on the sweet liquid, despite his terrible thirst. 'Just a little more, that's right. I'll give you a quick needle now, to make you more comfortable.'

A sting in his thigh, and the great tide of pain receded, but now Tom found it even harder to think. Why was he in hospital? Had he been shot down?

This was to be the pattern of his days. No sense of time. Three-hourly morphine shots making the pain tolerable, but keeping his mind in a confused stupor. Faceless nurses giving him agonising saline baths. Blind eyes itching under his bandages and not being able to scratch. Disgusting liquid feeds and umpteen bottles of lemonade and ginger beer that never quenched his unbearable thirst. Restless sleep peppered with nightmares of burning and falling.

'Wonderful news,' said a nurse one day; he couldn't say which nurse or which day. 'Mr McIndoe says you're well enough for visitors. They've been lining up: your aunts, RAF buddies, and somebody very special.' Her voice betrayed her excitement. 'Tom, your wife is here to see you. We've all been so excited. None of us girls have ever met a real life movie star.'

His wife. Were they talking about Emma? They must be married. Why couldn't he remember? And what did the nurse mean about a movie star?

'Tom,' said a woman with an American accent. Her heady perfume chased away the odour of disinfectant and the acrid stink of burnt, blistered flesh. 'It's me, Kitty. How are you, baby?'

Kitty? He didn't know anyone called Kitty.

Now a warm male voice that Tom couldn't place, speaking with the flat vowel sounds of a New Zealander. 'I'm Archie McIndoe, Tom, your surgeon. You're going to be fine. We're going to fix you up.'

He knew that name from somewhere.

'Did you hear that, baby?' Tom felt arms wrap around him, and cried out in pain.

'Don't touch him please, Mrs Abbott,' said the voice of Archie McIndoe. Mrs Abbott? It made no sense. Tom didn't know this woman. 'Your husband has burns over most of his upper body. The prognosis for recovery is good for the areas where his clothes protected him.'

'That's fabulous, doctor.' The voices moved away from Tom's bed and lowered a little, but he could still hear. 'My husband will be able to see, won't he, when you take off the bandages?'

Tom racked his fuddled brain for clues. His eyes might not work, but his nose did. That fragrance; a rich scent of jasmine and orange. Flashes of a girl with hair like spun gold and bright blue eyes. He grasped for the memories, yet they remained as elusive as shadows. One astonishing thing was clear from the conversation. He wasn't married to Emma at all. This woman with the American accent was his wife.

'With proper care Tom will not lose his sight,' said the doctor. 'However he has deep-dermal flame burns to his cheeks, nose and lips. Unfortunately he was not wearing goggles, and suffered full thickness skin loss around his eyes. When he's sufficiently recovered, I will need to replace his eyelids and rebuild his nose.'

A jolt of fear went through him, and there was no mistaking the woman's horrified intake of breath. Now he knew where he'd heard the name. McIndoe was a pioneering surgeon, famous in the RAF for restoring the disfigured bodies of badly burned pilots. And Tom was in the special plastic surgery ward of the Queen Victoria Hospital at East Grinstead. He'd visited a friend there once, a man who'd had his hands and face burned off when trapped in his downed Hurricane. Never had Tom seen such a chamber of horrors. Men with missing ears; melted, misshapen noses and holes where their eyes should be. Men with bulbous lips and distorted crimson gashes for mouths. The faces of those poor airmen had haunted his dreams for weeks. And now he'd joined their ranks.

'Understand, Mrs Abbott, that your husband must undergo some complicated facial reconstruction surgery in the next few months. He will require your unfailing support.'

It took a long time for her to respond. 'Of course, doctor,' she said at last. 'Nothing matters more to me than Tom's recovery.' He could sense her coming close again; the waft of perfume, the sound of a chair being pulled over.

'There's some great news, baby. I'm starring in a new movie. It's all settled; well, almost, but my agent says the part's perfect for me. I play a New York heiress who travels to the west and falls in love with a handsome rodeo star who doesn't know she's rich. It's a chance for me to do comedy. I've never done comedy, but I've always wanted to. You said I'd be good at it, remember?'

He didn't. He barely remembered anything about her, just a shadowy face. Yet this was his wife. What a shock it must be for her, seeing him like this.

'The thing is, I have to meet the producer in LA next week, so I'm flying out tomorrow. Don't worry, baby, I'll be back before you know it. Then, when you're better, you can come to America while I'm making the movie.'

She was speaking fast, barely drawing breath, as if she couldn't wait to be finished. The more she talked, the more he recalled. He couldn't remember how he'd been burned, but he knew the war was over. And he remembered a few snatches of his life with this woman. Dancing at a glittering party. Watching sunsets over the Thames. Nothing more substantial. He could hear murmuring voices in the background, people asking for autographs.

'Goodbye, Tom.' Something lightly brushed his bandaged face. 'I'll see you as soon as I get back. Love you, baby.'

Tom listened for the footsteps to recede, the doctor's matter of fact ones and the light trip-trap of his wife's high heels. Then he slumped back and the pain built again. Shutting his eyes behind the dressing was more of a psychological exercise than a physical one. Still, he did his best and tried to summon up an image of Kitty. But no matter how hard he tried, it was always Emma's lovely face that stubbornly came to mind.

CHAPTER 27

Emma read the news item with a sense of disbelief.

London, Friday: Australian RAF pilot, Wing Commander Thomas Abbott, was injured yesterday during a test flight. His aircraft flipped and burst into flames on crash landing. Abbott suffered serious burns to his face and body. His wife, Hollywood actress Kitty Munro, braved the media today, saying, 'My husband is badly hurt, but he has a courageous spirit. We must all pray for his full recovery. Nothing matters more to me than Tom's return to health.

Emma took the newspaper into the kitchen. Elsie, who'd become the family's cook, was pickling vegetables, and her mother was making a pot of tea. Harry was up to his elbows in flour, kneading a big ball of dough.

'How hungry are you lot?' Harry was surprisingly good at making scones, and had made it a Saturday morning tradition. He'd also made it a tradition to eat most of them himself as soon as they were out of the oven, slathered with raspberry jam and clotted cream.

Mum found Harry's penchant for Devonshire teas hugely amusing. 'Why do you love scones so much?' She strung her words together slowly, with a slight drawl, but was perfectly understandable.

'A throwback from childhood,' he said with a shrug. 'And I don't have to share this lot with my brother.' He expertly rolled out the dough. 'Tom always hogged the lot.'

'Not like you then, Harry.' Mum winked at Emma, but she was in no mood to appreciate the joke. Mum glanced at the wall clock. 'Will you take my cuppa in, Harry? It's time for my play.'

Harry obliged, and Emma was once again touched by how kind he was to her mother. Elsie sealed the last jar of pickled cucumbers and put it in the pantry. 'Think I'll join Eileen.' She poured herself a cup of tea. 'I'm hooked on those wireless serials of hers.'

'Harry,' said Emma, when Elsie had gone. 'Look at this.' She thrust the paper at him.

'Not now, Em.' He held up his freshly floured hands.

'It's about your brother.'

Harry paused. 'Show me.'

She folded the paper to make the headline about Tom stand out. Harry took his time, his expression bland and unreadable. A slight twitch in his cheek was the only emotional giveaway.

'He'll be all right,' said Harry at last. 'Tom always did have the luck of the Irish.'

Emma drew back in surprise. She knew things weren't right between the two brothers. She'd quickly learned not to talk about Tom, for fear of putting Harry into a black mood. But this was different. Tom could have been killed. He was seriously ill in hospital. Surely Harry could put aside childish animosities long enough to show some concern.

'It's hardly good luck to be burned in a plane crash,' she said. 'We should send a card, or a telegram. Maybe make a phone call to the hospital?'

Harry's face turned hard, his eyes accusing. 'You'd like that, wouldn't you? Having a chat with my war hero brother, telling him how brave he is, and how much you admire him.'

'I only meant—'

'Oh, I know what you meant, all right. Tom was always your first choice. And me? What was I? Some sort of consolation prize?'

His unexpected anger wrong-footed her, partly because it seemed so out of proportion to her perfectly reasonable suggestion, and partly because there was more than a grain of truth in what he said. 'If you'd been able to go to war, Harry, I'm sure you'd have been just as brave as your brother.'

'Just as brave as my brother?' His voice dripped with a bruising sarcasm and his face turned red. 'I guess I'll never know. Maybe I'd have ended up a snivelling coward, crying for my mother. But there's one thing I do know. If my perfect brother ever found out that you were a whore, he wouldn't touch you with a barge pole.'

Emma's breath caught in her throat, and the room began to swim. Why was Harry saying this?

'You see, Em, Tom's always had a lovely view from the moral high ground. He sees the world differently from us. With him, people are either black or white, good or bad, in or out,' he said, while savagely cutting out rounds of dough to the rhythm of his words. 'And I have a strong feeling that women who sell themselves to the highest bidder would most definitely be *out* where my brother is concerned.'

Emma ran from the kitchen, burning from the scorch of Harry's words. All she'd done was show him an article in the paper about Tom being hurt. Surely it was something a brother would want to know. Why had Harry reacted with such cruelty? He'd never thrown Hampton Hall in her face, not once – not until now. 'We all do things we're not proud of,' he'd told her on their wedding day. 'Especially when we're backed into a corner. I'll never hold that against you.'

How grateful she'd been for his acceptance and tolerance. How secure, sleeping in his non-judgemental arms every night. But today that sense of security had been turned upside down.

She would die if Tom ever found out she'd been a prostitute, but if Harry started holding that information over her, there were even worse scenarios, much closer to home. Her mother … Jack and Tim. How could she bear her family finding out the ugly truth? And Mrs Woolhouse? Emma had wangled a part-time position as a volunteer teacher at Campbell College, in return for taking the subjects she'd missed all those years ago.

The principal had warmly welcomed her back, patted her hand,

and given a conspiratorial wink. 'I know the university Dean very well, dear, and they're planning a mature age intake to medicine next year. Your dream may not be dead after all.'

A strict character test applied to medical students, requiring them to be of *high moral standing*. Any hint of scandal would immediately disqualify her. Harry knew how much this second chance meant, had said how proud he was. So, why, after more than a year of marriage, why this veiled threat to expose her?

A sharp sliver of fear pierced her belly. Emma hurried to the conservatory, lifted up the window seat and looked in vain for the little leather trunk containing her scrapbooks. It was gone.

Emma replaced the window seat and sank down on it, all the strength drained from her legs. So that was the reason for his anger. She tried to imagine how Harry would feel as he looked through the clippings. The general ones weren't so bad. Lots of people kept war scrap books, though hers were mainly about the RAF. The special Tom scrap book would be the problem.

She leafed through its pages in her mind's eye. The first newspaper cutting, May 1940, an article about Tom and another Australian pilot, Stuart Kennedy. His Spitfire was shot down over the channel during the Dunkirk rescue, yet miraculously he survived. A photo of the two young men smiling together, arms around each other's shoulders. They'd quoted Tom, and Emma remembered every word. *Stu's my best mate, like a brother, and he's a true hero. I nearly ran out of fuel searching for him.* She'd drawn hearts around the edge of the pages.

Then came the Battle of Britain section. The Australian press loved to highlight the part Australians played in defending the motherland. Reports of Tom clashing with German fighters and bombers during the Blitz, starring in the courageous air campaign that saved London. His *Ace In A Day* exploits, when he claimed five Messerschmitts in twenty-four hours, had the reporters in a spin. Later on, the part Tom and his squadron had played in the skies above Germany, defending the pilots of Bomber Command as they brought Germany to her knees.

By just imagining the scrapbook and its contents, Emma felt the old, familiar tingle of pride in Tom's achievements. But Harry wouldn't see it that way. Damn him. How could he still be so jealous of Tom? Tom, who she hadn't seen since she was fifteen years old; who was married to a glamourous actress and lived on the other side of the world. He was a fantasy, that was all. A fantasy that had helped keep her sane through the years she'd worked at Hampton Hall. A harmless fantasy that had become a habit. If she explained things properly, it wouldn't be too hard to make Harry understand.

But instead of going to find her husband, Emma stayed sitting where she was, staring out the window as if in a trance. She'd left a few roses in place to please her mother, but had dedicated the rest of the garden to natives. A honeyeater hovered among the first scarlet bottlebrushes of spring, flitting from flower to flower, heedless of human miseries.

Memories of another spring tumbled in. A magical childhood spring when the creek ran high with snowmelt. Building dams with her brothers as magpies and currawongs carolled overhead, and tadpoles skittered in the shallows. The bush alive with birds and animals and frogs and insects. Trees whispering ancient secrets to the wind. The very earth itself, bursting with life. How far she'd come from those carefree days.

And suddenly hot tears were streaming down her cheeks. Tears for poor burned Tom. Tears of shame and hurt and anger. She should have known. Every time she clawed her way back to a semblance of happiness, something or somebody always threatened to tear it down. She hadn't expected that this time the threat might come from her own husband. How foolish she'd been, how naive. Perhaps she deserved it. Perhaps it was her punishment for never having loved Harry properly. For having lied when she made her vows. For having talked herself into believing that gratitude and affection would do.

CHAPTER 28

Harry's hands trembled as he put the scones in the oven. He hadn't meant to react like that. He didn't like feeling out of control, but Emma had surprised him with that damn newspaper.

He could hear faint crying from the conservatory, and was grateful that Eileen and Elsie were still glued to the parlour wireless. So, Emma had discovered her missing scrap books. He'd found them yesterday while searching for an old boating magazine, and all the painful, conflicted feelings about his brother — feelings he'd tried so hard to suppress — had come rushing back.

So Tom was badly hurt, burned in a plane crash. Part of Harry was horrified — the boy in him who'd loved his brother, as a best friend, confidant and companion in grief. Part of him saw it as payback — the vengeful, jealous part of him who blamed Tom for stealing his grandmother's love and his wife's heart. Worst of all, for shattering his faith in their father on that fateful day at the waterfall, when everything between them had changed. And part of him wished that he could trade places. It would be worth the pain of a fiery plane crash, even worth the pain of dying, to do his duty and prove his courage – to himself, as much as to anybody.

Papa had been a naval officer during World War I, and part of the

Zeebrugge Raid, an attempt to block the Belgian port of Bruges-Zeebrugge by sinking obsolete ships in the entrance. For his efforts he received the Distinguished Service Cross for gallantry at sea in the presence of the enemy.

Harry was immensely proud of that medal, positive proof that his father was a hero; not just in his opinion, but in the objective opinion of the world. Sometimes he'd been allowed to play with the little silver cross. His finger would trace the circle at its centre with its engraved crown of George V. Harry would pin it on reverently by its blue and white ribbon, then do drills around the house, chest puffed out, feeling instantly taller and stronger. Or he'd take his fleet of toy boats to the pond, pretend the giant goldfish were German U-Boats and spend lazy afternoons trying to sink them.

He tried to involve his brother in these games, even offering to let him wear Papa's precious medal, but Tom wasn't interested. He preferred reading in the garden or watching birds or making paper planes. It annoyed Harry no end that Tom didn't appreciate the significance of that simple silver cross.

After Papa died, Harry pestered Grandma Bertha about the medal, insisting his father would want him to have it. However, Bertha shooed him away. 'I'm too busy to bother with trinkets,' she'd say. Trinkets! Seething with impotent anger, Harry complained to Tom who didn't seem to care a jot.

When the war came Harry tried to enlist, dreaming of following in his father's naval footsteps and perhaps earning his own medal for bravery. But he soon discovered that shipbuilding was a reserved occupation. It came as a bitter blow. For Harry there'd be no glory on the other side of the world. No joining his mates and brother in the adventure of a lifetime, no serving his country.

Instead there was a white feather in his letterbox, the first of many. White feathers were aimed at men not wearing uniform, branding them as shirkers and cowards, and designed to shame and offend. One seventeen-year-old shipyard apprentice, disqualified from enlisting both by age and occupation, received three white feathers in the course of a single week. One morning he put on his cadet uniform, took his rifle, and blew his brains out on the beach.

Harry grimly endured the misguided contempt of the public, and his own personal disappointment. He went back to the docks, striving to honour his father's memory by working tirelessly to reclaim the family shipyard. When he succeeded, when Abbott & Son finally became his, he thought he'd put his childhood demons to rest.

Yet when Harry looked through Emma's scrapbooks; when his brother's stellar war record was laid out so comprehensively before him, all his own accomplishments turned to dust. Tom had lived Harry's dream life. Emma loved him for it, and who could blame her? If Papa had lived, he'd have loved Tom too. He'd have recognised his mistake in favouring the wrong son.

Tom had everything now, everything that Harry wanted, and perhaps the worst thing was that Tom hadn't intended any of it. He'd acquired Binburra on a whim of their grandmother. He'd surpassed Harry in the estimation of their dead father, and wouldn't be the least bit interested that he'd done so. He'd unwittingly monopolised Emma's love from afar. It was all so damn innocent. Tom had made a mockery of Harry's life without even trying.

Harry sat and gripped the kitchen table hard enough to make his knuckles show white. Seething inside, while hot waves of emotion coursed through him. What to do about Emma? She was still in love with his brother, after all these years. Could he forgive such disloyalty?

Harry wasn't dishonest enough to be outraged. He wasn't blameless. If the truth be told, part of his wife's attraction was that Tom had cared for her. Harry had wanted to possess her. He'd wanted Tom to come home and discover that the girl he'd loved belonged to his brother, and Emma had wanted to escape the shame of Hampton Hall. An odd alliance from the start, both using each other, both with their own agenda, but an alliance built on genuine affection nevertheless.

The timer rang on the oven. Harry buried his face in his hands, wiped his eyes, and fetched the scones. Music was playing in the parlour, signalling the end of the radio play. He was glad Eileen and

Elsie hadn't heard the row. Harry was fond of those two. It felt like a proper family, living here, and he didn't want to give that up.

Harry didn't want to give Emma up either. A woman of rare strength, courage and intelligence. Flawed of course, and scarred by life, but then so was he. He admired her compassion, appreciated her beauty, craved her body when they were apart. Emma was a skilful lover, and knew tricks in bed that left him begging for more. He cared for her deeply, and Emma cared for him too, in her own way. It wasn't love, but it was enough.

Harry rarely apologised, and when he did, he wasn't very good at it, but today he decided to make an effort. He put the kettle on, went out to the garden and picked a fragrant yellow rose just starting to unfurl, aware Emma could see him through the window. He made a pot of tea, filled a dish with cream, and searched the pantry for her favourite blackberry jam. A silver tray, a crystal bud vase for the rose, and the Devonshire tea was ready.

When he took the tray in, Emma was sitting on the window seat with red eyes and a guarded look. Harry dropped a sugar cube into each cup and poured the tea. 'I didn't mean to frighten you.' He sat beside her and she moved slightly, increasing the space between them.

'Why are you so jealous of Tom?' she said.

'Oh, I don't know. Maybe because my wife keeps a secret scrapbook of his heroic exploits.'

'It didn't mean anything.'

'We both know that's not true.' Harry handed her a cup of tea, with a scone balanced on the saucer. 'I'm no monster, Em. I'm sorry Tom's hurt. When we were growing up, he was my other half, my best friend.'

'Please don't tell him about me. Don't tell anyone.'

Harry sighed and lit a cigarette. This wasn't the fearless woman he'd married. He hated the pleading note in her voice, and the apprehension on her face. He hated even more that he was the one who'd put it there.

'That telegram you were talking about, wishing Tom well? Go ahead and send it, Em. Send it from both of us.'

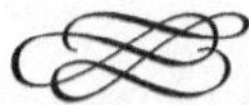

Tom seemed to have been lying in darkness forever. His body had been unwrapped weeks ago; a grim experience accompanied by the sort of pain that even an extra dose of morphine could not mask. Daily saline baths were doing their job, and he could now lie directly on the bed with a reasonable degree of comfort. Yet he was still blind, and found it difficult to distinguish between sleeping and waking, nightmares and reality.

Then one morning, after his liquid meal the staff called breakfast, Tom's nurse removed the bandages from his face and, for the first time, left them off. It was Jean – he knew all the nurses by voice now – and instead of wrapping him back up like a mummy, she slathered his lips with Vaseline and applied cool, saline compresses to his eyes.

What was the point when he was blind? Yet within hours those compresses soothed and lessened the angry swelling of his face. When next the nurse came to change his dressings, he tried for the millionth time to open his eyes. A crack of light appeared. He could see!

Tom hardly dared to believe it. Little by little, he drew back what was left of his eyelids, and widened his lens on the world. He could see the nurse bending over him; a pretty, red-headed girl with a freckled nose, fussing around with washers and salves. She looked like an angel, and he was thankful his first glimpse was of something so lovely.

He forced his tongue between his teeth, separating lips that he'd feared were fused together forever. 'Hello, Jean.' His voice sounded strange and unfamiliar in his ears and he seemed to have a mouthful of sawdust.

She stopped what she was doing, stared in astonishment and bent close. 'Tom, what colour are my eyes?'

'Green as emeralds.'

She gave him a radiant smile. 'Tom, how marvellous. Wait until I tell the others!'

Within half an hour the room was filled with excited nurses, and he began to put faces to voices. Wendy, the stern-faced senior burns nurse, who'd been in charge of his case all along. He knew her voice well. She'd been the one to read him the telegrams during his early days in hospital – so many that he couldn't take them all in. They'd merged into a confused blur of well-wishing. It seemed all of England and Australia were praying for his recovery. She read him Stu's letters, telling of his new life with Dolly in Canada, and Kitty's letters, full of news about how the film was going.

There was Daphne, his night nurse, who loved amateur theatrics and who practised her lines on him in the wee hours. Mary and Eve, volunteer aides who always stayed longer than they needed to, chatting about their love lives and making him feel that he did belong, after all, to the land of the living. Sometimes they forgot he was listening, and talked about Kitty in disapproving tones. 'They say she's only been in to see him once, right at the start. She may be a la-di-da Hollywood actress, but she's not much of a wife.'

Tom had wanted to defend her, wanted to say that Kitty didn't visit because she was making a movie in America. But he couldn't talk, and even if he could, it would have been like defending a stranger. He was still missing great swathes of memories about Kitty and their marriage. He couldn't remember how they met or where they lived. He couldn't even remember their wedding day.

'We'll need to irrigate your eyes hourly to keep them clean and healthy until you get new eyelids, but I expect you'll move next door now,' said Wendy. 'Much more fun in there; even a keg of beer on the ward.' He tried to smile, but it hurt too much. 'You can get up just as soon as the boss gives the okay. I'll go talk to him now.'

The gaggle of nurses left the room, chattering softly like birds. Tom watched them go, then gazed in wonder at the window. It framed a watercolour sky and a silver birch tree with freshly unfurled leaves and robins flitting through its branches. He could feel himself coming back to life. Lifting the sheets, he inspected his legs – blistered and discoloured, but perfectly serviceable. He swung them off the bed, gritting his teeth against the inevitable stiffness and pain, and waited for a wave of dizziness to pass.

A man from the next bed offered a cane. It helped Tom's wasted legs to bear his weight, and for the first time in weeks, or maybe months, he was standing.

Faint cheers, and a few calls of, 'good on you, mate,' came from nearby beds. Tom ignored them. He wasn't game to look too closely at his fellow patients, remembering all too well the ghastly, frightening faces from his former visit.

Dabbing at his aching, streaming eyes with still-bandaged hands, Tom staggered to the window for a better view of the birch tree. He recoiled as he glimpsed someone in the glass of the ward door. Poor devil. The skin of his melted face stretched taught over his skull, mouth fixed in a twisted smile. A shapeless lump for a nose. Monstrous eyes bulged, angry and red, from swollen sockets. It took Tom a few long seconds to realise he was looking at his own reflection.

Tom took to his bed and laid a cloth over his eyes. For days he wouldn't eat or speak to the nurses. He refused to see his aunts or friends, or read Kitty's letters. What was the point? His life was as good as over. He could face down enemy fighters in the air, but he couldn't look in the mirror down here on the ground.

On the third day Archie McIndoe himself came to see him. 'What's this I hear about you not eating?'

Tom kept his eyes firmly covered, and turned to the wall. He heard a chair being dragged across the floor and felt a hand on his shoulder.

'Self-pity is sabotage, Tom. Give me six months and I'll give you a new face, but to do that, I need your cooperation. What do you say? Get up, Tom. Get up and help me save your life.'

Tears spilled from his lidless eyes, but still he wouldn't turn around.

'Perhaps this will change your mind. A note from a young woman, not your wife. I took the liberty of opening your letters when I heard you wouldn't read them, and this one in particular moved me. Shall I read it?'

Tom shook his head.

'You can't very well stop me though, can you, so here goes. *My dearest Tom, it saddens me beyond measure to learn of your dreadful accident. I sent you a telegram when it first happened, but you may have been too ill to remember. I imagine that recovering from burns is a painful and traumatic ordeal, but if anybody has courage enough for the fight, it's you, Tom.*

If things ever become too much, maybe Karma can help you, as she has helped me. Shortly before your grandmother died, she sent the principal of Campbell College a sum of money to be held in trust for me, should I resume my studies. It is a generous sum, sufficient to fund my medical degree if I should ever be fortunate enough to qualify for the course. She also sent me a marvellous gift: a thylacine pendent on a silver chain. It's a figurine of Karma, who she knew we both loved. The note told me to wear Karma for good luck, and also that you had the twin of my necklace. The magic has worked for me, Tom. At my darkest times, I've held Karma, and felt her strong spirit running free again in her wild mountains. She gives me some of her strength, along with hope for a better future. I sincerely wish that she will do the same for you.

Congratulations on your marriage. I'm sure you and Kitty are a wonderful support for each other during this difficult time. You must bring your wife home to Tasmania soon to meet me and Harry. As you may know, Harry and I are married now, and it is my dearest wish that you two might one day mend the rift between you. Also, you are needed at Binburra. Mrs Mills and George are growing old, and I worry about those two, living out in the bush by themselves.

Please know that my thoughts and prayers are with you, as are those of your brother, Harry.

Your sincere friend and loving sister-in-law, Emma.'

Tom heard folding paper. He opened his eyes and shakily sat up. 'Give it here.' McIndoe handed the letter over and Tom read it once, then twice. 'No more tantrums,' Tom said at last. 'Just do what you need to fix my face.'

McIndoe beamed. 'Very good. We'll move you to the recovery ward and begin tomorrow.' He stood and pointed to the letter. 'Emma's a very special young lady.'

'Yes, she is.' And Harry's wife. Tom hated that, despite the fact of his own marriage. 'And doc?'

'I suppose you want the pendant mentioned in the letter, my boy. A most unusual piece, by the sound of it.'

Tom tried to smile.

'I'll see what I can do,' said McIndoe. 'We could all use a little good luck around here.

McIndoe kept his word. The pendant duly arrived, discovered after a meticulous search of Tom's possessions in storage. The silver thylacine hung once more around his neck. Whether it was coincidence, a psychological placebo or genuine magic, he didn't know, but Karma's arrival coincided with a period of remarkable recovery.

First, McIndoe replaced his eyelids, using tissue-thin skin taken from the inside of his upper arms. Tom was briefly blind again, but this time he could cope. The burns recovery unit at East Grinstead was unique, and full of comforting noises not usually associated with hospital wards. Music played all day on the wireless; Saturday night dance tunes on the gramophone. Loud voices, laughter, singing and the clink of glasses. Wendy hadn't been wrong about that keg, although she admitted the beer was watered down. They were happy sounds that helped drown out the inevitable moans of pain, and occasional eruptions of rage or despair.

Next McIndoe reconstructed Tom's cheeks, and built up the fleshy lump in the middle of his face with skin grafts and pig cartilage, until it looked more like a nose.

Tom launched into months of painful surgeries with such enthusiasm that he boosted the morale of the whole ward.

'I have a new burns patient,' McIndoe would say. 'I can restore his body, but only if he lets me. Talk to him, Tom. He's frightened, in shock. Nothing inspires these men like a good news story from someone who's suffered as they have.'

And Tom's *was* a good news story, although he thought his injuries mild compared to many. Some RAF aircrew burned in the war had been returning to the ward for years, enduring upwards of fifty operations. Mere boys whose hands had been burned to stumps. Young men who'd lost their ears and chins. In an earlier war they might have rotted as beggars by the road, shunned and reviled by the very people they'd sacrificed their youth and health for.

Part artist, part surgeon, McIndoe used pre-injury photographs to guide him. He rebuilt their bodies and their spirits, one operation at a time. He dispensed with the regulation RAF hospital clothes made of bright blue calico and resembling prison garb. The men could wear their service uniforms instead.

He restored their self-esteem, recognising the importance of socially reintegrating his patients. No longer were they hidden away so they wouldn't frighten the children. McIndoe convinced the locals to support his boys as heroic and deserving young men, who'd helped win the war and save all England. Instead of cringing, people welcomed them at the shops and pub. They invited them to dances and into their homes. Grinstead became known as *the town that does not stare.*

Much to Tom's disgust, McIndoe also overlooked the outrageous flirtations of these lonely young men with the nurses, flirtations that at times amounted to assault. McIndoe expected his female staff to be broadminded, and deliberately hired pretty women to make his 'naughty' boys' lives more cheerful. Their happiness was paramount, trumping the basic rights of his staff to a safe workplace.

Tom became a particular champion of the young Red Cross volunteers; naïve girls, many still in their teens. They didn't know how to deal with difficult, amorous patients, and were offered no protection. 'Save us from the heroes,' complained Eve one day, after a patient roughly grabbed her breast while she changed his dressings. It horrified Tom to think of Emma or Kitty in such a vulnerable position.

Tom's inclination to defend them made him a favourite among the nurses, who remained critical of his wife for staying away. 'Don't give us that rubbish about her making a movie. You're more important than some stupid film. She doesn't deserve you, she doesn't.'

They were wrong. It was the other way around. He still couldn't recall a lot about Kitty or their marriage. How could he expect her to love him under those circumstances? And he had another fear, one common to every man in the ward. His face was a vast improvement on the one he'd arrived with, but he'd never look the way he once did.

For some women, the disfigurements suffered by their loved ones were too much to bear. He'd seen wives and girlfriends turn from injured men on their first visit, never to return. He'd seen them faint clear away. He'd heard stories that during the war, some women failed to claim their unidentified, unconscious and badly-burned men, pretending not to know them. With distorted faces and fingerprints burned off, such patients remained nameless until they could speak for themselves, be identified by a process of elimination, or died.

Some women concealed their disgust and disappointment, putting on a brave face at first, then visiting less and less frequently before fading entirely away. Shattered engagements, broken hearts and broken marriages – all common enough.

Some women stayed out of duty. Some women stayed out of love. Some didn't stay at all. What sort of woman was Kitty?

CHAPTER 30

'Cut!'

Kitty swore under her breath and brushed the flies from her eyes. This heat was impossible. Sweat dripped from her brow, ruining her makeup. She climbed down from the top rail of the corral. Alan Duffy, the director of *Secret Heiress*, was an old-school nightmare to work with – demanding and uncompromising, criticising everything she did. Kitty glared at him. 'What now?'

'You don't know your lines, that's what. Your beloved Buck Carter is about to risk his life on the roughest, toughest, most dangerous Brahman bull in the west, and you just referred to it as a cow.'

'What's the difference?'

'A cow has no balls.'

'Well, do you think I'm going under there to check? It's an easy mistake.'

'No, Kitty … no it's not. And while we're on the subject of mistakes, I thought you said you could ride?'

'So?'

Alan snorted with contempt. 'A donkey at the seaside, maybe. I just talked to our head wrangler. He reckons you don't know a horse's head from its arse.'

Alan puffed on his black Sobranie while Thelma, his dowdy little assistant, gave him a weaselly smirk. How Kitty hated that po-faced bitch. Always trying to make trouble. According to the makeup girls, Alan was screwing her. God knows, he'd tried it on with every other female on set. Thelma was probably all he could get.

For the past fortnight Kitty had been shooting location scenes at Worldwide Studio's movie ranch in the Santa Monica Mountains. She hated the dust and flies. She hated the stark rocky peaks, standing lonely and forbidding against the horizon. There could be bears out there. Maybe wolves and mountain lions as well. She hated the isolation and the ranch's 'boy's own' culture. In short, it wasn't going well.

Thelma touched Alan on the arm. She kept her voice low, but Kitty could still hear. 'We'll need to use a double for Miss Munro in the cattle drive scenes. Shall I organise that for you, Mr Duffy?'

'Yes, Thelma. And while you're at it …' He gave her a conspiratorial wink. 'Save my life and get her a double for the rest of the whole damn movie.'

Their mocking laughter was the last straw. 'Fuck you!' screamed Kitty, hurling away her ridiculous Stetson hat. It landed in the corral, where the bull ground it into the dust with his horns. 'Get yourself another star.'

Kitty stalked off across the scorching yard that stank of horses and manure, to the shelter of her air-conditioned trailer. She'd made an empty threat. With an airtight contract and a half-finished movie, the studio couldn't afford to let her go. But maybe now Alan would treat her with some respect.

Kitty unbuckled the torturous leather belt that bit into her skin, cinching in her already tiny waist. She gulped in a delicious breath of cool air, and poured herself an icy drink. If only she could stay here all morning, drinking champagne and staying out of the withering sun. Out of Alan's line of fire.

This movie wasn't at all what she'd imagined. The studio had sold it as a sparkling romantic comedy, with a potentially award-winning script. Kitty had been so excited by the offer that she'd taken her agent's word for it without reading the part for herself. She was starring opposite Montgomery Grant, a Hollywood icon and someone she'd admired for years. He hadn't done a movie for some time, so she imagined *Secret Heiress* must be something special to lure him back to work. His casting had convinced her that the film would be taken seriously, by both industry pundits and audiences alike.

How wrong she'd been. The script was lightweight, lacklustre and predictable. The supporting cast consisted of no-names; hack actors, either on their way out, or too new to know what they were doing. Some of them were downright useless, always bungling their lines. And then there was Monty, the biggest disappointment of all.

Montgomery Grant and his square jaw had loomed large upon the silver screen all through her youth. Kitty had been star-struck, and why not? Dark-haired, dark-eyed and with a brooding sexuality that made women swoon. He'd played leading men to the finest: Rosalind Russell, Merle Oberon, Barbara Stanwyck. Being paired with him would surely catapult her to similar levels of fame.

The first day Monty had arrived on set, Kitty realised her mistake. He was ancient, for one thing. Almost fifty, and he looked it. Kitty could barely recognise the former heartthrob of her girlhood fantasies. On the contrary, he was the opposite of everything she admired in a man. Lecherous and egotistical, with bloodshot eyes and an almost manic intensity. Far shorter than he looked on screen. Bone thin and with groping arms, like a spider monkey. Alcohol and drugs had taken their physical toll. Monty lived on coffee and whisky, popped bennies like lollies, and there wasn't enough pancake makeup in the world to disguise the ugly cracks and pus-filled pimples in his craggy face and neck. He'd been criminally miscast as Buck Carter – her handsome, cowboy lover. Kitty found him repulsive in every respect.

Romantic scenes were the worst. She tried to imagine being with her beautiful Tom instead, tried to summon up some vestige of the unrestrained heat of their passion. Impossible. The lack of chemistry between her and Monty was plain for all to see. Kissing his slobbery lips was like kissing a wet ashtray, and he loved to force his tongue down her throat. She flinched when Monty held her, unable to disguise a shiver of disgust. He always pressed against her crotch or squeezed her breast, pretending it was accidental. They both knew it wasn't, but Kitty repelled every advance. Movie stars, even washed up ones like Montgomery Grant, weren't used to rejection and she could feel his cold resentment rising daily.

Kitty cast thoughts of Monty from her mind, lit a cigarette and sat down to wait. She picked up the latest *Modern Screen* magazine. A devastatingly handsome photo of Gregory Peck graced the cover. Now if *he'd* been her co-star, she'd have been tempted, marriage or no marriage. After all, her husband was in hospital, a world away. She loved Tom, she really did, but what he didn't know wouldn't hurt him, and she was a woman with a healthy sex drive.

Time ticked by. More than an hour passed before a rapid knock came at the door. She poured herself the last of the champagne. Probably Alan, coming crawling back. Or maybe prune-faced princess Thelma. Kitty took a deep breath, determined to stick to her guns. She'd come back on set in return for a full apology. Nothing less would do.

Kitty lounged on the bed at the end of the trailer, looking as stylish as it was possible to look in jeans and an ugly check shirt. 'Come in.'

But it wasn't Alan or Thelma standing on the step when the door opened. It was Monty, his face twitching and bloated and red. Even from that distance, she could smell the stink of whisky on his breath. Kitty shrank back on the bed, a swooping, sinking feeling in her stomach. She recognised that look. Her father had worn the same look on his scarred face when he'd come home late at night, drunk and angry, to tear the house apart. To beat up on her mother as Kitty and her sisters trembled in their beds.

Monty stumbled inside and slammed the door shut behind him. 'Know what you're doing, you dumb bitch?' He banged his fist on the table. 'You're ruining my fucking comeback. Have you seen the goddamn dailies?'

Kitty slowly shook her head. Alan hadn't invited her to view them, but in any case, like many actors, she believed it was bad luck to watch her performances back.

'That love scene yesterday made everybody cringe. No fucking wonder. You had all the sex appeal of a dead fish.'

Kitty wondered whether, if she made a dash, she could get past him before he could react. He was drunk, but then she was a bit drunk too. If only she hadn't opened that damned champagne.

'Know what you need, bitch?' Monty's tone, low and menacing, alarmed her as much as his words. 'You need a damn good rogering.' He swayed as he moved towards her, his bulk blocking her exit.

Kitty started rocking softly, blood hammering in her ears, as terrifying flashbacks of her father assaulted her senses. She had to act soon, or Monty would be upon her.

He peeled off his trousers, paused to empty some bennies into the palm of his hand, then washed the little pills down with a swig of whisky from a silver hip flask. Kitty's muscles tensed for flight. This was her chance to get past him while he was distracted.

She made a wild dash for the door. Not fast enough. Monty's arm snaked out with astonishing speed and latched on to her. 'Be nice to me, Kitty.' He fondled his groin and raised his eyebrows, urging her to make the next move. 'Otherwise I could make a lot of trouble for you at the studio.'

Kitty tried to twist away and he threw her onto the bed, pinned her arms over her head with one hand, and fumbled at her waist with the other. She lay still as a stone, but her mind was working overtime.

'Your belt's undone.' He thumped down on top of her. 'Were you expecting me?'

Her heart was racing, but she could feel Monty's beating faster still, as if it might explode from his chest. He bent over and licked her neck. She shuddered as his thick tongue trailed along on her sensitive skin.

Kitty spat in his eye. He released her arms to give her a double-handed slap. Seizing her chance, she brought her knee up hard between Monty's legs, and heaved him away. He fell off the bed onto his back, his head hitting the floor with a sickening clunk. Kitty leaped over him to escape, but when she reached the door, something made her turn.

Monty lay where he'd fallen, gurgling and clutching at his chest. Foam bubbled from between slack lips and glassy eyes stared at her, bulging from their sockets, as if beseeching her for help. Slowly she returned, horrified and fascinated all at once. Monty's mouth gaped open as she knelt down beside him. He was trying to say something, clawing at her arm.

Kitty leaned over and whispered in his ear. 'Screw you.' She took a pillow from the bed and held it over Montgomery Grant's face until she was sure he was dead.

CHAPTER 31

The rest of the day passed in a blur. Alan tried to keep a lid on it, but even way out here at the ranch, movie sets were busy places and riven with gossip. Within hours the news got out that Montgomery Grant had died in Kitty Munro's trailer – with his pants down.

Kitty waited in a corner of Alan's office while he made a frantic phone call to the producer. The conversation went back and forth for half an hour. What were they going to do? What if the press got wind of it? How on earth were they going to finish the movie now their star was dead? Easy, Kitty wanted to say. Hire a replacement for Monty, somebody she could work with this time, and reshoot the location scenes. But nobody bothered to ask her opinion. Thelma brought her cups of coffee, but otherwise people either ignored her, or cast brief, pitying glances her way.

When the police arrived, she told her story, between sobs. Monty shoved his way into her trailer, drinking and popping pills. He tried to rape her, and while she was struggling to fight him off, he collapsed. She ran to the first aid trailer for help, but by the time she returned with a medic, Monty was dead.

'It must have been a dreadful ordeal.' The sergeant nodded sympathetically, offering her a handkerchief and what must have been her tenth cup of coffee. 'If I could possibly have your autograph, Miss Munro? My wife is a big fan.'

The doctor arrived, a middle-aged man with kind brown eyes almost lost beneath a tangle of grey eyebrows. He talked to Kitty, then disappeared into her trailer to examine the body.

'A straightforward case,' he said afterwards in the office. 'Excessive doses of whisky and Benzedrine combined with, ah, imprudent physical activity has precipitated a fatal heart attack. I've taken blood samples, but I predict they will confirm my findings.'

The sergeant put the hip flask and bottle of pills on the table. 'These were found on the deceased's person.'

'Quite so,' said the doctor. 'It seems Mr Montgomery had a chronic problem with alcohol and drugs.'

'Yes, well … I'd appreciate no official mention of that, doctor,' said Alan. 'To preserve his reputation. For the sake of his family.'

The doctor nodded, sat down at Alan's desk, and proceeded to fill out the death certificate. 'I'm all finished here. Good day to you, Miss Munro. I suggest you get some rest.'

The death certificate lay on the table. Kitty sneaked a look as Alan escorted the sergeant and doctor outside. Under *Cause of Death* was written *Acute myocardial infarction due to underlying arterio-sclerotic heart disease.* She breathed a sigh of relief. The bastard probably would have died anyway. She'd just hurried him along.

Monty's threatening words came back to her. *I could make a lot of trouble for you at the studio.* Not any more he couldn't. Nothing and nobody was going to get in the way of her career. Father always said she and her sisters would amount to nothing. Hopeless, useless, stupid. Fat little good-for-nothings. Lazy little sluts who'd better hurry up and marry before they lost their looks.

Her two sisters had done just that, marrying at eighteen to escape the hell that was home. Choosing husbands so much like their father that they soon created their own fresh hells. Kitty had vowed never to fall into that trap, vowed never to throw her life away on some tosser to please that old bastard. And she hadn't. Tom and her father were as different as summer and winter.

Through the window she saw a black hearse arrive. Alan directed two men in dark suits to Kitty's trailer. Minutes later they emerged with Monty's body on a stretcher, and then he was gone, just like that. Problem solved. It was the same when her father died. He fell down the stairs when she was fifteen, with a little help, and she was free. Free of his violence, his insults, his scathing dismissal of all she might ever be. Though not entirely free perhaps. The boiling desire to succeed and prove him wrong remained, burning white-hot at the very core of her being. One day she'd quench it and the searing pain would stop. One day.

Alan came into the office, looking dejected. He took a numbered key from the desk draw and handed it to her. 'Take this spare trailer for tonight. The cleaner will need to go through yours. I'll have someone pack up your things.'

Kitty longed to ask him about the movie, and who might take over Monty's part. She had a few suggestions, and also some great ideas about how to play the re-shot ranch scenes to give them more comic effect. Finally *Secret Heiress* had a real chance of box office success, with a new co-star and a fresh direction. But she couldn't discuss it now. Alan's face said it wasn't the time. He'd been friends with Monty, for God knows what reason. Tomorrow would be soon enough.

Tom would be so happy for her. Kitty hadn't seen her husband for months. It was hard being apart, but she wrote whenever she could; long, rambling letters telling him all about how the movie was going. Tom promptly replied, although until his hands healed the nurses had to write the letters for him. He was always interested in her news. How lucky she was to have a husband that appreciated the impor-tance of her career, even if it meant she couldn't be there for him right now.

He was recovering so well, that recently they'd started talking on the phone. Naturally there was a certain strain in their conversations. They almost felt like strangers. But it wouldn't be long before Tom could join her in Los Angeles. Amazing what they could do with plastic surgery these days. Kitty was thinking of having a small procedure done herself. She'd always envied Marlene Dietrich's *retroussé* nose.

Closing her eyes, she pictured Tom's chiselled face. His classically even features and compelling brown eyes. That dimple. He was simply the most handsome man she'd ever met, and from all accounts an excellent horseman. If he could act as well, he'd make a perfect Buck Carter. Maybe she could talk him into a screen test.

Kitty yawned and felt in her pocket for the key Alan had given her. Time for a beauty nap. It had been an exhausting day, and she'd been up since five. Her new trailer better have champagne in the fridge. She could use a glass to celebrate.

First thing next morning, Thelma delivered a message. Howard Hawks, the producer, was coming to the set and wanted to see her. Kitty couldn't contain her excitement. Here was the perfect chance to make her own suggestions about recasting the movie and setting it on a new course. Alan was an experienced director, with plenty of box office hits under his belt, but so far he hadn't coaxed the best from his cast. She didn't blame him for Monty's abysmal acting. Nobody could extract blood from a stone. However Alan's blunt, acerbic manner was too often counter-productive, leading to boring scenes, flat performances and too many takes.

Kitty herself had ambitions to direct one day. Women were perfectly capable of the task, as demonstrated by her role model, Dorothy Arzner, the only major female film director Hollywood had so far known. Arzner's movie, *The Bride Wore Red*, where Joan Crawford played a nightclub singer posing as an aristocrat, was a comic masterpiece and a bit like *Secret Heiress* in reverse. Many of Arzner's techniques would work well in this movie, giving it a witty freshness that Alan's plodding, critical direction could never match. And now Kitty had the opportunity to share her thoughts and ideas with one of America's greatest film-makers.

Hawks wouldn't arrive until eleven o'clock, but Kitty was dressed and ready by ten, going for a glamourous but serious look. Eager for the famous producer to see past her beauty to the brains beneath. She regarded herself in the mirror. Tailored burgundy skirt suit with a mink-trimmed collar and dramatic padded shoulders. Hair pinned in an elegant half-wave. A stylish little hat secured at an angle by a sequinned pin. Perfect. With her confidence steadily rising, Kitty resisted the urge to break out the champagne. She didn't want Hawks to smell it on her breath. Instead she sat by the window to wait.

A mountain storm was brewing, and the trailer swayed and bounced in the wind. Two giant beetles climbed up either side of her mirror, and a big, black spider lay in wait on the wall above. She despatched the vile creatures with a rolled up magazine. Ugh! How she longed to get away from this godforsaken place and return to her home in West Hollywood.

Finally a maroon Cadillac convertible pulled into the yard. It matched her dress, surely a good sign. But when it was finally time to walk to Alan's office, the storm hit in earnest. Driving rain soaked her suit and the gale blew her carefully styled hair into a tangled mess. Kitty reached the shelter of the porch and did her best to rearrange herself. She put on her most sombre expression and stepped inside.

'You're doing *what?*' said Kitty.

'In the light of this dreadful tragedy,' Howard Hawks was expressionless, 'we're shelving *Secret Heiress* indefinitely.'

'But you can't.' Kitty shifted in her seat. 'I have some terrific ideas for recasting—'

'It's decided,' said Alan. 'We don't think it's worth persevering.' Alan seemed stern, almost hostile. 'Kitty, we're going to have to let you go too.'

She must have misunderstood. He handed her a typewritten sheet of paper. She held it gingerly, between her fingertips, as if it might any moment burst into flame.

'What's this?'

'The requisite five days' notice, informing you that the studio is cancelling its arrangement with you.'

'You can't do that. I have a contract.'

Hawks crossed his arms over his chest. 'Not any more. Yesterday you breached the morality clause.'

What? The injustice of the accusation was breathtaking. 'Monty barged into my trailer and tried to rape me. How am I responsible for that?'

'You wouldn't be,' said Alan. 'Not if that's what really happened. Unfortunately you smelled of alcohol, and your version of events doesn't tally with what we know of Montgomery Grant's good character.'

'Good character?' Kitty snorted with derision. 'Monty was a sleazy old lech who wouldn't take no for an answer. Ask practically any woman on set. Ask Sonia in makeup, she'll tell you.'

'Have some respect.' Alan flexed his fingers. 'A man is dead, here. A man who was my friend.'

'Little wonder.' Kitty stood, eyes blazing. 'You have so much in common. The same sort of *good character*.'

'People, people.' Hawks held up his hands. 'Enough. Miss Munro, please. Sit.'

Kitty caught her breath. Calm down, she thought. There must be a way to salvage this. 'I need to talk to my agent.'

'Suit yourself,' said Hawks, 'but it won't change anything. According to our lawyers, the studio has a watertight case for dismissal.' He picked up a document from the desk. 'Your contract, Miss Munro. Clause 23.

The actress agrees to conduct herself with due regard to public conventions and morals. She agrees not to do anything that might shock, insult or offend the community or outrage public decency. In the event that the actress violates any term or provision of this paragraph, then the Worldwide Film Company has the right to cancel this contract by giving five days' notice.

You are a married woman, and a married man died in your trailer without his trousers on, while you were drunk,' said Hawks. 'That constitutes an outrage to public decency by anyone's standard. You argue that he forced you, but there is no proof of that.'

'What about my bruised face?' She wished now she hadn't worn so much make-up.

'Sue if you want, Miss Munro, but I guarantee you'll lose,' said Hawks. 'And the studio will destroy your reputation in the process.'

Kitty felt sick. This couldn't be happening. 'What about my money?'

'You forfeited your entitlement when you violated the contract,' said Alan. 'However Mr Hawks has generously agreed to a modest severance payment.' He stood, as if she was already dismissed. 'We've packed up your trailer, Kitty. A taxi will be here in one hour.'

'The studio appreciates your cooperation in this matter,' said Hawks, smiling now, and perfectly businesslike. 'In return we'll keep your name out of the papers. Our goal is to avoid a scandal. The official line will be that Montgomery Grant died of a heart attack in his own trailer, not yours. We will compensate witnesses for maintaining their silence. No doubt at some stage the rumour mill will grind into action, but we will not feed it, I promise, and neither should you.'

Hawks stood and offered his hand. Kitty ignored it and rose unsteadily to her feet.

'Put this ugliness behind you, Miss Munro.' Howard Hawks opened the door for her to leave. 'Go home to your husband.'

The taxi moved off, leaving Kitty standing outside the modest single-storey hospital at East Grinstead. Freshly mowed lawns and colourful flower beds gave the place a tranquil air.

The last time she'd seen Tom, more than six months ago now, he'd been wrapped from head to toe like a mummy. She was ashamed to say that she'd been shocked and frightened to see him like that. Her imagination played tricks, conjuring visions of blindness and disfigurement beneath the bandages. Bringing back memories of her father's scarred face. She'd longed to get away.

But now Tom was much better, even leaving the hospital to enjoy evenings at the local pub, according to his letters. He'd never once complained of her absence during his long convalescence. In fact, he rarely wrote about himself at all. He always showed an interest in the filming, and had been furious when she told him about how the studio had treated her. In short, he'd been unfailingly loving and unselfish. It had been wrong to leave Tom alone all this time, and she wanted to make it up to him.

Kitty smoothed her skirt and checked her lipstick in her compact mirror. She was still determined to become a star again. The *Secret Heiress* debacle was only a setback to her ambition, not the end of it. However she did need a holiday, and time to reconnect with her husband. So when Tom had asked her to go with him to Tasmania, she'd agreed.

According to his doctor, Tom still had some mending to do. She rather liked the idea of playing the caring wife at his grand estate in the country. That would put paid to the vicious gossip rags. All those rumours about Monty. Accusations she'd abandoned her injured war hero husband for a part in a doomed B-grade movie. When Tom was completely well, and the media interest in Monty's death had settled, they'd move back to Los Angeles and she could resume her career. Tom would make a handsome addition to her arm at all those Hollywood parties.

Kitty entered the reception area with her pen at the ready. She'd been mobbed last time, but not today. A growing collection of nurses hovered in the corridor, whispering and looking her way, but nobody approached her or asked for an autograph.

The grey haired woman at the desk sniffed and peered at Kitty over her glasses. 'You're after our Tom, then,' she said in a cold voice. 'Wait over there. He'll be here directly.' She pointed to a hard bench by the wall as a murmur rippled through the group of nurses.

Kitty turned and saw him, her husband, coming towards her with his doctor. She tried to smother her shock. It was Tom, and then again it wasn't. Everything was there. He wasn't missing eyes or ears, like in some of the horrific photos she'd seen of burnt airmen. But it seemed as if someone had stretched a mask tight over his face, muting his features.

The taut skin of his cheeks shone in shiny shades of pink and white. Faint scar lines showed where sections of skin had been stitched on. And his nose ... not Tom's proud, straight nose at all. An angry red lump of a thing, that seemed to have randomly attached itself to his face. What was it about his eyelids? Of course — no lashes and no brows either. His lips looked paper thin, like those of an old man; like her father's lips. The adorable dimple on Tom's chin had disappeared altogether. Only his deep brown eyes, set in those grotesque but vaguely familiar features, remained unchanged.

Everyone was staring. Kitty knew she should hug her husband, give him a kiss, but she couldn't. She just couldn't. She wanted her beautiful Tom back, not this poor tortured man.

'Hello, Kitty.'

It was a shock to hear her husband's voice emerge from that ruined face. He didn't try to hug her, didn't press her. His eyes said he understood. That was Tom for you, always putting her feelings first. Following his example, she tried to do the same thing.

'Darling.' Kitty stepped forward and kissed him, to the cheers and applause of those gathered there. Only she and Tom knew it was an artfully disguised air kiss and that she kept her eyes squeezed shut. Things would be different when he looked normal again, but until then she couldn't bear to touch those misshapen lips.

Kitty turned to the doctor. 'How long before his face will be entirely healed?'

'Maturation will take two years or more, during which time the scarred and grafted tissue gradually returns to a more normal skin tone, and becomes softer and flatter. Tom may need more operations, but I predict an excellent result in the end.'

Kitty exhaled, all eyes upon her. A blinding flash lit the dark reception space. She turned to see a reporter by the window, and another coming in the door. This was better. It was second nature for Kitty to perform for the press. 'How marvellous to be together again,' she said, pasting on an instant smile. Tom would need a very good makeup artist for any magazine shoots. False eyelashes and lipstick. Powder to even out his blotchy skin, but it wouldn't be forever.

Kitty moved to stand beside him and tentatively touched his hand. She flinched at the feel of it – scaly and rough, like lizard skin. How was she supposed to hold it? Kitty opened her fingers and Tom's hand slipped away by an inch. He kept it so close to hers that nobody noticed.

She gazed into the caring eyes behind Tom's ugly face. Part of her wanted to run outside, leap into the taxi and flee, but where to go? She was out of money, luck and opportunities, and the papers would have a field day if she left Tom in his time of need. Her already tarnished reputation would be entirely destroyed.

'Give him another kiss,' someone yelled. 'For the camera.'

She steeled herself, shut her eyes, and this time their lips connected. Kitty shuddered a little on the inside, but didn't let it show. She had to find a way to do this, had to persevere with the marriage and go to Tasmania with her husband. Tom had been granted a medical discharge from the RAF, and all he wanted to do now was go home. It might work out for the best in the end. She needed time to decide her next career move, and Tom needed time to heal. Then they could move to Los Angeles as she'd planned.

The nurses came forward with cards, chocolates and great, heart-felt hugs for Tom. Some were crying as they said their farewells. It was as warm a show of affection as she'd ever seen. The cameras loved it.

A nurse with steel grey hair stepped forward with a bunch of mauve and white lilacs for Kitty. 'Your husband's won a fair few hearts,' she said. 'He'll be sorely missed.'

Kitty noted the name tag. 'Thank you, Wendy.' She buried her nose in the flowers, letting their heady fragrance chase away the smell of carbolic soap and disinfectant.

Wendy took her aside while Tom was busy with well-wishers. 'Look after our Tom, Miss Munro. This lot here will be gunning for you if we hear any different.'

It was obviously meant to be a joke, but for some reason Wendy wasn't smiling.

Kitty turned on her most dazzling smile. 'We'll be staying with Tom's aunt, Lady Ann Sinclair. After that we're going home to his country estate in Tasmania.' She put a gloved hand on the nurse's arm. 'Never fear, Wendy. I intend to devote myself entirely to my husband while he recovers.'

Wendy did not look convinced. 'No more movies then?'

A nearby reporter was eavesdropping and scribbling furiously on a notepad.

'Not for now. I'm taking time off until Tom's better. The studio was furious, of course, but I insisted.'

'He's not ill, you know,' said Wendy.

'What do you mean?'

'Taking time off until Tom's better? You speak as if he's an invalid. Miss Munro, your husband is a perfectly healthy young man ... in every respect, if you understand me.'

'Well, yes—' The thought of being intimate with Tom made her skin crawl.

'Wives often find it difficult to accept disfigurement. Some adjust, some don't.' Wendy fixed her with a probing stare, as if daring Kitty to search her soul. The reporter leaned closer.

'I love my husband,' said Kitty firmly, 'and we are both absolutely thrilled to be reunited.' Then, more quietly. 'It doesn't matter to me what Tom looks like. I'm not that shallow.'

Just then a group of men in RAF uniforms emerged from the corridor, joking and laughing and slapping Tom on the back. Men with missing fingers, lobster skin and bulbous lips. With crooked chins and no ears. Worst of all was a man with a trunk for a nose.

Kitty's mouth gaped in open horror. One of these monstrosities turned to look right at her. His twisted mouth grinned ghoulishly and he waved his stump of a hand in her direction. She backed away as a wave of dizziness swept in.

'Are you all right?' asked Wendy. 'Miss Munro?'

She turned towards the door, finding it hard to breathe. But before she had time to escape, Kitty fainted dead away.

CHAPTER 32

Emma arrived home to find a letter poked through the mail slot in the front door, addressed to Mr & Mrs Henry Abbott. She recognised the writing. Cheeky Tom — he knew Harry hated being called by his proper first name.

The note inside was brief. Tom was coming home; him and his wife, Kitty. They would arrive next Tuesday and looked forward to seeing Harry and Emma before travelling home to Binburra.

She read the letter again. After daydreaming about Tom's return for so long, Emma was oddly troubled by the news. Her life was settled now. Mum was well. Harry worked all the time but that was how he liked it, and the shipyard continued to grow and thrive. Their marriage was happy enough. Best of all, Emma had finished her prerequisite subjects at Campbell College and qualified for entry into medicine at the university next year.

Emma tried to talk herself out of her disquiet. Tom coming home would make no difference at all. She'd be delighted to see him, of course. Hopeful that he and Harry could finally put their differences behind them, and she was curious to meet Kitty Munro.

Emma had seen both of her films and followed her career in the movie magazines. The *scandal rags*, Mum called them. Kitty had been controversially linked to the mysterious death of Hollywood star Montgomery Grant on the set of the ill-fated *Secret Heiress*. She'd also been prime fodder for the gossip columns when she left her injured war hero husband and flew to Hollywood to make a movie. Emma had been outraged. It was what prompted her to write to Tom at the hospital.

They'd exchanged many letters since. She told him about her studies, and Harry, and how she'd joined the Tasmanian Field Naturalists Club. *We go for trips to places like Bruny Island and Coles Bay and meet each month in the Royal Society's rooms at the Hobart Museum. You'd love it, Tom. Last time Crosbie Morrison gave a lecture on Tasmania's marsupial predators. Your grandmother's name is on the big Roll of Honour board as you come in. Your great-grandfather is there too.*

Emma wanted to know about Tom's treatments, insisting that she wasn't the least bit squeamish. He wrote: *As a woman with a keen interest in medicine, you may be interested to know how McIndoe remade my nose. He raised a flap of living skin and flesh from my upper arm, twisted and rolled it into a tube known as a pedicle, and stitched it to my poor burned face. When the pedicle had established itself, he cut it free from my arm and used it to rebuild my nose. Until then you would have laughed to see me, Emma, as I looked like an elephant with a trunk.*

Although the letters were innocent enough, Harry didn't need to know about them. Emma had gone so far as to ask Tom to use the Campbell College address when he wrote to her, so the mail never came to the house.

Harry's animosity towards his brother had mellowed since the accident. He now agreed to sending the odd telegram, with his name included at the bottom. He read the telegrams sent in return. This new Harry might not object to her exchanging letters with Tom, but Emma wouldn't risk it. His one-off threat to expose her chequered past was never very far from her thoughts.

Emma's initial sense of unease was passing and she grew impatient for Harry to get home from work. How would he react to his brother's return? Would he be glad, like she was? No, that wasn't right. She was more than glad. The world seemed suddenly a much brighter place than it had been ten minutes ago.

Harry read the letter and snorted. 'So, my little brother is coming home with his tail between his legs.'

Emma bristled. 'It's not like that.'

Harry kissed her. 'Don't worry, sweet. No need to jump to his defence and tell me what a hero he is. I'm sure Tom will make a fine job of that himself.'

She pulled away and checked the bubbling copper kettle. 'You're impossible, Harry. You'd better behave when we meet them or I'll never speak to you again.'

He recaptured her, nibbling her ear. His finger traced the fine silver chain of her necklace, where it flashed against her smooth skin. 'Did I say we'd meet them?'

'Of course we will. It's been years since you've seen your brother, and he's been through so—'

'Uh uh.' He put his finger against her lips. 'What did I say?'

'Oh please, Harry.' The whistling kettle grew more demanding.

'I'm teasing, Em.' Harry turned off the gas. 'What's this Kitty like, do you think?'

Emma wanted to say that she sounded awful. That she'd deserted Tom for months while he was in hospital, and that someone like her would never fit here in Hobart, let alone in the wilds of Binburra. But instead she shrugged and made the tea. The last thing she wanted to do was sound jealous of Tom's wife.

'They can stay here,' she said. 'We've plenty of room.'

It was true. They'd recently bought a spacious, two-storey home in Sandy Bay, not far from Campbell College. The war had stimulated a burst of manufacturing growth in everything from motor vehicles to the mining machinery. It had put Tasmania's economy into overdrive and Harry was perfectly poised to capitalise on the opportunity. With the shipyard booming, unable to keep up with demand, the money rolled in. Harry began reclaiming the timber coupes, sheep stations and mining leases lost by his father. He bought back Canterbury Downs, the Abbott family estate not far from Binburra, where his father had lived as a child. Harry leased the land out to a neighbouring farmer and held onto the imposing blue-stone mansion as a weekend retreat. People said he had the Midas touch.

'Well?' said Emma. 'Shall we ask Tom and his wife to stay?'

'Whoa, let's not go overboard.' Their new house boasted six bedrooms, but Harry's new-found tolerance of his brother apparently did not extend that far. 'I said I'd see Tom, not fight over the toaster with him in the morning.'

Emma felt the unexpected sting of tears. 'Why does everything have to be a fight with you?'

'Tell you what. I'll book them a couple of nights in a fancy hotel in town. Call it a late wedding present.'

'Oh, yes, Harry. That's a wonderful idea.'

Mum walked in. She barely needed her stick these days. 'Did I hear the kettle?'

'Harry's twin brother is coming home with his new wife.' Emma's voice vibrated with excitement. 'Tom's the one in the RAF.'

'Oh, I know who he is all right.' Mum looked from her daughter to her son-in-law and back again. 'I thought there was some kind of rift between him and Harry.'

'My bloody oath there is,' said Harry. 'Miss sweetness-and-light here wants to pretend it never happened.'

Mum frowned. 'This isn't about Emma. Don't let her push you into something you're not comfortable with, Harry.'

'I *am* in the room, Mum.' Emma rarely became irritated with her mother, but this was one of those times. She'd worked hard to persuade Harry to see Tom. Effecting a reconciliation between the two brothers meant the world to her. It would have meant the world to their grandmother too, and here was Mum, sabotaging something she knew nothing about.

Harry seemed amused by Emma's agitation. 'I'm my own man, Eileen. Your charming daughter can convince me of many things, but reconnecting with my brother isn't one of them. The truth is I'm curious. It's been many long years since I've seen him.'

Mum poured him a cup of tea. 'What age were you?'

'Seventeen, at my grandmother's funeral, and the last thing we did was throw punches at each other.'

'Seventeen? You were just boys,' said Mum. 'But I'll admit that's not a good way to leave things.' Mum offered Emma a cup, but she shook her head. 'I hope you can patch things up. What was the fight about, love?'

'My grandmother left her house and land at Hills End entirely to my brother. Tom seemed as surprised as I was, and swore he knew nothing of her plan. Yet when I proposed that he transfer half the property back to me, he wouldn't. We grew up side by side on that rundown farm, each other's best friend. But in the end, greed apparently trumped brotherly love. How am I supposed to forgive him for that, Eileen? Binburra was my home too.'

She lifted her eyebrows. 'Sounds like you both have some soul-searching to do.'

'Not me.' Harry's voice rose a notch, taking on a defensive edge. 'Tom's the one who needs to make amends.'

He received that probing look usually reserved for Emma, when Mum knew her daughter was holding back. 'Are you sure about that, Harry? In my experience arguments have two sides, and are rarely about what people think they're about.'

Emma stood dumbstruck. She'd puzzled for years over Harry's estrangement from his brother. How many times had she quizzed him about it? How often had he stonewalled her, refusing even to speak Tom's name. And now her mother asks some vague, casual question and Harry pours his heart out.

So their row was over Binburra. When she and Harry weekended at Canterbury Downs, they often visited Mrs Mills and Old George there. Harry was very fond of them and Emma had fallen in love with the place. Exploring the big old house, seriously in need of repair, but brimming with wonderful books and old world charm. Riding through the nearby hills on horseback, discovering a pristine wilderness alive with rare birds and animals. Harry knew those mountains like the back of his hand. It was one of the most impressive things about him.

Emma had always assumed Binburra belonged equally to both brothers, and Harry had never corrected her. Though the property was vast, it was mainly inaccessible wilderness, and the house would be expensive to restore. It couldn't be worth a lot of money. Surely Tom could be persuaded to turn over Harry's half, if it could bring peace to the family.

A stirring orchestral theme sounded from the wireless in the lounge room. 'Ooh, time for The Lawsons.' Mum turned to go. 'Top up my tea will you Harry? I don't want to miss the start.'

Harry did as she asked, adding an extra sugar lump for good measure, and took the cup in for her.

'Why are you so good to Mum?' Emma asked when he came back.

It was a rhetorical question, one she'd asked many times before, but apparently Harry's forthright mood had not yet worn off. 'I still miss my own mother, Em. Eileen reminds me of her sometimes; her wisdom, her kindness.' He took his lucky gold nugget from his pocket and rubbed it idly between his fingers. 'I was only ten when Mama died. Maybe if I'd had her for longer …' His voice broke with emotion. 'Maybe then I'd be a better man.'

A great gush of warmth filled Emma's heart. She'd seen glimpses of this sensitive, vulnerable Harry. When he read *The Great Gatsby* and cried. When he took her sailing and watched an albatross soar across the leaden face of a storm. When he heard a news item on the wireless about a man who killed his wife and children before drowning himself.

'How could someone do that?' said Emma. 'To his own children.'

'Maybe in his own misguided mind it was an act of love.' Harry had slumped forward, laying his head in his arms. 'Who knows what's in another's heart?'

Emma treasured this softer, contemplative Harry, but could never predict when he would emerge. Her husband was usually such a cynic, with his clever, sarcastic tongue, ready to poke fun and scoff at any sentimentality. However, it seemed Tom's imminent return had breached his defences. That could only be a good thing. It meant a reconciliation was truly on the cards.

'You don't need to be a better man for me.' Emma put her arms around Harry's neck and kissed him. 'I want you just the way you are.'

'More fool you, then.' But behind his mocking eyes Emma could tell he was pleased. She had to stop thinking about Tom and concentrate more on her husband. Maybe then Harry would feel free to display his tender side more often. Maybe then she'd grow to love him the way he deserved to be loved.

Harry and Emma stood by the window at Cambridge Airport, watching the silver airliner touch down. A twin engine Douglas DC-3 Harry noted, glad he recognised the plane in case the question came up. He didn't want anybody, let alone Tom, thinking him ignorant.

A posse of reporters and photographers stood outside, waiting to pounce. What would Tom be thinking, coming home after all these years? He'd left this airport as a seventeen-year-old trainee mechanic, and was returning the conquering hero.

Harry's sweaty hands were due to more than spring sunshine streaming through the glass. He hadn't expected to be so nervous.

Emma touched his arm and pointed. 'There they are.'

Harry couldn't stop staring. Firstly at Kitty Munro, who was a knockout in her sleeveless white dress, killer heels and crown of golden ringlets. And then at Tom — thin and frail in his too-large uniform, scarred skin drawn tight over his skull, features warped almost beyond recognition. There seemed something mythic about the pair of them. Beauty and the beast.

As Tom and Kitty approached, Harry peered closer. The only original part of Tom's face were those deep-set brown eyes; eyes that Harry knew as well as his own. Eyes that shone with welcome.

'Hello little brother.' Harry extended his hand. 'It's been a while.' The skin of Tom's hand felt rough and strange. It had been burned too. *You poor bugger*, he wanted to say.

Harry looked across at Emma. What would she think of her handsome flyboy now? But Emma didn't seem to notice Tom's disfigurement. She wrapped him in a long, heartfelt hug and kissed his cheek. 'I can't believe you're back.'

Tom put a hand in the small of his wife's back, urging her forward as introductions were made. Harry wished it was his hand instead. Her blue eyes fell on him and he felt special, like the only man in the world. Harry looked away, bashful as a school boy. Kitty was simply the most mesmerising woman he'd ever seen. Emma was lovely in a subtle, elegant way, but Kitty's luminous beauty lit up the space around her. If Emma was Katharine Hepburn, Kitty was Jean Harlow times ten.

They collected the luggage and headed for the car, while airport security staff held back the press. Kitty and Emma walked on ahead. The two men trailed behind with the bags on a trolley.

'You copped it hard, mate,' said Harry.

Tom shrugged. 'That's life.' He stopped to light a cigarette. 'You and Emma, eh? You're a lucky man, Harry. She looks damned good.' Tom's mouth turned up in a twisted smile, but the rest of his face didn't follow. 'Remember those boy's trousers she used to wear? I barely recognised her in a dress.'

Harry didn't want to talk about Emma with his brother. 'I've booked you into the Grand.'

'Better cancel it then,' said Tom as they reached the car. 'I haven't come halfway round the world to stay in some hotel.'

A surge of irritation hit Harry. He'd gone out of his way to extend an olive branch and Tom was throwing it back in his face.

'Drop us at the station,' said Tom. 'Old George can pick us up at Hills End.'

Harry bit his tongue and opened the door for Kitty. She favoured him with a dazzling smile that took his breath away. He tried to imagine this glorious, high-heeled creature at Binburra. Hiking up the waterfall track or slogging through mud to feed the horses. He failed.

'You can't take someone like Kitty on the train,' he whispered.

'Why not?' said Tom. 'She's got two legs, hasn't she?'

Indeed she has, thought Harry, catching a glimpse of a trim, tanned thigh as Kitty took her seat in the back. 'She'd be used to chauffeur-driven limos, wouldn't she?'

'Maybe once,' said Tom. 'Right now, Kitty's as broke as I am.'

Harry filed that information away. 'I'll drive you,' he said. 'Emma would never forgive me otherwise.'

Kitty stared out the window as the pretty countryside slipped by. Budding orchards and green fields full of sheep. Graceful old manor houses. It could have been England. Kitty stifled a yawn. How tired she was of travelling and living out of suitcases. She frowned at her reflection in the window. Dark shadows under her eyes. Uneven complexion. Plane trips dried the skin and it was impossible to moisturise properly while travelling. The journey from London had been an ordeal; a week of connecting flights and stopovers. Tripoli, Cairo, Karachi, Calcutta, Singapore, Darwin, Sydney, Melbourne – she never knew if she was coming or going.

And being out in public with Tom had been a constant humiliation. Kitty was used to turning heads wherever she went. She expected to. But now her husband received all the attention, drawing looks of pity and disgust instead of admiration. Children pointed, too young to understand or pretend. Mothers moved away and held their babies close. Solicitous old ladies patted her hand, and asked in hushed tones if his condition was hereditary. Louts laughed and shouted insults: *monster face, monkey nose, bogey man, Frankenstein. Get back to the freak show. Go live in a zoo. Do your mother a favour and kill yourself.*

People at hotels and airport ticket counters assumed Tom was backward, and spoke to him in slow, exaggerated sentences. Or they ignored him altogether and wanted to deal directly with Kitty instead. Some shrank back and called their managers, thinking he was somehow dangerous.

It wasn't as bad when Tom was in uniform. Kitty insisted he wore it all the time but it wasn't a complete defence. He was like a rock, seemingly impervious to all the world could throw at him, but she wasn't so strong. The rudeness, rejection and endless stream of vitriol had worn her down. Things would be better when she could stop, breathe and get some sleep. Things would be better when she got to Binburra.

The landscape was changing; picturesque paddocks turning to wooded hills. 'Oh look, kangaroos.' She pointed out the mob to Emma, who sat beside her in the back seat.

'Lots of kangaroos at Binburra,' said Emma. 'Wombats and wallabies too. Devils, if you're lucky.'

'Devils? I don't much like the sound of them.'

Harry swung around to look at her. 'Emma's bound to find all sorts of strange creatures for you. The weirder the better.' Then his eyes were back on the road.

Kitty laughed. 'I might stick to kangaroos.' She liked Harry. He had a great sense of humour and looked very much like Tom before the plane crash. Not quite as handsome perhaps – his eyes a little closer together, his features not quite so symmetrical – but he came close.

Emma, she wasn't so sure about. Kitty was used to women envying her — *that* she could understand. But she didn't sense jealousy from Emma, more a general air of disapproval. Not that it mattered. Kitty didn't make a habit of cultivating friendships with women.

She lay back in the soft leather seat of the silver Bentley, closed her eyes and let the humming motor lull her into a half-sleep. She'd had her misgivings about coming, but maybe this was just what she needed. A country retreat at a stately home. A peaceful place with time to relax. A place where Tom's face could heal, with only the hired help to see. Servants wouldn't stare, they wouldn't dare. And while

Tom's health improved, she'd take stock and work out a way to rebuild her career.

Kitty yawned as Tom gently shook her awake. The weather had turned and rain streamed down the car window. 'Why have we stopped?'

'We're here, Kit.'

She looked around. There must be some mistake. A dark tangle of trees loomed through the mist. Where were the sweeping lawns? Where were the manicured gardens? Where was the house?

'Sorry, there's a bit of a walk.' Tom opened the door and the rain angled in, soaking her silk dress and making her shiver. 'The drive was washed away in a storm last week, apparently. If Harry drives any closer he'll get bogged.'

Kitty gingerly stepped from the car straight into a puddle. Harry appeared with a mohair blanket and slung it over her bare shoulders, then went to help Tom unload the bags.

'Oh no,' said Emma. 'Your lovely shoes.'

Kitty's stiletto heels had sunk into the sucking mud. The rain strengthened and, as she tried to move, she tripped hard onto her knees. Argh. The gravel burned her palms and muck splashed her white dress. Her carefully coiffed curls fell apart and lay plastered against her face. Kitty felt like a drowned rat and was close to tears.

Tom helped her to stand. 'My ankle hurts,' she said. He tried to pick her up, but skidded on the slippery clay and they both landed on their bottoms in the puddle.

Emma started giggling and Tom joined in. Harry swept Kitty out of the mud, into his arms, and went marching up the hill. 'Not much of a welcome to Binburra,' he said. 'Emma and Tom can be clowns sometimes.'

A few minutes later the house emerged from the mist. A good first impression. An imposing two-storey timber homestead with large windows, wide verandahs and wrap around balconies. Harry carried her up the porch steps, set her down, and went back to help with the bags. On second glance Kitty revised her opinion of the house. Peeling paint, splintered floor boards and eaves thick with cobwebs.

The front door flew open and a plump old woman emerged, wearing an apron over a shabby floral dress. 'Oh my lord, you must be Kitty. I'm Mrs Mills,' she said in a loud voice. 'Come in, get warm. Hurry up before you catch your death.'

Mrs Mills. The name rang a bell — the housekeeper, although she didn't behave like any housekeeper Kitty had ever known. More like a bossy grandmother. She led Kitty through the entrance hall to a parlour where a welcoming fire blazed in the hearth. 'Sit down there, girl.'

Kitty did as she was told. The room, though grandly furnished, had seen better days. Worn out carpet, tattered wallpaper and stuffing spilling from the threadbare cushion of her antique armchair. The very essence of faded glory.

Tom appeared in the doorway. Mrs Mills screamed. 'Oh, my poor Tom. Whatever's happened to your beautiful face?'

He gave the woman a long hug and then warmed his hands before the fire. 'It got burned, Mrs M. I wrote you a letter, remember?'

Mrs Mills began to cry, the loudest weeping Kitty had ever heard. 'I didn't think it would be so bad,' she managed between sobs. 'I prayed for you, Tom. I really did, but it wasn't enough.' She touched his face. 'Your nose. It's huge.' Mrs Mills traced his lips with an arthritic finger. 'And your mouth's all crooked, and your skin.' She paused with a shudder. 'Those doctors can't leave you like this. It's a crime.'

'You should have seen me before the surgeries. I didn't have a nose at all.'

She began wailing again. Astonishingly Tom silenced her with another affectionate hug. 'I've got a way to go, Mrs M. There's still room for improvement.'

'Oh lord, I do hope so, Tom.' Mrs Mills sniffed back a tide of tears. 'I'll get to more praying while I make the tea.'

Kitty looked on in disbelief. And here she was thinking the

servants wouldn't stare. What a rude old woman. She'd have to talk to Tom about letting her go.

An ancient man shuffled in, seventy at least, with a stout build and ruddy face. He removed his battered hat to reveal a bald head so shiny he must have polished it. 'Pleased to meet you, Miss Kitty. I'm George, the odd jobs man.'

He stepped forward to shake her hand. Kitty screwed up her nose. He smelled, and was that oil on his fingers?

George turned to Tom and his weathered face crinkled with pleasure. 'Good to see you, son.'

'You too, George.'

They shook hands as George took in Tom's gaunt figure and scarred face. 'You've paid your dues, my word you have. Done Australia and the mother country proud. You RAF fellers showed Hitler a thing or two, eh?'

'That we did, George.'

'Looks like you could use a good feed though. Between your wife and Mrs Mills here, there'll be no shortage of home cooked tucker to fatten you up.' He gave Tom a dig in the ribs with his elbow and grinned. 'Could be trouble in the kitchen, eh? Too many cooks.'

Kitty fumed. How dare he suggest she might work in the kitchen. She was an actress, not a cook. It was insulting. In spite of Tom's obvious affection for the old man, he needed to learn his place or leave. Kitty looked around. Were these two geriatrics the only servants?

Harry and Emma arrived with the bags, and the brothers launched into a boring conversation with George about rainfall totals.

'You'll want to change out of that soiled dress,' said Emma. 'I'll help take your things up.' Her air of faint disapproval remained.

Kitty followed her upstairs to a large and elegant bedroom. Rich oriental rugs on the floor. Silvery wallpaper of a delicate floral medallion design. A four poster bed with arched canopy of tasselled tan-and-gold brocade. But as with the lounge, an atmosphere of neglect and abandonment permeated the room. Dust lay thick on the dressing table and drapes. Spider webs festooned the ceiling corners and a musty smell tickled her nose.

'The bathroom is through there,' said Emma.

Kitty pulled the curtains and opened the window. The sun had broken through, but the view wasn't what she'd expected. No stately gardens and rolling pastured hills. Instead a wild forest grew close to the house, as if it might any moment reclaim it. The sight made her scalp prickle.

'When was the last time anyone slept in here?'

'Twelve years ago, I expect.' Emma thumped the largest suitcase on the bed. It raised a tiny cloud of dust, making Kitty sneeze. 'That's when Tom's grandmother passed away.'

Kitty felt a creeping horror. 'You mean she died on that bed?'

Emma gave the slightest shrug, watching her with cool, curious eyes.

'If you don't mind,' said Kitty, 'I'd like to change.'

'Of course.' Emma left without a word.

Kitty took a big breath and tried to steady her nerves. She couldn't sleep in this room. What if the ghost of Tom's grandmother came out at night? She wouldn't be surprised. In fact she wouldn't be surprised if the whole damn house was haunted.

She explored the bathroom. Tiny ants trailed along the window sill and fingers of mould spread up one wall. She found a bath sponge, turned on the tap and filled the basin. It took three goes before she managed to get a sinkful of water free of wrigglers. Kitty washed her legs and arms, dabbing at her painful grazed knees and palms. She brushed her hair, put on a smoky-blue pant suit that complemented her eyes, and went to find Mrs Mills.

'Mrs Buchanan's room? Well, I'll need to change the bedding first and give it a good dusting.'

'So that's not the bedroom you meant for Tom and me?'

'Oh no, love. I set up the front room upstairs, fresh flowers and all. A wee bit smaller but with a prettier outlook. Lovely views over what's left of the garden and on a clear day, all the way to Hills End. I think it's less lonely when you can see the town, knowing other people aren't too far away after all. But if you'd rather—'

'No, the front room sounds lovely,' said Kitty. 'But if you could prepare Mrs Buchanan's room for Tom, please. While he's recovering we're not supposed to … you know.' This wasn't true, but since the accident Kitty couldn't face sleeping with her husband.

Mrs Mill's eyes widened and she gave Kitty a knowing wink. 'Say no more, girl. I'll see to it right away.'

'One more thing,' said Kitty. 'Tom's grandmother. Did she … did she die in her bedroom? Tom might feel uncomfortable there if she did.'

Mrs Mills gave her an understanding smile. 'Tom's lucky to have such a thoughtful wife, but you needn't worry. Mrs Buchanan couldn't get up the stairs in the end. We set the library up as a sick room. Sounds strange, doesn't it, but it's what she wanted, to be near her books.'

Thank goodness. It would be easy to steer clear of library ghosts. Kitty didn't read.

She went out to the verandah, cursing as she skirted broken boards and a patch of slippery moss. Wind moaned through the trees, making her shiver. She hated this place. She hated the isolation, and the gloomy forest, and the eerie house. Her husband had lied to her. Binburra was no relaxing country retreat, with servants and gardens and a pool with a waterfall. Binburra was a nightmare.

CHAPTER 34

'Los Angeles?' Tom put down his forkful of scrambled eggs. 'But we've only just arrived. I thought you wanted to come here?'

'I've changed my mind.' Kitty lowered her voice. 'You tricked me. You said this was a mansion, but the house is falling down.'

'So it needs a bit of work—'

'It needs more than a bit of work. The kitchen roof leaks. The bathrooms are mouldy and there are rats under the floor.'

'Not rats. Bandicoots. They're harmless.'

'You said there were servants.'

'What do you call Mrs Mills and Old George?'

'I call them too old for the job. It's time they retired.'

'Come on, Kitty, have a heart.'

Kitty blinked back tears. 'I thought there'd be friends and garden parties and croquet games and, I don't know … riding to hounds. But that would be difficult wouldn't it, because the only two horses in the stable are as ancient as the servants. So instead of doing all those marvellous things, I'm stranded here in the middle of nowhere, bored stupid.'

'You've only been here a week.'

'That's long enough. I've packed our clothes. Tell George to get the car.'

'Wait a minute. I don't want to leave, and besides, we can't afford to.'

Kitty blinked at him, eyes wide. 'Stop it, Tom. That's not funny.'

'How much does it cost to rent houses in Los Angeles? We can get by on my RAF pension here, but I imagine it wouldn't go far in California.'

Kitty's mouth gaped open. 'A pension? What about your inheritance?' Tom looked blank. 'When we met in London, you said you had an inheritance. Or have you forgotten that too?'

Tom still had memory gaps. He couldn't recall much of their marriage and it remained a bone of contention between them. Sometimes he felt like he was married to a stranger. But he remembered their first night. The sumptuous hotel room, when his face was whole, and the beautiful Kitty lay willing in his bed. 'A boast,' he said. 'You told me to impress you.'

'Impress me, yes. Not lie to me.'

'I didn't lie. Nana left me five thousand pounds. Most of it went on us living the high life in London that first year.'

Kitty didn't look angry anymore. She looked close to tears. 'How much is left?'

'Maybe four hundred pounds.'

The colour drained from her face.

'Don't worry, Kit. Once my pension builds up we'll move to Hobart and I'll get a job as a pilot. But until then, unless you've got a fortune stashed away somewhere ...'

'We're stuck here?'

He shrugged. 'If you want to put it like that.'

'You could sell Binburra.'

'Not in a million years. I promised my grandmother to protect this land.'

'There's nothing to protect. It's just worthless forest.'

He cringed at her words, glad that Emma wasn't there to hear them. It wasn't Kitty's fault. She'd grown up in a big city. It was up to him to help her understand. 'Give us a chance, Kit. Let me take you on a trip into the mountains. Show you the real Binburra.' He stroked her arm and for once she didn't flinch. 'Come bushwalking with me for a few days, and I'll arrange a weekend in Hobart when I get back. We can visit my brother, go to the movies. *Key Largo* is playing. Humphrey Bogart and Lauren Bacall.'

Kitty's expression brightened. 'I've met Lauren. She's so serious. It wouldn't hurt her to smile once in a while.'

'So, do we have a deal?'

'Okay.' She squeezed his hand. 'We have a deal.'

Tom spent the rest of the day preparing for their trip. Being back home had brought with it a joyful sense of liberation. The steely shield he'd built around himself was dissolving. The shield that guarded him from disabling grief when his fellow pilots didn't come home. That warded off misery and despair during long, lonely nights in hospital. That helped him endure the pain of operation after operation. That defended him from endless taunts and jibes and pitying looks. But in protecting him, it had also shut him down, locking his heart away for safekeeping and diminishing him in the process.

Here in these wild mountains, his spirit was on the rise. Breaking free like the streams high with snowmelt, and the bursting buds of wattle and waratah. Remembering who he was, what was fundamentally important, and letting the rest slip away. Mrs Mills's prayers were working.

Tom loved sleeping in his grandmother's room. He felt her presence there so strongly, he half-expected to see her gazing out the window at her beloved ranges, or seated at the dressing table brushing her hair. In this peaceful place Tom found he could sleep again. His nightmares fled, and he awoke refreshed and restored. And for once his damaged face wasn't the first thing he thought about in the morning. Scars didn't matter here.

Tom's excitement built as he collected provisions and equipment for their trip. They would leave tomorrow at first light. He hoped to forge a connection with Kitty, one that was missing. Perhaps it was due to the gaps in his memory. He could remember their wedding night, but not why he'd married her. Sometimes it seemed like a complete mystery, as they had so little in common. But Kitty was his wife and he'd taken vows. He had a responsibility to bring them back together if he could.

On the back verandah Tom picked up a twisted branch he'd found stripped from an old Huon pine during last week's storm. It would make a fine hiking stick for Kitty. He trimmed it with a sharp machete, then whittled a curved handle and sanded it back. What better way to reconnect than alone together in the bush? Nothing and nobody to come between them. Nowhere to hide from each other. If the grandeur of Tiger Pass couldn't bring Kitty around, nothing could. Nana would forgive him for breaking his vow this once, for showing Kitty the lost valley. She was his wife, for better or worse.

A secret part of him wished he could be making the trip with Emma. What a delight it would be to share the valley's story with someone who loved and respected the thylacines as much as he did. She'd called a few days ago, urging him to patch up the differences on show that first day between him and Harry. And he thought they'd been on their best behaviour. 'Give him back his share of Binburra,' she said. 'It's rightfully his, morally if not legally.'

'Doesn't he own enough already? How much money does one man need?'

'This isn't about the money.'

He dragged his fingers through his hair. How little she knew her husband. With Harry, it was always about the money.

She tried again. 'Please, Tom. Harry loves Binburra, and it would mean the world to him. You two could be proper brothers again. Otherwise it will always come between you.'

Sweet, that Emma cared so much. She seemed to think that Binburra was the sole problem between him and Harry. If only it was that simple. She didn't know about the uneasy rivalry that had dogged them since children. Or about their father and mother, and the terrible day above the waterfall. She didn't know that Harry had married her so that Tom couldn't.

The plane crash had done more than disfigure him. It had taught him a lesson about human nature. There was a time when he took everybody at face value, never questioning their motives or second-guessing their actions. Gullible, Harry used to call him. Yet since the crash something strange had happened. He'd started seeing people for who they truly were, the ugliness and beauty beneath their skin.

Every day had been a new study. Some people insulted and ridiculed him because of their own insecurities, or sought out his company in order to prove how kind they were. Some treated him according to their mood or the company they kept. Some treated him well out of pity, or poorly out of fear. And some people accepted him for who he was. He'd learned to measure a person's sincerity by the look on their face when they first saw him.

When Tom met Harry at the airport there'd been some very mixed messages. He'd expected curiosity, surprise and pity, and he'd found them. But he hadn't expected to see their old rivalry burn as fiercely as ever in his brother's eyes. It was almost flattering that Harry still saw him as a contender. That's when Tom knew why he'd married Emma. And there was something else in Harry's eyes, something he hadn't expected to see. Love.

Next morning Tom was up at dawn, finalising preparations for their trip. A bitter-sweet experience. No Harry cracking jokes and sabotaging his packing. No Nana running in and out of the house with extra treats and telling him what animal or plant to look out for. No dogs. Rex and Shadow had often accompanied him on trips into the mountains, and Tom could almost see them bounding around, eager for the fun to begin. Their little packs, found among the old camping things in the stable, symbolised all he'd lost.

Tom shook his head to clear away the memories, and concentrated on the task at hand. He had to be especially careful not to forget anything they might need. Hiking into a wilderness with the inexperienced Kitty could prove a challenge.

At six-thirty Mrs Mills hailed him from the kitchen. 'You'd better wake your girl, Tom. She'll sleep until nine if you let her, and she needs to make time for breakfast today. I've done all her favourites.'

Tom smiled. Mrs Mills constantly worried about Kitty's finicky appetite and she was right about Kitty sleeping in. Nine was being generous. But to his surprise Kitty came down the stairs on time, looking fetching, if not entirely practical, in a cream knitted top, calf length rolled wool pants and suede leather boots. After she got used to the idea she'd become quite keen on this camping trip.

'I want you to take photos along the way,' she said, producing an expensive looking camera. 'For my portfolio. My agent thinks it will make me look more authentic for adventure roles. He says jungle movies will be big next year.'

'You look great,' said Tom, 'But I told you to wear full length pants.'

'I don't have any,' Kitty said breezily on her way into the kitchen. 'I hope Mrs Mills has made something I can eat, for once.'

Tom sighed. He didn't dare say that land leeches would make mincemeat of her bare legs. She might change her mind about coming. Still, he couldn't let his wife spend a week in the bush dressed like that. Tom himself was wearing sensible moleskin trousers tucked into his boots, and had soaked his socks in salty water. Some of Nana's clothes remained in her closet upstairs. He'd find some long trousers to take, for when Kitty came to her senses.

After breakfast they set off up the waterfall track on a perfect late spring day. The first few hours were easy going and Kitty enjoyed herself. Pointing out parrots and kookaburras. Paddling in the crystal streams and posing for photographs. Oo-ing and ah-ing over swarms of swallowtail butterflies that tumbled from the canopies of flowering sassafras. And her eyes almost lost that fleeting, involuntary start when she looked at him. Almost. Tom couldn't have hoped for a better beginning – but it came with a tinge of sadness. The ghosts of lost friends travelled with him.

As the sun climbed higher and the terrain grew rougher, Kitty's mood changed. It coincided with her first leech. Tom was walking on ahead, planning the easiest way up the next slope, when a scream alerted him to trouble.

'There's slimy things on me!'

He was surprised it had taken so long. He took a tiny bottle of tea tree oil from his pocket and ran to the rescue.

Kitty squirmed as Tom dabbed at the creatures, and one by one they dropped off. 'Land leeches?' she said. 'I've never heard of anything so disgusting in my life.'

'Yes, you have. I told you about them myself, but it seems you weren't listening.' She glared at him in silence. 'Here.' He pulled his grandmother's moleskins from his pack and offered them to her.

'What's that?'

'Your new trousers.'

Kitty took them warily and wrinkled her nose. 'They smell like mothballs.' She threw them back at him. 'I can't wear those.'

'Righto.' Tom stood up. 'But there'll be more leeches.'

Her eyes showed the struggle within. 'Oh, give them here.'

'Don't forget to tuck the legs into your socks.'

She slipped off her own trousers, close to tears. 'I swear, if you take one more photo—'

The day went downhill from there. Kitty imagined leeches every-where, checking behind each wild flower and fern frond, slowing their progress to a snail's pace. Once they saw a snake – the mere flicker of copper-coloured scales disappearing in the grass – but Kitty froze.

'It's gone, Kit. Come on.' It took half an hour before he could persuade her to move.

As the hills grew steeper, her pack grew heavier, and she complained constantly. It wasn't long before most of her things were in Tom's already overloaded pack. His fitness was down and he struggled with the added weight. By the time they made camp for the night they were both exhausted. Wearily he set up the tent, while Kitty sat on a log and took off her boots. He ventured away from the camp to collect firewood.

A familiar rocky outcrop, shaped like a dragon's head, told Tom they'd travelled only half the distance he'd hoped for. He was surprised how surely he remembered the way. To the west, a solitary eagle wheeled across the face of the range. Tom watched it with envy, just as he had as a boy. Oh to be that bird, soaring free above the mountains.

The setting sun turned the peaks to purple, while streamers of painted cloud scattered across the sky. A scene of overwhelming beauty. He glanced across at Kitty. Surely no one could remain untouched by such a lovely twilight? But she wasn't admiring the sunset. She couldn't even see it. She'd gone into the tent and zipped up the flap.

Tom set about lighting a fire, cooking the sausages and laying out his swag. He didn't expect to be invited to join his wife.

It took them four more days to reach the cliffs of Tiger Pass. Blisters plagued Kitty's feet and the sun burned her skin. Who knew her lovely tan was due more to soaking in baths full of tea than from being outdoors? But as their trip wore on and the distractions of everyday life faded away, a change came over her. The bush was working its magic, opening Kitty's eyes to the enchantment surrounding them. She spent less time complaining and more time paying attention. Watching out for baby wombats and wallabies. Photographing waratahs and wearing fragrant leatherwood flowers in her hair. Debating with him the best course to take up a rocky incline. Helping to pitch the tent at the end of the day and even trying her hand at cooking. It was the first time he could remember the two of them acting as a team. The first time she seemed to forget about his face.

This was what he'd been hoping for – just him and Kitty and a ten-thousand-year-old forest. If they were ever going to make a connection, it would be here.

On the last night before reaching Tiger Pass they talked, really talked. Sitting together on a fireside log, he told her about growing up with Harry, and how a love of birds had fuelled his passion for flight.

And for once Kitty listened. 'If you knew back then what would happen,' she said. 'That you'd be burned alive and almost die, would you still have become a pilot?'

'Of course. For good or bad, flying is my destiny.'

'Yes.' A soft smile of comprehension touched her lips. 'And acting is mine. I'll make more films, Tom. I was born for it, just like you were born to fly.'

A chill breeze sprang up. Kitty moved closer, leaning into him and trading warmth. And there, under a spangled sky ablaze with stars, she poured out her hopes and dreams in a great, gushing stream of consciousness. Her abusive childhood. Her unwavering ambition to be a famous actress. Her burning desire to succeed, no matter what it took. 'You understand, don't you?' said Kitty. 'How important this is to me?'

'If it's who you are, nobody can change that. Nobody should try. You're my wife, Kitty. I'll do what I can to make you happy.'

A high wind moaned through the celery topped pines. Tom sniffed the air; a mountain storm was on its way. A devil shrieked in the night and Kitty leaped onto his knee with her arms around his neck. She looked so lovely, eyes shining in the starlight. He kissed her, his face in shadow, and Kitty returned the kiss.

He felt the stirrings of love in his heart, a love he hadn't felt since the crash. Up until now he'd been holding back. This was how to connect with her. Share who he truly was, and she would do the same.

Stray raindrops fell as the stars went out. Darkness was his friend. Kitty took his hand and drew him into the tent.

CHAPTER 35

They broke camp next morning under a rain-washed sky. The jagged crags of Tiger Pass loomed large on the horizon. Soon they'd be there.

Tea tree oil had dried up Kitty's blisters, and she trod the trail ahead of him with an easy, hip-swinging walk. Skin glowing with a natural tan, soft curls bouncing in the sun. It was hard to believe this was the same grumpy, whining young woman of a few days earlier.

Kitty turned, yawning and smiling. Tom bounded forward to sling a supportive arm around her shoulder. 'Tired?' he asked. 'I know I am.'

'But in the most delicious way, right? I want to be *this* kind of tired every morning of my life.'

He bent to kiss her. Laughing, she turned away. Apparently their newfound intimacy did not extend to daytime. He could cope with that. A big improvement on those early days when Kitty gagged at the sight of him. He forged on ahead, born upon a tide of optimism and excitement. This trip had succeeded beyond his wildest expectations.

Making good time, they reached their destination in under two hours. With tentative steps they passed through the two high walls of stone that formed a natural gateway. For Tom, it was like stepping back in time. Massive cliffs, striped with shadows and fringed with jagged battlements. The stream running through the centre of the canyon, linking a chain of dark, rocky pools. The strange stillness. A place that had remained unchanged for thousands of years.

Kitty looked at him, her face one of awed reverence. Hallelujah! She could feel it too. He felt like singing.

Tom led her along the stream, past cliffs peppered with limestone caves, until they reached a high granite ledge. He helped Kitty up and waited for her gasp of delight. The stream plunged over the edge in a cascade of rainbow spray, tumbling hundreds of feet to the forested valley below. A valley that extended for miles like a vast, natural amphitheatre.

'Breathtaking,' she whispered. 'It feels like we're suspended in space.'

'Tiger Pass is a little hanging canyon,' he said. 'Carved out by long-vanished glaciers. Can you imagine how it was back then – one vast, glittering ocean of ice?'

Kitty stood, hand on her heart, lips slightly parted, clearly moved by the grandeur of the scene. Tom took her hand. He could love this woman, and maybe she could love him again too – but only if they trusted each other. She was his wife, and their marriage deserved a leap of faith.

'Is there a way down?' she said.

'Come on.' He helped her from the ledge. 'I'll show you.'

Tom found the old Huon pine tree that marked the cave entrance. Nothing had changed since he'd come here with his grandmother years ago. The ancient rock paintings, and that eerie likeness of a thylacine gazing from the ceiling.

They climbed down the narrow, tomb-like tunnel through the bowels of the mountain. The descent was almost too much for Kitty, especially the bats, but eventually they emerged onto the valley floor. A mob of wallabies bounded across a grassy clearing brimming with wildflowers: everlasting daisies, lilies and native cornflowers. Pretty green rosellas browsed on a curtain of crimson bottlebrush. A pair of shelducks, resplendent in shining chestnut waistcoats and white neckties, led their brood of fluffy ducklings down to the creek.

Behind them, perpendicular cliffs soared hundreds of feet into the blue — veined with quartz and gleaming feldspar. Patterned with lichen. An impenetrable, natural fortress.

'Oh, look,' said Kitty. 'A hedgehog. It's so cute.'

'An echidna,' said Tom, watching as it demolished a bull ant nest with powerful front claws. 'And yes, it's very cute.'

At the stream they took off their packs, refilled their canteens, and sat on the warm river sand to rest. A platypus emerged from the reeds by their feet, followed by twin babies. Kitty laughed as they dabbled about in the shallows, using their beaks as snorkels.

'Like a cross between a duck and an otter, but with a beaver's tail,' said Kitty. 'Don't you have normal animals here in Tasmania?'

The platypuses paddled into deeper water. 'They lay eggs, you know,' said Tom. 'So does that echidna we saw.'

Kitty frowned and wagged her finger at him. 'Now you're making fun of me.'

A warm flush passed through him and his doubts fled. How lovely Kitty was. How charming. They'd make camp at Fortune Cave and he'd lay himself bare. Tell her about his parents' death. Tell her what happened all those years ago with Harry at the waterfall, and the truth about his grandfather. He would even tell her about the tigers. Were they still here? It had been twelve years since he and Nana had heard that lonely cry in the night.

'Up you get.' He shouldered his pack and helped Kitty on with hers. 'Not much further now.'

They came to the foot of the falls. It cascaded into a deep water-hole, creating a curtain of shimmering spray. 'I told you Binburra had a pool.'

'Oh, Tom. What a perfect place to make a movie.' Kitty stripped down to her knickers and stood poised on the rocky bank. 'If my agent could only see me now!' she called. 'Tarzan, eat your heart out.' She looked surreal, like a statuesque goddess, as she dived into the water. His pampered city girl was becoming quite the adventurer.

. . .

From the waterfall it was an easy hike to Fortune Cave, following a broad animal track beside the stream. They walked in silence, the valley's grand stillness not conducive to small talk.

In his mind, Tom went over and over how the forthcoming conversation with Kitty might go. Where would he start? What if she didn't appreciate the significance of what he was telling her? He tried to put himself in Kitty's position. She'd be sympathetic, certainly, to learn how his mother really died. But the rest of it? Why should she care about the rivalry with Harry that had defined both of their lives? Why would she care who his grandfather was, or if there were tigers living in the valley? She wouldn't even know what a thylacine was, so why risk telling her?

Tom glanced back at Kitty, who had dropped far behind. He paused for her to catch up, kicking at a piece of driftwood with his boot. Damn it. He had to stop second guessing himself like this.

It was then he saw them in the damp river sand — the unmistakeable prints of a thylacine. No, not *a* thylacine, three or four of them. A chill ran up his spine. There'd been no verified sightings since Karma died twelve years earlier. Most scientists believed them extinct. Yet here was proof that they lived on, here in the remote reaches of Binburra's ranges, and he was the only person alive to know.

Tom's head was spinning. His grandfather had risked everything so that the thylacines might make one last improbable stand against extinction in this vast lost valley. The gamble had paid off. The rarest creatures on earth had found sanctuary here, and his grandmother had charged him with protecting them. He'd made a solemn oath. It was a sacred trust.

Tom felt for the pendant around his neck, hearing the beat of his own heart and the pulse of rushing blood in his ears. He exhaled slowly. Karma was warning him. Warning what a mistake it would be to betray the tigers' existence, even to his own wife. Warning that it was a false and foolish plan. There could be no cathartic outpouring, no matter how sweet it would be to unburden himself. His marriage would have to survive without it.

By mid-afternoon they reached Fortune Cave and Tom began setting up camp. Kitty looked around doubtfully at the damp walls and the uneven floor, strewn with rocks. 'Why are we staying here?' A mountain dragon darted out from between her feet, making her squeal. 'Let's go back.'

Tom shook his head. He could say that coming here was a pilgrimage to honour his grandfather, a great man that Tom dearly wished he'd known, however the mood for sharing secrets had deserted him. When he left to collect firewood Kitty was frowning. His decision to hold back was already spoiling things.

As Tom snapped a stick across his knee, a scream sounded from the camp site. He raced back to find Kitty running from cave. She leaped into his arms, but with no fear on her face. Instead it shone with delight.

'You naughty boy.' She kissed him full on the lips, eyes wide open. 'When were you going to tell me? You know I hate surprises.'

What on earth was she talking about?

Kitty took his hand and pulled him into the cave, past spider webs and a bleached wombat skull. A sinking feeling hit him. He'd underestimated his wife's newfound adventurous spirit, never imagining she'd explore so far inside. Kitty felt her way in the dim light until she reached the broad, shining band running diagonally across the rock.

Her fingers trailed along the bright seam. 'The gold, babe. I found the gold.'

Bacon and beans sizzled in the pan as the sun sank beyond the cliffs, casting the valley into shadow. Tom made a pot of coffee and toasted the bread. Going through the motions. Thinking furiously how best to contain the damage.

Kitty was still tapping away at the seam of gold with Tom's peg hammer. She'd been at it for an hour, and already had a pouchful of nuggets that must have been worth thousands of pounds.

'Kitty,' he called. 'Come have some dinner.'

Kitty emerged from the rear of the cave wearing his head torch, covered in dust and carrying that damn bag of gold.

He thrust a mug into her grimy hand. 'You must be exhausted.'

'I want to do my bit.' She kissed his cheek. 'We need some samples to take home.' She sank down onto the log beside him and took a gulp of sweet, black coffee. 'When can we get it officially assessed, you know, by proper mining engineers? Or have you already done that?'

Her excitement was palpable as she prattled away, talking a mile a minute about all the things she'd do when they were rich. 'I won't have to wait for those assholes at Worldwide to toss me a bone. I'll start my own movie studio, choose my own pictures, pick my own co-stars. We'll have a mansion in Hollywood.'

Tom stared at the ground, shell-shocked. How was he going to tell her?

Kitty put down her mug and grew suddenly serious. She took his hands in hers. 'Tom, thank you. Nobody's ever loved me like you — finding this gold, bringing me out here in the middle of nowhere to see for myself, all to make my dreams come true. How did you keep it a surprise for so long? And to think I almost didn't come.'

'You didn't?'

'I thought it was insane to go traipsing around in the woods for days on end. I came along because of that weekend you promised me in Hobart, and because I would have gone mad if you'd left me behind with those demented servants of yours. God, I hate those two.'

Tom served up the beans and bacon, not daring to speak. Kitty didn't seem to mind. She was doing enough talking for both of them.

'You can get your face fixed properly now. That English doctor made a mess of it, didn't he? But don't worry, we've got the world's best plastic surgeons in Beverly Hills. My friend had her nose made to look exactly like Olivia de Havilland's.' Kitty laughed. 'Can't have you on my arm, walking the red carpet, looking like that, can I? Even if you are filthy rich.'

'You've got it wrong, Kit.'

But Kitty wasn't listening; still talking about the house she'd buy, and the people she'd impress. The clothes she'd wear, the restaurants she'd go to – even the meals she'd order.

Tom studied his wife in a detached kind of way. The wild glint in her eyes, her rapid breathing and the manic tone to her voice. 'Stop it, Kit. Shut up!'

Kitty paused mid-sentence.

Tom shovelled the rest of his meal into his mouth, finished his coffee in two gulps, and quenched the campfire with a canteen of water.

'Babe, what's the matter?'

'We're leaving.' He rinsed their dishes and stowed them in his pack. 'Going back, like you wanted.'

'Don't be silly, Tom. That was before.'

He rolled up their swags.

'I've seen all those westerns,' she said. 'Don't we need to stake a claim or something?'

He rounded on her, eyes blazing, all his guilt and fear and disappointment boiling inside him. 'This place will *never* be mined — not by me, or you, or anyone else.'

'What are you talking about?' She picked out a gleaming nugget from her bag. 'We've hit the jackpot.'

'Forget the gold.' He snatched the bag from her, marched over to the stream, and tossed it in.

'No!'

Kitty hurled herself after it, but Tom caught her wrist and pulled her back to the campsite. She stood facing him, chest heaving, her face a mask of anger and confusion. 'Have you lost your mind? You bring me all this way to show me this gold — gold that will change our lives — and then you want me to forget about it?'

He lit a cigarette. 'Bringing you here was a mistake.'

'No, it wasn't,' she said, her tone wheedling now. 'It's the best thing that ever happened to us.' She moved nearer, laced her arms around his neck, briefly found his lips with hers. 'I'm your wife, Tom, and I love you. Let's go back for more samples.'

He pushed her away. 'No, Kit. We're leaving now, even if I have to carry you.'

She slumped down on a log and started to sob.

Tom sat beside her, taking a long drag on his smoke. What a monumental cock-up. He'd betrayed the tigers more surely than if he'd led Kitty to their den. He might have convinced her to overlook the miracle of their existence. But gold? Kitty would never let this go.

He no longer had any illusions about where he stood with his wife, and wouldn't waste any more time struggling to love her. She'd said too much and put too much greed on show. His 'demented servants' were like grandparents to him. And he wouldn't be 'fixing his face properly' so she could parade him at some Hollywood party. He'd decided against further operations. McIndoe's words came back to him. *Some people undergo endless surgeries, desperate to look normal again. But you'll never be normal, Tom. You must decide what is a good-enough face for you.* Kitty had helped him make his decision. Tom wouldn't be guilted or cajoled into chasing the impossible. He was content with who and what he was. Kitty would have to deal with it.

After a long time her sobbing subsided. He put a consoling hand on her shoulder.

She slapped it away. 'You're such a liar, Tom. Remember what you said to me just a few nights ago? *You're my wife, Kitty. I'll do what I can to make you happy, Kitty.* What a crock. I knew you were weak, but I never thought you were cruel.'

Tom stood to finish packing. To be fair, Kitty had a right to be confused, yet there was nothing he could say to help her. He shoved Kitty's hairbrush into her backpack.

She jumped to her feet and pummelled his chest, screaming, 'Leave my things alone!'

'Pack yourself then.' He held her at arm's length until the tantrum subsided. 'But if you don't, I will. It's a two-hour walk, plus the climb. If we don't leave soon, we'll lose the light.'

Kitty stepped back, panting, with an ugliness on her face that he'd refused to see before. She helped pack up the camp in sullen silence, and when they started back, she lagged twenty feet behind him He cast frequent glances over his shoulder to ensure she was still coming. 'Are you there, Kit?'

'Screw you!'

Tom groaned. It was going to be a very long walk home.

CHAPTER 36

By the time they made it back to the homestead, Tom and Kitty had reached something of an uneasy truce. Or perhaps more of a cold war. Barely civil when they spoke, which was seldom, and working hard at avoiding each other.

'Whatever happened with you two on that trip?' asked Mrs Mills the next day at breakfast.

Tom scowled. The last thing he wanted was to relive the disaster.

'Why does your girl walk out of the room when you walk in?'

He dropped his half-eaten piece of vegemite toast, and shoved his chair back. 'Mind your own business.'

Mrs Mills blinked at him in surprise. 'Rudeness won't solve your problems, Tom.'

'Then tell me what will, Mrs M,' he snapped. 'Tell me what will?'

Over the coming days, Tom threw himself into the work his grandmother had started, collecting unusual leaves and flowers to catalogue in the library. Kitty spent her days drinking the parlour bar dry, and subjecting Old George and Mrs Mills to torrents of foul abuse when they tried to intervene.

'This can't go on,' said Mrs Mills one morning, when she found vomit in the hallway. 'For God's sake, Tom, talk to the poor girl!'

Tom scrubbed his hands over his face. 'Ask George to put a lock on the parlour door,' he said. 'I'll give her a day to sober up.'

The next morning Tom knocked on his wife's bedroom door. No answer. He went in anyway. She sat huddled by the window with downcast eyes, clothes crumpled and stained, her once golden hair matted and oily, with dark roots showing through.

'Hello, Kitty.'

'What the fuck do you want?' She didn't look up.

'I hate seeing you like this.' He pulled up a chair beside her. 'Look at me.' She raised her gaze. Puffy face, splotchy skin, eyes bloodshot and red-rimmed. 'What can I do to help?'

'Change your mind about the gold.'

Tom shook his head.

'Why not?'

'Mines damage landscapes, Kit. I won't destroy such a beautiful place.'

'But you'd be rich, very rich. You could buy a hundred Binburras, save a hundred forests.'

She had a point. Sacrificing Tiger Pass might be worth it to protect many thousand more acres of wilderness — if it weren't for the tigers.

'Sorry, Kit. I won't do it.'

'Not even for me?'

'Not even for you.'

A subtle change came over her. Was it acceptance he saw on her face? Kitty was a good actress, hard to read, but acceptance would make living in this loveless marriage easier.

'I promised you a weekend in Hobart and tomorrow's Friday,' he said. 'We could leave first thing, find a nice hotel. Go to the movies. See a play? Do whatever you want. Then on Monday I'll head to the airport and see if someone needs a pilot. What do you say, Kit? Will you come?'

. . .

'We're here,' cried Kitty, winding down the window. Her face was flushed and she talked too fast. Tom wished he'd been able to stop her drinking at dinner. They alighted from the taxi at Hobart's Theatre Royal and joined the throng of people in the foyer. Colourful posters for *Show Boat* lined the walls. Kitty was in her element, looking stunning in her new dusty pink halter-neck gown of soft velvet and matching evening gloves. Her neck dripped with diamonds – well, quality paste ones at least – and an afternoon at the hairdressing salon had restored her crown of platinum curls. She looked every inch the film star.

Heads turned and people pointed. 'Isn't that Kitty Munro?' She put on a brilliant smile, like someone had turned the lights on, and subtly distanced herself from Tom.

Tom lit a cigarette and kept to the wings, letting Kitty have her moment. Men flocked around, casting admiring glances while she flirted outrageously. He had to admit, Kitty dazzled when she wanted to. He must be the only man in the room immune to her charms. What a thoroughly unsuitable husband he was.

A young girl of about twelve stopped to stare at him. Her mother hurried her away with a worried backward glance. He was a fish out of water here among the beautiful people. She'd have been better off by herself. Why ever had he agreed to come? The hotel, tickets and new clothes had set him back two month's pension. Kitty could try to disguise him in a tuxedo, waistcoat, bow tie and shiny Oxford shoes, but his getup wasn't fooling anybody. This crowd would still despise him and his ugly face.

'Tom?' Emma came hurrying over, subtly stylish in black Chantilly lace. 'Why didn't you tell us you were in town?' And there was his brother. She waved to Harry, but he'd already been drawn into Kitty's bright orbit. 'Why not stay with us? I'd love for my mother to meet you.'

'We have a hotel.'

'Come back for supper, then.'

The bell rang, telling the audience it was time to be seated. Emma slipped her arm into his and they headed for the stairs.

Harry pulled some strings so the four of them could sit together. Front row, dress circle – best seats in the house. Tom expected the sort of frivolous operetta that would bore him stupid. But *Show Boat,* with music by Jerome Kern and lyrics by Oscar Hammerstein, was neither frivolous nor boring. It told a deeply moving story of bigotry and tragic enduring love. Tom was transfixed. When Joe sang *Ol' Man River*, the haunting ballad moved him to tears.

Afterwards, in the foyer, Kitty wasn't so complimentary. 'Talk about depressing. When I was in Hollywood there was talk of MGM doing a new film version of *Show Boat* with Ava Gardner playing Julie LaVerne. I'll talk to my agent about it, tell him to get me an audition. I could add a little more fun, a little more glamour to the role.'

'Fun?' said Tom in disbelief. 'Julie is a tragic figure, destroyed by prejudice and abandoned by the man she loves.'

Kitty glared at him. 'You can lighten any role with a little imagination.'

'I've called a taxi,' said Harry. 'We're all going back to my place.'

Tom tried to refuse, but Kitty squealed and took Harry's arm.

'Come on,' said Emma, taking Tom's. 'When Harry makes his mind up …'

They sat in the grandly furnished supper room of Harry's Sandy Bay terrace house, drinking champagne and eating salmon mousse canapés.

Kitty and Harry talked and joked and ineptly played the piano, screaming with laughter. It was as if nobody else was in the room.

Emma moved to sit on the broad arm of Tom's leather chair. 'What's wrong? You've hardly said a word.'

He gave her a tight-lipped smile. Kitty was knocking back champagne at a great rate, already three sheets to the wind. Tom checked his watch, wondering how soon he could escape without appearing rude. Another ten minutes should do it.

'We're hopeless,' laughed Kitty after a particularly miserable attempt at a chopsticks duet. 'Play a record, Harry.' She spun around and around, sending her dress flying up her thighs. 'Let's dance.'

Harry put on Pee Wee Hunt's *Twelfth Street Rag.* Kitty slipped off her shoes and began to move, champagne in hand.

Even Tom was hypnotised. The way she rocked and swayed, without spilling a drop. The way she skipped and twirled, as if the beat was coming from inside her body. The tilt of her chin and the looseness of her knees, like a leaping cat. And all the while her eyes never left Harry's face. She was dancing for him alone.

When Kitty stumbled and nearly fell, Tom stood and took the needle off the record mid-tune. She gulped down her drink and hurled the empty glass at his face. Tom ducked, while the sudden silence magnified the tinkle of shattering crystal. He picked up her clutch purse, took her hand, and tried to lead her from the room.

Kitty snatched back her bag and slapped him. 'As if I'd go anywhere with a freak like you.'

Emma gasped and her hand flew to her mouth. Tom grabbed Kitty's arm. She kicked him, and fled behind the piano.

Emma attempted to intervene, approaching Kitty slowly, as she would a startled colt. 'You've had enough champagne. Your husband's trying to look out for you.'

Kitty laughed, a hollow mocking sound that gave Tom a chill. 'Looking out for me? That's a joke. Tom doesn't give a shit about me.'

'You know that's not true,' said Emma in a soothing voice. 'Tom loves you.'

Kitty snorted. 'I'll tell you how much he loves me.' She stared at him accusingly. 'He's found gold at Binburra and won't share one nugget of it with me.'

Tom forgot to breathe, praying the others would dismiss Kitty's remark as drunken nonsense.

Harry frowned. 'Is that true, little brother? Have you found gold at Binburra? Papa always said it could be there.'

All eyes were upon him. What to say? He'd promised Nana never to tell anyone, especially Harry. 'Fool's gold, nothing more. Kitty doesn't know what she's talking about.'

'You're so full of crap,' yelled Kitty.

Time stretched as Harry studied Tom's face. 'You never were a good liar. How about it, Kitty, did you see this gold for yourself?'

'I sure did. A big seam of it, right across a cave wall. I dug samples out with a hammer, but Tom took them. Wants it all for himself, he does.'

Harry fixed him with a knowing smile. 'Fool's gold doesn't come in seams.'

Tom's mouth turned to sawdust. 'It's not how she says, Harry. I don't care about the damn gold.'

But Harry wasn't listening. 'When did you know?' Tom could see his brother's mind working. 'As far back as the funeral? Is that why you wouldn't hand over my share?' His voice broke with anger. 'You're a dark horse, little brother. I work my guts out trying to make things right, trying to restore our family legacy, and all the while you've been sitting on an easy fortune. You must have thought it a great joke.'

The disappointment on Emma's face was hard to bear. 'I can explain,' said Tom, although he had no idea where to start.

'I have a better idea.' Harry opened the door to the front hall. 'Why don't you leave, before I throw you out.'

Tom pressed his lips together in a frown. 'Come on, Kit.'

Kitty poured herself another drink. 'Fuck off.'

Emma gave him his hat. 'We'll look after her.'

Tom nodded. What did it matter? The damage was done, and it would be a blessing, not having to deal with his wife tonight. He glanced back when he reached the door. Harry had laid a consoling arm around Kitty, who was leaning on his shoulder. Tom almost felt sorry for his brother.

Emma saw him out. 'You should have told him, Tom. He'll never forgive you.'

'If you knew my reasons—'

'Try me.' She gazed up at him, green eyes wide pools of concern.

Tom bit his lip, dying to unburden himself, yet fighting the temptation. If anyone in the world would understand his dilemma, Emma would. But she lived with Harry, and Tom knew his brother. Right now her husband was filled with a dangerous rage. If he suspected Emma of keeping secrets ...

'My hands are tied,' he said with an aching heart. 'Maybe one day.'

Emma's eyes brimmed with tears. 'Oh, Tom. One day might be too late.'

Tom returned to Binburra without his wife. Mrs Mills and Old George didn't ask questions.

He didn't miss Kitty, as such. He could do without her contempt, rudeness and constant complaining. He could do without her drinking, sullenness and dissatisfaction. But he did miss the idea of being married, of caring for somebody else. Of putting someone else's happiness ahead of his own.

Tom waited a week, but nobody rang; not Kitty nor Harry nor Emma. He didn't ring them either. There was a finality about what had happened that couldn't be fixed.

'I'm going camping,' he said a few days later over breakfast.

Mrs Mills stopped kneading bread dough and wiped floury hands on her apron. She came over and gave him a rare kiss, right on the top of his head. 'Should you be going off on your own like that, Tom? When you're feeling so down?'

He took her wrinkled hand in his own. 'I go bush to stop feeling down. You should know that by now.'

She forced a smile. 'Righto. I'll tell Old George to check your gear and get some supplies in. Make a list of what you might need.'

'I can do that myself, Mrs M.'

'He'll want to, Tom,' she said with a catch in her throat. 'George wants to look after you. We both do.' She gave him another kiss. 'Listen to me. I've come over all soppy. You make sure to be home for Christmas, you hear?'

Tom set out early next morning under a sky of perfect blue. What a pleasure, to just *be*. Be with the kookaburras, and bottlebrush and birdsong. With the ground and rocks and living forest. To feel and hear and smell the land as it had always been. But this wasn't a mere pleasure trip. The rugged Binburra ranges were criss-crossed with many canyons, creeks and waterfalls, but he'd be foolish to underestimate his brother. Kitty had enough information for a helicopter to possibly identify the lost valley from the air. Underground minerals belonged to the Crown, not to the landholder. If Harry tried to stake a claim, Tom needed to stake one first.

This trip to Tiger Pass was very different from the one he'd taken a few weeks ago. Travelling at his own pace, no Kitty to worry about, he could relax and fully appreciate the grandeur of the bush. His wife had complained that these mountains were a million miles from anywhere. She couldn't have been more wrong. Binburra's wilderness was at the centre of what mattered. Huon pine seedlings that could live for three thousand years, sprouting from their mossy beds. The purest air in the world. Devils and tigers, soaring eagles and crystal streams. Ghosts of the first people to roam these primal forests. This was a world older and greater and more important by far than the human world. This was a world of marvels. This was home.

On the third morning Tom reached Tiger Pass. Twice he'd heard the loud, *whup whup whup* of helicopter blades and hidden in the undergrowth until it passed. But today all was quiet. He made the descent, wondering as always who'd carved the ancient steps. Wishing he could go back in time to see.

Tom hadn't come solely to stake his claim. He'd come to map and record as much as possible, to continue the work his grandparents had begun. The lure of gold and timber would always attract greedy men. To properly protect the thylacines, Binburra must become a national park.

Tom had been reading the backlog of magazines, scientific journals and natural history publications that still arrived for his grandmother. Generous donations to organisations such as the Royal Society, Hobart Walking Club and the Tasmanian Field Naturalists, had given her life member status. She'd somehow remained on their mailing lists long after her death.

Tom spent hours in the library discovering the accomplishments of a small band of naturalists that had gone before him. Conservation stalwarts such as Evelyn Emmett, Leonard Rodway, Clive Lord and his own grandparents. Dedicated men and women who'd put the case for, and achieved, Tasmania's first national parks: Mount Field, Freycinet and Cradle Mountain.

Tom learned about the burgeoning American conservation movement pioneered by John Muir. Muir had founded the Sierra Club, with the goal of establishing nature reserves and preserving California's coastal redwoods. Glacier, Mount Rainier and Yosemite National Parks soon followed. When a dam threatened Yosemite, Muir argued the valley must be preserved for the sake of its beauty, as much as for anything else. *No holier temple has ever been consecrated by the heart of man.* He could just as well have been talking about Tiger Pass.

As Tom read through these inspirational accounts, an excitement built within him, as well as a purpose. Here was a mission every bit as important as any wartime battle. A fight for Binburra's forests; a fight his great-grandfather Daniel Campbell had begun, and one that he would finish and win.

Tom found what he was looking for when he climbed down into the valley and reached the waterfall — tiger tracks in the sand, leading to the mouth of a large cave. He took out his notebook, carefully sketched each print and photographed them. He planned to record and document everything.

Tom took his torch, put on his head lamp and ventured in, further and further, moving slowly, eyes peeled. The tracks continued, the musty smell grew stronger and a rustling noise came from the darkness. Tom stopped and trained his torch towards the sound. A low growl startled him. There, in the shadows, the red eyeshine of two large animals. He was about to move when it happened. A native tiger loomed from the gloom.

It bore little resemblance to Karma, the sad, half-starved creature with matted fur and staring ribs that Tom had met in the Hobart Zoo. This animal was powerfully built, as big as a mastiff and with a chunky head. Sleek of coat, well fed, striped fur gleaming with good health in the pale torchlight. How he wished Emma was here to see.

The tiger yawned wide in an intimidating display of threat. Tom stood transfixed. Here was more than stories and tracks and cries in the night. Here was a living, breathing thylacine, an animal that had walked the earth for millions of years longer than humans had. An animal the world believed to be extinct.

Tom took the tiger pendant from around his neck. 'You lot need good luck more than I do,' he whispered, and hung the silver chain from an exposed tree root in the cave wall. 'Here's an ancestor to look after you.'

A snarl rumbled in the back of the animal's throat.

Tom exhaled and backed away, wishing he could properly assess how many tigers lurked at the rear of the cave. But he was here as protector, not tormentor. Time to leave them in peace. He'd spend the afternoon pegging out Fortune Cave, then head to Hobart to register the claim.

'It's high time that awful woman left, Emma. Making eyes at Harry and drinking all day long. It's a disgrace.'

'We can't just throw her out.'

'Why not?' Mum scowled. 'If she tells me about how she lunched with Bob Hope one more time, I'll murder her myself. Let her go home to her husband where she belongs.'

If only it was that simple. Emma finished brushing her mother's hair and twisted it up in a neat bun. She didn't want Kitty back with Tom. He didn't deserve that, but she didn't want her living here any longer either.

Emma kissed her mother. 'See you tonight, Mum. Say goodbye to Elsie for me. I'm off to my course.'

It was three months now since Kitty had dropped her bombshell; setting Harry implacably against his brother, and unleashing in him a boiling hostility that frightened Emma. Kitty showed no sign of either remorse, nor of wanting to leave. She swanned around the house all day, taking endless bubble baths, reading movie magazines and drinking champagne. Full of condescension and veiled insults. Complaining about everything from the food to the brand of toilet paper. Waiting for Harry to get home from work.

Little wonder, for Harry was besotted with Kitty. He brought her chocolates and wine. Escorted her on walks along the waterfront. Laughed at her lame jokes. Listened to her stupid stories. Wanted to be in her company all of the time, even if it meant being late for work or missing meetings. When Emma demanded to know why he was so slavishly at Kitty's beck and call, Harry argued that he was merely consoling a broken-hearted woman.

'Kitty's devastated about the breakup,' he said. 'Tom's a heartless bastard. Hasn't rung her once.'

'Has she rung him?' Emma asked. 'Surely there's blame on both sides?'

Harry didn't see it that way. Blind to Kitty's faults, defending her at every turn, reproaching Emma for meanness and jealousy if she complained. So far she'd witnessed nothing physical between Harry and Kitty, but if he expected Emma to believe his fixation was mere concern for a troubled sister-in-law, he was mad. Emma might indeed have been jealous, if she wasn't already numb inside. Her marriage was over.

Emma recognised what had happened to Harry. She'd seen it before at Hampton Hall, the compulsive hold some girls had on particular men, and there was nothing platonic about it. It was a bond of powerful erotic attraction, strong enough to banish reason and make its victims act like fools. Abandoning families, losing jobs. Martha loved telling stories about men who'd been driven mad by their obsessive passions. Killed for them. Died for them. One client hanged himself from the wrought iron balustrade of the second floor verandah. A second kidnapped the object of his desire, hurled her off the high lift-span of the Hobart Bridge, and threw himself after her. Another dug up the grave of his dead lover, stole her decomposing corpse and kept it for months in his bedroom.

Her husband's erratic behaviour, combined with the fact that Kitty oozed sex appeal whenever he was around, convinced Emma that they were having an affair. Harry coveted whatever his brother had, and there were plenty of opportunities for the two of them to be alone together. It was a big house, and Mum couldn't manage the stairs. Or Kitty might be meeting Harry somewhere during the day.

Emma was determined to find out. She got ready for university as usual, packed her books, and said goodbye to Kitty in the sunroom.

Kitty looked up from her beauty magazine and Emma took time to study her. Looking gorgeous, as usual, with her hair already set, although she wasn't yet dressed. Wearing a bias-cut, sheer black negligee that showed off her voluptuous figure – Elsie was feeding her too well. A matching robe trimmed in lace and ribbons – and lipstick. Lipstick, for God's sake, and perfume, and winged eye-liner that made her look like a hungry cat.

'I might go into town today to do some shopping,' said Kitty, showing Emma a glossy advertisement for a new Revlon nail varnish called *Savage Thrill*. Kitty was always buying new things: clothes, hats, makeup. Where did her money come from? 'Will this colour suit me, do you think?'

'I've no idea.' Emma neatly stacked up the magazines that were strewn all over the table. 'I'll be home around five.' But Kitty had already gone back to her reading.

Emma went out the front door and shut it loudly behind her. She waited a few minutes before slipping quietly into the house again, and locking the back door, to which Harry had lost his key. If he wanted to get in, he'd have to use the front entrance. Then she waited in the upstairs sewing room with a good view of the street.

Time ticked by, measured by the longcase clock in the corner. Nine o'clock. She couldn't read her anatomy textbook, or she might miss Harry coming in. Nine-thirty. Her pharmacology lecture was half-way through. Ten o'clock. Was that his car? Ten-thirty. Madness, missing classes to sit alone in a room, waiting for something that might never happen. She'd give it one more hour. Eleven o'clock. She needed to go to the toilet.

Emma took off her shoes and crept down the hallway to the bathroom at the end of the landing. She froze as she shut the door. Footsteps coming up the stairs. Opening it a crack, she heard whispered voices. Harry and Kitty, and they were right outside.

Emma waited for them to pass, barely breathing, then took a peek. There they were, down the hall. Harry pushed Kitty against the wall, as she shrugged off her robe. His hands all over her, hungry lips on her mouth, her neck. He slipped the straps from Kitty's shoulders, exposing her breasts. She moaned as he cupped them roughly, teasing her nipples with his teeth.

Emma could take no more. She burst from the bathroom. 'Scraping the bottom of the barrel, aren't we, Harry?' She marched right up and slapped him hard. 'How stupid do you think I am?'

Kitty pulled up her straps, eyes wild. 'Leave him alone. Harry's with me now, so get used to it. He wants a divorce.' She stroked his reddened cheek. 'Don't you, babe?'

'Well, Harry, is this true?' Emma asked. 'Or don't you speak for yourself any more?'

At least he had the decency to look ashamed. 'Sorry Em. I love her.'

'More fool you then. Did you think you could keep us both? Get out,' she yelled. 'The two of you.'

Harry hung his head. 'I'll look for a place today.'

'Oh no, you won't. I don't mean leave later. I mean leave right now, or I'll turf your things out the window for all the neighbours to see.'

The pair of them stood staring, as if they didn't understand. Emma ran to the main bedroom, snatched an armful of Harry's suits from the wardrobe, and went back into the hall. 'You think I'm joking?' She shoved open the sash window at the front of the house and tossed the clothes onto the street.

'Stop it, Em. You're making a spectacle of yourself.'

'Me?' Emma managed a hollow laugh. 'I wasn't the one with my face buried in her tits.'

'You're such a prig,' said Kitty. 'Just lie on your back, do you? Open your legs and read a book. No wonder he's leaving. You wouldn't have the first idea how to satisfy a man.'

Emma did not dignify her words with a response. Thank God

Kitty didn't know about Hampton Hall. She turned her back and returned for more of Harry's clothes, saving time by simply tossing them out the bedroom window this time. A pair of long johns landed on the head of a woman walking along the street below, making her scream.

'You don't need to do this, Em.' She felt his hands on her shoulders and spun to face him. 'Kitty and I will leave immediately.'

She'd expected some sort of argument, some sort of foolish rationalisation to defend the indefensible. It wasn't like Harry to go down without a fight, however hopeless the odds. Yet her usually self-assured husband seemed uncertain. It was only when Kitty appeared in the doorway that he regained his confidence.

'You poor bugger,' said Emma. 'Kitty really does have you by the balls, doesn't she?' She dropped the bundle of shirts onto the floor. 'You have until one o'clock.'

An hour later, they were packed and ready to go.

'Why are you home?' asked Mum, coming out of the kitchen. The front door was open and a dozen bags and suitcases were lined up in the hall. 'What's all this?'

'Kitty's moving out,' said Emma.

'Good riddance.'

'And Harry's going with her.' Mum's face went white, and she put a hand on the wall. 'Come and sit down, Mum. I'll explain as best I can.'

A little while later, Harry came into the parlour to say goodbye.

'How dare you!' Mum's voice quivered with anger. 'How dare you dishonour my daughter this way.'

'I'm sorry, Eileen.' He was close to tears. 'You've been like a mother to me.'

'I trusted you to look after my Emma, always spoke up for you. And you let a bleached-blonde trollop like Kitty Munro tear apart your marriage and destroy your good name. Your own brother's wife no less.'

'Calm down, Mum.' Emma was frightened she might have another stroke.

Harry gulped hard and a pounding pulse started in his neck. 'We'll be staying at the Royal.' As he turned to go, he whispered in Emma's ear. 'I have a contact in the Mines Office. Your precious Tom registered a claim at Binburra this morning. So much for him not caring about the gold. This whole mess? My brother's fault.'

CHAPTER 39

Mrs Mills called from the verandah. 'Phone, Tom.'

He finished potting up the last myrtle-beech seeds that he'd found under the bench in the main greenhouse. There were dozens of other seeds too: leatherwood, celery-top pine, sassafras, waratah. A cornucopia of local flora. A rainforest in a box. Autumn was harvest time in the bush. Soon he'd be collecting seeds of his own.

It surprised Tom to hear Emma's voice at the end of the line. 'I have to talk to you. No, not on the phone. I'll drive up this afternoon.'

They sat outside, beers in hand, as the setting sun sent golden flares across the folds of the ranges. Mrs Mills brought out a platter of ham, cheese and red grapes, fresh from a local vineyard. 'I'm sorry to hear about you and Harry, Miss Emma. It's a scandal for him and Kitty to go dragging the Abbott name through the mud like that.'

Emma smiled. 'Those two deserve each other.'

'If you don't mind me saying so,' said Mrs Mills, 'nobody deserves that woman. Now if you'll excuse me, I need to start packing.'

'Going on a trip, Mrs Mills?'

'The first in fifteen years. My sister in Sydney isn't well, and Tom's

290

paying my fare to visit her.' She put an affectionate arm on his shoulder. 'He always was a good boy. Old George is coming too. I don't feel confident travelling that far by myself. George is like a kid looking forward to Christmas. He's never been to the mainland. I'm afraid Tom will have to look after himself for a while.'

'I'm thirty years old, Mrs M. I think I'll manage.'

As Mrs Mills returned to the house, Tom turned to Emma. 'So your dream's finally coming true. You're going to be a doctor.'

'I didn't come all this way to talk about me. It's truth time, Tom. Time for that explanation you wouldn't give me back in Hobart.'

He ran a finger around the rim of his glass.

'Tom, look at me. Before Harry left the house, he said you'd staked a claim. I thought you didn't care about the gold?'

The silver Karma gleamed against her neck. Sunset highlighted the curve of her cheek, the glow of her skin, the shine of her red-gold hair falling loose around her shoulders. Gone was the sophisticated woman he'd encountered second time around in Hobart. Without makeup she looked very young – like the freckle-faced girl he'd met at Campbell College fourteen years ago. The memory made him smile.

'Tom, I'm serious. Tell me.'

He knew what to do now. 'Can you keep a secret?'

'Truly?'

Tom handed her the small, warm bundle with its pointed whiskery nose, black-striped fur and bright eyes. 'Meet Karma junior.'

'A thylacine pup.' Emma laughed as Karma licked her nose with her neat pink tongue. 'I'm dreaming, of course, but please don't wake me.'

An enormous weight lifted from his shoulders. Somebody else knew. The burden of the tigers' existence was no longer his alone. And that somebody was Emma. Life couldn't be more perfect.

She examined the pup, gently parting its fur to reveal six deep welts that had started to scab over. 'Whatever happened to her?'

'An eagle is my guess. It must have dropped her. I found her bleeding and dehydrated half a mile from her den. Sick and covered in leeches. I brought her home in my backpack and luckily she was old enough to take solids. With a little penicillin and a lot of care, she'll soon be good as new and back with her parents, if they'll accept her.'

'Her parents?'

Tom couldn't stop grinning.

'You know where her parents are?'

'I do.' He paused for dramatic effect. 'Living smack bang in the middle of my mining claim.'

He studied Emma's lovely face, waiting for the penny to drop. There it was, that delicious flash of understanding.

'You staked that claim to stop Harry.'

'Bingo.' A warmth radiated through him from head to toe. He was invigorated, super-alert, like he'd woken from a deep sleep. This was the adrenaline-charged surge of energy he felt before a wartime mission, minus the fear.

'What did you do with Karma when you went to the Mines Office in Hobart?'

'I smuggled her into the hotel. Meet the first Tasmanian tiger to stay at the Dorchester. Their roast lamb is her favourite.'

She shook her head in disbelief. 'I was losing faith in you, Tom. Why didn't you tell me any of this?'

A mistake he intended to rectify. He explained everything, while Karma wriggled and chewed Emma's finger. He told her about his father, and his mother, and his true grandfather. He told her about Daniel Campbell's last ditch attempt to save the tigers by hiding them in an inaccessible rocky valley, and about the gold in its limestone cliffs and caves. And he told her about a solemn promise to a dying grandmother; a promise he'd just broken for the second time.

'You've done the right thing, telling me,' said Emma. 'If your grandmother was here, she'd say so too. You and I are the same, Tom. What matters to you, matters to me. I knew it that first day at the zoo, seeing your tenderness with the animals, your love for them.' She cradled Karma in one arm and reached for his hand with the other. He waited for her to flinch at the rough, scaly skin of his burned fingers, but she didn't seem to notice. 'Your secret is as safe with me as it is with you.' She kissed the little tiger on the head. It protested by growling and giving a wide threat yawn. 'My Karma used to do that.' Silent tears ran down her cheeks. 'I'd rather die than betray this little one.'

Wonderful as it was to hear, Emma didn't have to say it. He already knew, with a deep, abiding certainty, that he could trust her. He couldn't say that about another soul on earth, not even Mrs Mills and Old George. They wouldn't be intentionally disloyal of course, but a careless slip of the tongue? He couldn't risk it, which was one of the reasons he'd encouraged the two of them to take their trip. Little Karma was growing fast on a diet of rabbit and wallaby meat, and couldn't be concealed in the stable forever.

Tom closed the stable door. 'Put her down,' he said. 'She can walk, you know.'

Karma trotted about, digging in the straw, climbing the stacked hay bales, chewing on an ancient bridle that had fallen from its hook.

'Ah, how will I ever drag myself away from her?' Emma moved closer to Tom. 'I wish I could move into your stable.'

What an agreeable thought. She came closer still and his heart turned over. Her smooth throat, the rise and fall of her breasts, her perfect profile. His stomach tightened. Surely she could feel it too?

Slowly Emma turned to face him. Tom's body ached with desire, desperate to kiss her, but self-conscious about his face.

She smiled and traced the scars with her fingers — an unspoken understanding that made his heart hum. 'You're beautiful, Tom, and don't ever forget it. Beautiful inside and out.' The kiss that followed was a contradiction; full of future promise, yet as sweet as their first kiss all those years ago at the zoo.

Emma leaned into him, fitting perfectly. 'What a lot of time we've wasted. Do you think it's too late for us?'

'Not too late.' He kissed her again — a long, slow kiss that sang through his veins. 'We're right on time.'

. . .

Tom settled little Karma back in her pen with a fresh rabbit to eat and her ragged teddy bear to snuggle with. He lit the kerosene heater in the corner — contained in a wire netting cage for safety — and walked Emma back to the house. Arm in arm, careless of prying eyes. Proud to be seen with her.

Old George was mending a rail on the yard as they approached. 'We need to be careful,' said Emma, disengaging her arm from his. 'We're both facing divorces, most likely long and bitter ones. Let's not give them extra ammunition.'

'Bring it on,' said Tom, attempting to take her arm again. 'I won't live a lie because of my brother.'

Emma shrugged him off and moved away. Enduring the gap between them was like a physical pain.

'You know how it works,' she said. 'I risk everything financially if I'm found to be the adulterous party.'

'Stuff his money.'

'All right for you to say.' Emma's voice had a real edge to it. 'You're not supporting an invalid mother. You're not facing years of study with no income.' She took a deep breath. 'You're not burdened with an unsavoury past that Harry could drag through the courts to my eternal shame. There's so much you don't know about me.'

'Then tell me,' said Tom. 'It's truth time, remember? Now it's your turn.'

For a long while she didn't speak. The charged moment stretched between them. 'Very well,' she said at last. 'But if I'm going to do this, I'll need a very, very big drink.'

They sat on the verandah with a bottle of wine, while Emma told her story. Her near-destitution, her monster sister-in-law, Melvyn, Hampton Hall — everything.

Tom listened with a growing sense of outrage. How could the world have let his sweet Emma down so badly? His fiery ordeal faded to nothing when compared to the life of torment that she'd suffered.

He had half a mind to head for Launceston then and there, to exact revenge on the odious Melvyn Spriggs.

When Emma finished her story, she wouldn't meet his eye. Her lovely face wore an expression somewhere between apprehension and shame. A wave of compassion crashed over Tom. Melvyn could wait. This wasn't about him, or any of the low-life scum that had so cruelly exploited a vulnerable girl. This was about assuring Emma that nothing and nobody could ever shake his faith in her.

She stood up. 'Say something.' Her voice was no more than a whisper, and she choked back a sob.

What could he say? That she'd shocked and saddened him beyond belief? That he wished with all his heart that he'd been there? That he'd never stopped loving her?

Tom wrapped her in a powerful, protective embrace, while her body stood stiff and unyielding. 'You, Miss Emma Starr, are the bravest, cleverest, kindest, most inspiring person I've ever met.'

She relaxed a little in his arms. 'Does what I told you make a difference?'

He held her gently at arm's length to examine her tear-streaked face. 'Do my scars make a difference to you?'

She managed a faint smile. 'Truth is a tough game.'

'Maybe, but it's the only game worth playing. Living without secrets … it's liberating, like flying. Don't you feel it?'

'Yes.' She drained her glass. 'I feel it. Now, what about another drink?'

As the sun went down, Mrs Mills brought them a big pot of tea, along with a platter of cold lamb chops and salad. She eyed the empty wine bottle. They'd started on a second. 'That Kitty woman would drive me to drink too, Miss Emma, but how will you drive home? You can't very well stay here, not under the circumstances. What would people think?'

'What people?' asked Tom. 'There's nobody for miles.'

'Mrs Mills is right. I can't stay here, and I can't drive all the way back to Hobart, half-drunk.' She looked through her bag and produced a set of keys. 'I'll stay at Canterbury Downs tonight and leave first thing.'

Tom took her home, headlights carving twin beams of light through the blackness.

'What will you do about Karma?' she said as they drove through the bluestone gates and up the serpentine drive.

'Wait until her wounds heal and try to reintroduce her to her family.'

'And they live in the valley where the gold is.'

'That's right.'

'A condition of a mining lease is that you work the claim. How will you get around that?'

'I have three years,' he said. 'By then Binburra will be a national park and I'll give up the lease. At least that's the plan. I'm writing a proposal now and enlisting some high-profile supporters: Charles Barrett, Crosbie Morrison, David Fleay.'

'David Fleay? He's the scientist that Karma bit on the bottom,' said Emma with a laugh.

'Thank God he doesn't hold a grudge.'

'The Royal Society can help,' she said. 'We'll start a campaign. It shouldn't be hard, since you're willing to donate the land. It won't cost parliament a penny.' Emma smiled at him; one of those rare smiles that he'd seen only once or twice in his lifetime. It said she believed in him, and all he stood for.

He kissed her on the doorstep, brimming with gratitude and hope. 'Working together, how can we fail?'

Harry was in heaven, spending each night in Kitty's arms, careless of consequences, lost in a powerful passion that he couldn't control. He didn't want to. She was his drug. The more he had, the more he needed.

To his dismay, Kitty didn't feel the same way. She made him feel like a king in the bedroom, yet out of it, all she could talk of was moving to Hollywood and reviving her career. Obsessing over the lives of actresses in the movie magazines. Bombarding her agent with angry phone calls, demanding he find her a decent part.

'You don't need to bother with all that any more,' said Harry, as she lamented her lack of prospects. 'Stay here. Marry me. We'll have a good life.'

Kitty could not be dissuaded. 'Why is my agent ignoring me? I bet that prick Hawks is behind it. Time to get a new agent or better yet, start my own studio.' Harry knew where this was going. 'You have money, Harry. It would be a terrific investment. Think of it. I could choose my own script, hire a decent co-star. Really make my mark.'

He hated the faraway look in her eye, a look that said he didn't matter at all. 'I told you, honey. My money's all tied up.'

'Well, untie it. Sell something.'

He bit the inside of his cheek. How could he explain that every asset he owned had been strategically acquired according to a plan. Piece by piece he was rebuilding the empire that his father had lost. The shipyard, the timber coupes, the sheep stations, the Hills End gold mine – an atonement for the death of his parents. He wouldn't give up a single one, not even for Kitty.

'If you cared about me—'

'I do care about you.' He hated the pleading note in his voice. 'I love you, honey.'

'No, you don't.' Her beautiful face creased with anger. 'Why should I live in this godforsaken town at the end of the world, with a man who doesn't love me?'

His heart hammered against his ribs. He'd given up everything for Kitty. His home, his wife, his reputation. The gossip pages had them together at the Royal and were having a field day. The thought of Kitty leaving, after he'd sacrificed so much, terrified him.

'Give me some time,' he said. 'I'll come up with something.'

'I know something you can do today. Make Tom an offer he can't refuse,' she said. 'For Binburra and the mining claim both.'

'Don't you think I already have?' Harry took a sip of bitter black coffee and made a face. 'Bid after bid, each more generous than the last. Tom sends the letters back unopened and refuses to take my solicitor's calls.'

'Solicitor? That won't work with Tom. You need to talk to him yourself. He's literally sitting on a gold mine. Don't you care that he cheated you, made a fool of us both?'

Harry thought back to that evening when he'd discovered his brother's despicable deceit. Gold at Binburra. Gold that, by rights, belonged to them both. The memory made his jaw clench and his teeth grind together.

'I can't talk to him, honey. I don't even know him any more.' The Tom he knew wouldn't let money come between them, not even a fortune in gold.

'You're weak, Harry.' He looked away, unable to face the contempt in her eyes. 'Just like all men. Make Tom sell. Make him understand.'

'Jesus, Kitty. You're asking the impossible.'

'But you'll try, right?

He ran his hands over his face. 'Righto, I'll try, but it won't work. Tom's a stubborn bastard.'

'Then get rid of him.'

'How do you mean?'

Her eyes narrowed dangerously, and her mouth was set in a hard, determined line. 'You know what I mean.'

Harry stiffened. 'Be serious.'

'Don't forget, Tom's still my husband. If he dies, I inherit Binburra.'

Harry let that fact sink in. If she owned Binburra and they married, it would all be his. The land, the gold, Kitty – everything he wanted so badly that it hurt his chest to think of it. But murdering his brother?

'Listen to me,' said Kitty. 'Go to Tom, talk with him about old times, have a drink together. Try to convince him to sell. Up your offer if you have to. If he agrees, well and good.'

Harry tried to lick his lips, but had a mouth full of sand. 'And if he doesn't?'

Kitty glanced around, as if someone might hear, even in the privacy of their own suite. 'Drug his drink and burn the place down. Give him enough and he won't feel a thing.'

'What about Mrs Mills and Old George?'

'Do I have to think of everything? Find some way to get them out of the house.'

'I don't know—'

Kitty sprang to her feet. 'You have to do this!' Her breathing quickened and her eyes grew wild. 'Or I'll leave you, Harry. I swear I will. I'll go back to America and get rid of the baby. What choice would I have? I couldn't raise a child alone and still have a career.'

A baby? He stood blinking at her, too stunned to speak. How he'd longed for this, longed to be a father, as if it might somehow redress the tragedy of his past. It had never happened with Emma. Hampton Hall was as well run as a brothel could be, but there were inevitable health risks. She'd been to several gynaecologists. Their verdict? Bouts of venereal disease had destroyed her fertility.

Harry placed a tender hand on Kitty's belly, a belly that seemed more round and full than before. 'Are you sure?'

Her expression softened. 'The doctor confirmed it.'

A firecracker of joy exploded inside him, followed by a wave of fear. His world had narrowed suddenly to a single, burning need. Hold onto Kitty and protect his child. 'This changes everything.' He kissed her, long and hard.

'So you'll do it?' Kitty nibbled his ear, causing him to harden with desire.

He slipped a hand inside her robe, fondling a soft breast. 'Binburra will be ours,' he said. 'Whatever it takes.'

CHAPTER 41

Tom answered the ringing telephone. 'Hello, Harry.'

He hadn't spoken to his brother since Kitty's vindictive outburst in Hobart. He had, however, received a string of solicitors' letters, returning them unopened. Binburra wasn't for sale, so what was the point?

But the Harry on the phone wasn't the angry, resentful person he'd left behind on that fateful night. This was a much more reasonable Harry; a Harry suddenly interested in putting things right between them. It seemed an impossible task, even to Tom, but if his brother was willing to give it a go, so was he.

'I'll be at Canterbury Downs for a few days this week, inspecting the Hills End mine. Could I drop by one night, Tom? For dinner maybe.'

'Come if you like, but I'm warning you, Harry — if this is about Binburra you're wasting your time. And don't expect much of a meal. Mrs M's gone to Sydney with Old George.'

Harry drew into the driveway at Canterbury Downs as the sun dipped below the elm trees. He parked the car in front of the house and rested his head on the steering wheel. This was it. Tonight, one way or the other, he'd repair the wrong done to him by his grandmother.

He and Kitty had gone over the plan a hundred times. He'd come equipped with a powerful sedative, obtained from one of his shonkier connections. A few tablets dissolved in Tom's drink would knock him out for hours. Please God it wouldn't come to that.

Harry's heart hammered in his chest. He needed to stay calm, keep a clear head, but Kitty's pregnancy and her threat to end it constantly hijacked his thoughts. An empty bluff most likely, made in the heat of the moment. But part of him recognised that Kitty was unhinged enough to follow through. To leave him, abort their child, and go to Hollywood chasing fame.

Harry took a deep, steadying breath, grabbed his bag and headed for the house. His fears had rolled themselves into a heavy ball that sat like a cold, wet stone in his stomach. He shivered as he checked his watch, impatient for the waiting to be over. Eager and terrified in equal measure.

When he arrived at Binburra, Tom was waiting on the the verandah. Harry went to meet him, strung tight as a bow. His brother's ravaged face gave him momentary pause, and he steeled himself against an automatic surge of sympathy. This was no time for sentiment. He had to keep his eye on the goal.

They sat in the parlour before an open fire. Harry glanced around. The place was a mess. Empty glasses on the sideboard. Files and books and papers strewn across the table, spilling onto the floor. His brother was no housekeeper.

'I haven't had time to cook,' said Tom. 'Which is probably a good thing.' He cleared a place for a plate of cold lamb chops and roast beef sandwiches. 'I remembered you like chutney. What about a drink? Beer or whisky?'

'Beer.' Harry picked up a sheet of paper from the floor. On Commonwealth letterhead from the Director of National Parks. Acknowledging an application from Mr Thomas Abbott to have all his Tasmanian land known as Binburra, contained in Certificate of title Volume 8949 Folio 009, declared a national park.

Tom returned with the drinks.

'What's all this?' Harry held up the letter.

'Just what it says. You can read.'

Suddenly everything made sense. Until now, Harry had been on the back foot, confused by this strange new Tom. A Tom prepared to sacrifice their relationship for money. A Tom so far removed from the brother he remembered, that he barely recognised him, inside or out. But he'd been wrong. This was the true Tom after all, and therefore a far more formidable opponent.

Harry made his pitch for Binburra, without success.

'Missed opportunities,' said Harry. 'The story of your life, little brother. Remember the time you found the neighbour's pregnant sow in our bottom paddock? A reward of ten pounds for that porker, yet you kept her hidden in the stable. First thing Nana knew about it was when she escaped and ate out the greenhouse.'

'I remember, all right. Those piglets had the run of the place. Did they ever drive Old George mad? I wouldn't let him butcher them.'

'You never could turn a quid.'

'You had a knack for it, though.' Tom finished chewing on a chop, set the bone aside and poured himself a whisky. 'What about that time you went around town selling shares in the non-existent Binburra sawmill? You made fifty pounds before Nana found you out and made you give all the money back.'

'We could have made a fortune,' laughed Harry. 'Nana was as hopeless as you when it came to making a profit. Loved the trees too much.'

Tom grinned, and Harry could suddenly see the boy inside him. The fresh-faced boy who protected piglets and had once been his best friend.

He leaned forward in his chair. 'Sell me Binburra, Tom. I only want the gold. Any safeguards you want for protecting the forest, just ask. I could make you head ranger.'

'No you couldn't, Harry. Rangers work in parks, not mines.'

Harry smiled and raised his glass. 'Is there any point in discussing a new bid? How about triple my last offer?'

'Sorry.' Tom knocked back his whisky, then poured himself another, and one for Harry.

Harry lit a cigar. Tom wasn't going to sell, and was well on the way to being drunk. If he was going to drug his brother, this was the time to do it. But the plan suddenly seemed foolish and cruel. There must be some other way to give Kitty her bloody studio.

A gust of wind whistled down the chimney, sending a spray of sparks from the grate. Tom rose unsteadily to his feet and threw another log on the fire. 'How's my wife?'

Harry stiffened. Kitty wasn't up for discussion.

'Did she put you up to this?' asked Tom. 'Coming round here, having a cosy drink, acting like we're mates. Did she think you could convince me to sell out for old time's sake?'

'Give it a rest, Tom.'

'She's not what you think, Harry. Granted, she's gorgeous and charming. Utterly captivating actually, but it's just a beautiful façade. There's something missing on the inside.'

'Shut up, Tom. I'm going to marry her.'

'What about Emma?'

'I'll get a divorce.' Harry's chest tightened. 'Kitty's pregnant. It's important we get things settled before the child is born.'

'A baby.' Tom poured himself another drink. 'I never could quite picture Kitty as a mother. How far along is she?'

Harry didn't like the turn their conversation was taking. 'Why?'

Tom held up his hands. 'Forget I asked.'

Harry skulled his whisky. Tom wouldn't look him in the eye and then it hit him. Tom thought the baby might be his. Kitty had sworn blue murder that she hadn't slept with her husband since the accident, and he'd been fool enough to believe her. She was repulsed by him, she said. One glance at Tom's face told him that she'd lied.

Cold hatred rose like bile in his throat. Tom and Kitty were still married. If the baby was born before they divorced, it would legally be Tom's child. What was to stop him from claiming custody? A long, drawn out paternity suit wouldn't hurt Tom, especially when he'd look like the wronged party, but it would destroy what little was left of Harry's own reputation. And what if his brother won?

Tom picked up the empty platter. 'I'll make more sandwiches.'

Harry stood and wandered around the room, trying to quell his agitation. So many memories. The window sill where he'd scratched his initials. The pencilled dates and marks on the wall, where Nana measured heights on their birthdays. His favourite books still on the shelf: *The Sword In The Stone, Tarka the Otter, Emil and the Detectives.*

He took down a well-thumbed copy of *The Hobbit* with his name scrawled on the first page. The rug beneath his feet had burn marks from when he stole Old George's tobacco and smoked for the first time at eleven years old. The ceiling had a discoloured hole in the plaster where he'd let off a sky rocket one cracker night.

Reminders of childhood were everywhere. Kitty's plan was ridiculous. Doping Tom. Burning down the house. How could she ask him to kill his own brother? How could she ask him to destroy this beautiful homestead? A little worse for wear perhaps, but still so very dear to him. He had to find a better way.

It was then he saw it — a fringed, silk scarf with Egyptian motif. The same Dior scarf he'd given his wife for her last birthday. His legs turned to jelly and he put a hand on the wall. Emma had been here. When? How often? What if all the time he'd been with Kitty, racked with guilt and ruining his good name, Emma had been having an affair with his brother? It was perfectly plausible. She'd always been in love with him.

Harry closed his eyes, seeing down a dark tunnel into a bleak future. A future without Kitty. She'd leave him when he couldn't provide her with that damned movie studio. Without Emma. She'd go with his brother. Without his child, who'd grow up calling Tom *Papa*. Without Binburra and its gold. Without his reputation.

A wild panic hit him. Life would be worth nothing. But if he followed through with the plan? Kitty, Binburra, the gold, the child – it could all be his. Harry took the bottle of ground-up pills from his pocket and tipped it into his brother's half-empty whisky glass.

Tom came back with the sandwiches and drained his drink in one gulp.

Harry watched on with a kind of horrid fascination. Growing tauter and tighter until he thought he'd snap. He jumped to his feet. 'I've got to go. Goodbye, Tom.'

Harry could feel the sweat pouring from him, his palms slick and clammy. Tom went to rise, and Harry waved him back down. 'Stay there in front of the fire. I'll see myself out.'

He hurried from the house, not wanting to confront the first signs of Tom's drowsiness. Not wanting to confirm the awful reality of what he was about to do. Best to wait down the road a way, give the drug time to work, and then return when Tom was fully asleep. Twenty minutes would be enough, so he'd been told.

Harry took off too fast, wheels skidding on gravel, barely making the turn. He had to get hold of himself. Down the long, steep driveway, out the gate. He turned left, headed half-a-mile down the road and parked the car. It was a black night, black and starless with no moon. Time ticked by with inexorable slowness. He must have checked his watch a hundred times before the twenty minutes were up.

At last he turned on the ignition, and the engine's roar magnified the stillness. He was more determined now. Tom was the bane of his life. Time to finish what he'd started all those years ago at the waterfall.

His car crept back up to the house. The lights were still on, but there was no need to be quiet, not really, not if the pills had done their job. Harry took the can of petrol from the boot and searched his pockets for the matches. He planned to start a fire in the hall by the stairs. It would climb up the staircase, the spine of the house, and radiate out.

He splashed petrol over the floor and bannister with a fervent energy. No time for indecision, just get on with it. A tossed lit match. Shocking, the instant heat and flames. Shocking, how quickly it took hold. Harry ran from the house, dizzy and shaking. He collapsed to his knees, trying to shut out the image of Tom's face, which kept swimming into view. Not the ravaged post-war Tom, but the clear-eyed boy who'd once been his best mate. A boy who'd listened to him, protected him, who'd taken the blame for so many stupid stunts. A boy who'd grown into the kind of man Papa would have been proud of.

Was that it? Was he killing Tom out of jealousy? Harry desperately examined his own conscience. He'd loved their father, worshipped a man who'd committed a terrible crime. Had he been warped by Papa's example, convinced that murder was an acceptable way to deal with his problems?

The stained-glass panel in the front door glowed rosy red. Was Tom really knocked out in there? Harry had been too much of a coward to check. His heart pounded like the hydraulic hammer at the mine, and a voice screamed in his head to stop this madness now, to put out the fire. Tom had suffered ghastly burns in the plane crash. Could he let Tom feel those flames again? The fog of anger cleared. He'd left his brother for dead once before, an act that had haunted him half his life. He wouldn't make the same cruel mistake twice.

Harry dashed back, slammed open the front door and rushed headlong into hell. So much smoke that he couldn't see, couldn't find his bearings. Unbearable heat. A fire monster raged at the heart of the house, a towering pillar of flames that was once the stairs. Its hungry, burning tongue licked the ceiling, the walls, the floor.

He battled his way into the parlour, choked by smoke, deafened by the fire's roar. Feeling his way along the wall and shielding his eyes with his hands. This part of the house wasn't yet alight — there was still time. Out of the toxic grey void loomed the backs of the armchairs that he and Tom had been sitting on, only an hour before. Talking and drinking before the tame little fire in the grate. More like brothers than they'd been since children.

Choking and panting for breath, he reached the chairs, determined to drag Tom out, or die trying.

CHAPTER 42

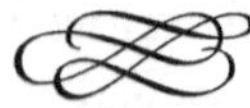

Kitty snatched up the phone, praying that it would be Harry. It was hotel reception instead. 'The police are here to see you, Mrs Abbott. Shall I send them up?'

The knock came at the door before she had time to put on her makeup. The mirror showed deep worry lines around her mouth, and shadows beneath her eyes. No wonder — she hadn't slept a wink. Why hadn't Harry called?

She opened the door to two officers, who introduced themselves, holding their hats and looking grim. 'You might want to sit down, Mrs Abbott.'

'No, just tell me.' Kitty tried to prepare herself. She'd been practising weeping all week, but all she could manage was a single tear.

The older man, Sergeant Shaw, gave her a searching look. 'Are you expecting bad news?'

'Of course I am. You're here, aren't you?'

Shaw glanced at his companion. 'The Binburra homestead at Hills End burned down last night. I'm afraid a body has been found inside. We believe it to be that of your husband, Thomas Abbott.'

Kitty made a choking cry. Oh, Jesus, Harry had actually done it.

She staggered backwards to the couch, replaying a scene from *The Moving Finger* when her character lost a brother in the war.

Shaw asked the young constable to fetch her a glass of water. 'You're estranged from your husband, are you not?'

'We've had some difficulties,' she managed between sobs. 'But that was all over. I was ready to move back to Binburra.' She put a hand on the small mound of her stomach. 'For the sake of the baby.'

Shaw raised his eyebrows. 'Where might we find your brother-in-law, Mr Harry Abbott? His wife says she hasn't seen him for some months.'

'Why ask me? I've no idea.'

'No idea, despite the fact that Mr Abbott is registered in the room next to yours.' He tested the connecting door to see if it was locked. It wasn't. 'Are you still telling me that you don't know where he is?'

'That's exactly what I'm telling you. Harry has been … supportive during my separation, nothing more.' This wasn't how it was supposed to be. Harry was supposed to be here so that she could give him an alibi.

Shaw wandered about the room, picking up objects and putting them down again. 'I'm sorry to be the bearer of such news. You won't be required to identify the body, Mrs Abbott. I'm afraid it's too badly burned for viewing. Is there anything your husband may have had on his person that will help us? The deceased wasn't wearing a wedding ring.'

Kitty glumly shook her head.

'We'll leave you in peace, then.' Shaw gave her a card with his phone number. 'If you should see your brother-in-law, let him know we need to talk to him.'

The officers saw themselves out. They were suspicious, no doubt about it. She had to speak to Harry and warn him. Kitty poured herself a double gin and tonic, then sat by the phone to wait.

Hours passed. Kitty jumped at each sound coming from the corridor; each footstep, each faint conversation, each muffled, unidentifiable noise. Hoping against hope that it would be Harry. Morning passed into afternoon. She'd been twenty-four hours without sleep, but was still too wired to rest or eat. All that gin on an empty stomach had made her sick and dizzy.

At four o'clock she finally heard footsteps outside the door. At last. She flung the door open to find Emma standing there. Her eyes were red and swollen, her face puffy from crying. Kitty tried to close the door in her face.

Emma shoved her foot inside to block it. 'The police came to see me.' She pushed past Kitty into the hotel room. 'Is it true? Is Tom dead?'

'They were here this morning,' said Kitty. 'They found someone in the burned out Binburra homestead, and they think it's Tom. That's all I know.'

'Then why are you sitting here? Why aren't you on your way to Binburra?'

'What good would that do? They'll have moved the body by now.'

'The body?' Emma was shaking, her face a combination of anger and grief. 'Don't you dare describe my beautiful Tom as *the body*. Not the sweetest, kindest, bravest man in the world.'

Kitty tried to make sense of Emma's reaction. This was more than the response of an affectionate sister-in-law. No, Emma was in love with Tom. Damn — even if the police ruled his death as accidental, Emma might not let it go.

Kitty pressed her hand against her forehead. She was getting the headache from hell. Where, oh where, was Harry? A knock came at the door. But Harry wouldn't knock, he'd use his key. The police again? A rising panic claimed her. Had Harry talked, implicated her somehow? None of this was her fault, she'd been at the hotel last night. She'd done nothing wrong.

Kitty felt a sudden urge to flee, but where to go? She had no connections in Hobart other than Harry, and he'd abandoned her. Her mind flashed back to that glorious time in London, when she'd first met Tom, when she'd been the toast of the town. The knock came again. Perhaps she could escape through the connecting suite? But before Kitty could move her frozen feet, Emma opened the door.

CHAPTER 43

Tom stood before them, dirty and dishevelled, covered in ash, with a wild look in his eyes. Emma screamed and threw herself into his arms, smothering his filthy face in kisses. He enfolded her in a fierce embrace while Kitty watched in disbelief.

She ran her tongue over chapped lips. If Tom had survived the fire, if he hadn't died in the house … Oh God. A strangled cry. Could the burned body be Old George or Mrs Mills? But Harry said they were in Sydney. She went numb with fear. If Harry was dead, she was lost. Pregnant, with no money, no job, no friends. All her eggs in one basket that had burned to cinders.

Tom turned to look at her. Kitty tried to smile, tried to make a convincing show of being happy to see him. But she couldn't do it. She was too frightened about tomorrow. Too heartbroken that her husband was alive, and Harry was dead.

Tom disengaged himself from Emma's arms, rage churning inside him. 'You don't look pleased to see me, Kitty. I'm disappointed. I thought you were a better actress than that.'

'Of course I'm happy. I'm still your wife, remember.'

'Oh, I remember. You're the one who forgot.'

'I'm sorry, babe.' Kitty's eyes darted to and fro, like a rat in a trap. 'I was confused. This thing with Harry — a crush, that's all. A stupid infatuation. It's you I truly love.' She ran to Tom and tried to kiss him.

He shoved her away. 'Has anyone seen Harry?'

Emma put a hand on his arm, face full of tenderness and concern. 'They found a body, Tom. In the burned out homestead. They thought it was you.'

Tom's bottom lip quivered. Unable to dam the flood of tears, he turned the full force of his rage and sorrow onto Kitty. 'If Harry's dead, it's all too late.' He tried to breathe, but couldn't fill his lungs. He was suffocating, choking as he had in the plane crash, choking the way Harry would have when the searing smoke filled his airways and the flames melted his flesh. 'We could have got through this, my brother and me. We could have made things right between us. Harry just needed help to see a way through, but you did the opposite. You poisoned everything good in him.'

Kitty turned to run, but he grabbed her arm and wrested her back. 'What about the baby?'

'You're hurting me.'

She wriggled and kicked and squirmed, but he held fast. 'We both know it could be mine.'

'Stop it, both of you!' Emma screamed. 'Let her go!'

He looked past his anger to the fear on Kitty's face. Tom allowed her wrist to slip from his fingers. She dashed for the door of the adjoining room, threw it open and slammed it shut behind her.

Tom gathered Emma to him.

'Thank God you're alive, Tom,' she whispered, over and over again.

It sounded like a prayer. Tom could feel her ragged breathing, hear the beat of her heart – wished they could stay like that forever. He brushed a tangled lock of hair from her face, which was damp with tears. Guiding Emma to the couch, he sat her down.

'What happened?' she managed. 'Tell me.'

Tom shut his eyes and steeled himself to tell the story. 'Harry came round last night with a cheque, three times what he'd offered before. I refused it, of course, but we talked. It mightn't have seemed much to you if you'd been there, but we talked about when we were children, and about Nana. Harry opened up. It was the sort of connection I'd craved for years. He told me Kitty was pregnant, and then I went to get us some sandwiches. When I came back Harry was different — cold and angry. He left in a hurry.'

Tom was shaking and Emma took his hand.

'I started to feel sick and dizzy. Thought it was the whisky, but now I reckon Harry put something in my drink.'

'No!'

'It's the only explanation for what happened. I went down to the stable to check on Karma, and couldn't keep my eyes open. I sat in her pen and nodded off, until the little mongrel bit me.' He pulled up his sleeve and showed Emma a crescent-shaped red wheal. 'Just in play, mind, but it was painful enough to wake me. I heard a kind of roaring noise and saw a red glow outside. I was so groggy it was a struggle to get to that door. Last thing I remember was seeing the house ablaze … and Harry.' His voice broke. 'Harry running back inside.'

'Oh my God. You didn't stop him?'

'I couldn't.' Tom could barely get the words out. His heart felt like somebody was twisting it in a vice. 'I passed out in the hay. Woke up this afternoon feeling like a train had hit me. Nana's beautiful home all gone, burned to the ground. Harry's car was still there, but I couldn't find him.'

Emma shook her head, tears streaming down her cheeks.

The ringing phone startled them both. Tom answered it. 'No, this is Tom, Harry's brother. There's been some confusion about my state of health … Yes, my brother always carried it with him.'

Tom put down the phone, chin trembling. 'They found something in the ruins beside the body — a small nugget of gold that survived the house fire. You know what this means, don't you? Harry changed his mind. He died trying to save me.'

'Do you think Kitty knew what he was planning?'

'My oath. I think she put him up to it.'

An anguished scream came from the adjoining suite. Tom tried the door. It was locked.

'Kick it in!' yelled Emma.

A terrible scene confronted them – Kitty lying on the bed in a flood of blood, her face snow-white and twisted in pain.

'Jesus Christ!' said Tom. 'What have you done?'

A bent wire coat hanger lay at Kitty's feet.

Emma threw a blanket over her. 'Call an ambulance.'

After an hour of waiting in the hospital corridor, a doctor came to see Tom.

'I'm here to discuss the treatment of Mrs Kitty Abbott. You're the husband, yes?' He pointed to the door of the consulting room. 'Come through.'

Emma squeezed his hand. 'I'll be right here.'

'Your wife is lucky to be alive,' said the doctor. 'She lost a lot of blood. It's miracle she didn't lose the baby as well.'

Tom slumped with relief. 'Can I see her?'

The doctor took off his glasses and twirled them between his fingers. 'How would you describe your wife's mental health?'

'Fragile,' said Tom. 'She's been having an affair with my brother, Harry. We think he died last night in a house fire.'

'I see.' The doctor took his time, seemed to be preparing his next words. 'The police have talked to me. Attempting to procure an unlawful abortion is a crime, a crime your wife is clearly guilty of. If she'd been successful, it could have resulted in twenty-one years' jail.'

'Kitty needs help, not jail.'

'I agree. It appears that she is delusional and unaware of the gravity of her situation. Kitty keeps talking about going to Hollywood and making a movie. She was an actress once, I take it?'

'Yes.' Tom took out his cigarette case. 'May I?' The doctor gave him a light. 'Since we married, her career has taken a downturn. Kitty is obsessed with reviving it.'

'That's very true. Your wife believes she's no longer pregnant, in spite of my contrary advice. She also believes she has a plane ticket booked to Los Angeles, and is making repeated attempts to leave the hospital. Quite frankly, in such a state, she presents a serious risk to both herself and her unborn child.'

'I see.'

'The police have agreed not to prosecute on the condition that Kitty is committed to a psychiatric hospital for the remainder of her pregnancy. Another four months, I imagine.'

Tom ran a hand over his face. Four months. The child could indeed be his. Not that it mattered. Daughter or niece, son or nephew — this baby was family and would be dearly loved.

'If your wife is no better after the birth, I assume you are prepared to take sole responsibility for the child?'

'Of course. Can I see her now?'

'I don't think that's wise. I'm afraid she doesn't want to see you. Kitty becomes quite violent at the mention of your name, and keeps asking for your brother, Harry.'

Neither of them spoke on the way back to the hotel.

'Will you stay here tonight?' asked Emma, when they arrived.

'You forget. I have to get back to Karma. I owe her a lot. That little tiger saved my life.'

The forest was purple with evening shadows by the time they drove up the hill to Binburra. Harry's car was there, parked where he'd left it the night before. Surreal, to see the remains of the house still smouldering. Tom picked through the ruins in the failing light for what remained: some pots and pans, a brass figurine, a few coins. Heartbreaking.

'You can't stay here,' said Emma. 'Get Karma and we'll go to Canterbury Downs.'

Tom wandered the grand rooms of the bluestone mansion. Dark, wood-panelled walls and formal portraits. His father had lived here until he was nine years old. He couldn't imagine a child running and playing in those gloomy halls.

Tom spread out a bale of hay and settled Karma in the old chook pen. Emma knelt beside him to feed the young tiger pieces of a rabbit that Tom had shot. He reached out to lay a hand on her knee, and in spite of their combined grief and weariness, a shock passed between them. His fingers travelled, ever so gently, up the curve of her back and down again. He stroked the hollow of her flank, and she shivered.

He took her hand and led her into the house, into the parlour, to the wide Chesterfield couch. Emma stretched out on the soft leather, eyes beckoning. This was a union years overdue. Tom lay beside her, unbuttoning her shirt, then the waist of her jeans – slowly and reverently, like he was unwrapping a costly gift. The hard, painful years of separation vanished and they were young again, sixteen and full of tomorrow.

With a quiver of pleasure he caressed her warm secret skin, her figure taut and fit beneath him, still the body of a girl. 'You're the most beautiful woman I've ever seen.'

She half-smiled and tugged at his belt, feeling his hardness, making it throb and grow. Love was a powerful aphrodisiac. He kissed Emma's neck, her breasts, her navel — and she made a small sweet sound in the back of her throat. 'Now,' she whispered. 'I can't wait.'

Tom had dreamed of this moment for years. He entered her gently, eager to make the moment last. They moved as one, conjoined in a whirlpool of feelings. Their shock and sadness and grief faded away, replaced with a sense of destiny.

.   .   .

Afterwards they warmed up cans of baked beans and soup for dinner, laughing at the modesty of their first romantic meal together.

'What will we do about Karma?' said Emma.

'Release her.' Tom scraped his plate clean and poured two mugs of black tea. 'Before she loses her wild instincts. We'll all go together.'

It took them three days to reach Tiger Pass. Tom feared Karma might run off, so for the first morning he kept her on a light chain. This didn't work. It was like trying to lead a stubborn cat. She fought and twisted and chewed at the chain, so they hardly made any progress at all. When he took the risk of letting her go, she followed along, exploring fallen trees and puddles and wombat holes, but never straying too far.

As they climbed higher, the world and its problems disappeared. At night they slept in a double swag beneath a dome of stars, secure in each other's arms — feeling like the last two people on earth. Tom grew impatient to reach their destination. Impatient to show Emma the magnificent lost valley; for her to experience its magic.

At last they walked in hushed silence through the rocky gateway to the pass. Tom led her along the bubbling stream to the stone ledge above the waterfall. A vantage point from where the true size of the hidden valley became apparent; forests and grassy clearings stretching for miles into the mist. Autumn had gilded the vast stands of deciduous beech below — it was a valley of gold in more ways than one.

'The tigers' own personal Shangri-La,' he whispered. 'Fresh water, all the game they could want and protection from prying eyes.'

'How do we get down there?

Tom helped her from the ledge, his heart cheering.

Into the Huon pine cave they went. Tom shone his torch at the low stone ceiling where the likeness of a thylacine gazed down at them. Emma's face showed her delight, and Tom burst with joy to see it.

They descended the ancient stone steps, with curious Karma

chasing after. Past glow worms and whirling bats, until they reached the valley floor.

Tom shrugged off his pack by the banks of the stream and filled his canteen.

'Rest here,' Tom said. 'While I give Karma a bath.'

'A bath,' laughed Emma. 'Whatever for?'

'To remove our scent.' He pointed to animal prints in the damp river sand, as a thrill nipped at his spine. 'Her family is close by.'

With Karma washed and rubbed with wombat droppings, they set off again. The young tiger grew more and more animated as they went, sniffing the ground and yipping with excitement. An hour later they reached the waterfall, where it plunged in a rainbow of spray from the cliffs above.

Karma whined, pricking up her ears, and Tom gestured for them to take cover in a low stand of beech trees. 'That cave at the base of the falls is the tigers' den.'

Karma seemed confused, running in circles, but never moving far from Tom. He pushed her with his foot whenever she came near. 'Go on,' he whispered. 'Go home.'

The pup uttered a series of high-pitched barks, not quite dog-like. It was then they heard it, an answering call. Karma stood to attention.

With one final shove of Tom's boot, Karma headed off towards the cave. She hesitated at the entrance, uncertainty evident in the lines of her bowed body and flattened ears.

Emma touched his arm and put a hand to her mouth. An animal emerged. An adult tiger; a male, judging by its size and large head. Karma's father? Its jaws opened impossibly wide and Karma sank to the ground, yipping and showing her belly, just as a puppy might. Tom's heart skipped with fear. What if it had all been for nothing? What if little Karma was snapped up in the big tiger's jaws?

He needn't have feared — it couldn't have been a gentler reunion. Karma crept to her father, who sniffed her from head to tail. He licked her mouth, turned around and waited for her to follow. The two of them vanished into the cave.

Emma sank to the ground in stunned silence, eyes wet with tears. Tom crouched down beside her, and kissed her like it was their first time.

CHAPTER 44

F our years later—

Tom sat with Emma on the garden swing at Canterbury Downs, while three-year-old Fraser tried to tip them out of it.

Emma shook with giggles as the little boy tickled her. 'That's enough.'

'Leave your mother alone.' Tom grabbed Fraser and held him upside down, provoking peals of laughter.

'Our guests will be here soon,' scolded Emma. 'Will you two behave yourselves?'

'Daddy,' piped Fraser as Tom put him down. 'Can I wear my nugget today? Please Daddy ... pleease?'

Tom frowned. He'd had the gold nugget made into a pendant, in memory of his brother, and had given it to Fraser. The little boy had started sleeping with it under his pillow — just as Harry had once done. Something about that made Tom uneasy. He'd retrieved the pendant with the excuse that Fraser might lose it, hoping his son would forget. No such luck. Fraser asked about it all the time.

'Let him have it,' said Emma. 'It's a special day.'

Reluctantly, Tom fished the pendant from his pocket and gave it to the delighted child.

Mrs Mills came down from the house. 'A phone call, Tom. From the hospital.' His heart sank. Today was not the day for bad news.

'About your wife,' said Kitty's doctor. 'In the considered opinion of our team, her delusions have subsided sufficiently for her to be released.' A pause. 'However she doesn't want to be reunited with either yourself or her son.'

'What does she want?'

'To return to America — and a divorce.'

'Tell her she may have both. I'll pay for her ticket and give her a monthly stipend. Or should I speak to her myself?'

'That won't be possible. Kitty still refuses to talk to you, but I think your offer will be most welcome.'

Emma came in as he hung up the phone, eyes wide with concern. 'Trouble?'

Tom picked her up and spun her around. 'Quite the reverse.'

What a joyful gathering, the culmination of four-and-a-half years' hard work. The 'who's who' of Hobart's Royal Society was there, along with the Premier, the press and many government members — all come to celebrate the gazetting of Binburra as Tasmania's newest National Park.

'A significant addition to the protection of our State's unique flora and fauna,' boomed Premier Cosgrove as a reporter took a photo.

'If people only knew how significant the protection really is,' whispered Emma.

She and Tom exchanged a swift kiss, feeling the full weight of both their achievement, and their responsibility.

Tom clinked his glass with Emma's. 'Here's to a lifetime of making sure that nobody ever finds out.'

ACKNOWLEDGEMENTS

Thanks go to the team at Pilyara Press, especially Kathryn Ledson, Sydney Smith and Kate Belle. Thanks also to Desney King for her eagle-eyed proofreading and more.

I pay tribute to pioneering naturalist, David Fleay (1907 - 1993), whose interest in the natural world coincided with the awakening of scientific interest in endangered species, and the realisation by the public that Australian animals were worthy of attention.

Fleay was the last person to photograph a Thylacine, also known as a Tasmanian tiger. He was bitten by the tiger on the buttocks in the process, and carried the scar proudly throughout his life.

I also pay tribute to Crosbie Morrison, another early naturalist, educator, journalist, broadcaster and conservationist. Morrison was one of the first Australians to promote the protection of wildlife, and the need to create and properly manage national parks

Thanks to my lovely agent, Clare Forster of Curtis Brown Australia.

Thanks to my talented writing friends, the Varuna Darklings and the Little Lonsdale Group, for their friendship and encouragement.

Finally, I'd like to thank my family for their patience and support. You are all stars!

ABOUT THE AUTHOR

Bestselling Aussie author Jennifer Scoullar writes page-turning fiction about the land, people and wildlife that she loves.

Scoullar is a lapsed lawyer who harbours a deep appreciation and respect for the natural world. She lives on a farm in Australia's southern Victorian ranges, and has ridden and bred horses all her life. Her passion for animals and the bush is the catalyst for her best-selling books, which are all inspired by different landscapes.

Visit Jennifer's website to enter the monthly prize draw! If you enjoyed this book and have a moment or two, please leave an online rating or review. Reviews are of great help to authors.

www.jenniferscoullar.com

THE MEMORY TREE

THE TASMANIAN TALES 3

For those fighting to protect the Tasmanian Devil

~

Matt spun the wheel hard, navigating another hair-raising bend in the narrow gravel road. He glanced at the clock on the dash. Midnight. His wife called it the witching hour – a time of ghosts and magic. He wasn't superstitious like Penny, but tonight, hemmed in by the dark forest, he could almost believe it. Matt stifled a yawn and turned on the radio. Music would help him stay awake. He'd been up since dawn.

What was that? Something swift crossed the corner of his vision and Matt slammed on the brakes. They gave a tortured squeal, but it was too late. He felt the sickening thud of metal on flesh. Matt cursed and stopped the car. Nothing showed in the headlights. No trace of the shadow that had raced across the road.

Shoulders hunched against the cold, Matt walked back along the corrugated track. The fog was a night shroud swallowing the torchlight. There – sprawled on the rutted roadside. He knelt down and felt its warmth, felt the final fragile flutters of life until the animal was beyond fear or care. It lay quite still now. Blood oozed from its mouth and nose, and moon shadows striped its coat.

Matt could barely breathe. This couldn't be. He shook his head, hot tears flowing as the impossible became reality. A dog? No – a phantom.

Penny brushed her long copper-coloured hair, and tugged it back into a practical ponytail. She buttoned her shirt, squeezed into jeans, frowning as she struggled to zip them.

'I'm starting a diet today,' she said, as usual.

'Don't,' said Matt, as always. 'You're perfect the way you are.'

Penny made a face and left the room. He found everything about her irresistible. Her ripe figure, her serious smile, her freckled dimples and clear blue eyes. But Penny couldn't take a compliment. She never believed him and he didn't know why. After all, he was no oil painting – tall and fit, for sure, but with an ugly hawkish nose like his father. It made him look arrogant.

Matt showered, thinking a little about the day ahead and a lot about the night before. He arched his neck and turned up the heat, let the water pummel his shoulders, knock some sense into him. Matt hated secrets, but he couldn't tell Penny what had happened. It was beyond him.

He found Penny in the kitchen.

'You'd better boil the kettle again,' she said, before disappearing into the lounge room with a brush-tailed possum curled around her neck like a stole. 'Can you muster the pademelons for me?' Penny asked when she came back in. 'We're weighing their joeys this afternoon.'

'Sorry,' said Matt. 'I promised Bernie to fly the falcons.' He combed his dark hair with his fingers. The purple bottlebrush outside the window quivered with honeyeaters. The sun shone. A spider wove its web across the sill. How could everything look so normal when nothing was?

'Dr Deville's coming this morning,' said Penny. 'Don't you want to meet her?'

Matt put the kettle back on the gas. 'It can wait.'

Penny nursed her mug and watched him. 'You didn't sleep much last night.'

That was an understatement. He'd lain restless in the dark, reliving each detail of his heartbreaking accident in the park. Reliving the shock, the amazement – the dreadful guilt and grief. Willing himself to wake from this living nightmare. As head ranger at Binburra National Park he'd pledged to protect it from harm. Instead he'd caused the greatest harm possible. He'd killed a Tasmanian tiger – an animal believed extinct for almost a hundred years.

The kettle screamed. Matt caught the edge of his hand on the scalding jet of steam and barely felt it. Penny's questioning eyes bored into him and he tried changing the subject. 'You're running an information session this morning, right? What's this one about?'

Penny didn't answer. Then Matt remembered and wished he'd never asked. The Devil Roadkill Count was Penny's pet project. Binburra was at the forefront of conserving Tasmanian devils. As scavengers, they were particularly vulnerable to being killed by cars. Matt had hit one himself last year – one of Penny's painstakingly hand-reared orphans. Released with radio collars and a great deal of hope, many perished on the roads within months. 'How could you be so careless?' she'd asked him. How indeed.

Matt kissed his wife and escaped to the verandah.

Their modest house was perched halfway up the hill above Binburra Wildlife Park's home compound. Covering several hectares, it stretched out before him under a sky of brilliant blue.

The buildings and enclosures were designed to blend seamlessly with the native trees and gardens, providing as natural an environment as possible for their residents. The main focus of the park was the breeding and conservation of Tasmanian devils, but Binburra also housed a wide variety of rescued birds and animals. Some would be rehabilitated and returned to the wild. For those too badly injured to fend for themselves, Binburra provided a permanent home.

Matt hurried down to the historic shearing shed that he'd converted into a mews. It housed Aquila and the peregrine falcons that he'd be flying today. First he checked on the other raptors: the masked owl with the wire-fence injury; the snow-white goshawk, his leg in a cast; and an old peregrine, blind in one eye, his retina detached by the force of a three-hundred-kilometre-an-hour dive. Last in line was a slim nankeen kestrel, victim of an inebriated and out-of-season duck hunter. Matt frowned as he fed the kestrel a mouse. Her hovering days were over, but at least she could fly from floor to perch now. It was time to move her to the flight aviary. But not today. Today was Hills End Cup Day.

Matt drew on a leather gauntlet and fetched the falcons. They hopped onto his arm in return for pieces of rabbit. First Sooty, the tiercel, and then Sweep, the larger female. The blue-black plumage of their heads and upper body gleamed with good health. Their breasts were the colour of rich King Island cream, and delicate buff bands extended with exquisite symmetry to the tips of their short tails. Their gaze, once wan and pale, now flashed clear and bright; eye rings vibrant yellow, golden beaks tipped glossy black. Matt encouraged the birds onto his homemade cadge, a portable frame fitted with perches, and whistled low while hooding them.

Jake, Binburra's only full-time keeper, came in with a trolley of road kill to restock the freezer. He was a gentle young man of twenty-five with sandy-blond hair, kind eyes and an impressive work ethic. Matt liked Jake a lot. Usually the two of them would stop for a chat, but today Matt merely grunted at Jake's cheerful, 'Good morning,' and busied himself with the falcons.

Jake finished packing the freezer. 'You off to the races? It's a nice sunny day to fly those birds.'

Matt ignored him, couldn't even look at him – caught up in an irrational fear that Jake would know what had happened last night if he made eye contact. When it became clear that Matt wasn't going to respond, Jake shrugged and left with the empty trolley. Matt let out his breath. More than anything, he wanted to be alone with his thoughts. His throat went dry. If he couldn't even face Jake, how on earth would he face crowds of strangers at the race track?

Once the peregrines were in the jeep, Matt fetched Aquila. She flew to a low branch at his approach. Matt braced against her weight as she stepped onto his arm, broad wings unfurled. The eagle bent her head, with its striking blonde nape, against his cheek. Matt laughed and rubbed her neck. 'All right, you floozy, that's enough. Save some love for Woorawa.'

With just eighty breeding pairs of giant wedgetails left in the wild, the sub-species was in serious trouble. Fingers crossed, Aquila would bond with Woorawa, a young male arriving next month, and the pair could be released along with the peregrines. But the birds required more free flight sessions before then to regain strength and stamina. Matt rewarded Aquila with a strip of rabbit, she consented to the hood, and they set off in the jeep for a day at the races.

CHAPTER 2

Penny watched the black Audi sweep into the carpark. That had to be her. Its driver, slim, dark-haired and stylish, walked over and introduced herself with a broad American accent. 'Dr Sarah Deville, UCLA.' She smiled and shook Penny's hand a little too hard. 'I've never seen a live devil. Really looking forward to this.'

Penny began the seminar, standing beneath a banner strung above the whiteboard – *Slow Down Between Dusk and Dawn*. It was more than a little overwhelming to have the renowned geneticist in the audience. If she pretended Dr Deville wasn't there, it might help. She cast her eye over the crowd. About thirty. A good number. Dr Deville sat at the back. Penny tried to concentrate.

'Welcome to Binburra Wildlife Park, thirty thousand hectares of World Heritage wilderness high on the rim of Tuggerah Valley. The property originally belonged to a founding member of Tasmania's environmental movement, Daniel Campbell. His family later bequeathed it to the state, to be gazetted as a national park.' Penny wet her lips. 'Binburra pioneered the captive management and breeding of Tasmanian devils. They're a lonely species – their close relatives already gone – and for the past two decades we've been fighting to save the devils themselves from extinction, because a cruel and mysterious disease is set to wipe them out.'

Penny winced. How stupid she sounded, going through her little spiel when the world expert on the devil genome sat right there in front of her. She tried not to look at Dr Deville and ended up staring slightly to the side, as if there was some sort of fascinating patch on the wall. Two women in the front row were looking sideways now too. For goodness sake, get a grip.

'A virulent contagious cancer known as Devil Facial Tumour Disease – DFTD for short – causes suppurating tumours in the animals. Those affected die agonising deaths within months, starving as disfiguring growths eat away their jaws and choke their throats.' She cleared her own throat. 'Binburra provides healthy animals to mainland and overseas zoos. These Project Ark founders are breeding safe from the threat of disease, but our wild devils could soon face extinction.' She was talking too fast, rushing it. She took a deep, steadying breath. 'And if we let that happen, nobody will understand, and nobody will forgive us.'

Penny reached into the box at her feet. She pulled out a squat black creature the size of a small bulldog, with round furry ears – cute like a teddy bear. It sniffed the air. She set the animal on the desk in front of her and it shuffled around to face the audience. With a collective gasp, people shrank back. The devil looked as if a hunk of raw, rotting meat had been slapped along the entire side of its head. Its jaw was disfigured by ulcerating growths that forced its lips apart and protruded through its mouth. A fleshy, bleeding tumour mushroomed from one eye.

'Meet Angel,' said Penny. 'A motorist killed her mother three years ago and thankfully stopped to check for pouch young. She found two dead babies and Angel here, barely clinging to life. I nursed her round the clock, took her with me everywhere.' Penny paused to fondle Angel's misshapen head. 'Angel stayed with me at the sanctuary until she was eighteen months old. I never met a sweeter, cleverer little devil. In winter she dragged logs to the fireplace, hinting for us to light it. She loved curling up by that fire. And she mothered the younger orphans, carrying them in her mouth if she thought they were in danger, putting them back in their baskets. She really is special. Last year I released her into what we hoped was a safe area of the park. We trapped her in the course of our regular monitoring program two weeks ago ... looking like this.'

A question came from the crowd. 'How did you know it was her?'

'All our animals are microchipped. But I'd know her anywhere, and she recognised me too, knew I was trying to help.' Penny kissed Angel's forehead and stretched out her hind legs, exposing an emaciated abdomen. More gasps from the audience. Three joeys clung to Angel's belly. 'Afflicted she-devils are extraordinarily devoted, never abandoning their young. Instead, a mother steadfastly feeds and protects her joeys until the very last moments of her life. We're just waiting for Angel's babies to be a few weeks older, closer to weaning. Then we'll euthanise her.' Penny tucked Angel's legs back in as comfortably as she could. 'You won't suffer anymore then, sweetheart.' The devil laid her poor, mutilated head in the crook of Penny's arm.

After the seminar, Penny sold a few souvenirs as people left. Sarah Deville stood by, watching a volunteer carry Angel out in a crate. 'Can you show me a healthy one?'

'Of course. Just let me lock up.'

Penny entered the shady enclosure where Bonny and her babies snored in a hollow log. She beckoned for Sarah to follow.

Sarah hesitated. 'Won't they bite?'

'Our devils are used to handling,' said Penny. 'And Bonny here, in particular, is a complete pushover.' As promised, sleepy Bonny let Penny pull her from the log to show off her four babies.

'Is it true they eat anything?' asked Sarah.

'Pretty much,' said Penny. 'We've found all sorts of things in their scat. Boot leather, bottle tops, cigarette butts. Even echidna quills. Their stomach acids have a bone-dissolving enzyme.' Sarah squealed as one little devil ran up Penny's arm and sat on her shoulder. Penny tickled the baby's tummy. 'These joeys really should be independent by now, but little Zoe here is a persistent late suckler, so they'll stay with mum a bit longer.' Penny placed Zoe in Sarah's arms. 'Some people call baby devils imps,' she said. 'For good reason.'

'Where's her white stripe?' asked Sarah. 'The others look like they're wearing football jerseys.'

'Sixteen percent of devils are melanic – all black.'

The tiny devil nestled in, examined Sarah's arm with her wet, pink nose then climbed up to chew her sunglasses. Sarah seemed charmed. 'Zoe's adorable, like a cute little kitten with a great big attitude. Nothing like I imagined.'

Penny couldn't resist asking. 'An international expert on devil genetics and you've never met one? Isn't that a bit odd?'

'I suppose so. At home I'm a human cancer geneticist. This devil gig started off as a purely intellectual exercise, but it's not anymore.' A flock of emerald rosellas landed in the bottlebrush branches above them. 'What a beautiful place to work. My lab in Hobart isn't quite so picturesque. Still, I'd love to show you around it some time.'

Penny grinned. She'd been silly to worry. Dr Deville was lovely.

'Why not stay back and have dinner with us tonight?' she said. 'If we're going to be working together, we may as well get to know each other.'

'Brilliant,' said Sarah. 'An invitation too good to refuse.'

CHAPTER 3

Matt drove to the Hills End racecourse feeling numb, last night's tragedy on repeat in his aching head. He missed the turn-off and arrived late, after the first race. Colourful marquees dotted the lawns on either side of the driveway. Crowds of people, with glasses of wine or cans of beer in hand, wandered around the grounds – men in penguin suits and women wearing ridiculous hats. Matt drove past, shaking his head, and parked next to the grandstand. A flock of pigeons circled the sky above. Dozens more cooed and strutted along steel stanchions beneath the roof. When patrons filled the stand, a steady stream of pigeon poo rained down on them. That's where the peregrines came in. Bernie Dobbs, chairman of the racing committee, walked over and slapped Matt on the back.

'Best get those birds in the air. The stand's filling up fast.' Bernie peered in the window at the raptors. 'Got a surprise for you today, Matt. Our special guest of honour.' Matt began arranging rabbit strips and lures. 'Fraser Abbott. He's donating money to redo the clubrooms. And he's interested in this hawk stunt of yours.'

'Falcons,' said Matt. 'They're falcons.'

'Catch up with us later in the members' marquee. Fraser's expecting you.'

Matt snorted and turned his back. Fat chance of that.

Bernie peered in the jeep window again and grinned. 'Good. You've brought the eagle. He puts on quite a show.'

'She does. *She* puts on a show,' said Matt through gritted teeth.

After Bernie left, Matt punched the jeep, startling the falcons. Of all the rotten luck. After the shock of last night he was finding it hard enough to concentrate. And now with this news about Fraser Abbott being at the track? Things had just got ten times worse. Perhaps he should simply pack up and go home. No, he wasn't ready to face Penny. So he set about preparing Sooty and Sweep for flight.

Falconry for falconry's sake was illegal in Tasmania. But it wasn't illegal to fly raptors for rehabilitation and education. After wing injuries or hospital stays, birds lacked stamina. They needed space to exercise, more space than flight aviaries allowed. Free flying was also the only way to teach orphaned young falcons to take live prey. This resident flock of plump, lazy pigeons presented the peregrines with a perfect opportunity to hone their hunting skills.

Falconers required the confidence of their haughty birds. This made training a tricky and demanding business. Matt dared not chastise Sooty or Sweep in any way for fear of breaching their trust. But, equally, falcons weren't inclined to please. He'd never come across any creature more proud or independent than a peregrine – except, perhaps, for Penny.

To elicit the birds' cooperation, Matt established daily routines – food rewards at random times, trying to recreate the hit and miss nature of hunting. After many months of training, Sooty and Sweep were moving ever closer to release, their focus subtly shifting. They paid more attention to their surrounds, noticed the overhead shadow of passing birds, kept a close watch on each other as a bonding pair should.

In a few weeks, Matt would drive them into the ranges to a remote rocky pass bordered by towering cliffs. There he would witness their freedom flight. Though not without regret. Peregrines were swift and courageous, the preferred birds for hawking. Once upon a time, Matt might have presented this expertly trained pair to a duke or a prince –

won acclaim for his skill, his finely-tuned falcons, his grasp of the craft. Successful release was a wonderful achievement, but part of him always mourned the loss of these special birds. All that training wasted, overcome by wild spirit, the birds' singular human connection forever forgotten.

Sooty and Sweep sat alert on their perches. Matt nodded approval at how they eyed the sky when he removed their hoods. Next, Matt fetched Aquila from the jeep. She'd been raised by carnies who took dodgem cars around agricultural shows. They'd handed her in when she ate their cat. After such a cosmopolitan upbringing, Aquila was quite at home with crowds. Matt used her in free-flight demonstrations on these sorts of occasions, hoping to attract corporate sponsors for the Raptor Rescue Program.

A few folk began to gather around the jeep.

'They're peregrines right? What does peregrine mean?' asked a boy.

An intelligent question, for a change. 'It's from the Latin, *Falco peregrinus*,' said Matt. 'It means wandering falcon.'

'So why are they called raptors?'

'They're not raptors. They're just birds,' said a skinny young woman in heels.

How disappointed they always were to discover raptors weren't bloodthirsty dinosaurs chasing Sam Neill around a movie set. Matt frowned and shuffled a little. He was no people person, and shouldered this promotional role with barely disguised distaste.

'Raptors are carnivorous birds with hooked beaks and talons. Birds of prey. The word *raptor* is also from Latin. *Rapio* – to seize.'

'Ooh, seize me any time, tiger,' cooed the skinny one. Her friends giggled.

Bernie came back over to see what was happening. 'Will you hurry up and get those hawks flying?'

Matt glared at him and untethered the falcons. He swung two colourful feathered lures at once. The pair dived in unison and each bird claimed a prize. The crowd clapped. Matt rewarded the falcons with scraps of food. Not too much now. He needed them keen enough to catch a meal.

Nervous pigeons wheeled in a grey cloud overhead. The flock abruptly split in two and fled the skies above the stand in opposite directions. A faint high-pitched whistle confirmed his fear. Of all the rotten luck. A wild peregrine hurtled from heaven and broadsided a straggling pigeon. Predator and prey crashed to earth in the grassy middle of the racecourse. Nobody else seemed to notice. The pigeons vanished into the distance. Sooty and Sweep chose this moment to fly from their perch up to the grandstand. Bernie beamed – all he saw was a sky clear of pigeons, and the falcons sitting on the roof.

'Great work, mate. Those birds of yours finished the job in record time.'

There was no point trying to explain what had really happened to a man as dense as Bernie. 'No problem,' said Matt. 'Raptor Rescue is here to help.' The wild falcon finished her meal, climbed the breeze and disappeared.

A field of horses swept along the rails. People roared. The ground trembled. Aquila spread her wings and hopped along the perch, proud head bowed. Matt removed her hood. The curious eagle always enjoyed the sight and sound of an audience. Sooty and Sweep hopped a little further away. He'd better bring the hungry falcons down from the roof before they grew too impatient. He reached for the lures. Now, children crowded too close to Aquila. Matt shooed them off. Where was his gauntlet? When he turned around, the falcons were gone.

A succession of screams rose from the far side of the grandstand. Matt sprinted around the corner. A sign before a roped-off section read Fashions on the Field. Everywhere, ladies in smart frocks, high heels and fancy hats were running for cover. Sooty and Sweep crouched on the dais in proud possession of a pair of plumed bonnets they'd mistaken for lures. Such pandemonium over two harmless little birds. The falcons eyed his approach, wings folded protectively over their hats, eager for their reward. Sweep's talons crushed a feathery fascinator. Matt edged closer, with clucks and low whistles. Slowly does it. But as he was about to reclaim his birds, an irate steward ran over, flapping a coat, shouting and shooing.

Sooty and Sweep flew away. Specks in the sky, soon vanishing altogether.

Matt turned on the man in a fury. 'Why the devil did you do that? Those birds aren't ready to fend for themselves.'

But now there were fresh screams. Matt whirled to see Aquila sail in low flight above the crowd, intent on something, hunting something. He scanned the ground ahead of her flight path.

There, in the centre of the racecourse. A small white poodle chewed on the remains of the pigeon taken minutes before by the wild falcon.

Matt raced for the dog, but his mission was hopeless. Aquila soared past Matt's head, banked and took precise aim. Seconds later her extended talons crushed the pet's skull. The eagle screeched and stood over the dead poodle, wings spread in defence of her prey. Matt approached with soothing words and rabbit strips. Aquila folded her wings, accepted the offering and consented to step onto Matt's ungauntleted arm. Razor claws sliced through his cotton sleeve. Bracing against the pain, Matt took her hood from his pocket, slipped it on and fastened her jesses. Angry race officials converged on the pair. Judging discretion to be the better part of valour, Matt hurried back to the jeep, leaving the bloodied corpse of the dog where it lay.

Matt and Bernie reached the jeep at the same time. 'I'm shooting that bird,' said Bernie, 'and suing you as well. Our anniversary race day ruined. Patrons terrified. Children traumatised ...'

'It's children who are to blame,' said a third voice. It came from the jeep. Fraser Burns Abbott climbed from the driver's seat. 'In particular this child.' Fraser pulled a sulky-looking boy of about twelve from the back. 'I saw him untie the eagle's tether.'

'Brodie?' said Bernie.

'Sorry, dad,' the boy mumbled miserably.

'So, seeing it's *your* son who's responsible,' said Fraser, 'I believe you owe mine an apology, eh?'

Both men looked at Matt, who stood by with the eagle, blood

streaming down his arm. 'There's still the Fashions On The Field fiasco. Not to mention the cost of two very expensive hats,' said Bernie.

Fraser took out his wallet and pressed a wad of notes into Bernie's hand. 'That should cover it.'

Bernie sputtered in protest, but not too hard.

'I'd hate to have to reconsider funding those clubrooms.'

Bernie conceded defeat and dragged his sulky son off by the collar of his shirt. Fraser laughed as he watched them go.

'I didn't need your help,' said Matt, transferring Aquila to the cadge and trying to wrap his injured arm in an old towel, without much success.

'Yes, you did, Matthew. Turn around so we can talk.'

Matt faced his father, who indicated a nearby bench. He frowned, then sat down. So did Fraser. It was odd to be beside this man again after so many years. Fraser looked older, thinner, smaller. But he retained that brusque, imperious manner that was so irritating – intimidating as well.

'Okay, talk,' said Matt. 'But make it quick.'

'Very well. I'm dying, son. Doctors say I may have a year, maybe not ...'

Matt silently digested the news.

Fraser narrowed his eyes, inspecting Matt's face. 'I have a proposition for you.'

'Not interested.'

'Have the companies, Matthew. Have the lot. Burns Timber and Hydro, Hills End Mining, Costain Constructions, their subsidiaries. The board will vote you CEO if you want.'

Fraser rushed his words as if he'd practised them, as if to spit them out before he changed his mind.

'What's the catch?'

'No catch. No strings.'

Matt didn't believe it. He didn't believe any of it. His father wasn't dying. This was some sort of malicious trick, one more attempt to rope him into the stinking family business. Matt stood up, packed the last of his gear into the jeep one-handed, and climbed behind the wheel.

'You'd best get that arm seen to,' said Fraser, his voice rising a notch.

Matt turned the engine over.

Fraser laid a hand on the car. 'I'll be damned if I'll let you leave like this!'

Matt leaned out the window. 'You're damned already, Dad.'

'Pity about that other falcon.'

This took Matt by surprise. He didn't think anyone else had spotted the wild bird who'd set off today's chain of disastrous events.

Fraser's eyes blazed with a strange intensity. '"Turning and turning in the widening gyre / The falcon cannot hear the falconer; / Things fall apart."'

Matt hesitated, then set his jaw, spun the wheel and sped away.

CHAPTER 4

Penny bustled about the table for the umpteenth time, straightening the cloth and rearranging the centrepiece. In a vase, spikes of golden lily and frail snowy pompoms of bushman's bootlace framed the dramatic heart of crimson waratahs.

'What's the big deal with this Yank anyway?' asked Matt, half-amused, half-annoyed by all the fuss. He did not need an impromptu social engagement tonight. He needed time to himself – time to think.

A cascade of unruly red curls swirled about Penny's freckled face, and he felt the familiar pull of attraction. How lovely his wife was. She hardly ever wore her hair loose like that anymore.

'Take the dips from the fridge and get three wine glasses. She'll be here any minute.'

'*Jawohl, mein Kommandant.* Don't worry that my arm's all torn up.'

'It's your left one, isn't it? Can you manage with the right?'

Matt saluted and did as she asked. Penny glanced at the clock, cast an appraising eye over the table and another out the window. Her eyes widened. 'Sarah's here. Quick, take this.' She thrust a heavy glass platter laden with olives, cheese and crackers at him.

Matt took it awkwardly and, as Penny whipped off her apron, he fumbled and dropped the platter. 'Sorry, Pen.' He held out his injured arm by way of explanation.

Sarah knocked on the door. Penny knelt to retrieve the cracked dish. Grapes rolled across the worn carpet. Chunks of soft cheese clung to bits of fluff. The knock came again. Matt reached for the door. 'No,' mouthed Penny.

Too late. Dr Sarah Deville stepped over the threshold, smiled and shook Matt's hand. After a full day's field work she still looked fresh, glamorous even. Penny got to her feet with the salvaged tray, feeling her face flush to match the colour of her hair. She kicked an olive under the couch.

'Just a little accident.' She forced a smile. 'Nothing to worry about. Would you like some wine?'

Sarah nodded. 'Red, if you have it.'

Penny escaped into the kitchen with the broken platter, and reappeared with a bottle of wine in one hand and a tea towel in the other. Not one of their regular tea towels, not faded with a stain or two. This one was brand new and more like a mini beach towel. It featured a devil print and boasted a terry towelling thickness worthy of the finest shag pile. She must have raided the souvenir stand.

Penny used it to give the sparkling glasses on the sideboard a final polish. Matt handed each woman a shiraz and poured one for himself. Sarah was staring at Matt's bandaged arm, or maybe she wasn't staring. Maybe she always watched the world with such singular intensity. Matt stopped himself from staring back. Dr Deville was quite a looker.

'This?' He raised his injured arm. 'I'm accident-prone, aren't I, Pen? This is from an eagle.'

As Sarah went to sit at the table, Penny's hand dived under her descending rear and wiped the chair with the glorious tea towel. Sarah jumped up like she'd been shot, spilling her drink. Beads of red wine rolled down her cream shirt.

'There was spilt milk on the seat,' said Penny in a tone of horrified apology. 'It must have been from when Matt fed Paddy. I didn't want you to sit on it.'

Sarah dabbed at her stained front with a paper serviette, and waved away Penny's offer of help. After a close examination of her chair, she cautiously sat down. An awkward silence ensued. Penny's embarrassment had rendered her speechless.

'What's a Yank doing out here, studying our devils?' asked Matt, trying to help.

Sarah fixed him with tawny eyes. 'I visited the Field Museum of Chicago a few years ago and came across this.' She scrolled through her phone, leaned close and showed him a photo. 'So peculiar. Like a little mutant wolverine.'

Penny came around from the other side of the table to see. In the jaundiced glow of a display case sat a stuffed devil. Its heavy head swung a fraction to the right. Tired jaws gaped, weary tongue protruded. Unseeing eyes bore an expression of eternal defeat. Fading forever on its fake rock, surrounded by strands of long-dead grass, the devil was sadness incarnate.

'I was curious about my namesake. *Such* an interesting study. Do you realise how rare contagious cancers are? There are only three ever recorded.' Sarah paused for a sip of wine. 'Canine transmissible tumour, a comparable cancer, was first described a century ago. It's intriguing to reinterpret that data in light of your devils' disease.'

Matt couldn't help grinning. 'You're as weird as my wife.'

Penny almost choked on her drink. But before long even Matt conceded that cancer was a fascinating malady, at least the way Sarah described it. Malignant cells, cloning themselves in an anarchy of spurned rules, theoretically immortal. But these rogues faced a dilemma. When their host died, so did they. Contagious cancers had learned to cheat death.

'It's quite a trick,' said Sarah. 'Take canine transmissible tumours. Diseased samples from fifty dogs across five continents share identical genetic markers. That means each tumour evolved from one single ancestor, from one diseased cell, in one ancient dog. The oldest lineage of mammalian cells on earth, unchanged for hundreds, maybe thousands of years, achieving eternal life by outliving their original host.'

'Real-life body-snatchers,' said Penny, going back to her seat opposite Sarah.

'Exactly.' Sarah finished her wine. 'By then I was hooked, and spent a year collaborating remotely with a team of Aussie scientists. We finally have a complete map of the devil's DNA.'

'The holy grail for marsupial biologists,' said Penny in an awed tone.

'Hardly,' said Sarah. 'That gong would go to a complete thylacine genome, don't you think?'

'Yes, of course, you're right.' Penny may as well have said *silly me*. Matt had never seen her so starstruck.

Sarah offered her glass and Matt refilled it. 'The more I learned about devils, the more I wondered about Tasmania. Somewhere unimaginable, somewhere far beyond the city lights that keep Los Angeles stars permanently at bay.' Penny sighed. Sarah did have a way with words. 'Anyway, having a year's leave up my sleeve, I agreed to head up this devil genotyping project. And that,' she said, 'is where you guys come in.' Sarah flashed an ivory smile. 'You're doing some amazing work here at Binburra. But my concern is your insurance devils. I'm not sure your animals have enough genetic variety.'

'We thought Winston did,' said Penny. 'Researchers inoculated three of our devils with dead cancer cells, then injected them with live ones.'

Matt heard the effort in Penny's voice, the effort to sound professional. She'd cried long and hard the night before that research team came. It didn't matter that it was for the good of the species in the long run. Those were her babies.

'Two died,' said Penny. 'But Winston produced antibodies. He was free of cancer for a whole year. Then they injected him with a different strain. He was fine for six months. The saviour of the species we thought – we hoped. But in July we found two tumours.' Her voice cracked. 'It broke my heart.'

'I know about Winston,' said Sarah.

Penny's face fell. 'Of *course* you do. Sorry, I—'

'Any resistance is encouraging.' Sarah's smile seemed a touch condescending. She took a folder from her bag and produced a chart. 'I've mapped the DNA of one hundred devils statewide. Each colour represents a genetically identical cohort. We don't have many samples from this region, but those we do have are all in the green group – meaning no genetic diversity at all.'

Matt frowned as he realised the significance of Sarah's words.

'But our insurance devils are from this region,' said Penny.

'There's the problem. Your gene pool is weak. Even if your ark animals do beat DFTD, the next thing will probably carry them off.'

Penny looked as though she was going to apologise again, as if inbred devils were somehow her fault. Matt came to the rescue. 'How can we help, Sarah?'

'I need hair samples from as many devils as possible. My goal is to test each captive animal in the state, and a lot of the wild ones. I'll run the samples through a genome sequencer and map them genetically. Then you guys can matchmake based on scientific principles, not guesswork. How does that sound?'

'Brilliant,' said Penny. 'What does a genome sequencer look like?'

'Like a fancy washing machine with a computer screen on top,' said Sarah. 'Back home, my lab looks like a high tech laundromat. Before the sequencers it was agonising work. Manual readings, a single genome divided between thousands of international project teams. Some scientists joked that they'd rather be executed than endure a stint on the sequencing chain gang. But today it's almost routine.'

'How does it work?'

'You take some DNA, the tiniest scrap will do: saliva, skin cells, even hair follicles from ancient hides. The machine chops it up in multiple ways, sequences the fragments, and jigsaws them back together.'

Penny leaned further across the table. It was a wonder she wasn't taking notes.

'Think about tearing up fifty copies of a book,' said Sarah. 'Then mixing them up and trying to put them back together. You can't imagine the sort of RAM it takes. But even so, the cost of sequencing keeps dropping and computers triple in speed each year. Before long, sequencers will sit in doctors' offices and give you a personal genetic read-out while you wait.'

The oven timer beeped a rude interruption. Penny headed to the kitchen with a disappointed expression on her face. 'Show Sarah our babies while I serve up,' she called over her shoulder. 'Let her feed Paddy if she likes.'

Sarah looked doubtfully at Matt's injured arm. 'I'm not entirely useless,' he assured her, and escorted Sarah to the dimly lit lounge room. A wood heater glowed in one corner. An owl hooted from atop a crowded bookshelf and a little wombat poked its nose out from under a frayed couch. A dozen pillowslips hung from low hooks along the wall, like Christmas stockings in an orphanage. Matt lifted a tiny wallaby from the nearest pouch and gave it to Sarah. The joey lay warm and wide-eyed, barely furred, cradled in the crook of her arm. Penny brought in a bottle of milk with an odd extended teat, handed it to Sarah and returned to the kitchen. Despite Sarah's best efforts, the little pademelon refused to suckle. It twisted its head from side to side, spattering milk all about.

'Here, let me.' Matt eased Paddy from Sarah's arms, sponged the joey clean, then expertly guided teat to mouth. Paddy fed in a greedy ecstasy of gangly legs and jutting tail. 'Take this, will you? And give me that.' Sarah took the empty bottle from his hand and substituted a tube of sorbolene. Matt massaged dollops of the cream into Paddy's soft skin, all the while whispering sweet nothings. His fingers worked with delicate care.

'Mum's pouch was humid,' he explained. 'It kept Paddy's skin supple. These artificial pouches are dry, so we need to use a lubricant.' He took a damp cotton ball, massaged Paddy's bottom, caught a smudge of faeces on a tissue and binned it. Then he washed the soiled fur, patted it dry, bundled Paddy up neatly in a clean bunny rug and replaced the sleepy youngster in its pouch.

'You certainly are *not* useless,' said Sarah as Penny came into the room and took the empty bottle. 'Your husband's amazing,' Sarah said to her. 'Such gentle hands.'

Penny's face softened and she favoured Matt with a smile. 'He's wonderful with the babies.'

Sarah and Matt followed Penny to the kitchen. 'You have such a lot of mouths to feed,' said Sarah. 'It must be hard work.'

'It is,' agreed Penny. 'Hard and complicated work, but I don't mind. I'm an orphan myself, so I know how they feel.' Penny lifted the lid from a pot of steaming rice. 'We need lots of different formulas. For possums, for wallabies, for wombats. Dasyurids like devils and quolls are different again.' Penny pointed to a bench cluttered with tins and teats and bottles. 'You've got four kinds of milk replacer for macropods, four for possums and gliders, more for echidnas and wombats. And another for the bats.'

'The bats?' asked Sarah.

Penny pulled a casserole dish and foil-wrapped loaf from the oven. 'Tasmania has eight species of bats. Only the little ones though, the microbats. We've six in the laundry right now. Matt, can you show Sarah the bats?'

In the large laundry, a fridge and two industrial-sized chest freezers stood against one wall. Rows of cotton-lined wooden boxes sat on a table, secured at the top with taut flyscreens. Matt slipped on gloves and extracted a small grey bat from a box. It had an odd squashed nose, prominent ears and sharp thumb-claws on each satin wing. 'Exhibit A … the large forest bat.'

'But it's so tiny,' said Sarah in wonder.

'As opposed to Exhibit B … the little forest bat.' He extracted an even smaller bat, barely five centimetres long, with the tiniest hands and feet imaginable. 'Montgomery's not weaned yet.' Matt held up a tiny syringe.

Sarah stifled a giggle. 'You're kidding me. You feed that flying mini-mouse milk? And he's called Montgomery?'

All through their dinner of vegetable curry, Sarah was full of batty questions.

'They fly around the lounge room at night to exercise their wings,' said Penny. 'Of course, we put Hedwig away first.' The bookshelf owl hooted on cue from the lounge room.

'They're rodents, right? Like mice?' said Sarah.

'Ever heard of a mouse with echo-location radar?' said Matt.

'Speaking of flying mice …' said Penny.

'Here we go.' Matt settled back in his chair.

Penny was a taxidermist. She held a licence to mount native animals, and wanted to set up a museum at the Sanctuary. State law meant she couldn't sell natives, but she was already earning extra money stuffing dead pets for grieving owners. She made jewellery from bits and pieces of non-natives, using rabbit tails and feathers and fins. Penny's bestselling brooch was a mouse, with rhinestones for eyes and a tail cast in bronze. At Christmas time she made tree decorations, picking the prettiest white mice from the reptile feeder packs, stuffing them with cotton balls and attaching tiny angel wings sourced from craft shops.

Penny jumped up from the table and returned with a container of tiny stuffed mice angels, not much bigger than Montgomery. Sarah examined one, stroked its snowy fur and traced the wire in its wings with her finger. 'These are cute,' said Sarah. 'Bizarre … but cute.' Penny looked pleased and fetched some trays of mouse jewellery to the table. Sarah oohed and aahed politely.

'Wherever did you get the idea?'

'My great-great-something-grandmother came here from England in 1856 to mount specimens for the Royal Society. She ended up a taxidermist at the Australian Museum in Sydney. Ten pounds a month, same pay as the men. She ran a business with her daughter. They won medals at all sorts of international shows. They might have even mounted that devil you saw in the Chicago museum.' From the sideboard drawer, Penny extracted a yellowed newspaper clipping in a plastic sleeve. The 1893 article about the World Taxidermy Exposition in Chicago announced Mrs Jane Tost and Mrs Ada Rohu as winner and runner-up of the Supreme Champion Exhibit. It went on to claim that '… a good deal of bird and animal stuffing in Australia is performed, oddly enough, by females.'

'Okay, but that was centuries ago,' said Sarah. 'What made *you* want to do it?'

Matt watched Penny check herself. Her strange passion wasn't something she usually talked about, for she rarely got a good response.

'Go on,' said Sarah. 'You *have* to tell me.'

'Well ... death and life go hand in hand, don't they? I want to create my own museum here at Binburra.'

Sarah considered this. 'What was it like the first time?'

'I thought I mightn't be able to do it, but it's not like there's blood and guts everywhere. When you strip the skin, the body's quite neat, contained in muscle. It's beautiful really ...'

Sarah had that look on her face, the one Matt had seen too often when Penny explained her odd hobby. A combination of distaste and incomprehension.

'I'll get dessert,' said Penny, and hurried to the kitchen.

'Let's hear about you then, Dr Deville,' said Matt. 'Why are you so interested in our little bats?'

'As a kid, at twilight, I'd watch little bats dip in and out of pools of lamplight in the park. I called them my shadow angels. Now they're gone. I still look for them, but haven't seen one in years.' She sounded suddenly sad. 'I think pesticides killed them off. City Hall uses a lot of pesticides these days. Climate change has people scared of mosquito-borne tropical diseases, like West Nile virus and malaria.'

Sarah picked up her wine glass, then put it back down as Matt began to speak. 'Bats are top insect predators. They'll eat their weight in mozzies each night. Without your shadow angels, mozzies will swarm back in ten times the numbers, and immune to pesticides to boot. The bats won't bounce back like that.'

'Don't they have big litters, like mice?'

Matt shook his head. 'I told you. They're not like mice. They're like us. Just one, maybe two babies at a time.'

Penny came in with cheesecake and coffee. She caught the end of the conversation. 'One out of every five mammals alive on earth at this very moment is a bat,' she said. 'People don't realise.' The conversation ground to a halt. Penny began to serve dessert.

Sarah waved her hand. 'None for me. It's late. I should let you guys get to bed.'

Penny looked bereft. 'Not even coffee?'

'No thanks,' said Sarah. 'Well, I'll see you in a few weeks when you come to Hobart. By the way, do you have a name for your little jewellery line?'

'Memento Mori,' said Penny

'And it means?'

'Aah … it means 'Remember you shall die.'

Sarah smiled a tight smile and turned to leave.

'I'll walk you to the car,' said Penny, finding a torch and turning on the outside light.

Sarah held up her hand. 'No need.' She let herself out.

Matt and Penny moved as one to the window and stood side by side, watching her leave. Sarah paused for a moment in the glow of a single cobwebbed verandah globe, then stepped into the darkness. A minute later her headlights blinked on.

'That went well,' said Matt, when she was finally gone.

Penny groaned and lay her head on his shoulder. 'You wash, I'll dry.'

CHAPTER 5

Penny had waited weeks for Sarah to ask her to Hobart, and the invitation had finally come. On the way into town they stopped at the old zoo site.

'I never did like it here,' said Penny.

Sarah gazed about and nodded. 'It's certainly not what I imagined.'

They stood beside a busy road, in front of a tall pair of padlocked gates on the edge of Hobart's Queens Domain parklands. Not the original gates – they were long gone. White letters, set in a high steel frame, spelt out *Beaumaris Zoo* across a blue-tiled background bordered in red.

Once upon a time this quiet place shook to the roar of lions, the screech of monkeys and the coughing barks of Tasmanian tigers. Once there were turnstiles and ticket collectors and Sunday families. Now, forlorn animal sculptures of beaten tin guarded the gates. One of them was a sad-looking thylacine.

Sarah peered through the iron bars, past a few derelict wooden buildings set in a bare, rocky hillside. A two-metre chain-link fence, topped with barbed wire, secured the grim site. 'So this is where the last one died?'

'In 1936. There's not much to see now,' said Penny. 'The site's contaminated. The Navy used it for fuel storage after the zoo closed.'

'What a wasted opportunity,' said Sarah, shaking her head. 'Back home this place would be a tourist attraction. There'd at least be some sort of memorial.' Sarah read a sign on the gate. 'It says here that a woman started the zoo?'

'Mary Grant Roberts – a real hero of mine. The first person to breed devils and publish the findings. That was back in 1915, and I still use her notes today. She really liked devils, tried to give them an image makeover.'

Sarah rattled the gates.

'It's private property,' said Penny. 'You can't go in.'

Sarah slipped through a break in the wire and headed up the hill. Penny looked around to see if anybody was watching, then climbed through the gap and set off after her. She caught up with Sarah high on the hill, at the ruins of a circular stone enclosure.

'The old polar bear pit,' said Penny. 'The thylacines were over there.' She pointed behind the wrecked walls. 'There's nothing left of their pen now.'

'Polar bears?' asked Sarah. 'I didn't realise.'

'The zoo held all sorts of exotics,' said Penny. 'Lions and tigers. Monkeys and zebras and elephants. A leopard that went for a daily walk on a leash around The Domain. Thylacines didn't attract much interest from the public back then.'

'The fools didn't realise what they had.' Sarah turned to face the sweeping panorama across the Derwent River. A cold wind whipped off the water. 'And now Tasmanian tigers are gone.'

'Is anything ever really gone?' said Penny. 'They were here just a blink ago. There are traces of them everywhere – in the rivers, in the trees. We're breathing the same air they did ...' She kicked at a rock. 'Walking the same ground. Look back in time and they're just behind us. Look too far ahead and we're gone too.'

'You make it sound like a ghost story,' said Sarah. 'I'm a scientist. I don't believe in ghosts.'

Penny couldn't bear it any longer – the air of neglect and squandered chance, the sense of loss. Tasmania could be the loveliest place on earth and the saddest all at once. She ran down the hill, squeezed back through the fence and waited in the car. Penny didn't like people to deliberately flout the rules, but she'd make an exception for Sarah, the way she had for Matt. He'd done the very same thing last time they were here.

No matter. Here came Sarah now, and in a few minutes they'd be in Macquarie Street, stepping into Penny's favourite place – the Tasmanian Museum and Art Gallery. It didn't matter how often she visited the eternal twilight of its corridors, its last-century dioramas and ancient art. She always got that delicious, anticipatory tingle, and today would be more special than usual. Today she was helping Sarah collect hair samples from the museum's historical devil collection.

Sarah reached the car. How did she manage to always look so good? Penny caught her own reflection in the mirror. Hair a mess, half out of its band. Frizzy, stray locks dangling down her face. Sarah's hair merely looked fashionably wind-swept.

Penny swung sharply into the light traffic stream, heading south into Hobart along the Domain Highway. Her mind wasn't really on the driving. A few impatient beeps didn't bother her, not on a day like today. Not when the fun was about to begin.

The basement vault smelled like a funeral home and was filled with treasures. They were onto their thirteenth devil; this one a joey, poorly preserved and thinly furred. Barely enough hair to collect a decent sample. Penny heaved a great contented sigh. What a privilege to have access to the specimen stacks, to dozens of devils she could otherwise have never hoped to see. Such an incredible range of taxidermies. Some good, some bad, some complete aberrations; hack jobs, turning the devils into freakish crosses between bug-eyed weasels and cringing beavers. Patrick Duff, curator of vertebrate zoology, was a sallow man, who looked half embalmed himself. He brought out the next specimen, a jewel by comparison to the rest. So real, it might at any moment escape its frame.

Penny couldn't resist a delighted squeal. 'That's an Alison Reid.'

Patrick's lips split in a bloodless smile.

'Alison Reid?' asked Sarah.

'Last person to run the Hobart Zoo, the one who walked that leopard round The Domain,' said Penny. 'Her father was the curator. When he died in 1935 she unofficially took over.'

'Miss Reid was also a brilliant taxidermist,' said Patrick, 'as evidenced by this mount.' He beamed at the stuffed devil. 'Years ahead of her time and an unfortunate victim of the patriarchy – denied the curatorship because nobody believed a woman could run the zoo. Truth was, she was the only person qualified to do so. It folded within months of her being forced out.'

Sarah placed the latest sample into her insulated bag. 'Enough morbid talk.' She smiled her perfect smile. 'Take me to lunch, Patrick.' Penny gave a little groan. 'Penny's hungry as well,' said Sarah. 'I heard her tummy rumble.'

It couldn't be lunchtime already. The last thing Penny wanted was to be dragged away from the collection.

'I know just the place.' Patrick peeled surgical gloves from his elegant white hands. 'Meet you at the cafe in a jiffy.' He disappeared up the stairs.

'Salamanca Market is on today,' said Penny. 'We could have a quick browse? Get something to eat there instead?'

Sarah looked unimpressed at the prospect of lunching at a street stall. 'Let's wait for Patrick. He already has a place in mind.'

On their way to the courtyard cafe they passed through the Indigenous gallery. Sarah stopped to stare at a portrait of an Aboriginal man holding a firestick.

'He looks so dignified,' said Sarah. 'I wonder who he was.'

'That's Mannalargenna,' said Penny. 'Chief of the Ben Lomond tribe. He led a guerrilla war against the British.'

Sarah peered at the sign. 'So it is.'

Why did she sound surprised? 'I should know,' said Penny. 'After all, Mannalargenna and me – we're related.'

Sarah shot her a sceptical look. 'That can't be. Aboriginal Tasmanians are all gone.'

'I told you, nothing's ever really gone.' Penny pointed to a grainy photo of a seated young woman with a Mona Lisa smile. 'Read the sign.'

'Dolly Dalrymple,' said Sarah. 'Born to George Briggs, a sealer, and Woretemoeteryenner, daughter of Mannalargenna.' She turned to Penny. 'I can't get my tongue around these names.'

'Keep reading,' said Penny.

'Dolly Dalrymple was the first child in Tasmania known to be born to an Aboriginal mother and a European father.'

'Dolly is my nanna's grandmother,' said Penny.

'But your red hair? Your freckles?'

Penny shrugged. 'You're the geneticist. We're talking just a drop of DNA.'

'Still, it's intriguing. To think you have the blood of an extinct race.'

Extinct? Penny sighed. Sarah wasn't the most perceptive person, that was for sure. 'Maybe I have an Irish complexion,' she said, 'and a black heart.'

Upstairs, in the cafe, Penny sipped a coffee and hoped Patrick would change his mind about lunch. Salamanca wasn't just any market. It was a world-famous showcase of Tasmanian products. All set near the waterfront, between spreading plane trees and the sandstone facades of historic Georgian warehouses. Far more interesting for an international visitor than one of Patrick's fine dining choices, aimed at people with more money than sense. Some place that charged twice as much, for half as much, and that Penny couldn't afford anyway.

'How did you meet Matt?' Sarah asked suddenly, taking Penny off guard. An odd question, and a little too personal. Penny wasn't sure she wanted to answer, but Sarah's expression was so expectant and friendly.

'We met at the show, the Hills End show.' Sarah looked blank. 'It's like a country fair. I was at the woodchop. My boyfriend back then,

Scott, he was state champion. Anyway, Matt came over. Asked me, if he won the woodchop, would I go on a date with him. I was that flattered. Fraser Abbott's son and all, and the best-looking bloke I'd ever seen. So I said yes. Matt entered the comp at the last minute and won.'

'And Scott?'

'Scott was furious. Accused Matt of being a spoilt silvertail, lording it over the rest of us. My uncle had to break up the fight. I kept my word, though, went on the date, and the rest is history. We were married six months later.'

'How old were you?'

'Eighteen.'

Sarah looked nonplussed. 'That's very romantic, but you were both so young. How could you possibly know?'

'Beats me,' said Penny. 'We just did.'

Patrick saved her from further questions. He arrived wearing his most unctuous smile, and expounded the wonders of a particularly wanky restaurant famed for *nouvelle cuisine*.

'I'm going for a walk instead.' Penny slipped away, down to the street, drawn by the smell of salt spray and the mellow aroma of coffee and croissants. The market was crowded and filled with music. Buskers strummed folk songs, stroked harps or sang the blues. Street performers did circus tricks in the sun. You could get a feed here for a song: pumpkin muffins, steamed dim sims, the freshest fish and chips possible. And then there was the art and jewellery and handcrafted local timbers. What a shame Sarah wasn't here to see it all.

Penny wandered along the stalls. Under the shade of a snow-white awning, a trestle table groaned with exquisite cupcakes, each an individual work of art. She stopped to admire their buttery adornments. The children's were the best: sugarplum fairies, ghosts, pigs and humpty dumpties. One was a bee. There was even a three-tiered christening cupcake. If she had a little boy or girl, she'd buy them. Shame she didn't have an excuse. Although there was Sarah. Cupcakes as a thank you? To show off what Salamanca had on offer, what she'd missed? Penny chose a classic foursome: zesty lemon drop, passionfruit obsession, butterscotch dream and triple-choc indulgence.

'Pop them cakes in the fridge soon as you get home, love,' said the beaming, big-bosomed woman as she handed over the neat box. 'It's a bit too warm for them today.' Penny nodded and turned to leave.

'Pen!' A tall man in a pirate hat waved wildly from the World Wildlife Fund stall further down. He vaulted his chair, sprinted to Penny and embraced her. 'It's been how long?'

'Drake! I didn't even know you were back. Matt never said.'

Drake gave her an inquisitorial look. 'How *is* Matt?'

Penny prepared to give the polite stock standard answer, but Drake's pale, penetrating eyes wouldn't tolerate the lie, so she said nothing at all.

'I've been trying to reach him for weeks now. He won't return calls. What's up, Pen?'

It was almost a relief to know that Matt was shutting other people out. It meant it wasn't just her. 'He seems to have a bit on his mind right now. I don't know … he won't talk to me.' She longed to tell Drake more. To tell him about Matt's black moods, about the nightmares that made his heart race beside her, and soaked their sheets with sweat.

Drake gave Penny a bear hug, then stood her at arm's length, holding her shoulders. 'I'll be in the Tuggerah next week.' The snake tattooed on his forearm seemed to stare at her. 'There are big plans afoot to stuff up Mum's re-election campaign.'

Penny smiled. Typical. Drake was always at loggerheads with his mother. Those two were as different as Matt and Fraser.

'Tell Matt I'll be seeing him soon, whether he likes it or not.'

'Good luck with that,' said Penny, gloomily. 'He's turned into a hermit. All he wants to do is go bush.'

'So what's new?'

Penny struggled to put her fears into words, loath to admit them even to herself. 'Matt's always been a loner, but this is different. He's up at dawn and disappears into the park without a word. Half the time I have no idea where he is or what he's doing. He's avoiding everyone.'

'I've noticed,' said Drake. 'Don't worry. I have a foolproof plan to grab his attention.'

'Of course you do.' Penny kissed his cheek. 'I hope it works.'

Drake bowed and returned to his stall. Within minutes he'd charmed donations from several passers-by. Drake certainly had charisma. He was also Matt's oldest friend, since primary school. Penny scrubbed a hand over her face. Time to admit that her marriage needed a circuit-breaker. Something was troubling Matt, and she had no idea what it was. He needed someone to talk to. Perhaps Drake would succeed where she had failed.

Penny returned to the museum and showed her pass to the man at the door. He pointed down a corridor leading to the basement. 'Last room on the left, miss. You can wait there for the others.'

Penny found herself in a small anteroom adjoining the vault's massive locked doors; an empty room save for two locked filing cabinets, a steel table and four chairs. She checked her watch. The others would still be ages. Patrick was renowned for his long lunches, even during the week, and this was Saturday.

Penny sat down and took a look at her cupcakes. Oh no … squashed … a gooey mess of crumbs and melted icing. What was she supposed to do? The room had no bin, and she couldn't bear for Sarah to see them now. Perhaps she could eat them. There was probably time.

Penny sat with her back to the door, scraped the lemon cupcake off the cardboard and jammed it into her mouth. Moist and delicious, the icing tingling like lemonade. Very rich, though. A cup of tea would be good. Penny finished the lemon cupcake and scooped up the disintegrated, triple-choc indulgence. Sublime. Was that a Lindt chocolate ball in the centre? How did they do that? Butterscotch dream next. In her haste to finish, she bit her tongue, and the cake's cloying sweetness made her gag.

'There you are.' Penny jumped at the sound of Sarah's voice. A jersey caramel flew from her mouth and hurtled across the room. She was choking on a shard of toffee, coughing and spluttering, as much with embarrassment as anything else.

Patrick galloped in, slapped her back several times, then rushed off for a glass of water. Sarah loomed before her, brows raised. Penny blanched. She must look a sight, face smeared with icing, like an animal feeding.

'They were for you,' said Penny, 'but they melted …' She was making things worse. Penny picked up the box and fled the room. She made a beeline for the ladies bathroom, stuffed the box into the bin, and washed her face and hands. She waited until her breath no longer came in shallow spurts, until her always-rosy face was no longer beet-root red.

For some reason the guard on the door escorted her down to the vault this time, as if she could no longer be trusted to wander the corridors alone.

Sarah looked up as she came in. 'Penny should have had lunch with us, shouldn't she, Patrick? The dessert trolley was to die for.'

'How would you know?' he said. 'You ate like a bird.'

Penny felt colour flare back up in her cheeks as Patrick drew on a pair of long white cotton gloves. 'I have a treat for you, Penny.'

'More cupcakes?' asked Sarah, sweetly.

Now that wasn't called for, thought Penny. That was just plain mean.

'Come on, both of you.' Out the door they went and around the corner. Patrick used his key card and they entered another room. 'The thylacine collection,' he announced, pulling covers off the glass cases at the back. 'Four mounted specimens by Alison Reid. Despite their age, they're still quite lifelike, don't you think? We also have record-ings of Alison talking about mounting these same tigers, saying how difficult it was, because they looked so different from placental mammals. I'll pull a few strings if you like, Penny, and get you a transcript.'

Penny was speechless. She threw her arms around Patrick's neck in a quick hug, then knelt down to examine the nearest thylacine. Such an unusual head – its muzzle longer and narrower than any wolf, its stripes like swift brushstrokes. And that broad kangaroo's tail looked quite wrong on a quadruped.

'Over here,' said Patrick, pointing to some jars on a shelf. 'Thylacine pouch young, pickled in ethanol. Candidates for DNA extraction.' They were tiny, the biggest no larger than a kitten. 'Only nine of these specimens in the world, and we have five of them right here. Each one is insured for millions.'

Penny peered at the biggest pup. Triangular head sprouting delicate whiskers, eyes closed as if in sleep. Wrinkly baby skin. Tiny claws emerged from tiny paws tucked under its chin. The pup was heartbreakingly beautiful.

'Have you ever seen anything like it?' whispered Penny.

'As a matter of fact, I have,' said Sarah. 'An older, much larger pup at the Australian Museum in Sydney.' She sounded impatient. 'This is all very fascinating, but we have a job to do.'

Penny looked up. She couldn't possibly leave, not yet. Two articulated skeletons still sat in the corner, and the fabled eight-pelt rug lay under a glass pane at the side of the room.

'I haven't had a chance to look at the rug,' said Penny.

Sarah crossed her arms.

'Next time,' said Patrick, his tone consoling.

Sarah tipped her chin a little higher. Penny forced her features into a smile and followed her from the room. However much she professionally admired the good Dr Sarah Deville, she wasn't sure that she liked her.

CHAPTER 6

LAZARUS

Lazarus stretched on a stone ledge above his den, basking in the late afternoon rays. Countless generations of devils had sheltered here before him – once upon a time, thylacines as well. The craggy buttress baffled even the wildest winds and the ledge retained the sun's heat. A bowed King Billy pine, lichened and twisted with age, obscured the den opening in a tangle of exposed roots. Below his den, sheer rock walls dropped to a tarn of darting minnows and choirs of frogs. Lazarus yawned and sat upright like a little black bear. He scratched his chest with a paw, blinked in pleasure and collapsed to toast his other side. Life was sweet in this peaceful stronghold.

As the sun went down, Lazarus began his nightly wanderings. He splashed across the corner of the tarn where it crept over pebbles, rippling with the dimpled reflection of a lopsided moon. He shook himself on the other side and headed at a shambling lope up the winding, well-worn trail through the beech forest. He planned on excavating a warren of rabbits. Baby rabbits were his second favourite food. His first was pademelons, but they were too large for him to bring down by himself. He only tasted his favourite meat at the remains of eagle kills or when one of the little wallabies died of old age or disease. Roadkill was rare on the remote Binburra roads.

His first stop was the sassafras gully devil latrine, up ahead at the creek crossing. It served as a noticeboard, with information about rival males, available females and general updates on community life. Lazarus duly noted the scats of a new female and her half-grown joeys and ... something else. Something at the same time familiar and strange, a scat with no scent Lazarus recognised. In size and shape it looked much like devil droppings, but the odour was so unsettling that Lazarus cut short his visit and followed the creek northwards, his large head swinging from side to side as he went. En route, Lazarus searched for nests of duck eggs, water rats beneath river banks, eels in shallows. No luck. His previous good temper was fast evaporating as he approached the warren, complete, he hoped, with a bounty of baby rabbits. He asked questions with his nose. It directed him to a mossy cave beneath a fallen pandanus palm. Ah ... not rabbits, but cats.

He poked his whiskered muzzle into the opening, only to have it raked by a wild cat's claws. Lazarus screamed, and the cat's tail bristled like a bottlebrush. She came at him like a she-devil, with explosive hisses and an angry singsong wail – all arched back, flattened ears and bared teeth. Her half-grown kittens stood behind their mother, spitting and snarling and yowling in imitation.

Lazarus backed away, rubbing his smarting nose with a forepaw. Although he was twice the weight of the feral cat, there was such a fierce courage about her that she may well have caused a tiger to tremble. Lazarus considered his options. He'd eaten and enjoyed kittens before – younger, unprotected kittens. These were another matter altogether. In a fight he might have their mother's life, but not before she had his eyes. Lazarus took another look at the cat, suicidal recklessness blazing in her own emerald eyes, then screamed in complaint and loped off east through the forest.

Now he was ravenous and in a really bad mood. On a good day Lazarus ate 40 percent of his body weight in one sitting and tonight he was way behind quota. The grumpy devil had stopped to clean his scratched face when his nostrils gathered an irresistible scent – fresh, dead pademelon. He followed his nose, padding aslant down a steep path. To his left, dappled tree ferns grew up the hillside. To his right, the ground plunged to a narrow moonlit valley swathed in honey-suckle-draped banksias and waratahs. He snapped up earthworms, beetles and a frog on his way. Soon he came to a road. Lazarus hesitated. He feared cars, but heard no motor roar, only the rhythmic mating call of a mopoke owl. By the time Lazarus reached the grassy clearing on the valley floor, the smell of fresh meat was overwhelming.

Lazarus zeroed in on the carcass, on alert for rival devils. Such a find was bound to attract freeloaders from miles around. But the pademelon tasted so fresh on his nose, so newly dead. Perhaps he'd be the first to find it? Lazarus paused. There was that scent again, the unidentifiable odour from the latrine. Soon it screamed as loud as the carrion smell. Lazarus saw the tantalising mound, lying hidden in moon shadow by the road. Throwing away caution, the famished devil advanced on the remains at a speedy canter, salivating in expectation of flesh on his tongue.

Lazarus was ready to sink his jaws into the wallaby when a large animal padded from the shadows, mouth agape in a threat display, teeth glinting in the moonlight. It gave a howling bark, and an answer echoed from the forest to the north. Lazarus cocked his ears at the unfamiliar sound and drew back.

In this vast highland wilderness, adult devils faced no natural predators – no four-legged ones anyway. Lazarus only recognised danger of the winged or wheeled variety. His gnawing hunger made him bold and he advanced on the carcass again, with a string of bloodcurdling shrieks and yowls. The animal sprang without warning and seized the unsuspecting devil in crushing jaws, shaking him like a terrier with a rat. Lazarus stopped struggling. The creature spat him out and watched for a while. But there was no fight left in Lazarus. Blood trickled from the injured devil's mouth. He struggled off. A punctured lung made it hard to breathe, so he rested for a while on a bed of cushion plants beside the road.

And early on a morning of blue sky and magpie song, Lazarus slipped from unconsciousness to death, releasing his spirit back to the bush.

CHAPTER 7

Sarah waved from Mrs Murphy's verandah as Matt pulled up. Her footprints tracked green across the frosty grass. 'Hop in,' he said. The old jeep's rear seat was cluttered with traps and tools, maps, empty crisp packets and cans of coke. The front seat wasn't much better. Matt turfed a pile of stuff into the back. Sarah slipped gingerly into the seat beside him, her small daypack perched on slim knees, goose-bumped from cold.

Matt looked bemused. Shorts, for a day on the range in a highland spring? 'We have a few hours' drive ahead of us,' he said, 'so get comfy.'

Sarah reached behind her back and extracted a spanner.

'Thanks.' Matt pitched it over the back seat. 'I was looking for that.'

Taking Sarah on a tour of Binburra's trapping sites had been Penny's idea. 'She's doing so much for us. Genetically mapping our devils. Revolutionising our entire breeding program. The least we can do is show her around.' Matt hadn't argued. He'd been avoiding people lately, keeping to himself, but in Sarah's case he'd make an exception. They owed her big time. Her work could save the entire species.

He switched on the radio for some music, drove through a small strip of shops, the main street of Hills End, and turned up Binburra

Road. Farms slipped by. Sheep dotted the grassy slopes below looming forest ridges. They passed a pair of wrought iron gates with the name Canterbury Downs inset in ornate lettering. Bronze eagles crouched atop the gateposts, which were flanked by massive bluestone walls.

'What an impressive property,' said Sarah, stretching her long, tanned legs. 'Do you know who lives there?'

Matt didn't answer, but it seemed Sarah was not the type to be easily ignored.

She turned down the radio. 'I said, do you know—'

'It's Fraser Abbott's place.'

'Fraser Abbott … he's your father, right? Is that where you grew up?'

'We spent a lot of time there when I was a kid. Dad's way of mixing business with pleasure. He owned the Hills End mine and timber operations. Still does.'

'And what about your mother?'

Did he really want to get into this with her? Matt glanced across at Sarah. Something in her open, expectant expression loosened his tongue. 'Mum loved that place, but after she died we stopped coming.' Sarah fell silent. It always happened when people found out. They were curious, but thought they shouldn't ask. Usually that suited him just fine, but Matt suddenly felt like talking. He'd been cooped up inside his own head for way too long. 'Mum died in a car accident when I was twelve, along with my twin sisters. Fraser was driving.'

'How awful,' said Sarah. 'What's your mum's name?'

Her question took Matt by surprise. Nobody ever asked him that. 'Charlotte. My mother's name is Charlotte.' It felt good to say it out loud after all this time. 'And my sisters? Christy and Cathy.' He gave Sarah a grateful sideways smile. She was easy to talk to, this Yank.

Matt took a left turn past the main entrance to Binburra Park. Penny was in there. He stopped the jeep, gripped by a sudden desire to see her, talk to her – confide in her. The urge was never very far away. It had come upon him that morning at dawn as he'd risen and dressed. He'd stood statue-still for minutes in their bedroom, wrestling with his conscience, caught between wanting to share his secret, and wanting to let Penny sleep. Watching the soft rise and fall of her breath, the curve of her throat, the curl of her lashes. How very beautiful she was – beautiful inside and out. How little he deserved her. He'd kissed her softly on her freckled cheek and escaped into the bright morning.

'Matt, what's wrong?'

As Sarah touched his arm, the urge to see Penny subsided. Now wasn't the time. She'd be taking school groups through the hospital ward to show them devils injured by cars. He was well out of it.

An hour passed. The road ran between blue gum canopies under a narrow ribbon of sky. It grew rougher and rougher as they climbed, causing the truck to pitch and slide. An iron rim of distant cliffs rose up ahead. Sarah seemed content to stare out the window, but she'd see no panorama. Trees hugged them too close, obscuring the view.

They were getting close now, close to where it had happened. Matt's knuckles showed white on the wheel and he swallowed hard, bracing himself for that sick, swooping feeling in his stomach. He tried to concentrate on driving, working hard to coax the vehicle up the steep, rutted track.

'Not much wildlife,' said Sarah.

Matt barely heard her. He was reliving that fateful night a month ago. Going over and over what he was doing, what he was thinking, in the seconds before the young thylacine died. He'd been listening to music. Cold Play. Viva La Vida. A song about a fall from grace. He liked to sing along to the song, but he didn't know all the words and was focused on the lyrics instead of the road. Is that what happened? Theo – the name he'd given the thylacine – died because he couldn't remember the words of a damned song? Matt thumped the steering wheel, alarming Sarah. She looked at him for an explanation, but he said nothing so she went back to staring out the window.

'Stop,' said Sarah. 'Is that a devil?'

Matt slammed on the brakes. He ran to a dark shape lying beside the road. Flies buzzed about. Congealed blood caked the animal's coat and ran in a line from its mouth. He examined the ear-tagged devil more closely – an all-black male, dead less than twenty-four hours by the look of him. Matt felt sick. Was this Lazarus?

He fetched his scanner with a sinking heart, hoping he was wrong, but the animal's microchip told the tale. Matt swore, feeling the prick of tears and a stomach-churning sense of déjà vu. This part of the park was closed to the public. Nobody else had access. He must have hit Lazarus last night on his way home from setting the camera traps. Matt examined his muzzle – healthy, with no deformity. If he was going to kill devils, couldn't he at least pick on diseased ones? Thank goodness it was a male. He didn't know how he or Penny would cope if he'd killed a female with pouch young.

'So sad.' Sarah squatted down for a closer look.

Matt gazed at the dead devil. In flashback he saw a bleeding Theo instead. The sense of loss was overwhelming.

'Who could have done this?' asked Sarah. 'Don't only park staff came up here?'

'It was me.' Matt could hear the pain, the tremor in his own voice. He fetched a specimen bag from the jeep and placed the stiff corpse inside. Then he bent over the bonnet, closed his eyes and clasped his hands behind his neck.

Sarah touched his shoulder, her fingers softly stroking. 'This wasn't your fault. It was an accident.'

Was it an accident though? Or was it criminal carelessness? He hadn't even noticed hitting the poor little devil. With first aid and a trip to Binburra's hospital, Lazarus might have been saved. Instead he'd bled to death on a lonely roadside, while Matt kept driving down the mountain.

How would he tell Penny? How could she forgive him? Lazarus carried precious genes from a rare, almost extinct west coast population. They'd hoped he might inject some desperately needed hybrid vigour into Binburra's devil colony. Penny's Uncle Ray had delivered Lazarus to their door last summer. He'd hit the wild devil with his log truck in the Tarkine and driven all day to bring it to Binburra. Matt hadn't realised Ray could be so sentimental. That bristly old bastard had taken a real shine to his rescued devil, bringing him marrow bones for treats while he recovered from his injuries and naming him Lazarus. Ray had never taken a shine to Matt, though, even at the best of times. Matt could only imagine what he'd say now.

'Matt?' asked Sarah. 'Are you okay?'

Her soothing fingers rubbed his shoulders. Unexpectedly, she ran her hand down his back. Matt let it linger for a second before standing upright. He was supposed to take Sarah to the main research sites. He was supposed to spend the day explaining how they monitored traps and recorded data, but he was too upset – too heavy with guilt and grief. He'd been living in a pressure cooker of his own making for weeks now, and Lazarus's death was the final straw. What he needed was time out, a chance to think things through, gain some perspective. What he needed was some peace, and he knew just where to find it. 'Do you mind a change of plans?'

'Where are we going?' asked Sarah simply.

'Loongana Warrawong,' said Matt. 'Tiger Pass.'

The road narrowed and narrowed again. Bracken and saplings punched through the track. Flattened by the jeep, they sprang back up behind, resilient, reclaiming the road. The country grew wilder, more rugged. Tall eucalypt forests gave way to sassafras, beech and leatherwood. The morning was cold and unnaturally calm. No wind tossed the trees or crumpled the light coverlet of cloud. They saw no bird or animal. The stiff plastic bag holding Lazarus crackled in the back, a constant reminder of his folly.

They rounded increasingly precarious hairpin bends, as the jeep climbed and climbed. An hour passed without a word. Somehow it wasn't awkward, being silent with Sarah. Now she'd get her view. Each twist of the road revealed spectacular scenes of the range, in turn blanketed by forest or scarred by jagged bluffs. The once-distant granite cliffs loomed in the windscreen.

Matt parked the jeep when the road ran out and they walked between high stone walls into a rocky gorge. Fat little wallabies bounced across their path. The air here was thick with a chorus of birdsong – magpie, butcherbird and currawong. Bright parrots foraged in treetops, and butterflies swarmed on swathes of wildflowers. The bush pulsed with life.

Sarah gazed around, her expression one of pure delight. 'Now this is more like it.'

Matt smiled. 'It helps to get out of the car.' Sarah made a face. Abruptly, he grabbed her arm. 'Don't move.'

Sarah froze mid-step. 'What is it? A snake?'

Matt pointed to the path ahead. 'See there?'

Sarah peered at the ground. 'There's nothing,' she said at last.

'It's not what you look at,' said Matt. 'It's what you see.' He crouched down, indicating that she should do the same.

'*Caladenia anthracina*. The black-tipped spider orchid.' He pointed out a fragile finger-high purple and white flower. It poked bravely through the leaf litter, with petals like tiny striped tuxedo tails. Matt lay prone on the ground for a closer look and beckoned for Sarah to join him. She hesitated, then lay down flat beside him.

'There aren't leeches, are there?' she asked, uncertainly. 'I heard there were leeches.' Her body, from hip to shoulder, pressed lightly against him.

'Shh.' A tiny wasp zigzagged its way to the delicate bloom, grasped it with its legs, and thrust its abdomen in and out of the flower's heart. 'Darwin's beautiful contrivance,' Matt whispered. 'The orchid mimics one specific species of female thynnine wasp. Frustrated males pollinate the flowers, whose seeds then germinate in symbiosis with one specific local soil fungus. These plants have evolved together with this particular place.' He breathed a long sigh. 'Perfect, isn't it?'

The unsuspecting wasp flew away and Matt helped Sarah to her feet.

'Is that orchid endangered?' she asked.

'Critically.'

'Shouldn't you make some sort of official report?'

'And tell the world? No chance. These spider orchids have lived here quite happily since dinosaurs roamed the earth. They don't need our interference. They need to to be left alone.'

Sarah frowned and began to argue the point. He put a forefinger to his lips. 'Now, there's something you don't see every day.' He pointed into the bushes. A line of spiny little echidnas trundled along, nose to tail. There must have been ten of them.

'What on earth?'

'That,' said Matt, 'is an echidna love train. A female leads the way. The rest are poor lovelorn males, hoping she'll take pity on them. It might take six weeks before she agrees to group sex. Only the strongest, most persistent males get lucky.'

They watched the strange procession waddle off into the scrub. Matt brushed a beetle from Sarah's hair as a long-legged bird with red eyes and slate grey wings stalked across their path.

'It looks like an overgrown chicken,' laughed Sarah.

Half a dozen more of the birds scooted past, one followed by fluffy black chicks. 'Tasmanian native hens,' said Matt. 'Known locally as turbo-chooks. That bird with the chicks? She's the single female in the group. Native hens are polyandrous.'

'Which means?'

'You know your Latin. *Poly* – many. *Andro* – men. The girls have harems of husbands.'

'Nice,' said Sarah. A laggard sprinted past, uttering a high, see-sawing alarm call. 'Tasmanian females seem very well provided for.'

'Come on,' said Matt, feeling lighter than he had in weeks. 'I have something to show you.'

'The mind boggles.'

He led Sarah down an overgrown path. They followed a fast-flowing stream punctuated by pools and fringed with ferns. The cliffs of Tiger Pass rose on either side, dark and forbidding, into a sky of broken blue. Small caves peppered the weathered parallel walls of stone. Ancient rainforest trees reached for the sun. Walking into the pass was like walking back in time.

After half an hour they came to the head of the gorge. The stream flowed even faster here, rushing through the rocks in a mini-maelstrom. Matt took Sarah's hand as they scrambled onto a rocky ledge above the water. Tiger Pass was really a little hanging valley, carved out by long-vanished glaciers and suspended high above a vast forest basin. The creek spilled over in an unbroken crystal band, shattering into rainbow shards of spray when it broke on boulders hundreds of metres below.

Matt gazed skywards, imagining a pair of peregrines soaring in the empty blue sky. This was the place where he'd planned to release Sooty and Sweep. They should be here. He ached with missing them.

'Ever been to the Grand Canyon?' Sarah's voice was a whisper. 'It's the same feeling – kind of holy.' She moved closer to the brink.

Matt took her arm, edged her back. 'Gaze not too long into the abyss ...'

'Lest the abyss gaze into thee,' she answered.

Matt inclined his head in acknowledgement. 'Not many people know that quote.'

She stared at the view a while longer. 'How do you get down to the valley?'

'You don't,' said Matt. 'Not without a helicopter. Five years ago we scraped together funding for one and set traps. Hoped to find some disease-free devils.'

'What happened?'

'We didn't catch a single devil and the state withdrew our grant. Either there are none down there, or they're unusually suspicious of carcass baits.'

'And you've never been back?'

Matt gazed longingly after the cascading water. 'Legend says there's a way down, but if there is, Penny and I have never found it. Lord knows we've tried.' Matt winced at the *we*. He and Penny didn't feel like a *we* at the moment.

'Working out here, being part of all this ... you must really love your job.'

'I don't have to wear a tie,' said Matt. 'And it's a living.' He indicated the magnificent scene before them with a wide-armed flourish. 'A living in the true sense of the word. The job doesn't pay much and the park gets next to no funding, but that suits me. It means they won't fix the roads.'

'But you're so far away from everything.'

'The way I see it, everything's right here.'

'What exactly do you do?' she asked.

'Take my time. Watch the clouds.'

'When you're not watching clouds.'

'Watch for idiots with trail bikes and four-wheel-drives tearing up the place. Watch for weeds, poachers, lost tourists.'

'I bet you don't like tourists.'

'They're all right, some of them, the ones who remember that their legs work. You'd need a crowbar to get others out of their cars.' He tossed a pebble into space. 'Last week I lost it with this couple taking photos through their windscreen. "Get out," I said. "Get those kids out of the car. Let them run around for Christ's sake. Let them loose."

'"Aren't there snakes?" That's what the woman said to me. "Of course there are snakes," I said. "And bull ants, and leeches. But there's also a creek and a mountain and a ten thousand-year-old-forest. There are sassafras leaves to chew and leatherwood flowers to smell and stones to skip on the river. There's mud to squelch between your toes and rocks to climb and birds to spot. There's the cleanest air in the world to breath, a whole frigging wilderness to explore – and you won't even wind down your window."'

'You said that?' Sarah's eyes were wide.

'Something like it.'

They looked at each other and burst out laughing.

'What happened?' asked Sarah.

'They took off. I'll probably get a complaint.'

'I asked you if there were leeches,' said Sarah, with mock indignation. Matt grinned and helped her down from the ledge.

As they walked back along the track, Sarah stopped to peer into several small caves.

Matt pointed up ahead to a big rocky opening at the foot of a massive Huon pine. 'We can go into that one.' He ducked his head, flicked on his torch and followed Sarah into the gloom. After a few metres she screamed and lashed out, as if fighting an invisible foe.

'Stay still. You'll hurt her.' Matt gently pinned Sarah's arms to her sides, then carefully unwrapped the transparent sheet of web, more than a metre in diameter, from her upper body. He accidentally brushed her breasts, which were small and firm beneath his fingers. 'There she is,' he murmured, coaxing an enormous spindly spider onto his hand. It was as big as his palm. '*Hickmania troglodytes*, the Tasmanian cave spider.' Sarah shrank back. 'A relict species dating all the way back to Gondwanaland. Her closest relatives are in South America. They can live for decades.' He brought the spider close to his face. 'You could be as old as we are, darling.'

'How can you tell it's a female?' asked Sarah.

'Her size, for one thing, and the fact that she's guarding this.' He pointed out a snow-white pear-shaped egg sac, suspended in a stony crevice by a silken thread.

'I suppose she has some strange sexual predilection as well?' said Sarah.

'Good guess. Her mating is highly ritualised. The smaller, weaker male courts her for hours, rhythmically plucking her web and stroking her into a kind of trance. The aim is to grip her head in a special kink on his legs and jam her jaws apart so he can safely have sex. Venom drips from her fangs the whole time they're doing it.'

He eased the spider back onto the wall, and trained the torch beam against the roof of rock high above their heads. The painted likeness of a striped animal stared down at them, surrounded by handprints, concentric rings and mysterious dot designs.

'A thylacine.' Sarah's awed voice returned to them in mocking echo.

She backed up to take in the paintings, and pulled her phone from her pocket.

Matt covered it with his hand. 'No pictures, for cultural reasons.'

Sarah resisted for a few moments, then put her phone away.

It felt strange to be at Last Stand Cave with anyone other than Penny. What would she think of him hijacking the day's carefully planned itinerary, of him bringing Sarah to this special place? In bed that morning, half asleep, Penny had embraced him. His body had responded, but his mind made him tense and shift ever so slowly out of reach.

Sarah touched his shoulder and Matt tried to put thoughts of Penny aside. He aimed the torch at the ground, revealing an engraved memorial plaque. 'There's quite a story attached to this cave,' he said. 'You want to hear it?'

CHAPTER 8

Penny watched Fraser work the blade with the precision of a surgeon and the delicacy of a lover. She'd never seen such a large animal skinned before, and was both squeamish and fascinated. It made no difference to the stag whether Fraser mounted its head or not, destined as it had always been for the butcher. But vegetarian Penny was still sad for its death, for its once graceful body now dangling from the gallows. She was still shocked when, after flaying down as far as he could, Fraser severed the stag's head with a meat saw. He used the antlers as handles, struggling to thump his gory prize onto the workbench. The deer had been dead long enough for rigor mortis to stem the free flow of blood, though it still congealed in occasional resinous pools. Fraser idly scraped them away.

'A head,' he said, 'should be skinned all in one piece, including the ears, eyelids and lips.'

He sawed across the top of the skull, using a screwdriver to prise stubborn skin from the base of one antler. Next, he made a cut along the neck, intersecting the first incision. When he sliced the ears, he expertly left them attached to the skin. Penny murmured in admiration, then grimaced as Fraser removed the eye and jammed his forefinger deep into the empty socket.

'The skin grows close to the skull here, Penelope,' he said without looking up. 'Which makes the eyelids tricky. But if you poke your finger into the back of the eye … just so … you'll feel where skin meets bone.' Penny held her breath. 'Done. Now for the nose.' Fraser's blade pierced the soft muzzle. This time he used his thumb, shoved hard into the deer's mouth, felt for the bulge and cut around it. Fraser deftly slit the lips and removed the fleshy interior, miraculously leaving the thin dark skin attached to the head. 'Save as much of the lips as you can. You'll need them later.'

He finished by splitting the nostrils, separating flesh and cartilage as he went. 'Fingers crossed.' With meticulous care Fraser peeled hide from head, inside out and all in one piece. The bloody skull remaining bore no resemblance to the noble-eyed, velvet-muzzled stag of an hour ago. With gaping sockets, flayed face and an incongruous crown of blood-spattered antlers, the head looked like something straight out of a horror movie.

'I tried to skin a wombat head last week and made a complete hash of it,' said Penny. 'If only I'd known that trick with your finger.'

'I have lots of tricks I could show you,' said Fraser, winking.

Penny lightly punched his arm. 'Behave yourself and show me how to do the ears.'

Fraser made two cuts and turned each ear inside out. 'Get the salt.'

As Penny reached for a jar on the top shelf, the earth rumbled.

'Here comes another one,' said Fraser.

The floor shifted beneath their feet, windows rattled and shelves shuddered. Penny caught the salt jar as it fell. Furniture clattered. The studio creaked and groaned, then everything was still again.

Six weeks ago, a violent quake had rocked Hills End. Houses shook. Windows broke. The verandah of the Royal Hotel collapsed, along with half a dozen inebriated patrons. Since then, a series of aftershocks had plagued the town.

Penny retrieved a screwdriver that had rolled off the table. 'Did that first quake cause you any problems?'

'It certainly did. It spilled a perfectly good glass of red.'

'Down your mine, I mean.'

'Nothing that can't be fixed,' said Fraser. 'Earthquakes happen.'

Penny gave Fraser a searching look. 'Matt says that blasting down the mine triggered the earthquake.'

'Does he? Well, I can assure you that Matt is quite wrong.'

Penny wasn't convinced. Plenty of people in Hills End blamed the mine.

A flicker of something like sadness crossed Fraser's usually impassive face. 'Tell me, Penelope, are you going to stand around and recite the gospel according to Matthew or shall we get on with it?'

'Get on with it,' said Penny.

Fraser nodded approval. He opened the salt jar, coated the stag's head and placed it in an empty sink to drain. He then washed his hands and arms in a basin of hot, sudsy water.

'Now, what do you have for me?' he said to Penny as he dried his hands. She pointed to a sack on the floor by the door, and Fraser opened it with an appreciative sigh. He covered an empty work table with thick layers of newspaper, and then lifted the limp body of the eagle. 'When did this bird die?'

'Last night.' Penny showed Fraser its shattered, swollen left wing. 'He didn't respond to antibiotics. It's happening a lot lately – wildlife just not healing.' She could have said more, but bit her tongue. Matt wasn't the only one who held Fraser's forestry practices responsible for the odd spike in ailing animals. Their vet did too, and some of the farmers, those with unusually high numbers of aborted and deformed lambs. They blamed herbicides like atrazine and triazine, sprayed from helicopters to prepare clear-fell sites for pine plantations. Herbicides banned in Europe for their links to birth defects and cancer.

Fraser examined the eagle's gunshot wound. 'I think we can disguise this under the feathers.'

'What about his missing talon?'

'Thermoset resin claws are most lifelike.' Fraser fixed his hawk-like gaze on her. 'Does Matthew know you've brought this bird here?'

Penny couldn't meet his eyes. She'd lied to Matt that morning. A day talking to school groups, she'd said. 'He thinks the vet cremated it. But I couldn't let that happen, Fraser. I just couldn't …'

Fraser held up his hand. 'Thanks to you, this splendid eagle will live forever in the hearts and minds of all who view him.' Fraser stroked the tawny head. 'An immortal ambassador for his kind. A bird of such beauty, such rarity.'

'Matt wouldn't agree,' said Penny.

'My son is a stubborn fool, like his father,' said Fraser. 'Worse, he has a hero complex. Where is he today? Capturing a ring of international poachers? Single-handedly replanting an entire forest? More likely reading the riot act to some poor tourist who took a wrong turn.'

Sometimes Penny hated Fraser, but he was like Matt in so many ways. His tongue protruded ever so slightly when he concentrated. He could hold opinions in dogged defiance of reason. They were both handsome, despite Roman noses and thin mouths. Fraser still had a full head of hair, now tinged with grey. Would Matt look as distinguished at sixty? But Matt certainly didn't have his father's arrogance, nor his sharp tongue. Fraser took such pleasure in finding fault. 'Matt's taking a scientist on a tour of the devil traps,' she said. 'He won't be back until late.'

'We have some hours then. Shall we begin?'

Penny hesitated. 'I haven't done a bird before.'

'Birds are the easiest of all,' said Fraser. 'They have such thin skins. You can mount a bird in one day, even a large raptor like this, and then leave it to cure on the model.'

'I don't have a model,' said Penny.

Fraser disappeared into the next room and returned with a polyurethane eagle form under one arm. 'He's bigger than I imagined, but I suspect we can build this up with some cottonwool.' From a drawer, Fraser produced a knife and a box of borax. He laid the eagle on its back and handed Penny a needle and thread. 'Sew up that wound before we start.'

Penny took a deep breath and began.

CHAPTER 9

M att began his story. 'In 1887, the richest bloke in Hills End was a man named Henry Abbott.'

'Any relation?' asked Sarah.

'I'm afraid so. Abbott pretty much owned the town. He owned the richest farmland, the most valuable timber, the most profitable businesses – and he owned the goldmine. One day an earthquake caused the mine to flood. Underground streams run deep around here. Dozens drowned, but a young miner known as Adam McCleod rescued seven men, including Henry Abbott's own son.'

A possum crept from a crevice above them and darted into the darkness, startling Sarah. She moved closer to Matt.

'Even though Adam was badly hurt himself, he collected as many injured men as he could, hauled them into a mine car, and ran them through rockfalls and rising water to the main shaft. They escaped just in time. Adam was the town hero.'

'What's that got to do with this cave?' asked Sarah.

'Well, apparently Adam wasn't who he said he was. He was really an escaped convict named Luke Tyler, jailed for assaulting none other than Henry Abbott himself, years before.' Sarah raised her perfect brows. 'It gets better. Not long after that, Luke murdered Henry

Abbott. Set his dog on him, so the story goes. Then Luke and the dog took off. The police hunted them down to this cave, but since Luke was such a hero, nobody wanted to shoot him.'

'He'd just murdered a man.'

'Maybe so, but apparently people hated Henry Abbott and were glad he was dead. So the local sergeant went into this cave and tried to get Luke to surrender. A few minutes later the police outside heard an explosion. The sergeant raced out, running for his life. Said a demon came out of the walls and attacked him. Then the back of the cave collapsed.' Matt paused for effect, aware of Sarah's rapt attention. 'No trace of Luke or his dog was ever found.' Matt pointed to the roof. 'Legend says those rock paintings mark a door to the spirit world, and that the two of them passed through. Whenever the earth trembles, Hills End locals call it the Abbott curse.'

Sarah looked around uneasily. 'What's on that plaque?' Matt shone the torch down and she knelt to read the words etched in stone-set brass. 'In loving memory of Luke Tyler and his loyal dog Bear. My heart is forever yours. Bluebell.' Sarah tilted her head, trailing fingers over the cold brass. 'Who put this here?'

'Nobody knows.' Matt peered into the murky depths of the cave, almost saw the desperate young man, almost felt the shudder of the cave collapse. Then, the ground beneath him really did shift. He grabbed Sarah's arm and pulled her to her feet. 'Aftershock.' They darted for daylight, followed by a cloud of dust.

'That's pretty creepy,' said Sarah, gasping for breath. '… just after that story.'

Matt looked up. Threatening grey clouds were gathering fast, piling high in the sky. His phone rang, a crowing cock. 'Matt here. Pallawarra? I can be there by five.' He put his phone back in his pocket. 'There's trouble in the Tuggerah. We'd better head back.'

'Fine by me,' said Sarah. 'I've had just about enough of your Australian bush for one day.'

.   .   .

The road home offered unparalleled views of the forest in breath-taking sweeps from the crest of the cliff. Sarah stared out the window until the forest closed back around them. She looked in the glove box, found a copy of the local newspaper and started to read. Time slipped away.

'Is it true,' asked Sarah, 'that people don't need permits for logging?'

'A uniquely Tasmanian idea, courtesy of my father. You need a permit to put up a new letterbox, but if your land is declared a private timber reserve, you don't need a permit for anything. Not for clear-felling, access roads, firebombing …'

'Firebombing? Why on earth would somebody firebomb their own place?'

'It's all the rage around here. First they woodchip the trees, then they drop a sort of napalm from helicopters and burn what's left. To top it off, they drop poisoned carrots to finish off the wildlife.'

'It sounds like war,' said Sarah.

'That's exactly what it is.'

A pause. 'Can I come with you to the Tuggerah.'

Matt turned to look at her. Dark hair escaping from its clasp, face and clothes smudged with dirt. She looked more alive than he'd seen her. 'Okay, but don't get in the way.'

'Of what?'

'Of the war.'

Sarah reached into her bag, extracted a lunch box and passed him a ham sandwich. Penny didn't buy ham. He'd forgotten how good it tasted.

They passed Binburra and turned left at Kingston Track. Their way dipped deep into the valley, crossed the wooden bridge over the dark, swift-running Charon River and led to a fork in the road. The left track climbed back to the park. They took the right fork leading down to the vast Tuggerah valley, whose forests stretched south for five hundred kilometres. Binburra's jagged quartzite peaks, iced with snow, stood in firm command of this place – a place little changed for fifty million years. Mountain ash, *Eucalyptus regnans*, ruled the mixed, temperate rainforest. The Tuggerah lay within a mountainous ring of World Heritage national parks, but it didn't share their protected status – it was classed as public land, nothing more. And now Matt's father had the go-ahead from Premier Logan to move industrial-scale woodchipping operations into the valley.

Matt had watched the decision polarise the previously peaceful Hills End community. Local sawmillers objected to the new clear-fell policy. It destroyed the precious rainforest understorey, which took hundreds of years to reach commercial size: celery top and Huon pine, sassafras, leatherwood, myrtle, native olive and cheesewood. Mountain ash trees regenerated quickly after fire, but the pockets of rainforest nestled at their feet did not. The last jungles of Gondwanaland were fast disappearing, along with people's livelihoods.

And it wasn't just the millers who were up in arms. Local furniture and instrument makers, wood-turners, sculptors and shingle splitters – all their jobs depended on sustainable harvesting of the Tuggerah and the few remaining places like her. They viewed with despair the neat rows of pine and eucalypt monoculture – the green deserts – that replaced the rainforest. Conversely, loggers and truck drivers like Uncle Ray saw these specialty timber workers as turncoats, betraying their own and throwing their lot in with the hated greenies. Matt loathed how his father had set worker against worker, friend against friend, brother against brother. Fraser had a lot to answer for.

Sarah craned her neck out the open window. 'Stop the car,' she said, pulling Matt out of his worries. He killed the motor in the middle of the track and they got out. There was something deeply primeval in the air.

'So this is the Tuggerah.' Sarah slowly spun around, taking it in. 'It's magnificent.'

Matt smiled. 'I thought you'd had enough of the Australian bush.' He'd seen it before, the effect this place had on first-timers. Like a fine piece of music or poetry, it moved people in profound and unusual ways. Matt pointed to a little seedling, weaving skywards from beneath leaf litter by the side of the road. 'A baby myrtle. It could live for a thousand years.'

Mist held them in a moist embrace. Filtered song, twitters, whistles and chirps betrayed invisible birds in the upper canopy: parrots and pardalotes, currawongs and cockatoos. Whipbirds whistled in stereo. Golden fungi and green moss clothed fallen logs on the forest floor, while orchids and ferns burst high on branches. Mountain ash trunks towered so high, their canopies were lost in the clouds.

'The tallest flowering trees in the world,' said Matt.

Sarah stared skywards for the longest time. 'I'm an ape in an earth odyssey.' She trailed her finger along a tree's rough bark. 'I should dance naked around the monolith.'

'You should get back in the car,' said Matt with a smile. 'Let's go.'

Sarah gasped when they rounded the next bend. To the left, the same soaring stands of ash interspersed with tree ferns and shady southern sassafras. But to the right? A splintered bombsite of woody debris, churned earth and shattered roots. Levelled pedestals of giant trees, broad as billiard tables, dotted the devastated scene.

'Look,' said Sarah. 'What's that?'

A pale animal, about the size of a small dog, crouched on a stump near the road. Matt stopped the car and they picked their way towards it through the carnage. The dazed creature didn't move. Its long whiskers and large ears were covered in mud, as was its blond coat. Its furry flaxen tail hung limp.

'A golden brush-tailed possum,' said Matt. 'A big one.'

'He's beautiful,' said Sarah. 'Why is he just sitting there?'

'He's in shock.' Matt kicked the broad stump. Sweet sherry-scented water still bled from its heart. 'This would have been his home tree. He shouldn't even be awake in daylight, but his hollow is gone. His whole bloody forest is gone.'

'We have to help.'

Matt swept his arm wide, indicating the ruin all around. 'Possums are territorial. I can't relocate a traumatised old male like him. I've tried it before. They never survive.'

Sarah stroked the possum's soft head. It was too far gone to care, barely noticing her touch. 'What will happen to him?'

'If we do nothing? He'll sit there until he dies, or burn when they torch the place.' Sarah kept stroking the traumatised animal until Matt took her small hand in his. 'We have to go. Get back in the car.'

Sarah stared at the motionless possum. She looked like she might cry.

'Please – get back in the car.'

'I thought you were going to help him.'

'I am.' Matt waited a little longer. When Sarah showed no sign of leaving, he went to the jeep and returned with a rifle. Matt briefly raised the animal by its bushy tail, confirming it was male, then shot it in the head. The possum toppled from the stump to rest on a bed of withered leaves. Matt covered it with a screen of myrtle branches.

Sarah had turned pale.

'It was the kindest thing,' he said.

Back at the jeep, the sound of approaching machinery ripped through the silence. A yellow bulldozer roared into view and pulled up behind them. A sticker on the window said *Fertilise the forest. Bull-doze in a greenie.* A burly man with a bushy grey beard and a sour expression leaned down from the cabin. 'Do you think you own the road, Matt? Get out of my way.'

'What a charming man,' said Sarah.

'That's Ray, Penny's uncle. Not exactly my greatest fan.' Matt pulled the jeep aside to let the dozer pass, acutely aware that Ray's rescued devil, Lazarus, lay dead in the back.

Ray glared at Sarah suspiciously as he pulled alongside them. 'Who's she?'

'Dr Deville. A scientist from UCLA.'

Ray snorted like he didn't believe it. 'How's Pen? I haven't seen her this week.'

'She's fine, Ray. You heading for the coupe?'

'What does it look like?' Ray gunned the engine. The dozer lurched off down the rutted road with Matt following behind in escort.

CHAPTER 10

Ray bumped past Matt's jeep and lit a cigarette. He'd promised Penny to cut back on his smoking, but was already onto his second packet for the day. A profound sense of failure, of letting her down, added to his dark mood. He shouldn't be driving this dozer. He should be in his truck heading up the highway with a load of logs for the Hobart mill. But the protestors had held things up for weeks now, blocking the chainsaws and preventing trucks from being loaded. So his Kenworth rig lay idle, although he still had to make the payments. His best mate, Charlie, had wangled him a few hours work on the bulldozer, for which he was grateful, because the bills were piling up.

There'd been nothing but trouble in the forest lately, even before the protest circus came to town. Breakdowns, accidents, injured men. Some folks blamed the greenies, but there wasn't any proof. It could be just a string of terrible luck, like the local sergeant said. Worst of all was what had happened to young Scott Marshall. A fellow log truck driver, he'd been crushed beneath a tonne of timber when his load somehow came loose. It had hit Penny hard when Scott died. They'd been at school together. Friends right from kindergarten, all the way through. They'd even dated for a while.

That was before Matt came along. After their whirlwind marriage,

Penny became the target of nasty gossip, accused of gold-digging – of throwing aside her local lad to marry the son of the wealthiest man in Tasmania. Hills End was a close-knit community, and Matt did himself no favours in the popularity stakes by keeping to himself the way he did. Ray had tried reaching out, but Matt wouldn't go on the fishing trips or join the other blokes down the pub on Friday nights for a beer. He wouldn't even go to the footy.

Even after twelve years of living in the town, Matt remained somewhat of an outsider. He wasn't quite the catch everyone had thought him either. He had no money after all, due to some sort of row with his dad. That park ranger job of his paid diddly squat. The way Pen told it, she earned more than he did. But Ray wouldn't hold that against a man. Truth be told, he didn't earn much himself these days, what with younger men happy to drive day and night – even if they were a hazard to themselves and everyone else on the road.

Ray had long ago learned to accept Matt, even though he didn't much like him. If Matt made Penny happy, that was all that mattered. What bothered Ray lately was that Penny no longer did seem happy. She complained that her husband was avoiding her, shutting her out. Ray had dismissed her concerns at first. 'Sometimes a man just needs some space, love,' he'd told her. For all his misgivings about their marriage, he'd never doubted Matt's love for Penny. But Penny had been miserable for weeks now, and Ray was getting worried.

Just who was the girl in the jeep with Matt? She was a pretty little thing – a scientist, he'd said. Penny had mentioned a visiting lady scientist. Could she be part of the problem between Penny and her husband? Ray frowned and changed gears as he approached the logging coupe. A flush of anger passed through him. If Matt was betraying Penny in any way, God help him.

Matt pulled into the coupe behind Ray's dozer. Police cars had formed a cordon around a row of logging machinery, and a few officers stood talking together by their vehicles.

'Stay here,' said Matt. Sarah got out and followed him anyway.

'Hey, Matt,' called a middle-aged policeman. 'Thank God you're here.'

Matt turned and glared at Sarah before introducing her. 'This is Sergeant Nick Byrne. Nick … Sarah.'

Nick acknowledged her with a nod. 'Well, Matt, better get to it.'

A pale sun was sinking below the treetops. Matt and the sergeant took off in a police car, leaving Sarah standing there. They were heading towards the forest margin on the far side of the clearing, where razed ground met standing trees. Giant logging machines stood parked by the road, great gobs of mud plastered in the broad tread of their monstrous tyres. A neat painted sign on the back of one said *Please don't damage this bulldozer.* Other signs weren't so polite. The bush crew formed a circle nearby, swapping stories and stamping feet. Hard hats and steel-capped boots. The forest here smelled of oil and diesel, cigarettes and sweat. The men took turns staring at Sarah. One of them wolf-whistled. She moved close to an officer.

'What's happening?' she asked him.

'Another bloody greenie up a tree.'

A logger yelled a lewd remark and blew Sarah a kiss. She went back to the jeep and locked herself in, straining to see what was happening at the edge of the coupe. The same logger pursed his lips and made an obscene gesture. Sarah wriggled across to the driver's seat, turned the key, let out the clutch and drove off down the perimeter track until she reached Nick Byrne's car.

Matt and Nick stood talking next to what must have been the tallest tree in the world. Its massive bole was covered with carvings. High in the canopy, almost too high to see, was a platform strung with banners. Sarah got out of the jeep and approached the two men. They ignored her.

'Says he won't budge unless you go and get him,' said Nick.

Matt peered up at the great tree.

'There's a gale warning tonight,' Nick added. 'If he won't come down, it'll serve the mad bugger right.'

'Don't worry, I'll get him.' Matt walked to the jeep and pulled out climbing equipment – ropes and pulleys and cinches.

Sarah looked from Matt to the top of the tree. Its sheer trunk soared impossibly high. 'You're not—' she started.

Matt smacked the tree. 'Don't worry. Me and Pallawarra here, we're old mates.' He selected some gear and put on a helmet and gloves.

'This tree has a name?'

Nick guided her away with a hand on her shoulder. 'He'll be fine. Stay out of the way. He needs to concentrate.'

Sarah stood open-mouthed as Matt looped a sling around his body, then around the trunk, and clipped in another strap. He bounced back twice into the sling, braced himself and was suddenly two metres up the trunk. For the life of her, Sarah couldn't quite make out how he'd managed it. He continued to scale the tree, making swift progress. She couldn't imagine the sort of upper body strength it took.

A cry rang out, making Sarah jump, and a rope snaked down from above. Matt grabbed it, and his ascent quickened. Ten minutes later, as the watchers held their breath, he clambered onto the platform sixty metres above the ground. Sarah exhaled and turned to Nick, who was rigging up a bank of portable floodlights. 'He made it,' she said.

'Don't count your chickens. I'd rather go up that tree than come down it.'

Daylight dimmed and dimmed again. Swirls of mist fell to earth, hiding the canopy, and dusk consumed the searchlights. A hush fell on the watchers below. Police and loggers melded, staring into the sky, all rendered blind by obscuring cloud. A young logger lit a cigarette and offered it to Sarah. She hadn't smoked in years, but accepted it for some reason and took a bottomless breath. The familiar acrid sensation deep in her lungs still retained its power to soothe.

A freshening breeze caused her cigarette to burn brighter. She shivered. A man removed his coat and draped it over her shoulders. She recognised him. It was Penny's uncle, Ray, who'd been driving the yellow dozer. She pointed up the tree. 'Shouldn't somebody call Penny to tell her what's happening?'

Ray shook his head. 'I'll not drag Pen down here just to see what a mad bastard her husband is.'

'Ray's right,' said Nick. 'Matt's got nine lives. Why worry Penny?'

Sarah turned to speak to Ray but he was no longer there. Upon some invisible signal the loggers were retreating to their machines. Their glowing cigarettes hovered like fireflies in the gloom. Sarah dropped her own cigarette and stamped it into the earth. If *she* was Matt's wife, *she'd* want to know.

CHAPTER 11

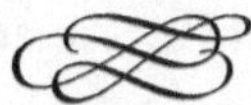

That precious, familiar calm. Tree climbing. Different from rock climbing. Trees lived. Even mighty Pallawarra gave with the wind. He moved. Matt moved too, away from the people and cars and the ravaged earth. He moved into another dimension. For the first time in a long time, Matt focused on the moment. On his breath, his feet, his fingers. A meditation. There was no choice. Any slip was death.

The darkening forest lay in mysterious degrees of light and shade. The more Matt looked at the tree, the more he saw the tree. Its position, its size and form – its unique structure and balance. He saw through its bark-dangled camouflage.

Now light rain began falling, deepening the colours. The auburns and browns, the greens and golds, the glistening mottled curls of stringybark streamers. Birds of the upper canopy had fled, leaving the forest unusually silent. Except for the sound of a strengthening breeze, like the seashell psalm of a distant sea.

With a loud tearing noise, a sudden gust ripped at a long piece of bark beside him. It peeled like a bandage from a healed wound, revealing the creamy porcelain perfection of trunk beneath. Sailing out on the current, the four-metre ribbon began its journey to the forest floor. Once upon a time, it might have caught in a forked branch with others of its kind, all gathered like lovely tassels on a giant Christmas tree. It might have floated further afield to help weave a blanket for the fragrant understorey of sassafras and myrtle. It might have taken months to find its final resting place on the ground, providing food and board for lichen and moss and tiny creatures of the leaf litter. But now there was nothing to break its fall. It reached earth in one long drift, destined to provide sustenance only for the foresters' fires.

Matt hoisted himself up onto the canvas-covered platform. A tall, lanky man with bleached blond dreadlocks watched him with amused eyes, from under a football beanie. Drake. He was lying at ease on a treeboat, a type of hammock climbers used to enjoy picnics or naps high in tree canopies. Anchored cables – emergency escape routes – disappeared into the forest. A dented exercise bike, hooked up to a generator, stood strapped to Pallawarra's giant trunk.

'It's about time you got here.' Drake took a drag on what looked like a joint, then offered it to his visitor.

Matt shook his head. 'What are you playing at, mate?'

'Just trying to get your attention,' said Drake. 'We're overdue for a chat.'

'Wouldn't the phone have been simpler?' Matt regretted those words as soon as they were out. Drake *had* used the phone. He'd texted him, called him, left messages. Plenty of them. It wasn't Drake who'd let their friendship lapse. Since Theo, Matt had let a lot of things slide.

He put that unwelcome thought aside and took a look around the roomy treetop camp. An impressive set-up: fridge, laptop, satellite phone – all the comforts of home. Quite a feat, to get all this up here unseen.

Drake followed Matt's gaze and gestured around them with a flourish. 'Hauled the platform up two months ago. Ken Murphy from the mill gave us the timber and second-hand steel. We hid sections in the bush and dragged them up, one by one, at night. Six radial supports, six floor sections.' Drake stamped his foot and smiled. 'See that? Solid as a rock.' He pointed to the roof. 'Gutters funnel rain into that poly tank.' He stroked the rough tree trunk with the tenderness of a lover and his expression grew grim. 'Pallawarra here was our tipping point. We planned to ramp up the campaign when the logging crews reached him. Truth is, none of us expected it to happen so soon.'

'You lot don't have much of a presence on the ground.' Matt peered into the gloom. 'Nothing but loggers and cops down there.'

'Just wait until tomorrow.' Drake clipped himself into a harness and sprang back once to test the rope. 'Aren't you ever going to talk me down from here? I'm freezing my arse off.'

Matt smiled and used his phone. 'We're on our way.' A faraway cheer and faint staccato applause drifted up through the branches.

'You know,' said Drake, 'more people have stood at the top of Mount Everest than at the top of this tree.' He saluted and kicked off. Mist closed fast around him. Matt took one last look at the dark canopy, then followed his friend back to earth.

The sergeant was talking to the first man who'd come down from the tree. Even at a distance in the dusk, Sarah could see the man wasn't Matt. About the same height, but slimmer and with a rope of pale hair. Instead of Steve Irwin khaki, he wore tatty jeans, a heavy homespun jumper two sizes too big and a black-and-white beanie. The man shook the sergeant's hand, then strolled towards her. Sarah looked past him to see Matt make a neat landing. The man blocked her view and extended his hand, forcing her to pay attention. He took off the beanie. A halo of dreadlocks swung free, revealing a rainbow headband.

'Drake Logan.'

'Dr Sarah Deville. UCLA.'

Drake arched his eyebrows, shook her offered hand with his right and cupped it with his left. 'You are an uncommonly beautiful doctor.' His eyes held hers for a long time. Then, like some sort of overgrown Mad Hatter, Drake pulled an enormous antique fob watch from his pocket. 'Goodness gracious, look at the time. You will be my guests for dinner. A night of fine food, finer conversation and a welcome to country.'

He behaved like the matter was settled. She had to admit he had a certain style. Good-looking too. Very. At the airport, Sarah's sister had made her customary *tick-tock body clock* remark, and then gone on and on about the hunks Sarah might find Down Under. Her sister was right. Most of the young loggers could have been male models back home. Not to mention Matt, who was absolutely her type. Sarah had lost interest in Los Angeles men. The pale, bookish academics at the University, wedded to their intellects and egos. Or the self-conscious gym junkies, all spray tan, body wax and hair product. They couldn't hold a candle to the simple rawness of these Aussie men. Penny had certainly had some talent to choose from.

Drake took a swig from a flask at his belt and announced that dinner would be at seven. Sarah checked her phone. Six forty-five. How on earth could Drake produce dinner by seven o'clock? They were in the middle of a forest, at least an hour's drive from Binburra, and by all accounts he'd spent the last twenty-four hours up a tree. 'Are you a magician?' she asked him as Matt strode over.

'Not a magician,' said Matt. 'But he's quite the performer. An artist too. A bullshit artist. How'd you talk your way out of this one, Drake? I expected the coppers to cart you off.'

'I simply made a pledge not to climb Pallawarra. Nick knows my word's good.'

'He does, but don't expect the same from the city coppers.' There was a grim set to Matt's jaw. 'As from today, this is an exclusion zone. You're trespassing, along with us and everybody at Camp Clementine. Word is that tomorrow they're bringing in a show of force from Hobart. Private security as well.'

Drake shook his head. 'I don't need advice from you, Matt. What I do need is a lift' – he paused theatrically – 'and to know more about this delectable young doctor.' Sarah surprised herself by blushing. 'Why haven't we been introduced?'

Matt grinned. 'Righto. Dr Sarah Deville, meet Dr Drake Logan.'

Now it was Sarah's turn for raised eyebrows. Drake took her hand, kissed it, then snapped shut the giant fob. 'Hurry folks, or we'll be late for cocktails.'

They piled into the jeep and bumped back past the police and heavy machinery. A small group of loggers were having some sort of a powwow with the officers. A few cries of *piss off* and *you need your heads read* followed them down the track. In a mere ten minutes, a crudely painted sign in the headlights announced their arrival at Camp Clementine.

'This protest camp is in the centre of the area to be logged,' said Drake. Sarah peered out the window, but couldn't see much in the dark. Drake plucked the watch from his pocket again and shrieked. He dived out the door, extracted Sarah, and hurried her off in the direction of a camp fire. Somewhere nearby a generator throbbed. Sarah crossed the threshold into the flame-lit circle. Silhouetted forms turned into people, sitting and eating by the fire, speculating quietly about the size of the force they might face in the morning.

'We acknowledge the traditional owners of the land upon which we gather today,' said Drake solemnly. 'We pay respect to their elders – past, present and emerging – and to the Lia Pootah and Palawa people, who are the custodians of this land.' Then Drake cuckooed loudly, declared the hour, and magically pressed a plastic glass of red wine into Sarah's hand. Vanishing for a moment, he reappeared with a paper plate full of golden-brown samosas, all delicately poised on a steaming mountain of jasmine rice. Drake slid a curled gumleaf of dipping sauce onto her plate.

Everything smelled delicious. Sarah hadn't realised how hungry she was. Balancing her wine on the arm of a folding chair, she jabbed a crisp samosa into the sauce and took a bite. Drake held his breath in fake anticipation, then pressed his palms together when she gave the nod. He really was a centre stage sort of person.

Matt joined them, plate piled high and with a can of Bundaberg Rum in his hand. A young woman followed him over to the fire. She had tangled, dirty-blond hair, gypsy earrings and intense blue eyes. Drake introduced her as Lisa Bade – singer, songwriter, photographer and tree-sitter. Sarah nodded hello. Lisa knelt down and held her hands out to the flames. She oozed charisma. These people were so full of passion. It dripped from their bodies and seeped through their clothes. Sarah admired their courage and indisputable resolve. There was something to be said for having a cause.

For a time they ate in silence. When Sarah finished, Drake sprang to his feet and gestured to her empty plate. 'Seconds?'

'You do know,' said Lisa, 'that our food comes from supermarket dumpster diving?'

Sarah looked to Drake for confirmation. 'Perfectly good tucker,' he said. 'It's a crime to waste it.'

The samosas didn't appeal quite so much anymore. 'No thanks, no seconds.' She raised her empty plate. 'Where's the bin?'

'There is no bin,' said Lisa.

'Where do you throw things away?'

Lisa rolled her eyes. 'There is no *away*, don't you get that? The concept of throwing things out, throwing things away – it's just shifting your rubbish somewhere else, making it someone else's problem.'

Sarah felt out of her depth, out of her comfort zone, as Drake took her plate. Beyond him, three children emerged from the fog and played a noisy game of chasey around the fire. 'How do children manage here?' she asked.

'As well as they manage anywhere. Probably better,' said Matt, accepting a second can of rum and coke from Drake, who seemed to have an endless supply tucked away in an icebox beneath his chair.

'But what about school?'

'What about it?'

'Don't they go to school?'

'Of course not.' Lisa made an expansive gesture. 'Their school is the forest. Their teachers are the trees.'

A shocked Sarah tried to keep her expression neutral. Drake and Matt burst out laughing.

'They go to Hills End Primary, every day,' said Drake. 'Their dad, Ken Murphy, owns the local sawmill. He's here to add numbers for tomorrow's stoush, and their mum's camp cook this week. As a matter of fact, I'm driving those little terrors to school myself in the morning, but they'll go to their aunty's afterwards. Things are going to escalate.'

The joke at her expense made Sarah feel foolish, excluded. 'You said their dad owns the sawmill. Why is he here?'

'What?' said Lisa. 'You think because Ken owns the sawmill that he'll automatically be on Burns's side?'

Everyone looked at Sarah. She'd clearly put her foot in it again, but didn't know how. 'Well, it stands to reason—'

Lisa exploded in a torrent of words.

'Enough,' said Drake and Lisa stormed off.

'What did I say wrong?' asked Sarah.

Drake crouched in the empty place beside her. 'There's old-fashioned logging and then there's what's happening here in the Tuggerah. Burns Timber clear fells old-growth forests and sells the lot for woodchips. Our rarest Tassie trees are being turned into Japanese toilet paper. Sawmills are closing down for lack of logs. According to Ken, if this keeps up, our famous craftsmen and furniture makers will run out of wood. There'll be no Wooden Boat Festival, and we'll be restoring historic Port Arthur with plantation pine.'

Lisa returned with a plate of food and sat next to Matt, while a broad-chested, middle-aged man joined the conversation. 'I'm Ken Murphy and I'll speak for myself. Used to be we let the small trees grow. We harvested the forest selectively, in patches, and we didn't waste one single piece of a tree. We sawed the best logs, tanned the bark … even the leaves went for oil. Now they chip the lot – myrtle, sassafras, leatherwood. Leatherwood's bloody priceless. It breaks my heart.'

'Sorry,' said Sarah. 'I didn't know.'

'That's our main problem – nobody bloody knows,' said Ken. 'Between Premier Logan and our sorry excuse for a union and the Hobart papers? You'd think Burns was the saviour of Tasmania's timber industry. We're labelled traitors if we speak out.' Ken spat in the fire. 'Well, not anymore. It's time to take a stand.' And with that he stomped away.

Sarah sighed. First she'd upset Lisa, now Ken. She couldn't take a trick with these people. Better change the subject. She turned to Drake. 'So, you're a doctor? What sort of a doctor?'

Drake gave her an amused look. 'What, don't you believe me?'

Sarah looked to Matt for help. He was standing nearby, spinning Lisa some sort of ghost story. Sarah took a second look at him – relaxed, happy, as though he was free of something. The fire flared and turned his hair to an attractive bronze. She liked his eyes, a sort of smudged brown. When they smiled it brought a pleasing balance to his face. His body was muscular, baked brown, with no hint of softness around the belly. He moved like an animal, swift and sure.

The rumble of approaching vehicles disturbed the quiet night. Several people left the fire's circle, including Lisa, who checked her watch and hurried off. Sarah reached over and touched Matt's leg. 'What kind of doctor is Drake?'

Matt sat down beside her. 'You wouldn't think it to look at him, but our friend Drake here has a seriously impressive resume. A medical degree for starters. A PhD in zoology and marine biology from Princeton. A Eureka Prize for entomological research. Um … and he's written two books. Have I left anything out, Dr Drake?'

'I do a bit of sailing.'

'Oh, yeah,' said Matt, drawing a noughts-and-crosses board in the dirt. 'Drake spent last year as chief research officer on the *Sea Steward*.'

'Shall I start?' Drake traced a cross.

Sarah whistled low. Wow, the *Sea Steward*. How different Tasmania was to home. With its curious culture of understatement, of not bignoting oneself. She wished she could transport all her Los Angeles friends to this dark camp. Have these odd people look straight through them, catch them out, see the plain truth behind their masks.

The *Sea Steward's* Captain Peter Weston was a hero among Sarah's neoliberal friends back at UCLA. He'd founded a group to take direct action against sealers and whalers and long-line fishing vessels. Other conservation groups distanced themselves from Weston's organisation, alarmed by the fearless tactics he used to disrupt Japanese whaling ships.

Matt frowned and drew a victory line in the dirt. 'Don't be too impressed. Drake was seasick for the first two months.'

Not missing a beat, Drake turned his weak stomach into a badge of honour. 'It doesn't matter if you're sick as a dog, not when the whalers go after a mother and calf. You put yourself on the line. That's just what you do.'

'How far south did you go?' asked Sarah.

'Right to the ice shelf.'

'I'm impressed.'

'I do hope so,' said Drake.

Headlights shone down the road past the campfire, spotlighting Lisa and another man, both dressed in climbing gear and carrying helmets.

'Where are they going?' asked Sarah.

'Up Pallawarra.'

'What, at night? In this weather?'

'Only way to get past the loggers,' said Drake. 'Don't worry. The storm won't hit properly until morning.'

Sarah was speechless. She couldn't imagine the zeal that sent Lisa off to risk her life in the dark, windy forest. She felt a sharp pang of envy and fear. Drake touched her knee and topped up her glass.

'Are you married?' she asked him.

For the first time that night, Drake seemed wrong-footed. 'I suppose you could call it that.'

He wore no ring, but for some reason she wasn't surprised. 'Children?'

'Tell her, Drake,' said Matt, his tone daring. 'This should be interesting.'

Sarah leapt abruptly to her feet, swatted her knee and flicked a large insect to the ground. With a little shiver, she ground it beneath her heel.

'Stay still.' Drake reached across and stroked her bare leg. Sarah shivered again, not from fear this time. He coaxed a second insect, a shining beetle, from her thigh onto his hand. 'A jewel beetle. Lovely, isn't he?'

Sarah took a closer look. 'Why, yes,' she admitted. The beetle's shell glowed electric blue or emerald green, depending on its angle. The beautiful beetle unfolded stained glass wings and flew away.

'Insects are evolution's greatest success story. They saw the dinosaurs come and go. But their numbers are plummeting all over the world, so we really shouldn't stomp on them.'

'I asked if you had children,' said Sarah, irritated by Drake's disapproval.

'No. I'm a voluntary extinctionist,' said Drake.

'A what?'

'Our motto. *May we live long and die out.*'

Matt grinned and cracked another can.

'The basic concept,' said Drake, 'is that we don't breed. The alternative to the extinction of millions of species is the voluntary extinction of just one – us.'

His words made Sarah's skin prickle. What on earth was he talking about? These people were utterly bewildering.

Drake went on. 'Deciding not to have children is the morally correct choice. Humans are a plague, doctor, a planetary disease like the tumours on your devils. Their actions over the past few hundred years exhibit all the characteristics of malignant process. Rapid, uncontrolled growth. Invasion and destruction of neighbouring ecosystems. For metastasise, read colonise and urbanise. For dedifferentiation, read loss of diversity. Read a McDonald's in every country on earth. And what are the usual implications of a malignancy?'

'Death of the host,' said Sarah.

'Exactly. As special as we think we are, humans present a clear and present danger to life on this planet. It's time we went extinct.'

'You'll never convince me,' said Sarah, although there was a certain insane logic to his position. But there was also a logic to survival. More than that, it was a biological imperative. Any extinction was a disaster. That was why she'd got involved with the devils in the first place – so they wouldn't go the way of their cousins, the thylacines, vanished from Tasmania within living memory.

'A woman at the post office swears that she once saw a thylacine,' said Sarah.

Drake laughed. 'Half the population of this island thinks they've seen one, but there's not a scrap of proof. No remains, no photos, not even a footprint.'

'What do you think, Matt?' Sarah turned to him in the firelight.

Matt took his time answering. 'People want to believe,' he said at last. 'But there are no thylacines anymore. And do you know what?' He snapped a stick in half. 'I'm glad.'

Sarah gasped. 'How can you say that?'

'Since it seems to be a day for stories, let me tell you the story of the last thylacine known to walk this earth. A young female called Benjamin – they couldn't even get her sex right. The only person who cared about this extraordinary animal was a woman called Alison Reid.'

'The museum curator told me about her,' said Sarah. 'Forced from her job running the Hobart Zoo because she was female.'

Matt nodded. 'After that Benjamin was left alone, twenty-four seven, in an open concrete cage without access to her den. No shade from the sun or shelter from the cold. Benjamin died of exposure sometime during the night of the seventh of September, 1936. They didn't even bother to preserve her body – it went to the tip. And Australia has the nerve to declare the seventh of September, National Endangered Species Day. Let's celebrate our grand indifference, shall we?' Matt hurled his can into the fire. It caused a little hissing explosion. 'Benjamin and her kind are better off dead. What's the point of all this striving for life anyway?'

Sarah was speechless.

'Matt's drunk,' said Drake. 'You two had better stay here tonight.'

Matt burped loudly. 'Fine by me.'

The three of them were the only ones left at the fire.

'And what about you, doctor? Is it fine by you?' Drake sneaked his arm around Sarah's waist.

She let it linger awhile before slipping sideways. 'I'd better turn in.'

Drake sighed. 'Come on then, Lisa's bunk is empty.'

Sarah wrapped herself tight in Ray's coat and followed him to the tents.

Drake returned as yet another vehicle arrived to help fill the camp.

'You're in quite a mood tonight.' He tossed Matt a swag. 'Want to talk about it?'

Matt looked away. Of course he wanted to. He longed to take up his friend's offer, longed to unburden himself. But he couldn't risk telling Drake about Theo. He couldn't risk telling anybody. So instead he shrugged and slapped a mosquito into oblivion.

'Does it have anything to do with our beautiful young doctor?'

'Mate, you know me. I'm happily married.'

Drake fixed him with searching blue eyes. 'So happily married that you haven't called Penny?'

Matt groaned and buried his head in his hands. He'd messaged her about going to the Tuggerah, but that was hours ago. He hadn't called to say he wouldn't be home tonight. The alcohol that had made him briefly forget about Theo, had also made him forget about Penny. It was unforgivable.

'Don't worry,' said Drake. 'I rang her for you – said your phone had no reception.'

Matt let out a great grateful breath. 'I owe you one.'

Drake offered him the last can from the icebox. 'All yours. I need to be good for the morning.'

'Bit late for that, isn't it?' Matt tossed the can in the air, caught it and opened it. He'd have a hangover tomorrow.

Drake tucked the camp chair under his arm and gave Matt a final look. 'Remember mate, I'm here when you want to talk.'

After Drake had retreated to the tents, Matt poked at the dying fire. Its embers flamed once and died in a sad twist of smoke. The black forest pressed in around him, eerie and quiet – not even the friendly call of a boobook owl to punctuate the night. According to Penny, boobook owls were spirit guides of the dreaming. Lucky charms. But Camp Clementine was on the rim of the logging coupe, and the wise little owls had fled. Good fortune would have fled with them. He sat for the longest time, drinking alone while a chill seeped into his bones. Only when his teeth began chattering did he zip up his jacket, climb into the swag and close his eyes.

Matt awoke in the dark with a searing jolt, burning up by the fire, unaware at first of where he was. He rolled away from the hot coals and lurched to his feet, the dream still vivid. His eyes slowly adjusted and objects emerged from the gloom. His scorched swag lay where he'd fought his way out of it, ripped at the zip, in a crumpled heap on the ground. Why was this happening again? This nightmare where he turned into a monster.

Matt shivered. He'd seen his reflection in the dream river. The square head of a lion stared back at him; a marsupial lion, with fangs bared in a snarl – a creature extinct for twenty thousand years. It always ended the same way, this dream. It always ended in a successful hunt. And it felt very right to pound through the spectral forest after his shrieking prey, so sure in the dark. To seize it in his jaws, to gut it with his clawed thumbs in a rain of blood. The face of his prey came into focus – his father's face.

It began to rain. Matt pulled his swag under the cover of a canvas awning near the tents, climbed back in and lay rigid. The wind moaned like a banshee through the trees, and he hoped sleep would not come to him again that night.

CHAPTER 13

Fraser took off his pyjama trousers in front of the mirror, and stared at the place where his balls used to be. They produced too much testosterone, that's what his specialist had said. They had to go. Bilateral orchiectomy, they called it. But that wasn't what it was. It was gelding. They'd turned Fraser Burns Abbott into a eunuch.

He studied the body that had so betrayed him. His body used to be a mere thing, like any other thing. Something to be pushed, to be used and abused as required. Its deadly mutiny took him by surprise. It was testosterone that fed the cancer, that gave it the energy to metastasise, to escape his diseased prostate gland and launch an imperial army of invading cells. He could feel them in his bones. Now, without its life-giving hormone, the tumour had shrunk, relieving Fraser's backache overnight. It was a temporary reprieve. Sooner or later, the frustrated cancer cells would evolve, discover new ways to rob his ravaged body of nourishment, resume their deadly duplication. But right now he was close to pain-free. Just a dull lumbar ache that never let him forget. It gave Fraser great satisfaction to know that when he died, so would the cancer.

Fraser stepped into the shower. Steady, hot and strong, no water-saving rose for him. He fingered his empty sac and wondered again about prostheses. His surgeon wanted to put implants in his scrotum, *'to maintain a natural appearance'.* But what was the point? There were no women in his life, no lovers. And since becoming impotent, there weren't likely to be any. Make no mistake, he still had desires. The mind was the seat of desire, he knew that now, and there was nothing wrong with his mind. If anything, his thinking had acquired an extra clarity since the surgery, like he'd emerged from some sort of mental fog. No sign of the depression his doctors had warned of. But physical sex was finished. Fraser was a realist. The old credentials didn't stack up, and no amount of desire could change that.

Fraser dried himself and dressed in one of the interchangeable suits that hung in his vast walk-in wardrobe. More of a suite, really, with chairs and mirrors and two dressing tables. One half of the space still contained Charlotte's things. Her clothes, her shoes, her eighteen-year-old scarves – as if any minute she might walk back in the door. There was more than enough room to keep the clothes, and it brought him some comfort to see them there. Fraser looked in the mirror again, pleased with his hair. That was one advantage to the surgery – he'd never go bald. The thought helped him overlook the fact that the suit was too big for his shrinking frame.

Fraser began his drive to Hobart, thoughts skipping ahead to his lunch appointment with Premier Kate Logan. What would his old friend say, he wondered, when he told her?

CHAPTER 14

Sarah woke with a stiff neck, freezing feet and no sense of place. Rough-hewn roof beams above her and warped tin walls. Lisa's bunk, that's where she was. Last night's memories returned in steady fragments, while rain beat a tattoo on the rusty roof. Outside, she heard a commotion, busy sounds, people. Sarah checked her watch. Almost six o'clock, barely light. She pulled her sleeves over her hands.

Drake poked his head in. 'Rise and shine, princess, or you'll miss the school bus.'

Sarah climbed from Lisa's bed. The ground was icy. A fierce wind whipped through the door, whipped through her clothes and made her shiver. She was glad for Ray's oversized coat, and wrapped it around her as she struggled out the door and took in Camp Clementine by dawn. Grey sky, picnic chairs blown about, billowing canvas shelters. Boxes of posters and leaflets, banners and badges, weighed down with bricks. Derelict cars lay half-buried in the earth. Dozens of people filled the outdoor bush kitchen and huddled by the camp fire, eating bowls of oatmeal and toasting chunks of bread on green twigs. She couldn't see Matt anywhere.

Drake pressed a mug of black tea and a slab of toast into her hands. 'Get this into you,' he said with a grin. Sarah didn't much care for tea. Wasn't there coffee? She took a tentative bite of the toast. Its oily black spread tasted as foul as it looked. She spat the mouthful out.

'What *is* that?'

'Vegemite,' said Drake. 'The health food of a nation.' He relieved her of the toast and crammed it into his own mouth. 'We'd better hurry.'

Sarah took his arm. 'I need to *go* first. You know …'

Drake pointed her in the direction of the less-than-private composting loo with a queue. 'It's that or pick a tree.' Sarah didn't do *primitive* well. A tree had sufficed last night under cover of darkness. But in daylight, in this crowded camp?

'I'll wait until we're down the road,' she said, miserably, and trailed after Drake. The three children from last night stood by the jeep, dressed in neat uniforms and clutching schoolbags.

'That's Matt's jeep,' said Sarah, looking round 'Where is he?'

'Young Matt overdid it last night,' said Drake. 'You saw him. He's in no condition to drive. He's not even conscious, actually. In the meantime, wasn't it you who were so concerned about these children's education? You don't want them to miss the morning bell.' The kids giggled. 'Sarah, meet Ben, Tyson and Matilda.'

They all climbed into the jeep and drove back past the battered Camp Clementine sign, back past the loggers' equipment. 'We want to see Dumbledore's Wand,' said Ben.

'That's what the kids call the tree I climbed yesterday,' said Drake. 'It has lots of names. Different things to different people. To me it's Pallawarra, the tipping tree. Matt says we shouldn't name it at all.'

'Why?'

'He says it's like the blind men trying to describe the elephant from just a leg or a tail. They all have a point of view, and they're all wrong. He says that it's a vanity, that the simple fact of the tree is enough. But even he calls it Pallawarra.' Drake spun the wheel and veered off the track. 'Some people call it the fairy tree, or the cupid tree. To Burns, it's Ereg T950. To the hippies, it's the Tree of Life. The witches call it Tapio, the fierce spirit that protects the forest.'

'Witches?' asked Sarah.

'White witches,' said Drake. 'You met one last night – Lisa. They're perfectly friendly, most of the time.'

'We call it Dumbledore's Wand because it's magic,' said Ben.

Sarah turned in her seat and smiled at the little boy. He was so cute. All blonde hair and big blue eyes, and such an imagination. If she had a child she'd want one just like him.

Drake detoured and pulled over by the tree. Sarah could see an ancient face in its bark, with a beard of lichen and eyebrows of moss. She'd missed it yesterday, but it was plain enough now. Sarah got out and peered up Pallawarra's trunk, leaning back until her spine hurt. The tree was so tall that, even in broad daylight, she could get no real perspective on it. A wave of vertigo turned her stomach and sent her head swimming. She closed her eyes tight to keep balance. Tangled hair whipped around her face. The wind felt different, warmer and wilder.

'Are Lucky and Lisa up there?' asked five-year-old Ben.

Drake nodded. 'Probably tucked up, sound asleep. Getting some rest before the fun begins.'

'Will they get blown down?' asked seven-year-old Tyson.

Good question. How could anybody stay put up there in this howling gale? Sarah imagined Lisa's slight form plummeting to earth.

'No way,' said Drake. 'They're roped in, snug as bugs in rugs. Nothing will get them out of that tree until they decide to come down.'

'Dumbledore's Wand wouldn't let them fall anyway,' Ben explained. 'Coz they're its friends. But it would be dangerous for enemies to climb up, wouldn't it, Tilda?'

'Oh yes,' said ten-year-old Matilda. 'They'd die.'

Sarah inhaled sharply. Such a strange thing to say.

It began to rain. As Drake drove back past the heavy logging machinery, all three children leaned from the window and shouted *BOO* at the top of their lungs. Sarah jumped. Drake took no notice.

'What was that for?' she asked.

'We're voking a deadly curse,' answered little Ben.

'He means *invoking*. It's just a bit of fun,' said Drake.

'No, it's not,' said Ben in an indignant voice. 'It's real.'

'It *is* real,' said Matilda solemnly. 'What about Scott?'

'Stop it, Tilda,' said Drake. 'Scott died in an accident.'

Nobody spoke. They passed the place where Matt had shot the possum. Sarah imagined it rotting beneath the leaves. She was tired of the crying wind and the children. Tired of the granite grey sky and the brooding *Lord of the Rings* forest. Drake swung left through a curtain of rain, over the rickety bridge, across the swollen Charon River.

'Why is the water so black?' asked Sarah.

'It's stained with tannin, leached from button-grass moorlands higher up,' said Drake.

'No, it's not,' said Matilda. 'It's black because it belongs to Charon the Ferryman. He rows dead souls to Hades.'

Sarah decided she didn't like Matilda anymore.

'You're clever, Tilda,' said Drake. 'Where did you learn about Charon?'

'We're doing myths and legends at school. I know the five rivers of the underworld as well. Acheron, the river of pain. Cocytus, the river of wailing. Styx, the river of hate. I can't pronounce the river of fire. It starts with P though.'

'Phlegethon,' said Drake.

'Yes,' said Matilda. 'And I think I've forgotten the last river.'

Drake laughed. 'You must have been drinking from it then. It's called Lethe, the river of forgetfulness.'

Matilda bounced up and down. 'That's it, that's it. Lethe. But our teacher calls it the river of oblivion.'

Sarah checked her watch. This was getting creepy. Like that first dinner at Matt's house, when Penny's talent for making pretty jewellery turned into a bizarre obsession with taxidermy.

'Do you have to pay the ferryman?' asked Ben. 'What if you don't have any money? I don't have any money.'

'Then you'll be a ghost for a hundred years,' said Matilda, firmly.

Ben started to cry. Tyson found some change in his pocket. 'Here, Ben. But don't spend it at the canteen. Save it for Charon.'

Sarah looked out the window at the giant trees. They were outlandish. These children were alien. So was Drake's easy acceptance of their superstitions. For the first time she felt homesick. Los Angeles made so much more sense.

'Here we go,' said Drake, as a procession of police cars, trail bikes and four-wheel-drive vehicles appeared through the sweeping windscreen wipers.

Drake pulled off the track to make a hurried call. Another phone lay on the dash. Matt's phone? Sarah picked it up and examined it. Turned off. She switched it on. The approaching convoy halted at their parked jeep. Drake explained that they were driving the children to school in Hills End. This satisfied the officers, and the convoy moved on. Drake jumped straight back on the phone, giving an estimate of police numbers.

'Come on, Drake,' said Matilda. 'We'll be late for school.'

Matt's phone crowed and Sarah picked it up. 'Hello. Is that Penny? It's Sarah here.'

CHAPTER 15

WOORAWA

Jake released the big black eagle into the aviary beside Aquila, under the watchful eye of a small boy. The boy didn't come when his father called him, or when his family moved on to the next exhibit. The eagle hopped and flapped to the highest perch and stared at the sky. What a beauty. Where was Matt? It wasn't like him to miss such an important arrival.

'What's his name?' the boy asked Jake.

'Woorawa. It's an Aboriginal word for eagle.'

'Woorawa,' the boy repeated. 'Why is he here?'

'Hit by a car. Happens to a lot of them. You'd think people would be more careful.'

The boy nodded, never taking his eyes off the bird. 'How old is he?'

'Sorry, kid. I've got to go.' Jake picked up his bucket of dead possums. 'Why not ask him yourself?'

Jake smiled as he walked away. 'Talk to me, Woorawa,' the boy was saying. 'Tell me your story.'

The eagle swivelled his head and fixed his gaze on the boy. After a moment, a man came and took the boy's hand, hurrying him away.

Woorawa looked back towards the sun, rising high in the morning sky.

Last night, he'd dreamed he was back in the Tarkine with his mother and father and Moon, his sister. He'd dreamed about the ancient eyrie of his birth …

His parents. Old eagles. Experienced. Thirty seasons of chicks had hatched in their broad nest high in the branches of a centuries-old myrtle beech. Each year, they cleaned and refurbished it with new stems and lined it with sprays of soft sassafras.

It was a good season, the season of his hatching. Woorawa's egg came first: an especially beautiful egg, splotched purple-brown and lavender. Moon's plain white egg arrived three days later. His parents shared incubation duties by day. At night, mother eagle brooded alone, her mate on watch, roosting in the canopy. Forty-two sunsets had passed since the laying of this clutch. Sometimes she stood and stared at the eggs, listening to her unhatched chicks.

For six weeks Woorawa lay curled around his yolk, never hungry. Brightness came and went. Then one day he felt an irrepressible urge to scratch at his shell. With his beak crammed awkwardly under his wing, he scraped and struggled and scraped, not knowing why. One more scrape. He punched through the membrane, drawing breath from a trapped bubble of air, filling his lungs. He peeped. He peeped again. The world grew bright as mother eagle leapt from her nest. She stared at the egg, touched it with her beak, uttering soft low encouraging calls. *Dirra-lich … dirra-lich … dirra-lich.*

Woorawa peeped and peeped. *I'm here. I'm coming.* Tap, tap, tap … tap, tap, tap.

Moon heard him in her ivory egg. Hour after hour, he chipped away. It was gruelling work. Only strong chicks hatch. All through that day he tapped, rested, and tapped again. The sun sank below the ridge. Mother eagle tucked her eggs under her warm brood pouch and they all slept.

Morning came. Tap, tap, tap … tap, tap, tap. Woorawa raised a little bump on the shell. Mother and father stood by in rapt attention. Sister heard him too, waiting for breath inside her ivory egg. He peeped and scraped and pecked and peeped, holding his entire family spellbound. He tapped in a circle, broke off a cap and pushed it away. Mother and father leaned close to see their son. The end of the egg came off. Woorawa wriggled free and fell in an exhausted heap. There was no hint of the strength to come. Father launched off, determined to provide his mate with a meal before dark.

Mother eagle swept her baby beneath her breast, drying his snowy down, warming his wet body. And Woorawa slept. He slept all that long afternoon. He slept through the evening. He slept all night. And when morning came he sat up, bleary-eyed, wobbly head held high, surveying a view as ancient as he was new.

Mother admired her hatchling. She knew when she saw the beautiful egg that he would be special. Special like the pair's firstborn, hatched when their nest was still small and shallow. Hatched when she was still young.

Her mate fought for her that first summer, all those years ago. The new breeding season had seen her cast out by her parents, last year's chick no longer welcome. For two years she'd roamed alone on thermals of the central plateau. Sometimes she strayed into the territory of the few adult eagles who shared the skies. Invariably, these pairs, including her own parents, evicted her with aggressive territorial displays.

And it wasn't just her own kind who despised her. She was a pariah of the avian world wherever she went, relentlessly hounded by smaller birds. Magpies and mudlarks. Crows and currawongs. Sometimes hawks and falcons mobbed her with shrill whistles, dashing in with claws and beaks. She mostly endured the indignity. Sometimes she rolled and plucked a too-bold raven from the air, making a meal of it. Other birds harassed her as she ate, even little robins and wagtails. Was she welcome nowhere in the world? Perhaps she should leave her hostile homeland.

Weeks of lonely, aimless flight brought her to the Tarkine, a vast wilderness in Tasmania's north-west. But prey was scarce and hard to catch for an eagle raised in the farmlands of the Central Highlands. No dead sheep. No paddocks full of cats and rabbits here on Tikkawoppa Plateau. Instead, myrtle beech rainforest and button grass moorland extended to the horizon. She'd never learned to hunt large prey, but plump little pademelons abounded in the cold grassy clearings below. How hard could it be?

Cloudy skies allowed her to drop lower and lower without fear of the prey detecting her shadow. Selecting her target now. One ... two ... three. With folded wings she plummeted earthwards. The pademelons heard the whine of wind in wings and leapt as one for the forest. Her intended victim reached shelter. She switched focus to a larger male, crashing onto his shoulders mid-bound before the trees swallowed him. Seizing her prey tight with beak and claws, beating broad wings in reverse, she hauled him back into the open.

But this was no rabbit. The struggling wallaby weighed ten times more than the inexperienced young eagle. And it fought, desperate for life, ignoring the pain of slashing talons, resisting the force of battering wings, dragging itself closer and closer to the haven of the forest where she dared not follow.

It threw itself on the ground, dislodging its attacker with powerful kicks of clawed hind legs, inflicting damage of its own. Discouraged, she retreated, while a flurry of buff breast feathers whirled about the battlefield. The wallaby regained its feet and gathered itself for one final bound to safety. She hung back, unsure if she possessed the strength to mount another assault.

Then, out of the blue, the cavalry arrived. A second bird screamed earthwards, slamming the pademelon with all the force and know-how of a born and bred Tarkine forest eagle. Now both birds went in for the kill. Beaks like knives. Rapier talons crushing with bone-piercing force. The stranger's claws gripped the wallaby's neck, throttling it. Soon their victim ceased struggling. The eagles fed in a spirit of companionship, gorging until their crops could hold no more. The male lifted off, roosting on a low bough, ruffling feathers and preening. He watched her. She joined him. Side by side they rested, digesting their meal.

Hours later, the stranger took off with a stick held in his beak, broad wing strokes struggling to restore him to the breezy skies. She followed without hesitation. Higher and higher they spiralled, riding updrafts where wind met mountain. Her companion was in a playful mood, dropping his stick over and over, only to sweep around and catch it again. She joined in the game, diving on the stick, snatching it in her claws.

The male bird abruptly plunged, wings folded, then looped into a vertical climb. Stalling, he hung suspended in space, striking a heroic pose in silhouette. She watched this virtuoso display with admiring eyes, sometimes mirroring his movements. Again and again, he demonstrated his acrobatic skill. Teasing, she swooped him. He fled in mock fear. First she pursued him, then he her, flying close above and behind, perfectly synchronised. She spun and hung upside down in the cold air, presenting her talons. Instantly he seized them in his own, and the pair fell from the sky in a spectacular, cartwheeling trust exercise.

They pulled from their giddy descent just metres from the tree-tops. Intoxicated with love and lust, the birds alighted on a broad branch in the upper canopy, making low, affectionate yelps. He preened his intended, nibbling her nape, caressing her bill, serenading in high tremulous yodels. She crouched, beginning a loud, demanding *choo ... choo ... choo*, reminiscent of the voice of a whining nestling. Her suitor mimicked the call. Rising a few metres in the air, he landed lightly on her broad back, balancing with clenched claws to avoid causing harm, wings beating in slow motion, beak agape. Bowing low, he curled his wedge-shaped tail aside ... and she had her wild mate.

When other male eagles strayed into the forest, he defended her honour. Hovering high on silent wings, he would arrow down, trying to knock his rival from the air. So fierce were these encounters that both birds sometimes crashed into the canopy, where the fight continued. No challenger ever matched his savage resolve. Each time he saw his opponent off, occasionally dropping down to strike the humiliated loser in the back as he fled. Master again of his skies.

Thirty springs had passed since the she-eagle hatched that first, lovely lavender egg. She remembered the love, the pride, at the sight of her chick. The sadness when tapping from her second egg grew weak and died. The joy of her son's first flight, of his first kill.

She'd laid many eggs since then. Speckled ochre ones, blotched green ones, dull grey ones, spotty brown ones. But never one to match the beauty of that splendid original egg. Until Woorawa.

Moon hatched three days after her brother. Father was such an enthusiastic provider that the nest soon groaned with uneaten prey. Discreetly waiting for his departure on the morning hunt, mother took to collecting old carcasses and dropping them away from the nest. A boon for devils and forest ravens.

At two weeks, the chicks shed their silky white down for sooty grey fuzz. By three weeks, mother brooded them only at night or during the wildest storms, shielding them with extended wings to keep them dry. At four weeks, the eaglets were strong enough for play. Tug of war with sticks and bones. Hop chasey. Pretend-to-fly games. Dark primary quills sprouted on stubby wings. Soon Woorawa managed little lift-offs, facing into the wind, flapping uncertainly until rising over his sister's head. Filled with envy and admiration for her accomplished brother, Moon practised too. The chicks grew bold, exploring branches beyond the nest, giving ungainly chase to yellow thornbills whose pretty nests adorned the eyrie's walls and understorey.

At three months, the eaglets were fully fledged. One hot afternoon Woorawa took his first flight. Moon tried to follow, flapping and leaping skywards. But she-eagles are larger than males, and Moon's weight put her at a disadvantage. It was more than a week before she joined him, flying clumsily about the canopy.

Soon they soared with their proud parents. Black Woorawa and his red sister, learning eagle lore. Like all youngsters they had much to learn. How to glide on still wings and fall like a stone on their prey. How to seize wayward daytime possums and pluck birds from mid-air. And how to steal meals at roadside kills.

When Woorawa's parents first took this territory, and for decades after, there were no cars. But then a rough road took shape, snaking through virgin wilderness, bisecting the beautiful forests of Donaldson Valley. The eagles learned to scavenge roadkill, scanning the looping track for carcasses.

Men and machines became increasingly common visitors to the Tarkine that year, as the southern beech coloured red and gold. The family sometimes trailed deerstalkers, claiming the headless carcasses of stags. One hunter released a group of sows with piglets, hoping to pursue them the following spring. The eagles picked off the piglets one by one, working in tandem to separate them from their mothers. Bold Woorawa, in particular, enjoyed these easy pickings.

One morning, as they began the hunt, he watched his father launch into high soaring flight, prospecting for prey over the forest. A waste of time. Woorawa screeched derision and veered north towards the road, Moon close behind. After a moment's indecision, mother followed her fledglings, leaving her mate tracing measured ever-widening arcs in the western sky.

It wasn't long before the eagles spied breakfast. A fat pademelon lay dead on a curve in the road. They dropped to earth in lazy circles. A motor sounded somewhere in the distance. Woorawa bounded to the carcass, perched on top and plucked at the belly. Mother and sister showed more caution. It took some minutes before they joined in the feast.

The motor grew louder. The preoccupied eagles barely turned their heads, unaware of the danger until a ute raced around the bend. Moon's take-off was too slow, too cumbersome. She barely made it to windscreen height before the impact sent her crashing into the cabin. Showers of glass and feathers and blood blinded the driver. The dying eagle's hooked beak reflexively seized his leg.

Screaming in pain and surprise, he let go of the wheel and swerved from the track towards the other eagles. On the ground their broad wings and short legs made them clumsy. Woorawa and his mother, flapping to the roadside, could not escape the careening vehicle. It snapped Woorawa's unfurled left wing and clipped his mother's head. The raptors collapsed in the dust.

A man in the passenger seat opened the door and hurled Moon's smashed corpse on top of Woorawa's prone body. 'What the hell?'

The shaken men got out and gazed at the carnage. Blood seeped from the driver's blue-jeaned thigh.

'They're bloody eagles,' said the passenger. 'I don't believe it.'

'Who cares what they are, Joe. Just get me to a doctor fast.' The driver hobbled to the car and hauled himself in.

'Hang on a minute.' Joe retrieved a long-bladed knife from the back of the ute. Since childhood he'd been impressed by his uncle's hunting trophies – including eagle skulls and claws. What about a collection of his own? Already Joe could see the display behind glass in his pool room. He reached down to sever Woorawa's feet.

But Woorawa wasn't dead. He reared back and seized the man's right wrist in his steel-clawed grasp. Joe dropped the knife. Woorawa's hind killer claw pierced bone. Three forward-facing talons sliced deep. His leg muscles automatically tightened his grip, ratchet-like. Joe stared at his trapped, mangled hand, too horrified at first to make a sound. Woorawa leaned forward and tore a strip of flesh from Joe's arm.

The man's scream roused Woorawa's mother from her stupor. She shook her head, regained her feet, and took off at a clumsy run along the road, skipping and hopping and flapping until airborne. She circled low, calling encouragement. Woorawa heard her. Releasing Joe, he struggled off, dragging his snapped wing behind him. Joe struggled off too, moaning. Mother watched the ute reverse and drive away. She planed back to earth, reassuring her crippled son with soft double-noted whistles. *Dirra-lich ... dirra-lich ... dirra-lich.*

Woorawa nibbled her bill, her nape, yodelling like a nestling. He flapped his good wing and fell unbalanced to the dirt. Mother walked over to Moon's body and pushed it. She picked up the knife and dropped it. She flew to a low branch and called him again.

As morning wore into afternoon she remained close by. Woorawa dragged himself a little closer to his sister's side, surprised and confused by the pain in his useless wing. He watched his mother, comforted by her presence. Now they both heard a motor's thrum.

With one wild, grief-stricken shriek, mother launched skywards, flying south, abandoning her son. Next year's brood would learn to stay shy of the shining eagle-slayers that hurtled along roads.

The ranger slowed his vehicle at the sight of Moon's crumpled corpse. He got out to examine it and spotted Woorawa huddled nearby on the roadside. He fetched a net and gloves. On the ground a man can run down an eagle, but Woorawa barely tried to escape. Dejected, in pain, in shock, he suffered the indignity of netting. That was two years ago. Two years of surgery and pins and more surgery at Hobart's Raptor Rehabilitation Centre, until Woorawa's left wing matched his right in suppleness and strength. And now he perched in Binburra's Number 3 aviary, waiting for his new mate and a second chance.

'Penny? Are you still there?' The phone went dead. 'That was Penny,' Sarah told Drake. 'She said to tell Matt that the eagle has arrived.'

'Okay.'

'She seemed upset.'

Drake gave her a knowing glance. 'Listen, princess. Matt never called Pen last night, and now you answer his phone? Why wouldn't she be upset?'

Matilda leaned forward and crossed her arms over the back of Sarah's seat. 'Are you trying to steal Penny's husband?'

'No, of course not.' Sarah felt a little sick in her stomach. 'Drop me off at Binburra. I'll sort this out.'

'Are you going to say you're sorry?' asked Matilda.

Drake grinned at her.

'Matilda, if you don't stop being rude, I might just put that curse on *you*,' said Sarah.

Ben started wailing.

'She didn't mean it, mate,' said Drake. 'You were joking, weren't you, princess?'

Ben's wails reduced to expectant sobs.

Sarah glared at Drake. 'All right, yes, I was joking.'

'It wasn't very funny,' said Matilda. 'It wasn't, was it, Drake?'

'Right, kids, a bit of shush.' To Sarah's amazement, the children obeyed. Drake pointed to the sign up ahead. 'Next stop, Binburra.'

Penny turned up her collar against an icy wind whipping round her ears. The weather was as bleak as her mood. Usually the park was filled with sound and colour and movement. Devils loping about their pens or screeching at each other over a carcass. Wallabies cropping the grass while their joeys played chasey. Bright parrots courting in the treetops. Magpies carolling, bees buzzing and honeyeaters swarming the crimson bottlebrush flowers. Not today. Today each bird and animal was seeking shelter from the coming storm.

Penny bit her lower lip and fiddled idly with her wedding ring. Matt hadn't come home last night. He hadn't even called. Drake had though. He'd explained how the two friends wanted to reconnect, how a night in the forest might get Matt to open up. He'd explained, apologised even, about their drinking. He hadn't mentioned Sarah.

Penny watched Matt's jeep speed towards her through myriad rivulets threatening to wash away the drive. What would she say? What would he say? There'd be a good explanation, she knew that. Putting on a brave face, Penny went to meet him. But it was Drake driving. No sign of Matt at all.

Her brave face fell when Sarah got out of the passenger seat. Penny was all too aware of her sodden clothes, her mud-stained coat and shoes. Although for once, Sarah didn't look much better. It gave Penny an unexpected shock of satisfaction to see Sarah's tangled hair and shabby oversized parka. The rain eased to a drizzle. Drake leaned his elbow out of the driver's window.

'Morning, Pen.'

'Where's Matt?'

'Sleeping it off back at the camp.'

Sarah handed Matt's phone to Penny. 'Sorry if you were worried,' she said in an offhand way. 'Matt took me out to Camp Clementine yesterday, and then Drake invited us to eat. We had a few drinks and decided to stay. I had no idea Matt didn't call you.'

Penny burned with humiliation, but worked hard not to show it. 'Why do you have his phone?'

'It was in the jeep,' said Sarah.

Penny turned to Drake. 'Why do you have Matt's jeep?'

'Had to borrow it, Pen, to get these kids to school. Mine's almost out of diesel. I'll have it back before he even wakes up.'

Matilda poked her head out the window. 'We'll be late for school.'

'Tilda's right,' said Drake. 'Climb back in, princess.'

Colour was creeping across Sarah's cheeks. A guilty blush? An embarrassed blush? Her imagination? Penny couldn't tell.

Sarah took off her coat and handed it to Penny. 'Give this back to your uncle,' she said. 'And thank him, will you?'

A wave of disquiet washed over Penny – a disquiet bordering on resentment. How did Sarah know her uncle? The woman seemed to be inserting herself into every aspect of Penny's life.

She ran her hand over her head and gave her ponytail a sharp tug. Stop being paranoid. Sarah and her genetic research represented the very best chance for the devils to beat their disease. This was a time for gratitude and optimism, not for conflicted feelings.

Penny forced a smile and took Ray's coat. 'Are you sure Matt's alright?' she asked Drake as he put the jeep into gear.

'Right as rain.'

'Wait.' Penny held up her hand. 'I need Matt's jeep. The raptor gear is in there. Take mine instead.'

They all dutifully piled out and climbed into Penny's vehicle. All except Ben.

'Ben, hurry up. We'll be late,' complained Matilda. 'I hate being late.'

'Miss Goody-Two-Shoes, Miss Goody-Two-Shoes, Miss Goody-Two-Shoes …' Ben's muffled chant came from beneath a blanket in the back of Matt's jeep. Then a yell. 'There's dead things in here.'

Drake strode over, extracted the screaming boy and deposited him unceremoniously into Penny's jeep. Then he took off down the drive.

Penny's mobile rang. Could it be Matt using someone else's phone? No, just Jake asking about the new eagle. 'I've put him in the aviary beside Aquila.'

'So?'

'Is that okay, do you think?'

'What the heck are you asking me for? I'm not in charge of the raptors. Work it out for yourself, why don't you?'

As Jake hung up, Penny gave a heavy sigh. This wasn't Jake's fault, so why had she yelled at him? She was overreacting over Matt's absence and she had to calm down. After all, it was just one drunken night. Wasn't it?

No, it was more than that. She was sick of pretending they were intact when they weren't. Matt worked late, rose early, avoided all but the most perfunctory conversations. Sometimes she caught him watching her, as if he wanted to say something. But when their eyes met, a brief, almost accusing glance wounded her before he turned away. What had she done? Or was it him who'd done something? She banished the thought. Loyalty was Matt's very strongest suit, and she was suddenly ashamed of her suspicions.

Penny had never had reason to doubt her husband's love. Not when she attended his swanky Hobart College reunion, along with Drake, marvelling at how Matt came to pick her over all those gorgeous, well-connected girls. Not when her family behaved like a pack of hillbillies, alternatively lampooning him and hitting him up for money. Not when her period turned up relentlessly, month after month, year after year, even though they wanted a family. There were times she'd questioned his discretion, his tolerance, his judgement, but never his fidelity. So why let the rats of doubt gnaw away at her confidence now?

She felt better, almost silly for worrying. Matt and Drake had gone bush plenty of times before. Penny took a deep breath. She'd go check on the new eagle, that's what she'd do. It was odd though, that Matt had missed its arrival. He'd worked so hard to find Aquila a mate. As an added bonus, a fledgling peregrine had also arrived that morning. A woman handed it in when she found the unfortunate falcon living in a budgie cage on top of her teenage son's wardrobe. Perhaps these new arrivals would help Matt get over the loss of Sooty and Sweep.

Penny gazed in admiration at the new eagle. It sat on the highest perch, separated from Aquila by a few metres and some chicken wire. The birds studiously ignored each other, though they couldn't resist taking the odd surreptitious peek. How impressed Matt would be with this beautiful black eagle. He should be here.

Despite her best efforts, the questions came crowding back, tying Penny's stomach in knots. When Drake rang last night, why hadn't he mentioned Sarah? And why on earth had Matt taken Sarah to the Tuggerah in the first place?

Penny hurried back to Matt's jeep. Flinging open the back, she began to pull things out, though she had no idea what she was looking for. She turfed out gloves, traps, weighing scales. Matilda's pink *My Little Pony* umbrella. She flicked through some notebooks, before they too hit the ground. Then she saw it, hiding beneath a pack of polythene tree guards – the bagged body of a devil.

Penny caught her breath as she recognised the ear tag. Oh, no, not Lazarus. Congealed blood matted the fur around his mouth and nose. At a guess, he'd died within the last forty-eight hours. What had happened to him? Apart from eagles, devils faced no natural predators in the park, and this was no eagle kill. Could Matt be responsible? Is that why he hadn't come home last night? He'd hit Lazarus on the road and couldn't face her.

Penny blinked back tears, extracted Lazarus from the bag with exaggerated care and examined him. Before long, her sadness gave way to professional curiosity. Methodically she parted sections of the devil's matted fur. There, behind the shoulders. A line of puncture wounds, bite wounds. Dismay and relief came together. Lazarus wasn't the victim of roadkill at all. This was a dog attack. Did Matt realise? She pulled out her phone and called him. A cock crowed in her pocket. Of course, she had his phone. Penny phoned Jake instead.

'Jake? Something's come up. You'll need to take the morning school groups for me.'

'But the vet's coming at ten.'

'Good. I have a dead devil for her to autopsy. I'll leave it in the reptile fridge.'

'Anything else?' asked Jake. 'I could dig some new dens with my bare hands?'

'That would be great,' said Penny, absentmindedly.

Consigning Lazarus to the refrigerator, she filled the jeep with diesel and headed for the Tuggerah.

CHAPTER 17

Shouting and roaring engines. Singing. Screaming? Matt struggled through foggy sleep towards consciousness. He was creased and stiff from cold, with a vile taste in his mouth. The hammer in his head didn't help. The sharp kick to the ribs did. He rose on one elbow, forced open his eyes and peered up at his attacker. A woman in police uniform peered back.

'Rise and shine, sweetheart,' she said.

As Matt stumbled to his feet he saw the full chaos surrounding him. It must have teemed overnight. The camp was drenched. Sodden people sat shackled to tree trunks. Some were firmly ensconced in the buried cars, their hands chained through holes in the floor to concrete blocks below. Others were clambering up trees or fleeing into the bush, defying the shrill orders of police and forestry officials. Half a dozen dragons – old bombs minus wheels – blocked the rough road into the forest, preventing effective pursuit. *We Shall Overcome* sounded in harmony from a group sitting cross-legged, arms linked, under the Camp Clementine sign. Swarms of police wandered the camp, some threatening, some cajoling. Matt didn't recognise any of them. He checked his watch. Nine o'clock already. The folly of yesterday filtered into his hangover-fuddled head. Where were Drake and Sarah? He couldn't see them.

'Name, address and driver's licence,' said the policewoman, pen and paper at the ready. She wasn't a local. Must be part of the Hobart force. All around him, charges of trespass were being read out. Sheepishly, he produced his ID. The policewoman examined it without comprehension.

'It's a park ranger's licence,' he said. She still looked puzzled. 'It means I'm allowed to be here.'

Matt sank into a soggy chair and put his head in his hands, while the woman called another policeman over to look at the licence. The wind had shifted north, warmer now, almost humid. He pulled back his hood and glanced skywards. A curious cloud bank was building in the north-east, boiling higher and higher.

Matt glanced about and saw Nick Byrne wend his way through the throng towards him. He flashed his badge and waved off the doubtful officers. 'What the devil are you doing here?'

Matt shrugged. His tongue lay thick and foul against his lips. Somewhere a chainsaw roared to life, then another. Over by the sign, muddy protesters were being dragged to paddy wagons, one by one. Matt's instinct was to help them.

Nick must have sensed trouble. 'It's not your fight,' he warned.

'Isn't it?' said Matt. Perhaps his father had made it his fight.

'Interfere with this, your job's as good as gone, mate.'

Nick was right, of course. Matt pulled himself together. 'I'm out of here,' he said, holding his palms in an open-handed sign that he was done. Nick nodded and marched off to help process the ever-growing queue of arrestees.

Matt looked about for his jeep, searched the lines of vehicles. It was gone. Bit by bit the realisation hit him. Drake had taken off with his jeep, and with Sarah, and left him stranded in the middle of a rout. Some friend. Matt groaned. Aquila's mate, Woorawa, was arriving this morning. And what about Penny? He flicked a leech from the soft skin of his wrist and explored his trouser pockets for his phone. Nothing but a few coins, some gum and a used tissue.

Matt racked his brain about the night before, disgusted with himself. He had little recollection of anything after arriving at the camp. The evening had vanished into a slab of Bundaberg Rum. For all he knew, he'd left the phone in his jeep or lost it altogether. Had he called Penny? He hoped so. Well, no use worrying about it. Right now he needed to find a lift home and some Panadol.

Ignoring the surrounding mayhem, he lurched to the kitchen tent and hunted around until he found a box of headache tablets. He swallowed three of them, along with some orange juice, and felt strength returning to his dehydrated body. He slapped a cold, fried egg between two slices of stale bread. Better than nothing. Matt pulled his coat tight around him and buried his hands in its pockets. At least the rain had stopped. He sat down to watch and wait. His best bet might be to cadge a ride back with Nick at the end of it all.

It soon became evident that this wasn't quite the rout he'd imagined. For one thing, dozens of cars full of protesters were still arriving. Film crews were arriving too, one from the national broadcaster and two more from commercial channels. They parked behind the police contingent, hemming them in. The silver *Save Tassie's Forests* banners would show up well on TV.

Police and protesters swarmed between the recently arrived vehicles and the camp site. Some people escaped back along the track, pursuable only by police on trail bikes. The city coppers seemed disorganised and out of their comfort zone, reluctant to slide through wet clay and roots to follow people into thick forest, or to struggle through the spiky barriers of branches around the camp perimeter.

The local police knew to soak their socks in salt water before scrambling through the bush. In contrast, the Hobart coppers stopped constantly to pick off leeches, and faltered at each mischievous cry of *tiger snake* or *copperhead*. Only a small proportion of activists seemed to be ending up in paddy wagons, and the roaming television crews were putting a dampener on the Forestry Department's famous enthusiasm for arrests. A petite elderly woman slipped over as they led her away, and the cameras were right there. A constable helped her to her feet. She leaned heavily on his arm, clutching a beaded handbag and looking dazed. Matt stood up. It was Margaret Murphy, Ken's grandmother. He moved within earshot.

'Are you okay?' a reporter asked her.

'I've hurt my ankle,' said Mrs Murphy. 'But it's my heart I'm worried about. My heart is sore.'

The alarmed constable called for first aid and the reporter found her a chair.

'Can you tell us your name?'

'Margaret Murphy.'

'And why are you here, Margaret?'

'I think these trees should be preserved. They're our grandchildren's heritage, after all.'

The reporter nodded. 'Are you a local?'

'Oh my word, yes,' said Mrs Murphy. 'I've run the tearooms in Hills End for forty years, with a little bed and breakfast attached. And now when tourists come, they ask me, "Why do you people let them cut down these lovely forests? It's what we come to see." And I thought to myself, they are entirely right. So I came out here to help.'

More press crowded around. Someone wrapped a blanket about Mrs Murphy's shoulders. A few drops of rain and someone else found her an umbrella. Matt smiled, enjoying himself now. Reporters loved a human angle, and his father would hate this little piece going to air. Sweet, silver-haired old ladies like Mrs Murphy hardly fitted the stereotype of ratbag mainland greenies. He guessed the police had only detained her because the able-bodied had fled. Another television crew joined the scrum.

'And what does this forest mean to you, Margaret?'

'Life,' she said simply. 'This forest has meant life to my family ever since I was a girl. My father owned the sawmill then and my grandson owns it now. My mother said Dad's occupation was a blessing, because during the war Hobart shipwrights built supply ships and minesweepers for the Pacific campaign. Sawmilling was a protected industry and timber workers weren't allowed to enlist. "This forest saved Dad's life," Mum would say to us kids. But he didn't chop down every tree in sight, not like they do now. He only logged what he needed, and he used everything. Swamp gum for hulls. Back then a single log could build an eighty-foot keel. Huon and celery top pine for decks. "Celery top needs to be at least two hundred years old," Dad used to say. "If you saw it under that, you're wasting it." We were the original greenies, I suppose, during the war. We had to preserve things, conserve things, make things last. My father would turn in his grave to see them chip all this wonderful wood.'

A young officer came over with a steaming mug of coffee. She wrapped her stiff fingers around the warm mug.

'Thank you, dear. Now, where was I?' Her voice, though low, commanded the attention of all those nearby. 'Sometimes my mother and brothers and me, we'd join Dad out here at the bush camp. We had marvellous times, absolutely marvellous. We just ran wild. Mum took us for picnics to the fairy tree and told us stories. That was my favourite place. A tree so tall its top was lost in cloud, so old its roots were lost in time. Dad carved make-believe animals and elves and goblins into its bark for us, and we believed it was enchanted. When I was grown, my husband carved our names in it as well. "As long as this tree stands strong, so will our love," he told me, and he was true to his word. You could never have met a finer husband and father than my Bob.'

'Your Bob sounds like quite the romantic,' said the officer with a smile.

'Oh, we weren't the only ones. Local sweethearts have been carving their names into that tree for over a hundred years. I remember one particular carving. *Belle and Luke*, etched inside an angel. A beautiful angel, very old and engraved with great care. I always prayed that those two lived a life as happy as mine and Bob's.'

'And do you know what happened to the fairy tree, Margaret?' asked a reporter.

'Of course I do. It's the same tree those young people have climbed today. They are very brave to risk themselves, defending their principles like that. I think they are the very best young people we have.' Margaret sipped her coffee. Nobody spoke. A medic arrived, helped her to her feet and guided her away.

'Matt! Matt, over here!'

He turned to see Penny, frantic, trying to push past an officer who had hold of her arm. Her copper hair lit the grey-skied morning. Matt's heart beat faster, and a rush of warmth washed over him at the sight of her. Yet fear lurked beneath his pleasure; fear of telling Penny about Lazarus and of the pain it would cause.

He hurried over. 'This is my wife.' Matt showed his ID, and the officer let Penny's arm go. Matt pulled her to him, wrapped her in his arms and kissed her lightly on the lips. She yielded at first, leaning into him, then stiffened.

'Come on.' She led him to the edge of the camp and into the forest, away from the shouting and milling people. Penny brushed a leaf and cobwebs from his hair. 'I know about Lazarus.'

Her words sent a raw jolt through his throbbing head. 'I found him yesterday,' said Matt. 'Beside the road, high in the park.' He licked his lips, which were rough and dry as sandpaper. 'Sorry Pen. It broke my heart, too. I don't remember hitting him, but no one else was up there this week.'

He saw no blame in Penny's eyes, and for some reason that made him feel worse. He deserved her anger.

'Is Lazarus the reason why you didn't come home last night?' He pressed his fingers to his temple. She gently pried them away, keeping hold of them. 'Listen to me. You had nothing to do with what happened.' He squeezed her hands, then dropped them and turned away. She pulled him back to her. 'Matt, I mean it. You didn't kill Lazarus. A dog did.'

'That's impossible.'

'The vet will confirm it later today. It was a large dog, definitely a dog.'

Matt struggled to make sense of it. There were no dogs in the park. Then a second, stunning possibility dawned in his foggy brain.

'I thought you'd be happy to know you weren't responsible.'

Matt said nothing, looked at his boots, and Penny shook him by the shoulders. 'Tell me what's wrong. We can't go on like this. Do you realise you missed Woorawa coming? And what's with the new chest freezer that arrived yesterday out of the blue. How much did that cost? Don't we talk about anything anymore?'

Matt burned with words that wouldn't come.

'Aargh, I give up.' Penny stamped her feet and marched off.

He followed her, weaving his way through the police throng, dodging timber workers who were sawing through the stumps of camp buildings and hauling down canvas and tin.

Nick waylaid him. 'They're going up after Lisa and Lucky,' he said.

'Who, the city coppers?' Matt snorted. 'They couldn't climb a ladder.'

'Nah, the state search-and-rescue boys. Those blokes know what they're doing.' Nick looked after Penny, stomping her way to the jeep, shoulders squared, fists tight by her side. He offered Matt some gum. Matt popped it in his mouth, but peppermint couldn't disguise the rank taste on his tongue. 'I reckon they'll be a lot safer going up that tree than you will be going home with her,' said Nick.

Matt grinned ruefully. 'I reckon you're right, mate.'

CHAPTER 18

By the time he reached the jeep, Penny was already sitting in the driver's seat. Pursed lips, stiff back, knuckle-white hands in charge of the wheel.

Matt climbed in beside her. 'Did Woorawa come? Does Aquila like her new boyfriend?'

Apparently it was Penny's turn not to talk. She took off, grinding gears, wheels hurling mud behind them.

'Remind me never to listen to Drake,' he said. 'Or drink Bundy and coke.' A tight smile this time, as though she was happy he had a hangover. He tried again. 'Hobart search-and-rescue are going up after Lisa and Lucky.'

Now he had her attention. 'Up where?'

'Up Pallawarra.'

Penny's eyes grew large. 'Nobody would dare cut down Pallawarra.'

'Not if Drake's mob can help it.'

The jeep emerged from the track into the flattened logging coupe. Penny stopped for a moment, grim-faced, unable to get her bearings in a forest so utterly changed. 'Our names are on that tree,' she said.

Matt let out a long breath, remembering their first date. It had been on the anniversary of her parents' death in a road accident. In a way, he and Penny were both orphans. They'd visited Pallawarra to look for her mother and father's name on the trunk. Matt had added their own, engraved within a large heart. When she saw what he'd done, she'd blushed and scolded him. But she hadn't meant it; she'd been happy. She wasn't happy now.

An officer stopped them when they reached a wide cordon set up around Pallawarra. Matt showed ID and they were through, with Nick and several news crews following close behind. They parked behind the high-angle search-and-rescue vehicle. It overflowed with equipment: nylon kernmantle ropes and lines, an array of anchoring and belaying devices, pulleys, harnesses, a capstan winch on a light aluminium frame. Paramedics stood by with stretchers and first aid supplies.

Matt hung his binoculars round his neck, leaned against the jeep and grinned at Nick as he got out of his own car. 'I don't think they've got enough gear.'

'Why don't they just climb the bloody tree, like you did?'

Penny turned to face Matt. 'You climbed Pallawarra?'

'I had to get Drake down,' he said sheepishly.

'Nick, is this true? Matt could have died, and nobody thought to tell me?' Penny looked close to tears as Nick and Matt mumbled apologies.

Pallawarra stood framed by an anvil of cloud. Minus the protection of his centuries-old companions, the tree looked as hurt and sad as Penny did.

'Two Hobart coppers from southern command have gone up first,' said Nick. 'Some sort of a turf war, I reckon. They wanted to beat the local search-and-rescue fellers up the tree. I tell you what, they're making it look like bloody hard work.'

Matt went for his binoculars. The two officers were barely ten metres above the ground, inching up the trunk, supported by lanyards and harnesses. They'd take forever at that rate. The tree-sitters' platform was a good sixty metres high.

The men wore vicious-looking tree spikes strapped to their boots.

Matt flinched each time the blades pierced Pallawarra, injuring the living tissue beneath his bark, making entry points for rot. It was like multiple stabbings. The wounds would bleed sap for days.

Now a member of the local search-and-rescue crew began his ascent with a sling. He was a first-rate lead climber who didn't use spikes. Those on the ground went quiet, backing up to take in the man's progress, ignoring a sprinkling of hail. When he overtook the Hobart team, a brief cheer rang out, before a sudden fierce rain squall forced everyone under the hoods of their jackets. Matt offered Penny the scant shelter of his hat, and she accepted without a word.

Ten thousand metres above the forest, warm winds were melting hail into solid shafts of rain. A narrow column of air chased after the downpour, plummeting earthwards, gathering momentum on the way. Thunder rumbled and Zeus himself might have been massing the clouds.

The tired climber reached a broad branch only fifteen metres beneath the platform. He fixed an anchor rope, known as a belay or top rope, and rappelled back down. Now two fresh men geared up, attaching their harnesses to the belay rope.

Matt was sweating. The air felt clammy and lightning streaked across the wine-dark sky. Wisps of virga hung like torn drapes beneath the thunderhead.

'We should head home,' said Penny.

Matt nodded, but neither of them moved. The news crews lay in wait, doing the occasional live-cross. Margaret Murphy sat in the front seat of the Channel 9 truck, running commentary. With the belay rope in place, the two new search-and-rescue men soon passed the Hobart team and reached the anchor branch. Matt peered through the binoculars. Metres above them, Lisa and Lucky stood braced and strapped together against the trunk running through the middle of the platform. Lucky had lowered a stout top rope to assist the climbers below, and the local boys now used it to reach the platform. Nobody wanted any accidents.

Matt checked his phone. Eleven o'clock, but the day felt older, worn through. He gave Penny the binoculars, then crossed his arms above his head against the rain: fat plopping drops, like Queensland rain.

'Will Lisa and Lucky try escaping?' asked Penny.

Matt had also noticed the swaying escape cable disappearing off into the canopy, but he shook his head. 'Too dangerous in this weather. What's happening now?'

'I don't believe it.' Penny handed the binoculars back to Matt.

The city coppers, who'd almost reached the anchor branch, were still using tree spikes, even though they had a top rope and branches to climb.

Lightning stabbed the peculiar grey-green sky, followed by close volleys of thunder. A violent wintry blast threatened to knock everyone off their feet. Above them, Lucky would be checking his straps, holding tight to the top rope, shouting encouragement to the climbers. *Stay calm and check your harness, your locking triggers. Keep your buckles tight, your carabiners secure. Don't worry, I've held plenty of falls.* But the wind would whip his words away, and what about this bloody weather?

Needles of icy rain stung Matt's face, as a sudden, plunging wall of water extinguished the sun. Thunder cracked like the snapping of giant bones. And a myrtle beech began, ever so slowly, to topple at the edge of the clearing. After five long centuries, its ancient roots could no longer cling to the newly eroded soil.

Screams pierced the loud creaking of its fall, and all across the coupe, onlookers ran for cover. Matt grabbed Penny's hand and pulled her down behind a big log. Huddled together, battling for breath, they watched the myrtle fall in slow motion, watched it collect the Hobart police climbers in its branches on the way down. Lucky's top rope swung free and Matt swallowed back bile.

A moment passed. Two. Then a freezing wind shear blasted the naked earth, turning logging debris into deadly missiles. Roots and jagged stumps hurtled in all directions. A snapped bough speared the leg of a cameraman filming the chaos. Matt pulled Penny lower, protecting her with his body, trying to melt into the log, as trees on the forest edge splintered and fell. The freak wind wrenched others right out of the ground, massive root balls and all. Horizontal sheets of rain fanned like spokes of a giant wheel, driving everything before them.

As abruptly as the storm arrived, it vanished. Five minutes had felt like five hours. The impossible rains eased. The improbable winds lost their strength, and swirled now in gentle curls. The day instantly brightened and warmed. One by one, people released their death grips and staggered into the open.

Pallawarra stood strong, framed by a brilliant double rainbow. Strewn at his feet, like so many pick-up sticks, lay a dozen of his fallen companions. The rest of the forest crowded round in silent witness. The rain-washed air was redolent with eucalyptus and sassafras, instead of diesel. The bodies of the police climbers lay trapped in the myrtle's branches. Even from a distance, Matt could see they were dead. Their bloodied limbs lay at strange angles. Their heads lolled limp.

Penny and Matt unfolded themselves from each other and ventured into the open. They squinted skywards, buoyed to see Lisa and Lucky safe on the platform, along with the two search-and-rescue men. Paramedics picked their way to the site of the fatal fall and the grisly task of untangling the bodies began. Penny and Matt helped Nick drag a downed sassafras away from their vehicles.

'What on earth just happened?' asked Nick, giving the splintered trunk one last heave.

'A microburst,' said Matt. 'They don't usually happen this far south, but with climate change ...' He stepped back and wiped muddy hands on his trousers. Shock had driven his headache and hangover away. 'Drake and I dodged one at sea once. A shelf of cumulus cloud rolled in, lit up by lightning, then everything went black. We hove-to, unplugged the instruments and kept our heads down. The wind and rain lasted just a minute, but it was the wildest thing.'

An officer came to tell Nick what they'd already guessed – the climbers were dead. Matt hugged Penny to him, his legs weak. He stared about at the stunned, uncomprehending crowd. The air was heavy with collective grief; grief that could easily turn to anger. Two police officers killed because of the protest – what would happen now?

Out of respect for the fallen, Lucky and Lisa were descending the tree.

'Should we stay?' asked Penny.

'Nah,' said Nick. 'You two clear off.'

Matt and Penny climbed into the jeep and manoeuvred along the storm-strewn track until they reached the open road. Matt thought about the dead men, about their families. He couldn't help being glad that Pallawarra remained standing, despite the terrible price paid.

CHAPTER 19

Sarah mounted the flight of granite steps leading to the broad bluestone verandah of Canterbury Downs. Black shutters guarded the mansion's windows. From the enormous oak-panelled front door, to the profusion of marble garden statues, the place oozed old money. She tried to imagine a little boy bouncing balls off the dark walls or playing in the manicured garden. She failed. It seemed no place for children.

Sarah raised the big bronze door knocker cast in the shape of a boar's head. It fell with a dead thud. Muffled barking came from the rear of the house. A chorus of dogs, big ones by the sound of them. Sarah frowned. She didn't like dogs. After waiting for a few moments, she tried the handle. The heavy door swung in on well-oiled hinges. Sarah knocked again, this time on the jamb.

'Mr Abbott?' Her voice echoed in the great space.

No answer.

The foyer was dominated by a monstrous wall-mounted moose head beside a cantilevered stone staircase.

Sarah wandered in, admiring the artwork, avoiding the hulking moose. Her favourite painting was a luminous forest scene of exotic animals in pairs, with an ark waiting in the hazy distance. Quite charming. Peering close she could make out a signature, Brueghel, and a faint date. The painting was five hundred years old. The next four paintings were equally ancient: scenes of four seasons by the same artist. What must they be worth?

The only contemporary piece was a portrait of a young woman. She bore a striking resemblance to Matt. A certain shyness, the same unsettling brown eyes, the nose softer, though. Now she'd met his mother, she was more curious than ever to meet Matt's father.

Sarah held a breath and listened. There, a series of soft pops coming from somewhere at the back of the house. She went through the door on her right into an elegant lounge room with a snow-white marble fireplace in classic columns. Then into a breakfast room, beneath a hemispherical dome pierced by lunettes. Floor-to-ceiling cedar shutters on French doors led to a stone-flagged verandah. Sarah looked across the sweeping lawns to the stately elms, across the ornamental lake and serpentine paths. A low rock wall, topped with a hedge of lavender, separated the orchard from the formal gardens. The pops sounded loudly from that direction.

Sarah crossed a stone bridge over the wall, and there he was. A tall man, wearing headphones and goggles – firing a pistol at a curved grass berm. Baffles topped the embankment. Six steel target plates stood bolted to a cast iron stand, solid black circles on white backgrounds. Red flags fluttered, positioned between the firing line and the target. With each pop, a target spun around and automatically reset itself. The shooter didn't miss once.

At last Fraser Burns Abbott lowered his weapon and leaned on a timber bench topped with sandbags. His shoulders sagged, yet when he turned and saw her he no longer looked weary. Fraser offered his hand on her approach, his expression unfathomable behind dark glasses. He took Sarah's hand and pressed it to his lips while she stared at his weapon. It looked like a fancy toy. 'May I touch it?'

'A woman of taste.' He slid the gun onto her open palm. It felt cool and heavy.

'An 1880 Colt 45 single-action six-shooter, factory-engraved with walrus ivory grips. A beauty, eh? It belonged to my great-grandfather.' He pointed out the name *Henry Abbott* imprinted on the gold-plated back strap beneath the barrel. 'I gave this gun to Matthew on his sixteenth birthday.'

It really was exquisite. Each inch of steel boasted engravings of bears. A gold inlaid boar charged from the ivory handle. Fraser turned the pistol over in her hand. On the other side was a carved bull's head with gold-tipped horns. Sarah looked up into eyes that might have been Matt's eyes, and closed curious fingers on the gun.

Fraser gently pried it from her. 'Dr Sarah Deville, I presume?'

'Mr Abbott.'

'Fraser, please.'

Sarah smiled. 'Your home is magnificent.'

'Indeed, although the plumbing remains a riddle.' He rubbed the barrel of his pistol. 'To what do I owe this pleasure?'

'I'm simply here to thank you,' said Sarah. 'For that amazing donation. To be honest, you've more than doubled our budget.'

He pinned her in his intense gaze. 'I hope we can always be honest with each other, Sarah.' An unearthly howling started up behind her. She turned to see two massive black dogs bounding at the fence of a grassy run. 'My newfoundlands, Sasha and Bruno,' said Fraser. 'It's traditional to keep a pair here at Canterbury Downs.'

Sarah stared at the baying, leaping dogs. Thank goodness the great creatures were behind the fence. She followed Fraser back into the house, across the polished parquet floors and into the library, with its walnut wainscoting and high-beamed ceilings. He flicked a switch on the wall and soft classical music sounded through the house.

'Brahms,' said Fraser. 'His second piano concerto, almost a symphony.'

'Third movement,' said Sarah. 'This cello solo is quite unique.'

Fraser inclined his head, approvingly.

Sarah took in the library: the white tiger skin on the floor, the tall grandfather clock. 'That clock is gorgeous. What are those tiny spinning moons?'

'Lunar dials,' said Fraser. 'They show the precise phase of the moon at a glance. In days gone by, if you planned to travel at night by horseback or coach, the journey was far safer by the light of a full moon. Bushrangers and other scoundrels liked to operate under the cover of new moon darkness.'

One whole wall of the library was lined with a grand cherry-wood gun cabinet boasting maple inlays and glass doors. Strip lighting cast a soft, even glow over the collection of rifles and pistols. One velvet rest lay empty.

'Excuse me, my dear.' Fraser cleaned his ivory six-shooter, then put it back in place.

An old man in a suit arrived, announcing, 'Afternoon tea is served in the breakfast room.'

'Thank you, McGregor.'

'Is he an actual butler?' whispered Sarah, as Fraser led her next door to coffee and a selection of cakes.

'Butler, confidant and friend.'

Sarah picked up a squat skull from a side table as Fraser handed her a cup of coffee. 'A devil?'

Fraser nodded and indicated the powerful jawbone. 'Very like a hyena. Our devils generate the strongest bite per body mass unit of any living mammal.'

The butler came in and handed Fraser a glossy magazine with a twelve-tyned stag's head on the cover. 'Your new *Van Dyke's Review*, sir.'

'Thank you, McGregor. How very exciting.' He turned to Sarah. 'It's a catalogue of the latest taxidermy supplies. Forms, tools, glass eyes …'

What was it with Tasmanians and stuffing animals? 'May I see?' Sarah flipped through page after page of featureless polyurethane animals forms. Pale, eyeless, earless ghosts in various poses: crouching, leaping, climbing, running, attacking. 'A hippopotamus?' said Sarah. 'Who stuffs an entire hippo?'

'A younger man than myself, I suspect,' said Fraser. 'I did once mount a baby humpback for Hobart Museum. Now that was a challenge.'

'Where on earth did you find a baby whale?'

'The unfortunate youngster was an orphan, or perhaps merely lost. He mistook a yacht for his mother and wouldn't leave its side – even trying to suckle. I had the devil of a time getting a custom model made for him.'

'How awful. Couldn't he be saved?'

'I don't think even my son would be foolish enough to try raising a two-tonne whale calf, requiring six hundred litres of milk a day. I'm sorry if I sound harsh, Sarah, but it really was for the best. The baby had suffered shark bites and was weak and infected. I donated the money to have it sedated and euthanised.' Fraser put away the catalogue. 'Enough gloomy talk. Tell me about your work, Sarah. I'm a tremendous admirer.'

'Thank you.' She tried to put the sad story of the whale out of her mind. 'We're really improving the devils' chance of survival.'

'I meant your other work,' said Fraser. 'Your human disease research.'

Sarah brightened. 'That's my main passion. Next generation gene sequencing is changing the whole face of medical science. I'm analysing entire chains of prostate cancer DNA. Imagine if we could genetically engineer a cancer cell. Turn it off, so to speak. Or a body cell, turn on its immune response. Imagine if we could accurately predict the probability of the disease based on genetic testing? Early stage prostate cancer has an excellent prognosis, but so many men find out too late.'

'Indeed,' said Fraser.

'Devil cancer may serve as a model to help explain prostate cancer growth. Perhaps I'm being optimistic, but I think a real cure is close. Did you know that Matt is helping?'

'How so?' Fraser offered Sarah a lemon slice.

'Collecting devil hair samples so I can widen my DNA database. Have you heard of museomics? No? It's the large-scale analysis of the DNA content in whole museum collections. I must admit that I find your interest in stuffing animals macabre, but thanks to taxidermists, museums are turning out to be treasure troves for molecular zoologists. I consulted with a team who have even sequenced part of the thylacine genome.' Sarah sipped her coffee. 'They extracted DNA from the hair of two museum specimens.'

'Will they ever clone thylacines back to life, I wonder?'

'Sadly, no,' said Sarah. 'We don't have enough genetic material.'

'Pity. It has always been a dream of mine to mount a thylacine and display it in my studio,' said Fraser. 'Father told me stories about his grandmother, Isabelle Abbott. She kept three thylacine pups as pets when she was a girl. Her father made her release them when they grew up. Apparently they were quite charming.'

'I'm sure they were – like Penny's devils are charming. I'd rather see one alive than stuffed, though.'

'Of course, just a foolish fancy of mine. Finish your coffee and come see my work. Perhaps you'll become a convert.'

He took her to a sandstone studio in the garden. It was the size of a small house and was crammed with hunting trophies. Bears and boars and birds, all in lifelike poses. A snow leopard reclined on a high log. A lion seized an impala by the neck, while a warthog raced to safety, tail in the air. Sarah could almost hear it squeal. The animals looked absolutely alive, as if they might leap at her any minute. She remembered the worn-out little devil back at the Field Museum of Chicago that had originally sparked her interest in this project. Chalk and cheese. Fraser hadn't just captured the physical bodies of these animals. He'd captured their spirits as well.

Fraser watched Sarah, anticipating the thrill that would come when she appreciated the truth of his work, the excellence of it. *There it was.* Fraser sighed with satisfaction and led her into the next room. 'My work in progress.' A crouching three-metre tiger prepared to strike. Sarah took an instinctive step backwards. 'A Siberian tiger, the world's largest cat,' said Fraser.

Sarah paled. 'And critically endangered. Wherever did you get this animal?'

'Shot him in China last year. Quite legally. I have all the required paperwork.'

'I know rather a lot about these tigers,' said Sarah, her voice taut. 'We use them as models to predict devil population outcomes. Because, just like devils, Siberian tigers are on the genetic brink of extinction. Do you know how many are left in the wild?'

'Fewer than five hundred,' said Fraser, fondling the tiger's ears.

'But if you know that, how could you possibly …'

'This is a ten-year-old male, superfluous to the Chinese breeding program. For a fee, an extravagant fee, such tigers can be released into private parks and hunted. These fees help fund the Daqing Centre, housing over eight hundred Siberian tigers. Eighty cubs were born there last year alone. There are gene variants found in captivity that no longer persist in the wild, isn't that so?'

'Yes, but canned hunts? Shooting fish in a barrel? That's cruel and pointless.'

Fraser still stroked his tiger. 'My old friend here was removed from the concrete cage in which he'd lived his entire life, and released into a two-thousand-hectare reserve. Forty feeding stations scattered throughout the park were randomly baited once a week with carcasses, encouraging him to range far and wide. He swam in the Tai Shan river and sharpened his claws on century-old birch trees in the forests of his native Manchuria, lived a winter in the snow.' Fraser ran a finger along a narrow tan stripe in the shaggy pale-gold mane. 'He even learned to hunt. Not all of them do, you know. Wild boar and red deer. It made quite a challenge, tracking him down. He died from a single bullet to the head after nine months of freedom. Alternatively, he could have been euthanised in his cage. Tell me, if I asked him, which death would he choose?'

Sarah's next argument died on her lips. She turned away from the tiger. 'What's this one's story then?' She pointed to an eagle with a two-metre wingspan, frozen as it landed on a branch.

'Gunshot injuries. Not, I might add, inflicted by me.'

'It looks so real,' said Sarah. 'You're a great artist.'

'Well, thank you, Sarah, but I'm afraid I can't take credit for this one. It's the work of a talented student of mine.'

'There are more taxidermists in this town?'

'You already know her. This eagle is the work of my daughter-in-law, Penelope. No need to mention it to Matthew. I'm afraid my son is not a fan of mine.'

CHAPTER 20

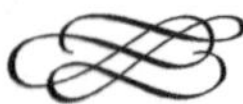

Premier Kate Logan tossed the keys of her sleek bronze Mercedes to the valet, and took the lift to the seventeenth floor of Pierpont Casino. She was not in a good mood. This morning, as she walked through Salamanca Market, a street performer had called her a bitch. Just like that, for no reason at all. He spat out the insult with such venom it quite unnerved her. Of course plenty more people had stopped to shake her hand and tell her what a terrific job she was doing. But that one fool had left a foul taste in her mouth, and she'd decided to hide behind too-large-to-be-fashionable shades. Then she'd listened to a race call on her way in, and her hot tip had come last.

Paul waddled over from the bar, florid face beaming and double chins wobbling. His Italian suit struggled to bridge the obstacle of his stomach. He looked like a fat, red toad. 'Good to see you, Kate.' A handsome young waiter, dressed in a dinner jacket, escorted them to a table complete with French champagne and harbour views.

Kate sipped her wine and watched the waiter strut away. 'When did we lose our youth, Paul?' She raised her glass and frowned. Was that a new age spot on her hand? She'd need to get her dermatologist onto it.

'Stop it. You're still a beautiful woman, Kate.'

'Flattery will get you everywhere, Paul. So, how many new gaming tables are we looking at?'

'Two hundred, for now.'

'And you currently have?'

'Three hundred.'

'And poker machines?'

'Let's double them.'

Kate gazed out the window. It really was a spectacular view, looking north up the sparkling Derwent river to a flotilla of yachts bobbing on the picture perfect harbour – her harbour.

'And the quid pro quo?' she asked.

'We'll pay a 5 percent higher tax rate on our profits.'

'The anti-gambling lobby will demand more,' she said. 'A social or economic impact study perhaps?'

'Even with our tame research groups that will take weeks, and I'm in a hurry. Tell you what, I'll throw in a fifty-thousand-dollar anti-gambling package. It won't make much difference, but it will look good. I'll also support your re-election campaign with a free media blitz, and host your victory party here on the night. What do you say?'

'I think that will be sufficient,' said Kate, coolly, looking first at the menu, then to catch a waiter's eye. The good-looking one appeared by her side. 'I'll have the twice-roasted duck. And for dessert ... bitter chocolate tart.' She favoured the young man with her most dazzling smile. He winked. Kate blushed just enough to be charming.

'If Madam Premier is free after lunch, it will be my pleasure to escort her to the Diamond Room.' The waiter spoke with an intriguing, faintly European inflection.

'That bloke fancies you,' said Paul with a lewd grin. 'Of course he does. Everybody loves you. Beats me why they bother with elections at all. They should just crown you Queen of Tasmania and be done with it.'

Kate tried to ignore Paul's dancing chins.

'I'm afraid the electorate is not as convinced as you are, Paul. Do you know how much I've spent on consultants this year? Nine million. Boost employment, they said, and my government has tried, we truly have. I've mightily subsidised the big employers, thrown hundreds of millions at the timber and hydropower companies. Telcom threatened to close its call centre, so I gave them five million to stay. Saved four hundred jobs right there, but do you think I get any credit?'

Paul swilled his champagne and regarded her with shrewd eyes. 'Cashing up call centres is a mug's game, Kate.' The meals arrived. Paul took a forkful of spaghetti and continued talking with his mouth full. 'Ireland gave billions of tax breaks and subsidies to call centre operators, who then went off-shore anyway and left the country broke. They'll bleed you dry and send your jobs to Manila.' Kate rolled her eyes. 'Didn't any of your flash advisers tell you that?'

No, but plenty of people from her own finance department had. Kate had brushed off their protests, their warnings of budget disasters and credit rating slides. She'd chosen to believe her army of costly private consultants over a few disgruntled treasury officials. If she'd been wrong, she did not appreciate Paul pointing that out. 'Careful, Paul. My gaming commission is more than generous to this casino. I wouldn't bite the hand if I were you.'

Paul guffawed and Kate glared at him. There was nothing to laugh about. The latest polls confirmed she was out of favour with the voters.

Kate picked at her duck. It was a little dry. 'Let us finish our meal with no more talk of politics,' she said. A mistake. Paul droned on instead about some boring holiday he'd had in Bali.

Kate interrupted. 'I'm off myself soon – two weeks of sunshine in Antigua.' She put a hand to her heart, closed her eyes and sighed. 'Bliss.'

'The Caribbean?' Paul raised his brows. 'I saw Gerard at the club last night. I'm surprised he didn't mention it.'

'My husband will not be joining me.'

Paul couldn't conceal a small smirk.

'What? You know Gerard can't stand humidity.' Could Paul be any more tiresome?

Kate's phone rang. She pushed away her half-eaten duck and answered it. More trouble. 'But, Drake, darling, you absolutely must come. It's our biggest fundraiser for the year. Go play in the forest another day. Your father and I will be expecting you.' Kate waved her dessert away. Paul called the waiter back and added Kate's portion of tart to his own plate. 'Drake *is* irresponsible,' she said. 'Why can't he understand how damaging his little causes are to my re-election prospects.' Kate smoothed her blouse, hands lingering over her breasts.

'Is madam ready for the Diamond Room?' asked the waiter.

'Madam is, Karl,' she said, reading his name tag. 'The state may govern itself for a while.' Kate took Karl's arm and gave Paul a peck on the cheek. 'You shall have your expansion, and I shall have my fun.'

'Enjoy,' said Paul, with his mouth stuffed full of tart. Kate left and he snapped his fingers. An assistant hurried to his side. 'A penthouse for the Premier,' he said. The penthouse suite was quite a freebie, with its gold taps and personal butlers, but then Kate was worth her weight in gold. 'And tell Karl to keep her chips flowing.'

CHAPTER 21

Drake was late. Matt waited for him on the verandah, with sandwiches and a lunchtime beer. He loved Mondays, when the park was closed to visitors. Binburra stretched out before him, basking in the warmth of the early summer afternoon. Though a shelf of dark sky building in the south said the sunshine wouldn't last. He'd enjoy it while he could. A light morning rain had left the bush gardens sparkling and fragrant. Animals and birds were out enjoying the sunshine. Even nocturnal devils lay sunbaking on the grass of their pens. They had nothing to fear in this peaceful place.

In the distance, proud purple peaks rose into a sky of brilliant blue – a view unchanged for thousands of years. Time had stood still here. One-hundred-and-fifty years ago, his forefather, naturalist Daniel Campbell, must have gazed out on the very same scene. Matt marvelled again at the foresight it had taken for Daniel to preserve this place, at a time when farmers still shot thylacines as pests. He'd been a man way ahead of his time.

Matt had read Daniel Campbell's journals, read of the Englishman's love for his adopted home and his despair at the wholesale destruction of Tasmania's native flora and fauna. There was one diary entry that Matt particularly loved. He knew the date by heart – the sixth of November 1880. *Perhaps the best way to protect the forest is to own the forest.* Daniel had purchased Binburra two months later. How proud Matt was to be related to a man of such vision, and to be carrying on his legacy. It made up a little for Fraser.

Drake arrived, wearing a wide smile, and settled himself into a canvas chair. 'We've won,' he said. 'Pallawarra will be safe in time for Christmas.'

Matt offered him a beer and cast him a sceptical glance. Maybe. It was true that logging crews had temporarily retreated from the Tuggerah, but Fraser was no quitter. He was bound to move an even bigger force into the forest eventually. Still, Matt had to admit that for the time being, the protesters had triumphed.

They'd fought a fierce fight, backed by Drake's clever and far-reaching international media campaign. The tragedy of the two officers who fell to their deaths was on one hand a public relations disaster, but it also drew the world's attention to what was happening in the forest. It fuelled debate on the very issues that Burns Timber wanted to suppress.

With some strategic encouragement, the media enthusiastically personified Pallawarra. They played up the curse angle, turning the tree into a celebrity, even a hero to many. Drake used donations and his considerable personal wealth to produce figurines, along with a story book and computer game, in which the characters defended their home from wicked Mr Woodchip. King Pallawarra fought alongside Bertie Blackwood, Henrietta Huon Pine, Larry Leatherwood and Captain Sally Sassafras to protect their forest. Drake distributed the toys, books and games for free at schools, shopping centres and hospitals. Politically correct they were not – King Pallawarra wielded a sword and ray gun – but they were a hit with the kids. The scheme even attracted sponsors.

Save The Tuggerah rallies in Hobart drew thousands of supporters, including mainland and overseas celebrities. A televised fundraising concert proved to be a big hit. A host of foot soldiers in the trenches maintained a relentless pressure on the logging operations. They winched logs across roads, poured glue into padlocks, chained themselves to trees and bulldozers. They befriended bored journalists.

Bold breakaway groups took radical, even violent, action. They drained diesel tanks, and drove spikes into trees to tear apart high-speed saws with potentially lethal consequences. They cut through the supports of Charon River bridge, causing a fully-laden log truck to topple in, hurting the driver. Jammed tight between the narrow banks, the truck blocked the road for days. They damaged equipment and strung fine wire cables between trees, thirty metres above the ground, so increasingly jumpy loggers couldn't predict how their trees might fall.

The gloves were off on both sides. Timber workers took sledge-hammers to a protester's car, injuring a terrified woman and child who were trapped inside. A published video of the incident sparked outrage. Accusations flew fast and furious on both sides. A girl disappeared from the forest, and Drake ran a media beat-up, highlighting the threats made against the protesters by some of Burns's men. The police were ready to drag the Charon. 'Why bother with that muddy ditch?' said one of the logging crew. 'When there's a thousand old mine shafts where we could dump a body?' A young dozer driver went missing at the same time. Wild, superstitious talk had him sacrificed by a coven of witches. When the two of them turned up together in a Nandena motel room, there were red faces all round.

Drake's publicity campaign was so effective that as fast as protesters were arrested, more arrived. The contractors couldn't make a living in this snail's pace operation. 'By the time we'd finished, they needed fifty police to guard each convoy,' said Drake, sipping his beer. 'Half a dozen coppers around each truck so the tyres wouldn't get spiked. Then, get this, they *walked* beside the trucks to the police camp. From there they moved out with one police car in front, one in back, a copper in the passenger seat of every truck, and another on the driver's side running board. The convoy crawled along so slowly that Joey Hancock spiked two rear tyres while the trucks were still moving.'

'Joey Hancock. One of Ken Murphy's apprentices?'

Drake nodded. 'All the guys at the sawmill are fired up. Everyone is, even the press. Pallawarra is publicity gold. Public opinion has well and truly swung our way.'

'What about your mother?'

Drake gave a rueful smile. 'I'm no miracle worker. Some challenges are beyond me.' He leaned forward in his chair. 'Like convincing Sarah to go on a date. She only has eyes for you.'

Matt didn't deny it. Sarah always stood very close to him. Sometimes she touched him – butterfly light. When Matt spoke, Sarah listened with a singular intensity, as if his words brimmed with special meaning. He was flattered, of course, by the admiration of a beautiful woman. Yet, it did not compensate for the fact that Penny was barely speaking to him. Not that Matt blamed her. He'd built a wall to guard his secret and left his wife on the other side.

A knock came at the door. 'Speak of the devil,' said Drake as he caught the scent of Sarah's perfume.

Penny wasn't home. How did Sarah always know? Her work at the park was finished. She was living and researching in Hobart now, but she'd taken to spending weekends at Hills End when she could.

'Welcome, Doc,' said Drake. 'As you can see, we're celebrating.'

'I heard the loggers have pulled out,' said Sarah, joining them on the verandah. 'Congratulations.' Her lacy singlet didn't quite reach the top of her shorts, showing off her tanned stomach, complete with a gold belly-button ring. Matt glanced at the sky, at the black clouds rolling in, wondering idly if Sarah had brought a coat. She was going to need one. Storms blew in quickly over the mountains.

'I'd better head off.' Drake jumped up. 'Come on, Doc. There's a celebration bash at my place.'

Sarah's amber eyes found Matt's. 'Are you coming?'

He finished his beer. 'Maybe later. I still have to feed the eagles.'

'Can I help?'

Matt looked from Sarah's expectant expression to Drake's *I told you so* face.

'Sure,' he said. 'Catch you later, Drake.'

'Remember to tell Penny about the party,' Drake called after them.

Binburra had six flight aviaries, sponsored by Eagle Insurance. The two largest had fifty-metre flight paths running side by side. Opening the gates at each end converted them into a single elliptical hundred-metre flyway. Sarah followed Matt down to the mews. A battered fridge and freezer stood near the door, with the new chest freezer right at the back beside the coolroom. Sarah wrinkled her nose as Matt took two possums and a little wallaby from the fridge. He foraged around in the old freezer and extracted a number of frozen rabbits to defrost.

'I'm hoping those lovebirds might share this wallaby.' He sharpened a cleaver.

'These freezers are full of dead animals?' asked Sarah.

Matt nodded, slicing great gashes in the carcasses and sprinkling in vitamin and mineral powder. 'Mainly roadkill. Penny picks out a few she wants to stuff and the rest go in the freezer. Woorawa and Aquila are fed only what they'll find in the wild.'

With the meat bucket ready, they headed for the aviaries – towering spaces constructed of trawler netting and eleven-metre-tall telegraph poles. The two eagles were perched close together on high branches, framed by the darkening sky. Matt placed the possums on separate stumps, and the wallaby on the ground. The birds observed him with keen eyes. When Matt left the enclosure, they descended as one, in measured flight, to feed on the little wallaby.

'The black one,' said Matt, 'that's Woorawa. He'd have me if he could. See him watching? Two years in care before he arrived, but he's not tame. Never will be. Without that sort of a mate, Aquila could never be set free. She needs something truly wild to teach her.'

'Look.' Sarah touched his arm. 'How sweet.'

Aquila had reached out to tentatively nibble Woorawa's neck, just as she used to do to him. It was the first time Matt had seen Aquila make this gesture to her new mate, and he felt an absurd prickle of jealousy. Ridiculous, to be jealous of an eagle, but he sure could use some affection himself right now. He imagined Penny's freckled arms around his neck, the warmth of her soft lips on his, and a wave of loneliness crashed in. One way or another, he had to find a way to resolve things with his wife.

'It must have been hard losing your other eagle,' said Sarah.

'What other eagle?'

'You lost one a few months ago, didn't you?' said Sarah. 'Another male? Not quite as big and black as Woorawa, but beautiful just the same.'

'Some idiot hunter shot that bird from the sky for no reason at all. A farmer found him half-dead in a paddock, too sick to save. Did Pen tell you?'

'No.'

'Then how did you—?'

'Your father. He told me that he helped Penny mount that eagle. She's done a fantastic job, hasn't she? Really made him come alive.'

Matt stared at her, disbelieving. His throat refused to swallow. 'That's impossible.'

Sarah pressed on, speaking quickly as if she thought he would interrupt. 'The bird was hit twice; once high in the left wing, and again in the leg. One talon was shot off, so Penny substituted a replica. You'd never know.' Sarah paused for breath. 'Didn't she tell you?'

His heart lurched at the betrayal. Penny knew how much this would hurt him, knew that he'd never forgiven Fraser for the car crash that killed his mother and sisters. Fraser had been drunk the afternoon that he ran off the road and hit a tree. Matt could still smell the alcohol on his father's breath, still hear his mother asking to let her drive instead.

He survived because he'd been forbidden to attend the Christmas Eve party thrown each year for the mineworkers' families. That morning Matt had sneaked the keys to the gun cabinet from his father's desk, and Fraser had discovered him playing with a rifle. He'd been grounded, left at home with the gardener and maid.

Matt saw the scene like he was standing outside his own body. Him as a twelve-year-old boy, sitting disconsolate on the stone steps of the verandah. His little sisters skipping to the car, all laughter and bouncing curls. His mother, running back at the last moment, kissing him and promising to bring back a show bag. He never saw them again.

Fraser survived with barely a scratch. He was charged with dangerous driving; it was in all the papers. But somehow the results of his breath test went missing, courtesy, Matt guessed, of a police minister in Fraser's pocket. The case fell apart, and Fraser never faced justice for his crime. But his relationship with his son was shattered; a son filled with so much misery and grief that it swallowed him whole. Matt left home at sixteen to work on the scallop boats up north.

Two years later, homesick for the mountains, he returned to Hills End and found a job at Binburra. That's when he met Penny. That's when love and light returned to his life. Her parents had died in a car crash, and it served as a powerful point of connection between them. She of all people should understand his bitterness towards Fraser – should understand why he'd washed his hands of his father and wanted them to have nothing to do with him.

Matt left the buckets where they were and strode to the house. Sarah followed him, running to keep up. Penny still wasn't home. He tried her phone. It was turned off. He rang Fraser, his fingers so unsteady that he could barely press the digits, annoyed that he still knew the number.

'Is Penny there?'

'Ah, Matthew.' His father sounded unsurprised, despite this being the first call from his son in fourteen years. 'It's conventional to begin a conversation with *hello.*'

Matt repeated the question, his voice thick with fury.

'No, your wife is not here, Matthew. Why, is something wrong?'

Matt ended the call and glared at Sarah. He wished that she'd stayed away, that she'd never dropped her bombshell. But the concern on her face tempered his anger. Blaming Sarah was shooting the messenger. She couldn't have known the trouble her news would cause.

'That party at Drake's,' he said. 'You want to go?' When she nodded, Matt steered her out to the jeep, and took off down the track.

Sarah sat silent beside him. Banks of low cloud erupted in torrents, inundating the road. The speeding jeep slipped and slid.

When they reached the broad gates of Canterbury Downs, Matt turned into the driveway. Curtains of rain obscured the front of the house. He hadn't been here since he was sixteen years old, but could still picture the dark shutters and the shape of each blue stone. His chest tightened, just to be there.

Matt peered through the downpour, searching for Penny's car, hoping not to find it. Was it parked around the back? He leapt from his seat, head bent against the blast, and ran to the house. His father stood in the open doorway, his face inscrutable. He looked scrawny, easy to snap.

'Is it true about Penny? Has she been coming to see you.' Matt was shivering and dripping water on the porch.

Fraser's eyes narrowed. 'Your wife is my student, yes. Does she not have the right?'

'It's *you* who doesn't have the right,' yelled Matt. 'You don't have the right to come anywhere near my wife. Not after killing my mother and sisters. Not after splitting this town in half with your special brand of bribery and vandalism. You destroy everything fine that you touch, Dad. I tried to get away, begin again, create some sort of a life for myself. But you're always there, aren't you, lurking in the shadows to ruin things?'

For a moment Fraser looked hurt, but only for a moment. Then he shrugged – a one-shouldered shrug as if his son warranted nothing more. 'Don't blame me if you've lost your wife, Matthew. I suggest you look for her elsewhere.' Fraser closed the door hard, just short of a slam.

Matt stood there for a minute, wrestling with his rage. Then he headed for the jeep with an unfamiliar stinging behind his eyes. He didn't make it. He sank down on the ground in the driveway, barely aware of the storm slapping him in the face. Elbows on knees. Head in hands. Tears mingling with the rain.

Someone tapped him on the shoulder – Sarah, carrying Matilda's sparkly *My Little Pony* umbrella. She held it over his head, sacrificing herself to the downpour. Water streamed down her face, her chest, and plastered her clothes to her body. The whole thing seemed suddenly ridiculous. Penny. Fraser. Himself. Soggy Sarah with the pretty pink umbrella.

'Let's go.' She offered her hand to help him stand, and he took it. Matt looked back at the house as he drove away, and saw the curtain fall back into place at the window.

CHAPTER 22

Matt watched Penny walk into the party wearing her best blue dress. She was also wearing her sad face, the one that always got her sympathy. Not this time. She'd probably already spoken to Fraser. Perhaps they talked every day? Penny turned this way and that through the crowd, past benches groaning with drinks and snacks, past the trestle-table bar, seeking him out. Matt neither withdrew nor advanced. The edge was gone from his fury, but it smouldered beneath, red-hot, ready to ignite. Sarah had retreated to where Drake was holding court in the garden.

'Where were you?' Matt asked, when she found him.

'At Uncle Ray's. I'm worried about him.'

Matt stared at his wife, expecting her to somehow look different, surprised when she didn't. He took her arm, pulled her into Drake's bedroom and shut the door.

'I know about you and Fraser.'

Penny took a step backwards. 'What's the harm?' she said. 'I could travel halfway around the world and still not find a better taxidermy teacher. It's stupid to let your dad's knowledge go to waste.'

'Don't call him that.' Matt raised his forefinger to her. 'Don't you ever call him that.' A clock ticked on the wall, the noise unnaturally loud. They held their positions, characters frozen in a vignette. He yielded first. 'You knew this would kill me, Pen.'

She exploded with the force of a flood. 'And you don't think it's been killing me, these last few months? Wondering why you avoid me, ignore me, make me feel completely alone? I wanted to talk to you about Fraser, but I can't tell you anything. You're … absent.'

Her anguish was so plain, so genuine – so justified – it completely disarmed him. 'There's a reason, Pen.' He turned away and leaned against the window, staring into the dark of Drake's yard.

Penny forced herself between him and the sill, forced him to come back. 'Please, Matt, tell me what's wrong.'

His cheek began to pulse and blood pounded in his ears. Could he do this? Could he free himself from his secret? The possibility screamed louder and louder, and one final look at Penny's anguished face convinced him. Whatever happened next, he owed his wife the truth.

'I'll do more than tell you what's wrong,' he said. 'I'll show you.'

The mews. Matt was emptying out the new freezer in front of her. He'd driven like a madman back home, unable to stand one more moment of her not knowing.

Penny looked on in confusion. Sweat beaded Matt's face, and soon a pile of frozen bodies littered the concrete floor. He lifted out a large bag from right at the bottom and placed it on the bench with extravagant care.

'Meet Theo.'

Penny pressed her spread fingers against the frosted plastic.

'What on earth?' She turned to Matt with widening eyes and a slow, disbelieving shake of her head.

Back in the house, Penny examined Theo under the harsh fluorescent glare of the kitchen light. 'A young male,' she said. 'Almost grown, I'd say.'

'So, he's real?'

She laughed in delight. 'I've no idea how, but yes, he's real.'

For the first time since that dreadful night, Matt touched Theo. Touched his impossible head, traced the stripes of his coat, stroked his powerful tail. And Matt's imagination gave the young thylacine back his life.

There he was, shifting through the foggy forest, full of promise and youthful curiosity, following his family to the unfamiliar roadside. So young and inquisitive and inexperienced. So exceptional. Had he paused in the headlights' beam, wondering what to make of the twin moons hurtling towards him? Or perhaps he'd crouched by the track, intending to lie low. Had his family crossed the road? Had Theo leapt up to follow them at precisely the wrong moment? Matt didn't know. He'd barely seen Theo – only the familiar thud of another roadkill had caused him to brake. Most wouldn't have even bothered, and the remarkable, unimaginable young thylacine would have perished, unnoticed by man, as if he'd never lived. Perhaps it would have been better that way.

Penny inspected the body, poring over each tiny detail. She scribbled elaborate notes about coat colour and genital size. 'The scrotum really is in a little pouch. Come look.'

At her request Matt took photos. Until it started to feel sacrilegious. Until he began to cry.

Penny wrapped her arms about his shoulders. 'Honey, what's done is done. It was an accident. A terrible, inconceivable, heartbreaking accident, but an accident just the same.'

'I was going too fast.' He lowered his eyes. They'd had that argument before.

'You should have told me.'

Yes, but there'd been no words. Not when Theo lay dead and bleeding. Not when Matt tenderly bagged his body and buried it at the bottom of the freezer. Not afterwards, as the awful weight of guilt bore down on him.

'Tell me now, then,' said Penny.

So he did. He told her how he'd shone the torch along Theo's body, challenged by the evidence of his eyes. But there'd been no mistaking the pattern of dark bands across the animal's biscuit-coloured coat, running from shoulder to the base of its stiff tail. He'd counted the sixteen stripes. Reached out, hardly daring to touch. He'd felt Theo's coat, the ebbing warmth of his body, stroked Theo's damp head, while his tears mingled with the mizzle. He'd cradled the body in his arms and carried it to the jeep. He'd gone back to look for tracks and found them too. Dog-like imprints on the soft verge, more than one set. With a bag of dental stone, he'd gone to work, setting each cast, then prying it from the earth. By four, he'd slipped into bed beside his sleeping wife and lain sleepless till morning. He still struggled to think of that night.

'I can't believe you kept it to yourself all these months. Something as monumental as this. Why?' Silence. 'Matt?' He turned away and she slapped his arm. 'Matt, you're doing it again.'

Why hadn't he told her? He knew why he hadn't told Parks Tasmania. Theo's family needed protection. Beautiful Binburra was mainly remote and inaccessible, one of the few truly wild places on earth. The department directed its resources to the more popular parks, the ones that attracted the most tourist dollars. It was good at producing brochures and flashy websites. The minister was good at cocktail parties and sponsorship deals, and not much else. Matt didn't mind. Binburra was better off being left alone.

Theo would change all that.

Rediscovering Tasmanian tigers would be the ultimate publicity jackpot. Some years ago, a ranger reported a possible thylacine sighting near Togari, in the north-west. Dozens of Parks Tasmania officers swept in to search three hundred square kilometres of surrounding bushland. They rigged up cameras and laid sand patches along trails. They set traps, monitored potential den sites, collected hundreds of scats for chemical analysis. All based on one uncertain sighting in the dark. Matt could imagine the pandemonium an actual specimen would cause.

He'd spent weeks agonising over it; weighing up the pros and cons of revealing his astonishing discovery. And he'd decided that Binburra

National Park should not be disturbed. Could one man's opinion justify such a serious betrayal of the international scientific community? And that's precisely what it was, keeping this secret – a betrayal. Maybe of the tigers themselves. Publicity might bring the animals safety and support. In a perfect world, maybe, with a decent government. Not with this government. This one was rotten from Premier Logan down, walking hand in hand with big business and vested interests. It would sell out the tigers, nothing surer.

But all this didn't explain why he hadn't told Penny, and she knew that.

'You didn't trust me.' Her voice was full of hurt. 'That's why you didn't say anything.'

He had no defence. It was true. Penny would expect him to share Theo, to tell the scientists, the people of the state, the people of the world. For her there would be no choice. So it had become his job to protect the tigers, even from his own wife.

Penny's large accusing eyes shone with tears, and she left the room. He almost followed, but it seemed wrong to leave Theo alone. Matt stood, confused, listening to Penny moving around in their bedroom. He didn't know how to fix this. Ten minutes later she appeared with a duffel bag, eyes puffy and red. 'I'll be at Uncle Ray's when you're ready to talk.'

She zipped up her bag, went to the door and turned one last time. 'This isn't your call, Matt. You have to tell somebody.'

He wanted to take her in his arms and beg her to stay. He wanted to kiss her, reassure her, wipe away her pain. But too much remained unresolved. Penny seeing Fraser behind his back, for instance. Remembering her disloyalty hardened his heart.

'Why don't you then?' he said. 'I'm sure my father will be fascinated.'

Penny looked as if she'd been struck. 'I won't do this for you, Matt. You killed Theo. You decide.'

It was almost dark. Penny drove past the string of run-down cottages, past the sagging fences and *For Sale* signs, and parked in the street outside her uncle's home. By the light of a street lamp it looked more run down than ever. Fibro-cement walls begging for paint. Rusted roof. The unkempt lawns sprouting yellow clumps of dandelions. Scarlet geraniums, escapees from their beds, strangled straggly azaleas, once the pride of the garden. Ray's battered ute slumped in the carport. She sat awhile, determined to stop crying before going inside.

Penny had only left Ray a few hours ago and had not expected to be back so soon. He'd seemed fragile and depressed when she left him, not like her uncle at all. Not like her rock. For that's what he'd been all of her life. Ever since a drunk driver slammed into her parents' car when she was a baby. Somehow she'd survived; six months old, strapped into the carnage. Trapped in the shattered wreck with her dead parents. It was a blessing, people always said, to be too young to remember. And it was true – she didn't. But Penny's dreams invented memories at least as terrible as the truth.

She found tissues in the glove box and blew her nose – a great honking blow. How to compose herself? Matt had taken her so completely by surprise. With Theo. With his overwhelming lack of trust in her. It was as if she didn't know her husband at all. Penny's thoughts ran helter-skelter, searching for answers. Keep Matt's astonishing secret or expose him? These were her impossible choices. Her mind was racing. She couldn't dump this problem on her fragile uncle, and she missed Matt already, and she craved to touch Theo again. And she dreaded the pregnancy test lying in the bottom of her bag.

For months she'd suspected. For almost as many months, it turned out, as Theo had lain hidden in their freezer. Theo was why Matt had pulled away, why she hadn't been able to share her baby hopes. Why she couldn't face mornings anymore and why Matt turned from her at night. Theo was the albatross around the neck of their marriage.

The porch light was on. Penny hauled her bag from the jeep, stomach still coiled in knots, and walked up the cracked concrete path. The screen door squeaked open and banged shut, the signal for Ray to sing out *Come in if you're good-looking*. But today he did no such thing. Penny found him sitting in his favourite armchair before the fire. Just sitting. No television. No radio. No stereo. It wasn't like her uncle. He couldn't abide silence – he always had to fill the modest house with music and sport broadcasts and Jackie Chan movies turned up too loud.

'Hullo, love.'

'You're sure I can stay?'

Ray heaved his barrel of a body from the low chair and kissed her cheek, his lined face softening. 'My girl is home.' He picked up her bag and led the way.

Nothing had changed in the house since she was a child. The framed grainy photograph of a young Ray with a crosscut saw hanging in the hallway. The prancing pony wallpaper in her room. The frayed patch of carpet where she'd swung her feet out of bed each morning. The homemade shelves spilling children's books and old *Dolly* magazines. Soft toys crowding the top bunk.

Penny sank down on the lacy white bedspread, adorned with pink roses. Ray put down her bag and smiled with such warmth that Penny forgot her misery for one sweet moment. But when he left the room, the waves of worry crashed back in. She fished the pregnancy test from her bag. How many times had she taken one of them, only to be disappointed? Yet, right now, if the strip showed positive, she'd surely drown in her own doubts.

Penny crossed the hall to the little linoleum bathroom, with its cracked basin and ridiculous fluffy toilet seat cover. Mouthing a silent apology, Penny turfed Ray's razor out of the chipped china mug. She used the mug to collect a urine sample, then returned to her room to wait. According to the instructions, the results took an excruciating five minutes. Apparently a watched stick never changes colour, so she wound up her old puppy alarm clock and tracked the second hand as it marched past the different breeds of dogs. When the time was up and she finally dared to look, two bright red bars showed stark on the strip. Positive.

Penny collapsed on her bed and hugged the bunny pillow. A concerned camellia, older than her uncle, swayed outside the dark window, scratching at the glass. She turned on the lamp and made shadow puppets across the pony wallpaper. Their familiar forms reassured her. Everything about this small room, where she'd known only comfort and love, reassured her. All that past pressing down on the present. Waggles peered from her top bunk, so she pulled the little toy down and fondled the dog's floppy ears, inhaled his musty scent.

And at last it happened. Her pain and resentment fled, replaced with a sense of overwhelming love. A child. She was having a child. She imagined Waggles snuggled in a bassinet beside her sleeping baby. She imagined soothing tiny tears, and whispering *Don't cry, my baby, Mummy's here* – just as her mother must have done for her long ago. Penny forgot about Matt and Theo. 'My baby,' she said aloud. It sounded good. Good enough for now, anyway. Saying *'our baby'* would have to wait.

Penny went to the lounge room, where her uncle sat staring at the flames. The air hung stale and smoky. How sad he looked. Ray covered the hand she laid on his shoulder with his own.

'Is there something I can do, love?'

'Yes,' said Penny, pulling him to his feet and sitting him down at the dining table. 'You can tell me what's wrong. Why doesn't anybody tell me what's wrong?' She turned on the lights and the kettle and put the television news on low. She emptied the ashtray. A grey residue of cigarette ash lay in a mound on the floor beside his armchair. Ray followed her gaze.

'It keeps the moths out of the carpet,' he said, apologetically.

Penny opened the window, took his knobbly hands in hers and waited for Ray to speak.

'They laid me off this morning,' he said at last. 'For a whole month. That new conveyer belt at Kemp Cove? Never worked properly from the start, it didn't. Five ships are held up at the wharf and their wood-chip pile's full. So they put off half the drivers, just like that. I suppose it's worse for them with families ...'

'And what exactly am I?' asked Penny.

Ray squeezed her hands and gave her a grateful smile. 'I shouldn't be bothering you with this, love. You've got enough on your plate.' But his words found their own momentum. 'Log carting's a mug's game these days. Four in the morning until six at night. They gave us these new logbooks to keep track of our hours, to make sure we don't drive for too long, but we've thrown them out the window. Paying the fines is cheaper than not hauling enough loads. Dog-tired, I've been, I don't mind admitting it, and how do they thank you? With a kick in the teeth.'

Penny knew the drill. She'd grown up with the big trucks, knew the strain of forty-five tonnes of logs in the back, of mountain roads with centimetres to spare between you and the guard rail. One wrong move and you're over the edge. A car veers in front, you hit the brakes ... but the big trucks take time to stop. And you can't afford break-downs either, or flat tyres, nothing like that. Two, sometimes three jobs a day. Each load a six-hour return trip to the bush. She'd seen her uncle worn out after just one run. But tonight was different. Tonight, his weariness was of despair. Penny made them a cup of tea.

'If it's all the same, love, I'll have a beer.' He fetched one from the fridge and sat back down. 'Some people hate us now, especially in the towns. This woman had a go at me last week, said I shouldn't be driving log trucks. I told her I don't know nothing else. Forty years in the game. But, for once, I knew what she meant.' Penny kissed his cheek. 'There are days I hate to see those trees come down myself. I'm thinking … how in heck do they manage it? Clearing a whole hill in six hours? One feller knocked down a stag tree when he found an eagle nest in it, just so he didn't have to go through the bloody paper-work. I couldn't come at that.' Ray sat up straighter. 'A lot of truckies think like me. Some don't. Some don't think twice. But others do, especially us oldies.'

'You're not old—'

'No, love. Let me finish.' Ray rose to his feet and paced the faded floral carpet in his work boots. 'Blokes like me, we remember. We know what it used to look like, but if you're young, driving them big trucks, it's just a job. Don't get me wrong. Young and old, every one of us feels like a robot, 'cause you have no say anymore. And it's not just us, it's all the contractors. Pete bought a Timberpro harvester last year. Beautiful machine, but there's no change from four hundred thousand quid, and that's second-hand. Now the Tuggerah's on hold, he has to go farther afield for work. If they put him off, he still pays the loan. A bundle of nerves, he is, ever since that bunch in Opposi-tion said they'd cut down on logging if they get in. Reckons if the Greens get their way, they'll stop it altogether, along with the new pulp mill. On top of all that, his Mary's having twins.'

'Twins?' Penny reached for her belly. Images of twin prams and twin jumpsuits hijacked her thoughts, and she almost blurted out her news.

Ray went on. 'There's fool talk of a strike, talk of every driver and logger stopping work.'

'Sounds good,' said Penny.

Ray shook his head and lit a cigarette. 'Us poor buggers couldn't run a chook raffle, and we haven't got the balls besides, pardon my French.' He slumped in his chair, as if the burst of dissent had winded him. Penny had never heard this sort of talk from her uncle before.

'What about the union?'

Ray snorted like a wounded bull. 'The union? Bloody useless. That mob's not for the workers. They're in Burns's pocket. Everything's upside down these days.' He sculled his beer, hurled his empty can at the overflowing kitchen tidy, then went and helped himself to another. 'Want one, love?'

'No thanks, Unkie. Might turn in.'

'Righto.' Ray settled back into his armchair. A current affairs show was coming on the television. Good, he seemed calmer.

Penny retreated to her bed, exhausted, but that wasn't the same as sleepy. She got up, slipped out the front door and padded barefoot in the cold to the jeep. A quick rummage in the back turned up Matt's jacket. Penny hurried back to bed and buried her face in it. His smell was in the weave.

Ray tried to concentrate on the telly. *'Tonight, the Premier predicts savage job losses in the timber industry should her party lose power.'* He felt the throb of blood in his ears, the ropes of veins rising on his throat. Ray turned off the television and went to the kitchen. He poked around behind the coffee tin until he found the little bottle of pills Pete had given him. Helped you sleep, that's what Pete said. Ray swallowed three with his beer, turned off the light and sat at the dark window, staring into the void.

CHAPTER 24

'Here comes another one,' said Jake, as he helped Matt load Woorawa onto the jeep beside Aquila. The vibration finished almost as soon as it began, a brief wobbly sensation in Matt's legs. It would have been different inside, where shivering shelves and creaking walls revealed the most minor of tremors. It was always the rigid, the manmade, that bore the brunt of damage when the earth moved. Pity those poor blokes down the mine.

Matt took a deep breath of pure morning. The powder-blue sky was streaked with sunrise streamers of coral cloud. They unfurled southwards, betraying a high wind. Perfect. The hooded eagles, quiet in their carriers, would sail the summer breezes by noon.

'Good luck,' said Jake, and waved goodbye.

Matt pulled out onto Binburra Road just as Penny pulled in. The vehicles paused, as if their drivers considered stopping, winding down windows, having a chat. But on some invisible signal, both continued on their way. Penny was staying at Ray's until Matt made a decision about Theo. They'd decided Matt would have the final say. Well, Penny had decided, like it was some kind of test. 'You need thinking space,' she'd said. Neither of them knew he'd need so much.

Matt searched one-handed in the glove box. Darn it, no gum.

Chewing gum stopped him from grinding his teeth. The adolescent habit had returned recently. He mouth-breathed in shallow pants, jaws ajar until he forgot about fighting it. His molars clenched together and began their inexorable grind.

Matt tried to focus on the day ahead, but his thoughts inevitably returned to Theo. There were more thylacines. Where? Did he even have the right to wonder? After releasing Aquila and Woorawa, he would revisit the place where Theo died. Re-examine it in the light of the little bit of emotional distance he'd achieved. Maybe his course would become clearer.

'You'll make the right decision,' Penny had said on the phone yesterday. How would it feel to be Penny? Everything so cut and dried, so black and white. Never in doubt, whether wrong or right. Weren't women supposed to be the ones who crippled themselves with guilt? Not in this marriage. Penny had somehow absolved herself of blame, overlooked her own culpability with Fraser. Overlooked her deceit. Instead, she'd loaded both barrels with righteous resentment and blasted him at point-blank range. The hypocrisy of it.

From the back, Aquila chirruped and ruffled her wings. She liked him to take it slow. Matt lightened his foot on the throttle.

'Not long now,' he told her. Aquila settled at the sound of his voice. Not so Woorawa. He uttered a rasping *kark*, the call he made when threatened. Woorawa had maintained a healthy hatred of humans throughout his rehabilitation. This wild instinct would serve as the best possible protection for him and his over-friendly mate. But still, such a hard-earned release was nerve-racking as well as elating. Binburra's budget didn't stretch to radio trackers for eagles, only devils. He imagined Aquila with a mobile phone tucked under her wing, wished he could ring and say, 'How're you going, darling? Have you had a good feed?' But all he'd be able to do was wonder and hope.

Woorawa had demonstrated in the last few weeks that he was ready to return to the sky. Freshly moulted, new feathers gleaming, black as sable. Five or six times a day he completed a dozen laps of the aviaries' hundred-metre flight path, his playful mate chasing after him. The birds, with their two-metre wingspans, negotiated the twists and turns with extraordinary precision. Matt never tired of the display. Some captive raptors were lazy, but not Woorawa. He revelled in his increasing strength and pinion power, maintaining a self-imposed training regime worthy of the finest athlete.

Matt had planned to release Aquila at Tiger Pass ever since she arrived as a yearling three years ago. It was ideal eagle territory. Remote, unoccupied by other pairs. He glanced at the time. Nine o'clock. Halfway. By eleven they'd be there.

As they climbed higher and higher, Matt forgot his worries. There was only him and the eagles and the wilderness. Last year Penny had accused him of taming Aquila, and to be honest, it had been a challenge not to. The bird had a crush on him. Not his fault. Aquila had been raised by humans. It could take years to dehumanise an animal, particularly a carnivore. To make it aware of its own species, and ensure it could hunt without human support. To make it frightened of strangers. The job demanded a style of animal husbandry designed to preserve the sanctity of wild behaviour, a style specific to wildlife rehabilitation. It was wrong to care too much, or at least to show it. Successful release required animals to span the gap between two radically different worlds. Sometimes they failed. Matt had done his best.

The sun sailed high in a neon blue sky when Matt parked the jeep. Pet carriers in hand, he followed a rough track to the head of the rocky pass. Sheer walls of stone enclosed the way, tops fringed with jagged sandstone battlements. How good to feel the weight of the birds in his hands this one last time.

What would it be like to be an eagle? To be Woorawa? Fierce and faithful. Ever-vigilant. To possess vision of unimaginable clarity. Humans may have invented Google Earth, but their vision was fuzzy rabbit-eared antennae reception compared to the eagles' glorious high-definition colour. What would it be like, to bear unblinking the full force of noonday summer sunshine and still be able to read a newspaper headline a kilometre away? To see without doubt?

He'd like to fly. Just glide away and leave the old world behind, as the eagles were about to do. The odd stillness of the pass moved him as it always did. No breeze stirred the sassafras that clung to the sides of the cracked stone cliffs. Yet high winds swirled the myrtle beech forest canopy above the escarpment. Matt followed a barely rippling stream, a dark chain of rocky pools. Half-an-hour's walk brought them to the falls, and he swung the cages onto the broad stone ledge jutting over the water. Liberation point.

Release was always bittersweet. Aquila would go first. Matt had free-flown her at this place many times before, watched her spiral and dive and soar close to the sun. Always she'd returned to him. Not this time. He was just a man now, no longer her keeper.

'Okay, darling, let's get this hood off you.' Matt kissed her head. Aquila whistled with excitement, ready for what would come. Gathering her in his arms, wings tucked in tight, Matt tossed her to the sky. Up and up she flew, higher and higher, until Matt could barely see her. Then she banked and wheeled in a tight circle, the wedge of her tail in sharp silhouette against the bright sky. Matt breathed a big sigh and turned his attention to her mate. He was something else altogether. Matt peered into the carrier. Woorawa was quiet within an eagle sleeve – a homemade canvas and velcro restraint. Penny herself designed and sewed the unique sleeves, which were attracting interest from mainland zoos.

Penny. He missed her, wished she was there to share this special moment. Matt's phone rang, making him smile. How had she known he was thinking about her? But it wasn't Penny. It was Sarah.

He answered the call. 'I'm kind of busy.'

'What are you doing?'

'Releasing the eagles.'

'What, right this minute?'

'Aquila's already circling and Woorawa's just about ready to fly. I've got to go.'

'Let me stay on the line,' said Sarah. 'It will be like I'm there.'

'Righto. I'll switch my phone to speaker.'

Matt extracted Woorawa from the carrier. The bird felt heavy, muscular, tense with anticipation as a wild bird should. Matt removed the hood. The eagle gazed at him with cold agate eyes. Slowly, carefully, Matt opened the sleeve, grasping Woorawa's legs and body tight.

The bird held him for a minute in a magnetic stare, beak agape. *I fear nothing in the earth or sky*, he seemed to say. Then he turned to face the blue.

'What's happening,' asked Sarah.

'I'm about to let him go.'

'Tell me.'

'I'm holding his legs and letting him flap for a minute to stretch his wings. Now I'm lifting him over my head. Here's your second chance, mate. Good luck, and don't blow it. One, two, three – and there he goes.'

This was where Matt's well-laid plans could come unstuck. Aquila had to follow her wild mate. If she returned to Matt, it wouldn't be the end of the world; secretly, he might even be pleased. But if she headed off alone, her chances of survival were bleak.

'What's happening now?' asked Sarah.

'I wish you could see it. Woorawa's a few metres above Aquila, and he's circling too. They're in unison. This is brilliant. You'd think they'd done this all their lives. It almost looks like they're hunting.'

'Congratulations,' said Sarah. 'You must be proud. You worked so hard for this.'

He *was* proud, and exhilarated, and terrified watching the soaring eagles. Perfect mates. They didn't compare notes, didn't plan ahead. Their bond was intuitive, their strategy instinctive. There were no lies or misunderstandings.

Woorawa suddenly dived. A split second later, Aquila plunged after him. Matt almost fell from his perch high above the falls.

'They *are* hunting,' said Matt. 'I don't believe this.'

'What can you see?'

'Not a thing. They've dropped out of sight.'

Matt ended the call. He craned his neck towards the faraway valley floor, but saw nothing. Clouds of spray from the waterfall obscured his view. What was happening down there? Matt kicked at a rock. It made a graceful arc over the cascade, then plummeted, just like the eagles. He swore. Even a lifeless stone could reach the valley, but not him. For a long time he watched the sky, but the birds didn't reappear.

After an hour Matt collected his gear and walked back along the track, his mind working overtime. Then he rang Penny, crossing his fingers for reception. If anybody could understand what he was going through, it was his wife. Yes. Penny's soothing voice was echoing in his ear. 'I'd love to get down there and see what's happening,' he said. 'You don't have a helicopter on standby by any chance?'

Penny hung silent on the phone.

'Pen? Are you still there?'

'I'm here,' she said after a while, 'and I have an idea. Promise you won't get mad, though.'

'Why would I get mad?'

'It has to do with your father. Everything to do with your father makes you mad.'

He'd left himself wide open for that one. 'Forget it.'

'Don't go, just listen.'

Matt stayed, too wound up to speak, too curious to bail.

'Fraser says there was once a way down to the valley.'

'We already knew that.'

'Yes, but he knows where it was – through the back of Last Stand Cave. Fraser could never find a way through, but you're an expert caver. It might be worth a try.'

'He told you this?'

'Yes,' said Penny.

'When?'

A long pause. 'Two months ago, maybe?'

'He never told me.' The satellite phone crackled.

'I know. He should have.'

And so should have you, he thought. Matt felt like screaming. How many times had the two of them searched for a way down to the valley?

Matt switched off the phone, looked across to the ancient Huon pine tree, guardian of Last Stand Cave. He dropped the cages, pulled a flashlight from his pocket and hurried over, too impatient to head back to the jeep for ropes. He'd been in that cave dozens of times. There was nothing at the back except a ceiling-high pile of rocks and thousands of tickling cave crickets. The walls seethed with them.

He ventured in, further and further again, his small torch struggling to light the recesses. Hadn't he normally hit rocks by now? The floor abruptly gave way, plunging him down a muddy hole. Only a braced forearm saved his head from striking stone. The narrow beam of the torch illuminated a steep rockslide in front of him that had not been there before. It looked like the entire rear wall of the cave had collapsed into the earth.

Matt took a leap of faith and started down the incline, skidding and sliding with the torch between his teeth. One minute. Two minutes. Ten minutes. It grew brighter and Matt propped on a ledge just in time. Fifty metres below him, the shaly slope yawned into space – a heart-stalling ski jump to nowhere. The arm he'd used to save himself had received a painful twist. Why hadn't he gone back for the ropes? With deliberate, measured lungfuls of breath, he calmed his nerves. To his left gaped a vertical fissure in the cliff, as wide and tall as a man.

Matt scrambled across to the narrow passage and squeezed inside. Flutters in the dark – a cloud of bats swarming around his head. He knew about bats, how harmless they were, but still a primal fear gripped him. The fear of the dark, of the unknown. The fear of creatures crawling in his mouth, of wings beating about his face. As quickly as he'd felt them, the horde vanished into the void and Matt reclaimed his breath. Water was dripping on his head. He stepped forward, slipped and hit his face on the rock, tasting blood.

Torchlight revealed a shallow stream at his feet. It led down through the cliff tunnel. Carpets of green and gold lichen adorned the clammy walls and, beyond the bright beam, rocks glimmered with glow-worms. The path steepened and, astonishingly, his feet found crude steps carved in the stone. This was it: the fabled passage down. A passage to the underworld. An irrational fear prickled the nape of his neck. The legends he'd loved as a child said it was forbidden to go to the land of the dead. The underworld protected its secrets.

However no mythical guardian waylaid him, and before long Matt stood on the valley floor. His legs went to jelly and he felt the unfamiliar sting of tears behind his eyes. He'd dreamed of this moment for years – of finding his way down to this lost valley – and the wonder of it overwhelmed him.

The desolate voice of a crow sounded from high on the rim. He looked up at the ring of granite cliffs soaring hundreds of metres into the sky, making the valley a fortress against the modern world; a place where Woorawa and Aquila could live untroubled by man.

Matt peered through a screen of sassafras, a perfect natural hide, to the clearing beyond. And there on the ground, in the middle of a button-grass meadow, his eagles were ripping and tearing at a dead pademelon. Woorawa was perched atop the carcass, with Aquila taking tentative tastes from the side.

Woorawa had done well to bring down a wallaby. Aquila wouldn't have been much help. She was unaccustomed to hunting anything larger than rabbits. Curiosity overcame his caution and Matt separated himself from the shadows. Aquila stayed put, but Woorawa launched himself skywards. It was reckless, what he was doing. It could drive Woorawa away, separate the pair he'd worked so hard to match, but he had to know.

He approached, one careful step at a time. Woorawa circled low, then alighted on the bough of a swamp gum bordering the clearing. His gaze never left Aquila, who hissed and then returned to her meal. Their bond was strong. Reassured by Woorawa's proximity, Matt drew close enough to see what he was looking for.

Eagles hadn't killed this wallaby. Its teeth-torn throat and missing flank said as much. Matt scanned the ground with rising excitement, and paw prints confirmed his hunch. This was a tiger kill. He almost took photos, but thought better of it. He'd already deleted the shots of Theo from his camera. Why leave evidence when he hadn't yet made his decision? Instead, he backed off, unwilling to interfere anymore. Some tiger tracks led north into the forest. Some led south, straight to the sassafras thicket from which he'd emerged. They told the story, plain as day. Tigers were using the path opened up by the earthquake to exit the valley.

Did they return at dawn to shelter here? Perhaps, at this very moment, tigers slept close by in one of the cavities peppering the cliff face. In that one, or that one? Or this one? Matt explored the nearest cave, disturbing a sleepy tiger quoll, nothing more. He crept back out and peeked through the sassafras curtain. Woorawa was again perched atop the carcass. Aquila reached up, caressed his nape with her beak. Thank goodness for that. He should never have jeopardised their release. Penny would be unhappy if she knew.

But then after what Penny had done, keeping her friendship with Fraser a secret, who was she to judge him? A sour resentment rose in his throat. How hard were Penny's releases anyway? Find a run-down farm infested with cats and rabbits. An easy-to-monitor moorland plain. Some boggy regrowth forest. Simply let the devil go, often with the luxury of a radio collar. It was worlds away from freeing eagles in the wilderness on a wing and a prayer.

Matt glanced up. The jagged clifftop broke the sky like knuckles on a row of clenched fists. His arm throbbed. It would be a hard return journey.

The climb back up to Tiger Pass took three times longer than the descent. The lower section of the tunnel appeared to be in original condition, parts of it worn smooth by the passage of ancient feet. Who carved the steps and when? So many questions. Now he was looking for them, tiger tracks weren't hard to find. They hugged the inner wall at the edge of the treacherous rockfall, guiding his own steps, making his scramble up the stony slope easier.

Matt finally emerged from Last Stand Cave, squinting and blinking at the sun, drawing ragged breaths. He retrieved the carriers and headed back to the jeep, mind abuzz. Why had Penny kept this news about the valley to herself for so long? Only one explanation made sense. Fraser had told her, and she wanted to conceal the fact that she'd been speaking to him. It was disconcerting to discover a secret side to her, and he was not ready to forgive, despite his earlier softening. Maybe you could never really know another person. The possibility made his chest hurt. He wanted *his* Penny back. The honest one, the one he could trust.

He reached the jeep, packed away his gear and slumped in the driver's seat. His arm was aching more and more. Matt tried to focus on the day's astounding discoveries, but loneliness was swamping his elation. He missed the eagles, missed his wife, missed having someone to talk to. He checked the clock. If he headed back now, he might still have time to help Jake feed up. Matt turned the ignition key, wondering how he would bear being alone tonight. Then his phone rang.

'Matt? It's Sarah. I have to see you.'

CHAPTER 25

Penny struggled beneath the dead weight of the wallaby, feeling the strain across her stomach and shoulders. Seeing the blood on her shirt.

'I'll take that one for you, love,' said Ray's friend, Charlie. 'He's a big 'un.' They stowed the six bodies in the coolroom beside the mews. 'If it weren't me doing the culling, it'd be some other bugger,' he said, defensively. 'At least you knows I don't let them suffer.'

'I do know that, Charlie. And I also know you could sell them to the processor at Eaglehawk Neck instead of giving them to me.' She gave him a quick kiss. He rubbed his cheek and smiled, revealing the stubs of his front teeth. 'You're very generous, Charlie, considering you and Ray aren't flush with cash right now.'

'You're not wrong there, love. Log runs are thin on the ground this summer.' He took off his hat and looked sheepish. 'Seeing as I am a bit short, like you was saying, I was wondering about the skins? I know a bloke who takes them.'

'Of course, Charlie. Have the skins.'

He grinned and checked his watch. 'Still time to make a few quid to spend at the pub. They have footy on the telly Saturday nights.'

Charlie took a murderous-looking set of flaying knives from his truck and marched back to the coolroom.

Late afternoon shadows striped the paths as Penny made her way down to the front gate. It was time to feed the joeys, but the volunteers could do that today. She waved the last visitor goodbye and locked up.

'Should I feed the raptors?' Jake sang out from the mews. 'Matt's still not back.'

'Go ahead,' said Penny. 'He had some problems with the eagles up at the pass. He might be late.'

It felt good to report on Matt's whereabouts like a wife would. Penny hadn't felt like his wife for far too long. They'd even spent Christmas apart. It was such a difficult holiday for Matt. He'd lost his mother and sisters on Christmas Eve, and he struggled with the date every year. She'd hoped he might turn up for a feed of roast pork and salmon and her uncle's homemade plum pudding icecream. Instead, she'd found her present lying on Ray's doorstep, with a note from Matt to say he was spending the day alone on the range. They'd been behaving like strangers, each too full of pain and pride to bridge the yawning gulf between them.

Penny hoped to change that tonight. Leaving Matt had been a big mistake. Giving him space wasn't working. Matt seemed paralysed, unable to make the decision about Theo that she'd demanded of him. All she was doing was driving him further away at a time when she desperately needed him. Enough was enough.

It boded well that Matt had rung her today, turning to her like he used to. And she'd come through for him, even though it had meant raising the thorny subject of Fraser. Never mind, Matt would have to get over it, just as she'd have to get over him keeping Theo a secret.

Penny put the bottle of non-alcoholic champagne in the fridge in preparation for tonight. She gave the kitchen a quick tidy, cleaning benches and piling dishes in the sink, too distracted to do a proper job. Had Matt found his way down to the valley? If anyone could, he could. She played with her phone again, dying to ring him. No, not the right tactic. Let Matt do the calling.

Penny showered and towel-dried her hair before the mirror. Leaving it loose, she changed her clothes, all the while keeping watch for Matt. Her good jeans felt a little tight. This top? No. That one? Trying too hard. This one? Low-cut plum satin. It would do. She donned a lacy black bra that Matt liked. Where was he, anyway? Penny popped a tray of cheese and spinach cannelloni into the oven. On second thoughts, she pulled it out, and grated more and more cheese on top, until the pan could barely contain the fluffy yellow mountain. Matt loved cheese.

Just on dark, the jeep pulled into the driveway and Matt disappeared into the mews. A few minutes later he emerged, talked briefly to Jake, and walked up the path to the back door. Penny ducked away from the window. She could hear him in the laundry and stared impatiently at the door. When Matt finally came into the kitchen, she could see he'd been climbing. Dried blood caked his arms and the stubble of his cheeks.

He stopped abruptly, clearly surprised to see her. It was the first time since their separation that she'd stayed back after work instead of going to Ray's. Perhaps she should have let him know.

'Don't keep me in suspense,' she said. 'Did you make it down to the valley?'

'I did.' His dark eyebrows slanted into a frown. 'You can tell Fraser he was right.'

Penny ignored the dig. 'Fantastic, and what about the eagles?'

'They're fine. They stayed together.'

He went past her to the sink and washed his hands. She waited for him to continue, but apparently the subject was closed. Penny took a step back. She hadn't known what to expect, but it wasn't cold indifference. Matt wasn't making this easy.

'I've made dinner,' said Penny. 'Want a beer?'

'I can't.'

Why did Matt seem in a hurry? 'We need to talk,' she said.

'Sorry, Pen, not tonight. I'm going out.'

'Going out?'

He couldn't even look at her. 'It's to do with work.'

Penny felt like she'd been slapped. Here she was humiliating herself, agonising over their separation, struggling to put their marriage back together – and Matt was going out. It was too much. She hurried to the bedroom to get her overnight bag.

Matt wasn't in the kitchen when she returned. Penny could hear the shower running. She turned off the oven and slipped away without saying goodbye. Weak with disappointment, she stumbled down to her jeep, taking huge, heaving breaths to calm herself. Against her better judgement, she looked up at the house and willed Matt to come after her. Fool. She found a rag on the back seat, blew her nose and mopped her face. What was she going to do now? The thought of going home to Ray's *I told you so* was unbearable.

The open gates of Canterbury Downs loomed from the dusk. Why not? She'd never visited Fraser this late before, but now there was no pretence, so what did it matter? Matt was off goodness-knows-where with goodness-knows-who and she didn't have to answer to him anyway.

She hit the brakes hard to make the turn and parked behind Fraser's Lexus. Penny inspected herself in the sun visor mirror; puffy eyes and a postbox red nose. So what? She poked around in the glove box. That would do, that disgusting fluff-laden rubber band. With a savage twist, Penny jammed her hair back into a tight ponytail. She skirted the front door and slipped along the dark verandah, her body feeling weak from the disappointment.

Light shone from the studio and strains of opera, of a sad, sweet soprano, sounded through the still night. Fraser often worked to music and Penny could think of nothing she'd like more at this moment than to lose herself in a taxidermic fervour. The newfound-lands were barking up a storm. Fraser stepped into the porch light, silenced his dogs with a frown and beckoned her in, for all the world like he knew she was coming.

'I have something for you – a surprise.'

Penny gave the big dogs a hug and followed Fraser inside.

He paused and cocked his head towards the wall speakers. 'Wagner's *Die Fliegende Holländer*. Senta's ballad. A beautiful maiden, such as yourself. Can you hear? She sings to her phantom captain, prays she might be the one to save him.'

'Why does he need saving?'

'He's cursed, Penelope. Cursed to wander the sea in a ghostly schooner laden with treasure, in search of a woman who will redeem him with her fidelity. *What good is wealth,* he asks himself, *without wife or child to bind me to this earth?* The man has a point.'

'How does it end?'

Fraser shrugged. 'In melodrama. It's Wagner.'

'Is this my surprise? This music?'

'No, no.' He threw her a glossy magazine. 'Have a look.'

It was the new Van Dyke's annual catalogue, with an astounding range of animal forms. There were the usual deer, boar and buffalo. But there were also dozens of rare species. Bears and baboons. Bobcats and beavers. Otters, cheetahs, a mongoose. For twenty thousand dollars you could buy a full-size polyurethane elephant model. Standing trunk up, right foot forward. Elastomer reproduction tusks were an extra two thousand.

'Why didn't you show me this before?'

'There's a rhino in there this year. You wouldn't approve. But tell me, which artist appeals the most?'

Penny returned to the catalogue. Jody Green did wonderful deer. John Schmidt captured movement and was a consistent award-winner for anatomically correct sculpting. John Roffers had a way with moose. But for Penny's money, the standout was Dan Bolt, not only for the sheer number of species he worked with, but for his realism, his intricate muscle structure, his breathtaking range of natural poses. Penny pointed to the stalking form of a wolverine.

'This guy's a genius.'

'Excellent choice,' said Fraser, beaming. 'It so happens I commissioned Bolt to do some work for me.' He disappeared into the storeroom, returning with a medium-sized animal form, which he handed to her. It took Penny a moment to appreciate what she was seeing. It was a devil. Light as a feather, beautifully crafted, posed in a lope with head swung left. She laughed with pleasure.

'I have ten forms in five different positions,' he said. 'This one, of course. Also standing upright, sitting, head raised sniffing, and lying down. There are others too, available on request.'

Penny threw her arms around Fraser's neck. Until now she'd struggled to make her own devil moulds. Freezing dead animals in particular poses, then laboriously making plaster casts, half a carcass at a time. The results had been mediocre at best, laughable at worst. One time, her devil looked remarkably like a sausage dog.

'I don't know how to thank you,' said Penny.

'Yes, you do.' Fraser's expression turned solemn. 'End this ridiculous separation, Penelope, and help me talk some sense into Matthew.' His voice had an uncharacteristic quiver to it. 'I want my son back before I die, perhaps even a grandchild …'

She sank down on the couch, on the zebra-skin throw rug, and burst into tears.

'Now I've upset you.' Fraser looked lost. 'Let me get you something. Brandy?' Penny cried harder. 'I'll fetch some from the house.' He escaped out the door.

Like father like son. Matt would have done the same thing. At least she had a chance to compose herself. By the time Fraser returned with a bottle and a pair of brandy balloons, she was merely sniffing.

Penny refused the brandy, slid to one end of the couch, feet curled beneath her and patted the seat beside her. 'Sit.' Fraser poured himself a generous glass and complied. 'I'm already pregnant,' she said. 'Four months gone.'

Fraser dropped his drink. The glass shattered under the table, and the smell of brandy filled the air. His wide, shining smile made him look ten years younger. 'My dear, this is wonderful, wonderful news.'

How she wished it was Matt sitting beside her with joy on his face.

Fraser's smile morphed into a puzzled frown, and he laced his fingers together. 'What's all this separation nonsense? Why isn't Matthew by your side?'

'Matt doesn't know.'

Fraser drew back. 'Why ever not?

'I haven't found the right time ...'

'I can help with that.' Fraser reached for his phone. 'My son deserves the truth.'

Teary now, Penny pulled the phone from him. 'He's mad at me right now because he's mad at you,' she said. 'He always has been, ever since I've known him.'

Fraser found some tissues, wiped her eyes and his own and took her hands in his. 'Then we must change his mind, eh? You and I together? How could he resist us?' Penny smiled, despite herself. 'Aha,' said Fraser. 'I'm winning you over.'

He surprised her by extracting a cigar from an ornate box on the sideboard, and snapping the seal with his thumb. Since when did Fraser smoke? 'I suspect Matthew is keeping his own secrets,' he said, lighting up. 'Some months ago I put a proposition to your husband.' Penny shook her head in disbelief. As far as she knew, Matt hadn't spoken to his father in years. 'I offered to resign my position as company CEO and transfer my shares to Matthew, effectively giving him control of Burns and all its subsidiaries. He turned me down flat.'

'I had no idea,' said Penny. 'But with respect, Fraser, Matt wouldn't want to run a company like yours.'

'He wouldn't have to. He could run it his own way, grind it into the ground if he wants. Torpedo the pulp mill. Halt all logging and close the mine. Convert my priceless timber reserves into national parks. Matthew will be a wealthy man when I die, whatever he decides. It would be entirely up to him.'

'I don't understand. Why would you give away your companies?'

Fraser sighed with the sadness of the ages. 'To atone for a misspent life,' he said. 'A life lived with a kind of moral blindness.'

Penny stared, open-mouthed.

'I'm facing my own personal extinction, Penelope. I may not have a year.' His voice was grave, but free from self pity.

Penny shook her head, in shock. Oh no, poor Fraser. She tried to say she was sorry, but he frowned and held up his hand. 'I won't have platitudes. After all, nobody gets out of here alive. But I *will* have my son back. And thanks to you, darling girl, I will have my grandchild as well.'

Penny hugged her knees, mind folding around what she'd learned. How had her world become so false, so riddled with secrets? She tried to summon indignation about Matt keeping Fraser's offer from her, but the hypocrisy was too much. Her hand strayed to her plump stomach. She was beginning to show. Sins of omission. Had she and Matt convinced themselves they were less destructive than outright lies?

'Help me, Penelope.' Fraser looked hopeful now, even happy. 'I'm not the man I used to be.'

Penny studied his eager face, and her heart went out to him. 'Prove it, then,' she said. 'Prove you've changed. Save Pallawarra for a start.' Fraser looked blank. 'Don't you know anything about what's been going on in the forest?'

'I don't micromanage.' His brow furrowed. 'But I know the gist. There's a formal halt on logging in Tuggerah Valley until after the election. Then state cabinet will meet to reverse the ban.'

'What? As cut and dried as that? Already decided?'

'I'm afraid so. Kate wants to avoid a fuss on the eve of the poll. Afterwards, she'll pass a Peaceful Assembly Act to criminalise forest protests and shut them down for good.'

'How can you possibly know that?'

Fraser sighed. 'Because it was my idea.'

Penny felt suddenly sick, dizzy, as though the ground was shifting beneath her. Was it the pregnancy – feeling things she'd never felt before? Or was it Fraser, what he'd done? Matt was right, the man was a monster. 'What about our right to freedom of assembly?'

'We are not America, Penelope. There are no such entitlements in our constitution. Our rights in this regard amount to whatever the law states, so they amount to nothing.' He blew a smoke ring. 'Kate's legislation will not be popular, hence her decision to wait.'

'But that's outrageous. She's lying to the electorate. Doesn't the truth matter?'

'My dear child, someone famously said that a lie told a hundred times becomes the truth.'

'No, it doesn't.' Penny's voice grew shrill. 'No it doesn't!' She rose to leave.

He stood and blocked her way. Staying upright was costing him a noticeable effort, and his expression was one of uncharacteristic desperation. 'Please Penelope?' The plea sounded strange coming from Fraser – a man normally in total control.

Penny took in the lines on his face, the sag of his cheeks, the hope in his eyes. She drew a deep breath. 'Will you do whatever I ask of you?'

Fraser's hand found his heart.

CHAPTER 26

The sun was setting in a nest of purple clouds when Matt pulled up at the bed and breakfast attached to Mrs Murphy's tearooms. Sarah was waiting out the front, clad in a tight black dress with a chain around her hips, holding a document wallet. Matt pulled over, disconcerted by how glamorous she looked. He was dressed in his ranger's uniform. She was dressed for a date.

'Hop in.'

'Whatever have you done to your face?' she asked.

'I told you I was accident-prone.' He drove past the local hotel and took the road to Nandena. There might be a band playing there tonight. Ha, who was he kidding? He didn't want to be seen with Sarah in town, not looking the way she did.

The road ran between plantations of pine, which clung to the slopes and valleys like a dark fog. Ahead, a wombat lay slumped on the verge. Matt pulled over, checked its pouch and dragged the dead marsupial into the scrub. 'You have to get them off the roads,' he said. 'They attract devils.' A few minutes later it was a possum. Next was a young pademelon, with a flattened black corpse beside it. Matt swore, bagged the remains of the devil, and hurled the wallaby into the bushes. 'See what I mean?'

'Ew,' said Sarah. There was now a ripe odour in the jeep.

'You're lucky I don't take them all back to put in Binburra's freezer. That's what I usually do.'

Sarah screwed up her nose. Opening her document wallet as he drove, she pulled out some papers. 'Matt, this really can't wait,' she said. 'I've identified a genetically different population of devils, and – guess where? In the Tuggerah Valley.'

'Different how?'

'Different in the best possible way. In their major histocompatibility complex genes – their MHC genes.'

Did she expect him to know what that meant?

'MHC genes help the immune system to recognise and attack foreign cells. They're what causes a patient's body to reject a donor liver, for example. Most devils have MHC genes so similar to the cancer, that they can't identify or fight their tumours. But I've found a population whose MHC genes are very different to DFTD cells.'

'But you said local devils were close to immunological clones,' said Matt.

'I was wrong,' said Sarah. 'Thanks to Penny's roadkill count project, I'm getting a lot more samples, widening my data base.'

A rabbit dashed across the road and Matt braked to avoid it. Sarah's voice grew high with excitement. 'I re-ran my tests. Devils with this different MHC genotype, I've named it MHC2, should be able to recognise the cancer and mount a defence against it.'

The significance of her words sank in. Sarah's research might not only save the devils, but the Tuggerah as well. A critically endangered population of tumour-resistant devils could permanently halt all logging.

Matt pulled the jeep off the road, grabbed Sarah and kissed her. It was meant to be a congratulatory kiss on the cheek, but she turned her head and their lips met. 'You're a genius,' he said, and he meant it. This was by far the biggest breakthrough they'd had. If Binburra could breed up these special devils? If their MHC2 genes were dominant and prevailed in their offspring? The possibilities were too marvellous to think about.

Sarah was still talking, but Matt was no longer listening. He was imagining the joy on Penny's face when he told her the news. He should have asked her to come along tonight, but he'd been mad at her – again. A sudden flash of insight told him he was blaming the wrong person. His father was the culprit. Fraser had lured Penny into visiting him at Canterbury Downs. He'd encouraged her to bring him specimens from Binburra, behind Matt's back. He'd told Penny about the way down to the valley, when, as lifelong protector of Binburra, that information belonged to Matt by right. Fraser was deliberately causing trouble. Well, no more. Matt would put his marriage back together, and Sarah's breakthrough could be the catalyst for doing it.

'I need to do more testing, that's the main thing,' Sarah was saying. 'Almost twenty-five percent of Tuggerah devils tested so far have the MHC2 genotype. Penny's frozen samples are next. I can't *wait* to get started.'

'Of course, of course. Whatever you want.' Matt hugged her, laughing, overcome with excitement. For one glorious moment his worries evaporated. 'Come on,' he said. 'We're celebrating.'

The Top Pub at Nandena was a historic two-storey Georgian building with a graceful twin-gabled roof line.

'How gorgeous,' said Sarah, admiring the hotel's sandstone Regency façade.

Matt hopped out and opened Sarah's door for her. 'This place was built by convicts in 1840,' he said. 'Martin Cash, Tasmania's own Robin Hood, among them.'

They took seats at the bar, Sarah still clutching her document wallet. She unzipped it, zipped it back up again and put it down. 'Tell me about Martin Cash,' she said, pouring them both a glass of water.

Matt stretched his arms over his head, feeling happier and more relaxed than he could remember. 'Cash was an Irish hothead. Women loved him, but they were his downfall, all of his life.'

'Ooh,' said Sarah. 'Do tell.'

Matt rearranged his long legs. 'Cash was only eighteen years old when he looked through a Dublin hotel window and saw someone hitting on his girlfriend. The two men got into a fight. Cash shot the other bloke and was sentenced to seven years' transportation here to Van Diemen's Land. But no jail could hold him. Cash even broke out of Port Arthur, and that was some achievement. Completely escape-proof, they reckoned, like Alcatraz. Armed sentries everywhere. Only connected to the mainland by a narrow strip of land – Eaglehawk Neck – and a line of savage, starving dogs chained across it. Convicts believed the water both sides was infested with sharks.' Matt sipped his beer. 'Cash didn't care. He tied his clothes round his neck in a bundle and swam for it. Got clean away, first man ever. Lost his clothes though. Did his first hold-up starkers.'

'Naked?'

'As the day he was born.' Matt was enjoying himself. 'Nicknamed Cash and Co, him and a couple of mates had short but spectacular careers as bushrangers.' Matt leaned forward in his chair. 'Dodged five hundred constables and soldiers sent to bring them in. Survived six shoot-outs, escaped dozens of traps, outwitted everybody. They only robbed the rich – squatters, hotels, mail coaches – and they left the poor alone, didn't rape or shoot people. The gentleman bushranger, that's what they called Cash. Quite the gallant.'

'Did they ever catch him?'

'Betrayed by the woman he loved, so the story goes.' Matt picked up the menu. 'Do you want to order yet?'

Sarah slapped his arm playfully. 'Finish the story.'

'In 1843 word reached Cash that his girlfriend, Bessie Clifford, was having an affair with a man called Joe Pratt in Hobart. Cash was on his way into town to kill Joe, when Bessie found out and tipped off the police. There was a shoot-out. Cash fatally wounded a young constable before he was captured. But – get this – he's such a legend, the press mounted a campaign to pardon him. Loads of Cash's victims interceded on his behalf. The court sentenced him to death anyway.'

Sarah was sitting forward too. She licked a drop of water from her lip. 'Did he die bravely?'

Matt grinned. 'The slippery bastard won a reprieve an hour before he was due to hang. They transported him to Norfolk Island where he became a model prisoner, won a pardon and headed straight back to Tasmania. Cash married, bought a farm and died in bed.'

She laughed. 'Are you sure it happened like that?'

'As God is my witness.'

While they waited for their meals, Matt led Sarah out the back to see the hotel's historic stone wishing well. 'It's over a hundred and fifty years old.'

Sarah looked unimpressed. 'Yours is such a young country. You don't have anything really old here. Well, you don't,' she said, at Matt's amused smile. 'You can't. You haven't been here long enough.'

Matt tossed a coin into the well and wished that his falcons, Sooty and Sweep, had found their way in the wild.

'Go on then, name something,' she said. 'Name something really old.'

'The forest,' he said, without turning around. 'The rivers. That rock art I showed you. Our Indigenous culture.' Matt thought of the carved stone steps at Tiger Pass. How old were they?

Sarah blushed through her tan. 'Sorry, I was thinking small.'

'Most people are.' Matt tossed in another coin. 'What do you know about wishing wells?'

'Nothing.'

'Copper or silver coins stopped the water going sour - that's the practical explanation. But the idea that wishes would be granted came from believing that tiny gods lived down wells. It's a form of ancient pagan sacrifice.'

Sarah leaned against the well close beside him, and tossed in a coin. 'I wish …'

'Shh … it won't come true if you tell.'

A sudden screech from a nearby tree sent Sarah rocketing into his arms. For a moment he held her, smelled her sweet perfume, felt the warmth of her body and her willingness for something more.

'Just a masked owl.' He stepped back and glanced inside. 'Our meals are ready.'

. . .

They were both quiet during dinner. It wasn't until the tiramisu that Sarah said, 'I heard that Penny moved out.'

Matt twisted a paper serviette. He toyed with his beer and watched the band set up on stage. He wasn't enjoying himself anymore. The pub was filling up, and the blonde girl on stage with her back to him looked familiar. Of course, it was Lisa.

'G'day Matthew … Doctor.' Drake peered over Sarah's shoulder. Just what Matt didn't need. The evening was bound to get back to Penny now. 'Mind if I join you?'

Matt sighed. 'Suit yourself.' He felt a sudden urge to get away.

Drake slid his chair in beside Sarah and began a low conversation, too low for Matt to hear, now that the band was tuning up. Sarah laughed and nodded, eyes smiling at some joke. Tawny eyes, with a hint of green, like ripe hazelnuts.

Lisa and the band launched into their first number.

When Drake left to order drinks, Matt put his hand on Sarah's arm. 'Sorry to be a party pooper, but I'm off,' he said. 'Drake will give you a lift back.'

'But why? The music's just started.'

'I might not have shut the laundry door at home. I'd hate Hedwig to get in with the baby bandicoots.'

Sarah thought for a moment, then picked up her bag. 'I'll come with you. There are some research notes I want to pick up from Binburra anyway.'

'I'd love a drink,' said Sarah, as they walked inside. 'And can we put on some music? I haven't finished celebrating.'

'My iPod doesn't work.'

'Don't you have Spotify? Never mind. Let's be old-fashioned.' Sarah began rifling through a shelf of dusty CDs. Soon Sade's smooth sound filled the house.

Matt cracked a bottle of champagne he found in the fridge. When he read the label, he put it back with a stopper. Non-alcoholic. Where had that come from? He opened a bottle of red wine instead and poured them both a glass. 'I'd better look in on the babies.' Sarah trailed after him, sipping her drink. He moved about, checking on the wallaby joeys and the bats and the bandicoots. A family of half-grown quolls, who regarded night-time as playtime, escaped from their pen in the corner and darted about the laundry.

'That's the second time they've done that,' he said. 'There must be something wrong with the latch.'

'How adorable,' said Sarah, as Matt retrieved a wayward youngster from his head. She lifted the lid of a freezer. 'Are there devils in here?'

'I don't know.' Matt snatched a quoll from the curtain. 'See for yourself if you want.'

Sarah put down her glass and started sorting through the carcasses. A wide variety of plastic-wrapped, frozen Tasmanian wildlife soon littered the floor, from giant freshwater crayfish to hairless wombat joeys.

'I can't find the devils.'

Matt put away the last quoll and frowned. What a mess. Did she have to be so careless with Penny's animals? 'Come on. I'll help you pack this up.' There was an edge to his voice. He was tired, that was all, and his arm throbbed where he'd twisted it in the descent. It wasn't fair to take it out on Sarah.

Some fresh air would help. He took the bottle of wine and some cheese out to the verandah, poured their drinks and watched a bushfire moon break free of the distant mountain. Stars pricked through the roof of the sky.

'What an enchanting evening.' Sarah's face was in shadow, but he could feel her eyes upon him. 'Isn't starlight romantic?' Her voice was low and silky.

Was she coming onto him? Matt was clueless about women other than Penny. And given the state of their marriage, it turned out he was pretty clueless about her too. He moved his chair to better see Sarah's eyes. Maybe he shouldn't have brought her back to Binburra.

But his disquiet evaporated when Sarah began talking about her work. She positively shone with passion for it. 'Genetic tagging is the key to protecting endangered species,' she said. 'Imagine tracking your devils by their DNA signatures instead of by ear tags and microchips and electronic collars. You'd hugely reduce your own workload. Reduce the stress caused to the animals from handling them. All you'd need is a sample of hair, scat or saliva.'

'Have there been field trials?'

'Absolutely, from humpback whales to grizzly bears. It's early days, of course, but genetic tagging is the future of conservation.'

Matt was riveted. With Sarah's help, Binburra would stand on the cutting edge of devil research. They opened another bottle of red and moved onto theories of wildlife management. Sarah held a pragmatic view, believing that animals should be intensely managed, and individuals sacrificed to science if needed for the good of the population as a whole.

'You do whatever you must to protect a species, right?'

Matt remembered Winston, Penny's resistant devil that had been injected with different strains of cancer cells until he finally succumbed; remembered his suffering. 'A species is more than a biological construct,' said Matt. 'It's a collection of feeling individuals, who are entitled to enjoy their one and only life on this earth without human interference. I say leave them alone.'

'But your job involves actively managing this park.'

'Does it?'

'So, that's why you didn't make a report about the rare orchid.'

He grinned. Sarah rolled her eyes and the debate continued.

It was after midnight when Sarah yawned. Matt yawned too. 'Time I took you home.'

'After all those drinks?' she said. 'I don't think so.'

'You're right.' He stretched his legs, stood up and started collecting plates and glasses. 'I'll sleep on the couch.'

'No need.' When he looked up, Sarah had slipped out of her little black dress. She stood before him, naked apart from lacy red briefs. Her slim body was toned and olive-skinned, with small, high breasts like a girl's.

He took a step backwards. 'Now look …'

A loud crash came from inside the house, followed by the sound of breaking glass. Matt swore and went to investigate. A series of thumps and screeches were coming from the lounge room. Hedwig was flapping from bookshelf to dresser to table, pursued by a posse of fugitive quolls. A lamp lay smashed on the floor. Only Matt's quick reflexes rescued rows of glass photo frames from the same fate. He fetched a net from the laundry and set about recapturing the absconders. Half an hour later, when he'd finally caught them all, the lounge looked like a bombsite. Overturned chairs, broken glass, furniture pulled away from the wall. Matt replaced the tired youngsters in their pen, complete with a bonus supper of rabbit, and set about cleaning the room.

He kept a close eye on the door, expecting a naked Sarah to come stalking in any moment, but there was no sign of her. It was one o'clock by the time he'd finished. He made a cup of coffee, mainly to delay dealing with Sarah, then crept into the hall. Where was she? He peeked into the bedroom.

Sarah lay on the bed, hugging a pillow – fast asleep. What a relief. Matt fetched a spare blanket, took off his shirt and lay down on the couch, his mind racing. Thank goodness Penny hadn't arrived in the middle of Sarah's little striptease. Matt tossed and turned on the too-short couch trying to get comfortable. He yawned again, his eyes grew heavy and sleep claimed him in the middle of a thought.

Matt woke sometime later in a sweat, and with a sense that something was terribly wrong. He got up, groggy with sleep, and moved through the quiet house, searching for whatever had disturbed him.

Somewhere outside a motor started up and wheels crunched on gravel. A jeep flew past the moonlit window. What on earth? A swift check of the bedroom revealed that Sarah had gone. Matt sprinted to the verandah and peered into the night. A light shone in the old shearing shed and a sick feeling grew in the pit of his stomach.

Matt took the verandah steps in one, long stride and ran barefoot to the open shed door. Sleepy raptors shuffled feathers, restless in the light. At first glance all appeared normal and he allowed himself some hope. But when he lifted the lid of the new freezer, his hope vanished. Carcasses piled higgledy-piggledy. He hadn't left them in such a jumble. Dreading what he might find, Matt turfed out the bodies in a frantic search. 'No!' he roared. Theo was gone.

Matt ran back to the house, trying to make sense of what had happened. Decide. He needed to decide right now what to do. The clock on the wall said five o'clock. He still had time before the park opened. Okay. Shoes. Car keys? Dammit. Sarah had his jeep keys, which meant she also had the office keys, and keys to the other park vehicles were kept in the locked office. He searched the bedside table draw. Bingo, his bike key.

He'd bought the Enduro last month. A beautiful bike, 654 cc, six gears. Smooth-as-silk clutch, as at home on the highway as in the bush, and a steal at the price, even with its dodgy brakes. The front one made a sickening grinding noise and caused the bike to veer alarmingly to one side. The rear brake felt spongy and offered little resistance. He'd tinkered with it, but not fixed it. Too late now. Matt wheeled out the bike and prayed for a quick start. The machine roared to life and he sped off down the drive.

Matt hadn't ridden the bike at night before. It was more disconcerting than he'd imagined, hurtling through the dark, uncertain which way the road turned, despite knowing it so well. The darkness confused him, disguised tight corners, left him unsure of how to lean. His high beam provided just a narrow tunnel of light, and the screaming brakes aimed him at trees – more dangerous than no brakes at all. A combination of gear shifts and sheer dumb luck kept him on the track. Sarah couldn't be far ahead. She was bound to be slow in an unfamiliar vehicle on these rough roads.

Matt raced on, body thrust forward, hand heavy on the throttle. He owed Theo this much. If anyone would decide the dead tiger's fate, it would be him. Where the heck was Sarah anyway? It wasn't until the road left the forest and approached town that he spotted tail-lights up ahead. Matt honked the horn and increased his speed. She must have noticed him, but the jeep showed no signs of slowing.

Matt rounded the next turn, eased on the rear brake and timed his acceleration just right. Only a few metres behind her now. They tore into town, towards a concrete roundabout with a lamp post in the middle. Matt took a deep breath and shot around on the wrong side of the road, diving in ahead of the jeep as it exited the intersection. Sarah slammed on the brakes. Her front bumper collected the rear of his bike, threatening to drag it under the chassis. He spun sideways – no helmet, not even a shirt. This wouldn't be pretty. Matt leapt from the saddle, jumped the handlebars and rolled as he crashed to the ground.

He lay winded, feeling as if he'd been skinned. When he could breathe again, he drew in great lungfuls of air that stank of burning rubber. Matt looked back at the jeep, half-expecting it to be gone. There was no telling with Sarah, he knew that now. But the jeep was still there with the driver's door wide open. Suddenly Sarah was there too, kneeling beside him.

'Are you okay? I could have killed you.'

Matt hauled himself to his feet, with wobbly legs and a painful shoulder. It hurt to breathe.

'Where is he?' said Matt, surprised he could speak.

Sarah pointed to the jeep. Matt staggered over and checked the back. Theo was there alright. He snatched the keys from the ignition.

'What will you do?' he asked.

'I'll ask the questions, that's what I'll do,' said Sarah. 'First one. Whatever possessed you to hide this?'

Matt licked his split lip. How on earth was he going to silence Sarah? He hunted for a strategy that didn't involve throttling her on the spot. 'Get in,' he said.

A faint brightness tinged the sky. They sat in the jeep, eyeing each other in the pre-dawn light.

'Don't ask me to keep this secret,' said Sarah. 'Don't ask me that.'

'What will it take?'

'We should be shouting this from the rooftops. The entire world will sit up and take notice.'

'Exactly. There's the problem.'

Sarah's voice hardened. 'You have no right, Matt, to play God like this.'

'Me play God?' His temple throbbed and he checked the impulse to scream each word. 'I won't be the one pulling Theo apart, molecule by molecule. I won't create squirming, suffering, not-quite-right copies of him for science. I won't hunt down his family to turn them into a freak show. That'll be your job. Whose side do you reckon Theo would be on?'

Sarah slapped him, hard. Good, he was getting to her. 'Haven't you ever questioned what you do?' he asked. 'The ethics of what you bloody do? Have you even thought about it?'

'I want to help these animals however I can.'

Matt reached for her hand. 'Devils, yes. Devils still have a place, a chance. But you can't help these last few tigers. They'll be inbred, right?'

'Severely so. We've completed DNA hair analysis on every museum hide we could find. Even prior to 1900, tigers had hit a genetic bottleneck – practically no diversity at all.'

'Then what chance do they have of being anything besides short-lived curiosities? Of surviving long-term outside zoos and molecular biology labs?'

'Matt … they're already surviving outside zoos. Your animal is proof of that, and with it as a genetic template …'

'Theo. His name is Theo.'

'All right,' said Sarah. 'With Theo as a genetic template, we have a real shot at cloning him.'

Matt snorted. 'Great idea. Why bust our guts protecting anything if we can just clone it back into existence? The Premier will love that.'

The dawn was bright enough now to show him Sarah's frown. 'You're saying the government could use my work as an excuse to abandon threatened species.'

'In the mistaken belief that they can be resurrected by science whenever it suits them. Yes. Show them a rathole and they'll run down it.'

For the first time, Matt saw Sarah's resolve falter. On an impulse he leaned across and kissed her. 'Give me some space, Sarah. Please.'

She opened her eyes and breathed. 'Maybe we do need time to think this through, to be strategic with our announcement – but I won't sit on it for long.'

Matt was dizzy with relief.

Sarah touched his grazed cheek. 'Telling the world is the right thing.'

He forced a smile. 'Neither of us have had much sleep. I'll take you home.'

'Put on a shirt first,' she said. 'I don't mind, but Mrs Murphy might.'

Matt found a windcheater in the back and pulled it on. A few cars were already on the road. He dropped Sarah off outside the tearoom in the full light of a Hills End morning. Doris Briggs nodded to him as she went past. Of all the rotten luck. Who knew why she was out and about this early?

'Promise me.' Matt held Sarah's shoulders with an intensity that seemed to send old Doris into a flutter. 'Promise you won't tell anyone, not yet.'

'I promise.' Sarah kissed him goodbye on the lips, slow and lingering. 'From now on we're in this together.'

Doris flew as fast as her walking frame would allow to take the news to town.

CHAPTER 27

Matt did a quick U-turn, then barrelled out of town. He braked when he spotted his damaged bike by the side of the road, got out and hauled it into the bushes. Then he drove a few hundred metres up a side track, parked and closed his eyes. He felt paralysed, the events of the past twenty-four hours tearing through his aching head. What a fool. So many ways he could have averted disaster; not answering Sarah's call in the first place, having dinner with Penny last night instead, leaving Sarah at the pub with Drake or taking her straight home or being sober enough at midnight to drive.

Matt had no idea how long he'd been sitting there. He checked again that Theo was safely stowed in the back. He could hear the occasional car heading east along Binburra Rd. One of them would be Penny's. After some Panadol and a long drink of water he knew what to do.

By the time Matt arrived at Binburra, Penny was briefing staff and volunteers about the day ahead. He joined the small group on the steps of the visitors centre. When Penny saw him she dropped her notes. He picked them up and handed them to her. She seemed so unsure around him. It hurt.

'What happened to you?' She took in his fresh cuts and bruises. Blood had soaked through the sleeve of his windcheater, causing a dark stain. 'You're a mess.'

'I have to speak to you.'

Penny's eyebrows rose in disbelief. 'What, so *now* you want to talk?'

He scrubbed his hands over his eyes and waited.

'Go on then.'

'Somewhere private?'

She gave him a guarded look. 'Meet you up at the house in a few minutes. I have to feed the babies anyway, but you'll need to be quick. I'm going home to cook Ray a Sunday roast. He needs cheering up.'

'This won't take long.'

Penny resumed the briefing while Matt headed for the house. Uh-oh – the empty wine bottles. The two unwashed glasses. Sade on the stereo … the unmade bed. Penny could get the wrong idea.

Matt sprinted up the hill, burst in the door and threw the bottles under the sink. He rinsed the glasses, ejected Sade from the stereo and hid the offending CD under a couch cushion. His injured arm grew stiffer and sorer by the second. The bedroom next. Whoa, Sarah's phone, there on the floor beside the bed. What a find. He checked it for photos. In the back of his mind was the fear that she'd already sent images of Theo into the ether. But there was nothing more recent than the two of them together at the pub. He deleted the shots and slipped the phone into his pocket.

Matt was in the process of plumping pillows and pulling up the doona when Penny came in. 'Are you actually tidying up?'

He reached out his good arm, threaded his fingers through hers and led her to the kitchen. 'I need your help, Pen.' A weight was already sliding from his shoulders.

Penny's eyes bored into him for what seemed like forever. She pulled out a chair from the rough-hewn kitchen table. 'Sit down. You look like you need some coffee.'

. . .

He stared into his mug, throat so tight he could barely swallow the hot liquid.

'Matt?' said Penny softly, encouragingly.

He looked up. For pity's sake, just say it. 'Sarah knows about Theo.'

Penny slowly pushed back her chair. He endured the stunned expression that crossed her face. 'You didn't trust your own wife, but you let a hotshot molecular biologist in on the secret? Yeah, you sure can rely on her not to tell anyone.'

'I can't. Of course I can't.' He wrung his fingers together, rubbed his cheek. It set his cuts bleeding. 'We need to move Theo.'

'Sarah knows where he is?' said Penny. 'I don't understand. How? Why?'

These were good questions. Last night flashed in fast motion across his mind's eye. The laundry floor strewn with Penny's frozen specimens. Sarah's disappointment at not finding devils in the house freezer. Her nakedness as she slipped out of her dress. Sarah was bold and brash and impulsive. Disrespectful of Penny's work and single-minded about her own. He should have locked the shearing shed before going to sleep. No, he should never have taken her to Binburra at all.

'Matt, answer me.'

He ran his finger along the table. 'It's complicated.'

She glared at him with reproachful eyes. 'If you want my help, I need to know everything.' She was right, she deserved to know. Most of it, anyway.

'Sarah and I went to Nandena last night to see Lisa's band.'

Pain showed in the crease of her brow, and he hated knowing that he'd put it there. Hated that pride and anger had made him choose Sarah over his wife last night.

'You said you were doing something *work-related*.'

'We were. Sort of. I guess we ended up celebrating. There's good news, Pen. Wonderful news. Sarah found a population of devils with different MHC genes, right here in the Tuggerah. She wants to test your frozen samples next.'

'So …' He could see Penny's mind ticking over, processing what he'd told her. 'These devils might be able to mount an immune response to DFTD cells?'

'It's possible, yes.'

Her mouth curved into a slow smile. 'If we can identify some of them, we can begin a targeted genetic rescue program.'

How beautiful she was. Sapphire eyes, bright with delight. Soft, full lips with that slight gap between her teeth. High, freckled forehead, framed by wayward copper curls. He felt the magnetic pull of his wife, like he was falling in love all over again.

'This is great news,' she said. 'But it doesn't explain why you told Sarah about Theo.'

'I didn't. After dinner last night I brought Sarah back to Binburra to collect some research notes. I knew she was impatient to DNA test hair samples from your frozen devils, but I had no idea that she'd go looking for herself.'

'You mean she poked around in the freezers without asking? Where were you?'

He wanted to say that he'd been asleep, and that Sarah had stayed the night at Binburra. He wanted to explain about the kiss in the jeep outside Mrs Murphy's. But that explanation could ruin the precious reconnection they were making. He'd tell Penny the gist of it, that would do for now.

'Matt, I asked you where were you while Sarah was in the shed?'

'Aah … busy with the babies.' He felt a little sick as he said it.

The answer seemed to satisfy Penny. 'What a nerve that woman has. She must have been blown away to find Theo.' Penny gave him a searching look. 'You know Sarah will go to the press. We've lost the chance to do this our way.'

'I don't think she'll go public, not yet.'

'Why not?'

Matt's mouth went dry. 'I asked her very nicely not to.'

There was a heavy moment of silence. Penny buried her chin in her hand, and stared at Matt until he squirmed. 'You do know she has a crush on you.' More squirming. It wouldn't take long now. Penny's eyes grew large. 'She made a play for you, didn't she?'

'Maybe.'

'Sarah's keeping this secret as a personal favour. Keeping your spectacular science-shattering secret because she fancies you.' Penny sank down on a kitchen chair. 'Do you fancy her too?'

'No,' he said. 'I don't, and I also don't know how long she'll keep quiet. I need you to take Theo to Ray's right now. Hide him in the bait chest.'

Penny studied him awhile, then tossed her head. 'I'll be damned if that fake-tanned Yankee home-wrecker will make the announcement before we do. Are there photos?' Matt hesitated, then extracted Sarah's phone and handed it to his wife. She grinned. 'I won't ask you how you got that.' Her search revealed nothing untoward. 'Well, then, let's get to it. I'll feed the babies while you put Theo in the jeep.'

Matt gave his wife a swift kiss, and a familiar flash of desire stirred his blood – a flash of hope too. Together they'd get through this.

McGregor placed two large cardboard boxes on the breakfast table beside Fraser's coffee and scrambled eggs. 'Your homework arrived this morning, sir,' he said with a wry smile. 'Courtesy of Miss Penelope.' He handed Fraser an envelope. The note inside said, *Read everything. Watch everything. Love, Penny xx.*

Fraser opened the first box and took out a stack of books, journals and David Attenborough DVDs. Yesterday he'd agreed to do whatever she asked of him. Was this what she meant? Fraser opened a little book that had slipped from the pile, an ancient children's reader titled *Legends of Greece and Rome.* He recognised it as one of his old schoolbooks, with his name written on the first page in a childish scrawl. How curious. He turned to the page she'd bookmarked for him. The Punishment of Erysicthon. He sighed. What was the point of doing this? Still, he'd promised her. There was no harm in reading a simple story.

'There was once a lovely grove belonging to Demeter, a goddess with dominion over the fruits and riches of the earth. This sacred ground was filled with pear and apple trees, mighty elms and oaks. They grew so thickly, an archer could not shoot an arrow through the forest. Its meadows teemed with fat deer. Its creeks ran with silver waters. Demeter loved this place to the point of madness.

'There was also a Thessalian king, named Erysicthon, Tearer of the Earth. He planned to fell the trees in the sacred grove, and with their fine timber build a great banquet and pleasure house for himself. Erysicthon took with him twenty mighty giants, strong enough to lift whole cities, armed with double axes and hatchets.

'Among the trees stood a colossal oak, centuries old. Its broad branches reached to Olympus, towering as high above the other trees as they did above the grass. Around it hung wreaths and garlands and scrolls, with proof of prayers fulfilled. Yet even so, the wicked king refused to spare the blade. The holy tree shuddered and groaned as the gigantic axemen began their work. Each bough and leaf and acorn paled with fear, and blood flowed from its wounded bark.

'In death the holy tree cried out to Demeter, who heard its pain. She took the guise of a simple priestess and begged Erysicthon to stop his destruction, "... lest you anger the lady Demeter, whose grove you now make desolate."

'But the king was greedy and foolish. "Begone," he said. "Or my axe will bite your flesh." The giants rained blow after blow on the holy tree and hauled it down with ropes. At last the mighty oak crashed to earth, laying low its companions for miles around.

'Demeter, furious beyond telling, put on her goddess shape. Her steps touched the earth but her head reached heaven. Dryads of the grove, heartbroken for their loss and clothed in mourning black, prayed for punishment on the king. "Go build your banquet hall," she said to Erysicthon. "You who never tire of the feast."

'That night, Hunger wafted on the wind to the palace and entered the king's chamber. She wrapped him in her arms as he slept, became his breath, channelled her craving emptiness through his hollow veins. When the king awoke, a furious appetite reigned in his burning belly, an appetite that could not be satisfied. Whatever the wretched Erysicthon ate, that much he desired again. He feasted until the fields were bare and the flocks all devoured. Yet he gained no nourishment and wasted away to sinew and bone. The deep pit of his belly exhausted the royal wealth. His only daughter he sold to slavery for more gold to buy food. But the king's hunger remained unabated, the flame of his greed unappeased. He ate the mules, and the racehorses and his faithful war charger. He even ate his cat. And when his gluttony had consumed all the kingdom had to offer, Erysicthon gnawed at himself, devouring his own flesh and died, one bite at a time.'

Fraser closed the book. We are creatures of consequence, his Charlotte used to say. How she would have loved Penelope.

CHAPTER 28

Penny checked on Theo for the tenth time, threw a few more bags of whitebait over the top of him, then went into the kitchen. It was almost more than her life was worth, trying to ignite the ancient gas oven, but she persevered. She didn't want to bother her uncle. Watching football on TV was one of the few things that still seemed to give him pleasure. Penny nestled the beef shoulder in a bed of parsnips, pumpkin and potatoes, then put extra vegetables in an oiled pan for herself. The 1940s kitchen was pre-rangehood, so Penny opened the window, then frowned. Ray wasn't watching TV at all. He was standing in the driveway, smoking, staring at the road. She studied him. Once upon a time, he would comb his few thin wisps of hair over his bald pate. Lately, he'd forgone this small conceit, and the remnant strands hung like limp mouse tails around his ears. A fully-laden log truck was approaching, and Ray shrank back as it roared past, air brakes screaming, rattling the windows.

Penny rinsed her hands and joined him out the front. 'What's the score?'

Ray stamped the butt of his cigarette into the withered lawn. 'I lost track, love.'

Penny hugged him. He was skinnier than she remembered. 'Come on, Unk. Let's have a talk.'

Ray followed her inside and sat at the kitchen table. 'Something smells good,' he said.

'What were you thinking about when you were outside?'

Ray wasn't much of a talker, more of a listener, but he gave Penny's hand an affectionate squeeze. 'I was thinking how things have changed. You know Pete, stood down the same time as me? He's depressed something chronic, is Pete. The bastards repossessed his harvester and you'd think he'd lost his missus. To the bank she was just a tractor, but she wasn't. She was family. Pete and Big Valma were partners, they looked after each other.'

Penny nodded. Bush crews relied on their machines, even loved them. A man's machine conferred on him his status in the forest. Penny knew Big Valma, a giant harvester painted red and black like a dangerous spider, a pinnacle of mechanised logging. Pete never had to leave her comfortable, tinted, air-conditioned cabin. Valma weighed thirty tonnes, and boasted a Cummins 300 horsepower diesel engine. Her felling head cut a fifty-metre swathe of destruction in all directions. Hydraulic chainsaw teeth sliced through trees with shocking speed. Curved blades, like talons, seized them in a deadly embrace. Finally, rotating roller wheels forced the trunks inexorably through the de-limbing knives.

Penny had seen this monster at work and it gave her nightmares. But to Pete, Big Valma was a cherished workmate and ally. Early on in the forest wars, someone had smeared human excrement over her cabin doors. Although far worse was done to equipment later on – sliced electrics, gravel in drives, sugar in fuel tanks – the greenies couldn't understand how profoundly that first insult had hurt the loggers. It provoked an enmity deeper than they could ever have imagined. Still, in spite of Pete's grief, Penny couldn't help but be pleased to see the back of Big Valma.

'Know just how Pete feels, love. I miss the old Kenworth something shocking.' Ray had leased his truck to Johnno for the layoff, unable to afford to let it lie idle. Penny had a soft spot for the big rigs herself. As a child she'd loved to ride them, perched high above the road beside her uncle, lulled by the engine drone, cocooned from harm. Later on, she got her own heavy vehicle licence and gained a new respect for what it took to drive them.

Truck drivers needed to keep up punishing speeds to meet their quotas, and she'd been blind to so many things that suddenly mattered: bridge heights, sharp turns, telephone wires. She had to rely a great deal more on other road users. How grateful Penny was for a courtesy flash of the headlights when overtaking, letting her know that her truck had cleared the car, and there was room to safely move back into the left lane.

When hungry or needing to pee, she couldn't pull over wherever she wanted. She needed a truck stop with enough room to turn, and better meals than day-old hamburgers. Experiencing the road through a truckie's eyes made her appreciate the considerable difficulties they faced in simply getting from point A to point B.

'Johnno reckons this layoff's all part of the curse,' said Ray.

'That's silly. There's no curse, you know that.'

'No I don't, love.' His voice raised an octave. 'What about Scott?'

Penny felt a chill. She was glad that Ray was opening up, but her chest ached at the mention of Scott's name. He'd been her dearest friend forever and ever. One day last year he'd been taking tie-down cables off his load, when a log stacked too high above the stake tops rolled off and killed him. Scott's death had spawned a confusion of superstitious stories. But Penny hadn't blamed any curse. She'd blamed Burns Timber for tempting drivers to overload their trucks. She'd even tackled Fraser about it.

'A terrible business, what happened to your friend,' Fraser had said. 'Simply terrible. But be assured, my company's official policy warns contractors to comply with weight thresholds.'

'Maybe so, but unofficially it encourages them not to by paying for loads two tonnes or more above the limit. Some mill managers even hand out fat bonuses.'

'I can't be responsible for a few rogue managers,' said Fraser. 'But I'll do more to enforce the rules.'

For a while log weight limits were policed, but the drivers themselves had objected, complaining they couldn't make a living without the extra payments. Within months things had returned to the dangerous status quo.

Ray was pacing the kitchen now, more agitated than she'd ever seen him. 'It's not just Scott. There's trouble in that bloody forest every way you turn. The protests, the breakdowns, the accidents. Those poor coppers that fell from that tree. One of them hippy girls told Johnno she were a white witch.' Ray looked a little shame-faced for spreading this rumour. 'Reckoned her coven cast a spell to protect the Tuggerah.'

Penny sighed and put the kettle on. 'Remember in grade six when my rabbit died, I broke my arm, and I had to have my tonsils out all in first term? Fiona Williams said that she'd put a hex on me. You told me not to confuse bad luck with superstitious mumbo jumbo.'

Ray finally stopped his pacing. 'I remember.' He smiled at the memory, and sat back down at the kitchen table. 'You must think me a silly old fool.'

'Never.' Penny kissed his cheek.

'All I know for sure, love, is that Johnno bloody well better be looking after me old mate, or he'll have more than the curse to worry about.'

Ray's old mate was his twenty-year-old Kenworth rig. He knew its moods, and it knew his. It must have felt like abandoning a friend to turn his faithful truck over to someone else. The crowd roared in the lounge room. Penny went to check the score. 'Carlton's ahead by six points. Only a few minutes left, come and see.'

Ray trailed in after her, scowling. 'It's time this state had its own AFL team. Who cares about bloody Carlton?' With that he rolled another cigarette and went back outside.

Penny couldn't believe it. Ray was a rusted-on Carlton supporter, had been all his life. Sure he wanted a Tasmanian team. Everybody did, everybody always had. But that had never killed his passion for the game before. No, this was something else, a kind of general dissatisfaction with life itself. It had Penny very worried.

Trifle. Trifle always cheered him up. 'I'm going down the street. Want anything?'

'Tobacco,' he said. 'And a few packets of papers. I'm a bit short today, love. Can I fix you up later?'

It wasn't like him to ask. Ray knew how much she hated him smoking, but anything to make him happy. As she walked over the narrow bridge into town, a log truck thundered by. It barely slowed. Penny cowered against the railing, watching the towering load of logs sway alarmingly as it sped around the bend. Ray wouldn't drive like that, no matter how punishing his roster.

A group of children were playing in the civic park beside the bakery. A girl waved and sang out to her. Matilda Murphy and her little brothers, Ben and Tyson, ran over, clutching cinnamon doughnuts.

'Hello,' said Penny. 'Those look yummy.'

'We're here with Great Gran.' Ben pointed to where Margaret Murphy and Doris Briggs were sitting on a park bench, their heads together.

'Good morning, ladies,' called Penny, and they nodded a greeting. Why were they staring at her like that? Emily Bourke, exiting the shop, did the same thing.

'Are you getting divorced?' asked Matilda.

'No,' said Penny. 'What a question, Tilda.'

The children giggled and ran off.

Inside, Penny handed over her string bag. 'I'll have one of those sponges and a pipe loaf please, Colleen.'

'Of course, dear. I'll pop in some scrolls as well. They're on the house. And an apple turnover for your uncle. He loves them, he does, and you have quite enough on your plate without having to cook his favourites.'

Colleen packed the bag high with goodies. How curious.

'Colleen, I have no more on my plate today than I did last week, and I don't remember you handing out free cakes then.'

'Oh, but we didn't know then, dear, did we? Although some of us suspected, of course.'

Penny spotted the Murphy children peering in the window. Her throat was suddenly dry. 'I really don't know what you're talking about, Colleen, but I wish you'd tell me.'

'Oh, you poor love. They say the wife's always the last to know. But it's not really my place, is it?'

Penny's smile stiffened. 'Just tell me.'

Colleen beckoned Penny forward with a conspiratorial air. 'Your Matt dropped that Yank off at Margaret's, bold as brass, right in front of Doris …'

Penny tossed her head. 'So?'

'At seven o'clock this morning.'

The shop seemed airless and Penny had to steady herself against the counter. 'Thank you, Colleen.' She took her bag and fled down the street, combing through the conversation she'd had with Matt that morning. She examined every word, every nuance. He hadn't said that Sarah stayed overnight at Binburra, but he hadn't said that she didn't either. Sins of omission, sins of commission. How had the game really been played? Then it struck her: Matt's uncharacteristic desire to clean up the house before she got there … to make the bed.

CHAPTER 29

'I'm going for a drive, Unkie.' No point hanging around. Ray had hardly touched his meal, or the trifle, even with his favourite crushed walnuts on top. Pushed the food around the plate was all, and his gloom was infectious. Penny had no appetite either. Her head ached and her stomach churned. Whether it was Colleen's gossip, or her pregnancy, or a virus, she didn't know and she didn't care. She took the Binburra Road, glad to be out of the house.

Fraser was waiting for her on the verandah, looking frailer than the last time she'd seen him. McGregor hovered protectively nearby. Fraser beckoned her inside, and Penny followed him to the lounge room, barely noticing the enormous white marble fireplace that she usually marvelled at. A giant's fireplace. As far as she knew it had never held a fire. If ever she saw one in its monstrous grate she'd call the fire brigade. Something about Canterbury Downs suggested things could get out of control.

'I need your help,' said Penny. She glared at McGregor as he came in, and Fraser waved him out again. 'What I'm about to tell you can't leave this room,' she said. 'If it does, I swear I'll never speak to you again.'

'You have my word.'

Penny wet her lips. 'I have the frozen body of a thylacine in my jeep. Matt accidentally hit and killed it on the road.' She waited, expecting scepticism, shock, amazement. Instead, Fraser just looked stern.

'Who else knows?'

'Sarah Deville.'

'Sarah? She's the last person you should have told.'

'We didn't tell her,' said Penny. 'She sort of found out by herself.'

Fraser took Penny's arm and hurried her to the front of the house. 'I'm surprised you've kept this quiet.'

'So am I. It's Matt who's holding out. If it was up to me we'd go public right away.'

'No. No, that would not be wise. So, I have my son to thank. I've misjudged him. Now, let's have a look at your find.'

Penny glanced around to confirm nobody was about. Then she opened the jeep door and pushed the bags of frozen fish aside from Theo's body. Fraser heaved a happy sigh and traced a frosty stripe with his finger.

'Remarkable,' he said. 'Is there much damage to the hide?'

'No,' said Penny, still astonished that Fraser was taking it all in his stride.

'Well, don't dawdle. Let's get him inside. You take his shoulders.' Fraser grimaced, visibly struggling with the tiger's dead weight. They stowed Theo in the studio freezer, then went to the breakfast room where fresh coffee and cakes had materialised, although there was no sign of the butler.

'Do you think McGregor saw us?' asked Penny.

'Undoubtedly, but you have nothing to fear. McGregor and I are the last people on earth who would betray your secret.'

'Why? And why are you so … so unsurprised.'

'That, Penelope, is because it has been our secret for far longer than it has been yours.'

Penny put down her cup and stared at him. Now she knew where Matt got it from. Holding tight to secrets ran in the family. 'How on earth could you know anything about this?'

'An explanation that is long overdue and, I'm afraid my dear, one that is for Matthew's ears alone. But how to make him listen?'

Penny picked up her coffee cup and stared into the dregs, as if reading tea leaves. Fraser knew about the baby. He knew about Theo. It was time he knew of her suspicions about Sarah too. Her father-in-law was an unlikely confidant, but the truth was she badly needed someone to talk to. Perhaps she and Fraser could help each other.

'It's quite straightforward,' he said when she finished her story. 'Tell my son you're pregnant. He'll abandon the affair – if, indeed, that's what it is – and I'll arrange for Deville's funding to dry up. She'll be on a plane back to Los Angeles before you know it.'

Penny shook her head, a tight smile on her face. 'Eliminate my opposition and use the baby to emotionally blackmail my husband. I guess I asked for that, coming to you for relationship advice.'

'Don't be foolish, Penelope. My advice is perfectly sound. You walk out on a whim and leave the field open for another woman. A highly intelligent and desirable woman, I might add. Then you complain about the inevitable.'

Penny's face reddened. 'So it's inevitable that Matt has an affair the minute I turn my back? Is that what you think?'

'It's inevitable that he will feel deserted by his wife. Try to think like a man. I don't doubt that Matthew loves you and, I suspect, neither do you. The question is, Penelope, do you want to repair the marriage? If the answer is yes, I've proposed a practical course forward.'

This was outrageous advice, shallow even for Fraser. Did she want Matt? Yes. A thousand times yes. Had she thrown away her marriage on a whim?

'It's not quite so simple,' said Penny. 'Sarah's made a breakthrough with her research. A percentage of Tuggerah's devils may be tumour-resistant. She mustn't leave before she's genotyped all the samples.'

Fraser beamed. 'We understand each other then.'

Penny swallowed hard, afraid that they did. Her smug certainty about right and wrong was fast deserting her.

'Sometimes,' said Fraser, like he knew what she was thinking, 'the right thing is just the wrong thing in disguise. Leave the details to me. Miss Deville will ship out whenever you say the word.'

'You can do that?' asked Penny.

'You'd be staggered at the things I can do. Telling Matthew he is to be a father, however, is not one of them. Don't wait, my dear. I learned too late that a life ruled by secrets is no life at all.'

Penny hugged his skinny frame, not wanting to let go, and for once he didn't stiffen. It felt good having him as an ally, despite his dubious ethics. 'Now,' she said at last. 'My turn to help. If you want to please Matt, start by saving Pallawarra. It will mean a lot to him. It will mean a lot to this entire community.'

Fraser looked blank.

'You must know Pallawarra. The giant mountain ash above the old Charon River picnic ground? Local couples have carved their names on its trunk for more than a hundred years. Those two cops died trying to bring protesters down from it.'

Penny sensed Fraser's thoughts spiral off from the here-and-now. His eyes were unfocused. 'Yes, I do know your tree, but by another name – the fairy tree.'

'That's what Margaret Murphy calls it,' said Penny.

Fraser shut his eyes, and rested his forehead on the heel of his hand. 'My Charlotte's name is on that tree,' he said, 'alongside my own, although I doubt I'd find it after all this time. Forty years.'

'You can still read most of the carvings,' said Penny. 'Even the old ones.'

'They'll be so high up the trunk.'

'Trees grow by forming new layers of wood at the top, not by pushing up from below. Your names will be exactly where you left them.'

'Is that so? For somebody who's made a fortune from forests, I don't seem to know very much about trees. That should change, don't you think?' Penny smiled, feeling better, hungry even. She tackled a fat vanilla slice. 'Do you know what my Charlotte used to say? That my wealth was like fairy gold. Fairy gold appears precious at first, but soon turns into coal or weeds or stale gingerbread. In the end, she said, it would be quite useless to me.' He brushed a flake of pastry from Penny's cheek. 'We'll save your tree.'

'It's already been measured,' said Penny. 'One metre too short to be spared under the big tree policy.'

Fraser laughed, a not very pleasant laugh, and selected a square of bitter chocolate. Penny was glad she was on his side.

'I predict a more favourable outcome for the new assessment. Tuggerah's much-loved icon will receive the permanent protection it deserves. And do you know what? It makes me happy to say it. Happy,' he said with an emphatic nod. 'I haven't been happy for a very long time.'

K ate floated on her back in a tank at Hobart's new Gravity Centre. The pitch-black, soundproof pod normally offered a rare sense of meditative calm, but today she couldn't clear her mind. She couldn't stop thinking about politics. Wedge politics.

That's what she paid her hard-line backroom strategists for, and that's what had always worked. It wasn't about playing dirty, no matter what Robert Hellgrun said. It was simply about playing the game. Announce a big policy, back your enemies into a corner, leave them nowhere to run without being exposed as frauds and hypocrites. Then … checkmate. A tried and true recipe for success.

Kate had followed the winning formula, announcing a multi-million-dollar assistance package for timber companies and their workers. If Hellgrun and his dimwits didn't back it, she'd accuse them of abandoning jobs and the Tasmanian economy. If they did back it, she'd accuse them of having no ideas of their own. Win-win. And as it panned out, it 'appalled' the Premier that Hellgrun refused to match her party's commitment to industry. She branded the Opposition Leader as anti-development, anti-logging and anti-worker. But, for some reason, the strategy had backfired, at least that's what the darn polls said.

For years Kate had ridden high on those polls. She'd lost a few deputies to scandal, but she herself had always remained unsullied. Critics unkindly called her Teflon Kate, but that wasn't who she was. She was Tasmania's golden girl, the queen of feel-good politics, off on a never-ending honeymoon with the electorate. No Iron Lady. She had grace. She had style, flare, all the editorials said so. Her first two terms oversaw a rise in employment and a real estate boom. A by-product of the buoyant national economy, the Opposition said, but her constituents knew better.

'Our economic fortunes,' she'd famously said, 'reflect a new era of optimism and growth that makes Tasmania Australia's own Camelot.' She later regretted that remark, having been accused of hubris, of comparing herself to the charmed Kennedy administration. *Her* reference was to the vaguely remembered 1967 film version of the Lerner and Loewe musical. All that happy-ever-aftering in rousing chorus. The music had blared from loudspeakers at her rallies ever since.

But recently, for whatever reason, the polls kept tracking downwards. They still showed her winning, of course, but by a narrowing margin. She'd probably lose a few ministers this time around. Always difficult to find replacements from such a poor gene pool, and it didn't help having Drake running around hugging trees. Silly boy. He could have inherited political power, been preselected for a safe seat. He could have gone far, but he was too pig-headed, too critical. And he wasn't the only one. There were rumours that even her own environment minister privately disapproved of her forests policy. Though he hadn't disapproved when she raised politicians' salaries by 20 percent. He had no balls.

The most astonishing thing was that her personal approval rating was also down. It was so hard to please everybody. The party room had run their focus groups and blamed her presidential style. It smacked of elitism, they said, and was beginning to alienate voters. A humiliating series of political ads and photo opportunities followed. She frowned to think of them. Kate on a bus. Kate in an apple orchard, at a school, visiting tiresome children in hospital. Lots of sparkling white teeth, promises to listen, to share the pain, to admit mistakes. Mistakes? She hadn't made any. All this phony contrition was embarrassing, and not at all what the electorate expected from their leader.

What she needed was a showcase for her policies, and that's exactly what *Inquest* was. The question-and-answer style panel program suited her, as did the live studio audience. Tonight she'd appear alongside her old friend, Fraser Abbott, and the Opposition's Robert Hellgrun. With only a week until election day, this was the perfect opportunity for a popularity boost. Kate almost pitied Hellgrun. She and Fraser would wipe the floor with him.

The girl stroked Sassy's hooded head. She kept asking questions, although it was already late afternoon and the final flight demonstration had ended.

'What's the lure for?'

'It brings the falcon back. I feed her from it each day.' Matt let the girl hold the lure. 'See? It's made of leather, filled with rice, and a pair of pigeon wings attached.'

'Real pigeon wings? Wow. What does stoop mean? You said Sassy was learning to stoop.'

'That's falconry language. It means to dive down on prey with closed wings. When she circles overhead she "waits on". When she catches birds in mid-air she "carries". When she climbs high above her prey, she "towers".'

The girl stood on her toes. 'What's the hood for?'

'To keep her calm. Without it, she might become scared by the strange people, flutter about and break her feathers. Broken flight feathers are a death sentence for a wild falcon.'

Penny walked down from the mews. 'Enough for today,' she told the girl. 'Sassy needs her rest.' The girl ran off to find her parents as the last park visitors wandered to the gate. 'You're good with the children,' said Penny.

'With some of them,' said Matt, carrying Sassy back to the mews. 'Those that aren't idiots.' He settled the little falcon on her perch, then turned to find Penny's eyes upon him, studying him. 'Is Drake coming over tonight?'

'He'll be here,' said Matt. 'They should rename tonight's show *A Family Affair*. He'd invited Penny and Drake around to watch the *Inquest* election special on television that evening. The program was to feature Fraser and Premier Kate Logan, Drake's mother.

'You should stay tonight,' he said, 'so you can have a few drinks.' Penny said nothing. She watched Sassy tear a mouse apart, before heading for the house.

Matt sighed, and settled the other raptors. It would be fun seeing Kate squirm tonight in response to the latest polls. He was even prepared to suffer Fraser. Fraser – once so predictable. Not anymore. What about that tree business? Pallawarra was being fast-tracked onto the Giant Tree Registry. Fraser had sent him a copy of the assessment, a *with compliments* slip attached. The envelope contained something more. A black-and-white polaroid of names carved into a tree trunk: Charlotte and Fraser. On the back of the photo Fraser had written *Pallawarra*. Strange, confronting even, to think of his parents all those years ago. Not so different to him and Pen back in the day. Young, romantic, anticipating a shared future.

Matt had never thought of them that way before, and he liked it. Liked to think of his mother in the context of something other than her death. Liked to think of his father as more than the man to blame. So Matt had gone to see for himself. Flowers and cards from well-wishers spilled out around Pallawarra's trunk. Protecting this particular tree had been a popular move, even among forest contractors, many of whom had their own sentimental attachments. He'd found his parents' names, and those forty-year-old scratches had moved him more than he could have imagined. Helped to place things in perspective. Made him more determined than ever to put his own marriage back together.

His life was currently a mess. Sarah was in Hobart, all caught up in her work, genotyping devil samples. But she still wanted a romantic involvement with him, her flirty texts made that clear. And she was still trying to convince him to go public with Theo. Matt was avoiding her, without being too obvious about it. He posted Sarah her phone, so that she wouldn't come and pick it up. When she offered to spend a weekend in Hills End, he invented a camping trip. But Sarah wouldn't be put off forever. Eventually he'd have to deal with her.

And Penny was still living at Ray's. The reconnection that he'd been so excited about last week, hadn't happened as he'd hoped. Penny was friendly, but distant. Something was holding her back.

Matt's life remained on hold, in limbo. Maybe that would change tonight. Drake's presence would help keep things emotionally light while Matt gauged Penny's mood. When Drake left, Matt would have a heart-to-heart with his wife.

The early part of the evening passed in a happy blur. Drake brought fish and chips from town, and beer. This was like old times. Penny laughing, teasing Drake, playing daggy eighties power ballads. But she was cool with Matt, and wouldn't drink the wine he'd bought her, sticking instead to lemonade. At eight-thirty they turned on the television and settled down to watch. Drake snagged the spot beside Penny on the frayed couch. Matt made a face and sat in an armchair. He turned off the lamp as the host appeared on the screen.

'I'm Tom Munro and this is *Inquest*. On my right, Premier Kate Logan. On my left, Opposition Leader Robert Hellgrun. Also joining us tonight is a man whose critics call him The Puppet-Master. CEO of the Burns conglomerate, Fraser Burns Abbott.' Enthusiastic applause, but some boos as well from the audience. 'With the election only days away, polls indicate a mood for change. Everything depends on the undecided voters and there are still plenty of them out there. Tonight, you have a final chance to ask the big questions.'

'Mum can't smile properly,' said Drake. 'I reckon she's had another facelift.'

'Shush,' scolded Penny. 'Let's listen.'

Kate was a consummate performer, hogging the limelight right from the start. Even Munro's expert hosting skills were inadequate to prevent her from seizing the initiative on every question. Hellgrun complained about Kate's interruptions. Fraser sipped his water and listened.

'... so according to our internal polling, the momentum remains with the government,' said Kate, with a confident smile.

'We must move on,' said Munro. 'Let's hear from the gentleman at the back with his hand up.'

'Can the economy keep growing forever?' the man asked.

'That's a question for the fiscal philosophers among us,' said Munro. 'Fraser Abbott. You've been called the Gordon Gekko of Tasmania. Is economic growth always good?'

'No,' said Fraser. 'It's not.' A low murmur came from the audience.

'Perhaps you can explain your answer,' said Munro. 'Your pro-growth views are on the record.'

'If I may paraphrase David Attenborough ...' Penny gave a small delighted cry. Munro's brow furrowed as Kate Logan shifted in her chair, glaring at Fraser like he'd lost his mind. 'Someone who believes in infinite growth is either a madman or an economist.'

A louder murmur from the crowd this time and some scattered applause.

'With respect,' said Munro, 'that seems to be a total abrogation of your former views.'

Fraser shrugged. 'A man can change his mind.'

'Indeed he can,' said Munro. 'Let me ask the obvious question. *Why* have you changed your mind?'

Kate cut in. 'My government *does* stand on the principle of continued economic growth. Growth equals jobs. Growth creates wealth and opportunity for the people of this state. Record investment, record population increase, record employment and record consumer confidence. These are the trademarks of my leadership.'

'Fraser is quoting David Attenborough now?' said Matt with a shake of his head. 'I don't get it.'

'Your old man's changed.' Drake grinned. 'He's opened his mind, man.'

'Unbelievable. First Penny and now you? Am I the only one who still can't stand him?' Drake and Penny exchanged smiles. 'What, so we're all one big, happy dysfunctional family now, are we?' He hurled a cushion at Drake. It hit Penny.

'Shut up, you two,' she said. 'I want to listen.'

Munro waited for Kate to finish speaking, then went straight back to Fraser. 'I must ask you again, Mr Abbott. Why this remarkable change of heart?'

'Let's just say I've done my homework.'

Munro must have been dying to question Fraser further, but he couldn't ignore the sea of raised hands in the audience. 'A question from the lady in red.'

The woman stood up and waited for the microphone to reach her. 'Is it true that Pallawarra will be permanently protected?'

'Ah. That's the tree used by conservationists as a focus for their anti-woodchip campaign,' Munro told the broader audience. 'It was earmarked for felling. A very unpopular decision, I might add.'

'A new measurement shows the tree's volume to be two hundred and eighty-five cubic metres,' said Fraser. 'Any tree over two hundred and eighty cubic metres must be protected. The government will breach its own policy if the tree is felled.'

The audience clapped, with a few cheers thrown in. 'Sounds like you've won some friends,' said Munro. 'Next, can we have the gentleman here in the front row.'

The man read self-consciously from a sheet of paper. 'When will we see an inquiry into the shadowy role played by lobbyists in securing lucrative contracts and subverting proper planning processes?'

'I think the questioner is referring to calls from the Opposition for an independent anti-corruption commission,' said Munro. 'Premier?'

'These calls are a cheap political stunt,' said Kate. 'My leadership is, and has always been, completely transparent.'

'Ha,' said Drake. 'Mum's about as transparent as a round of lead. And just as deadly.'

Kate went on. 'We already have in place a comprehensive set of checks and balances to prevent any improper influence on government business.'

'We'll go to the Opposition Leader for a comment. Robert Hellgrun?'

'This government is riddled with a culture of secret deals for mates,' said Hellgrun. 'The Premier and Mr Abbott here are prime examples. They're as thick as thieves.'

Kate tried to interject, but Munro stood firm. 'We'll hear from Fraser Abbott himself. Have you or your companies ever received improper favours from this government?'

'Yes,' said Fraser.

Kate's smile fled. The audience gasped collectively.

'You're saying yes?'

Fraser sipped from his water glass. 'I'm saying, yes.'

Munro sat forward in his chair. 'What sort of favours?'

Fraser reached beneath his seat and dropped a fat brown envelope on the desk. 'For years I've transferred money into a chain of trusts whose ultimate beneficiary … is Kate Logan.'

Kate yelled out, but Munro held up his hand to silence her. 'You mean donations in addition to those listed on the official register?' He straightened his shirt sleeves, looking like he could barely believe his luck. Hellgrun, beside him, was still and watchful.

'I'm not talking about political donations,' said Fraser. 'I'm talking about personal bribes.'

A rising chatter was travelling through the studio audience. 'Go on,' said Munro.

'My company, Costain Constructions, renovated Kate's house here in Hobart, and built her holiday home on Freycinet Peninsula, along with apartments for her family in Sydney and on the Gold Coast. All at a fraction of their true cost.'

Kate stood up. 'That's a lie! Fraser, what are you doing?'

Fraser gave her an apologetic smile. 'Ridding my life of secrets.' His voice grew louder, loud enough to overcome Kate's protests. 'In return, the Premier set peppercorn royalty payments for Burns Timber to log state forests and legislated to remove planning restrictions on private ones. There's more. I won't go into every-thing now.'

'How dare you!' Kate's voice shook with fury.

Fraser looked genuinely remorseful. 'I'm sorry, my dear, but it's over.'

Munro licked his lips. 'These are extraordinary claims. Will you prove them?'

Fraser gestured to the envelope. 'It's all there. Evidence that our Premier is keeping two sets of books. Evidence also that she received gifts and hospitality from Pierpont Casino by way of accommodation, meals and gambling money. In return, she granted the Pierpont Consortium a gratis thirty-year gaming monopoly. She ignored breaches of the Responsible Gambling Code, and allowed the casino to increase gaming tables and poker machines numbers without due process.'

'An army of lawyers will be working as we speak,' said Kate, threat dripping from each word, 'to ensure these slanderous allegations are not repeated.'

Fraser shrugged. 'Truth is a defence, Kate.'

'For the time being I'd ask you, Fraser Abbott, to confine your comments to ones that won't give our legal department a heart attack,' said a concerned looking Munro. 'If I may, though, I'd very much like to examine the evidence for these claims.'

Fraser rose to his feet, glass of water in one hand, envelope in the other. He gave Kate a wide berth, as if he thought she might snatch the documents from him. Then he dropped the envelope on the desk in front of Munro. 'If you'll excuse me, I don't want to upset Kate any further. We've been friends for a lifetime and are equally guilty of treating this state like a magic pudding.' He looked straight at the camera and raised his glass. 'Matthew, this one's for you, son.'

With that, Fraser sculled his water and left the set. Audience and panel alike looked shell-shocked. Kate tried valiantly to defend herself, but it was no use. She was mortally wounded and Hellgrun tasted blood in the water. He went in for the kill with uncharacteristic brutality.

.   .   .

Drake scrubbed a hand over his eyes, as if he couldn't bear to watch. 'I don't believe it. I actually feel sorry for my mother.' Penny and Matt murmured assent. The woman was withering before their eyes. 'I'd better get down to Hobart,' said Drake. 'See how my parents are doing.' He stood to leave.

Penny hugged him goodbye. Matt didn't know what to say so he didn't say anything. Drake turned at the door and caught Matt's gaze. 'Your dad did a brave thing, my friend. I hope Mum survives his sudden attack of courage.'

Matt remained on the couch as Drake left, too stunned to recognise at first what he was feeling. He struggled to admit it, but the improbable certainty grew stronger by the second. It was pride. Pride in his father. It hurled him back in time, back to a childhood when that kind of emotion was a common feeling. It smashed through a bricked-off corner of his mind, contradicted his carefully constructed picture of Fraser.

Long forgotten film clips of his family were now playing. They made his insides tremble. Mum and his sisters, him and his dad. A wide-screen warmth embraced them all. His father's hand on his shoulder, echoes of whispered well dones. The taste of salt as they sailed Kemp Cove's black waters. Then tragedy. Fraser slumped in a chair or working nonstop, day after day, month after month. His impenetrable detachment. But what sort of witness is a boy? Matt saw now that grief had crushed his father, left him helpless to respond to the sorrow-stricken accusing child that was his son. His eyes filled with unexpected tears and he knuckled them away.

Penny sat down beside him and Matt gave her a hollow smile. 'So Fraser really is dying. I didn't believe him.'

She took his hand as tears streamed from his eyes. He wrapped his arms around his wife and rocked back and forth, back and forth. Penny held him tight, like she would a child, while he wept.

.   .   .

Later, they sat on the verandah with drinks in hand, watching a new moon sail over Binburra's mountains. 'I know Sarah stayed here overnight,' said Penny.

Oh. He burned with shame. 'I didn't want you to think …'

'Did something happen between you and Sarah that I should know about?'

Matt had learned his lesson. He told her everything. He told her about the wine and the music and Sarah's little striptease. He told her about falling asleep on the couch and waking to find Sarah and Theo gone. He told her about the chase in the dark, and the kiss and the flirty texts.

Penny listened quietly. When he finished, silence yawned between them, broken only by the night-time chorus of frogs in the dam. Matt wasn't sure how long they sat like that – it felt like hours.

'This has certainly been a night of surprises,' Penny said at last. She held his gaze, eyes drilling into him. 'Swear to me there's nothing more. That you're not holding things back this time.'

'I swear.' His voice rang with truth, and he felt suddenly lighter, freer, younger.

Penny gulped down a big breath. 'Then I believe you.' A slight smile softened the lines of her serious face. 'Not even you could make up that crazy story.'

Matt felt like singing. He reached for her hand but she moved it away. 'Not yet Matt. Give me time.'

CHAPTER 32

PALLAWARRA

Dawn – a pale pink smudge in the sky over Tuggerah's jagged cliffs. Local tribes are camping in the tangled temperate jungle below, feasting on the forest's seasonal bounty. Nectar-filled myrtle oranges. Tree fern hearts, good for roasting. Dried manna sap drops, good for satisfying a sweet tooth. And ice-cold creeks, good for escaping the mid-summer heat.

People abandon the valley at the first tang of smoke. They join an assortment of animals marching to the rocky southern ridge tops where fire can't follow. Wallabies and wombats. Devils scuttle past. A wary thylacine and her mate follow them up the cliff track, maintaining their distance. Sleepy possums brave the day to treetop their way to safety. Steady streams of birds fly ahead of the haze, higher and higher, until they emerge from the cauldron and vanish above the escarpment. A woman and child pause to look back down the valley. The sky darkens with unnatural storm clouds, an eerie roar begins and they are glad they acted quickly. Fire advances faster than they can run.

But the forest can't flee. Soft-foliaged southern sassafras and beech wither in the fierce north winds, before the flames even begin to lick at their leaves. Only the mighty mountain ash, *Eucalyptus regnans,* stands firm before the blast. Four hundred years. Four hundred years since the last great burning. Four hundred years of paradise for the cool rainforest understorey. It has flourished in the long absence of fire, reclaiming its ancient origins, reclaiming ancestral Gondwanaland dominance over the Tuggerah. Here and there, great pillars of trees soar a hundred metres high. All of an age, a great age. And now, nearing death, they prepare for life.

High in the open canopy of sickle-shaped leaves, clusters of white blossom lose their stamens to the whipping winds. Stamens, not petals, millions of fine flying filaments like incongruous flurries of snow. For the multitude of ripe gumnuts that set seed last year, or the year before, or the year before that repeating, their time has finally come.

On the forest floor things are heating up. Falling leaves and twigs and bark have pattered down here, day and night, century after long century. The vast accumulation of leaf litter feeds the fire racing through the valley. It pauses now and then, lingers on logs, incinerates arching fern fronds and starbursts of richea, engulfs defenceless sassafras and myrtle. But try as it might, it can't quite reach the mountain ash crown. Frustrated fireballs fling themselves skywards, like great, dazzling Catherine wheels. But the trunks are so smooth and tall, bare of branches until the very top. There is no foothold for the flames.

Blistering winds howl in disappointment. Never mind – an entire rainforest is theirs for the taking. Sap simmers and boils. A true inferno now, creating its own weather. A pyrocumulus cloud thunders over the forest, spawning a towering vortex of super-heated air. It rips long ribbons of bark from trunks, sets them ablaze, hurls them aloft like flares. Gumnuts crackle and pop, releasing millions of seeds into updrafts pungent with the smell of smoke and seared eucalyptus. Thousands of firebrands bombard the canopy. Eventually victory is theirs. The crowns of the mountain ash explode and the doomed giants of the Tuggerah burn like titanic torches in this day turned to night.

Hours pass. The front moves on. The sky clears. A cool change comes, the kind so beloved of the rainforest. But the rainforest is gone, replaced by a landscape of black spires and white earth. For the first time in centuries, sunlight touches the ground. A steady rain of seeds drifts down to rest in the fertile ash bed. No ants to plunder them. No understorey plants to challenge them. No fungus to invade them. Two million seedlings per hectare germinate in just a few days. Somewhere in this crush of shoots is Pallawarra. He grows swiftly, opening to the sun above the river. His peers grow too. They rise around their dead parents' trunks as thick and straight as a crop of young corn.

Fifty years pass. Adolescent Pallawarra is in furious good health. Only twenty mountain ash remain in this hectare of forest. Twenty from two million. From the outset, Pallawarra is blessed with good fortune – good soil, good light, good genes. He outstrips his companions, two metres a year, stealing their sun. Beneath his emergent crown, the rainforest stages a comeback, wet and green and mossy, dappled once more with luminous fungi. People visit this place in summer and claim Pallawarra, call him countryman.

Two centuries pass. Pallawarra is a mature tree. Grand. There is no forest commission or farmer to cut him down. Europeans barely dream of this far-flung forest. But there is a consensus of creatures who declare him top-end real estate, that most prized property of all – a hollow-bearer. For the first century of his life, Pallawarra was too healthy for hollows, his bark too smooth and unblemished. But ageing skin loses resilience. Shedding lower branches cause self-inflicted wounds. Bacteria and fungi invade the breach. Termites march in through splinters of a lightning strike. Beetles and borers launch direct assaults on his trunk. Wind and rain and heat batter his bark, and here comes the rot. An army of excavators take advantage of weakened wood, expanding cavities with teeth and beaks and claws. Soon, mighty Pallawarra provides high-rise apartment living for a multitude of forest dwellers: parrots and possums, spiders, skinks and tiger snakes, owls and bats and quolls. Composting bacteria do their work, generating warmth, centrally heating the hollows. Thylacines den beneath his buttressed roots. A pair of wedge-tailed eagles take the penthouse suite. Their eyrie commands a matchless view of the resurgent rainforest. Two pygmy possums scrap for the same nest, scattering swarms of swallowtails. Beautiful butterfly orchids and emerald shield ferns decorate his mossy branches as they rise inexorably towards the sky. Pallawarra is no longer just a tree. He is a place, a world.

Five centuries pass. 'That big bastard,' says a man from Hobart. A day much like any other for the man, but not for Pallawarra. Today his good fortune has run out.

Hundreds of cards and posies of flowers ringed Pallawarra. A second man stepped back to look at a trunk scarred with dates and names, hearts and initials. Some could not be read, for time had dulled the blade's course. Their meaning, like the carvings themselves, forever lost. He picked up some of the cards. 'Crikey, these cards are all for the tree. Prayers, kids' poems, everything. Even curses.' He picked up an ornate scroll.

'What are you talking about?' said the first man.

The second man read the scroll:

> 'Demeter's Curse –
> Those who harm the sacred tree,
> By hunger plagued will ever be,
> A hunger nought can satisfy.
> They sell their souls to find relief,
> Abandon honour and belief,
> Consuming their own flesh – they die.'

'Here's another,' he said in a worried voice. 'Let he who harms this tree be doomed. May evil return to its source tenfold.'

'Superstitious claptrap,' said the first man. 'Come on. We've got direct orders from the Premier's department.' He tossed the scroll, shovelled the offerings into the mud and sized up the tree. Too large for any harvester, this one. 'It'll be a single rider, if they can even load it on the truck. You don't see many of them anymore.'

A few years ago they'd have put aside their dozers and chainsaws and used explosives. But everything had to be done by the book these days. So instead, the men wielded Stihl 880 Magnums, the most powerful production chainsaws in the world. Their lethal fifty-inch cutting bars gleamed in the sun.

The first man started the saw, picked the lay, dropped his helmet visor and angled into Pallawarra's trunk. The saw chewed through outer bark, Pallawarra's thin skin. Then through inner bark, his tender phloem, transporting photosynthesised food down from the canopy to nourish his roots. The pulsing saw roared and muttered, roared and muttered. It severed vital cambium tissue, the green sheath of cells which generated new shoots, tirelessly healing wounds, century after century. Not this time.

The man braced his back and shifted his feet. The blade struck sapwood, jerking and screeching, cutting the lifeline to Pallawarra's high crown. His leaves still transpired, though nothing would replenish them now. Tree-dwellers huddled deep in hollows that offered no sanctuary. The motor howled as it hit the dark heartwood at Pallawarra's core. Sawdust fanned a perfect arc in air thick with fumes. A second saw screamed to life. It sliced through a wind shake, a canopy-high crack between Pallawarra's concentric growth rings, caused by centuries of straining against the weather. Trapped rain-water streamed from the wound, soaking the second man. 'The bugger's full of rot,' he said. 'Good for nothing but woodchips.' The thousands of tree creatures cowered deeper in their homes.

A massive wedge of wood was gone from the belly of the tree. The men went in for the kill from the back, slicing towards the gaping, weeping hole in his trunk. Their chainsaws reached a roaring climax. Pallawarra struggled to stand on one narrow hinge of wood. He lost balance. Splintering timber cracked like rifle shots in the still air. The men stood back. The bush held its breath, and Pallawarra toppled in slow motion. Sticks and leaves and gumnuts rained from the sky like nuclear fallout. In a rush of branches, in a blink of time, with a deafening roar, Pallawarra crashed to the ground. The earth trembled at his passing. For a moment, even the men were impressed.

Then the first man snorted and looked around. 'So much for the curse.'

It had been half an hour since he first set eyes on Pallawarra.

'How about lunch,' he said. 'I'm starving.'

'Me too,' said the second man. 'I could eat a horse.'

Then they were gone. Hours passed. Butcherbird sang a requiem. Evening closed in. Deep underground, disembodied roots remained on duty, feeding nutrient-rich fluid skywards. In vain, they sought their centuries-old connection with their crown. And in the silent forest, blood-red sap drip, drip, dripped from Pallawarra's shattered core.

CHAPTER 33

Matt sat with Penny and Fraser in the dining room at Canterbury Downs. Afternoon sunshine streamed in the French doors, highlighting the glossy brochures spread out on the table before them.

'That unfortunate tree business,' said Fraser. 'That was Kate settling the score. I want to make it up to you.'

Matt and Penny had been devastated by Pallawarra's passing, along with the rest of Hills End. Such an iconic part of the town's history, central to so many stories, connecting so many families. And it wasn't just locals who mourned him. Pallawarra had become a symbol of the natural world throughout Tasmania and beyond, beloved of children and adults alike. If the Government's election campaign was in trouble beforehand, Pallawarra's demise hammered the final nail into its coffin.

'I can't believe it,' said Penny, crying and smiling all at once.

Matt couldn't believe it either. He took the glossy brochure his father handed him. A photo of Pallawarra in his prime graced the cover. *The Pallawarra Project: Challenging current principles of forest management.*

'You wrote this?' asked Matt.

'My marketing department did, yes,' said Fraser. 'What do you think?'

Matt read the first paragraph.

This visionary project aims to demonstrate the true value of our state forests by showcasing products shaped from a single tree. Fifty specialty timber workers will create pieces ranging from musical instruments and sculptures to fine furniture. Everything will be used, right down to the branches, leaves and gumnuts. An iconic, centuries-old Eucalyptus regnans, mistakenly felled in the Tuggerah forest, has been selected to provide the materials. Burns Timber released the tree – affectionately known to Tasmanians as Pallawarra – into the care of local sawmiller and project administrator Ken Murphy, who will be operating under the guidance of the Tasmanian Timber Design School. Their challenge is to increase the value of a tree destined for the woodchip pile by 1000 percent. The Pallawarra Project aims to show how wasteful woodchipping is, and demonstrate the enormous potential for industry in downstream processing of our forest resources.

Matt skipped ahead: *Complete carbon content to be recorded ... piles of branch wood left behind to provide homes for wildlife ... Pallawarra's seeds harvested and germinated at Hobart's botanic gardens.*

'Well?' asked Fraser.

'I'm impressed, I'll admit it,' said Matt. 'But not convinced.'

'How can you say that?' said Penny. 'This is the most wonderful tribute to Pallawarra.'

'If you don't mind, Penelope,' said Fraser, 'I have something private to discuss with my son.' He gestured towards the library. 'Matthew, if you don't mind?'

After a moment's hesitation, he followed his father from the room.

Fraser gestured for Matt to sit on the couch, then settled himself into a chair opposite. 'What will it take to convince you that my change of heart is genuine?'

Matt didn't know. An explanation that fitted with what he knew of his father, maybe? Something to show this epiphany was real?

Dying or not, Fraser's sudden turnaround was too far out of character.

Fraser stroked his chin. 'The share price of Burns Timber is way down.'

'Hallelujah.'

'Our half-yearly profit report is due at the end of the month.' Fraser poured himself a scotch and raised the bottle to Matt.

Matt shook his head. 'What's any of this got to do with me?'

Strings of tendons stood out on Fraser's scrawny neck as he drank. 'It will show a substantial drop in returns.' Matt could see the wheels spinning in his father's head. 'On Friday I'm closing down the wood-chip mills.'

'Permanently?'

'Permanently.'

Matt was too suspicious to be pleased. What was Fraser's angle? 'That will mean laying off contractors in time for Saturday's election. Haven't you done Kate Logan enough damage?'

'I'm not trying to hurt Kate.'

'Well, you're doing a bloody good job of it.'

'The writing's on the wall, Matthew. Woodchip revenue has crashed. By comparison, value-added timber profits are rising. Do the sums.' Fraser rubbed his eyes. 'Burns can't compete anymore in the world woodchip market.'

There was a ring of truth to his father's words and he'd dropped his standard patronising tone. Fraser took another drink and slumped in his chair. The skin of his face shone with an odd translucent pallor, and his face was pinched. He looked ancient. A sarcastic response died on Matt's tongue.

Fraser handed him a pamphlet. *The FSC is an international organisation, established to promote responsible management of the world's forests. It sets standards, including independent certification and labelling of timber products.*

Things were getting clearer.

'Our biggest market, Japan, will no longer buy woodchips without FSC certification. Others will soon follow,' said Fraser. 'It's as simple as that. If we continue to woodchip old-growth forests, we can't get FSC approval, and we won't be able to sell a darned thing.'

There it was at last. Matt laughed, a great, grateful belly laugh. This was what he'd wanted all along, what he'd been waiting for. An answer that made sense, a reason to trust his father.

'So that's why those ridiculous stockpiles of woodchips just keep on growing. Why didn't you tell me that in the first place?'

'You know the answer to that already, Matthew.'

'I want to hear it. Why didn't you tell me?'

Fraser sighed. He looked tired and resigned. 'You may have thought there was an ulterior motive behind my change of heart.'

Matt whooped with satisfaction. 'As if I didn't anyway. You're a practical man, Dad. I knew there was something you weren't telling me. Think I'll have that drink now.'

As Fraser poured him a scotch, Matt's phone vibrated in his pocket, startling him. Another text from Sarah. A photo in lingerie this time.

'Problems?' asked Fraser.

That was an understatement. Ever since Sarah had found out about Theo, Matt had been playing a dangerous game. Sarah was still furiously genotyping devil samples at the University of Hobart, weaving them a DNA lifeline – the enormity of the task keeping her away from Hills End. But it was a temporary reprieve, and it had not prevented her from waging an intense phone campaign. Bring Theo to the zoology department, she urged him. They could take it from there.

Matt had walked a fine line between keeping her hopes up and holding his ground. He longed to come clean with Sarah, tell her that he had no romantic interest in her. Tell her that he wanted his wife. But he dared not provoke her, so he flirted, dissembled and dutifully listened to Sarah's plans for Theo, even while planning ways to thwart them. Fraser would have been proud of him. He couldn't go on like this forever, but if he stopped stalling, what then? Matt turned off his phone.

'It must be difficult,' said Fraser, studying him with shrewd eyes. 'Convincing Dr Deville to stay quiet.'

'Quiet?' He wouldn't let Fraser get him on the back foot again. 'Just say what you mean for once, Dad. It will make a nice change.'

'Very well, I'll be blunt. What does it take to convince a molecular biologist to conceal a thylacine?'

The improbable question sucked all the oxygen from the room. Okay, so he was on the back foot after all. Was there anything Fraser didn't know? Perhaps it was too late to protect Theo's family, Matt thought wearily. Too many people knew. Perhaps he should just step back and let the cards fall.

'So Penny told you about Theo.'

'She did,' said Fraser. 'But I knew long before that. I've known for most of my life. You should have known too. It was a mistake not to trust you, Matthew. It's time to set things right.'

His father's words were impossible to fathom, as if he'd just pronounced the earth flat or the moon made of green cheese.

Penny peeped through the door. Matt beckoned her in, holding up a hand against his father's protests. 'I will keep no more secrets from my wife.' He patted the seat beside him.

Fraser looked from Matt to Penny, and back again. 'Very well.' He opened a drawer in the sideboard and took out a leather-bound journal. It looked ancient, with intricate lacing, ornate engravings and a shining jewel set in the cover. He handed the journal to Matt. 'The diary of Isabelle Abbott, Daniel Campbell's daughter. It's yours.'

Matt accepted it with great reverence, almost afraid to touch. 'Is that a real diamond?' He ran his forefinger over the jewel, which seemed to burn with a fierce internal fire.

'Some history.' Fraser cracked the knuckles of each hand, readying himself. 'Our family is not descended from Tasmania's founding industrialist, Henry Abbott, as you and the world believe. Yes.' Fraser smiled. 'That was my reaction too, when I found out. Our true forebear is Luke Tyler, the young convict immortalised by the legend of Last Stand Cave.' The longcase clock ticked like a time bomb in the still room. Its lunar dial showed the moon was full. 'Isabelle conceived a child with Tyler when she was just seventeen. She married Henry Abbott's son under sufferance to conceal the out-of-wedlock pregnancy. That child, Luke Tyler's child, is my grandfather.'

Matt was rooted to his chair, couldn't move even if he'd wanted to. He'd always loathed his connection to Henry Abbott, who was by all accounts a monster. And now, it turned out, he was the descendant of a convict instead, like half the population of Tasmania. But … 'Is that it?' he asked. 'Is that what you're so sorry you didn't tell me?'

Fraser heaved a great creaking sigh, like a big tree in the wind. 'Old secrets cast long shadows, Matthew.' His father's face was anguished. He was finding this, whatever *this* was, genuinely gruelling. 'Daniel Campbell fought against the passage of the Thylacine Bounty Scheme back in the 1880s.'

'I know that,' said Matt.

'When his lobbying failed, he and Isabelle conspired to hide a group of thylacines away from the bounty hunters – in the secret valley up at Tiger Pass. Campbell's protégé, Luke Tyler, dynamited the entrance to seal them safely in. The creatures have lived there ever since, thriving for more than a century. Tyler was a brave man, Matthew, a champion. Our family owes him a great debt. More than one actually.'

Fraser poured himself a fresh drink, and opened the French doors leading to the garden. Bruno and Sasha trotted in, plumed tails waving. 'Bruno here is descended from Tyler's dog, Bear, just as we are descended from Tyler.' He pointed to Isabelle's diary. 'It's all in there. Read it carefully and privately, my boy. You'll find more surprises. That Luke Tyler did not die at Last Stand Cave, for example.'

'He didn't?' The world Matt knew was shifting.

'He escaped, reinvented himself and returned to Tasmania as the wealthy Colonel Buchanan to marry Isabelle, the only woman he ever loved.'

Matt stroked Bruno's great head, his mind spinning. The famous family scandal when Isabelle Abbott ran off with a South African millionaire – that was Tyler?

'But I digress,' said Fraser. 'The thylacines' existence has been a closely guarded secret through the generations. Your grandfather told me the story when I was fifteen. I was charged to pass it on to my oldest child in turn.' A pause. 'I failed in my duty.'

'You think?' Matt felt hurt flooding his body, like he'd been flayed. Penny reached for his hand. 'How exactly did I qualify to be the only one in my family kept in the dark? The only one, through a hundred and fifty years of history? Me of all people. Daniel Campbell is my hero, Dad. He's why I'm so passionate about Binburra, about the land that he fought to protect. I did a project on him at school once, although you wouldn't remember.

'*The Person Who Most Inspires Me*,' said Fraser. 'That was the topic.'

'I chose Daniel Campbell. You could have told me about the tigers then. What a perfect time to have told me, but do you know what you said instead? "Stop daydreaming about working at Binburra. A dead-end job," you said. Bloody hell, Dad, I've dedicated my life to that place. I had a right to know.'

'You did, absolutely.'

'So why, Dad? Why did you keep the tigers from me?'

Fraser looked to be in pain as he spoke. 'In the aftermath of your mother's death … your sisters. You know how I was. Many things were left undone.'

'That's not enough,' said Matt. 'I need more.'

'Perhaps I was jealous. How I would have loved for you to admire me in such a way, to want to follow in *my* footsteps.' Fraser sculled another scotch and put the glass down with a trembling hand. 'But it was more than that. You were such an honest boy; you hated keeping secrets. I didn't believe you could be trusted.' Fraser's hand was still shaking. He studied it dispassionately. 'I misjudged you, Matthew. Forgive me. You kept this secret of your own accord, and at great personal cost. You have lied, compromised your marriage, misled Sarah Deville – all to protect our thylacines.'

Was Fraser crying? Small sobs graduated to open weeping. Matt had never seen Fraser cry. It disarmed him and he hugged this strange father he'd never known, felt his thin bones, soaked him up.

'Shut up, will you, Dad. McGregor will think I'm murdering you. I suppose he knows everything?' Fraser nodded, and buried his face in Matt's shoulder. 'Of course he does. We wouldn't want McGregor to be the odd man out here, would we? That distinction must be reserved for me.'

His father gave another muffled apology.

'I tell you what,' said Matt, gently disengaging Fraser from his shoulder. 'I forgive you. I forgive you for every unfair, rotten thing you ever did. I forgive you for Mum. I forgive you for Christy and Cathy. I forgive you for not being there, for not trusting me. I flat out forgive you. I'm doing this as much for me as for you.'

Fraser pulled a handkerchief from his coat pocket. Matt took it and softly wiped his father's face.

Penny was staring at them both, astonished.

'Right,' said Matt. 'Is there anything else I don't know about? Anything at all? I'm warning you, Dad, you'd better tell me now.' Matt looked hard at Penny. Something flitted across her face, a sort of shadow. She smoothed her hands down the front of her green cotton dress. 'That includes you, Pen.'

'A bit rich, coming from …' she began, but something in Matt's expression silenced her.

'Anyone?' asked Matt.

Fraser blew his nose. 'Theo is stowed in my studio freezer.'

'Bloody marvellous,' said Matt. Both Fraser and Penny hung their heads, contrite like caught-out schoolkids. 'Now, Dad, if you'll pull yourself together, we have a lot to talk about.'

CHAPTER 34

Someone was banging on the door. Matt clutched for his happy dream.

'Rise and shine.' Drake's voice came into the bedroom. 'I need a favour.'

Matt dragged the pillow over his head and made a rude gesture. His mind ran over last night's events, struggling at first to separate fact from fiction. What he needed was time to make sense of it, but Drake kept talking, his words relentless – hunting Matt into the new day.

'Give me a minute,' said Matt with a groan.

'I don't have a minute.' Drake's tone was far too cheerful for so early in the morning.

Matt sat up, scratched his head and glared at Drake. The whistling kettle lured him into the kitchen. Cardboard boxes stood stacked by the door.

'How-to-vote cards,' said Drake. 'It's election day.'

Matt vaguely remembered Drake telling him that he'd started his own political party in opposition to his mother. He picked up a leaflet. *Vote 1 Sustainable Tasmania.*

'Since Mum committed electoral suicide on national television, we're only manning the main polling places. Hellgrun should walk it in. I'm driving down to Hobart to be with my folks. They're going to have a rough night.'

'So?'

'So can you run these how-to-vote cards out to the local booths?' Drake handed Matt a list, then went outside and came back with some large laminated posters of his own smiling face. 'Just string one of these up and leave a box of cards underneath. Oh, and remember to vote for me.'

Matt made himself a coffee while Drake waited expectantly. 'Sure,' he said at last. 'Why not?'

'I owe you one,' said Drake.

'Just one?'

Drake took a sip of Matt's coffee. 'What are you doing tonight?'

'Going to Fraser's to watch the election. Pen's coming too.'

'You and Pen? You're good?'

'I'm going to beg her to move back in.'

'About bloody time. So Sarah's finally fair game. You do know she thinks you and her are some sort of thing, don't you? She almost had me convinced of it.' Matt drained his coffee down to the dregs. 'Shall I set her straight for you?' said Drake.

'No,' Matt answered, quickly. 'I should do it myself.'

'Okay,' said Drake. 'But hurry up, will you? I plan to drop in on her when I'm in Hobart. If I'm lucky she'll pick me up on the rebound.'

Matt ran through the morning chores with Jake, then packed the boxes and posters into the car and set off on his grand tour. The government had pulled out all the stops. At each polling place, no matter how tiny the school or how remote the hall, their spruikers were out in force. On the payroll, according to Drake. Matt had never seen anything like it. Banners and placards and posters and streamers, all bearing Kate's chic smile. The actual candidate didn't rate a photo. Kate was billed as the star of the show, and since Fraser's revelations, that presidential strategy had backfired badly on the Government.

Although still running in her own electorate, she'd been forced to resign as Premier, and there hadn't been time to print new signage.

At Tancurry, Kate's bountiful bunting seemed to be the only thing holding up the run-down hall. Just as well the polling officials were already there. Without protection, his flimsy posters and brave little cardboard boxes might well have met with foul play. Matt set up his final booth, voted for Drake and glanced at his watch. Still time to stop at the bakery for breakfast and buy something to bring for tonight. A cake to celebrate maybe? What was the etiquette for a first dinner in more than a decade at your father's house?

Matt pulled up outside the bakery. The car parked in front of him looked familiar. Matt froze, but apparently Sarah's vision wasn't based on movement. She turned and waved, called out his name. Doris Briggs, sitting outside the shops, waved at him too. Interfering old biddy. Matt wondered if he could simply drive away. Too late. Sarah was at the window. He wound it down halfway

'I've taken the weekend off,' she said. 'To surprise you.' She looked relaxed, happy, unaware there was a problem.

'Great,' said Matt, forcing a smile.

'Want to do something later?'

'I'm not working this afternoon,' he lied. 'How about I take you to lunch?' He was already winding up the glass.

'Brilliant.' Sarah blew him a kiss as the jeep moved off.

Matt drove straight to Ray's house and rang Penny.

'Matt, is that you I can see out in the street? Come on in. Ray won't bite.'

He wasn't so sure. The word going around town had him and Sarah in the middle of a full-blown affair. Thankfully Penny believed him, despite the rumours. At the pub last Saturday night, Ray had got himself so drunk and worked up that he'd tried to round up some sort of posse to go out to Binburra. Nick Byrne had calmed him down, headed off the trouble. But Nick had visited on Sunday morning in his official police capacity and warned Matt to steer clear of Ray.

Penny herself had told Matt she was worried about her uncle, thought he was erratic and depressed, but couldn't get him to the doctor.

'No thanks,' said Matt. 'Can you come out here?'

A few minutes later Penny slipped out through the side gate and Matt drove them a hundred metres down the road.

'Sarah turned up this morning,' he said. 'I bumped into her in Main Street. Doris saw me, so I thought I'd better get to you first.'

Penny held up her right hand. 'I solemnly swear I won't listen to gossip.'

'Good,' said Matt. 'Because I'm taking Sarah to lunch today, and somebody's bound to tell you. I've asked Jake to fill in for me this afternoon. It's time to tell her where I stand.'

'And where is that?' asked Penny.

'With you, of course, Pen. Always with you.' He moved closer to her, close enough to hear her breathe. 'You backing my decision about Theo, understanding why I can't go public? It means everything.'

'What was I supposed to do?' said Penny with a smile. 'You and your dad ganged up on me.'

The thread of separateness, of strangeness that had run between them was unravelling. A surge of hope coursed through him, desire too, and he knew there was no answer for him anywhere in the world, but her.

Matt pulled Penny close, her body soft and yielding. She looked lovelier than he'd ever seen her, radiant, with shining hair fanning her shoulders and her complexion glowing with happiness.

They kissed, slow and tender, the seal on an unspoken promise. 'Move back in today, Pen,' he said, hoarsely. 'Right now.'

Concern clouded her face. 'I need to make sure my uncle is okay first.'

Matt groaned inwardly. Ray was sure to do everything possible to undermine a reconciliation.

Penny stroked his cheek. 'Don't worry. I can handle him.' She opened his palm and stroked his lifeline. 'You have something to tell Sarah, and I have something to tell you.'

'Lay it on me.'

'Later. Tonight.'

'Is it something you've done?'

'Kind of.'

'Is it a good thing or a bad thing?' Her smile reassured him. 'Even if it is a bad thing, I forgive you.'

She laughed. 'What, before you even know what it is?'

'I'll forgive anything if you'll just come home. And before you say it, I know there's plenty you need to forgive me for too.'

'That's a lot of forgiveness. I hope we have enough to go round.' Penny slid from her seat, laughing, and walked back to the house.

Matt watched her go, his heart bursting with hope and happiness.

CHAPTER 35

Sarah looked particularly fetching. Skin-tight jeans, soft cotton shirt clinging in all the right places, but Matt was immune to her charms. For lunch he'd picked out a modern, functional bistro several towns away. A tourist stopover, all glass and stainless steel.

'What a romantic little spot.' Sarah touched Matt's arm and moved closer.

'What would you like to drink?' He pushed back his chair.

Sarah frowned, withdrawing her hand. She fixed him with hazel eyes, searching now, not smiling. Matt dodged her stare and headed for the bar saying he'd choose for them both. A scotch for him and a gin and tonic for her. No, a bottle of champagne to butter her up. No, mineral water for them both. In the end he bought two light beers. Sarah grimaced at the first sip.

'We've finished the gene sequencing program,' she said. 'You're the first one outside the department to know.'

This was exciting news, and he was a complete bastard. What could he say to her?

'The results bear out our early findings. Almost 30 percent of test animals from the Tuggerah region have the MHC2 genotype.'

'That's fantastic,' said Matt.

'Your breeding program must urgently take this into account. I wouldn't arrange any more matings until the department analyses these results.'

She was right. A population of local animals with built-in genetic defences shouldn't be out-crossed to at-risk individuals. Isolation and protection of the Tuggerah was the obvious next step, which was fabulous news for both the devils and the forest. He should be expressing his profoundest gratitude to Sarah for what she'd done. Instead, he nodded and picked up the menu. 'The trout looks good.'

Sarah smiled a rather unpleasant smile. She took the menu from his hand. 'Is this about Theo, the way you're acting? You've made up your mind, haven't you, and I'm not going to like it.'

'Sarah, I've agonised over this, but I always come to the same conclusion. I'm not prepared to go public.'

The battle lines were drawn. Sarah opened her mouth to speak, then seemed to think better of it. She sculled her beer and thrust the empty glass at Matt. 'I'll have another ... and the trout will do.'

'Would you rather wine?'

She scowled. Strands of hair had slipped from her silver clip onto her face. 'Just hurry up.'

The lull before the storm, that's what this was. The bartender served Matt way too fast.

'Hear me out,' she said, laying a hand on his arm when he returned with the drinks. She was calm, too calm. 'Humans exterminated thylacines, that's what we all thought. But now there's Theo. It means we can fix our mistakes. It wasn't the thylacine's time, Matt. They have a right to this second chance.'

'You can't *fix* this, Sarah. You can't take it back. Not the stupidity, not the brutality. I won't give humans, who made the mess in the first place, the power to make another one. You want to talk about rights? What about the tigers' right to a peaceful enjoyment of life.'

Sarah's mask of composure slipped a little. 'Restoring Tasmania's apex predator isn't interference, Matt. It's an act of redemption. An implicit acknowledgement that we'll handle the species better this time around.'

'It's an experiment, and these experiments are always at the expense of the animals. Listen to your language. "Handle the species." I have a better idea. Let's not handle them at all.'

'We're morally bound to handle them.' Sarah removed her hand from his arm, knocking over her beer. She barely seemed to notice. A dark stain spread over the tablecloth.

'Why? To make us feel better?' asked Matt.

'To ensure their future. It's our responsibility.'

'These thylacines only survived *because* nobody handled them. Isn't it ironic? So inept at handling our own population, yet we presume to manage theirs. The problem lies in the very idea that we know better than nature. We don't.'

Sarah went quiet, regrouped, and launched another assault. But there was nothing she could say, no possible angle she could find to change his mind. She wheedled, cajoled, threatened, teared up. Matt was implacable. He wanted to leave, but he was already a heel. Better not compound the crime.

'Two trouts.' The waitress put the plates down.

Sarah left for the ladies room. Matt's face was sweaty, he could taste it on his tongue. She'd try to force his hand if she could. But how? Who'd believe her crazy story about stealing frozen thylacines from freezers? She had no evidence, and Theo was safely stowed away at Fraser's. Whatever Sarah did next, all he had to do was hold his nerve.

Here she came, stalking back across the room. Matt held his breath, fighting the feeling that Sarah was somehow about to wrest back control of the game. She sat across from him with an ugly smirk, as his phone rang. It was Penny. He gave Sarah an apologetic smile and left the table.

'Are you with Sarah?' she asked. 'Matt, be careful. Fraser and I examined Theo. There's a piece of his ear missing.'

Tension began its slow crawl up his spine. 'Ring me in fifteen minutes, so I can get out of here.' Matt snapped the phone shut. No wonder Sarah looked so smug; she was about to turn the tables. There was nothing else for it but to revert to his most tried and true strategy. Stall.

'I don't know,' said Matt when he returned to the table. He took a steadying breath and allowed his face no expression at all. 'Maybe you're right.' His words sounded thin and unconvincing.

'Really?' Sarah's eyes locked onto his. She was surprised, certainly. Suspicious, probably. He watched for a sign that she'd perceived the falsehood, for any telltale shift in her shoulders or tilt of her head.

'Like you said, it's not really my call.' Now Sarah just looked confused. Matt reached for her hand. 'I suppose I'm a bit thrown by the enormity of what we're about to do.' He was making himself sick, but the only way to the other side was through and, anyway, it seemed to be working. Sarah's expression softened, misgivings slipping from her face. She squeezed his hand. He tried a smile.

'Of course you're a bit spooked,' said Sarah. 'This is huge. For a while there, I thought you'd never come around.'

Matt forced himself to laugh along with her, and it really was pretty funny. Digging such a big hole and then hurling himself into it.

'Now, tell me everything. Where did you find your sample? Do you know about any others? You'll need to come to Hobart with me so we can meet with Professor Chang on Monday morning. I can't believe this is really happening, can you?'

'No,' said Matt. At least that was honest.

'So ...' Sarah gave him a dazzling smile, 'where did you find the specimen?'

'His name is Theo,' said Matt, wondering if under that soft cotton shirt she was wearing a wire. If her phone was on, recording their conversation. 'I can trust you, can't I?'

'Absolutely,' said Sarah. 'I was worried that I couldn't trust *you*. I even took out a little insurance, just in case. A tissue sample from Theo's ear. It seems silly now.'

Matt sipped his drink. The mouthful of beer went down the wrong way, and bile rose in his throat. Sarah asked him again where he'd found Theo. Oh well, might as well be hanged for a sheep as a lamb. 'At a camp site in the Tarkine, about three hundred kilometres north-west of here.' This wasn't so hard after all. When she went public with her story, at least he'd have put her off the scent. His fanciful account became more and more elaborate, more and more detailed, each word leaping straight from brain to mouth. His mother said that if you tell the truth, you don't need a good memory. He was going to need the memory of an elephant. Perhaps he should take notes?

'What happened when you seized their rifles?' asked Sarah.

'The cowards took off down that track like the devil was after them. It was only afterwards, when I inspected the camp, that I found Theo. Their truck had no number plate, so unfortunately I've no way of identifying them.'

'What sort of a person kills a thylacine and then hides it? You'd have to have absolutely no morals at all.' Matt nodded, wishing it really had happened the way he said. It felt good to not feel responsible.

'How many more are there, do you think?'

'Can't say,' said Matt. 'Didn't see any tracks. Those blokes could have shot Theo anywhere.'

'I didn't notice the bullet wound,' said Sarah. 'Still, there wasn't much time to examine Theo before you came racing after me.'

Matt tried the trout. It sat next to a few wilted lettuce leaves, two cherry tomatoes and a mountain of soggy chips. The food stuck in his throat.

Their waitress came over with two little pots on a tray. 'Forgot your tartare sauce. You American?' she asked, when Sarah thanked her. 'Best get you ketchup then.' She duly returned with a saucer of tomato sauce.

'What am I supposed to do with this?' laughed Sarah.

Matt dipped a cold chip in the sauce and ate it. He dipped another and offered it to Sarah. She opened her mouth and he popped it inside, as if it was a chocolate-coated strawberry in a soap opera love scene. Sarah was smiling, temporarily neutralised.

Matt's phone rang. Finally. He pretended to be talking to Jake. 'They need me at the park,' he told her. 'Sorry, we have to go.'

On the way home, Sarah was full of plans that horrified him. 'Be ready for a whirlwind of publicity. We'd better get you some media training.'

What a relief to drop her off at Mrs Murphy's. Matt escorted her through the gate, then propped at the door.

'When will I see you?' she asked. 'I could come by Binburra this afternoon. I'm dying to examine Theo.'

Matt counted to five before responding. 'I'll be flat out today.'

But she wouldn't be put off. 'You don't realise the significance of what we're about to do, the international implications. I can see that now. Anyway, it's Saturday and you can't work all the time.' She slipped her arms around his neck and kissed him. The blind at Margaret Murphy's window lifted. 'I've booked a room for us tonight in Nandena, at the Ashwood Inn.'

Matt tried to look pleased. 'Okay. I'll be there.'

'When?'

'By eight?'

Sarah shook her head and pouted. 'Too late.' She traced his lips with her little finger.

'Six then,' said Matt.

'You're your own boss, aren't you? If you're not there by five, I'll come looking.'

'Five it is.'

Margaret leaned out of the kitchen window. 'Lovely day.'

'Perfect, Mrs Murphy,' said Sarah. 'Simply perfect.'

CHAPTER 36

Sarah waltzed a frowning Mrs Murphy once around the kitchen, then ran to her room and threw open the suitcase on the bed. It was hard to know what was more exciting – the thylacine news or the upcoming night with Matt. She'd wanted them both, so very much, for so very long, and at times it had seemed that she might have neither. She shouldn't have doubted him.

Sarah showered, then laid out clothes on the bed. She tried on the new lingerie and inspected herself in the mirror. It was hard to buy decent labels in Hobart. The purple set was pretty, but Matt was a no-fuss kind of man. Better stick with basic black. The frantic pace she'd set at the lab had left her little time for anything else, not even for eating. It showed in her skinny ribs and jutting collarbone, and she looked tired. She *was* tired. A spa would be good when she got there, to unwind a bit before Matt arrived. She checked her watch. Better hurry. She packed an overnight bag and headed to the car.

'Don't worry about breakfast for me, Mrs Murphy,' she called on her way out. 'I won't be back tonight.'

'Suit yourself, dear. Where are you off to?'

But Sarah was already gone.

. . .

An elegant elm-lined driveway led to a collection of sandstone buildings, all set in a formal English garden. What was it with Tasmania's obsession with Britain?

'Welcome to Ashwood Inn.' The woman at reception spoke with a plum in her mouth. 'Would you prefer the library suite or the loft?'

'What's the difference?'

'The library is French provincial and includes a shared-table evening dining experience.'

'We're looking for privacy,' said Sarah.

'The loft then.' She reached for a set of keys on the board behind her. 'The original stable has been converted into a couple's suite. The bathroom is on the ground floor next to the water garden. The bedroom is upstairs, beneath the overhanging willow tree. All the privacy in the world. What time is your young man arriving?'

Sarah felt her face redden, as though she was sixteen again. 'Around five.'

'I'll send over a bottle of bubbly when he gets here.'

Sarah explored the loft, set the air-conditioning a little colder, then turned on the taps in the spa. What music? She knew nothing of Matt's taste. A quick flip through the offerings. She'd try Sade again and hope for better luck than last time. The pretty casement window looked out onto a private courtyard with a little creek splashing through. The suite was quite charming. She slipped from her clothes and climbed into the half-full tub. Maybe a drink to relax.

She dripped water all the way to the minibar, chose a bottle of sparkling wine and a cute little box of chocolates. She popped a sticky caramel into her mouth and a sachet of lavender bath salts into the water. It was almost too hot to bear. She fired up the spa. The jets unravelled each tense muscle. The wine was delicious. It slipped down so easily. A wave of weariness hit her. Sarah closed her eyes. Very calm. Very drowsy. Dreaming of Matt ...

Penny stood in her bedroom at Ray's, dressed only in a bra and briefs, studying her baby bump in the mirror. She'd always had a plump belly, and in her park uniform the bulge showed as little more than a thicker middle, barely noticeable. But tonight she wanted to show it off. Penny pulled on a green cotton shift, cut straight enough to skim her waist, but with enough room to be comfortable. She slipped on her best sandals and turned to the mirror. Hmm, the bump wasn't very obvious, but it would have to do.

Uncle Ray's house was a furnace in the afternoon. She fetched a glass of water from the jug in the fridge. The kitchen looked so much brighter now, with the corner cobwebs gone, and fresh curtains and flowers. Every inch of chrome and linoleum was polished to within an inch of its life. If only she could perform the same sort of makeover on her uncle.

Ray was sitting on the back porch with his battered Akubra and his best friend Charlie. They were chain-smoking and drinking whisky and coke, more whisky than coke. They'd been laid off for weeks now. Ray waited every day until noon, seven days a week, for a phone call that never came. At lunchtime he sought Penny out, or phoned her at work, sounding just as surprised each time.

'We're not getting back on the job today, love. Not me or Charlie.'

From what Penny knew, it was unlikely that they ever would. So each time, she made comforting noises that she didn't believe. It wasn't all bad news. If the mills stayed closed, she'd find him work with Ken Murphy, transporting dressed timber, on a proper wage, with proper hours.

Penny tried to put Ray out of her mind. There were other things to think of, like telling Matt about the baby. She grabbed two packets of potato crisps from the cupboard, put one in her bag and delivered the other to the men on the verandah.

'Thanks, love. You on your way out?'

Ray was a shamble of unwashed clothes, stubble and tangled grey hair. A box of medication lay beside his drink. She picked it up: *Rest-Rite.* 'What's this?'

'Something from the doc to help me sleep.'

Penny frowned. 'Don't you go mixing that stuff with alcohol.'

'Don't worry.' Ray burped. 'Charlie's whisky works better than any sleeping pills.'

Penny put the box down. 'I'm going round to see Matt, and I may not be home tonight.' She could hear the excitement in her voice.

Ray stood up, flush-faced and a little wobbly on his feet. He kissed her cheek. 'Hope it works out for you, love. I really do. Tell that bastard that if he does the wrong thing by my girl, he'll answer to me.'

Even at six o'clock, with the sun low in the western sky, the car's steering wheel was too hot to handle. Penny wrapped a cloth around it and started the engine. First stop, damage control at Canterbury Downs before going to see Matt.

The dogs met her in the driveway, waving their great plumed tails in welcome. Penny hugged Bruno's huge head. 'Where's Fraser?' They set off around the back and headed straight for the studio. Fraser was bent over a polyurethane form with a measuring tape. He jumped when he heard her come in. When she got a good look at the form, she understood why.

'Is that what I think it is?' asked Penny. Fraser said nothing. She ran her hand down the neck of the model. 'No wonder you look guilty.'

'Custom-made when I ordered your devils. It's extraordinarily difficult, you know, to produce the form of an animal that nobody has seen alive.'

'You want to stuff Theo?' Penny was stunned at the audacity of the idea.

Fraser opened his spindly arms in supplication. 'He'd be the first in almost a century. Maybe the last.'

'It's not me you'll have to convince.'

Fraser smiled. 'My stubborn son will be the sticking point, eh? An old man's dying wish?'

'Matt will never go for it.'

Fraser chuckled. 'Perhaps not. Now, to what do I owe this pleasure? The party won't begin for another hour.'

Penny hesitated, a little ashamed to tell Fraser her news, half-pretending to herself that she didn't know what it would mean. 'Um … Sarah has finished her genotyping project.'

'Yes, my dear,' said Fraser, brightly. 'Plans are already afoot to send the good doctor packing.'

'Just like that?'

'Just like that.' He scrubbed his hands together. 'Now is there something else? McGregor wants me in the cellar to choose the wines.'

'I'm taking your advice,' she said. 'About the baby. I'm going home to tell Matt now.'

'And I must appear to be ignorant until the formal announcement.'

'If you wouldn't mind.'

'Of course.' Fraser beamed. 'Nothing shall spoil tonight.'

Penny gave him a wry smile. 'You do know the Government won't win. All the polls say so. How many of your mates will lose their jobs?'

'*Que sera sera*. They've made their beds. If the result pleases Matthew, it will please me.' There was an unusual quality to Fraser's voice, an authentic resonance. For a moment the mask of illness dropped away, transforming his features, turning the pallid grey into a guileless warmth. Love for his son was stamped all over his face.

'Wish me luck,' she said, picking up her bag.

Fraser kissed her cheek. 'That baby you're carrying is all the luck you need – all the luck any of us need.'

They were interrupted by the barking dogs. Penny hurried from the studio in time to see Matt's jeep pull into the circular driveway at the front of the house. No, she'd wanted to tell him about the baby in their own cosy kitchen, not here at Canterbury Downs – a place where Matt had known a great deal of pain. A place from which he'd been estranged for years. Well, it couldn't be helped and she'd waited long enough. But still, the change in plans felt like a bad sign.

Sarah Deville woke, bleary-eyed, to a knocking at the door. The spa had turned itself off and the tub water was cold. A hair floated on its surface. Her fingers were wrinkled and grey. She stepped out and almost slipped. Ow, her toe. The champagne flute lay smashed on the floor beneath her foot. Blood trickled across the tiles.

'Just a minute, Matt.' Sarah staggered to the closet and put on a bathrobe. A quick glance in the mirror. Hair hanging in rat-tails. Scrubbed face revealing each dark circle and line. The knock came again. She rushed to the bathroom, applied a little powder, then dragged a comb through her lank, wet hair. That would have to do. Wait. The sexy underwear. A third knock. No, naked under the robe would be sexy enough. Sarah opened the door.

The woman from reception stood holding a bottle of champagne in an ice bucket. She peered past Sarah into the room. 'I didn't notice your friend arrive, but I've brought the wine anyway. Did I miss him?'

Sarah snatched the bucket and slammed the door. She checked the time. Past six-thirty. A text message from Matt. *Sorry Sarah. I can't make it. We'll talk tomorrow.* Short and sour, speaking volumes. Sarah hurled her clothes on and headed for the car. He wasn't getting away with this.

CHAPTER 37

Television coverage of the election had already begun when Fraser, Penny and Matt settled down on the oversized leather suite in the lounge room. Penny had been watching for a moment to take Matt aside, but an excited Fraser was monopolising him. Father and son were talking for the first time in years, and she didn't want to get in the way of that.

Penny emptied the potato crisps she'd brought into a bowl, and put them on the coffee table. They looked out of place beside the plates of gourmet hors d'oeuvres brought in by the butler. 'Anything vegetarian?'

McGregor materialised at her shoulder. 'Of course, Miss Penny.' He pointed to this or that appetiser, rattling off ingredients. 'Polenta wedges with bocconcini and basil pesto, leek and charred bell pepper tartlets, crunchy red lentil fritters with fresh mint …'

Despite the delicious food, Penny had little appetite. Nerves had the better of her. 'Did you really cook all this?' McGregor seemed mortified by the question.

'Stop showing off,' said Fraser, 'and fetch us something to drink.'

McGregor returned with a refrigerated trolley. 'Champagne, Miss

Penny? A great vintage. Veuve Clicquot Ponsardin Brut 1998.' The French words sounded strange in his thick Scottish brogue.

Penny shook her head, keeping a careful eye on Matt. She loved champagne. Would he wonder why she refused the glass of bubbly? But he didn't notice. He was listening to Fraser talk about Matt's American grandmother, a woman she knew he'd always wondered about.

'I went to live with my mother in Los Angeles when I was sixteen,' said Fraser. 'You know how teenagers are. I'd had a row with my father, Thomas Abbott, and she sent me a plane ticket. Kitty Monroe was a very glamourous lady, a movie star, married to a famous Hollywood director. It was an exciting life for a young man.'

'Didn't your dad try to bring you back?' asked Matt.

'He did, but I didn't want to go home, and Mother fought him in the US courts. She had money and influence and wasn't afraid to fight dirty.'

Fraser cleared his throat. Something of the joy had gone out of him. By now Penny was also riveted by Fraser's story.

'Kitty hated my father – I still don't know why. She did all she could to turn me against him, and I'm afraid she succeeded. I remained estranged from him almost until his death.'

'How awful,' said Penny.

'Yes, very sad.' There was a faraway look on Fraser's face. 'I'd forgotten how much I loved that man until I returned to Tasmania. But by then Mother's fondness for money had rubbed off on me.' He traced a Scotch thistle pattern in the tablecloth. 'Dad was a war hero, you know, a Battle of Britain fighter pilot. Also a passionate conservationist like yourself, Matthew. It seems I was the only one in the family not to follow in that proud tradition.' He clapped his son on the back. 'Until now, eh?'

Penny's heart melted. How wonderful for Matt to hear these stories from his father, before it was too late.

Fraser turned up the television. 'Come join us, McGregor, for history in the making.'

'No, thank you, sir. I've never placed much stock in politics. And on top of that I feel sorry for Miss Kate.'

Penny glanced at the television, which showed a large tally board divided into the five state electorates. Host Tom Munro was speaking. 'If you've just tuned in, we're coming live from the floor of the Pierpont Casino tally room for what's shaping up to be a fascinating night. We should see some figures from the smaller booths any time now. Polling places were packed out early, with people queuing to have their say.' The first results were coming in, and colourful graphs appeared on the screen. 'Things are already taking shape, with a substantial swing against the government. Remember, the swing will be stronger in the large metropolitan booths that come in later tonight.'

Well, what did they expect? Kate had lost her premiership in a sensational fashion and was likely to face corruption charges as well. It hadn't been a gracious leave-taking. Recriminations had flown in all directions. Kate seemed determined to take her colleagues down with her, and not without cause. She hadn't been the only one with her snout in the trough, so why should she be the only one to pay? The vicious blame game had mortally wounded the Government days out from the election. They didn't have a hope. Penny squirmed whenever she saw one of their pundits rationalise the party's chances, clinging to this or that false hope. It was sad to see people so reduced, whatever their politics.

Matt and Fraser, on the other hand, were watching the ruling party crumble with unashamed glee. There was some heavy father and son bonding going on. Although Penny was happy for them, she was beginning to wonder if she'd ever get her husband to herself.

Matt topped up Fraser's glass. 'If Kate broke the law by taking bribes, didn't you break the law by making them?'

'I did, but I also handed Hellgrun victory on a plate. Do you imagine his newly-minted government will pursue me?'

Matt chuckled. 'They're more likely to give you a medal.'

McGregor called them to the dining room for dinner.

'Let's eat in here,' Matt suggested.

'Yes,' said Fraser. 'Like old times.'

They clinked their glasses together in a toast. Who were they? Tweedledum and Tweedledee? Had Matt forgotten she had something to tell him? Now Penny really did want that glass of wine. McGregor cleared away the appetisers and brought in two T-bone steaks, and a large salmon portion with a baked potato and spinach on the side for Penny.

'Sorry, I don't eat fish,' she said. McGregor looked pained. 'Never mind, I'll just eat the vegetables.'

They started on their dinners. Matt attacked his steak with gusto.

'That's my boy,' said Fraser. 'You always did eat me out of house and home.'

Penny watched her husband with dismay. She didn't expect him to be enjoying all that meat so much.

The night wore on and the swing against the government grew. Matt and Fraser began acting out an incomprehensible comedy skit in posh English accents. Some sort of spoof election broadcast about a silly party and its ridiculous candidates.

'Do we have a swing in Luton?' asked Fraser, hand cupped to his right ear.

'Not a swing,' Matt answered, with a grin. 'But we do have a swong, right here in this box and it's looking fine.'

'What are you two doing?' asked Penny. Fraser was laughing, a great booming belly laugh. A laugh too big for his skinny body. She stood up, shouting to break through the hilarity. 'I don't get it.'

They stopped laughing and looked at her.

'Monty Python,' said Matt. 'Dad and I used to watch it together.'

'The election night parody? You must know it,' said Fraser. 'The Sensible Party and the Silly Party? It's priceless.'

'No, I don't know it,' she said. 'I don't know anything about it. Might have been nice if somebody had bothered to explain it to me.' Penny plopped back down on the couch as McGregor brought in a platter of poached pears and cream.

'If it's any consolation, Miss Penny, I've not seen that particular sketch myself.'

Matt looked apologetic and reached for her hand. She moved it away. Aargh, what a fool. All night she'd hoped he would do that. Why was she annoyed anyway? She should be thrilled that father and son, so long divided, had shared a lovely moment.

Fraser attempted in his clumsy way to help her out. 'Your wife seems a little more emotional than usual, Matthew. Why is that, I wonder?'

What was he trying to do? Announce her pregnancy himself? She wouldn't be surprised.

Loud cheering came from the television. It was just nine o'clock, but Robert Hellgrun was on the tally room floor claiming victory. 'Today the people of Tasmania have spoken – and spoken decisively.'

Matt raised his glass. 'Let the great shredderthon begin.'

Hellgrun told the noisy throng that this was a historic and trans-forming day, that he would govern for all Tasmanians and set sail for the future.

Fraser stood and took a bow. 'Come, my boy,' he said, with an expansive sweep of his arm. 'We'll look at the guns. Some new toys, plus all your old favourites. I still have your Colt, you know.'

Matt lit up. 'The Equaliser? I loved that gun.' He turned to Penny, eyes bright with excitement. 'Do you mind, Pen? I know how you hate guns.'

He looked so happy, so shiningly handsome. A jolt of love crashed through her. 'You go on,' she said, as McGregor came in with coffee and pastries. 'While I eat all the best cakes.'

Ten minutes later Fraser returned to the lounge room alone. 'Matthew had to go. Something he'd forgotten to do at Binburra. Said he wouldn't be long.' Penny's face fell. Fraser sat down beside her and squeezed her hand. 'It's like herding cats, eh, being married to Matt?' She was too upset to respond. 'Forgive me, Penelope, I haven't been helping your cause tonight. I became lost in the joy of being with my son.'

'It's fine,' she said, with a tight smile.

They sat awhile in silence. Matt's absence had left them both deflated. Penny tried to imagine what sort of task couldn't wait until morning. What would prompt him to rush off this late without saying goodbye?

At last Fraser spoke. 'I can't bear that long face, Penelope. Why not go after him?' He shooed her with pale hands. 'Go on, my dear, go home to your husband and tell him your long-overdue news.'

Penny hugged him tight around his bony shoulders. 'I love you,' she said. 'And I'm so glad you and Matt are finding your way back to each other.' Then she hurried into the starry night.

It was clear and still outside, so still that sound was magnified. A shrieking owl. The squeal of distant wheels somewhere out on the road. Frogs in the dam. A deafening clamour exploded from the trees all around. She usually liked cicada song, but tonight the wild discord unnerved her.

Penny started the car and swung onto the road; her foot heavy on the throttle, her imagination racing ahead. The expression on Matt's face when she told him about the baby, his gestures, his words. She needed to hear those words, and a drive that should take twenty minutes seemed to be taking forever.

Penny didn't see the dead pademelon and the devil darting towards it until the very last moment. She swerved just in time. What a hypocrite, always blaming others for this very thing – for speeding, for not concentrating. It was going to just about kill her, though, taking the time to pull over, go back and check the dead wallaby for pouch young. Nevertheless she dutifully stopped. A male, dead a few hours at least, which meant Matt hadn't killed it. Struck on the road to Binburra, though. Who then? Hunters? Penny got back into the car. It didn't matter. All that mattered was talking to Matt.

CHAPTER 38

Sarah stepped out of the house and onto the verandah, into a square of light. She must have found the key, let herself in, even turned on the radio. She spoke before Matt had a foot on the step.

'Guess what? It's my call now.' Yes. No more games, no pretence. Just the naked truth between them. 'I'd still like to bring you in on this,' she said. 'You have the local knowledge. But I don't need you.'

True enough. Hidden somewhere in the bowels of Sarah's UTAS laboratory, a tissue sample of Theo's ear held him hostage. It was all she needed to blow his denial out of the water. Matt didn't speak. Instead, he watched a huntsman spider ambush a pretty moth that had been lured to the cobweb-strewn light on the verandah.

'I've learned something about you,' said Sarah. 'There's what you say, and there's what you don't say. It's what you don't say that matters.'

Matt went into the house. Sarah followed him and took a seat at the kitchen table.

'I can hear the wheels turning, Matt, but don't waste your time.'

He sat opposite her. 'Four living tigers.'

'I thought you didn't know about any others.'

'Well, I do. I found tracks.'

'Four could be enough to save the species, and who knows, there might be more.' Sarah chattered on about scientific breakthroughs and molecular biology and answering the big questions.

Matt listened, feeling nothing but shame. His family had been the tigers' shield for one hundred and fifty years. From the meddlers, the scientists, the profiteers. Their shield from the Sarahs of this world. Even Fraser had been their protector, but now it was the end of the road, and it was all because of him. Trapped in a blind alley of his own idiocy; the only one in that long line of champions to fail them. And what of his forefather, Daniel Campbell, who'd had the foresight to plan this such a long time ago? A man so far ahead of his time that he worried over the fate of tigers when farmers still shot them as pests. What would Daniel Campbell think of him now if he knew? Matt tasted salty water on his tongue, though he didn't know he was crying.

'Tears now?' said Sarah. 'Nice try. More tricks up your sleeve than Drake.' She folded her arms across her chest. 'You made a complete fool out of me, Matt.' Her hand trembled. 'I didn't deserve that.'

'No,' said Matt. 'You didn't.'

Sarah inclined her head. 'Thank you for that at least. Now, where are the tigers?'

'You do know that if their location gets out, every idiot under the sun will go after them. Plenty would shoot them on sight.'

'True – that's why they must be captured. The animals are too valuable to be left to fend for themselves.'

'Valuable to who exactly? Zoos? Laboratories? Then forgive me if I can't see captivity being any great improvement in their lifestyle. And what about the cloning experiments that go wrong? There's a fair serve of suffering in that. And if you succeed, what happens when we don't only have ten, or twenty. What happens when we have hundreds?'

'We'll stock international zoos,' said Sarah. 'We could reintroduce them to the wild. You could have some here at Binburra.'

A pulse started in his neck. 'And if their numbers built up in the wild? What would happen if tigers started taking sheep?'

'They could be culled.'

'Are you kidding me?' It was like talking to a small child. 'That's what drove them to the brink in the first place.' He worked his jaw back and forth to relieve a painful cramp. 'You say humans will decide how many tigers there should be, and where they should live or die. You say it's fine to resurrect a species solely to be used as zoo exhibits or for experiments or to be killed down the track when it suits. That's hardly in the thylacines' best interests, and it's a questionable moral position to boot.'

'We've had this argument before.' Sarah's voice was low.

'Then we're bloody well going to have it again. Why can't we let nature be? Not conservation, but preservation. Not management, but protection. Please, Sarah. Please don't do this.'

Penny couldn't believe it. Sarah's car parked right next to Matt's. She grabbed a torch from the glove box and checked to make sure, but there was no mistake. Same model, same colour. Penny shone the torch in the window. A UTAS key ring dangled from the ignition. The beam caught something else, a dark smear on the bumper. Blood and fur. Sarah had killed the pademelon. It had been dead for hours, which meant Sarah had been here for hours. All that time. During appetisers, during dinner, during Hellgrun's victory speech. All that time, while Penny agonised over how to tell Matt of her pregnancy, Sarah had been at Binburra. Waiting. Waiting for another woman's husband, for her husband.

Penny's breath came shallow and strained. Her body hurt. Thank heavens she hadn't mentioned the baby. Would Matt have been pleased, or only pretended. A masochistic urge sent her sneaking up to the house. Her home, where she'd lived for twelve years, where she'd known so much happiness. It looked almost sinister tonight, crouched halfway up the hill. Some poor cursed creature, made ugly by a witch.

The verandah radio was on, sounding loud in the stillness, playing some silly love song. Penny hid in the shadows and held onto her breath, wanting proof. Something that meant there'd be no misgivings, no doubt about the fullness, the completeness, of Matt's betrayal. For once, Penny approved of the full-length glass that sucked in summer's heat and winter's cold. Of the tattered, threadbare curtains, their bottom edges ripped ragged by the teeth and claws of quolls and devils. They afforded no privacy to those inside, so long as the lights were on.

Closer and closer she crept, on tiptoes to her bedroom window, and knelt beneath the waratah Matt had planted for her birthday. Penny stared at the black glass. Maybe she was wrong. But even as this faint, hopeful thought dawned, she knew that way danger lay. There was no defence against an unacknowledged truth. Safety lay in facing it. So Penny stayed moth-quiet, watching in the night for her worst fear to reveal itself.

Sarah was an immoveable object. Their discussion was getting nowhere. Frustration boiled over, causing him to slam the table with his fist, startling her. Get a grip. Frightening Sarah wouldn't help.

He withdrew to the dark bedroom and switched on the lamp. Light flooded from the window through the unkempt bush garden beyond. He sat on the bed and stared at the night. Something was out there, a moving shadow. Or maybe not. He stood up, stood close to the glass for a better look.

Sarah knocked on the door and entered without an invitation. Matt sat back down and she sat beside him, resting a hand on his knee. 'My visits to your bed are always so disappointing.'

Matt laughed a hollow laugh. Sarah smoothed the candlewick coverlet then kissed him. He was too surprised to resist. 'That's for what might have been,' she said, stroking his cheek. 'I wanted to kill you when you stood me up tonight.' She looked so grim he didn't doubt it. 'But now? Now I'm just sad. It was going to be you and me and the discovery of a lifetime. It was going to be perfect.'

'I'm sorry,' said Matt, and he was. He owed Sarah, and he understood her. She'd played the game as hard as he had. She believed she was right, just as he did, and in the end she'd outsmarted him. If it had mattered less to either of them, they'd be shaking hands.

'Try to see the big picture,' she said. 'You keep devils here in cages.'

'That's different,' he said. 'There's still a viable wild population out there. Devils who know how to be devils. There's more to an animal than its DNA, Sarah. Remove those last precious apex predators from the wild and the species will be culturally extinct, even if you do have a few bewildered exiles running around in zoos.'

'Culturally extinct?' Sarah was half-smiling. 'Now you're having me on.'

'Do your research. Read Laland and Janik. Read Brower. He says wild species are 2 percent flesh and bone and 98 percent place. Like that orchid I showed you, they exist in the most important way, only in relationship to their habitat. How do you suppose those tigers have survived all this time? I'll tell you how. Through their local knowledge, their tried and tested hunting techniques, their intergenerational learning. Through vocalisations passed down and a thousand things that aren't innate – a rich social life that we can't even guess at.'

'Even if I accept that thylacine culture will die out, does it matter? Is it really that important?'

Matt ran a hand through his hair. 'How long have humans lived in Tasmania? Not Europeans – human beings.' Sarah shook her head. 'Fifty thousand years,' said Matt. 'And thylacines? Twenty million years. Twenty million years of thylacine culture on this island, and some blow-in Yank thinks she has the right to deem it unimportant.'

Sarah stared at him. For the first time that night, she had no counterargument ready. When she finally spoke, there was a quiver in her voice. 'I need a drink.'

Penny blinked as the bedroom light came on, turning the window into a cinema screen. If only this was a movie. There, Matt moving towards the bed, sitting down. He stared straight at her. Stood up, moved closer. He must have seen her, must know she was hiding out here in the gloom. Penny tensed, wanting to rush inside, waiting for a gesture, a sign. But Matt turned away. She was wrong. He hadn't seen her, hadn't felt her presence at all.

Sarah suddenly appeared in the room, a distortion of that familiar space. She crossed over to Matt. He sat down. She sat close beside him. Close enough to smell his aftershave, to hear him breathe. Any closer and Sarah would feel the beat of his heart. Then, in Penny's own bedroom, on her own bed, Sarah laid a hand on Matt's knee and kissed him. Penny lurched as a jolt of pain shot through her. How far would Matt go to neutralise Sarah? How far had he already gone?

Penny had seen enough. She fled back down the path. Her fingers fumbled at the gears, forgetting the handbrake, stalling twice before coaxing the car to life. She flew down the drive, wincing at the sickening sound of scraping metal as she misjudged Binburra's gatepost.

What she wanted was her uncle. Somebody who loved her for sure, for no reason. Loved her just because. That's what she needed now, unfailing love. Penny shivered in the warm night and eased her foot from the accelerator. Her unborn baby required unfailing love, too, from her. She could not crash on this lonely road with nobody to notice or come looking. Her unborn baby required to live.

Ray and Charlie were still in the backyard when she arrived. She could hear her uncle's raised voice, holding forth on some subject or other. Charlie would be sitting on a picnic chair, drunk as a skunk, nodding agreement no matter what Ray said. An unfailing friendship, that one. Penny felt a pang of envy as she burst onto the porch.

Ray looked up. 'What's the matter, love?'

He brought her a chair, and she confessed everything in a gushing stream of consciousness, as dark as the Charon itself. It was safe to cry, here with Ray, here with Charlie. Safe to vent her heartbreak. She told them of Theo and Sarah and her suspicions about Matt. When she got to the bit about the baby, Ray stood up.

'How far along, love? You should have told me.' He lit a cigarette and paced up and down the weedy strip of grass.

'I haven't even told Matt. I was going to tell him tonight, but she's there. Sarah's there at Binburra,' said Penny. 'I saw her and Matt together in the bedroom.'

Ray stopped pacing. He muttered something, but she couldn't catch his words in that strange, fierce growl of a voice. It hadn't struck her at first, but she saw it now. He was too restless, too alert. His eyes, reflected in the porch light, were wild and intense – not their usual rheumy self. His posture was stiff and erect. It was as if he was on the edge of something. The muttering increased, aimed not at her or Charlie. Aimed at the night. The oddness of his behaviour cut through Penny's misery and she tried to pull herself together.

Thankfully there was nothing strange about Charlie. He sat in the plastic picnic chair, murmuring sympathy. 'That's a real rough deal, love. You deserve better. I'd like to tan his hide. A tiger, eh? Didn't I always say there was tigers?'

The whisky bottle was almost empty. Charlie would sleep it off on the couch and never remember a thing in the morning. That was the way of these things.

But something was wrong with her uncle. She'd expected, she'd needed, consoling words and a soft place to fall. Instead, he seemed to be working himself into a private fury. Penny took his arm and he shoved her aside. She steadied herself on a chair, almost falling. Ray stared at her, as if surprised by what he'd done, then he strode off into the house.

Penny watched him go. Everything she held dear was deserting her. No, that wasn't true. She still had the baby, so hang the rest of them. She ran inside and lay face down on her bed, dry-eyed, all cried out. There were noises in the hall, raised voices. Then Charlie at the door, calling, knocking, calling again.

'He keeps saying as he's going to sort them two out. I think you'd better come, Pen. He ain't fit to drive.'

'Go away.'

Charlie knocked harder. 'You should come, Pen. He's taken my ute.' A motor revved up out front. Penny dragged her weary body from the bed and opened the door.

'I don't care, Charlie,' she said. 'I just don't care.'

'He went and got my rifle from the back and put it beside him before he left. I tried to stop him.'

Penny hadn't really been listening. 'Say that again, Charlie.'

'I said he's got my rifle. Worked up something terrible, he was. Reckon it must have been them new pills.'

'What pills?' Penny struggled to recall any detail of that night before her world caved in. But when Charlie handed her the box, she remembered – sleeping pills or something. She turned it over. No chemist label. 'Where did he get these, Charlie?'

Charlie fidgeted, seeming suddenly sober.

'Come on, Charlie.'

'From a bloke at the pub this arvo. Ray said the pills he got from Pete weren't working no more.'

Penny opened the box - three caplets were missing. She looked for the medical information leaflet. There, neatly folded and unread. That was something. It meant the pills weren't from some backyard laboratory. At least they'd know what they were dealing with.

Penny flattened out the leaflet. *Active ingredient Zolpidem tartrate. Standard adult dose of RestRite is one 10 mg tablet.* Ray had taken three. *For those over sixty-five years of age the dose is half a tablet – 5 mg.* Ray would be sixty-five next month. He could be on six times the proper dose. *Do not take RestRite if you have been drinking alcohol. It may increase side effects.* No surprise there. She read on through the range of reactions. *Dizziness. Drowsiness.* Why hadn't she tried to stop him leaving? *Less common adverse effects include psychiatric and paradoxical reactions.* Oh no. *Confusion. Agitation. Hallucinations. Other forms of unwanted behaviour including rage reactions.* Penny went into the lounge room. A fist-sized hole that wasn't there before gaped in the plaster by the door. Her mouth went dry.

'Charlie. Did he say why he wanted the rifle?'

'To kill them. That's what I've been trying to tell you. Matt and that other sheila. Ray said he was going to kill them both.'

An icy shiver ran through her. She fumbled in her bag for her mobile and rang Matt. His phone was turned off. The message she left was so long it dropped out just at the important part. Penny tried again, sticking to the essentials this time. *Matt. Get out of there. Ray's on his way with a rifle. He wants to kill you.* It sounded ridiculous. She steeled herself and rang Sarah. The phone rang and rang and went to message bank. Penny hung on until after the beep, then couldn't bring herself to speak.

She dialled the Hills End police station and got Sergeant Byrne's voice on a recorded message. Station unattended. For emergencies, ring Campbellfield. Campbellfield was an hour away. Matt might not have that long. Penny made the call in any case, sounding like somebody else on the phone, telling her absurd tale. Charlie stood by, wringing his hat in his wrinkled hands. He'd better come too. Ray might listen to Charlie. Penny urged him out of the door.

'What about Matt's old man?' said Charlie. 'Lives along Binburra Road, doesn't he? He'd have a fair head start on us.'

Thank goodness for Charlie. Penny gave him a swift kiss and made the call. Fraser didn't answer his mobile. Try the house phone. It rang and rang. At last McGregor picked up and she gave him a quick rundown. The story sounded outlandish, even to her.

McGregor interrupted halfway through her spiel. 'I'll fetch Mr Abbott.'

It took an eternity for Fraser's voice to sound on the end of the line. Penny started all over again. There was a fine distinction between rapid speech and garbled speech. She prayed she had the balance right.

CHAPTER 39

Matt poured them both a glass of Scotch.

'I could be prepared to negotiate,' said Sarah, 'if you tell me where the other thylacines are.'

Negotiate? He pulled a kitchen chair away from the table, spun it around, straddled it and rested his arms on its bentwood back. So this was no lay down misère, after all. What was he ready to gamble? His reputation? Certainly. His job? Yes. His integrity? She might be surprised at how much he was prepared to forfeit.

'I'll bet Penny could tell me where those thylacines are,' said Sarah. 'How about I ask her?'

'Be my guest,' said Matt, like a man with nothing to lose.

'Well, if you won't give me the others, will you at least give me Theo?' There was a desperate edge to her voice.

'And what do I get?'

Sarah's clever eyes studied him as he threw back his drink. Penny was waiting back at Canterbury Downs. What would she be thinking, with him disappearing like that? He took his phone from his pocket.

'Don't,' said Sarah.

Matt played with it for a moment, then put it down.

'Keeping Theo in a domestic freezer is no good,' she said. 'He'll deteriorate.'

Matt shrugged. 'It hardly matters. I'll bury him soon with a little eulogy.'

Sarah paled. 'Give him to me and I'll guarantee your anonymity.' The words came out in a rush. 'You get to protect your job and the living thylacines. I get more than a piece of ear.'

Matt weighed up his options. That might be a compromise he could live with. If he trusted her, which he didn't. Yet perhaps he'd have to take that risk. For Sarah, one thylacine in the hand was bound to be worth more than a few lost in the bush. Her natural habitat was the laboratory, not the field or zoo, and Sarah's research project held biological samples from all over the state. If she kept her mouth shut, there'd be no reason for anyone to suspect that Theo came from Binburra.

He reached out his arm. 'It's a deal.'

Sarah heaved a great sigh and shook his hand. She looked just like he felt, brimming with mistrust and doubt. Neither of them had exactly been straight shooters.

The radio still played on the verandah. Matt went outside and turned it off. Had the night changed? Had the music masked the sound of the wind whipping up, its thrum through the trees? No, the ficofolia flowers still hung like still life paintings beyond the railing. It wasn't the wind at all. It was a distant car, down on Binburra Road. Was Penny coming? Noise carried far in the mountains. The car could be ten minutes away, maybe more. Though Matt would tell Penny everything when she arrived, it would be better if she didn't find Sarah there.

'Penny's on her way,' he told her inside.

Sarah's mouth had a bitter twist to it. 'It was always her, wasn't it? You never cared about me.'

'Get the keys,' he said. 'You have to go.'

Sarah stood her ground. 'As long as we have that deal.'

'We do,' said Matt. 'You get Theo. Now hurry, please.'

With agonising slowness, Sarah collected her things. Matt

escorted her down to the car park, torch shining on the path ahead. He gripped her arm when she lagged. A round, ruddy moon broke free of the horizon. It hung sullenly in the emptiness between mountain and stars. The motor droned louder. It didn't sound like Penny's jeep.

Matt opened Sarah's car door. At last she got in and turned on the ignition. Her window slid open. What now?

'We'll talk tomorrow, yeah?'

'I'll ring you,' said Matt.

'That's a laugh,' said Sarah. 'I think I'll ring you.'

Somewhere out in the darkness, the sound of the motor dropped to a low hum. The engine changed gears, grinding back to life as wheels gained traction on the steep Binburra drive. Sarah's car reversed and moved off. Now headlights climbed the hill. Matt recognised the vehicle in the moonlight. Charlie Cook's ute. What the heck was he doing here?

The headlights were approaching fast. Too fast. A trick of the night, perhaps, but there wasn't much room for error on the narrow track. The speeding ute kept coming, AC/DC booming through the open window. Couldn't Charlie see Sarah's car? He was heading straight for it, driving like a bloody fool.

Sarah must have seen the danger, for her red tail-lights swung right and stopped a distance off the track. Charlie's headlights raced on faster than ever, then blinked off as clouds covered the moon. Where was he? It was hard to see in the darkness.

Then Matt heard it. No screeching of brakes, just the sudden ear-splitting crunch of metal on metal. What on earth? If anything, the revs had risen before the impact. Charlie must be drunk to run off the road like that on a clear night, to smash into Sarah's stationary car. Matt grabbed a torch and sprinted down the hill.

The close crack of a rifle stopped him short. There was no mistaking the sound. It cracked again through the blare of music. Charlie's shouts for help spurred him on again. Near enough now to see what was happening. It may have been Charlie's ute, but the man standing beside it was too tall for Charlie. It looked more like Ray.

What was up with him? He wasn't shouting for help at all. He was ranting – screaming at the night.

Despite Matt's confusion, one thing was clear. The ute had nose-dived into the side of Sarah's sedan. He was too far away to see if she was still in there. Matt trained his torch on the car and then on Ray, who turned and saw him.

What on earth? Ray had a rifle. He raised the weapon and aimed it straight at Matt.

Matt switched off his torch and ran. Another fire cracker of a shot. Charlie's ute roared to life and reversed away from Sarah's car, its headlights searching. The slope of native grassland offered Matt no shelter, only silver-grey tufts of tussock grass and clumps of heath. He could double back to the trees along the driveway, or make a break across the clearing to the woodland beyond. Ray decided the point, hurtling straight down the hill, forcing Matt to bolt towards the forest. The music made for a nightmare soundtrack.

Matt ran, crouching low, unable to properly judge distances in the dark. Yet his legs had a mind of their own and he trusted them. The rough ground felt solid beneath his feet, but didn't things feel like that in dreams? Was this even real?

There was no way he'd reach the trees in time. Matt dodged sharply left and set off down the hill, gambling that Ray's wild driving wouldn't allow for any quick swing-arounds. The bet paid off and the headlights swept past. He listened for the grind of brakes, but couldn't hear a thing beyond the blasting sound system.

Matt seized a breath and wiped sweat from his eyes. The advantage was his now. With the moon behind a cloud, Ray had lost him in the dark. Matt ducked as twin silver blades swung across the clearing. It wouldn't be too hard to dodge them, and he had his night eyes now. If he could reach the trees down by the gate, Ray wouldn't be able to follow.

He was heading downhill in a stooped run, when the night turned suddenly bright, and he was pinioned in the blinding wedge of a spotlight's beam. Matt shielded his eyes. He'd need a miracle now.

Solo spotlighting was a tricky sport. A hunter had to swing hard when he found his target. He had mere seconds to aim his light, turn ninety degrees, and position the rifle in the window rest. Only then could he shoot, relying on dazzled animals to freeze. But Matt couldn't be hunted like a scared wallaby. Now Ray could see him, Ray's best bet would be to just run him down.

As if reading his mind, the ute lurched into gear and took aim. Matt careened headlong down the hill, his way lit by the spotlight's beam. No point looking back. This would either work or it wouldn't. He veered right, towards the forest of moon shadows cast by trees on the clearing's edge. To judge by the tearing noise of the ute, it must be almost upon him. He braced himself. There, a wide trench after that dead gum, invisible to a high beam. Matt leaped like a spring released, flying through the air for as long as he could, knowing there'd be no second chance.

A dull crash sounded behind him, and the screaming engine fell silent. Matt's ankle rolled when he hit the ground, but he scrambled to his feet, limp-running to a line of trees. His breath came in painful rasps. The trunks of white peppermints loomed like rows of ghosts on the edge of the forest. Matt grasped the nearest tree, hugged the rough collar at its base, rubbed the pale, papery smoothness of bark above. The tree was an anchor, a proof of life. He dared to look around.

The ute lay upended in the drainage ditch on such a steep angle that he couldn't see its headlights. The music still blared, Meatloaf's *Bat Out of Hell*, and the spotlight on the cabin roof still shone. It was surreal, a movie set. Matt stayed quietly watching. If only the bloody music would stop. A startled owl flapped past his head. Matt jumped in fright, forgetting about his injured ankle and collapsed to the ground. He'd be a sitting duck if Ray ever climbed out of that ditch.

Matt found a stout stick for a crutch. His foot had swollen in the boot and his ankle couldn't bear his weight. He managed to hobble a few more metres when the boom, boom of the stereo suddenly stopped.

Fear settled on him like rain, seeped through his clothes, through his skin. He tried to lick his lips, but no spit would come. When he looked back, nothing had changed. He should keep going, but he couldn't drag his gaze away from the ute. Was it his imagination or could he see movement? Yes, a faint beam danced within the halo of light around the stranded vehicle.

Ray's dark figure hauled itself from the ditch, rifle in hand. Matt knew now what that faint light was. A deadly firefly: a scope-mounted spotlight. Ray began to bellow: insults and curses and threats – along with confounding accusations.

'Think you'd get away with cheating on my little girl? With her pregnant and all? Well think again, you bastard.'

Pregnant? A jolt of joy broke through his fear. Was that what Penny had wanted to tell him? He thought back to the evening at Fraser's. Why had he made it so difficult for her?

Ray took a random shot in his direction. 'You're a dead man.'

Matt prayed that Penny wouldn't come home, that she wouldn't come looking for him.

Matt's twisted ankle burned, but adrenaline was a fine painkiller. Quiet now. Even his breathing must be quiet. He focused on slowing down each breath, on its passage in and out of his lungs. In and out. In and out. Better.

Clouds still covered the moon, leaving him blind, but the pale peppermint gums supported and guided him as he edged between them. He could hear Ray stomping around, getting nearer then moving away. Careful now, Ray sounded close.

Suddenly Matt's good foot stepped into thin air. It was the second drain, a disastrous misjudgement. Matt teetered on the bank for a moment, struggling for equilibrium. Then he crashed down, rolling through bracken before coming to a stop with a thud. He'd made about as much noise as an elephant and lost his walking stick as well. Matt lay still, listening to the rush of blood in his ears. He couldn't hear Ray anymore. The moon emerged from behind the clouds to brighten the night. Footsteps. Matt held his breath.

And there Ray stood, looming over him, silhouetted by moonlight. Matt heard a strangled sound escape his own throat.

Ray's silence was more unnerving than all his mad ranting. Should he talk to Ray, deny the charge of cheating? Should he plead for his life? But since when had Ray ever listened to him? Ray would shoot him if he wanted. Nothing would change that. If he was going to die, he wouldn't die begging.

Time seemed to stretch. So many regrets. That he hadn't listened to Penny tell her news, and said that he loved her. That he'd lose his father as soon as he found him. That he hadn't safely buried Theo up at Tiger Pass. That he'd never know his child.

Moonlight flooded the scene. Matt watched Ray with a detached curiosity as he raised the rifle and nestled the butt high on his shoulder. He was having trouble getting his legs right. He shuffled about, trying to get his weight equal on both feet. At last he seemed happy. Ray aimed the barrel. At his head? At his chest? Matt couldn't tell. Ray tucked his cheek into the walnut stock. Matt closed his eyes. He had not expected to hear the shot.

What happened next was impossible. Matt opened his eyes. He moved his toes, his fingers, raised himself up on an elbow, amazed that his body responded. He was alive.

A figure armed with a rifle loomed against the moon. Not Ray this time, but a smaller man. His father. Fraser dropped the rifle, clambered into the drain and knelt beside his son. Tears glistened in his eyes. To their left, a flannel-sleeved arm dangled limp down the side of the ditch.

Matt grasped Fraser's hand and staggered to his feet.

'Lean on me.'

'Sarah … she was in her car,' Matt pointed, 'over there.'

Fraser shone his torch up the hill in that direction. 'Wait here.' He scrambled from the ditch. Matt found his walking stick and struggled after him.

Ray lay on his back at the edge of the bank. Moonlight showed the dark bullet wound in the centre of his chest. Matt turned away, the vile taste of vomit on his tongue.

When Fraser returned, he shook his head. 'I'm sorry, Matt. Sarah's dead.'

. . .

Matt stood with crutches out on the verandah, surveying the bizarre scene below him. Four in the morning, and the medical examiner's van was finally leaving to take Ray and Sarah to Hobart. The remote paddock beside the Binburra track was ablaze with floodlights. Police cars lined the driveway and yellow tape crisscrossed the grass. Crime scene tents covered the places where Ray and Sarah had died, and white-suited forensic investigators still wandered about.

Penny was inside giving her statement to the police. She'd spent the past few hours sitting on the ground as close to where Ray's body lay as the officers would allow, shell-shocked with grief. Matt had stayed beside her. He'd been afraid that she might turn him away; that she might blame him for this tragedy. But instead she'd clung to him, murmuring her thanks to God for his survival. Don't thank God, he'd wanted to stay. Thank my father.

A young policewoman came out of the house. 'Mr Abbott? Your turn now.'

Penny was huddled at the kitchen table, staring at a hot mug of coffee that Sergeant Nick Byrne had placed in front of her.

Nick caught Matt's eye and pointed to the lounge room. 'Shall we do this in there?'

'I have nothing to say that my wife can't hear.' Matt gave a long and detailed statement, leaving nothing out, except the reason for Sarah's visit. He'd already told Penny about that. She remained stony-faced throughout, but he could tell she was listening.

'What about my father?' asked Matt, when he'd finished. 'Where is he? What will happen to him?'

'Fraser gave his statement at Campbellfield hours ago. McGregor took him home.' Nick put on his hat and laid a hand on Matt's shoulder. 'Your dad will be alright. Ray had already killed once. It was a clear case of your father acting in defence of another – namely you.'

'I don't understand why my uncle had to die,' said Penny in a shaky voice. 'Couldn't Fraser have shot him in the leg instead?'

Nick took off his hat and sat down beside her. 'Shooting to wound is a myth, Pen. Same as shooting the gun from someone's hand. It's Hollywood movie hype.' She gazed at him with anguished, uncomprehending eyes. 'Fraser was out there in the dark, confronting a man intent on using deadly force. He aimed at the chest because he couldn't afford to miss. I would have done the same thing.' Nick stood up and put his hat back on. 'From the sound of it, if Fraser had shot Ray in the leg, your husband would be dead right now.'

Penny was staring into space, unfocused, as the officers moved around the room, collecting their things. Matt's gaze never left her face. At last she looked at him and he took hold of her hands. 'Pen … wasn't there something you wanted to tell me?'

CHAPTER 40

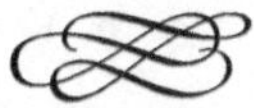

Aflautist played a tune in wavering vibrato, the sweet sound hovering between enlightenment and sorrow. Matt gazed with pride at the people around him – at Fraser and Drake, Lisa and Lucky, the Murphy family. And most importantly at Penny, who was pushing little Ray and Charlotte in their twin stroller. All the people who'd worked so hard to make this day possible were here to celebrate.

A crowd was gathering before the platform, where Premier Hellgrun stood in front of a microphone. 'The Pallawarra Lone Tree Expo,' he said, 'is a permanent exhibition that marks a fundamental shift in Tasmanian forest policy.' There was a burst of applause. 'This fresh paradigm unites, at last, both sides of a deeply divisive debate. The wonderful displays you can see around you were created from the body of a single tree. They demonstrate the true importance of value-adding, for employment, and for the environment.' A bevy of press photographers jostled for the best view. 'It is with great pleasure that I declare this visionary exhibition … open.' More applause.

Penny was talking earnestly to a tall, sallow man wearing a bow tie.

'Let me take the kids,' said Matt.

She shot him a grateful smile.

Matt and Drake drifted away from the crowd, trying to take it all in. Not only was the beauty of Pallawarra's timber showcased in the astonishing range of pieces on display, it was featured in the very construction of the vast purpose-built auditorium. Matt gazed up in awe at the high, vaulted ceiling beams. 'I have to hand it to Fraser. He really came through.'

'Did you know he made a huge donation to Sustainable Tasmania? It helped us buy loads of advertising. Your dad is the main reason we pulled in so many votes.'

'So Tasmania is stuck with another party leader with Logan for a surname,' said Matt, grinning.

The building was packed with traditional wood-crafted furniture, sculptures, bark wall-hangings, toys and musical instruments. It looked like the entire Hills End community was there as well. Young Ben Murphy was patting a sculpted eagle, perched on a stand with wings unfurled, ready to take flight. 'Don't touch,' said Matilda. 'I'll tell Dad.' Ben ran to the dappled rocking horse, its arched neck stippled with the mottle of natural grain. He climbed aboard. 'You're too big,' said Matilda. 'I'll tell Dad.' Ben dashed off to the jewellery display cases, his bossy sister in hot pursuit.

Matt and Drake laughed at the children and went for a wander. Past an inverted timber dome, lined with mirrors, designed to boil water with the reflected rays of the sun. Past a broad dining table made from just two solid planks, cut bark to bark. Past a gallery of Indigenous art. Past a range of stringed instruments: ukuleles, violins, flutes and even a lyre.

An elegant Celtic-style floor harp took pride of place. Children played with rhythm sticks and taut bark tambourines at little wooden tables. Folk music, played on limited edition Pallawarra brand guitars, sounded through loudspeakers. Luthiers plied their trade on a low stage, steaming plywood on jigs to bend it just so, sanding sound boxes to resonate with perfect pitch.

Matt stopped to watch someone string a guitar. He squatted down. 'Look, kids.' Little Ray and Charlotte watched solemnly from their stroller as the craftsman threaded the string, looped it under, pulled it taut and wrapped the first wind back over again. Charlotte reached both arms out to her father. 'Not yet, honey,' said Matt and they moved on to the indisputable star of the exhibition.

It was as if mighty Pallawarra lived again. His immense bole dominated the entire building. It served as the central pillar, load bearing, giving an unusual organic feel to the architecture. A jagged horizontal gash still scarred the tree where the chainsaws had torn through his twenty-five-metre circumference. Drips of congealed red sap showed where climbing spikes had pierced his trunk like crucifixion nails. Matt marvelled at the logistics. For Pallawarra's trunk soared, whole again, twenty metres to the domed ceiling and extended many more metres beneath the floor.

Epiphytes sprouted from high cracks and crevices. Swathes of hand-painted butterflies, authentic to the last detail, adorned his stringy bark streamers. Ramps and tunnels let visitors explore his labyrinthine root system, and tiny LED glow-worms lent a magical quality to this underground maze. Child-sized burrows and secret chambers, carved in his base, revealed all sorts of interactive wonders celebrating the life of the tree. Light spilled from strategic ceiling skylights to illuminate the carvings on the bark.

Matt released the twins. They toddled to the tree, crawled under a root and peek-a-booed from a low hollow. Matt pointed out Grandpa and Grandma's names in a heart. Then he showed them Mummy and Daddy's.

'Isn't Mummy clever?' he said, pointing to the collection of stuffed native animals and birds inhabiting the tree. A brush-tailed possum, baby on board, peered out of its nest. A wombat escaped down its burrow, and a devil played with its joeys. An eagle added a stick to its lofty eyrie. Penny had done a spectacular job. Everybody had, including his own father. They'd all worked together to bring the grand vitality of the Tuggerah to town.

Penny appeared and swept up her delighted children in a bountiful hug.

'I can't believe it,' she said. The children gazed in rapt attention at her shining face. 'The amount of interest in my Memento Mori line?

Three buyers from Hobart stores have put in orders. And that man in the bow tie, Patrick Duff? He's the curator of vertebrate zoology at the Hobart Museum. Know what he said?' Penny was off and running before he could respond, sparkling right along with her jewellery. 'He said he's impressed by my work – my devil mounts in particular. He says they're embarking on a project in conjunction with the university. Cataloguing DNA and restoring mounted specimens.' Her voice quivered and tracked higher. 'Thylacines as well. He wants me to consult. They say I have a way with marsupial carnivores.' Penny punched Matt's arm in excitement, causing little Charlotte to punch Ray, who started to cry. 'I'll actually be a museum consultant.'

Matt rescued Ray. 'Congratulations, honey.'

McGregor wheeled Fraser's chair over. He was physically frail now, with the return of the cancer, but his spirit seemed strong and his eyes shone with pleasure. Charlotte and Ray climbed onto his knee and searched his pockets for sherbet bombs. He pretended not to have any, then produced one from behind each child's ear, to peals of laughter.

'The museum is lucky to have you,' said Fraser when he heard Penny's news. 'It's not the other way around. Remember that.' She hugged him. Hugged the children. Hugged Matt. Hugged the jewellery store sales rep who came to retrieve her.

'I've got the kids,' said Matt. 'You go back to your wheeling and dealing.'

Penny gave him a dazzling smile and hurried off.

Fraser was correct; the museum was lucky to have her, more than it knew. Nobody alive was more qualified for the job. For back at Canterbury Downs, in a climate-controlled extension to Fraser's studio, Penny had restored Theo to life, or so it seemed. He stood at attention, forepaw raised, facing the steel door, ready to flee back to his mountains given half a chance. A security system guarded the room's concealed entrance, and its existence was known to just four people. It had come at a terrible cost. Sarah was gone, and Matt couldn't put that right. He would never shed the guilt he felt over her death.

There was something important that he *had* been able to put right though. With immense perseverance and the use of strategically placed camera traps, he and Penny had discovered precisely how many tigers were using the tunnel in and out of the secret valley. The number exceeded a dozen, more than they could have hoped for.

After hundreds of hours of observations, and months of field work, Matt knew the tigers well. He knew every stripe on each animal; every scar and limp and pawprint and torn ear. He knew their habits and routines, when they climbed up in the evening to go hunting, and when they stole back down to the safety of their valley to sleep.

Last week he'd spent a few days camping up at Tiger Pass. One bright morning, when Matt had established beyond doubt that every animal had safely passed down through the tunnel, he dynamited the rear of Last Stand Cave, just as Luke Tyler had done one hundred and fifty years before him. How proud he was to restore the sanctuary his forefathers had created for the tigers. Their secret was secure once more.

In the basement laboratory at UTAS, a scientist unlocked a tall freezer cabinet. She'd been set the task of reviewing the ground-breaking work of the late Dr Sarah Deville – the brilliant American researcher who uncovered the key to tackling facial tumour disease in devils, and then died in such violent and tragic circumstances.

The scientist commenced her morning's work, sliding out trays, identifying and cataloguing the samples she found. Each sample was neatly numbered and labelled. Except for one. One curious piece of ear.

ACKNOWLEDGEMENTS

Firstly I'd like to thank Inga Simpson, Australia's foremost nature writer, for mentoring me on this project. I can't believe how much I learned from Inga and I will be forever grateful.

Thanks go to the team at Pilyara Press, including Kathryn Ledson, Sydney Smith, Kate Belle, Desney King and Monique Mulligan.

Special thanks go to Kathryn Ledson and Desney King for their eagle-eyed editorial and proofreading help.

Thanks to my insightful editor, Alison Arnold, who has now worked with me on seven books.

Thanks to my lovely agent, Clare Forster of Curtis Brown Australia.

I pay tribute to the various Tasmanian Devil Conservation organisations. Without their dedication and hard work, our devils might already be extinct.

Thanks to my talented writing friends, the Varuna Darklings and the Little Lonsdale Group, for their friendship and encouragement.

Finally, I'd like to thank my family for their patience and support. Once again, you are all stars!

ABOUT THE AUTHOR

Bestselling Aussie author Jennifer Scoullar writes page-turning fiction about the land, people and wildlife that she loves.

Scoullar is a lapsed lawyer who harbours a deep appreciation and respect for the natural world. She lives on a farm in Australia's southern Victorian ranges, and has ridden and bred horses all her life. Her passion for animals and the bush is the inspiration behind her best-selling books.

Visit Jennifer's website to receive a free book, and also enter the monthly prize draw! If you enjoyed this novel and have a moment or two, please leave an online rating or review. Reviews are of great help to authors.

www.jenniferscoullar.com